Forge Books by Elmer Kelton

HOT IRON

—— AND ——

THE TIME IT NEVER RAINED

Elmer Kelton

FORGE®

A TOM DOHERTY ASSOCIATES BOOK | NEW YORK

This is a work of fiction. All of the characters, organizations, and events portrayed in these novels are either products of the author's imagination or are used fictitiously.

HOT IRON AND THE TIME IT NEVER RAINED

Hot Iron copyright © 1956 by Elmer Stephen Kelton Estate

The Time It Never Rained copyright © 1973, 1984 by Elmer Stephen Kelton Estate

A Forge Book
Published by Tom Doherty Associates
120 Broadway
New York, NY 10271

www.tor-forge.com

Forge® is a registered trademark of Macmillan Publishing Group, LLC.

ISBN 978-1-250-17786-5

Our books may be purchased in bulk for promotional, educational, or business use. Please contact your local bookseller or the Macmillan Corporate and Premium Sales Department at 1-800-221-7945, extension 5442, or by email at MacmillanSpecialMarkets@macmillan.com.

First Edition: December 2019

Printed in the United States of America

10 9 8 7 6 5 4 3 2 1

CONTENTS

HOT
IRON

1

Espy Norwood found Matt Ollinger's herd just about the way he had figured he would. He put his horse down the gentle slope in an easy trot and rode in toward the railroad shipping pens. His bay horse shied off like a raw bronc and rolled its nose excitedly at the steaming locomotive which waited there, a tendril of coal smoke spiraling up from its high smokestack into the open Kansas sky. A long string of stock cars stretched out behind it on the cinder-stained spur track.

Norwood edged his horse through the shadow of the tall water tower and circled around the sprawling railroad pens. Five years under the blazing sun had bleached the raw color from the rough-sawed lumber and left it a leaden gray.

Spring grass inside the pens had made its full growth and now was curing under the summer sky, undisturbed by trampling hoofs. These out-of-the-way pens were not used much, Norwood observed.

That would be Ollinger's reason for bringing the cattle here.

Beyond the corrals Norwood saw what he had expected, a dusty veil hovering brown over a bunched-up herd of rangy cattle. There was little bawling. Had there been, the easy drift of the earth-warm breeze would have carried it to him. No, this was a quiet bunch, a steer herd.

Norwood stood in his stirrups, squinting his gray eyes to count the men who ringed the cattle. Dressed in saddle-worn, brush-ripped range clothes with the dust and grime rubbed deep into the fabric, he was a medium-tall man with back as straight as the barrel of a Winchester. His unshaven chin set rigid and grave. His uncompromising gray eyes right now were blunt as bullet ends. He looked his thirty-five years and more, a man on whom the years had burned a deep brand.

With one quick glance behind him, he reached down and pulled the saddle gun out of its scabbard. He loaded it, placed it across the pommel in front of him, and gently touched spurs to the bay's grain-swelled sides. Out yonder, on the near side of the herd, he saw the man he wanted.

Warily watching the riders who held the herd, Norwood nevertheless let his eyes search over the gathering of steers. They were stockman's eyes, appraising the cattle out of long habit and the knowledge accumulated through years on horseback. These were Texas stock, not what the settlers called "American cattle." They were long of leg and horn, and sprinkled with every color a beef animal could have. Likely they had come up the trail from Texas the year before and spent the winter on a northern range. They didn't carry the flesh that a full summer would give them. But they were fat enough to do.

Norwood's gaze searched over the brands he saw on the rangy hips and stretchy sides. He pulled up short at the sight of one. It was meant to be a cloverleaf. For the time it takes to draw a deep breath, Norwood's gray eyes narrowed with the promise of anger.

Burnt cattle, he thought.

Then he edged away again, eyes leveling on the man who rode out to meet him.

Matt Ollinger reined up so that his horse and Norwood's were touching heads. Ollinger was a heavy-shouldered man with a bristly black beard sprinkled gray by dust, and with washed-out eyes that seemed to look through a man. His hostile gaze dropped to Norwood's saddle gun.

Its muzzle pointed at his stomach.

His expression never altered. He cupped huge hands over the high horn of his saddle.

"We're grown men, Norwood," he said evenly. "There's no reason for us to pretend anything to each other. I don't like you and you don't like me. I'm working cattle here. I'd be much obliged if you just kept a-riding."

Espy Norwood leaned forward, his hand tight on the saddle gun. "I figure on doing a little cattle work myself. With *these* cattle."

Ollinger's eyes were bottomless pools. His hands eased backward on the saddle horn. He bore a hard name, and he knew it better than anyone. The name Matt Ollinger brought a quiver of fear to many men. There were five notches on his gun, some said. Others declared it was more.

Ollinger said, "There's no call for trouble between us, Norwood."

Norwood gave him a brittle smile. "There needn't be any, Matt. But somebody stole a bunch of Colonel Judkins's steers up north. I'm checking this herd for them."

Ollinger's hand edged back toward the six-shooter that rested in a greasy holster at his hip. It lifted quickly again as Norwood's knuckles whitened against his saddle gun.

"You'll find no Judkins cattle here," Ollinger gritted.

"Maybe not. But we're going to look."

Color squeezed into Ollinger's face. "Nobody's cutting this herd. I got six men here, besides myself. You can't buck seven of us, Norwood. Not alone."

Norwood said, "I'm not alone." He pointed his chin northward.

Ollinger turned in the saddle, then stiffened. Down from a low ridge eight men came riding. Eight men, riding abreast. Even through the restless dust, it was easy to tell that they were well-armed.

Yes, Matt Ollinger had a reputation. Man with nerves like rawhide, they said. Fearless. A killer.

But Espy Norwood could smell the fear that rose in the man, that rippled just beneath the skin. And he knew the reputation for what it was—a hoax.

Norwood said, "Four hundred and fifty head, maybe five hundred, the colonel lost off of his winter range in Wyoming. You took them, Matt. You didn't know it, but we've watched you. We let you winter them, let you drive them down here.

"You were afraid to risk loading them at Dodge, where somebody might take too close a look. So you picked this place."

Ollinger shook his head. "You're wrong, Norwood. All wrong."

Norwood's eight men had reached the herd. They scattered, one man reining up beside each of Ollinger's men. Espy could see the guns drop. The two extra riders jogged around to Norwood. One of them pointed his long jaw toward the cattle.

"That cloverleaf or whatever it is—looks to me like somebody took a running iron to the JB Connected that was on them Texas steers the colonel bought last fall."

Norwood nodded. "That's the way I saw it. Rope one out, Tommy. We'll make sure."

Tommy Jensen shook down his rope and settled the loop around the horns of a rangy, motley-faced steer. The steer crow-hopped, slinging his head and fighting the rope as the cowboy dragged him away from the other cattle. The second man roped the steer's heels. They stretched him out.

Kneeling on the steer's side, Jensen fingered the brand, peering closely at it. He looked up, frowning. "Hard to tell, Espy."

"If the brand's been altered, it'll show under the hide. Shoot him."

Ollinger exploded. "Them's *my* cattle, Norwood. Kill one and I'll have the marshal on you."

Norwood said evenly, "If we're wrong, we'll pay you for him. If we're right . . ."

He let it hang there. Ollinger's jaw ridged under a dirt-crusted beard.

Tommy Jensen aimed at the base of the steer's horns. The animal jerked and fell limp. Jensen skinned down a big flap of hide, exposing the back side of the brand. He swore gently, then cut off the piece of hide.

"You don't owe him a nickel, Espy."

Norwood's eyes hardened. He reached into his pocket and pulled out a small book. "How many steers in this herd, Matt?"

Ollinger hesitated. "Seven hundred and thirty."

Norwood handed him the book and a stub pencil, keeping one hand on the saddle gun all the time.

"Write out a bill of sale to the colonel. Seven hundred and thirty steers."

Ollinger's eyes crackled. He hurled the book to the ground. "You can't get away with this. I know you, Espy Norwood. You're nothing but a sodden, whisky-soaked . . ."

The butt of Norwood's saddle gun struck him across the mouth. The sound of it was like the breaking of a dry mesquite stick. Ollinger tumbled from the saddle, landing in a heap. Groggily he struggled to his knees, the blood trickling down his beard in a crooked, dirty line.

"Get up, Matt," Norwood breathed. Slowly Ollinger got to his feet, his face aflame. He flexed his gun hand, weighing his chances.

But he saw something in Norwood's eyes, something that stopped him. He saw death pushing hard against a restraining will.

And Ollinger's counterfeit metal crumbled before the keen steel of Norwood's stare. His shoulders slumped. He reached down and picked up the book where it had fallen. He took the pencil and began to scrawl.

Norwood reached into his pocket and withdrew two gold pieces. "Make it for ten dollars and considerations," he said.

In a minute Ollinger handed him the book. Norwood pitched the coins to the ground at his feet.

Futile anger rippling in his face, Ollinger asked, "What about the considerations?"

Norwood stared levelly at him. "The considerations are that we don't leave you hanging from that water tower yonder. We ought to. Now take your men and get away from here, Matt."

Ollinger looked at the steers, his shoulders sagging in defeat. Six months he had spent working up to this day. Now he had lost everything in six minutes. Frustration and anger darkened his face. But outweighing them was the realization that he was whipped. "All right, Norwood," he spoke quietly, rubbing his mouth where blood still trickled, and a deep blue splotch was growing. "But there'll be another time."

"There'd better not be," Norwood told him. "Next time, I'll kill you."

2

Colonel Walter Judkins's outer office was a reflection of the man himself. Expansive and comfortable. Just well enough kept to prevent it from looking disreputable. It was one place in this crazy, sprawling Kansas City where a man just in off the prairie and the smoky cattle trains could stretch out and feel halfway at ease.

Espy Norwood slacked on a well-stuffed divan, waiting, his legs crossed. He was clean-shaven now, and the shave had taken much of the hard look from him. He could still smell the soap from the hotel bath. He wore a new-bought shirt, its clean collar a gleaming white against the walnut brown of his skin.

His gray eyes leisurely roamed over the familiar room. A great man for books, the colonel was. All around the place, broad shelves bulged with them. And between the shelves, framed pictures covered up the walls. The old colonel's love of livestock showed in most of them. Here was a painting of a Thoroughbred stallion, unlike any real horse that ever lived. Yonder was a glorified version of a Durham bull pawing sand, his huge head lowered in lusty challenge.

And there in the center, over the heavy mahogany desk, hung the framed U.S. Army commission which had carried the colonel through from Shiloh and Gettysburg to the finish at Appomattox, a long time ago. Directly above that yellowing piece of paper were the portraits of Abraham Lincoln and Ulysses S. Grant, joined in a single gilded frame.

Time was when such as that would have set the blood aboil in many a Texas man. But Espy Norwood was long since used to it and accepted it in stride. He had been but a gangling boy when the war was fought. His father had ridden off with the men of the gray, leaving Espy to take care of a mother and six little brothers and sisters. Biggest job he had was to burn the Norwood brand on the increase from the cattle herd each year, and to keep the Norwood cattle from scattering all over the coastal country of South Texas, as other war-neglected herds were doing.

He had done a good job of it, for a kid. But by the time his father came riding home with an empty sleeve and an age far beyond his years, the cattle weren't worth the powder it would take to shoot them. The family's shack was small, and the larder was smaller. So Espy Norwood rolled his scant belongings into a warbag and set forth to forage for himself. He had become a wandering, homeless kid in a land of wandering, homeless people, a restless people, aggressive, proud in poverty, never admitting defeat.

A loud argument was shaking the thin walls of Colonel Judkins's inner office. Espy knew it was none of his business, but he couldn't help hearing it, even through the closed door. He easily recognized the old colonel's thundering voice.

"You've made a profit every year, gentlemen. Not always a big profit, but a profit, at least. The way I see it, you haven't got any kick coming."

The answer snapped back in a sharp, piercing voice that Espy knew came from somewhere far east. "The Great Plains Land and Cattle Company came up with a twenty per cent return for its investors last year. Our syndicate made only five per cent. We're being cheated, Colonel. And we're going to put a stop to it."

Espy could almost hear the colonel's sudden, sharp intake of breath. "Slagel, are you trying to say that I've been cheating you?"

The answer was as cold and unwavering as a steel blade. "Perhaps you, Colonel, perhaps someone else. But we're being cheated."

An angry hand flung the office door open. The colonel stood there stiffly, his arm outstretched. "Get out, Slagel. Get out before I take a horsewhip to you."

The man named Slagel walked out, holding a soft fedora in his long hands and a cane under his arm. He was a tall, spidery man with a sharp, malevolent face that matched his voice. He was immaculately dressed in long, closely-tailored black coat and gray striped trousers which broke correctly across his expensive shoes.

He was followed by another, much shorter, man dressed in much the same manner, a self-important little man whose own indignation seemed to be merely a careful copy of Slagel's.

Slagel stopped and faced the colonel again. "We have better and safer investments for our money, Judkins. We will be more than happy to pull out of your wild scheme."

The portly colonel stood there with his short beard bristling. "Let me remind you, sir, that you signed binding contracts."

"Those contracts protected us as well as bound us, Colonel. One sign of fraud anywhere will relieve us of obligation. And mark my word, Judkins, we'll find fraud. Next month I'm going to take a group of our directors and attorneys to that ranch. If we find anything amiss, Colonel, you'll answer for it. We'll pull our money out of that company—every last dime!"

Espy had gotten to his feet as the men came out of the office. He stood in front of the outer door, anger nettling him. Nobody had the right to accuse the colonel of fraud.

Slagel noticed Espy for the first time. Fixing a hostile gaze upon him, he slipped the cane from under his arm. He pointed it at Espy, making a quick, sideward motion with it.

"Step aside there," he ordered sharply.

A stubborn thrust of anger made Espy hold back a moment, glaring. Then he eased to one side just enough that Slagel could edge by. The shorter man followed closely with a frowning glance at Espy.

Colonel Judkins walked up to the door and slammed it after the men, slammed it so hard that the picture frames rattled against the wall. He stood a moment, staring at the closed door, his fists clenched. Then some of the angry color drained from his full face. He turned to Espy, forcing a weak smile that quickly died. "Hello, Espy." He grasped the range man's rough hand in his own, his left hand on Espy's arm. "I've been expecting you, Espy. Sorry you had to come at a time like this."

He looked out the open window toward the stockyards, from which came drifting the sound of bawling cattle. "Been a hard day, Espy. I need a drink."

Worriedly he glanced at the man with the saddle-warped frame. "Would it bother you if I took one?"

Espy shook his head, a slow smile on his face. "It's been a year since I had the last one, Colonel. Go right ahead. It won't bother me."

Tiredly Colonel Judkins walked into his inner office. He reached into a heavy cabinet and took out two bottles. He studied them intently, then decided upon one with a firm nod of his gray head. He put the other one back and poured a healthy-sized drink into a glass. He downed it, his face tightening, then relaxing slowly.

"Funny," he observed, "how different this stuff can be for different people. For some, like you, it's poison. For some, like me, it's a real tonic." He strode to his desk and picked up a small cedar box. He opened the lid and held the box out for Espy. "Straight from Havana."

Espy took one, and the colonel got one for himself. He bit the end off and missed the spittoon with it by a foot and a half. He struck a sulphur match on the underside of the expensive mahogany desk and drew long and hard until the end of the cigar began to glow. He flipped the smoking match at the spittoon and missed again.

He savored the cigar a moment, his anger slowly dwindling away. A mild pleasure tugged upward at the corners of his gray-shot beard, which he kept clipped in the style of Ulysses S. Grant. "How's your son getting along, Espy?" he asked after a bit.

Espy Norwood's face tightened suddenly. "Well, I guess. I haven't been to see him yet."

"Good kid. Nine years old now, isn't he?"

"Ten."

The colonel smiled ironically. "That's the trouble

when you start getting old. Every time you turn around, there's another year gone." He fished in his pocket and brought out a silver dollar. "When you see him, Espy, give him this for me."

Then the colonel's face was serious again. "That was quite a stroke you pulled off with Matt Ollinger out there. Everybody on the Kansas City yards had the story inside of a day."

Seated, Espy Norwood drew thoughtfully on his cigar, not answering. The colonel went on.

"Worries me, though. Matt Ollinger has a hard name."

A deep frown darkened Espy's square face. "A name given to him by men he's managed to buffalo. He's a four-flusher, a bluffer."

"Sometimes it's the coward who's the most dangerous."

Espy nodded. "I know. Might be I ought to've killed him."

Pensively the colonel rolled the cigar around in his mouth. "I'm glad you didn't. Somebody else will, in due time. There's no reason it should be us. I had enough of that a long time ago, Espy."

"I know, sir."

An uneasy silence hovered about the colonel then.

Now's the time to tell him, Espy thought. But after all these years, he dreaded it, and he held back.

The thought struck Espy that the old man had aged a lot in the months since he had last seen him. Certainly the worry lines in his high forehead had pinched a little deeper, and a broodiness had taken the old spark out of the coffee-bean brown of his eyes.

"Espy," Colonel Judkins spoke abruptly, looking out the window again, "how would you like to go back to Texas?"

Espy straightened. His first reaction was a quick warmth of pleasure. It had been a long time. "Some cattle you want bought down there?"

The colonel still faced the window, his wrinkled hands clasped behind his black coat and the cigar smoke forming a soft cloud over his head. "Not this time, Espy. This job is bigger. I want you to save me from going bankrupt!" The old man turned to see Espy's jaw drop with surprise. "Yes, Espy, that's what I said. Bankrupt."

Espy's hands seemed to weaken, and the cigar lost its taste. Bankrupt. He'd seen other big speculators like the colonel go that way. But somehow the colonel was something special. Espy had never seriously considered that it could happen to the old man. He winced at a genuine touch of pain. The colonel was a good Yankee.

Pointing his chin at the outer door, Espy asked, "Is that what the argument was all about?"

The colonel nodded, sinking his heavy frame into a leather-covered chair. Judkins's worried brown eyes fastened themselves on Espy's. "You remember the ranch I helped an English syndicate to buy a half interest in? The Figure 4 outfit down below the Canadian?

"Well, there may not be anything wrong, Espy. It may be just imagination. But on the other hand, there may be a lot wrong. You've got to find out for me. Safest deal in the world, it looked like when we went down there. A broad, open, new grassland in the Texas Panhandle. Good country, good as you'll find anywhere on the Staked Plains. Frank Bowman had gotten there among the first, and he had taken over lots of land. He had good cattle, and he had the reputation of being a good manager. But he needed cash for one reason or another, and the syndicate was in the heat to invest some English capital. So we bought in with Bowman.

"But we haven't made as much money as they thought we ought to. You know how it is. All over Europe, promoters have been painting a bright green picture about all the money that's to be made in the cow business. Like that stuff about the Great Plains Land and Cattle Company. Twenty per cent. Horsefeathers!

"Now Slagel's a New York lawyer for the syndicate, and he's found some new scheme he wants to sink the syndicate money into. But he can't get at it if he can't pull it out of the Figure 4. He's fanned up a lot of unrest among the stockholders. When he hits that ranch next month, he'll go over it with a fine-tooth comb. He'd give his right arm to find something I can't explain."

His brown eyes were clouded with worry. "If the syndicate does pull out from under me, Espy, I'm ruined. Broke."

Espy fidgeted. *Tell him now,* he said to himself, *before he asks you to do something and you can't refuse him.* But instead, he queried, "What could I do about it?"

"Maybe a lot, Espy. You see, when we bought in with Frank Bowman, we consented to let him go on being the manager. But in event of his death, the syndicate was to be allowed to name the new manager. Frank Bowman is dead. Died of a stroke four weeks ago. Now I'm sending *you* down there as manager."

Espy swallowed hard. He arose unsteadily, then sat down again. He took the cigar from his mouth and noted distractedly that it was dead. "Colonel, I'm just a cattle buyer, not a ranch manager. The boots are too big for me. I can't do it."

The colonel's face puckered. "Espy," he said at length, "you've had it in mind for years to buy a place of your own some day, a place to take your son. If you had a chance to get such a place, you'd grab it in a hurry, wouldn't you? You wouldn't worry about whether or not you could manage it."

Espy's guard came up instinctively. He could feel himself being hazed into a blind trap. "No, sir, I reckon I wouldn't."

"Then, Espy, if you could do it for yourself, you could do it for *me*." The colonel was pointing his cigar like he would point a gun. "There's more to this than just managing a ranch. Much as I hate to admit it, there may be a little something in what Slagel says. That ranch hasn't paid off like it should have. Maybe we've been cheated. Maybe the management is just a little loose.

"I liked Frank Bowman. He seemed like a prince of a man to me. Capable, hard-working, ambitious. And as kind a man as you'd ever run into. But if something's wrong, I want to know about it. And I want it straightened out before Slagel gets there with his wrecking crew."

Espy still shook his head. "It's too big for me, Colonel. You ought to send somebody else."

"We have, Espy. The syndicate's had first one man, then another one down there half the time. They weren't of my choosing. Mostly they were just black sheep that some English family wanted to be shed of for a while. All most of them could ever do was get drunk and make obnoxious asses of themselves.

"Geoffrey Spence was the only one of them who was ever worth a dime. He went there about a month before Bowman died. He was smart, that Spence was. Had a way of looking right through you, like he could read everything that was on your mind. He wrote me a couple of letters. There was something down there he didn't like, Espy. He didn't say what it was, but he indicated that he was on the trail of something. Trouble was, he didn't get to finish."

"What happened to him?"

"Well, he was a great hand for hunting. That was his only weakness, I guess. Had a whole set of guns with him. One day he went out to shoot some prairie chickens and didn't come back. They found him dead, shot by his own gun."

"Accident?"

"Looked that way. Must have tripped and shot himself."

Thoughtfully Espy tugged at his ear. "Still, Colonel, if he *had* found out something, there's always a chance it wasn't an accident."

Colonel Judkins nodded. "That's why I want you to go down there. If there's anything wrong, you're the man who can straighten it out. And you're the man who will come back in one piece."

Espy wanted to go. The thought of a return to Texas started needles to prickling his skin, and he could almost taste the sharp, tangy air of the Texas high country, the great, sweeping plains of the Llano Estacado.

But he shook his head. His gaze touched the cabinet where Judkins kept his whisky. "Aren't you forgetting one thing, Colonel?"

Judkins saw what he was looking at. "A year ago, Espy, I wouldn't have dreamed of it. But today, I'd never be afraid of you. Not a bit. I'm willing to bet on you, if you're willing to bet on yourself."

This time it was Espy who walked to the window and stood looking out, his hands clenched. He tasted the gentle drift of dust that came in from over the stockyards, and his mind ran back to other days, and other cattle, and other times he'd tasted that dust. There had been a time he would have taken a job like this on the fly, without ever looking back. That was when Jeannie had been alive, and he had been a reckless young cowboy with the world by the tail on a downhill pull.

Lots of things were different now. He wished he had the confidence in himself that the colonel seemed to have in him. That matter of the colonel's whisky. It *had* bothered him, watching the colonel empty that glass. Even after a year or more, it still beckoned him like the legendary mermaids he had read about, luring ships to the rocks. Even now there were times he wrestled with it, wrestled harder than he could admit even to himself.

For there was something a man could do about most of his enemies. He could whip them, kill them, or drive them away. But when his biggest enemy was himself, what was a man to do? He could run and run, yet always his enemy was there, a coyote lurking in the shadows just beyond the campfire, biding its time.

Memory brought the taste of Texas back to him, an early-spring taste, cool and fresh, and sweet with the promise of rain.

But his mind settled on something else, a boy ten years old, a boy who had barely known his father the last three or four years.

"Colonel," Espy said at length, "I hate to turn you down, but you've got to find you somebody else. For a long time now I've had my mind made up. I've promised myself I was going to start staying close to Kenny. I've been on the go a way too much these last few years. Always on the trail, or fixing to leave, or just getting back. But I'm going to change that.

"I'm going to get me a job that'll let me stay here. Something on the stockyards maybe. I'm going to get to know my boy again, the way I used to a long time ago when his mother was living."

There was more he could have said, but that he would have told no man. Like the worrisome reserve that held back the love from Kenny's thin face when Espy went to see him nowadays. It was as if this rough, sun-browned man with the long-reaching look of the plains in his eyes was not his father at all, but, instead, a stranger who occasionally dropped in from some strange land, then rode away again, leaving him as always, in the care of his Aunt Margaret.

There was that night more than a year ago, a memory that always brought an upward surge of shame. Espy Norwood had been in Dodge City, taking delivery on cattle he had bought for the colonel. The hot, dusty day's work over, he had slumped into a chair at a table in the Alhambra and taken his supper from a bottle. That was his habit often in those days, when the only way he knew to stop memories from tearing at his soul was to keep them drowned in whisky.

Sometime far into the night he had gripped the bottle, shouldered his way through the milling throng that crowded the smoky room, and staggered up the street to the frame hotel. He had been singing some raucous ditty as he weaved up the stairs and shoved open his door, his big hand clenched on the neck of the bottle.

Somehow he got it through his thickened brain that the lamp was burning. Then his cloudy eyes saw them sitting there waiting for him—Jeannie's sister

Margaret, and little Kenny. She had brought the boy out from Kansas City for a surprise visit.

Sight of them sobered him the way cold water settles the grounds in a boiling pot of coffee. But it was already too late. As long as he lived, he would never forget the stricken look that chilled the gray eyes of his son.

He had babbled some explanation, but Margaret angrily led the boy out of the room and out of the hotel. In fury at himself, Espy hurled the bottle through the open window. It was the last one he had ever touched.

Espy could see the colonel's shoulders slump in disappointment. "I'm sorry, Colonel," Espy said. "You can find someone better than me. I've got a lot to make up to Kenny for. And I'm going to start now."

3

Margaret Tellison owned a fine two-story brick home in a fashionable part of the city. To her views, she had married much better than had her younger sister Jeannie. Her husband was a wealthy merchant who now had three stores in Kansas City and was about to acquire a fourth. The name of Tellison was rapidly rising. It should, for Margaret spent most of her waking hours working toward that end. Who could tell? With the proper social background, Edgar Tellison someday might become a councilman. Even a mayor.

The couple never had had any children. Espy Norwood had often tried to picture Margaret Tellison as a mother. Somehow, the picture never did seem to fit.

But she had offered to give Espy's son a home after Jeannie had died. Bewildered in his loss, Espy had gratefully accepted. And, true to her word, she was bringing him up to be a proper little gentleman. Best private school in Kansas City. Clothes as good as those worn by any rich man's son in town. Manners just as correct as the book could specify.

Wherever they went, Margaret introduced him as "my sister's son." Never a word about the hard-drinking, half-wild Texan who was his father. Kenny Norwood was growing up to be more like Edgar Tellison than like the man whose name he bore.

Espy Norwood stepped down from the horse-drawn cab and handed three jingling coins to the driver. He watched as the cabbie turned his horse around and took the vehicle back down the street in a rolling drift of dust.

Something about the Tellison home always made Espy freeze up inside. Looking at its tall brick walls, its many cupolas, and the two big bay windows that bulged in front, he felt out of place. Times like this, he almost wished Edgar Tellison were a poor man and lived somewhere close to the stockyards. Then maybe Espy could feel at home.

More than that, somehow it took time now to work up the courage to see his son. A cold hand gripped his stomach as he visualized the distrust he would see in Kenny's eyes. It would be there, he knew. It seemed that the gulf which separated them grew wider after every visit, so wide that soon he no longer would be able to bridge it.

"No sense in a grown man being afraid of a little boy," he chided himself. "Just go on in there." Espy held a big box in his hands. He tucked it under his arm and started up the long red brick walk toward the house.

A white-aproned maid answered his nervous knock on the carved front door. Her eyes widened. Espy knew she had to force her smile. "Why, Mr. Norwood. Come in, sir. I'll take your hat."

The hat was brand-new, not even well shaped yet. But she carried it out with her fingertips, as if afraid it would get dirt on her hands.

Espy waited in the parlor, pacing nervously along the wall, looking distractedly at stiff, painted family portraits he had seen twenty times. Officers and gentlemen, probably as farfetched as the horse and bull pictures which the colonel kept on his walls. Espy found that his fingers were shredding the paper in which the box was wrapped, and he set it down.

"Good afternoon, Espy," a woman's voice spoke evenly. He turned.

Margaret Tellison stepped into the parlor, closing a door behind her. She wore a prim, floor-length, black dress with white lace collar. Her back was straight as a diamond-studded walking cane. Her eyes were chilly and without friendliness.

"Hello, Margaret," he spoke politely. "You're looking well."

"Thank you." She motioned toward a chair. "Sit down." She seated herself upon a hard, straight-backed chair, looking like a grim hostess at some painfully formal social affair.

He tried to make some small talk. "Edgar's business is doing well, I guess. See you've done the house over. It looks fine."

She sat with hands in her lap, staring at him, saying no more than was necessary to answer his questions. And he quickly ran out of those.

In facial features, Espy could see her resemblance to Jeannie. The nose was the same. The shape of the chin. The color of the eyes. Margaret Tellison was a pretty woman, in a severe kind of way. Espy had often puzzled over it. How could sisters look so much alike, yet be so completely different?

He had waited as long as he could without asking her. "Where's Kenny? I'm anxious to see him."

She shook her head. "He's not here."

Espy's heart quickened. "Not here? But where is he?"

"We sent him to visit some friends of ours in Chicago. We thought the trip would be broadening for him. He'll be gone another week, or perhaps two."

Espy's breath slowly went out of him. He looked at the floor, an emptiness in him.

Margaret said, "When he returns, I'll tell him you were here."

Espy swallowed his disappointment. "No need. I'll be here to tell him myself."

Alarm began to push into her eyes.

He went on, "I've been away from Kenny too long. I'm going to work in the city from now on, so I can be close to him. It's not right for a boy to grow up a stranger from his own dad."

Incredulous, displeasure evident in her face, she stood up. "Are you serious, Espy?"

"Dead serious."

"Would you take him out of this house?"

He could see what she was driving at. "I'll give him a good home, Margaret, I promise you that. I'll work hard and send him to a good school. And I'll be close, all the time."

Abruptly she turned away from him. She stared out the window, her fingers flexing quickly, angrily. Then she faced him again, her eyes sharp. "I'm going to be blunt, Espy." Her words were chips of ice. "We're giving Kenny a fine opportunity. With us, he has a chance to become someone important, to acquire property and station. What chance has he with you?"

Stung, Espy started to interrupt. She held up her hand impatiently. "No, wait. Hear me out, Espy.

"What could he ever be? A two-bit cowboy, or a down-at-the-heels cattle trader, hanging around the yards? That's not good enough for him, Espy. It may be good enough for you, but not for my sister's son."

Espy strained against the anger that swelled in him. "It won't be that way, Margaret. I have some money saved. I'll give him a good education, and some day we'll have a ranch of our own. All the important people don't live in town."

She started to answer him angrily. But suddenly a voice lifted in another room. It was a boy's voice.

"Aunt Margaret. Aunt Margaret, where are you?"

Espy stiffened. He saw red flush into Margaret Tellison's face.

"I thought you said he was gone."

A door opened, and the boy walked in. "Aunt Margaret, may I—"

He broke off, seeing Espy. He stood there with his mouth open, uncertain as to what to do or say.

Espy warmed at the sight of him. He yearned to draw the youngster to him, to hug him tightly the way he had done when Kenny was a tiny boy, when such a thing wouldn't flush a boy's face with shame.

"Hello, son," Espy said, his voice tight.

"Hello, Daddy."

That's all there was. The warmth in Espy quickly died, and a chill came in its place. He saw in Kenny's eyes the reserve he had dreaded so much. Espy looked down, unsure of himself, cold fear a drag on him. Then he thought of the box.

Forcing a smile, he said, "Say, son, I brought you something."

He handed his son the box and waited tensely while the youngster broke the string and unwrapped the paper. Kenny's eyes lighted up momentarily at the sight of a handsome pair of handmade boots.

Eagerly Espy spoke, "If they don't fit, we can take them back and change them for another pair."

But the light in the boy's eyes died down. He looked at the boots, then at his aunt, his eyes asking if it would be all right to accept the present.

"Take them on up to your room, Kenny," Margaret Tellison said coldly. "Your father and I need to talk."

"Yes, ma'am," the boy said. He left without another glance at Espy. Then he reopened the door. Poking his head in, he said, "Oh, yes, thank you for the boots."

Espy sagged as if a cold, wet blanket had been thrown across him. "You're welcome, son," he breathed, trying to hold back his disappointment.

Silence stretched taut between Espy and Margaret Tellison. He stared at her, his mouth hardening.

"Well?" she spoke harshly.

"You lied to me, Margaret. You tried to keep me from seeing my boy."

Sharply she replied, "That seems to me the best thing to do. He saw you once before, to his sorrow. That night in Dodge City."

A suspicion had worked in Espy for a long time. Now it struck him again as a dead certainty. "You knew what you would find that night," he said, his voice hardening. "You took Kenny there on purpose."

She squared her shoulders. Anger sent her voice to a higher pitch. "Yes. Yes, I did. It was hard on him. You have no idea how much it hurt him, Espy. But it served its purpose. It drew him away from you, and it made him abandon whatever reserve he had kept up against the kind of life we were trying to give him."

Espy's fists knotted. His eyes were narrowing. "I haven't touched a drop of liquor since that night, Margaret. You know that."

"But you're still Espy Norwood. Because you've been straight for a year doesn't mean you can do it forever. You're the kind that has to quit completely, or not at all. Someday one foot will slip, and nothing will break your fall.

"Besides that, you still live in a world of horses and cattle and sweat and dirt. You live in a world of coarse men and coarse women. I've turned Kenny away from that world, Espy. You won't take him back to it!"

Espy trembled in fury. "He's my son, Margaret, my son. And you've been teaching him to hate me! But that's all over with. I'm taking him with me. Now!"

He started for the door that led out toward the stairs. Margaret stepped in front of him. "No, Espy, I won't allow it."

Roughly he pushed her aside. He took the steps two at a time and shoved into Kenny's room. "Pack your clothes, Kenny. You're going with me."

Eyes wide, the boy started to protest. In angry impatience Espy threw open the closet door and started ramming clothes into two traveling bags he found there. Kenny watched him, tears brimming in his eyes. Then, resignedly, he began picking up the articles of which he was fondest and putting them into a box.

White-faced, Margaret Tellison stood in the door. "You can't do this, Espy. I'll have the law on you."

"No you won't, Margaret. He's *my* son."

She stood in the doorway, shouting after him as he left. "You won't get away with it, Espy. I'll have him back, you'll see. I'll have him back!"

Two hours later Espy was hammering on Colonel

Judkins's door, looking back apprehensively at the forlorn boy who sat in the waiting cab on the street.

A sleepy-eyed colonel opened the door, shoving a lamp out in front of him. "Oh, Espy, it's you. What the devil's gone wrong at this time of night?"

"Nothing wrong, sir. Maybe it's right for the first time. I'll take that Texas job. And Kenny's going with me."

4

The frontier town of Mobeetie was taking on some of the appearances of civilization, although not all the realities of it. Frame buildings were beginning to rise among the low-built adobes and picket houses which huddled along Sweetwater Creek. There was a hotel now, as good as a man was apt to find way down here this far from the railroad. There was a livery barn, operated by the big freighting outfit of Lee & Reynolds.

And it hadn't been long since the citizenry, mostly buffalo hunters, gamblers, and saloon people, had organized the county. They'd done a quick job of it, without the sanction or even the knowledge of most of the ranchmen who had moved into the territory and set their huge herds of cattle to grazing the free state-owned range. As long as law and order was inevitable, the townspeople wanted to be sure they could administer it according to their own lights, and keep it friendly.

Sighting the scattered settlement at the end of the

wagon trail below him, Espy Norwood hauled up on the reins and stopped the buckboard. He waved his hand toward the town and glanced at the boy who sat beside him in silence.

"Mobeetie, son," he said. "We sleep in a real bed tonight."

The boy nodded wearily. Espy flipped the reins. His fine team of matched little mules trotted on down old Charlie Rath's trail that the heavy iron rims of freight and buffalo-hide wagons had ground to soft powder. Inwardly, he was at least partly pleased.

From the time they had left Kansas City, a fear had ridden heavy and cold in the bottom of his stomach. But there hadn't been a whimper out of Kenny, not one. Kenny's thin face, normally tending to paleness, was blistered a fiery red by the hot sun and the constant wind which never halted in its restless search across the broad reaches of the Llano Estacado. The boy's gray eyes were dulled with weariness. The man and the boy had been polishing the hard, flat seat of the buckboard from sunup to dark every day since they had stepped down off the train at Dodge and turned their faces south.

It had been a long, monotonous, almost endless trip down across the plains, where the horizon was the same, hour after hour, almost as if a man had been standing still.

"It's a mighty big land," somebody had said once, speaking of the great Staked Plains. "It just goes on and on and on, without ever an end to it. It's like looking into Eternity itself."

There hadn't been a word of complaint from Kenny.

But there had been few words of any kind, and that was bothering Espy as he watched the youngster's

tired eyes taking in the raw town ahead. He sensed
the boy's immediate disappointment.

"Not much like Kansas City, son," he admitted.
"But you'll like this country, once you get used to it."

Kenny said nothing. His thin lips had been tight
and silent since the day Espy had stormed into his
room and hauled him out of Aunt Margaret's house.

Espy thought of Colonel Judkins—how tickled
the old man had been when Espy told him he would
come to Texas after all, and bring Kenny with him.

"Give that boy a month of fresh air and Texas sunshine," Judkins had smiled, "and he'll never want to
see the city again."

His short beard spread wide by a grin, the colonel
had then admitted, "You don't know how worried I
was for a while today, Espy. I was so sure you'd go,
I wrote a letter to Frank Bowman's daughter a week
ago. Told her you'd be there to take over the managership."

Espy Norwood hauled up the buckboard in front
of Huselby's hotel. Stiffly he stepped down, wrapping
the reins around the front wheel. He reached up to
help Kenny. But the boy climbed down on the off
side, alone.

Espy stood there scanning the irregular rows of
indifferent buildings, some of them frame but most
of them rude adobe or picket shacks. The sun was a
flaming red, low in the west, like a candle flickering
bright just before going out. This was an awkward
hour for the town, caught in the transition between
the business activity of the day and the boisterous
playtime of night.

Down toward the end of the street he sighted a
settler with a wagonload of buffalo bones. Not a
great many settlers here yet, he knew. But there were

enough to set the pattern. It wouldn't be many years before they would control a big part of this country, and the free range days would be gone. The man who didn't own his land or have a lease on it would find himself shoved out.

Down the powdery street Espy's eye caught the name painted on a sign above a long, narrow frame building. "Buffalo Bar. Best Bourbon in Texas. Arch McCavitt, Prop."

The name brightened Espy's leathery, stubbled face with the pleasure of remembered days, a time long ago when there hadn't been any trouble in the world, and everything worth having was free.

Espy turned back to the buckboard. He gripped Kenny's suitcase and flung his own warbag over his shoulder.

"Come on, son," he said, walking up to the big front door of the hotel. "Let's go see about that bed."

The hotel had a bathtub, and Espy used it. He sharpened his long straight razor and shaved off the rough whiskers that had grown on the trail down from Dodge. Watching Kenny splashing in the tub, washing himself with the rough slab of poor soap, Espy remembered how much of a fight he had used to put up when he was a kid, any time Ma brought up the subject of a bath. But Kenny had been eager to wash the trail dust off. Kansas City training, Espy thought. Bath twice a week, and oftener if necessary. That didn't hurt a boy any. But baths were likely to come more seldom out here.

They started to the dining room together. Espy placed his big hand on his son's shoulder, then ruefully removed it when he felt the boy begin to pull away.

A heavy-set, middle-aged woman came out of the

kitchen to wait on them, her long skirt sweeping the floor behind her.

Espy said, "This boy here's been doing on canned tomatoes and sardines and stuff like that all the way down from Dodge. I want you to fill him up on some good Texas beef tonight, ma'am."

He felt a quick pleasure at the shy smile which flickered on the boy's face. The first he had seen.

While they waited, two more customers came in. They were young women, and Espy knew at a glance that they weren't of the kind most numerous in towns like this. He immediately placed them as women in from a ranch.

One of them, wearing a wedding band, he judged to be a little younger than himself. She wasn't pretty. Some men might even call her plain. But her face bore a compelling friendliness, and permanent laugh wrinkles had settled comfortably at the corners of her eyes.

Espy knew cowboys. He was certain that wherever she lived, cowboys probably would ride miles out of their way to happen by the house at mealtime. It was an unquestioned custom out here that drifting cowhands be fed. He knew by instinct that she would be one who would feed them cheerfully. In return they would fetch water for her, and see that the woodbox behind the stove was as full as it would go. And maybe they would whittle out a toy gun or a doll for her kids, if she had any. To see a good woman once in a while, to hear the lilt of her pleasant talk, filled a need for cowboys on the woman-shy plains that no number of trips to a ribald town could ever do.

Espy's gaze turned to the other woman. She was a few years younger, in her mid-twenties, he guessed. His interest rose. Here *was* a pretty one. He liked the mature features on her soft-skinned face. Her nose tilted upward at the end, a saucy tilt that suggested good humor. But the lamplight picked up a glint of red from her smooth-brushed auburn hair, and her blue eyes looked as if they could snap like a whip when the occasion called for it.

The blue eyes lifted to his face, and he quickly dropped his gaze, feeling the color rise under his skin. A man could stare all he wanted to at the girls in a dance hall. But here it was different.

He remembered how it had been with Jeannie, the first time he had met her. His mind drifted back in pleasant memory while his gaze fastened on the frayed edge of the tablecloth. The lamplight seemed to close in around him. He remembered himself and Arch McCavitt, wild young cowboys still on the sunny side of their twenties, headed for town in high good humor to see the elephant and buck the tiger. Two month's pay was burning in their pockets, and a dozen dance-hall girls were waiting to help them put out the fire.

Riding into town, they had spurred their horses into a hard lope and commenced shooting the sky full of holes to serve notice on all and sundry that the team of Norwood & McCavitt had arrived. Ahead of them two girls were riding in a buggy. Their horses misunderstood the cowboys' intentions and headed for the high country as fast as the buggy could bounce.

It was Espy who managed to catch up with them and pull the runaways to a reluctant halt. He took a tight grip on the buggy reins and spoke softly to the boogered, eye-rolling team. In the buggy seat, one girl was shaking her fist and speaking none too softly to Espy and to the late-arriving Arch McCavitt. That was Margaret.

But as shame flooded hot into Espy's face, he had looked at the other girl, and caught the spark of laughter in her eyes. She winked while her sister rattled on and on. This was Jeannie.

Now a thin smile came to Espy's face as he remembered. It had been a long time. It had taken years to do, but finally, through a stern will, he had put the grief and loss behind him. Now he could remember with pleasure, and without regret.

The clatter of a heavy plate jarred him out of his reverie. The plump woman set down two thick, pan-fried steaks in front of him and Kenny. She brought a chipped platter full of fried potatoes and a plate of hot biscuits, followed by a cup of coffee for Espy. In a moment she set down a pitcher of milk for the boy, and Espy wondered idly where she got it. Not many milk cows in this country. Not many people would've drunk milk even if they'd had the chance.

A desperate trail-born hunger temporarily robbed Kenny of his reserve. Discarding the gentle manners his Aunt Margaret had drilled into him, he dug into the steak like a half-starved puppy tearing at a caught rabbit. Espy watched him with a lingering smile of pleasure.

Two men came into the dining room together. Espy first noticed the quick frown of displeasure in the face of the plump old woman. He glanced across his shoulder.

Both men bore a rough, back-trail look, with a careless growth of whiskers you couldn't rightly call a beard. The shortest of the two weaved slightly as he walked. His hip pocket bulged. Although his pulled-out shirttail covered most of it, it was obvious what caused the bulge. Seeing the women, he pulled off his shapeless hat. Beneath it a mop of rusty-colored hair sprang up like a careless growth of weeds, with strands of silver shining in the lamplight.

The other man was taller, with shoulders as broad across as the length of a shotgun barrel. His dirty blue shirt, buttoned to the collar, fit snugly across a powerful chest. His eyes touched Espy, eyes black as the thick stubble of barbed-wire whiskers bristling on his big chin. They were belligerent eyes, the kind that were perpetually looking for a fight.

The shorter man stumbled against a table, caught himself, then weaved up beside the table where the two women sat. "Good evening, Mary," he said thickly to the younger woman.

She studiously ignored him, a splotch of angry color in her cheeks. The man stared at her, turning sullen. He had the florid face and swimmy eyes of the habitual drunkard.

"You getting too good to speak to your kinfolks anymore?"

She gave him a quick, raking glance. "You don't belong in here. You're drunk, and you're making a fool of yourself. Now get out."

His blood-laced eyes stared at the girl while his lips trembled with angry words unsaid. After a moment he turned and tromped out, walking into a chair and knocking it over, and sending another one clattering back in precarious balance against a table. The broad-shouldered, black-whiskered man followed him, his dark face unmoved.

The young woman buried her anger in the eating of her meal, while the other one sat in silent understanding.

Kenny had watched the scene with wide eyes. Now it was forgotten again, as far as he was concerned, and he hungrily dug into his steak. That done, he got around a big slab of pie which the elderly woman had brought.

Espy sensed that the two women were watching the boy, too. The younger one's eyes met Espy's, and he saw the gentle amusement that had come into them, displacing her anger. He warmed to her, wondering why. The answer hit him suddenly and hard. Those were the same eyes Jeannie used to have.

The young woman picked up her piece of pie and brought it over to Espy's table. "Somehow I'm not very hungry tonight," she smiled. "Maybe this young man would like to eat my pie."

Kenny's eyes lighted up. He looked to Espy for permission.

"Thank the lady, son," Espy said.

Kenny did, and piled into the pie.

Supper finished, Espy could see that some of the weariness had drained from the kid's blistered face. More contentment showed there now than at any time since they had left Kansas City.

"You're doing fine, son," Espy thought. "And someday maybe you'll even like me again."

As the dark blanket of twilight settled over the prairie town, a new and vibrant life began to surge down its crooked, dusty course. Horses plodded up and down the street. Spurs jingled, and boots clumped heavily on what plank porches there were. High-spirited talk rose with the moon, and somewhere off yonder a fiddle began to saw away.

Espy stayed in the room until Kenny crawled into the hard bed and dropped off to sleep. He pulled the blanket up over the boy. His eyes were soft as he watched a long moment the gentle rise and fall of the boy's breathing. Then he stepped back to the door, trimmed the lamp, and blew out the flame.

Outside, he stood a moment in front of the hotel, watching the lively foot and horse traffic up and down the street. He stepped into the sand and angled across to the place where he had seen the sign.

The Buffalo Bar was a long, narrow building with a pine bar running along one wall, up toward the front. Down the other wall was a careless scattering of card tables. In back were closed doors leading, Espy figured, to small private rooms. These could be used for big-stake games where the players didn't want a crowd hanging around, watching over their shoulders. Or they could be used for other purposes, too. But, looking around, Espy saw no girls.

A loud cowboy whoop ripped loose down at the far end of the room. Arch McCavitt came striding toward him, hand outstretched, his face glowing. "Espy Norwood! I wouldn't even have thought of you for a five-dollar gold piece!"

Espy pumped McCavitt's hand, enjoying the sight of that happy-go-lucky face. He bent forward for a close look at McCavitt's flaming red hair.

"Not a streak of gray in it, Arch. The years've been kind to you."

McCavitt laughed. "Aw, I just rinse it now and again with that stuff the girls use down at Kansas Kate's place."

He slapped Espy's shoulder and led him back toward a table at the far end. He made a quick signal to the bartender. "Lord, Espy, it's sure good to see you. Been a lot of years, a lot of years. Where've you been? How's Jeannie?"

Espy's face pinched. "Jeannie's dead, Arch. Been dead for five years."

Arch McCavitt's grip tightened on Espy's shoulder. Espy quickly changed the subject. "Well, Arch, looks like the only thing different about you is that you're a little older. You haven't changed a bit."

The bartender brought a bottle and two glasses. Arch started to fill them. Espy reached out and covered one of the glasses with his big hand. "None for me, Arch. I'm not using it anymore."

McCavitt looked quizzically at him. "Man, *you've* sure changed." To the bartender, McCavitt called, "Jud, come back here and get this stuff. You know I don't ever drink this early."

The two sat back, silent a while, enjoying each other's company the way old friends will. Arch rolled a cigarette with one hand, like he used to do as a young hell-for-leather cowboy, to show off. He had done it so long that it was second nature with him now. Espy was sure a lot of the old recklessness still clung to him. It showed in his face, his eyes, and the bright, clean cut of the fancy clothes he wore. It wouldn't all be burned out of him if he lived to be ninety.

Espy said, "I never would've thought about running into you here, Arch. But it looks like you've found you a good spot."

Arch's gaze swept the raw frame saloon, a warm pride glowing in his face. "Not the ritziest joint in the country, and I don't keep girls here like some of them do. But I still have a lot of business, Espy. Drinks and games. I try to keep an honest place. Man comes here, he knows he's not fixing to get cheated."

Curiosity burned in Arch McCavitt's dancing blue eyes. "What brings *you* down here, anyway? Last I heard, you were up in Wyoming, working for Colonel Judkins."

Espy nodded. "I'm still working for him, Arch. Going to manage the Figure 4 outfit for him and for the syndicate."

McCavitt suddenly frowned, his fingers pinching the cigarette so hard that it went out.

Espy saw it. "What's the matter, Arch? Maybe you can tell me what I'm getting into."

McCavitt dropped the cigarette into an empty sardine can that served as an ash tray. "Getting into? I wouldn't say that you're getting into anything in particular. The Figure 4's pretty much the same as the rest of the ranches around here. Bigger than most. Better cow country."

Espy sensed something evasive in Arch's answer. "Arch, the colonel and some of the stockholders seem to have an idea there's something wrong out there. You know this country. What do you think?"

Arch studied the tabletop, his face puckering. "I wouldn't say there's anything wrong. A little cow stealing along, of course. They'll always steal from an English outfit. You can't stop them."

"I can stop them. There's a law."

A touch of humor flickered in McCavitt's eyes. "Espy, you can read your lawbooks from Apple to Zebra, and you won't find any law there against stealing cows from an Englishman."

Espy pointed out, "Frank Bowman was half owner, and his daughter still is. They're just as American as a Rebel yell."

He waited for an answer to that and got none. He leaned forward, studying McCavitt's face. "Tell me about Frank Bowman. Was he honest?"

McCavitt said, "I've never known a man I liked any better. Heart as big as a barn door. Ride from one end of the Panhandle to the other and you'll never find a man who'll say a word against him."

Espy eased back into his chair, chewing his lip. Maybe the colonel's suspicions were wrong. Lots of things could account for a ranch not making the money it ought to, even with a good manager. Cattle thieves, storms, dry spells. Sometimes the very size of an outfit made it hard to operate efficiently. On a big, unwieldy spread, often it was impossible to keep the right hand posted as to what the left hand was doing.

"What do you think of his daughter, Arch?"

McCavitt smiled, his eyes softening. "Mary? She's . . . she's . . . Well, the only time I ever wish I was something besides a saloonman is when I see her." He pointed his finger at Espy. "Don't you ever do anything to hurt Mary. If you do, you'll have me to whip."

He said it good-naturedly. But Espy knew he meant it. "Look, Arch," he said with a smile, "I'm not here to try to make anybody out a thief. I'm just here to see if we can get the outfit to making a little more money. Got to keep the Bank of England strong, you know."

A girl stepped out of one of the rooms in the back of McCavitt's saloon, closing the door behind her. She looked around, spotted McCavitt, and came walking toward him, smiling. She wore a gray silk dress, cut low at the neck and clinging tightly to an amply-rounded figure. Espy had no trouble in classifying her, although he knew that she fitted in somewhere near the top of her class.

Arch stood up quickly, catching her hand and leading her to the table. "Lilybelle," he said, grinning, "I want you to meet an old *compadre* of mine, Espy Norwood. We used to cowboy together, way back when the Guadalupe Mountains were just holes in the ground. Espy, this is Lilybelle."

No, sir, Espy thought, Arch hadn't changed a bit. But his taste wasn't bad. Lilybelle was strikingly pretty. And her blue eyes were bright and intelligent, not empty and dumb as in so many such girls.

"I have to come in and check up on Arch occasionally," she said, her fingers running gently through Arch's reddish hair. Real affection softened her voice. "His arithmetic never was much good. He forgets to count his drinks sometimes."

Arch shrugged. "Lilybelle watches after me. She henpecks me like an old wife."

And Espy could tell that Arch liked it.

When Lilybelle had returned to the back room, Espy chuckled. "Thought you said there weren't any girls in here."

Arch flushed, still grinning. "There aren't. Not for the general public, anyway. That's strictly the property of the house."

As Espy started to leave, Arch took his hand. "You be careful, cowboy. I remember the last syndicate man who went out there. He's dead."

"But that was an accident—wasn't it?"

Arch frowned, then nodded. "Yeah. Yeah, I guess it was. But just the same, you be careful."

A deep worry dragged heavily at Espy as he walked out into the sandy street and started back afoot toward the lantern-lit hotel. Arch had been cautious about it, but he had made it plain—Espy had better watch his step. So there *was* something wrong, somewhere.

In his room, Espy struck a match on the sole of his boot and relighted the lamp, his face twisting to the sharp bite of burning sulphur in his nostrils. He straightened suddenly, in alarm. Kenny's bed was empty.

At a glance Espy saw that the boy's clothes were

gone from where he had draped them across the straight back of a rawhide-bottomed chair. He swung out into the hall, his heartbeat quickening.

Down the short hall he saw the yellow flicker of lamplight through an open doorway. Maybe somebody there had seen the kid. Espy strode hurriedly to the door, then stopped abruptly. There Kenny sat, comfortable in a high-backed rocking chair. Talking pleasantly to him were the two young women Espy had seen in the dining room.

The older of the two saw Espy first. Arising, she smiled warmly. Somehow, she didn't look so plain now as she had at first. There was a fetching comeliness to her face. "Come in, Mr. Norwood. We've been trying to make friends with your son."

Relief eased through Espy. He relaxed, returning her smile. "What happened, Kenny?"

The boy hesitated in answering him. The woman said, "Some cowboys were racing their horses down the street a while ago, hollering and raising Cain. The noise woke the boy up. He found himself in the dark, in a strange room. Naturally he was scared.

"We saw him come out into the hall, and we invited him to come in and talk with us till his father got back."

Espy smiled. "You get much conversation out of him?"

The younger woman answered that. "Not much. He's pretty shy. About all we found out was that you all are on your way to the Figure 4."

Her blue eyes studied him with interest. "Are you a cattle buyer?"

Espy stood there awkwardly, his hat heavy in his hands. "Well, yes and no. That's my usual business. But I'm not down here to buy cattle this time."

The girl made a mock frown. "Oh? That's too bad. We always welcome a cattle buyer out at the Figure 4."

The surprise showed in his face. Apologetically she said, "I'm sorry, I forgot to tell you who we are. Mr. Norwood, this is Helen Kirk." She swung her slender hand back toward the older woman, the one with the easy, warming smile. Espy bowed, bending slightly forward from the waist with the inborn chivalry of the old-time cowboy.

"Helen's husband is Sam Kirk, foreman of the Figure 4 for a good many years now," the girl said.

Espy waited for the girl's name, but he guessed it even before she spoke again.

"I'm Mary Bowman. Frank Bowman was my father."

Espy studied her a moment. "Then you're the one I want to see, I guess. Colonel Judkins sent me."

"The colonel?" Her eyes widened. "You're not English. I had begun to believe the syndicate employed nothing but Englishmen."

Espy told her, "They slipped this time. I've never been east of Kansas City."

Solemnly she said, "I'm sorry the colonel didn't send me word, but I can guess why he sent you. And I think you can take a good report back to him.

"I'll be a good manager, Mr. Norwood. I worked with Dad enough to know pretty well how he ran things. The colonel will have nothing to worry about."

Suddenly uneasy, Espy asked, "Didn't you get a letter from the colonel, about me?"

She shook her head.

She doesn't know why I'm here, he thought bleakly. And he knew suddenly that she would take it hard when she *did* find out.

In her blue eyes he saw a silent strength, a driving determination. He knew instinctively that she had stepped into her father's boots with firm resolution. Having someone wrest the managership from her now, without warning, would hit her like the strike of a club. Somehow, Espy knew she wouldn't break easily. She probably wouldn't break at all. She'd fight.

Just as well tell her now, he argued with himself. He had the words, but he couldn't say them. Tomorrow, maybe. Or later, at the ranch. He'd wait until the time was right. For he found himself liking this girl, liking the solid strength he saw in her. Maybe he could find a way that wouldn't hurt so much.

Walking with Kenny back to their room, Espy passed a man in the nearly-dark hallway. Wobbly on his feet, the man stopped, propping himself against the wall to stare at Espy. His heavy breath reached far out ahead of him. Espy recognized him as the man who had come weaving into the dining room earlier. Espy gave him a cold passing glance, then turned in through his open door, Kenny following closely behind him.

When Espy's door closed, the whiskered man staggered on down the hall. He stopped and pounded on the women's door. Mary Bowman opened it cautiously. Seeing him, she let the door swing open. Her eyes brittle, she placed her hands on her slim hips. "All right, Uncle Gid, what do you want? Money?"

He blustered with a thick tongue, "Do you think I'm one to go begging off of my kinfolks?"

Her answer was crisp. "Yes! You sponged off of Dad for years. How much do you want?"

He shook his head, muttering something under his breath. "I ain't looking for money. I just wanted to know something. That man who left here—was his name Norwood?"

"Yes, Espy Norwood. The colonel sent him."

"Did he tell you why?"

A worried tone edged into her voice. "Not exactly. I guess he's here to see how things are going since Dad died."

Gid Bowman shook his shaggy head, looking down the hall toward Norwood's door. "I didn't figure he'd tell you right off. He's come to take the place away from you. He didn't tell you that, did he, Mary?"

She grabbed him by the shoulders and shook him sharply. "What are you talking about?"

"He's here to take over the ranch. He's going to be the manager now. *Him*, Mary, not you. You're out. For ten years that ranch was yours and your dad's. Now he's going to shove you out.

"The syndicate's been trying to do it ever since they bought in. Your dad finally saw that. You better wake up too, Mary. Wake up before you find yourself without that ranch."

Her lips drew thin. Color flooded her cheeks. "You're lying."

He shook his head. "Ask *him*. Ask him if I'm lying."

She stood uncertainly in the doorway, her fists clenched. Then determinedly she shoved past the half-drunken man and strode angrily down the hall. She pounded on Espy Norwood's door.

Espy saw at a glance the way her blue eyes were crackling. It took him by surprise.

"Are you sure you told me all of it, Mr. Norwood?"

"All of it? I'm afraid I don't savvy, ma'am."

Her finger pointed straight at him, like a bayonet. "Did the colonel send you here to take the manager-ship away from me?"

Uncomfortably Espy tried to feel out his ground like a horse in deep mud. "It's not exactly that way,

Miss Bowman. He didn't know you'd figured on being the manager yourself. He figured . . ."

She cut him off, her voice sharp as barbed wire. "He figured that with Dad gone he could run this place to suit himself—that it wouldn't be hard to take it away from a woman. But he'll find out differently, Norwood, I promise you that."

Her eyes blazed. "This is one woman who knows what belongs to her. And she knows how to keep it. You'd better go back where you came from, mister. You've never seen trouble like the trouble you'll run into if you try to take my ranch away from me!"

And while Espy stood there open-mouthed, trying to think of an answer, she turned and strode back down the hall.

5

Espy headed the mules southeastward, down a wagon road the livery stable hostler had pointed out to him. The road was a plain one, well-carved in the prairie sod by the wide iron tires of freight wagons that had found the shortest, yet the easiest, route for their teams of mules and oxen.

The morning carried them across a gentle rolling country which fell back toward the broken ground and the brushy draws of the cap rock. Far as a man could see, there was little or no timber to break the easy swell and fall of the great domain of grass. It was a cow country. Spring rains had brought the short grass up to boot-top level and more. The flag tops bent downward in reverence to the ever-searching wind, the ceaseless wind working southward from an endless sweep of open prairie that stretched most of the way to Canada.

By a wagon-seat guess, Espy figured they were about halfway to the Figure 4 headquarters by the time he reached into a box and brought out the cold lunch he had fixed up in the hotel dining room.

Kenny wolfed cold steak and cold biscuits. Watching him, Espy smiled. There was a heap of satisfaction in watching a hungry boy eat. Made a man remember how good some things had tasted to him once. Made him wish the maturity of years hadn't robbed him of the simple pleasure which a boy could get out of a meal, be it hot, cold, or indifferent.

"Twenty-five or thirty miles out, the trail skirts by the west side of a big lake," the hostler had said. "It forks two ways there. You just take the right-hand fork and keep bearing south. You'll get there by and by."

Espy found the lake, or rather the lake bed. Weeds stood green and rank, and the grass was far taller than on the sloping land that shed its water into the sprawling natural basin. There was no water in it now, however. Spring rains had been good, that much was apparent. But there had been no rain in the last couple of months. The prairie grass had begun to burn a light brown under the summer sun, and the team's hoofs stirred up a nose-pinching smell of dry dust.

The right-hand fork led on into rougher country, where the green foliage of scattered mesquite and cedar brush broke into the even brown of the curing grass.

The mules sensed the horsemen before Espy saw them. The animals poked their long ears forward and lifted their heads in sudden interest. Just ahead, the wagon road skirted the edge of a mesquite thicket, which followed down a long draw toward another dry lake. Four horsemen moved out from the thicket and reined up in the trail, a hundred yards ahead.

One of the men swung down easily and dropped

the reins. He leaned his shoulder lazily against his saddle and waited there, watching Espy's buckboard. He was a big man, six feet tall, and maybe an inch or so more. He was broad-shouldered and black-bearded, and instantly Espy remembered him. This man had walked into the dining room last night with the florid-faced drunk.

The man's eyes challenged Espy. They were eyes black as the thick mat of whiskers on his square jaw. Espy reined up almost abreast of him. The man took a step forward. The black eyes raked Espy, shifted a second to the boy, then lifted to Espy's face again. His voice was almost a growl.

"You're another Englishman on your way to the Figure 4, ain't you?"

A quick resentment moved in Espy. "I'm on my way to the Figure 4."

The black-bearded man scowled. "We got no place for foreigners here. This country is for Americans. So turn that rig around and head it back to where you came from."

Anger smoldered in Espy, waiting for one quick breath to explode it into flame. "I've come a long way to get here. I don't intend to quit now."

The big man rocked back on his high heels, the beginnings of a hard grin breaking across his broad mouth, his knotty fists lifting. "Been hoping you'd say that," he spoke. "I been looking forward to thrashing me an Englishman. Git down from that rig."

Espy made no move. The three horsemen drew guns. The big man jerked his head sideways, motioning toward them. "They mean business. No telling what might happen if guns was to go to popping. Might even hurt that boy there. You better climb down, like I told you."

Boxed. There was no way out of this, Espy knew. And the big man outweighed him by forty pounds.

Kenny spoke out in a frightened, high-pitched voice. "Daddy, tell him you're not . . ."

"Hush, son."

Climbing down, Espy wondered how the big man had known of his coming.

He stood little chance, he knew, unless his lighter weight might make him quicker on his feet. And unless he could use surprise . . .

As his foot touched the ground, Espy's hand reached behind the buckboard seat. His fingers closed upon the handle of a traveling bag. With all the strength in him he hurled the bag right into the big man's face. He sprang in behind it, driving a hard right fist straight into the rider's eye. In the two seconds that the man staggered back, Espy drove one blow into his prickly jaw and another into his stomach.

His opponent cried out in rage and surged at him, his fists swinging like a pair of sledges. This was a bulldog kind of fighter. He would use his weight and his mighty strength to win. He could afford to swap blows because his own would be the hardest.

Espy managed to dodge the first swinging fists and crowd in. He landed some hard licks to the big face which was reddened with blistering rage. But he didn't expect that luck to hold. The big fists began to rock him. Pain ripped him. Half the breath was jarred out of him. It was as if a big bull had pinned him against a fence and was slamming its huge head into him. Espy's fists weren't hitting so hard now.

But the other man was slower, too. His lips were broken, and blood explored the heavy black whiskers. One eye was swelling shut.

Then, suddenly, Espy got his chance. The big man

missed him with a broad swing of his fist, and the dark face was wide open for a hard wallop. Espy swung. He felt a savage exultation as his fist drove into the other eye.

The big rider squalled out and doubled over against the slashing pain. Breathing hard, Espy pressed what advantage he had won, driving the man back, and back again, until he fell against the buckboard. The mules, badly boogered, jumped in the traces and rocked the rig. Then Espy had a new worry, that they would run away, dragging the helpless boy with them.

Blindly the big man rushed Espy. Espy stepped aside far enough to take nothing worse than a glancing lick. Almost exhausted, he swayed back in then and started slashing his tired fists mercilessly into the big man's face and stomach. He realized he had won. There was grim satisfaction in the knowledge. But he knew they wouldn't leave him alone. One of the other riders would take up the fight, and Espy couldn't last. He was almost ready to cave in now.

He saw one rider step down from the saddle, and he swayed around to face him. But he was powerless to help himself. He saw the gun barrel lift and arc toward his head, and he couldn't dodge it. Pain exploded in him. He dropped to his hands and knees and tried to stop himself there. But the gun struck him again, and he toppled forward into a black hole that had no bottom.

The rider holstered his gun and looked at Espy Norwood, sprawled limply in the dry grass.

"Got a head as hard as a rock," he muttered, half in admiration. "That's the fightingest Englishman ever I saw."

The black-bearded man was still down on one knee, rubbing his bruised and battered face and leaving angry smears of red. His coarse hair was tousled like the shaggy coat of a big black dog. He was talking to himself under his breath.

The smaller rider caught him under the arms and helped him sway to his feet. "Git up, Quirt. The fight's over, and you'd just as well run up the Union Jack. The Englishman whipped you."

Kenny Norwood had sat on the buckboard seat in ashen-faced silence. Now an old loyalty came rushing back to him, mixed with a flood of anger.

"He's *not* an Englishman," he bawled. "He's from Texas. And he'll whip all of you, you just wait and see!"

"Shut up!" the big man scowled. Cursing, he kicked Espy Norwood in the ribs.

"By God, he'll wish he'd never even heard of the Figure 4," he exploded. "You, Jake, unhitch them mules. Mose, you and Pete throw down that stuff from the buckboard. Scatter it from hell to breakfast."

Kenny jumped down and knelt beside his father. His widened eyes watched in terror while the men wreaked havoc with the clothes, the bedding, the saddles and gear on the buckboard.

Finally satisfied, the four men climbed back upon their horses. The big man had to have help. His eyes swollen almost shut, he reined in close to the boy. "Listen now, kid. When your old man wakes up, tell him this is only a sample. We're taking the mules. Maybe the long walk back to Mobeetie will give him time to do a little thinking. Tell him he better not come back. Next time, they'll have to carry him away in a box."

The four men wheeled their horses around and disappeared into the thicket, driving the two mules before them. Kenny listened until the hoofbeats faded away to the southwest. Then he got up and hunted for the water jug. He found it on the ground. Luckily, they hadn't broken it. He took a handkerchief from his pocket, poured water on it, and started wiping his father's face, fighting the panic that throbbed in his quick heartbeat and held a tight grip on his small throat.

"Daddy," he pleaded, "Daddy, wake up."

Full consciousness was slow in coming back to Espy. Nausea came with it. He clasped his hands over his stomach, where pain cut like the sharp swipe of a bowie knife. He turned away from Kenny and let the sickness come up out of him. The nausea ebbed then, but the pain throbbed on, numbing pain that beat at every part of him.

He took the wet handkerchief from his son's hand. Kenny knelt in front of him, dumb with shock, his eyes sick as they stared at his father's raw, bruised face.

"It's all right, son," Espy said in a low, tight voice. "It's over with now. Everything's going to be all right."

Kenny blurted it out in a voice shrill with excitement. "They took our mules, Daddy. They scattered out everything we had. They said if we ever came back they'd kill you."

With Kenny's help, Espy swayed to his feet. He leaned heavily against the buckboard, waiting for strength. It was slow in returning.

"Made a right smart of a mess, didn't they?" he said, forcing a grin for the boy's benefit. It hurt, and he let it go. "We better get started cleaning it up."

Espy made an effort, but it was no use. He sat on the ground, leaning back against a buckboard

wheel, his arms folded tightly across his middle. He
watched while Kenny gathered up their belongings,
scattered out over two acres of grass. Grunting, the
boy lifted Espy's saddle up into the buckboard. Then
he picked up his own, a boy's-size saddle which still
smelled strongly of new leather. Espy had bought it
for him in Dodge City. He had wondered at the time
if Kenny would ever use it. The boy had shown no
such inclination.

Kenny began picking up their clothes and shoving
them back into the traveling bags. He held up one of
Espy's shirts which had been ripped in two.

"Might as well throw it away, son," Espy said,
shaking his head. "And anything else that's torn up
that bad."

A good part of the clothing was. Mentally Espy
marked it off as a loss. Not a bad one, though. Aside
from the beating, it was the loss of the little mules
which bothered him most. They had cost a hundred
dollars in Dodge. Man didn't find a team like that
just anywhere.

When their gear had been placed back in the buckboard, Kenny asked worriedly, "What are we going
to do now?"

"We might wait here a week and not see anybody,
son. We just as well start walking."

"Back to town?"

Espy shook his head. "We're about as close to the
Figure 4 as we are to town. We'll go that way."

Fear looked out of Kenny's eyes. "But, Daddy, they
said—" He swallowed the rest of it in resignation.

Espy slung a canteen over his shoulder, dropped a
little food into a sack, and started walking. Kenny
was close behind him.

By the time he had gone a hundred yards, Espy

knew it was no use. He let the canteen slip from his shoulder, then eased himself to the ground, breathing hard.

"It's no go, son. I couldn't walk from here to that rise yonder." He grinned crookedly. "Looks like another dry camp for us tonight."

Aching, Espy stretched out in the shade under the buckboard to rest. Tomorrow he might be able to make it. Not today.

He had lain there perhaps half an hour when Kenny looked up, then jumped to his feet. The boy pointed back down the Mobeetie trail. "Somebody's coming."

Espy sat up and looked. A buckboard. He squinted, trying to see better. But his eyes were bruised and watery.

Kenny said, "It's the two ladies, Daddy."

Mary Bowman was driving. She reined her buckboard to a halt. She took in the whole scene in one glance. Her eyes were wide for just a moment. Then they hardened.

"What happened?"

Espy said, "Reception committee."

Mrs. Kirk's face was white. Her eyes softened in quick sympathy. Instantly she climbed down, looking apprehensively at the boy.

"Are you all right, son?"

Kenny nodded. "But they hurt Daddy."

The kindly woman turned her sympathetic gaze toward Espy. "How bad? Any bones broken?"

He shook his head. "No. There's nothing that won't heal."

She looked at Espy's face, gently searching over it with her fingers. "Couple of bad cuts there," she said softly. "We'll fix those soon as we get to the ranch."

Espy said pointedly, "Miss Bowman hasn't said she was going to take us."

He glanced up at the girl. She gave him a rocky look, one that set him to wondering.

"We'll take you," said the girl. "If it was just you, I'd leave you. But we can't leave that boy. Throw your things on the back. One of the cowboys will come tomorrow and get the rig."

Kenny transferred their belongings. There was barely room for them all because the women were bringing several packages from town, along with a couple of traveling bags.

Mrs. Kirk asked wonderingly, "Now, why would anybody want to do a thing like this to you?"

"They talked like they figured I was an Englishman, and they just don't like Englishmen." Espy watched Mary Bowman's face for a reaction. He saw none. He hadn't been fooled by that business about being English. He knew that was just an excuse. Briefly he described the men.

Helen Kirk mused. "Big man, black eyes, black beard. A good many men around here could fit a description like that."

Kenny spoke up. "One of them called him Quirt."

Helen Kirk glanced quickly at Mary Bowman. Something flickered in the girl's blue eyes, then covered up again.

"Quirt Wolford," Mrs. Kirk said. "There are a good many tough men around here, but there's a difference between tough and bad. Quirt Wolford's bad."

Kenny squeezed onto the seat beside the women. Espy hunched in the back, his legs hanging over. The bouncing over the rough spots in the trail doubled the ache that throbbed through him.

Presently Mary Bowman looked back at him. "You must be a tough man yourself, Norwood."

"Why?"

"If you hadn't been, you'd have turned back after what happened to you. Didn't you want to?"

Espy narrowed his eyes, studying her. "No. If anything, it just settled a few doubts."

She looked away from him, to the trail ahead of her. He stared at the back of the wide, flowered bonnet she wore. He wondered, and the wonder changed to a half-angry certainty. Someone had sicked Quirt Wolford onto him. Who else could it have been?

6

Frank Bowman had chosen his ranch site well when he had come here ten years or more before. The Panhandle had been almost wide open then, and he had been able to make his own choice. The northern part of his vast range was mostly open, rolling plains, with a vast sweep of grass stretching on and on, losing itself against a clear, blue sky. The southern part began with the breaks. The headquarters had been built up toward the head of a great, wide canyon. From there, the farther southward a rider went the rougher and brushier the land became.

It was to this country that cattle could drift for protection against the howling blue blizzards that would come roaring down from the high plains. Again, it was here that they could come when rainfall was short and the natural lakes went dry in the higher country. Here several springs burst forth from broken land and gave birth to welcome creeks which carried their precious water by tortuous routes through the rough country.

At near dusk, Helen Kirk turned in the seat. "We're almost there. Around that next hill, you can see it."

Rounding the hill, they heard a boy's shrill yelping and the sharp, frightened bawl of a calf. A brown and white spotted calf rushed toward them, fast as it could run. Right on its heels a young cowboy came spurring, swinging a rope over his head. The rope sailed out over the calf's shoulder and missed. The boy checked his horse's speed, disappointed. Then he saw the buckboard. He jerked up on the reins, half scared.

"Joe," Helen Kirk called sharply, "you stop running that calf. Come here!"

Head down, the boy nudged the horse with his heel and started toward them in a slow walk. Taking a long time about it, he coiled his rope, letting the loop drag on the ground behind him until he pulled it up and finished the coils.

He was ten, maybe eleven. He had a freckled face and bowl haircut, and he looked to be as full of mischief as a cat in a sewing box. One front tooth was chipped just a little.

Mrs. Kirk said firmly, "Joe, you know your dad has told you twenty times not to be running these calves and roping everything that moves."

Hanging his head, the boy answered, "Aw, Mom, I wasn't hurting anything. Besides—"

The woman cut in, her voice suddenly anxious. "Joe, what's that cut across your face?"

It was only a little scratch. "Got it chasing an old wild cow through the brush. It don't amount to nothing."

Her voice carried a world of love and worry. "You've got to be more careful, son. A thing like that could get you hurt badly. Now you follow along with us. We're going home."

Freckled Joe Kirk stared at Kenny Norwood. His mischievous brown eyes studied Kenny from head to toe, and a crooked grin broke across his wide mouth. Kenny shrank back a little.

As the buckboard rolled on into the big ranch headquarters, Helen Kirk pointed out the various buildings. "That," she told Espy, pointing to the big rock house which stood on a small knoll, overlooking the rest of the place, "is the one Mr. Frank built. It's Mary's now. Down there, that long half-dugout, is the bunkhouse. And next to it is the kitchen."

Two frame houses had risen up between the old dugouts and the big rock house. "That one nearest the bunkhouse is ours, Sam's, Joe's, and mine. Mr. Frank built it for us three years ago, and moved us out of one of the dugouts."

She pointed. "That other lumber building, nearest to the rock house, will be yours, I guess. It's the syndicate quarters. The lumber came down by freight wagon all the way from the railroad at Dodge City. You could have a big brick home in the city for what those two cost, with the freight and all. But a woman sets a lot of store in having a frame house instead of a dugout. Not many houses like them in this country."

Espy nodded. For his own money he had rather have had a snug dugout than a raw house set up on blocks, at the mercy of the everlasting prairie wind. Good dugout was warmer in the winter and cooler in the summer. But, like Mrs. Kirk said, a frame house was the measure of well-being out here.

Mary Bowman stopped the buckboard in front of the house that would be Espy's and Kenny's. They unloaded it.

"I'll go down and tell the cook you're coming," she

said. Her voice still held a chill. She flipped the reins, and the buckboard pulled away.

Mrs. Kirk went into the house with Espy and Kenny. It was almost dark. She found a lamp and lighted it. The house had only two rooms, a front room, or parlor, and a bedroom with two beds in it. Bedding was stacked on an open shelf. Mrs. Kirk pulled away a quilt. She sneezed at the settled dust which came drifting down.

"Hasn't been anyone in here since we gathered up Geoffrey Spence's belongings and shipped them to his people. You heard about Mr. Spence?"

Espy nodded.

Helen Kirk shook her head sympathetically. "He was a nice man. I can't say that for the others who came out here. Most of them have been . . . Well, they were a real burden to bear. Acted as if they were going to take over the whole place, as if no one else had any rights at all.

"That's what's really the matter with Mary. I hope you'll have patience with her. She learned to hate the others, and she can't believe that you'll be any different."

Espy's eyes met hers. "How do *you* know I will?"

The question was a little too direct. She dropped her gaze, her cheeks coloring. "I'm a pretty good judge of people, Mr. Norwood. And I like you."

She busied herself in inspecting the room. She shook her head. "It's hopeless until I get it swept out," she said. "I'll do that while you're eating supper. But first you'd better come over to our house, Mr. Norwood. I'll tend to those cuts on your face."

At the front door she paused. Embarrassed, she said, "If . . . if the boy needs to go out back, there's a lantern hanging outside, by the door."

Helen Kirk's house was built much like the other. It was bigger, with a kitchen, a bedroom, and a front room. Espy knew the wind would sometimes come whistling through the stripping of the outside walls. But a layer of bright, flowered wallpaper helped seal the house.

In one corner of the front room was a rumpled cot, evidently the boy's. Cheery curtains hung about the windows. Although dust had settled during her absence, and the cluttered kitchen showed the results of a short period of batching by a man and a boy, Espy knew the house was always expertly and lovingly kept.

Helen Kirk went into the kitchen to get some antiseptic from a cabinet. Espy looked over the furnishings. Most of them were plain, simple, and built for utility. Rawhide-bottomed chairs. Brightly-dyed throw rugs, made of strips of sacking. But there were evidences of a generous husband—a fine heavy china cabinet, and a huge Charter Oak stove.

Espy flinched against the burning of the antiseptic. Kenny, watching from a respectable distance, flinched with him. Mrs. Kirk's fingers were gentle and sure, and Espy found himself enjoying their touch, even though they brought momentary pain as she treated the abrasions on his face. Somehow he felt comfortable here. Comfortable like he had been with Jeannie, a long time ago. This home was much like their own had been.

A boy's footsteps clumped loudly on the porch outside. Young Joe Kirk shoved through the door. A little brown dog nosed right in behind him. Joe opened the door wider and gently shoved the dog back outside. "No, Slats," he said softly, "Mom's back now."

Espy saw Helen Kirk strain to hold back her laughter. But she managed to make her voice firm. "You've been letting that dog in while I've been gone, haven't you?"

"No, Mom. Well, not much, anyway."

"The woodbox is almost empty. You'd better go right on out back and bring in some more wood. I want the box full this time. Right to the brim."

Espy looked at Kenny. "You go on out and help him, son. You boys had just as well start getting acquainted."

Kenny wasn't enthusiastic about it. He held back until Espy told him a second time. Then he went out with worry in his face. Espy knew what the trouble was. Kid like Joe could throw a scare into a city boy pretty easily, if he wanted to. Joe looked as if he would probably want to.

"That's a healthy-looking son you have," Espy said when the boys were gone. "Favors you some."

She smiled. "Thank you. But the way Joe looks right now, I don't know if that's much of a compliment or not."

Espy said, "He looks just like a growing cowboy ought to look. I wouldn't worry about him. Now, if he was neat and clean and quiet all the time, I *might* worry about him."

Neat, and clean, and quiet. Like Kenny Norwood.

Mrs. Kirk replied, "Well, Joe surely won't fit that description. But what boy wouldn't be on the wild side, way out here like this? Why, he's never even had a friend his own age to play with."

"What about schooling?"

"I teach him. I was a schoolteacher when I met Sam."

A happy thought struck Espy. "Say, maybe you could teach Kenny, too. I'd pay you."

She smiled, shaking her head. She was almost pretty

when she smiled. A man never noticed her plainness the second time.

"I'd be glad to teach him, right along with Joe. And I won't take a nickel. It'll be worth it, just to get a playmate for our boy."

When she had finished doctoring his face, Espy stood up, his hat in his hands. "I sure do like your place here, Mrs. Kirk. It probably makes you the envy of every woman in the country. Your husband must be very good to you."

"Sam's a good husband," she replied. "I'm a lucky woman."

Espy smiled at her, meaning exactly what he said. "And he's a lucky man."

The kitchen was a long half-dugout, running along the edge of a slope. Its back wall was solid earth, where the structure had been carved out of the ground. The front was of pickets and sod. Four small windows had been placed along the long front wall. The door hung open.

Espy had to duck to walk through it. He saw the cook standing beside a big iron stove, sharpening a long butcher knife and scowling. They eyed each other for a minute. The cook was a short, slender man whose pants were two sizes too big for him and who wouldn't weigh a hundred and thirty pounds soaking wet. He looked as if he had acid in his veins instead of blood.

"You're the new syndicate man." It was a question, but the way he said it made it a stated fact. Resentment was evident in his rasp-rough voice.

Espy nodded. "I'm Espy Norwood. This is my son, Kenny."

The cook grunted. "My name's Jess Cooley." He stared in disapproval. "You're another Englishman, I guess. Well, I hope you brung your own tea with you. If you didn't, by Jasper, you ain't agonna git any."

Espy grinned then. He'd known half a hundred wagon cooks, and most of them were like this. Grouchiness was expected of them, and they generally obliged. It was more in pretense than in earnest. Let a cook get too easy and first thing he knew the cowboys would be running over him. Keep them at a distance and keep them about half boogered. That was the cook's theory. That way, he got along fine.

Espy said, "My preference runs to coffee, Jess. Black coffee, and not much water in it."

Cooley paused in his sharpening of the knife. His scowl eased. "You don't talk like the rest of them. You talk plain, sensible English."

"Maybe that's because I learned my English in Texas. I was born here."

Cooley blinked and laid down the knife. "A Texas man, by Jasper. Well now, that's an improvement."

The cook's hard shell crumbled away. He walked over and shook Espy's hand. "Miss Mary came storming in here a while ago and told me to fix supper for the new syndicate man. She was too mad to talk, so I naturally figured it was another one of them kind."

Jess Cooley reached into a bucket and brought out some eggs. "Don't you let on to the cowboys, but I'll fry you some hen fruit. Mighty few outfits in this country have got a flock of laying hens. Between the coyotes and these chicken-hungry cowboys, it's all I can do to keep them."

Shortly he set down a platter of eggs and fried steak, along with some warmed-over biscuits. Kenny cleaned up two eggs and a piece of steak and asked for more, thereby earning the cook's undying friendship.

"Nothing I like better than a boy with a good appetite," he grinned, breaking another egg into his skillet. "You'll have to go some to outeat Sam Kirk's boy, though. He can get around more food than six good men."

The door swung open and a young cowboy stepped in, ducking to keep from bumping his head on the jamb. "Hey there, Greasy, what you got cooked that a man could hold down?"

Cooley scowled at him. He pulled out his shiny old pocket watch and pointed at it. "Supper's at six-thirty. You missed it. Now, Cotton Dulaney, you just hitch up your belt a notch and wait till morning."

The kid named Cotton sailed his hat into a corner, rubbing white from the gyprock plaster of the earth wall. He ate a cold biscuit, then grimaced. "A man could lose a tooth on one of these. Say, what's that, eggs? I like mine with the sunny side up."

The cook grunted, "I'll kick you out of here with *your* sunny side up. How come you not to be here when you was supposed to?"

"Had an errand to run for Sam. I found where somebody had chased some cattle off. I'd've trailed them myself, only Sam said no. He said just go to town and get the deputy sheriff."

"You weren't gone long enough to get to town."

Dulaney shook his head. His hair was almost cottony in color. Plain enough where he got his name.

"No, I just rode down to Gid's ranch and found the deputy there. He always is. Helps Gid try to drink up all the whisky that Lee & Reynolds can freight down from the railroad."

In disgust Jess Cooley grunted, "And I reckon he promised he'd find the cattle."

"Sure. He'll get right on it. Soon's he sobers up, about the middle of next week."

Cooley scowled. "Someday maybe this outfit will start hunting down cow thieves itself instead of waiting around for a deputy sheriff that don't even know which way is up."

He broke two more eggs into the skillet. He growled at Cotton, "You tell any of them other yahoos that I fixed you some eggs, and next time I'll just let you go hungry."

Cotton turned to face Espy. Kidlike, he made no effort to conceal his curiosity. "What happened to you, feller? Fall out of a wagon or something?"

Espy replied, "Something like that."

The young cowboy studied Espy's face, "Well, I hope the other feller looks worse," he grinned.

He jerked his thumb at Cooley. "This old horned toad's too impolite to introduce anybody. Cotton Dulaney's my name. I'm one of the top hands around here."

Jess Cooley growled. "Top hand, my left hind foot. He can't pour water out of a bucket if the instructions are printed on the bottom."

Espy shook the young puncher's hand. "I'm Espy Norwood. I'm here for the syndicate."

"What's the matter," Cotton asked, "they run out of Englishmen?"

Then he frowned. "I oughtn't to've said that, I reckon. I got along fine with Geoffrey Spence. Fact is, it was me that found him . . . after the accident."

Espy looked up sharply. He filed that information away in his mind. He might want to use it later.

"You said Sam Kirk sent you for the deputy. Have you ever trailed any stolen cattle yourself?"

Cotton nodded, his mouth full of egg. "Yeah, but I lost the trail. And Sam gave me hell about it, afterwards. He's like Mr. Frank used to be. Says trailing cow thieves is a job for the law. He doesn't want any Figure 4 cowboys getting killed doing it."

"Has that ever happened?"

"No, but there was one old boy got shot in the arm a couple of years ago. Mr. Frank never did let us chase rustlers again."

Espy wondered at that. Not many ranchmen would restrain their cowboys from trailing thieves, and even administering quick justice beneath a cottonwood limb or an uptilted wagon tongue. "Does the law ever catch any?"

"Now and again. It don't do much to them, though. Tells them to leave the country and not come back. Some do, some don't."

Espy had finished his supper. He hadn't been able to eat much. Now he toyed with his coffee cup, pouring more coffee although he didn't really have a taste for it.

"Cotton," he said presently, "I'd like to have somebody show me over the ranch. Could I get you to do it?"

Behind the words was an unspoken curiosity about stolen cattle, and about things in general. Lots of times a man found out more from an observant kid cowboy than he could from the owner or even the foreman.

"Sure," Cotton said, "suits me fine. You better ask Sam Kirk first, though. After all, he's the boss."

Espy nodded. "Sure, I'll square it with him."

He knew he really wouldn't, however, not until

he had come back. He didn't want anybody coaching Cotton as to what to say and what to keep quiet about.

"All right," Cotton said, pulling away from the table. "I'll be ready just as soon as this old slouch here can get breakfast in the morning."

Jess Cooley shook his butcher knife at the cowboy, his voice tough as rawhide. "You watch how you talk about your betters, boy, or I'll get you put on the wood wagon, helping old Pancho."

But he was grinning when Cotton Dulaney walked whistling out of the kitchen. "A good boy, that Cotton. He'll make a real ranch foreman someday, if he doesn't break his neck first in some kid foolishness."

Mary Bowman was waiting beside the saddle shed when Sam Kirk wearily rode in. Swinging stiffly down from his bay horse, Kirk looked at her in surprise.

"Why, hello, Mary. You sure must've hurried. Didn't expect you two back for a couple more days."

Medium tall, Sam Kirk was a few years short of forty, but he looked older. He had been handsome once, and was handsome still, in a way. He had a strong, angular face that might have been carved out of oak. There was a directness about him, and a kind of basic honesty that Mary had always liked.

He peered closer at the girl, then frowned. "What's the matter, Mary?"

She tried to keep control of herself. "Sam, they're . . . they're . . ."

Then she was sobbing. She leaned against the pole fence, digging her fingernails into the dead bark and trying to choke down her emotion. Sam Kirk stepped up beside her, placing his hands comfortingly on her shoulders. She was thankful for his strength. Times like this, he was almost a big brother to her. She got hold of her voice in a minute.

"Sam, they're trying to take my ranch away from me."

"They?" He puzzled a moment. "The syndicate?"

She nodded, her jaw setting firmly. "I'm sorry to break down like this. All day I've been trying to hold on, trying to be tough. The glove just won't fit."

Kirk nodded sympathetically. "Maybe you'd better tell me about it, Mary."

She told him about Espy Norwood. "He says the syndicate has the right to name the manager. But that can't be, Sam, can it? This place was Dad's—Dad's and mine—for years before the syndicate was even heard of. What right have they got to come in here now and take the reins right out of my hands?"

Kirk shook his head, shock evident in his voice. "They can, Mary. It's in the contract."

"But how? How could Dad have let them do it?"

Deeply troubled, Kirk replied, "Mary, at the time, he never dreamed . . ." He hesitated. "It's a long story, and it's too late now to change it. One way or another, we'll just have to make the best of it." His voice tightened. "I promise you this—if he gets too troublesome, Mary, I'll run him off."

She shook her head. "That's already been tried. He didn't scare."

She told him about Quirt Wolford's reception. Kirk stared at her in disbelief. "Mary, *you* didn't—"

"No, I didn't have anything to do with it. But next time, maybe I will."

Kirk grinned, a cold, humorless grin. "I think that glove *could* fit you, Mary. If it comes to that, I'll help you make it fit."

After turning his horse loose and hanging up his saddle, Kirk started up the slope toward his house. He glanced once at the bunkhouse, thinking he might see if Cotton Dulaney had come back. But he changed his mind. He knew the deputy. Didn't matter much whether Cotton had found him or not. Nothing would ever come of it anyway.

He found the cookstove hot and a pan of biscuits baking in the oven. But Helen was not in the house. Glancing out the window, he could see lamplight in the syndicate house. He saw Helen step out onto the little front porch and shake dust out of a blanket.

Anger rippled in him. His wife didn't have to work for them too. If they wanted to have somebody clean up for them, why didn't they bring a valet?

He eased into his tall, hard-backed rocking chair, just now realizing how tired he really was. He pulled out his watch and checked the time. He started to slip it back into his pocket, then changed his mind. For a time he studied the inscription on the back:

"To Sam Kirk, fine foreman, fine friend. From Frank Bowman."

A veil of sadness settled over him. His fingers gently caressed the silver case. It was a new watch. Mr. Frank had given it to him only a few weeks before his death.

At the sound of Helen's footsteps, Kirk slipped the watch into his pocket and stiffly pushed to his feet.

Just inside the door, Helen Kirk stopped in surprise, joy spreading over her face. "Sam. I watched for you, but I didn't see you come in. Too dark, I guess."

"I guess."

Helen's heartbeat picked up. She took an eager step forward, hoping he would take her into his arms, this time.

But Sam placed his hands on her shoulders and gave her a quick kiss on the forehead. She took hold of his hand and squeezed it hard, covering her disappointment. She gazed fondly in his face, which was baked a deep brown by a lifetime in the sun. She wanted to run her hand through his dark hair and the glistening gray that streaked it.

"Have a good trip?" he asked her.

"Fine. But I'm glad to be home, Sam. I always miss you."

He gave her a tired smile, then dropped wearily into his chair.

"You've been working too hard again, Sam," she said worriedly. "But supper'll be ready in a few minutes. You'll feel better when you eat."

He nodded. "I'm just weary, Helen, that's all. Just tired."

She turned away, pain sharpening her face. Tired. Yes, he was terribly tired. But there was more to it than that. Much more. She had been watching it build in him for more than a year now. Like some malignant growth, the worry had eaten and burned within him, deepening the furrows in his forehead, setting new strands of gray to shining in his hair.

Yet when she had tried to help him, he had always drawn away. His answer was always the same. "Just tired, Helen. Just tired."

7

Kenny Norwood sat forlornly alone in the little frame house which was to be his home. His throat was tight, and he had fought hard to keep from sobbing in his loneliness. Looking about him in the raw, barren little room, he remembered the house where he had lived so long in Kansas City, the huge brick house with its massive furniture, its deep rugs, and the big windows which seemed to bring everything right indoors.

He had grown used to the noise which was always part of a city, even the residential areas. There were always the servants moving about downstairs, or back in the kitchen. Here there was nothing. No sound except the prairie wind whistling through a crack in the wall, and somewhere out yonder the melancholy bawling of a cow whose calf had been butchered for meat.

Espy had gotten the boy up before daylight and had taken him down to the dugout cookshack. Kenny had shrunk back from the bearded, rough-talking cowboys. He had disliked the way they all eyed him and his clean clothes with their city cut. He had winced when the one called Cotton had laughingly accused him of being a little Englishman.

"Don't let them get your goat, son," Espy had smiled later. "It's cowboy nature to hooraw a kid. They don't mean anything by it. Show them you can take it, and they'll do anything in the world for you."

Kenny hadn't answered him, for he still felt ill at ease even with his father. A stubborn resentment clung to him whenever his mind drifted back to Kansas City, and the comfortable home from which his father had dragged him.

But, even so, he had had to fight back a helpless panic when his father had saddled a horse this morning and ridden southward with the young cowboy, Cotton.

"We may be late getting back, son," Espy had said. "When it comes dinnertime, you just go on over to the cookshack. You might as well look the place over today, and get acquainted."

Kenny hadn't done much looking. Soon after his father left, he had high-tailed it back to the house. Now he sat there alone, sick at heart, loneliness a dull ache in him. He wished for a friendly word from somebody. Anybody.

It was Mrs. Kirk who brought it. She came over with a mop and a broom under her arm and a bucket of water in her hand.

"Why, Kenny," she said in surprise, "Whatever are you doing sitting here all by yourself? It's a pretty morning. You ought to go outside and play."

Kenny instinctively liked this woman. He liked the way she smiled at him, and patted him on the head. Somewhere, far back in his memory, was a vague picture of another woman who had done it that way. It had been a long time ago. He couldn't remember exactly what she looked like. But he remembered the softness of her voice when she spoke to him, and the way she smiled at him and ran her hand through his hair. Aunt Margaret had loved him, he knew that, but she hadn't been given to this kind of tenderness. It was not fitting for a person of dignity, she had once said.

"My Joe's playing out around the barn," Mrs. Kirk told Kenny. "Why don't you go out and find him? You two boys can have a lot of fun together, once you get acquainted."

Heart heavy with misgivings, Kenny left the house. He didn't think he liked Joe. He hadn't liked the way the boy had stared at him last night when they were packing in wood. Kenny turned once and looked back to see Mrs. Kirk sweeping dirt through the front door. With halting steps he moved on out to the barn. His heart was tripping with every step he took. He was like a frightened rabbit, ready to sprint for the brush.

"You look like a sissy to me!"

The voice hauled him up short. He spun on his heel. Joe Kirk was watching him from the top of a big stack of lake hay.

Joe leered belligerently at him for a full minute before he slid down in a dusty shower of hay and came striding forward, barefoot. Kenny froze. He thought of the boys he had known in private school. None of them looked like this.

The freckled boy stopped an arm's length from him and stood there regarding him solemnly, his hands on his hips. His mouth was open so Kenny could see where one front tooth was chipped a little. Kenny's heart was thumping.

"Hello," he managed to say.

"I betcha I can whip you," Joe said.

Kenny's tongue flicked out over his dry lips. "Your mother said I should come down here and get acquainted with you."

Joe wasn't going to be sidetracked. "Don't you think I can whip you?"

Kenny didn't know what to do. He had never run into a situation like this. Joe Kirk didn't look any bigger than Kenny Norwood. But the thought of a fist fight made Kenny shrink back.

"Fisticuffs are for common young ruffians," Aunt Margaret had scolded him once after he and another little boy had shoved each other into a hole of mud. Kenny had won that fight. But this one . . .

"Come on, dude," Joe Kirk challenged, bringing up his hard little fists. "Put up your dukes."

Kenny took a step backward. Joe followed him.

Then, courage leaving him, Kenny turned and ran, out past the barn and on toward the corrals that stretched beyond it. He ran and ran, and kept running until his lungs were ready to burst.

He stopped finally, humiliation spilling through him in a flood. He sat down on the ground there, chest aheave, a desperate loneliness gripping him. And with it came a rising anger, at himself, at Joe Kirk, at his father, at this whole wild country.

Far behind him, Joe Kirk stood with hands on his hips, jeering at him.

"Fraidy cat! Fraidy cat!"

A predawn start and a steady, mile-eating trot carried Espy Norwood and Cotton Dulaney to the south end of Frank Norwood's Figure 4 range by late morning. Down here it was rougher country than that farther north. It was still good grass land, but it was chopped by running creeks, by dry creek beds, and by sudden canyons with steep walls that pitched downward to rocky, broken floors. Lacing back and forth across all of it were the brushy thickets, mesquite, cedar, and in places wild china and hackberries.

Once they topped a rise and flushed a little bunch of antelope, grazing the strong, short grass. Laughing, Cotton Dulaney stepped out of the saddle and pulled his saddle gun out of its scabbard in one quick motion.

Espy wanted to stop him, hating to see anything killed without reason. But he held still, yesterday's soreness slowing him.

Cotton dropped to one knee and took careful aim at the flash of a broad white tail. The gun clicked harmlessly.

The young cowboy arose with a grin. "I don't ever really shoot them, not unless we need the meat. I just get a big kick out of knowing I could, if I wanted to."

Espy grinned with him, and a new sense of relief eased through him. He really liked this kid cowboy now. Cotton might still have his share of wild oats, but beneath it all was a basic horse sense that steadied him. He would be a really good man bye and bye, when the kid in him had worn itself away.

"Not far from here to the south line camp," Cotton said, pointing westward. "I had taken a string of horses over there and was on my way back when I cut the sign."

"Follow it far?"

"Just far enough to be sure I wasn't wrong. Last time I followed a bunch like that, Sam Kirk chewed me out so that my ears rang for a week. The way he sees it, I'm still just a kid."

A spark of humor played in Espy's gray eyes. "How old *are* you?"

"I'm . . . well, I'll be twenty-one my next birthday."

"And how long is that?"

Cotton colored. "Not quite a year."

Not much was left of the tracks. They were three days old, maybe four. Hard to tell anymore how many cattle there had been. Thirty head. Maybe forty.

A cold, hard anger began to grow in Espy, the anger that thieves always aroused. "Let's follow the trail a ways. See where they headed."

Cotton was more than ready. Grinning, he drew his six-gun and checked the load in the cylinder.

Espy shook his head. "Put that thing up, son. The trail's old. If I thought we'd run into anything dangerous, I wouldn't take you."

Cotton put the gun back where it belonged. The two rode along the old trail in silence, watching the ground.

Espy remarked, "Frank Bowman must not have been very worried about cow thieves, or he wouldn't have left it all to some sorry deputy."

Cotton shook his head. "I'm afraid Mr. Frank never realized how many cattle were being hazed off down into this brush country. His health got bad, and he never rode much the last couple of years. Never saw it for himself."

"Were there many cattle lost?"

Cotton said, "I've been working for this outfit for three years. I can tell. There aren't as many cattle down here as there used to be. It shows up some at branding time. Doesn't take as long to brand out a camp and move the chuckwagon as it used to."

After an hour or so, the dim, blown-out trail led

down into a creek. It didn't come out on the other side.

"Driving them in the water to kill the trail," Espy commented.

They followed the crooked creek an hour. Finally Espy reined up, shaking his head in slow anger. "They came out back up the creek somewhere. We missed it. Probably on one of those dry, rocky creek beds."

Without having to ask, he knew it would be easy for rustlers to get away with cattle once they got them down here to the rough country. There would be hundreds of places they could hide livestock. And from here there were several directions they could go to market them—northeast to the Oklahoma country, east to the settled parts of Texas, or west across the Panhandle to New Mexico.

"We'd just as well head back, Cotton," he said.

He knew it had been futile, following this old trail. But it had satisfied his curiosity. And it had fanned up an anger.

"Nobody's followed this trail but us," he told Cotton when they again reached the point where it had led into the creek. "No horse tracks but ours."

Cotton spat disgustedly. "Like I said, that deputy's probably still over there helping Gid drink up his whisky."

Espy's fist knotted. "How far is it to this Gid's place?"

Cotton's eyes widened, and he began to grin in anticipation, "From right here, it's three or four miles. We can be there before you know it."

"All right, then. Let's go."

Espy's face twisted as soon as he saw the place, and he spat disgustedly. "Looks like an old boar's nest," he muttered.

Not a single building stood much above ground

level. The barn was no barn at all, but only a dug-out shed in front of disintegrating pole corrals which had been thrown up with mesquite and cedar. It faced toward a larger dugout, carved into the side of a hill. This one obviously was home for the ranch owner. A tin chimney shoved up out of a sod-covered roof. Most of the structure was below ground level. There was just room enough for one small window between the ground and the roof. A set of steps led down to the door.

A man stood on these steps. As Espy and Cotton rode in, he quickly ducked through the door and out of sight. But not so quickly that Espy did not get a sudden impression of wide shoulders and coal-black whiskers. Quirt Wolford? Maybe, maybe not. But excitement began to play through him.

"Cotton," he asked, "who is this Gid?"

Cotton dropped his head. "I kind of hate to tell you. Every family's apt to have a black sheep in it, some time or other. Mr. Frank's family too. Gid Bowman is Frank Bowman's brother."

Gid Bowman's place was like a bad taste in the mouth. Everything about ready to fall in. A careless scattering of tin cans and bottles and trash all over. More bottles than anything else.

"What does he do to make a living?" Espy asked in a low voice.

Cotton grunted. "He has a few cattle. Mostly he just sponges off of Mr. Frank. Or did. I don't know what he'll do now."

They stepped down. Espy looped his reins around one wheel of an old broken-down wagon which was slowly falling to pieces under the relentless weathering of sun and wind and rain. Cotton followed suit, then turned toward the steps.

"Hey there, Gid," Cotton hollered.

A rusty-colored head appeared in the doorway. The man stood there hatless, squinting at the two visitors. Espy took a close look at him, and surprise hit him like a club across the shoulders.

Gid Bowman was the drunken man he had seen at Mobeetie that night, in the hotel. He was the man who had walked in with Quirt Wolford, and had tried to talk to Mary Bowman.

Several loose strings were beginning to tie up into one piece.

"Howdy, Gid," Cotton said. "We're looking for Llewellyn."

Bowman was staring up at Espy, his gaze raking him from boot heels to hat. After a moment he said, "The new syndicate man, ain't you?"

"How did you know?"

Gid Bowman only grinned crookedly. He took a step back into the dugout. "Llewellyn's in here, if you want him. But he don't feel so good."

A prescient tingle worked down the back of Espy's neck. That might have been Quirt Wolford he had seen, or it might not. His hand was close to his gun as he walked down the plank steps. The boards were rotted. One of them sagged dangerously under his weight.

The stench of the dugout slapped him across the face like a sweaty saddle blanket. The air was heavy and thick with the mingled smells of cheap whisky and tobacco, man-sweat and burned food.

Espy's gaze instantly swept the little room which had been dug into a hillside. No sign of Quirt Wolford. He could have been wrong, he admitted to himself. That could have been Gid Bowman he had seen.

There was little furniture. Two rumpled, smelly

cots. A few cluttered shelves. A two-lid bachelor stove with a drum inserted around the stovepipe to serve as an oven. Espy saw a small door at the back of the room, a door which could only lead back into the earth from which the dugout was cut. Probably it hid a pantry.

The deputy appeared lifeless, slumped in a chair pulled up to a stained table. His face was flushed against the pale, washed-out blue of his eyes. The long fingers of his right hand toyed listlessly with an almost-empty glass. He looked past Espy to the young Figure 4 cowboy.

"Awright, Cotton," he mumbled, "what is it now?"

Espy spoke for Cotton. His words bore the keen edge of his anger. "Cotton told you about some stolen cattle yesterday. We want to know what you found out."

The deputy shook his head. "I didn't find out nothing. Followed the tracks, but they played out. Too old."

Espy's voice cracked like a whip. "You're a liar!"

The deputy straightened and tried to focus his gaze on Espy's face. He drew in a sharp, quick breath. "Now you looky here, stranger . . ."

Gid Bowman broke in, his face clouded. "Listen, syndicate man, you can do what you want to on my brother's place, but this outfit is mine."

Espy's eyes were still on the deputy. "You're a liar," he repeated sharply. "You never made any effort to follow that trail. You never even left this place."

In drunken rage the deputy swayed to his feet and made a clumsy effort to draw his gun. Espy jerked it out of his hand. He gave Llewellyn a shove that sent him floundering backward into his chair. He hurled the gun through the little window. The dirty glass shattered.

Shaken and scared, the deputy was suddenly half
sober.

Espy faced him, his breath coming rapidly. "I
haven't got any control over the county government,
Llewellyn," he said flatly. "But if I were you, I'd turn
in my badge and move on along. Don't ever let me see
you again, because every time I see you, I'm going to
kick you right in the seat of the britches. I won't care
where it is, or who sees it. I'll kick your lazy rump so
hard you can't sit down for a week and a half."

Llewellyn made no answer. He just sat there with
chin sagging, hands aquiver.

Sullen defiance glared out of Gid Bowman's red-
veined eyes. "A little overbearing, aren't you, Norwood? You forget that this is *my* place, not yours. Now
you better leave."

Espy nodded, his blood still aboil. "All right, Bowman. But I want you to know one thing. From now
on the Figure 4 is my responsibility. If we ever need
a deputy again, we'd better not find him over here,
drunk. Let it happen again and I'll pull this boar's
nest right down around your ears. Let's go, Cotton!"

As he turned sharply toward the door, his angry
gaze fell upon an open letter lying on a dusty shelf.
He knew that handwriting. Espy picked up the letter.
It was from Colonel Judkins. And it was addressed to
Mary Bowman. Without having to read it, he knew
what letter it was.

Shoving it into his pocket, he stalked out, the grinning young cowboy two steps behind him. Outside,
Espy stopped so abruptly that Cotton bumped into
him. He was looking beyond the barn. "My mules,"
he exclaimed.

Walking toward the dugout barn in their free-
swinging gait were the two mules he had bought in

Dodge City, the two Quirt Wolford and his men had driven off yesterday.

Espy whirled back, facing the surprised Gid Bowman. "Those are my mules. What are they doing here?"

Bowman was suddenly flustered, his anger shoved aside. "*Your* mules?" Then, shrugging his shoulders, he said, "They strayed into camp this morning. I didn't know the brand on them, so I left them alone."

Espy stared hard at him. He knew within reason that the man was lying. "I'm taking them with me."

Bowman shrugged again. "Sure. Sure, if they're your mules, then take them on along."

The rusty-haired, short-bearded man stood in the doorway, his nerves tingling, watching Espy Norwood and Cotton spur northward, driving the mules ahead of them. He stepped back into the dugout and sighed.

The pantry door swung open, and a man moved out from his hiding place behind it. He was a broad-shouldered man with hair black as an Indian's, his face almost hidden behind a stubble of black, coarse beard.

Gid Bowman glanced at him, then sagged into a chair and poured a glass partly full from a bottle at the table. He downed it in one gulp.

"Damn it, Quirt," he said sharply, frowning at the whisky's fire, "you ought to've shot them mules. Mistake like that could spill all the beans in the pot."

Wolford growled. "Them mules was too good to shoot. They'd be worth a right smart of money. I aimed to send them west and sell them."

Bowman poured another drink. He glanced at the half-sobered deputy, then at Wolford's bruised, swollen face. "That Norwood's a tough man. I can see now how he whipped you."

Wolford jerked his head around in sudden fury and slammed his gun onto the table. He had held it in his hand the whole time he had stood behind the door. "He *didn't* whip me, Gid. You got that? He *didn't* whip me."

Bowman shrugged, fingering his glass. "Have it your way. All I know is what the boys said."

Wolford sat down, nursing his anger. He toyed with the gun. "I could've shot him a while ago, right through the door. He'd never've known what hit him."

Gid Bowman frowned. "Be patient, Quirt. Maybe you'll have to do it yet."

8

The Kansas City streets rumbled with activity this warm summer afternoon. But Margaret Tellison's driver was a good one, and he maneuvered her carriage expertly through the trying tangle of horses, vehicles, and foot traffic. Presently he pulled over to the curb in front of the dressmaker's shop and in studied deference helped Margaret down from the carriage.

"You may go now, Stevens," she said. "I shall be ready at four o'clock."

"Yes, Mrs. Tellison." The driver tipped his hat, climbed back into the carriage, and eased it out into the busy street.

Margaret Tellison stepped up to the door of the shop and waited there. When she knew the driver was out of sight of her, she moved out upon the brick sidewalk again and walked briskly around the corner, nervously twirling her parasol in black-gloved hands.

She saw the man she expected, leaning lazily against a brightly-painted carriage, idly twirling a gold chain.

He was expensively dressed, a little on the flashy side. Seeing her, he straightened.

"You found him?" she asked quickly.

He nodded. "I found him."

Impatience sharpened her voice. "Where is he, then? Why didn't you bring him?"

Dan Carver grunted. "Man like him is as independent as a hog on ice, Mrs. Tellison. He don't go running just because somebody wants to see him. He says if you've got business, you can go to him. He won't come to you."

She tapped the parasol handle impatiently against her palm, her lips tightening. "Very well, I'll go. Do you know where he is?"

Carver nodded. "I've got my rig here. I'll take you."

Hand on her elbow, he gave her a lift into the back seat of his double carriage. Margaret Tellison quickly looked about her, hoping she was not being watched by anyone who knew her. Her wide hat had a black veil. She pulled it down over her face for what protection it might give her against recognition. Then she sank deep into the seat while Carver flipped his whip at the team and pulled out into the horse-drawn traffic.

Revulsion brought a tremor to her as she looked at the back of Carver's fat neck. To think that Mrs. Edgar Tellison should ever have to conduct business with a man of this type, and of the type of the man to whom Carver was taking her.

Once a Kansas City police officer, Carver had been caught taking his share of bribe money from a well-known madam of the city. Not that such bribery was an unusual occurrence, but most policemen were discreet enough not to get caught at it. Now Carver continued to do work of a police type on a private basis. Suspicious wives sent him on the trail of errant husbands. Gamblers sent him to search for debtors who had left town without mentioning their destination. Politicians paid him well for digging up useful slander against their opponents.

For Margaret Tellison, he had found out where Espy Norwood had gone with his son. Now he had found a man who nursed a burning hatred of Espy.

Margaret's frown deepened as the carriage took her into the bawdier section of the city. Nervously she fingered the veil and wished it were heavier.

Carver finally pulled the carriage up in front of a nondescript two-story frame hotel. Margaret accepted his help in stepping down. She felt her face warming under the shameless stare of two rumpled-looking men slouched on a bench in front.

"I'll go in with you," Carver offered.

She shook her head quickly. "No. You wait out here."

The first time she had seen Carver she had had a disturbing thought that the payment for a detective service rendered might be only the first in an endless series of payments. She had had imagination enough to realize how ideal his situation was for eventual and eternal blackmail. That Carver would stoop to blackmail, she had not the slightest doubt. The best way to keep him honest, then, was to let him know as little as possible of her plans.

A balding, seedy little man sat behind the hotel desk, reading an old newspaper. He lowered the paper and stared at Margaret Tellison.

"I'm looking for a Mr. Ollinger," she said. "Matt Ollinger."

He gave her a long and thorough look before he answered, his eyes starting low and working up. Then he jerked his head toward the stairs. "Room two-twelve. Just go on up."

From the sly grin which creased his face, she guessed what he was thinking. Flame rose in her cheeks. "I'll see him down here," she said shortly. "Go get him."

He made no move until she told him the second time. "All right, all right," he said. "Just set yourself down there. I'll go."

An uncomfortable chill shook Margaret's thin shoulders as she watched Matt Ollinger walk heavily down the stairs. He was about what she had expected. Worse, perhaps. A dull fear began to beat in her as his bottomless eyes touched her. His rough black beard and his dark scowl made her think uncomfortably of a bear.

"You the woman that wanted to see me?" he demanded.

Swallowing, she nodded. She looked at the hotel clerk, then back to Ollinger. "I want to talk to you in private."

He led her into a small dining room that was almost stifling with the clinging odor of burned grease. At this time of day it was not in use. He let her pull out her own chair, seating himself across the table where he could look at her.

"All right, now," he spoke roughly, "what is it?"

Not quite sure of herself, Margaret began, "I understand you've had some trouble with a man named Espy Norwood."

His eyes cut back to sudden narrowness, and his big fist clenched on the table. He leaned forward angrily, half rising.

"If you've come to talk to me about Espy Norwood, you'd just as well leave."

"Wait," she said anxiously, "I have an offer to make."

He eased back into his chair, his fist still clenched.

Hurriedly she went on. "I've had trouble with him, too. I know a way you can even up for both of us, and make some money as well."

He listened with interest while she told him about Espy's taking Kenny away.

"Now I've found out where he's gone," she said.

His eyes widened, and his jaw squared. "Where?"

"Texas."

Ollinger's hand eased back from the table, near the butt of the gun he wore at his hip. He looked past Margaret Tellison, some violent dream building behind his washed-out eyes.

"Texas," he spoke softly. "It'd almost be worth a ride down there . . ."

He dropped it at that. His gaze returned to the woman. "What's this proposition you were talking about?"

"I'll give you five hundred dollars to steal that boy from him for me."

Pleasure warmed Ollinger's dark face. "You got you a deal. I'll get the boy for you. And I'll get Espy Norwood while I'm at it."

Her eyes went wide with fear. "No, no, nothing like that. I don't want Espy hurt. Just get the boy back. That's all I want."

"But we couldn't just let Norwood alone," he argued. "What's to keep him from coming right back up here and taking the button away from you again?"

Confidently she answered, "I have a lot of influence in this town. Once I get Kenny back here, the law will help me keep him. I'll show the court that Espy Norwood is unfit to rear a boy. I'll have him sent to jail if he even so much as tries to see Kenny again."

Ollinger eyed her with curiosity. "What else did this Norwood do to you—even before he took the boy away?"

Her breath cut short. "What do you mean?"

"He must have done something else to you. I see it in your eyes. Did he ever jilt you or something?"

She recoiled as if he had hit her. Her cheeks flamed. She tried to say something, but it didn't come out.

He shrugged. "Forget it. None of my business, I reckon. Just how do you want me to handle this job?"

After a time she got a tight rein on her anger. "I don't care, so long as you don't shoot anybody. Just get Kenny to me in Mobeetie. I'll wait there."

Ollinger rubbed his whiskered chin. "Why don't I bring him all the way back to Kansas City? I wouldn't charge you much more for that. Say two-fifty."

She shook her head. She had considered that possibility when she had first come upon the whole idea. But the thought of gently-reared Kenny having to spend days or weeks in the care of this ruffian . . .

She said, "No, I'll go to Mobeetie and wait. I'll pay you when you bring the boy to me."

"All right. Any way you want to do it. What does your husband think about this, Mrs. Tellison?"

In alarm she said, "He mustn't know anything of it, not until it's over. I'll tell him I'm going to Chicago to spend a few weeks."

Ollinger nodded. "But I'd still like to take care of Norwood."

"No," she repeated strongly, "I don't want him killed. You have to promise me you won't hurt him. That's part of the deal."

Ollinger gave in easily enough. "Sure," he shrugged, "it's your money. If stealing his boy is all the revenge you want, then that's where we stop."

Margaret Tellison was glad to be through, to be able to leave this somber man whose black reputation had reached over half of the West. She was glad to be able to get out of this evil building, and away from the baldish clerk whose beady eyes dwelt so indecently upon her.

Through a window Matt Ollinger watched her step hurriedly into Dan Carver's carriage, and watched the carriage pull away. He drew his gun. His fingers roved lovingly over it while the corners of his mouth pulled upward. The clerk walked in and leaned lazily against the doorjamb.

"Good-looking woman, Matt," he said. "If it'd been me, I wouldn't've let her get away."

"Good-looking women come cheap. This one was strictly business."

"What're you going to do?"

"I'm going to earn me five hundred dollars." He aimed the gun at a picture on the wall, smiling harshly. "And then, when I've got that money in my pocket, I'm going to pay a man off. Pay him for seven hundred and thirty steers!"

9

A smoky dusk had settled when Espy Norwood and Cotton Dulaney rode up to the Figure 4 barns and hazed the two little mules into a corral. Stiff, Espy swung down. A deep soreness still lay in him from the beating he had taken the day before.

"I'll unsaddle your horse for you," Cotton offered, seeing Espy's bone-weariness.

Espy nodded, leaning against the fence. "I'd be much obliged."

A man stepped out of the barn and walked leisurely toward them.

"Howdy, Sam," Cotton greeted him, letting Espy's saddle slide to the ground while he slipped the bridle off and turned the horse loose.

"Evening, Cotton," Sam Kirk replied. He walked on up to Espy. He extended his hand. "Mr. Norwood? I'm Sam Kirk. You all got out so early this morning, I didn't get a chance to meet you."

Espy measured the ranch foreman with his eyes and was not displeased by what he saw. There's something about a real stockman that another stockman can tell as far as he can see. Espy saw it in Sam Kirk.

"Glad to know you, Sam." This was his bid for friendship, the immediate use of Kirk's first name. It was not said in the patronizing tone of a man toward those he believes to be his inferiors, the way some men would talk to a bootblack.

Kirk glanced back toward the kid cowboy. "Cotton, the next time you go off like this, I wish you'd tell me. I'd figured on sending you to the Todd line camp today."

Espy spoke for Cotton. "I asked Cotton to show me over part of the ranch. I'd intended to tell you about it, but I never got the chance."

That was a little of a lie, and Espy had a feeling that Kirk knew it.

"Where did you go?"

"Over part of the south end."

Cotton piped up. "We took a look at those cow tracks I was telling you about, Sam. We followed them but didn't jump nothing. Then we went over to Gid's place and found Mr. Norwood's mules. You ought to've seen—"

Kirk stiffened. "You followed those tracks?"

Cotton's face fell with sudden uncertainty. "Yeah. I figured that with Mr. Norwood along, it ought to be all right."

Hands on his hips, Kirk stalked up to Cotton. His voice was tight with anger. "Kid, if I've told you once, I've told you ten times. Don't you ever go following stolen cattle like that. Those cow thieves are a desperate bunch, don't you know that? They'll put a bullet in your back. They'll leave you lying in a mesquite thicket, and nobody'll ever find you but the coyotes.

"If you can't follow orders, then you can't work

for me. One more time, Cotton. One more time and you'll just have to hunt you a new job!"

Cotton's head bent downward, and his face darkened with shame. "All right, Sam. I'll remember."

Cotton carried his and Espy's saddles into the barn. "See you tomorrow, Mr. Norwood," he said in a subdued voice.

"All right, Cotton," Espy answered. When the boy was gone, he turned back to Sam Kirk. "You were a little rough on him, Sam. I wish you'd taken that out on me instead. After all, it was me that asked him to go."

Kirk shook his head firmly. "I like that boy, Norwood. That's why I was rough on him. He's a good kid, but he's got a reckless streak in him that could get him killed. I'll be just as rough on him as necessary to keep that from happening. He knew better. And you're a grown man, Norwood. You ought to've known better too."

Espy straightened. "There wasn't any danger down there, Sam. If I'd thought there was, I'd never have taken the kid."

"How could you know there wasn't any danger?" Kirk demanded. "You're a stranger here. You might've ridden into an ambush. And you'd've gotten that kid killed right along with you.

"There's one thing I want understood, Norwood. It's none of my business what you do, yourself. But I don't want you getting my cowboys killed."

Espy's gray eyes narrowed. His voice sharpened to a finer edge. "I hate having to remind you, Sam, but I'm the manager here now. The syndicate sent me down here with full authority. I'll use it if I have to, till I find out how things stand."

Kirk still faced him, hands on his hips. "And I'll

remind *you,* Norwood. A manager's job is to make decisions. It's up to the foreman to handle the men. I'm the foreman here. And as long as I am, *I'll* be the one who tells the men where they're to go, and what they're to do."

The two men stood there, their eyes challenging each other. Kirk's belligerence was a surprise to Espy. He knew instinctively that it hadn't flared on the spur of the moment. It must have been the result of a long building-up.

An impulse moved in Espy. Fire him right now, it said. Fire him right now and save yourself a heap of trouble. But he managed to hold his tongue. He thought of Mrs. Kirk. He had liked that woman. For her sake, then, he would wait—and watch.

"All right, Sam. Bossing the men is your job, and I'll respect it. But I'll tell you this. If I see a man doing something I don't like, I'll fire him."

Kirk stared levelly at him a moment before he answered. "Fair enough, Norwood. I reckon we'll get along."

Espy raised his hand, but he was too late for Kirk to clasp it. Kirk already had turned and started walking up the slope toward the lamplight which shone a welcome in the windows of his frame house.

Espy frowned and kicked at a small rock which lay in the dust at his feet. This whole thing had turned out cockeyed. Bad enough to be on the outs with the woman who owned a half-interest in the ranch. Now to make it worse, he had to get off on the wrong foot with the foreman.

He looked toward the frame house which was his. It was dark. He glanced at the friendly glow of lamplight in the Kirk house. He knew a sudden envy of Sam Kirk, and a momentary loneliness took him.

He shrugged then and set out wearily for the kitchen.

Kenny sat at one end of the long table in the dugout cookshack, morosely watching the cook put the washed and dried supper dishes back onto the open shelves.

"Did you enjoy yourself today, son?" Espy asked him.

Kenny never answered, and that was answer enough.

Cotton Dulaney sat in silence, eating a warmedover supper, his shoulders hunched and his head low over the plate.

Hand on Cotton's shoulder, Espy said, "Sorry I got you that chewing-out. I wouldn't have had it happen for the world."

Soberly Cotton said, "Wasn't your fault, Mr. Norwood. Sam just can't see that I'm grown. He figures I'm due a scolding now and again, like a little old puppy."

Espy smiled. "You just hang on. He'll see things differently, if you give him time enough."

Later, in the syndicate house, Espy tried without luck to get Kenny to tell what he had seen and done during the day. He had just as well have tried to talk to a sorrel colt. Kenny answered him only when he asked a direct question, and the answers were short. "Yes," or "No," or "I guess so."

But Espy could see the bitter frost of unhappiness which lay in the boy's gray eyes. He finally gave up trying to talk to Kenny. Frowning worriedly, he turned away and began digging into the duplicate Figure 4 record books the colonel had sent with him.

Long after Kenny went to bed, Espy bent over the tally books, figuring with a stub pencil under the flickering glow of a kerosene table lamp.

Yes sir, they tallied up a hundred per cent, any way he went at them. Correct right down to a T.

Yet there was something here which caused the rat-gnaw of uncertainty in him. These records didn't show the kind of reduction in numbers that Cotton Dulaney had described. Sure, Cotton was just a kid, and kids let their imagination run away with them sometimes. But he was an observant button; Espy had seen that.

Next morning, after breakfast, Espy watched the big house until he knew Mary Bowman was up and about. He saw the slender girl step down off her back porch and shake out a tablecloth. Smiling, she folded the cloth against the full apron she wore and watched the cook's chickens running to grab the crumbs.

Espy felt a stirring of pleasure. There was a fresh prettiness to this girl, a prettiness he found hard to associate with men like Quirt Wolford and Gid Bowman. She looked like a happy young housewife this morning—yes, like Helen Kirk. She didn't look like a girl who two days ago had sent a brutal half-outlaw like Wolford to beat a man senseless and try to run him out of the country.

She was still wearing the apron when she answered his knock on the front door. Her friendly eyes hardened as she saw him standing there.

"Oh. Good morning, Mr. Norwood." Her voice was crisp.

Man might as well try to be friendly, Espy decided. Smiling, he said, "You sure look domestic today."

She never eased up a bit. "I'm awfully busy. Is that all you came to say, or are you here on business?"

Espy began to redden. "Business, Miss Bowman."

She stepped aside and beckoned him to come into the house. She watched him like a tired store clerk being painfully civil to a customer he wishes would finish his business and get out.

Espy decided to make one more try for a truce. "Look, Miss Bowman, I don't like us to be at odds with each other, and I don't expect you do, either. I didn't know I was shoving you out of a job you thought was yours. I'm sorry it happened that way. But there's not much we can do about it now except take things the way they are and make the best of them.

"We could get along fine, and I'd like to try. What say we just mark off our grievances and start fresh?"

She rubbed her hands together thoughtfully a long moment, looking out the open door. Then she turned, a sign of humor in her face. "All right, Mr. Norwood, I'll give it a try."

Espy smiled. "Fine. And from now on it's not Mr. Norwood. It's Espy."

A wariness still showed in her eyes, but she said, "How about some coffee to seal the bargain over? There's some on the stove in the kitchen."

She was back in half a minute, carrying cups and a pot of coffee. She had removed the apron.

Sipping the coffee, Espy caught himself enjoying the sight of her, the gentle curves and soft roundness which filled the upper part of her high-buttoned house dress, narrowing down to a tiny waist before losing its form in the full flow of ankle-length skirt.

"You said you had business," she reminded him shortly.

He nodded, pointing his chin toward a roll-top desk in one corner of the room. "I wondered if I could borrow your dad's records and tally books awhile. I'd like to go over them."

"That'd be all right, I guess. But he sent the syndicate complete copies of all of them."

Espy began to squirm in discomfort. "I know."

For a time she stared at him, her eyebrows knitting. She set down her coffee cup and saucer so hard that they rattled.

"So that's it." Her voice tightened again. "You want to see if the syndicate was sent false copies. Well, I can assure you it was not, Mr. Norwood. They are exact copies of the books Dad kept."

Espy faltered. "Miss Bowman, I didn't mean it that way."

"How else could you have meant it?" Anger leapt into her eyes. "You came over here talking truce, then the first thing you did was imply that we've been cheating the syndicate with false records."

"I didn't say that. I didn't say that at all."

"You didn't have to. You made it plain enough."

In quick strides she marched to the desk, rolled up the top, and grabbed up four ledger books. She shoved them toward Espy, almost throwing them at him.

"Here they are, all of them. Check them all you want to. You won't find a mistake. But *you've* made a mistake, Norwood. You made your mistake in ever coming out here."

Espy didn't want to be angry with her. But now the heat began to crackle in him. He reached in his shirt pocket and pulled out the letter he had found at Gid Bowman's.

"You tried hard enough to convince me of that when you sicked Quirt Wolford onto me."

Her eyes widened. "I put Quirt Wolford onto you? That's a lie, Norwood. I didn't even know you were coming till you were in Mobeetie."

Espy's jaw clenched. "You told me that. You said you didn't get the colonel's letter. But I found it. It was in your Uncle Gid's dugout. How did it get over there unless you sent it? And your uncle is a friend of Quirt Wolford. It all adds up pretty handily, Miss Bowman."

She grabbed the letter. Her face colored deeply as she glanced over it and saw what it was.

"I didn't send this to my uncle. I never even saw it before."

He stared levelly at her. "You're a very pretty girl, Miss Bowman. But I learned a lesson about pretty girls a long time ago. The reddest roses have always got the sharpest thorns."

Her hands trembled, and her lips were tight as a bowstring. "Get out, Norwood," she gritted, pointing at the door. "Get out before I throw something at you and break it."

Seething, she stood in the doorway, watching him stomp along the footworn path leading down the slope. He carried her father's record books under his arm. His back was rigid and straight as a poker.

Mary Bowman whirled on her heel. She grabbed a coffee cup and hurled it. It smashed on a doorjamb, sending a brown trickle of coffee running down to the floor.

A portly old Mexican woman came hurrying into the room, her eyes bulging with concern. She saw the smashed cup, then looked questioningly toward Mary Bowman.

"*Es nada*, Delfina," Mary said in a low voice, suddenly shamed by her uncontrolled anger. "It's nothing."

As the old woman left the room, Mary once again looked at the letter, puzzlement in her worried frown.

But her wonder over the letter quickly gave way to the fury which still smoldered beneath the surface.

She looked out the window toward the syndicate house down the slope.

"You'd better watch yourself, Espy Norwood," she breathed. "One way or another, I'll get you!"

10

Espy Norwood and his son Kenny had no particular trouble in finding what was known as the Todd line camp. The prairie wind was warm in their faces. The morning sun was hot and high, the shadows edging closer under the two easy-trotting horses, showing that it was only an hour or so until noon.

Espy glanced around often to look at the boy, who usually trailed a half length behind. It had surprised him a little when Kenny had decided to go with him.

"Tired, son?" he asked.

Kenny shook his head, but the sag of his young face showed that he was. He squirmed one way, then another, obviously sore and saddle-rubbed. An easy smile lifted the heaviness from Espy's countenance. Once over his soreness this time, Kenny would be all right from now on.

The Todd camp, on the upper part of Figure 4 range, was a small picket house, picket shed, and a set of pole corrals, built upon a gentle knoll amid a broad, rolling vista of short grass. It faced down toward a big shallow natural lake that shimmered lazily in the sun, the tall green tules at the lake's edge shoving upward like a million thin bayonets.

Kenny edged his horse over toward the tules, full of curiosity. He laughed as a big bullfrog leaped into the water with a loud and frightened splash.

Espy took deep pleasure from the boy's laugh. He had heard few of them the last couple of years.

A cowboy lounging in the shade on the shack's small front porch arose without haste as the man and the boy rode up. The puncher dropped his feet to the ground and sat up on the porch edge. He eyed the riders with lazy curiosity a minute before he spoke.

"Howdy. Git down and come in."

Espy raised his hand in greeting and swung to the ground. He heard the squeak of a bedspring inside the house. Another cowboy came to the door, sleepy-headed, his hair tousled. He was in stocking feet.

"Company," he observed. "Come on into the shade and rest yourselves. We'll have dinner in a little while, if old Dolph ever decides to leave them cattle alone and come in."

Espy told them his name, but not what he was. They showed no sign of recognition. They hadn't heard about the new manager yet. The way it looked to Espy, it was just as well.

"Hadn't really expected to find anybody around the house at this time of day," he said. "Figured you'd be out working."

Evidently they took him for someone just passing through the country.

"Why, mister," spoke the cowboy who had been lying on the porch, "this is the best outfit to work for that you ever saw. Work one hour, sleep the rest of the day if you want to. And if you've got some old hardhead like Dolph around, you can sleep the other hour too. He'll do the work."

Espy turned his attention to loosening his cinch, holding back the disgust which was beginning to rub against his grain.

"I'd like to work for an outfit like that," he said.

The other cowboy spoke up. "Then you ought to've come before Frank Bowman passed on. Tell him you were broke and needed work, and he'd put you right on. Once you get on with the Figure 4, you just stay on. Frank Bowman never fired a man."

"Even if he didn't work?"

"Aw," said the puncher, "we work if Sam Kirk comes over. He's the foreman. Way this house sits, we can see Sam before he can see us. Gives us time to get out and get busy."

"What about this Dolph you mentioned?"

The cowboy laughed. "He's one of these old moss-backs who thinks the only thing a man was born for was to work. So if he wants to work, we just let him. Makes it easier on us."

Espy felt the tingle of anger putting its splotch of color into his face. The cook, Jess Cooley, had told him there would be three men at this camp. He knew two of them who wouldn't be here much longer.

It was well past one o'clock on Espy's stem-winding pocket watch before the middle-aged puncher named Dolph came riding in wearily on a tired, sweat-streaked dun horse. On his way through the fenced horse pasture he had tossed a loop around the neck of a fresh sorrel and was leading him up to the shed at the end of his rope. This would be his afternoon mount, Espy knew.

Espy pitched in and helped the old puncher whip up a noon meal. The other two cowboys were not much help, except at eating it. After dinner Dolph saddled the sorrel and rode out again.

Anger tugging downward at the corners of his mouth, Espy said to his son, "Come on, Kenny. Time we were going."

He cast a sharp glance at the two lazy cowboys. Impulse urged him to fire them right now, right here. But judgment told him to wait. What was true here might be true at other line camps. Even the headquarters itself. He'd wait a few days, then. He'd wait until he had had a chance to observe all the men quietly, and make his own judgment. Then, when the axe did fall, he'd make it one fast, smooth stroke.

He waited even longer than he had expected to. He watched, he asked careful questions, and he listened. Then one day he sent Cotton and a couple of other cowboys out to the line camps to fetch in all the men who could possibly get away.

They all hunkered under the shade of a big chinaberry tree in the early afternoon sun, patiently curious. Stepping off the syndicate house porch and walking calmly down toward the tree, Espy could see the sudden surprise in some of the faces as men from the line camps realized who he was. In some of the faces he caught the sick flush of dismay.

He stopped in front of the men, still standing in the sun. He stood silently for the space of a minute or two, his eyes drifting from one man to another, catching curiosity in some faces, amusement, shame in a couple, and resentment in two or three.

At the big house, Mary Bowman stood watching. And at one edge of the group of men, barely inside the shade of the big tree, Sam Kirk waited worriedly.

"Men," Espy said, "I've met everyone who's here. And you've all met me, even if some of you didn't know who I was. I'm the new manager of the Figure 4. I haven't been here long, but I've already seen some things I liked, and lots of things I didn't like. I've seen some men who'd be a credit to any outfit they worked for. And I've seen some who aren't worth killing."

He reached in his shirt pocket. "I've got a list of names here. These men can draw their pay at the kitchen. I've already given Jess Cooley the checks. I want these men off the Figure 4 by sundown tomorrow. And I don't ever want them to come back."

He read the names, nine of them. He saw shock strike in the group, one man after another, like a hard-swung hickory singletree.

Finished with the names, he paused a moment. Sullenness had settled in some of the nine faces. One man had already arisen and was walking stiffly toward the barn, to get his horse.

"As for the rest," Espy said, "I'm pleased with most of you. There's nothing that makes a man's job better than to be able to work with good men. There are a few borderline cases here, though, some I might ought to've fired but didn't. If you're one of them, you likely know it.

"I'm giving you another chance. But I'll be watching you. From now on, any man who works for the Figure 4 will *work* for it. I don't drive men, but I want every one to do his share, the same way I'll try to do mine. I'll expect loyalty to the ranch and full obedience to Sam Kirk and myself."

He unfolded another sheet of paper. "I've got a list of rules drawn up here, to be posted in the bunkhouse. The same kind of rules that some of the other

Panhandle outfits are making. If you don't think you can live up to them, I want you to quit now."

Turning his back, he walked briskly toward the syndicate house. Mary Bowman stepped down off her porch and quartered across to intercept him. Scarlet worked in her oval face. Her slender hands were at her sides, flexing in hard anger.

"That was a little raw, don't you think? Even for a syndicate man."

"Raw? Maybe it was. But it was long overdue."

"My father hired those men."

"And *I* fired them." He tipped his hat to her and went on into his house.

Among the names he had read was that of a cowboy named Claude Hatch. Hatch stood six feet tall in his polished, knee-high black boots. A year short of thirty, he was kid-proud of his broad, strong shoulders. He shaved every night, a highly uncommon practice among the Panhandle cowpunchers. He kept his black hair trimmed neatly, and he spent many an hour before the cracked bunkhouse mirror, combing his hair down slick and neat.

Potentially a good cowhand, the way Sam Kirk saw him. But the trouble was, the only thing he ever worked hard at was catching Mary Bowman's attention. He figured his bearing and his natural good looks ought to go right well with a pretty girl and her big, fine ranch. Sometimes, out of sight of Sam Kirk and everybody else, he sat down under the shade of a cottonwood and dreamed about it.

Mr. Claude Hatch—maybe they'd call him "Colonel" —a prominent figure anywhere he went in Texas, from Tascosa to Austin. Owner of the Figure 4, biggest ranch in the state. Sure, it'd be the biggest some day. Give him a chance. And there'd be a pretty woman on his arm to charm the senators who paused in their work to come to him and ask his advice.

Far-fetched? Not for Claude Hatch. He'd won many a pleasant smile from Mary Bowman. He'd even taken her to a couple of dances. And afterward she'd taken him into the big house and brewed up a pot of coffee for him. He'd sit there and talk with her father as if he were as big a cowman as Bowman, and not just a ranch hand who in a few minutes would crawl into a hard cot in the same bunkhouse with upward of a dozen other men.

Hatch had been biding his time. He'd dropped her a few broad hints that he had marriage on his mind, and she hadn't turned him away. That was all the sign he needed.

Now, suddenly, everything had exploded in his face. Hatch stood helplessly, the shock draining down through him like a slow-burning acid. Then the anger began to rise, and it turned into a searing fury.

"He can't do it," Hatch declared.

A lazy kid named Choate snickered at him. Choate's name had been called too. "The hell he can't. He just did. Shine up your boots, Claude boy, and we'll head for town."

"He's not going to fire me," Hatch thundered, "not by a damn sight."

Hatch's narrowed eyes saw Mary Bowman standing on her porch. In long, angry strides he started her way.

"Mary," he said quickly, stepping hurriedly onto the porch, "you heard him call my name? You heard him fire me?"

Her voice was strained. "I heard him."

Hatch said, "You're not really going to let him do

it, are you, Mary? You're going to stop him, aren't you?"

She shrugged. "I don't know how I can."

"But you're still half-owner of this ranch. He can't do something like this if you don't want him to."

Levelly she said, "You're just partly right, Claude. Yes, it's still half my ranch. But I haven't a word of say left in the way it's run. Espy Norwood is the boss here now, the only one. I don't suppose I could even ride my own horses anymore if he said no."

Incredulously Hatch said, "You can't mean that, Mary."

She nodded. "I do mean it. I'm no better now than if I had been hired to scrub floors here."

He stood silent a moment, his mind racing with a dozen wild and desperate schemes. "I won't let him do this, Mary. You know how I feel about you. You know I don't want to leave this ranch—and you."

She watched him, half in pity. She had always liked Claude, in a way. He was pleasant company. But that was all he was, and all he was ever likely to be. Behind his handsome face and his proud smile, she knew he was empty. He was a man to dream big dreams, but he was a man who could never bring those dreams to reality.

In a way, then, she thought, it was probably best that he go. She didn't want to keep leading him on, yet she didn't want to make an outright break with him.

"I won't let him separate us, Mary," Hatch went on earnestly. "I'll run him out of the country before I'll let him do that to us."

Run him out of the country. A sudden idea set her to tingling. She measured Hatch's shoulders with her eyes. Here was a chance, a big chance.

"That might be the way," she said, covering her quick excitement. Then she cautioned. "But Norwood is no weakling. He's a stubborn man. Quirt Wolford tried to stop him and couldn't."

Hatch's shoulders squared, fists knotting. *"I'll* stop him, Mary."

A new determination driving him, he stepped down from the porch and strode down the slope toward the syndicate house. He stopped in front of it, hands on his hips. "Norwood," he called loudly, "come out here."

Espy Norwood came out onto the porch. He eyed Hatch sternly. "Your check's over at the cookshack, Hatch."

Hatch took a deep breath, swelling his broad chest. "I'm not picking up that check, Norwood. You're not man enough to fire me."

Disappointment was bitter as ashes in Espy's mouth. He had hoped this wouldn't happen. But all along, he had known it probably would. Out of nine men, at least one was bound to come looking for trouble.

Espy stared at Hatch, trying to weigh him, trying to decide how much of this was bluster and how much was fight. "I *have* fired you, Hatch."

The cowboys had begun to scatter. Now the angry lift of fight-talk started drawing them back. They gathered well behind Claude Hatch, none of them taking a hand, but all of them watching. Hatch looked back and saw them, and their presence strengthened his determination.

"And I say I'm not going, Norwood. Come down off that porch. Come down and I'll show you whether you can fire me or not."

Espy drew a long, deep breath, regret lying heavily

within him. He'd have to make his word good now. Back up, and he'd lose all control of this ranch.

Kenny edged worriedly out onto the porch. Espy glanced at him, then back to Hatch. "Go back in the house, son," he said quietly to the boy.

He walked down the steps and out toward Hatch. Two paces from the tall cowboy, he stopped. He set his feet solidly, his weight hard upon his heels.

The flare in Hatch's eyes betrayed him before he stepped forward and lashed out with his fist. Espy ducked back just enough, then caught Hatch in the stomach with a quick, hard punch. A gust of breath tore from the cowboy. He doubled, caught himself, and launched a smashing right that struck Espy's shoulder, spinning him back.

Regaining balance, Espy crouched defensively. Hatch rushed him, fists closed. He was a different kind of fighter from Quirt Wolford. He was a show fighter, a man who considered himself a boxer.

Espy struck at him and missed. Hatch's fist stabbed forward while his left stayed in close to his face, covering himself. Espy caught part of the blow on his chin. He staggered, while two or three of the fired cowboys yipped in glee and urged Hatch on. Hatch came in punching.

Espy warded off the blows. A hard anger began to rise as his tongue caught the warm salt taste of blood on his lips. Deliberately he stepped closer, almost chin to chin, taking two body blows in return for a chance to bring up a savage uppercut at Hatch's jaw.

Hatch reeled, his hands flying up to cover his face. Jaw ridged, Espy dealt him a breath-jarring blow to the ribs, and another to Hatch's stomach.

Blood fury exploded in Hatch's eyes. He flung away his technique, his caution. He waded in, fists driving like pump handles. Espy almost went down under their bludgeoning attack. But he caught himself and held. He went after the weak spots, the spots that Hatch was leaving uncovered in his blind rage. Striking at these, he wore the cowboy down.

Fatigue dragged on Espy's arms like sacks of lead. But he knew now that he had the fight won. He methodically forced Hatch back, putting his whole body behind the blows that became weaker and weaker, until Espy felt he could swing his arms no more.

But just when Espy was ready to fall exhausted on the steps of his house, Hatch went down and stayed down. He lay twisted, half on his side, half on his stomach. Espy swayed, then dropped weakly upon the steps, his breath labored and slow.

The watching cowboys had made no move to join in the fight. Through burning eyes, Espy watched them, wondering which way they would lean. Then two of the fired punchers stepped forward, violence in their eyes. Espy sat still, helpless to stand and defend himself.

Cotton Dulaney took several long strides and stopped in front of Espy, his fists clenched. "The boss man's give out," he said. "And if anybody thinks they can take advantage of him now, they'll have to whip me first."

The two cowboys stared menacingly at the kid, pondering whether or not to jump him. When it appeared that they would, old Jess Cooley stepped up beside the kid, his gnarled hand tight on a long chunk of stove-wood.

"You're nuttier than a fruitcake, button," he said quietly. "But you got the right idea. Any of them jumps you, he'll have to jump me too."

Espy could see the scales begin to tip. The other

cowboys began to crowd closer. Most of them were backing up Cotton and the cook. The two fired cow-hands sensed it, and the fight drained out of them.

Espy Norwood had regained enough breath that he could speak. He pushed to his feet. "The fight's over. Jess, you go on back to the cookshack, and pay off the men I told you to. Cotton, you go on about your business. The rest of you men too."

To the two cowboys who had moved to fight him, he said, "Hatch'll need help. Take him down to the bunkhouse. When he's able, you'd better travel."

The cowboys grudgingly helped the bloody-faced Hatch to his feet. Once standing, he angrily shoved them aside and stood swaying, alone. He tried to fasten his swollen eyes upon Espy. Hatred roiled in them like red-hot tar in a bucket.

"You haven't whipped me, Norwood, not by a gutful. I'll mark this up as a debt I owe you. And by God, I'll pay it, Norwood. With interest."

He staggered off toward the bunkhouse. One of the cowboys tried to help him. Hatch shoved him away and went it alone, the color boiling in his bruised and bloody face.

He turned once and shouted, "I'll be back, Norwood, you watch. I'll be back."

Espy said nothing, hoping this was the end of it but knowing it wouldn't be.

On the porch of the big house, Mary Bowman also watched, her face drained of color. Without her realizing it, her right hand gripped tensely the lace on her blouse. She watched Claude Hatch go, and she wished she hadn't urged him on.

If it hadn't been for me, she was thinking, he wouldn't have done it. But I pushed him, and now it's gone too far. There can't be any backing up.

The cords in her slender throat went tight with anxiety and with shame. Suddenly she was sorry for Hatch, and sorry for Espy Norwood too.

"What have I done?" The question kept driving at her stricken mind. "I've started something and now I can't stop it. Oh, Dad, I wish you were here. I wish you could tell me what to do."

11

Espy Norwood sat at Jess Cooley's long dining table, sipping fire-hot black coffee and studying Sam Kirk across the table. Kirk fingered a steaming cup, his eyes following the movements of the ranch cook as Cooley prepared supper.

"Yep," Kirk was saying, "I was as surprised as the rest of them. But I'll admit that you did a first-class job of culling. They're the same ones I'd've gotten rid of, if I'd thought Mary would stand for it."

"Why wouldn't she have stood for it?"

"Sentiment, mostly. Her dad hired them. She wouldn't fire them."

Espy rubbed his sore jaw, flinching as his rough hand grated across a mean bruise. "From all accounts, Frank Bowman was a good ranchman, Sam. Then how did he let himself get saddled down with all this deadwood? There's plenty of *good* cowboys needing work."

Sam shook his head. "Trouble with Mr. Frank was that he had too soft a heart. Let somebody come to him broke, down-and-out, and Mr. Frank would give him a job whether he needed him or not. And once a man got on with Mr. Frank, he had a job as long as he wanted to stay. I don't reckon Mary's dad ever fired a man in his life."

Espy came close to smiling. "He must've been a good man, Sam. I wish I could've come along soon enough to get to know him."

Kirk looked at the tabletop, memory misting his eyes a moment. "They've just about lost the mold nowadays."

Then he changed the subject. "We're going to need some men. This has left us mighty short-handed."

Espy nodded. "I thought about that even before I called in the men. I'll get some new hands, Sam. I think I know how to get some good ones."

He was thinking of Arch McCavitt. Arch was in a position to know most of the cowboys in the country. He would know which ones could be hired, and he'd know the good ones.

"I'll go to Mobeetie in a couple of days," he said. He knew the soreness from the fight would settle its full weight upon him by tomorrow. He'd wait until it waned. "We can make out a little longer."

Kenny Norwood knew the awful pangs of loneliness as he stood in front of the barn in the rosy glow of dawn and watched his father ride off toward Mobeetie. He wouldn't be back till tomorrow night, he had told Kenny.

"You go play with Joe Kirk," Espy had told him. "He can teach you lots of things."

Joe had, all right. He had taught Kenny not to

stand too close to a water trough. Fellow was apt to get pushed into it. Kenny had.

He had taught Kenny a couple of wrestling holds, too, painful holds that had brought the rush of angry, helpless tears to Kenny's eyes.

Stand and fight him! That was what the chorus of outraged voices within Kenny had roared every time Joe started to run another whizzer on him. But something had kept holding Kenny back. Not fear, exactly. He'd gotten over most of his real fear of Joe Kirk. But even yet, he knew a dull dread of physical combat. Aunt Margaret had drilled that into him too deeply for him to forget it easily.

Kenny watched his father ride away, and he wished he could have gone with him. He had thought he could never like his father again. But now Kenny found himself listening for Espy's footsteps with a quick thrill of gladness. He took a deep pleasure in the way Espy's voice always went quiet for him, and the way Espy's eyes softened as they dwelt upon his son. Kenny's heart stirred with pride at the confident way his father went about doing the things that had to be done.

Most especially had he swelled with pride when Cotton Dulaney had come to the syndicate house after Hatch and the fired riders had gone. Cotton had stood uncertainly, looking at the floor, trying to say what was on his mind without making it sound like soft soap.

"The boys asked me to speak for them, Mr. Norwood," Cotton had said. "We all talked it over, and we want you to know we'll back up anything you say, a hundred per cent."

Kenny hadn't missed the happy glow in Espy's eyes.

This morning Cotton had roped out the best horse in his company mount and turned him over to Espy. "This here is old Baldy," he had said. "You need a good horse, and this is him."

Four other cowboys had then done likewise. And now Espy had a first-rate mount of company horses. Kenny had sensed that Espy couldn't be prouder of them if he had bought them all for five hundred dollars apiece.

Shortly after Espy left, the cowboys began to rope out their horses and scatter for work. Kenny watched them, his eyes dwelling mostly upon cocky young Joe Kirk.

Aunt Margaret had preached to him against envy, but he could not resist the envy which burned in him now. He had seen the way the cowboys kidded Joe, joshing him around, pranking him, treating him like an equal with the men. They didn't do that for Kenny. They were polite, but that was all. Even with a crowd of cowboys around him, Kenny felt alone, hopelessly alone. Maybe if he had spent his life out here, like Joe had, instead of living in the city . . .

Joe Kirk saddled his own horse and mounted him without a footlift from anybody. He rode out with three cowboys to make a hand just as if he were a grown man. Kenny knew that, and the envy burned deeper.

Joe's eyes lit upon Kenny, and mischief flickered devilishly in them. Shaking down the rope from his saddle horn, he kneed his horse toward Kenny. "Run, calf, run!" he shouted.

Kenny's heart leaped. Joe was going to ride him down! He turned and ran for the safety of the fence. He heard the swish of Joe's rope. The loop jerked tight around Kenny's feet and yanked them out from under him. He sprawled face down in the sand. His cheeks were burning hot as Joe's taunting laughter reached him.

He got to his feet and kicked the rope off, his teeth clenched tight. Laughing, Joe coiled his rope and rode off after the cowboys. Kenny choked with shame as he heard one of the cowboys chiding Joe. "You oughtn't to treat the city boy that way. Not his fault he don't know nothing. They just don't teach them in the city."

It hadn't been meant for Kenny's ears. But it had reached them just the same. His blood ran hot. He couldn't let this go on much longer.

He turned back toward the cookshack. He stopped short as he discovered old Jess Cooley standing in the doorway, watching. Jess had seen it all. Shame touched Kenny again. He'd rather anyone had seen it than Jess. Jess or his father.

Jess was diplomat enough not to mention the incident. Not directly, anyway.

"How about some cold biscuits and some fruit, cowboy?" Jess asked him in a friendly voice.

With nowhere else to go, Kenny followed the cook into the kitchen. Cooley set down a bowl with a remnant of stewed apricots in it.

"Eat them up. I need the bowl, and them apricots is too good to feed to the chickens."

Eating them, Kenny lost his anger. He watched Cooley bring down a huge crock jar off a shelf, check it, and shove it back. Rising sourdough swelled up over the top of it, dough that soon would be biscuits on the table. Cooley started mixing up another batch of dough for a second jar that he had emptied in making breakfast biscuits. Kenny watched, fascinated, while Cooley punched dough into the jar. It was far short of the top.

"Aren't you going to fill it up?" he asked.

Cooley shook his head. "It'll rise like that other one yonder. Put any more dough in it and it'd get all over the kitchen."

Kenny's mouth was wide open. "Gosh."

He squirmed a minute, wanting to ask a question and hoping it wouldn't sound too foolish. "Say, Jess, what do you do to make it swell up that way?"

Furtively Jess looked all around him as if making sure there weren't any cowboys around to hear. Then he leaned close to Kenny's ear and whispered:

"I wouldn't want them finicky cowpunchers to find out my secret. You won't tell anybody."

"I won't tell."

"Well," the cook said cautiously, "I keep two big old bullfrogs in the bottom of each of them jars. They puff up the dough for me."

Kenny's mouth dropped wider open. "Gosh!"

Then doubt crowded in, and he grinned uncertainly. "Aw, Jess, you're just loading me. That's not the truth."

Cooley went on kneading the dough, snaggle teeth showing in his broad grin. "Well, son," he said shortly, "I reckon I *was* pulling your leg a little. Truth of the matter is, I only got *one* frog in each of them crocks."

Cooley waited awhile before he brought up the touchy subject. "Joe Kirk's thrown a booger into you, hasn't he, kid?"

Hotly Kenny said, "I'm not scared of him."

Cooley frowned, not making any comment.

Deeply disturbed, Kenny asked, "What's the matter with Joe? I try to get along with him, honest I do.

But every time I try to make friends with him he pulls something on me. Has he always been this mean?"

The cook said patiently, "He's not mean, Kenny. Oh, he's got more mischief in him than a dozen pet 'coons, but he's not mean. It's just that ever since he's been big enough to wean, cowboys have been hoorawing him. Cowboys will always bedevil a kid.

"Now you've come along. This is the first time he's ever had a chance to bedevil anybody else the way they've done him. And he's gone clear off the deep end with it."

"What can I do, Jess?"

"Well, sir, the Book says that if a man smites you on one cheek, you're supposed to turn him the other one. Now it looks to me like you've run plumb out of cheeks. So, it's about time to beat the everlasting whey out of him."

Kenny looked away, distaste wrinkling up his nose. This wasn't the first time he'd considered that possibility. He'd thought about it a lot.

"Maybe I could do it, Jess. I don't know. But I don't want to fight him. I hate to fight."

The cook's eyes were sympathetic. "Sure, son. Most people hate to fight. But sometimes there's no other way out. Look at your daddy now. You don't think he wanted to fight Quirt Wolford, do you? But he had to. It was either that or run. And he's no man for running. He didn't want to fight Claude Hatch, either. You could see that in his face. He hated it. But he had to fight or quit, and he's no quitter.

"You're in the same place, kid. It's either fight or keep on running. And I'm going to be mighty disappointed in you if you run. Mighty disappointed."

With that, Cooley hushed up, his face grave. Kenny's pulse quickened. He felt the blood begin rushing to his face. This was an ultimatum. Either he stood his ground now, or Jess was through with him.

Kenny walked outside, his hands suddenly cold and sweaty, and a million needles prickling the seat of his pants.

All morning long he paced around the barn, his mind running away with him in countless wild daydreams of vicious combat. He was a gladiator, his huge iron sword slashing Joe to the ground while the Romans cheered. He was an armored knight of King Arthur, his heavy lance sending the evil knight, Joe, spinning from his saddle. He was a marshal in Dodge City, blasting outlaw Joe full of holes with the two six-guns he wore at his sides.

And then Joe came riding in alone, ahead of the cowboys, and he was plain Kenny Norwood again, his heart thumping like that of a caught rabbit. Kenny watched Joe, near-panic surging in him. Not now, a weak voice cried within him. Another time, not now. But in the doorway of the cookshack, Jess Cooley stood with arms folded, waiting.

It *had* to be now.

How was he to do it? He knew he couldn't bring himself to start a fight. Once it started, he might be all right. But to start it himself . . .

Watching Joe, he almost backed into the water trough. The water trough! That's what would swing it.

Pulse hammering, he waited beside the trough, trying to act as if he didn't see Joe coming. He heard Joe swing down, heard the slap of leather as the youngster tied his bridle reins to the fence. There was a moment of hesitation. Then Joe was moving toward him, footsteps almost silent in the sand.

Tensely Kenny watched Joe's shadow. Not long before noon, the shadow was a short one. But Kenny saw it, and he saw it suddenly move forward as Joe lunged to push Kenny into the trough.

Kenny stepped aside. He grabbed Joe's shoulder and gave the startled boy a hard shove, straight into the trough. Face down, Joe floundered and gasped and choked. Then he came up, spouting water, his clothes soaked. Eyes raging, he rushed at Kenny, swinging his fists wildly. He hit Kenny twice.

Then Kenny hit him, right on the nose. And suddenly all Kenny's fear was gone. He'd started now, and he was mad, mad clear through. He thrust aside all the restraint that Aunt Margaret had drilled into him. He was going to finish this thing, right here and right now.

Everything he had, he put behind his tight-clenched fists. He drove them into Joe like the kick of a mule. His fury crackled and burned in him like brush afire. Joe was hitting him, too, but he hardly felt the blows. Desperation driving him, he kept pounding, forcing Joe back, and back, and back.

Sobbing in pain and anger, the surprised Joe Kirk gave ground until at last he stood with his back against a picket shed. Kenny's arms were tired and heavy, but he went on with it. At last Joe slid down, and lay on his back in the sand.

Kenny dropped to his knees, astraddle Joe Kirk. Bloody-nosed and bruised, Joe was choked, half crying, his weak hands fighting futilely to hold back Kenny's tight fists.

Kenny stopped hitting him. With both hands he grabbed Joe's hair and started beating the boy's head against the side of the shed. Joe cried for him to stop.

"Holler 'calf rope,'" Kenny demanded.

Joe was a little slow about it. Kenny bumped his head some more. Tears streaming down his sand-crusted cheeks, Joe finally gave in.

"Calf rope," he cried weakly.

Kenny stood up, knees wobbly. He leaned on the shed for support. For the first time he saw Jess Cooley standing there watching, the edges of his droopy mustache trying hard to lift in a grin.

Cooley reached down and helped Joe to a stand. Sniffling, Joe took one weak swing at Kenny, missed him, and stepped back quickly to keep from being hit in return.

"Now, Joe," Cooley said, "it looks to me like you've had about enough."

With his big hand he tried to wipe off some of the sand which had clung to Joe's wet clothing. It was useless.

The cook said, "You've done your hoorawing and gotten your comeuppance for it. From now on, you'll know better than to pick at Kenny Norwood."

Joe didn't answer. He sniffled, his eyes misty, his face still flushed with rage.

"Now then," Cooley went on, "Kenny wants to be friends with you. He's tried ever since he's been here. Why don't you shake hands with him?"

Stubbornly Joe put his hands behind him.

Cooley frowned darkly. "There's nobody seen this but me. You want me to tell the cowboys how bad this town kid whipped you?"

That brought a quick alarm to Joe's freckled face.

"Then you go on and shake hands. And if you don't make friends with Kenny, I'll tell the cowboys everything. I'll even tell them you cried and hollered 'calf rope.'"

With great reluctance, Joe Kirk brought his right hand forward. Kenny's own hand was beginning to hurt, his knuckles torn and bruised. But he shook Joe's hand and grinned.

Cooley smiled. "That's better. Now, Joe, you get back in that water trough and wash the sand off of you, and the blood. You can tell your mother your horse threw you in it. If she asks me, I'll tell her the same thing."

Joe crawled back into the trough and began rinsing off the sand. The water seemed to cool his temper. Out of the trough, he pulled off his clothes and wrung them out. Kenny helped him.

"Joe," Kenny experimented in a friendly voice, "I've watched you riding calves. I wonder if you could teach me?"

Joe grunted. "I doubt it."

"I bet you could. You're an awfully good rider."

The unexpected compliment got to Joe where he lived. After a time he said, "You really think so? Honest Injun?"

"Sure."

Joe rubbed his aching jaw. His resistance melted. He started to grin. "All right, Kenny, I'll teach you. Only you better not bawl when the big ones throw you off."

A bruise was beginning to darken around one of Kenny's eyes. But both eyes were shining like silver dollars.

"I won't bawl, Joe, you'll see. I won't bawl."

12

Gid Bowman saw that Claude Hatch's glass was nearly empty. He reached across the table and filled it from his bottle. And on second thought, he filled his own as well. Hatch had taken care of the better part of the bottle already. Now he hunched in his chair in Arch McCavitt's Mobeetie saloon, his eyes swollen, his face florid, from too much whisky.

Bowman dipped the chewing end of his cigar into his glass, then shoved it into his mouth. He hadn't allowed himself to take too much today. He had business to attend to. "So Norwood just flat run you off, did he?" he prodded Hatch.

"Not for good, he didn't," Hatch declared. He spoke with a little difficulty, his tongue thick. "Mary won't stand for it."

"I guess she will," Bowman commented. "She could've stopped him if she'd really wanted to."

Hatch leaned forward heatedly, his face threateningly close. "I tell you, there wasn't anything she could do about it."

Bowman frowned, biting hard on his cigar and drawing back from Hatch's anger. "You don't really believe that, do you, Claude? If she'd demanded that Norwood keep you, he'd've done it. But she didn't. And you know why? I think Norwood's stealing her from you, boy."

Hatch jumped up, his hands grabbing for Bowman's collar. Bowman leaned backward. Dizziness caught Hatch and made him slump into his chair again. He knotted his fists, but he couldn't bring his eyes to meet Bowman's.

A flicker of a smile tugged at Bowman's mouth, and he covered it. Why, he'd soon have this hollow-headed kid eating out of his hand.

"See there, boy," Bowman said, "you knew it too. You just wouldn't admit it to yourself. That sneaking syndicate man is taking Mary over, just like he's taken over the ranch."

Face sick, Hatch rubbed his shaky hands, hard. "I'll kill him, Gid."

Bowman shook his head. "They'd just hang you, and what good would it do you then? Naw, Claude, that's not the way to settle up with Norwood."

"What would *you* do?" Hatch asked in misery.

"You really want to even up with him?"

Hatch nodded. "Anything I can do."

Bowman leaned forward to speak, then settled back and waited. Arch McCavitt was walking his way. From what Bowman had heard, McCavitt was some kind of old *compadre* of Norwood's.

When McCavitt had gone on past, Bowman said quietly, "You just come along with me, Claude. We got plans for our friend Norwood. And you can help. We can use a good levelheaded man like you."

Hatch half snickered. "You? You can't do anything but drink whisky."

Bowman's lips flattened a moment, red spurting into his face. Then he caught himself. "It's not just me, Claude. Quirt Wolford is in on it, too. Don't you think Quirt Wolford will know what to do about Norwood?"

Hatch stared, surprised. "Wolford? Yeah, I reckon he would."

Bowman stood up, smiling thinly. "Well, then, come on along with me, Claude. We'll start out for my camp tonight. Tomorrow we'll see Quirt."

He helped Hatch to his feet. He slipped Hatch's arm over his shoulder to give the drunken cowboy support. Hatch was near collapse. It was hard work for Bowman, half-carrying and half-dragging Hatch toward the door.

Bowman stopped cold as a man walked in and stood before the door, letting his eyes accustom themselves to the dimmer light. Espy Norwood!

Bowman and Norwood quietly eyed each other a moment. Bowman was the first to speak. "Howdy, Norwood."

Norwood answered him with a short and simple "Howdy," his eyes on Hatch.

Bowman said, "Just helping the boy out, Norwood. Some fellers never do know when they've had enough."

Espy watched the two men labor out the wide door and into the sandy street. Then he turned toward the bar, worried. What in the dickens was Gid Bowman doing with Claude Hatch?

He shrugged, shoving the question aside as red-haired Arch McCavitt came from behind the bar, his hand outstretched. "Have they chased you off already?" Arch grinned, knowing better. "I hear they've tried."

Sitting at a table with McCavitt, Espy told what all had happened. McCavitt nodded quietly. He'd heard most of it.

Espy said, "So we need some new hands, Arch. I hoped you could help me find some."

Mischief played in Arch's eyes. "Maybe I can. I'll find you some men just as good as I am."

Espy grinned. "That's what I'm afraid of. You'll have to do a right smart better than that."

He headed back toward the ranch the next morning, confident in Arch's promise to help.

"It may take a few days," Arch had said, "but I'll find you some men. I'll send them out as they get ready."

Espy had asked Arch something else. "Do you know who usually takes count for the Figure 4 when it's on roundup?"

Arch's eyebrows had lifted. "Why?"

"Just curious. Wanted to do a little checking."

Bowman's tally books had continued to worry him, even though they had been exactly the same as those the colonel had, and balanced out letter-perfect. Espy still hadn't been able to shake off the doubt which Cotton Dulaney had started in him.

He'd seen Arch's obvious reluctance in answering and had wondered about it. "Well," Arch said, "I went out to the Figure 4 camp a couple of times this spring. The counters were Sam Kirk and old Charlie Burnside."

Espy hadn't heard the name before.

"Charlie's an old bachelor," Arch explained. "Got

him a little ranch out yonder toward the Figure 4, a little to the north. Good stockman, and the best hand at counting cattle you ever saw. Frank Bowman always liked to use him. Besides, Charlie generally needed a little extra money."

Riding out of Mobeetie under the rosy light of sunup, Espy bore a little north of the Figure 4. By noon he reached Charlie Burnside's camp. An old man stood beside the open door of a dugout, where woodsmoke curled upward from a crooked chimney in the sod roof. The prairie wind played through his long gray whiskers.

"Git down," the old man greeted him openhandedly. "Git down and come in. Chuck'll be ready pretty soon now."

Espy introduced himself. Burnside pumped his hand. Age had weakened the old ranchman's grip, but it hadn't dimmed his smile.

"Sure am pleased to meet you. Hadn't heard they'd gotten them a new manager over there yet. Just figured Mary was going to handle it."

Espy didn't know what answer to give to that, so he gave none. The old man added, "We don't hear much, just me and old Ramon on this place by ourselves. Ain't often either one of us gits to town."

Espy didn't ask him about the cattle counts until the two of them and Burnside's Mexican helper had finished eating. Espy and the old ranchman sat in the shade of a brush arbor that had been built beside the dugout to substitute for a porch.

Holding a tight rein on his eagerness, Espy asked, "They tell me you helped count the Figure 4 stock during the spring roundup." He made it sound almost as if he wasn't really interested—just making conversation.

"That I did, that I did. Been doing it for three or four years now." He added with a bit of pride, "May not be good for much else anymore, but I'm still the best cattle counter hereabouts."

Espy's hand was nervously flexing, open and shut, open and shut. "Would you remember what those counts were?"

The old man studied a moment, his eyes fixed on the broad horizon, where not a single tree broke the gentle swell of the prairie. "Well, sir, I couldn't rightly say anymore. I handed all the tally books over to Sam Kirk, for Frank Bowman. Frank's health was failing him last spring. He didn't get out to the roundup much."

Espy's eyes sharpened. "You mean he gave Sam Kirk full authority?"

Burnside nodded. "Sure. Sam always was Frank Bowman's right-hand man. There never was a better foreman. He'd've made the syndicate a good manager, if they'd had sense enough to hire him."

The old man reddened a little then. "No offense meant, Norwood. I judge you to be a pretty good cowman yourself."

"Thanks."

Espy frowned, a growing knot of suspicion tightening in him. "I wonder why they didn't keep your tally books?"

Burnside shrugged. "Sam always took count same as I did. I reckon he checked my books against his, then turned his own in to Mr. Frank. Chances are he just threw mine away. No sense in keeping two sets anyhow."

A tingle of excitement began to work through Espy. Here at last was something to put his finger on.

"Have the cattle numbers gone down much since you've been helping the Figure 4?"

Burnside nodded. "A right smart. You can probably find that in Mr. Frank's books." No use telling the old man it *didn't* show on Mr. Frank's books.

Espy pressed, "Taking the south end of the ranch for example, how much would you say the cattle have been cut down?"

"Down there, I reckon they've been trimmed way more than half in the last couple of years. Over the rest of the ranch, a little less. Seems to me like I remember the tally down on the lower end, what Mr. Frank always called the south ranch. There was something over a thousand head, maybe twelve hundred, last branding. Used to be a sight more than that. One year we worked three thousand head on the south ranch."

Anger filled Espy's eyes. Twelve hundred head. Yet the tally books showed twenty-seven hundred. He remembered that.

And Sam Kirk had handled the books!

A slow-burning anger ate at Espy all the way back to the Figure 4 headquarters. He knew a vague disappointment, too. He'd liked Sam Kirk. He had seen readily enough that Sam was a first-class stockman. And Frank Bowman evidently had trusted Sam through the years. But this business about the tally books was going to be hard to explain.

Espy rode in above the barns. Boyish laughter reached out to him long before he got there. The high-spirited shouting of youngsters led him around the back side of the barn.

In a pole corral Joe Kirk had snubbed a big bawling calf to a post. Kenny Norwood sat astraddle the struggling calf while Joe drew a rope tight around the calf's belly and over Kenny's hands.

"Ready," Kenny said, and Joe turned the calf loose.

Bawling, the calf bucked and plunged. Kenny bounced from one side to the other, laughing at the top of his voice. Then he lost balance and began to slip low off one side. He hung precariously there for two jumps, then sailed off and rolled in the sand.

Joe Kirk ran to him and helped him up. "You're doing better, Tex. You rode him six jumps that time. I counted them."

Grinning, Kenny wiped the sand from his face. It was a bruised face, and there was a big black ring around one eye. "Six jumps? Did I, really?"

"You sure 'nuff did. Want to give her another whirl?"

"You bet your boots."

They saw Espy sitting his horse, watching them. Kenny walked hurriedly to the fence. His exuberance spilled forth in a flood of words. "Hello, Daddy. I'm learning to ride calves. I'm doing pretty good, too, because Joe says so himself. And you know what else? He calls me Tex."

Espy's throat was tight, but he managed a smile. He hadn't heard Kenny laughing like that since he was a tiny boy. And Kenny hadn't looked at Espy this way in years.

Espy's eyes stung him, and he blinked hard. This durned sand . . .

Turning his horse loose, Espy walked up the slope toward Sam Kirk's house. Sam sat on the front porch, braiding a set of rawhide bridle reins. Sam nodded at Espy, then rolled the reins even under the weight of his boot. "Find us some men?" he asked.

Espy nodded, his mouth tight. "We'll get the men. Found something else, too. I want to talk to you, Sam. Is Helen in the house?"

Sam shook his head, curious. "No, she's out back, watering her flower beds."

"Good," Espy said. "No use for her to hear this."

Espy's hands were nervous. He rubbed them along the seams of his pants. "I want you to answer me straight, Sam. Did you turn in a true set of tallies to Frank Bowman after the spring roundup?"

Sudden harshness rushed to Kirk's brown face. "What do you mean by that?"

"Just what I asked you. Did you? Or were those tallies doctored up?"

Sam Kirk moved to his feet. He stepped down off the porch to the same level as Espy Norwood. His nostrils flared. "Nobody's ever called me a crook, Norwood."

Espy stared levelly into Kirk's brittle-turned eyes. "And *I* don't want to. But I had a talk with Charlie Burnside. What he told me doesn't check out with the tally books you turned in to Frank Bowman."

"What did he tell you?"

"He said he counted only about twelve hundred head on the south ranch. Tally books place the count close to twenty-seven hundred. You turned those figures in, Sam. I want to know why they're wrong."

Espy could see the pulse beating in Sam Kirk's throat. Kirk's chin was high and steady. "Charlie Burnside is wrong."

"He's got a reputation as a top counter."

"As a counter, yes. But he's got the poorest memory in the state of Texas. If he doesn't write a count down in a hurry, he forgets it. He probably can't tell you how old he is without looking it up."

For a moment Espy weakened under a serious doubt. What if the old man *was* wrong?

But he knew within reason that Burnside couldn't be that far wrong. The fault lay elsewhere. And it could only be in Sam Kirk.

"That all you've got to say, Sam?"

Kirk nodded. "That's all there is to say."

Stiffly Sam Kirk stood and watched as Espy strode off toward his house. Sam's jaw was ridged, his face red. Then his hands began to tremble. His shoulders slumped as he climbed the steps to the porch. He stopped abruptly.

Helen stood just inside the door, her face drained white. "Sam!" she breathed. "Sam, what's wrong? What's this all about?"

It was a moment before he answered her. "It was nothing, Helen. I wish you hadn't heard it."

She stepped out onto the porch. Her right hand gripped his arm. "Sam, there *is* something wrong. I can see it in your face. Maybe if you'd tell me, I could help."

He shook his head emphatically. "I said there's nothing to tell."

Before she could speak again, he turned quickly, stepped down off the porch, and headed for the barn in long, stiff strides.

Helen Kirk clutched one of the porch posts, watching him until he was out of sight. Her eyes glistened, near tears. She hesitated, trying to make up her mind. Then she stepped down off the porch and hurried toward Norwood's house.

Espy looked up in surprise as she came in. "Helen." One look at her, and he knew she had heard.

Her hands were clasped fearfully against her breast. "Espy," she said, "what is it? What has Sam done?"

Espy almost wished he'd never come to the Figure 4. He felt his heart tighten. He waited a moment, mustering up courage. "I'm not sure just what all he's done, Helen. But I do know that the spring tallies are false, and that he wrote them. The rest of it, you'll have to guess, just the way I'm guessing."

Helen looked at him with stricken eyes. A sob welled up in her throat. "Oh, Espy, Espy, what can I do for him?" she cried.

Espy's throat swelled. He did not answer, for he knew no answer to give.

13

The procession strung out for three hundred yards, twenty horses and four riders. In an easy, jogging trot, they followed an old wagon trail, two narrow ruts worn into the prairie sod, two ruts that were the only visible break in a great swelling, rolling ocean of short grass stretching to the horizon and far beyond.

A long-legged, loose-gaited *grulla* gelding was out in the lead, setting the pace, his head held high and proud. They were headed for the south camp of the Figure 4. The big *grulla* had spent much of his life there, and the homing instinct was strong in him. The other horses followed along, each in the place into which he had settled. Younger horses earlier in the morning had tried to take the lead, but the cantankerous *grulla* wasn't having it. With his ears backed down and his sharp teeth seeking blood, he had put them all in their place.

Espy Norwood and Sam Kirk followed a little way behind the loose horses. They had ridden almost stirrup to stirrup since shortly after daylight. Now it was two hours short of noon, and hardly a dozen words had passed from one man to the other. The tight barrier of silence between them was almost as solid as an adobe wall.

Far back, bringing up the rear, Kenny Norwood and freckled-faced Joe Kirk laughed and talked and played. For an hour one had been a Comanche Indian and the other an Indian fighter. A curt warning from Sam Kirk to Joe finally had ended that game.

The boys had dropped back, slowing their horses to a walk. They let their fathers get three hundred yards ahead of them. Then, yelling like two wild Indians, they raked spurs along their horses' sides and plunged into a breakneck race.

Over his shoulder, Espy watched the two youngsters thundering down upon him. His face relaxed momentarily, and a grin played at the corners of his mouth.

Joe pulled his horse to a sudden, sliding stop, the dust swirling past him. He looked back proudly at the two parallel marks the sharp hind hoofs had cut into the ground.

Sam Kirk twisted half around in the saddle, his eyes impatient. "Joe, if you buttons don't quit running those horses like that, you'll both be afoot before we get to the south camp."

Joe said, "All right, Papa." And in three minutes he would forget again.

Espy gave Kenny a sharp, reproving glance. But inwardly he was smiling. Kenny's happy laughter had been like music to him. He had spent hours puzzling about the change which had come to Kenny. He didn't rightly know the reason, and Kenny wasn't talking. One thing sure, Espy was proud of that boy.

They rode another mile, working into the rougher

ground. Behind him Espy could hear the earnest talk and the high-lifting laughter of the youngsters.

At last he broke the long silence between himself and Sam Kirk. "We haven't run across many cattle the last few miles," he pointed out.

Kirk made no immediate answer. It had been the better part of a week now since Espy had ridden in from Charlie Burnside's ranch and demanded an explanation about the tallies. He still hadn't gotten one that satisfied him.

Presently Kirk said, "You still don't believe me, do you?"

Espy didn't answer. Kirk added, "They don't value a man's word the way they used to."

Bluntly Espy replied, "Sometimes a man's word doesn't carry the value that it used to."

The fury in Kirk's eyes leaped at Espy. Then Kirk touched spurs to his mount and circled around to the side of the long string of horses. There he stayed, nursing his anger.

Espy asked himself for the twentieth time why he hadn't fired Sam Kirk the day he rode in from Burnside's. But he knew. It was Kenny, and reckless young Joe Kirk. And perhaps most of all, it was warm-eyed Helen Kirk.

There was one answer. A roundup, and a full count. But a roundup took time, and there wouldn't be enough before the lawyer Slagel arrived with the syndicate directors, dead set on wrecking the colonel.

And even if he did prove the numbers short, would that help the colonel? No, chances were it would hurt, and hurt bad.

Deeply troubled, he rode with his gaze on the ground.

Ahead, the trail pitched abruptly into broken

ground, into a brush-lined draw where a downpour
of rain would sometimes bring a violent rush of mud-
red floodwater that could sweep a whole herd of cattle away.

The horses bunched up closer as they slanted off
into the draw. Sam Kirk yelled at the drags. Espy
heard the two boys riding just behind him as he
started down the slope.

He saw the two horsemen almost as quickly as
they saw him. Two horsemen, working down along
the fringe of the brush, pushing a small bunch of cattle ahead of them. Cattle with the Figure 4 brand.
And these weren't Figure 4 men.

For a long moment, surprise was the master of all
the men. Then the rustlers' hands streaked upward,
and fire belched from their guns.

Espy's first thought was of the boys behind him. He
turned and yelled for them to get away.

Terror swept through the loose horses. They stam-
peded, breaking away from the thunder of the guns.
Their panic seized Kenny's horse. He bolted, racing
along the edge of the brush. Kenny tried to hold him,
but the horse had cold-jawed. Then it was all Kenny
could do to hold tight to the saddle horn and try to
duck the heavy branches that plucked at him.

Espy's horse panicked, dropping his head and beginning to buck. Espy struggled to hold the mount's
head up. And all the time Espy's eyes were on the
helpless boy, his heart high in his throat.

He managed somehow to get the horse straightened out and to spur off after Kenny. But by that time
Sam Kirk was ahead of him, sinking spurs into his
horse's ribs.

Espy saw the heavy branch hit Kenny and knock him
spinning from the saddle. But Kenny didn't fall clear.

Espy heard a sharp cry of despair and knew it was his own voice. Kenny's foot was hung in the stirrup!

"Kenny!" Espy cried out again, but his voice was lost in the rush of the wind. He spurred harder, but he saw the lift of dust as the boy's head and shoulders struck the ground. The heart and hope went out of Espy. He was too far behind. He could never save his boy now.

But Sam Kirk was not too far behind. Spurring hard, he closed the gap. Then his strong hand closed on the trailing bridle reins. He took a quick wrap around his saddle horn and eased the scared horse down to a trot, then to a walk, careful that in his fright the horse did not kick the dragging boy.

Espy pulled in beside him, reached down, and with a quick, firm grip yanked Kenny's boot free of the stirrup. The boy slumped to the ground and lay still.

Espy dropped beside him, weakness washing through him, his throat blocked. Gently he lifted the boy's head and brushed the dirt from the still face. His hand was warm and sticky, and not from his own blood.

Sam Kirk had stepped down beside him, while a wide-eyed Joe Kirk sat his horse and held the other three mounts. The loose horses had scattered out into the brush, and the tremor of their hoofbeats still echoed down the draw.

"He's alive." It was Sam Kirk who spoke.

With gentle hands Espy felt over the boy's body. If there were any broken bones, he couldn't find them. But the boy's head was bruised and bleeding.

Sam Kirk stood up, taking the reins of the three held horses. "Joe, you hightail it on to camp. You and the boys throw a mattress and some blankets into the wagon there and get back here just as fast as you can run."

"Yes, sir!" Joe wheeled his horse around and spurred across the draw.

Sam tied the horses to nearby bushes, then returned and knelt beside Espy. "Maybe he's just knocked out," he offered in sympathy.

Espy was a long time in finding his voice. "Maybe."

And then there was nothing to do but wait. Wait and think. "I'm obliged to you, Sam. Much obliged."

Yes, he *was* obliged. Whatever he'd intended to do about Sam Kirk would have to wait now. And somehow, Espy was glad.

Espy lifted his head from his hands as Helen Kirk stepped out onto the porch. "He's coming to, Espy."

Espy stood up quickly and pushed through the door after her. He leaned over the bed and took hold of the boy's hand. He forced a smile as Kenny fought to open his eyes.

"How's it going, son?" he spoke, his voice strained.

Kenny's first effort at talking was painful and without success. Finally he managed, "I didn't get thrown off, Dad." Pride was in his voice. "He couldn't have thrown me off . . . if it hadn't been for that big old branch."

Espy squeezed the boy's hand, his eyes burning. "No, son, it was a good ride. He'd've never thrown you off by himself."

Helen Kirk's hand was on Espy's arm, the fingers holding tight. Espy was acutely conscious of them, and he liked them there.

"I think he's going to be all right, Espy," she reassured him. "He's going to hurt for several days, but I think that's all it'll be."

He looked at her warmly. "Thank you, Helen. You've been wonderful."

She smiled, not answering. She walked to the kitchen cabinet and got a bottle. "Sam keeps this around the house for colds and such," she said. "I brought it over. A good stiff drink now might do you a heap of good."

She poured an inch of it into a glass and handed it to him. Hands trembling, Espy took it. It had been a long time, and maybe it would settle his jumbled, tortured nerves.

But something stopped him as the glass touched his lips. The strong, bracing smell of the whisky jerked his head back. He hesitated a moment, then set the glass down.

"No," he said, "for somebody else, maybe. But not for me."

Answering the question in her eyes, he told her, "I fought a long, hard fight with that stuff, Helen, and I won it. But I've got a feeling about it. If I ever took a drink of it, I know I couldn't hold myself back. I'd face that battle all over again."

She nodded sympathetically, putting the bottle back out of sight. "I'm sorry, Espy. I didn't know."

The worry slid away, and weakness rushed in to fill its place. Espy slumped into his chair.

"I'll stay here with him awhile, if you'd like me to, Espy," Helen offered.

Espy nodded. "Thank you, Helen. I'd like you to."

He watched her, and old memories reached up to him, warm, beloved memories.

Mary Bowman had kept to herself since Espy Norwood had arrived, and most especially since the fight.

Now, looking out her window, she sensed something amiss at the syndicate house, and sent plump old Delfina to find out.

Still watching out the window, she felt the strong tug of worry, and she wondered about it. Why should she feel any worry about Espy Norwood?

She had every reason to hate him. And indeed she had hated him, or thought so, at least. But somewhere things had changed. Somewhere she had begun to admit to herself that everything he had done so far was in the best interest of the ranch. Not a move could she see that was selfish, or done purely out of malice.

She thought she knew when the change had begun in her. It was the day she had encouraged Claude Hatch to fight Norwood. From her front porch she had watched, had seen the deep regret which had weighted Norwood's tired face. He had hated the fight, and yet he had gone into it because he had had to, because he was not a coward.

Watching him, she had realized that. And suddenly shame had reached her, a deep, sobering, burning shame. Never had she done such a thing before.

Since that day, she had spent hours at her window, looking for Norwood, and having found him, following him with her penitent eyes. She had wanted him to understand, but never had she been able to make herself go to him and explain. Somehow, perhaps, he would sense what she wanted to say, and would find it in him to forgive her.

When Delfina returned with her report about Kenny, Mary Bowman knew it was time to talk to Norwood, time to empty her heart to him and ease her tortured conscience.

A wave of sympathy swept over her as she walked through the syndicate house door and saw Espy Norwood, his face mirroring the anxious, heartbreaking hours through which he had gone.

Her heart quickening, she said, "I just heard about your boy."

Norwood's eyes lifted to her. She thought she saw softness in them. She hoped she did. "I hope he's not too badly hurt," she said.

He shook his head. "He's going to be all right."

Some of the tension left her in a long breath. "I'm glad of that." Her voice was quiet but earnest. "I'm sorry about a lot of things, Espy. I'm sorry for the way I acted when you first came here."

Norwood's eyes smiled at her. She felt a quick thrill of pleasure.

"I've stayed burrowed up like a badger or something," she went on. "But now I'd like to work with you, help wherever I can."

Visibly surprised, he was pleased nevertheless. She could see that in his gray eyes. It gave her hope. "And, Espy, please forgive me for Claude Hatch."

His head jerked upward. He flinched as if she had hit him. "What do you mean?"

She said, "It was my fault that he fought you. I egged him on. I just didn't realize what I was doing. But I know now, and I'm sorry."

He arose stiffly. No smile was left in his eyes. Of a sudden they had gone hard and cold. "You're sorry." He said it almost like a curse word. "That's easy to say now, that you've almost killed my son."

She took a step backward, her hand raised to her mouth in surprise.

Espy said, "Who do you think it was that we jumped today, running off Figure 4 cattle? I saw them, and so did Sam Kirk.

"One of them was a Wolford man. He was there

the day Wolford intercepted me on my way out here. And the other one, Miss Bowman, was Claude Hatch!"

A quick sob clutched her throat. "Espy, I didn't have any idea—"

His fists clenched tightly. His voice cut at her like the sharp edge of a knife. "I forgave you for what you did to me. But how can I forgive you for what you did to my son?"

Tears rushed hot into Mary Bowman's eyes. She whirled and hurried out the door. She shoved into her house, into her room. She fell down across the bed and let the anguished tears come.

She knew now what the matter was. Without wanting to, without even realizing what was happening to her, she had fallen in love with Espy Norwood.

14

The word quietly passed through the bunkhouse an hour before daybreak. Only a little muttered conversation rose above the sound of the cowboys pulling on their spurred boots, and the metallic clicking of buckles. Someone threw the bolt on a rifle, and a quiet voice said, "Don't load that thing in here. You're liable to shoot somebody."

Breakfast in the cookshack was unusually quiet. No joking, no hoorawing. Jess Cooley never had a sarcastic word to say.

The men looked up expectantly as Espy Norwood ducked through the low dugout door. Quietly he took his place at the table, the reddish lamplight harshly flickering against his drawn face. A grim determination seemed to be driving him.

Sam Kirk's eyes lifted to the manager's. His shoulders shrugged slightly, and he busied himself with breakfast.

The sound of horses shoving noisily into the corral brought several cowboys to their feet. Finished eating, they moved on out. In a moment the two horse jinglers came in for breakfast.

Most mornings there would be some raucous comment about their horse handling ability, and a quick answer about some puncher's favorite horse that was going to get forefooted and thrown flat on his back if he didn't quit trying to run off with the whole remuda. This morning nobody said anything.

Roping out the morning's mount was accomplished quickly, methodically, and quietly. For several moments Espy had sensed Sam Kirk's eyes upon him. Cinching up, he said over his shoulder, "You don't like this, do you, Sam?"

"Am I supposed to?"

"You don't have to go if you don't want to."

Kirk's answer was blunt. "I'll go wherever my men do."

A slight figure stood at the gate, dimly outlined against the dark sky. Espy led his horse outside, and the figure moved close to him.

Mary Bowman said, "Are you sure you know what you're doing, Espy? Are you sure you're not letting anger over your son drive you into making a mistake?"

He gazed sternly at her. "Who told you what we're going to do?"

"Never mind who. I just want to know if you really think you're right. Has my uncle been stealing Figure 4 cattle?"

Espy said, "I think he has. That's why we're going over there."

"What do you expect to find?"

"Cattle with the Figure 4 on them. Or burnt cattle with the Figure 4 blotted over by some other brand."

Her lips tightened. "And if you find them, what will you do?"

"We'll bring them back. And we'll bring Gid Bowman, too. He'll pay, Mary. Even if he *is* your uncle."

Her gaze was level and unwavering. "He's a leech, Espy. Ever since I was a child, I've hated him. Dad stood for it because they were brothers. The tie was too strong for him to break, I guess. But *I've* broken it."

Her hand hesitantly reached forward, touching his arm. "I'm not worried about Gid Bowman, Espy. I'm worried about *you*."

Espy found himself warming to the touch of her hand, and he didn't want to. Uneasily he pulled his arm back.

She said, "Gid may have Quirt Wolford backing him up."

Espy thought of the beating he had taken, and of the helpless boy who lay in pain at the syndicate house because of Quirt Wolford.

"I hope he does," he said.

Espy swung into the saddle. He tried not to, but he couldn't keep from looking back at her as he swung into a stiff jog trot. The men strung out behind him, two and three abreast. Mary Bowman was left standing alone by the gate, the dust drifting about her. She faded into the predawn darkness.

Espy set an easy pace, one at which the horses could last all day. This was one day they surely would have to.

Try as he might to dismiss her from his mind, his thoughts dwelt stubbornly upon Mary Bowman. Again and again he heard her phantom voice. There had been a worrisome sincerity in the way she spoke, worrisome because it didn't fit with her sending Wolford to beat him.

More than once she had denied having done that.

Now Espy was finding it harder and harder to convince himself that she had.

In some obscure way, it had pleased him that she had walked out to talk to him this morning. He could almost imagine he still felt the touch of her hand upon his arm. He forgot for a while about her being Mary Bowman, an enemy to him. He found himself thinking of her only as a woman, a very desirable woman. And the thought eased the hard-set lines in his face, bringing warmth to his chill gray eyes.

The morning was far gone when Espy reined in and waited for the stragglers to catch up. To Sam Kirk he said, "This is about where Gid's country starts, isn't it?"

When Sam nodded, Espy went on, "All right, we'll drop the first man off right here. Next man a quarter mile farther, and so on till we're strung out all the way across. Then we'll ride due south, taking it slow and easy and combing the brush for cattle. If you find anything that looks halfway kin to a Figure 4, push it along.

"We'll work south ten miles, then all shove whatever we find toward the center, at the south end of Gid's range. If anybody stumbles into trouble, fire into the air. The rest of us will come running. Any questions?"

There were none. Espy nodded to the old puncher named Dolph. "Dolph, if you'll drop off here—" It was always wise to have a steady hand on the outside of a drive.

Espy struck due west then, dropping the men off one by one. In time he reached the western end of Gid Bowman's range, and only Sam Kirk was left with him. For quite a while Sam had eyed him expectantly every time he had stopped. But never had Espy chosen to drop the foreman off.

For Espy, the reason was simple enough. He didn't trust Sam. And from the frosty reserve in the foreman's face, he knew Kirk sensed it.

Espy edged his horse southward. "Let's go, Sam. We've got the longest ride to make."

He hadn't expected to find anything right at first, so it didn't worry him. But when he had ridden an hour, then two, without finding anything but a few scattered cattle carrying Bowman's brand, it began to nettle him. From an occasional high point he would watch for the other riders, and having found them, try to see whether or not they were pushing any cattle along. So far as he could tell, they weren't.

He took off his hat and wiped his forehead with his sleeve, wondering whether it was the heat or the growing tug of worry that brought the sweat.

The sun was beginning to edge downward from its peak when Espy saw the single rider angling across toward him, his horse in a lope. For one moment Espy's pulse quickened. *They've found something,* he thought.

Then the rider drew closer, and recognition came. Espy's mouth pulled downward at the corners. He stopped, his hand fisted on the reins.

Gid Bowman hauled up so close that he could almost reach out and strike Espy. "What the hell do you think you're doing, Norwood? Get your men off of my range!" Though red-eyed and flushed, he was stone sober this time. And he was madder than a cat in a washtub.

Espy said flatly, "We're looking for Figure 4 cattle."

"If any of your cattle stray onto my land, I'll send them back to you. You don't catch me on *your* range."

Espy almost smiled at that. "No, but we've tried

to." Bowman flamed at the insult. "Get your men off, Norwood. Get them off before I go fetch the law."

Espy said, "What law—Llewellyn? We'll be through and gone before you can sober him up."

Bowman's hand trembled on his bridle reins. "Norwood, I warn you—" His eyes cut sharply to Sam Kirk. "Make him leave, Sam. If you don't, you'll wish *you'd* left a long time ago."

Kirk stiffened.

Espy sensed the angry understanding that passed between the two men. "What do you mean by that, Bowman?"

Bowman said, "Sam knows."

Kirk's eyes blazed, but they avoided Espy. Espy vainly studied the foreman's rigid face. He found no answer there, but he thought he knew the answer, just the same.

His voice cut like a razor, "We're going to ride your ranch out, Bowman. I know you've been stealing Figure 4 cattle. Frank Bowman must've known it, too, but he wouldn't take action because you were his brother. So you got away with it. But not anymore. If we find any stolen cattle here, we'll be back, looking for *you*. Come on, Sam."

He pulled his horse away and headed south again, leaving the bristling Gid Bowman to mutter to himself.

Espy and Kirk rode another hour, and still they found nothing. Espy paused often to listen for the bawl of cattle to the east of him, sound which would indicate that other riders were pushing along Figure 4 cattle. He heard nothing except the breathing of his horse and the quiet creak of his saddle.

He started the circle, swinging eastward again, sweeping the lower end of Bowman's range. But even as he did, he knew instinctively that the drive had been for nothing. He squinted hard, hoping he would see cattle gathering far up yonder. But somehow, he knew he wouldn't.

One by one the cowboys began falling in closer to him as they worked toward the center. Past mid-afternoon, they all met. Espy's eyes swept them. He didn't have to ask. He could tell.

His jaw clenched, and he slapped his saddle horn with the flat of his hand, jarring loose at least a little of the galling anger. He could taste the frustration, sour as vinegar.

"There *had* to be something," he gritted in protest. "Didn't anybody find *anything?*"

Some of the men shook their heads, the rest didn't have to. Espy glanced at Sam Kirk and thought he saw relief ease into the foreman's face.

The breath went out of Espy in a long, almost inaudible sigh. He shrugged helplessly. "They've moved south, then. And I reckon we're whipped for now. Let's get started home."

Instead of taking the lead this time, he dropped back to the rear, his shoulders slumped.

Damn it, he knew he'd been right. Gid Bowman was guilty, that was as certain as the prairie wind. And they hadn't found a thing. But one of them *had* found something.

Cotton Dulaney hipped around in the saddle and looked back at Espy. The kid could see the bitter twist of frustration in the manager's face.

Maybe I ought to tell him, he thought.

But he wouldn't. He'd made up his mind to that. This was *his* discovery, Cotton's alone.

He'd get a chance in a day or two. Then he'd ease back down here and follow up what he had found.

A big bunch of riders could never hope to slip up on those cow thieves. But one man, alone, might.

The thought of it brought a happy surge of warmth. *I won't ever be the kid of this outfit again.*

For two days Matt Ollinger had roamed what passed for streets in Mobeetie. He had been in every bar, and there were several of them. He had listened to all the gossip he could pick up concerning Espy Norwood and the Figure 4. And all the time he expectantly watched the trail which led in from the north, and wondered why in sin a woman had to be so damn slow.

The more he heard about the Figure 4, the more worried he got. A big outfit, and a long way from town. It wouldn't be easy to slip in there, steal a kid, and get clean away. Especially when you didn't know the country. It began to look like he was going to have to enlist some help.

Then Lady Luck dealt him a royal flush. Standing by the grimy front window of one of the saloons, he saw a rider knee a big brown horse toward a hitch rack. Ollinger's whiskers lifted in a slow grin as his boot heel ground his cigarette on the dirt floor, and he walked out into the morning sun.

"Jake!" he said, his voice hardly lifting above a normal tone. "Jake Claymore!"

The rider hauled up short, quickly on the defensive. Recognition came and he relaxed, reining in beside Ollinger. He reached down to take the man's hand.

"Name's Smith now," Claymore said pleasantly. "Just plain old Smith. How you doing, Matt?"

"Still using my own name."

Early though it was, they had a drink together, and then two. Ollinger pumped Claymore for information, and he finally got it out of him that he was working with Quirt Wolford.

"Wolford," Ollinger mused, fingering his dark whiskers. "I've been hearing about him. Might be he's just the man to help me with a deal I got rigged up."

Claymore shrugged. "I don't know. Quirt's got his hands pretty full right now. But if there was money in it . . ."

"There's not any money in the deal," Ollinger lied. "But I thought maybe Wolford might like to help me with it anyhow. It'd give him a chance to even up with Norwood. Sometimes there's things you can't just put a price tag on. Some things are worth doing when there ain't a nickel in them."

Claymore skeptically shook his head. "I don't know. You can't ever tell about Quirt Wolford. He's a smart man, Matt, a mighty smart man. Yet once in a while he acts like he's crazy."

Ollinger signaled for another drink. "Take me to him, Jake. Let me talk with him."

Worriedly Claymore said, "I don't dare do that, Matt. Quirt would shoot us both if I took a stranger to his camp."

"I'm not a stranger, Jake, not to you. You can vouch for me. If he likes the idea, fine. If he doesn't, I'll leave. You know how I stand with the law. You know I wouldn't tell anybody a thing I seen."

Claymore frowned deeply. With misgivings he finally gave in. "All right, Matt. But just remember it was your own idea."

Ollinger grinned. "Stop worrying. There ain't nothing going to happen."

* * *

Cotton Dulaney paused in the edge of the brush, trying to get his bearings. He looked wistfully at the hill yonder. If he could get on top of that, he could find his way for sure. But he'd be seen for sure, too. He had to keep to the brush.

He could find the place all right, if he could just spot that old dead cottonwood he'd seen beside a creek bed. The giant tree had been split down the middle by a bolt of lightning sometime in the past. Now its gaunt, stricken branches stood starkly against the skyline like a lonely grave marker far out on the prairie.

Cotton kept riding, sticking close to the protecting brush and watching carefully for the tree. He smiled as he thought how pleased Espy Norwood and Sam Kirk were going to be. Oh, they might paw a little sand because he went out alone. But at least they would have to accept him as a man now.

He found the fire-struck tree. Excitement began to play through him like electricity through a cat's fur in storm time. Straight east, a quarter of a mile.

He made the quarter mile with his hand on his .44. He had long since checked his saddle gun. It too was loaded and ready.

He found the place. It was just as he had left it the other day. Here was a small clearing in the midst of the brush. Inside it was a single pole corral, built of cedar and mesquite and anything else that had come to hand.

Quickly Cotton's eyes searched for sign that anyone had been here since he had discovered the place. Evidently no one had.

Disappointment was keen and painful. He *had* to find something.

Cotton kicked at the old trace of branding fires. A thin layer of dust had settled over the black ashes. The place hadn't been used in several days, maybe several weeks. It might even have been left for good.

He found the smoke-blackened running iron lying just where he had seen it before. He picked it up and knocked the loose dirt off against the fence. This was a typical rustler's iron, all right. Short enough that a man could carry it on his saddle without trouble, without its even being particularly noticeable. And the curved, J-shaped end of it was made for running a new brand over an old one.

For a moment Cotton considered taking the running iron back for his proof. But he could have done *that* well the other day. No, it wasn't enough. All he would get would be a thorough chewing-out for coming back here by himself. He had to do better.

He tied the running iron to his saddle and headed south. By George, he *would* find something, or he wouldn't go back. He'd ride all the way down to the Colorado River, if he had to.

He didn't have to. At dusk he hobbled his horse, ate a little from the sack of food he had stolen out of Jess Cooley's kitchen, and lay down on the ground, his head against his saddle. At sunup he was in the saddle again. Before long he began to run across cattle sign—fresh sign.

The sound of bawling cattle reached him. He'd cowboyed long enough to know that cattle being driven don't sound like cattle free on the range. And these were being driven.

Staying in the brush, he got close enough to see the herd. It was a little bunch, mostly young heifers, some cows with their first calves. He couldn't see the brand, but he knew the underbit earmark. Figure 4!

Cotton's heartbeat quickened. For the first time he knew the sudden grip of real fear, and a true realization of his position here began to sink in. Gone was the kid excitement, the lighthearted search for glory. Soberly he admitted to himself that he stood a good chance of getting killed.

Now was the time to turn back, to go for help.

But he couldn't do it, not yet. He had to see where these cattle were being taken. What good was it to know where they came from, but not where they went?

He licked dry lips and edged his horse forward. He'd dealt into the game. Now he would play out his hand.

Matt Ollinger rubbed a sleeve across his sweaty face. "You said it was a far piece, Jake," he grumbled, "but you didn't say it was halfway to Mexico."

Jake Claymore—or Smith—shifted his weight in the saddle. "It's not far now. Just around that hill a little ways."

Ollinger grunted. He was beginning to think it had been a mistake to come all the way out here. What if he couldn't get Wolford interested? One thing sure, he wasn't going to split any money with him. Five hundred dollars wasn't much when you had to share it.

Claymore said, "Wonder whose horse that is yonder?"

Ollinger's eyes followed his. He had almost missed the animal, tied out in the brush. Riding in close, he saw that it was a young pony, probably not much more than a bronc. And burned on its hip was a Figure 4.

Claymore jumped to the ground, gun in his hand, and began to move swiftly afoot, following the boot tracks that led away from the horse. Ollinger tied his own horse and followed.

The bawling of the cattle grew louder as they cautiously traced the tracks. They both saw the cowboy at the same time. Bellied down under a thick, low-growing mesquite, he was watching men in a corral a hundred or so yards away, changing Figure 4 brands into something that looked like an arrowhead.

Ollinger said sharply, "Get up slow and turn this way."

The cowboy jerked in surprise. He saw two guns leveled in his face. The color drained from his cheeks. Why, this was nothing more than a kid, Ollinger saw.

"Get up," he said.

The young cowboy slowly complied, his hands unsteady. His eyes were wild, and Ollinger read the thought behind them.

"Don't try it, kid. We'd kill you before you took two steps."

Cotton Dulaney gave up then. Ollinger saw the .44 at the boy's hip and the saddle gun he had leaned against a low limb of the tree. The youngster's hardware had been ready, but the boy hadn't.

With an old back-trail instinct, Ollinger knew Quirt Wolford without having to be told. Jake Claymore quickly explained to Wolford how they had come upon Cotton's horse.

Glaring malevolently, Wolford struck the boy across the face with the back of his hand. The impact knocked the kid's hat off, exposing a tangle of cottony hair. "How many others out there?" he demanded.

Cotton involuntarily raised his hand to his mouth, in an effort to hold the pain. "They're all there," he said desperately. "Enough of them to wipe you out. You better let me go."

Wolford studied him. "You're lying." He slapped the boy again. "You came by yourself."

That blow drew blood. Cotton stood silent, his hand over his mouth. Wolford ordered a couple of his men to go after Cotton's horse, as well as Claymore's and Ollinger's. In a few minutes they were back.

"Any sign of others?" Wolford asked. They shook their heads.

Wolford turned back to the boy. "Just got a little too big for your britches, didn't you, kid? You should've stayed home, where you belonged. Now you're never going back."

He reached for Cotton's rope and shook it down.

One of Wolford's men stepped forward. "Wait a minute, Wolford. What're you fixing to do?"

Wolford turned on him angrily. "Go back to the branding pen, Hatch."

Fear looked out of Claude Hatch's eyes. "He's just a kid, Quirt. Let him go."

"Let him go and get us hung?" Wolford stepped into Cotton's saddle. He dropped a loop over the boy's shoulders and spurred the horse. Cotton cried out once, and only once.

Moments later Wolford came back, dragging the limp body. The excited bronc stepped along fearfully, its eyes rolling. A couple of the men turned their backs and walked away. Even Matt Ollinger felt a flutter at the pit of his stomach. He carefully avoided looking down the rope.

Quirt Wolford was the only man who seemed unaffected. His voice was even as he dismounted. "Jake, we got to take this kid back to Figure 4 range and dump him. Turn the horse loose and leave the rope dragging. It'll look like an accident."

Claymore's face was the color of clabber. "Like that Englishman Spence?"

"Yes. Just like him."

The sound of a horse's hoofs jerked Wolford around. Claude Hatch had mounted and was riding away. "Come back here," Wolford bawled at him.

The cowboy rode on, unmindful. Wolford drew his gun and fired just over Hatch's head. Hatch hauled up. He pulled the horse around and came back at a slow walk. His whole frame was atremble with horror at what he had seen.

Wolford pointed to the torn body of Cotton Dulaney. "Take a look, Hatch, a good look. If you ever try to run out on me, that's what'll happen to *you!*"

Hatch dragged back to the branding pen and leaned over the fence, sick.

Wolford's angry eyes flicked over the rest of the men. "All right, now, get on back to the pen and finish up. We got a lot to do."

When the rest had gone to work, Wolford walked up to Ollinger. "Matt Ollinger," he said evenly. "I've heard of you. Now, what kind of a deal have you got?"

15

Cotton Dulaney was carried to the Figure 4's little burial ground atop a hill overlooking the headquarters. The circuit-riding minister finished his short funeral sermon, and the solemn cowboys filed by one by one to empty a shovel of dirt into the grave. With them was Arch McCavitt, his red hair bared to the gentle wind.

Jess Cooley stood off to one side, his back turned. Espy placed his hand on the cook's shoulder and felt the thin old frame shake.

The Kirk family stood together. Kenny Norwood was with them, beside Joe Kirk. Except for a little lingering soreness, Kenny had recovered.

Mary Bowman stood alone, by the wooden cross which had been erected over her father's grave not many weeks before. Her small hands crumpled a handkerchief. Several times Espy had sensed her eyes touching him. Now he felt compelled to stand beside her.

"The service is over, Mary," he said presently. "I'd like to walk back down with you."

Her eyes lifted to him. They brimmed with tears, unreserved and unashamed.

"Thank you, Espy. I'd like you to."

For half the distance down the hill they walked without speaking. Espy felt her nearness bringing an awakening warmth.

"He was a good kid," Espy said.

Mary nodded. "Dad was always fond of him. Next to Sam Kirk and Jess Cooley, I guess Cotton was his favorite."

Memory brought a near smile, momentarily relaxing her pretty face. "I'll never forget when Cotton came here, about three years ago. Just a half-starved, freckle-faced kid who didn't have a home anywhere until Dad gave him one. He had turned up in Mobeetie with a freight outfit, ragged and hungry, and somehow he had wound up at Arch McCavitt's. They always do. Arch fed him a few days, bought him new clothes, and set him up to an old saddle somebody had left there. Then Arch sent Cotton out here."

Her slight shoulders slacked. Espy put his arm around them. Touching her sent an electric tingle through him. He started to take his arm away but didn't. He wondered vaguely what had happened to the bitterness he had borne toward her. It was gone. Now all he had was an aching desire to hold her tighter. With some effort, he restrained that.

At her door she turned to face him, and regretfully he drew his arm away. But her warm fingers closed upon his hand. Her eyes leveled softly with his. "Espy," she said, "I wish . . ."

"Wish what?"

She hesitated. "Nothing, I guess. Please come in, Espy. I'll fix some coffee."

He followed her into the big rock house and back into the kitchen. He leaned against the cabinet, letting his eyes trail her as she ground coffee beans, dipped water into the small coffeepot, and put it on the stove. Watching her, he felt an old loneliness sweep over him again. Helen Kirk had awakened it in him, bringing up old and comfortable memories that had long remained unstirred. He hadn't been in love with Helen Kirk, he knew that. It was simply that with her he had realized more keenly than ever before how gray and empty life had become for him the last few years, how empty it was likely to be as time went on. Sure, he had a son, and that was a great help. But a man needed more—much more.

He didn't intend to do it. But without realizing what he was doing until he had done it, he caught the girl's shoulders and pulled her into his arms.

For a second her lips were tight with surprise. Then they softened. She answered his kiss with warmth, her loving hands tight on his back, her breasts soft against him.

When their lips parted, she pressed her cheek to his chest, her hands still holding him. Espy's arms remained tight around her.

"I didn't intend to do that, Mary," he said. "I don't know what came over me."

Softly she said, "I think I know, Espy. And I'm glad."

After a while Arch McCavitt came looking for him. Standing in the front door, he stared first at Mary, then at Espy, as if he didn't know whether to grin or frown.

"Jess Cooley's got something to tell you, Espy," he said in a solemn voice. "You better go with me."

Jess Cooley didn't see them as they first walked into the saddle shed. The old cook was talking quietly to the two boys, Joe and Kenny. Cooley fondly placed his hand on Joe Kirk's head, tousling the sandy-colored hair.

"Joe," he said, "that old saddle of yours is a worn-out wreck. Cotton thought a heap of you, and he'd have wanted you to have his. Take it, son."

Joe's eyes were shining. Reverently he reached out and touched Cotton's saddle. It was almost a new one. Choking, he said, "Gosh, Jess. Thanks."

The old cook's voice wavered. "Don't thank me. Just always remember Cotton, and try to be as good a hand as he was. That'll be thanks enough."

He became aware of Espy and Arch. His face went grim. "Let's go outside, Espy. I've found something."

The old man's hand clasped a short piece of iron. Outside, away from the boys, Jess Cooley suddenly turned and said, "It wasn't no accident, Espy. Cotton was murdered!"

Espy stopped abruptly, missing a breath. Chilling, he stared at Cooley. "How do you know, Jess?"

Cooley's narrowed eyes were crackling. "After the funeral, Dolph and me stayed on the hill to put up a cross. Dolph got to telling me how he found Cotton. I hadn't heard it before, because I hadn't been able to listen. This time I *did* listen.

"Dolph found the kid down toward the south end, on that big, open flat. There wasn't no brush there, Espy. None for a long ways. But it was me that dressed the kid for burial, and I could tell he'd been drug through the brush. There was thorns and twigs and . . ."

The old man's throat bobbed. His tough old fists drew up like mesquite knots. "He didn't die where Dolph found him. He was drug to death someplace else, and his body was moved."

Espy stared at the ground, fury scorching his face like a white-hot iron.

Cooley steadied his voice. "Something else, Espy. I found this tied to his saddle." He held forth the short object he had kept in his hand.

"A running iron," Espy said.

Cooley nodded. "I didn't think much of it at first. It ain't uncommon for folks to carry them. I figured he just happened to find it someplace. But now—I reckon we all know where he found it."

Espy's flaming eyes met Cooley's, then flicked to Arch. His hand went back to his hip, where the pistol usually rode. "We'll find him, Jess," he spoke grimly. "I'll get the boys together, and we won't come back till Quirt Wolford is dead!"

He whirled and started for the bunkhouse. Arch grabbed his arm, jerking him to a halt. "Wait a minute, Espy. That's not the way. I've already talked it over with Jess and made him see. Now *you've* got to see. This is for the law to handle."

Angrily Espy snapped, "The law? Like that sot Llewellyn?"

Earnestly Arch said, "Yes, the law, but not like Llewellyn. We've had an election in town since you were there. The old sheriff resigned. The new one's been hoping for a chance to get something on Wolford. This is his chance. Leave it to him, Espy. Wolford will hang, all right. Let him hang legal.

"That'll show we've finally got a law that means something. It'll do more to run the thieves out than a dozen lynching bees could."

Although his face was dark, Espy studied that. "Arch, I wouldn't've thought *you'd* ever be the one to give me a speech like that."

Arch said, "I'd never've thought I'd ever have to."

Espy could see that Arch was dead serious about this. He looked at Jess. The cook seemed to have been convinced. After a minute Espy gave in. "All right, Arch. I'll send somebody after the sheriff."

Arch shook his head. "You won't have to. I've already sent the minister."

Wryly Espy said, "You're ahead of me every jump."

"I figured it was better if we didn't let the cowboys know till the sheriff was here. You know what they'd want to do. Just exactly what you'd started to, Espy."

Espy rubbed the back of his neck. "I reckon you're right, Arch. We'll give the law a try. But just once. If it doesn't pan out in a hurry, we'll handle this ourselves."

Arch nodded. "Fair enough, I guess. The new sheriff is a friend of mine, Espy. This'll give him a chance to prove himself."

After a bit, Jess Cooley hobbled off toward the cookshack. Espy looked toward Sam Kirk's house up the slope. He straightened in resignation, knowing what he had to do.

"I'll see you after a while, Arch. Right now I've got a job."

Helen Kirk answered his knock. "I'm looking for Sam," he told her.

She managed a smile, though her face was drawn. "He's here, Espy."

Sam stepped out upon the porch, and Espy motioned for him to follow. They walked together to the syndicate house. Sam's face was haggard. It was evident that Cotton's death had hit him hard.

Espy made it quick and blunt. "Cotton didn't die by accident, Sam. Quirt Wolford murdered him. We've got the proof."

Sam's chin hardened, but he didn't look too surprised. "I guess I knew it. I tried to believe it wasn't so."

Espy tightened his fist. "I want you to leave, Sam. Now. Today!"

Sam's leathery cheeks lost their color.

Espy said, "I know you're tied in with Wolford some way, Sam. There's no need for you to deny it. But I know you wouldn't have had a hand in getting Cotton killed. And I owe you something, for Kenny. So I'm giving you a chance to get away, before the sheriff gets here."

Whatever was going on in Sam's mind, his guarded eyes never betrayed it.

"I hate to leave, Espy."

"But you will, Sam. If you don't, I won't protect you."

"I'd have to tell Helen something . . . and Joe."

"That's up to you. But tell them something and get out of here. Now!"

For a long time Sam stared out the open door, his hands flat against the seams of his saddle-worn trousers. Evidently reaching a decision, he faced Espy again. "You're a good man, Espy. I'd like to've been friends with you, if things had been different. Now it's too late, I reckon."

He extended his hand. "*Adios,* Espy."

Espy's throat tightened as he watched Sam go. Yes, Sam was right. If things *had* been different . . .

Espy walked out of the house and down toward the saddle shed again. Arch fell in beside him. Each sensed the melancholy that gripped the other. There was no need for talk between them. It was enough just to walk side by side, tied by a bond from long ago.

Aimlessly they moved past the saddle shed and up the slope to the bubbling spring that had drawn Frank Bowman to this place years ago, when this was still grazing ground for the buffalo, and when the Comanche still hunted here for meat, and for horses, and even for scalps. For a long while Espy and Arch sat there upon a big stone and stared silently at the rushing water, each with his own thoughts.

Restlessly Arch pitched pebbles into the water, watching the tiny splash of white after each one. Presently he said, "Mary Bowman's in love with you, isn't she, Espy?"

Half-startled, Espy said, "Why?"

"I saw her watching you at the funeral today. I could tell. And a while ago at her house, when I went to get you . . ."

He paused. "I think a lot of that girl, Espy. I hope you're not going to hurt her. Are you in love with her?"

Espy colored. "Arch, I don't know. I think I am. But I can't be sure. How can I know if it's really her, or if it's just that I'm lonely—that it's been so long since I've had any real interest in a woman that I'm letting my imagination run away with me?"

"Hasn't any woman ever stirred you since you lost Jeannie?"

"Sure, I've found myself interested several times, the way any man is apt to be drawn to a pretty woman. But it takes more than that, Arch. For me it does. There's never been one since Jeannie that hit me like this girl has."

Arch gripped Espy's shoulder. "Well, Espy, I hope this is the one. For you and for her. You both deserve the best. And I think you've both got it."

Arch stood up and stretched his long frame. Looking down toward the buildings, he suddenly frowned. "Here comes Helen Kirk. And something's got her excited."

Espy quickly arose and turned around. Helen was half running up the slope toward them, her face stricken. In long strides Espy hurried down to meet her.

Breathing heavily, she cried, "Espy, I've been looking everywhere for you. Sam's gone."

Regretfully Espy nodded. "I know." So Sam hadn't told her.

"But his guns, Espy. Why did he take his guns?"

"Guns?"

Trying desperately to keep from sobbing, she said, "Yes, his guns. He's gone to kill somebody, Espy. I could tell by the way he acted. He said he was going to do a job he should have done a long time ago."

Espy's blood chilled. His eyes met Arch's, and both men had the same answer.

"I tried to stop him," Helen cried, "but he wouldn't listen. He said someday I'd understand."

Espy gripped her cold hand. "Don't worry, Helen. I'll catch up with him and bring him back."

"He has a long start," she said. "It took me a while to find you."

"I'll bring him back," Espy said again. Then he struck into a long run down the slope and toward the saddle shed. Arch was right behind him.

While Espy roped a loose horse out of a corral, Arch asked him, "How did you know Sam was gone?"

"Because I fired him. I told him to leave. But I didn't count on a thing like this."

Briefly he explained what had happened. Arch listened patiently, then shook his head.

"You shouldn't have done it, Espy. You were wrong, dead wrong."

Incredulous, Espy stared, trying to read what was in Arch's mind.

Arch said, "Sam Kirk is a good man, Espy, a better man than you know."

"But the tallies, Arch."

Arch thought, *I know about the tallies. I know a lot more too. But the people out here have been my friends for years, Espy. It's not my place to tell you what I know. You'll have to find out for yourself.*

He said, "Believe me, Espy, you've made a mistake about Sam Kirk."

Looking into his friend's face, Espy realized Arch was telling the truth even though he hadn't given his reasons. He felt a quick wash of relief. He knew that, all along, he had wanted to believe Sam innocent.

Arch's horse was in the corral, too. Quickly Arch caught and saddled him.

Espy demanded, "What do you think *you're* doing?"

"Sam's *my* friend as well as yours. I'm going to help you find him and bring him back."

A thin smile came to Espy's face. "Been a long time since we've ridden together, Arch."

Arch nodded. "And let's get at it."

16

The approach of darkness never slowed Sam Kirk's determined pace. As daylight faded, a blood-red moon slowly arose. The stars blinked into view—one, two, half a dozen, and then the whole sky glittered. Sam knew his direction.

The full moon had risen high and night had polished it to a bright silver when Sam at last struck Gid Bowman's town trail. He reined in upon it and followed its southward course in an easy jog trot. The prairie wind had diminished to a cooling night breeze, carrying with it the warbling call of a night bird and the brittle staccato of a cricket.

As he rode, Sam's mind dwelt upon Cotton Dulaney. His hand went to his gun again and again.

At last Gid Bowman's cluttered camp broke into view before him, the low-built dugouts hardly casting a shadow in the brilliant moonlight. Sam dismounted, leading his horse to keep him from kicking up a racket among the cast-away tin cans and rubbish that littered the place. He tied the horse to an abandoned wagon, then went on to Bowman's living quarters afoot. Gun in hand, he cautiously walked down the shaky steps and ducked through the open door. For a moment he stood still, trying to identify the vague black shapes he could see scattered about the stuffy room. From the corner came the rasping sound of one man's snoring. *One man.*

Sam struck a match and lighted a smoky lamp. One glance in the flickering light confirmed that Bowman was alone.

"Wake up, Gid," he spoke curtly.

The snoring broke off abruptly. Gid Bowman sat up sleepy-eyed on his cot.

"Get your pants on, Gid," Sam said. "We're going for a ride."

It took a moment for the idea to force its way into Bowman's muddled brain. "A ride? In the middle of the night? Anyway, what in the hell do you think you're doing here, Sam?"

Kirk's voice was grim. "You're going to take me to Quirt Wolford. We're leaving right now. Get your pants on or you'll go in your underwear."

Grumbling, Gid Bowman swung his legs over the side of the cot. He scratched his sides, put on his hat and his boots, then pulled on his pants. Lastly he put on his shirt, shoving the tail of it into the ample waistband of his low-fitting trousers.

"You're crazy, Sam," he said, his eyes on the gun in the foreman's hand. "Quirt won't ever let you get to his camp."

Sam said, "He'll let me, because you're going to take me."

"And if I don't?"

Sam's eyes were brittle. He poked the gun into Bowman's soft belly. "You will."

Bowman had left a night horse in a corral. Punched up by Sam's gun, he saddled him and the two men rode southward. Sam pitched his rope around Gid's middle and knotted it. The other end he dallied around his own saddle horn.

"Try anything and I'll bounce your fat rump all over this ranch."

Gid Bowman no longer blustered. Fear put a tremor in his voice. "What do you say we at least wait for daylight?"

"No. There'll be men following me. And they can't follow in the dark."

Much later, far up in the dead hours after midnight, they halted to rest the horses. Sam never slept, watching Bowman. And Bowman never slept, watching Sam's gun.

"Sam," he asked once, "just what do you figure to do if we get there?"

Sam's voice was deadly as the rattle of a diamondback. "I'm going to kill Quirt Wolford!"

As daylight came, Sam pulled back into the brush, following Gid Bowman southward. "How much farther, Gid?"

"A good ride yet. But you better turn back while you can, Sam. You'll never make it."

"I'll make it." Sam frowned. "You know what happened to Cotton Dulaney?"

Cautiously Bowman said, "I've heard tell."

"He was dragged to death. It was an awful sight." Sam jerked at the rope around Gid's belly, jerked hard enough to make the heavy man grunt.

"I'm tying the rope to my saddle horn, Gid. If anything happens to me, my horse will run away. And he'll drag you with him, just the way Cotton was drug. So you better see that nothing happens to me."

Bowman's heavy face went the color of flour paste. His wide shoulders slumped. The hope went out of him.

They stopped and rested for one long period during the day, under the cover of brush. They had changed directions frequently, Bowman insisting that they were going the right way. When Sam figured the horses had had enough rest, he swung into his saddle. Bowman started to remount.

"No, Gid," Sam said curtly, taking the bridle reins. "You've led me miles out of the way. But you're not going to do it again. You're going to walk and lead me. Every extra mile you go means blisters on your feet."

Rage bubbled into Bowman's helpless face. He hobbled southwestward, Sam trailing behind him, the rope still on his saddle horn. Sam knew that this time they were headed the right way.

It was near night when Gid Bowman nervously reined up. Sam had finally let him mount again and ride.

"We're almost there," Bowman spoke nervously. "About three or four hundred yards ahead yonder, just off of the draw."

Sam swung down. "All right, then, we'll go the rest of the way afoot. You tie your horse here."

Bowman did. "Now, how about this rope?" he asked querulously.

Sam shook his head. "It stays on till I know you're not trying to trick me. I'll lead my horse. And don't you forget for a minute, he's plenty shy."

Staying well within the cover of the brush, they slowly worked forward. Sam stayed ready to cover the horse's nostrils at any sign it might nicker. The clanging of iron reached Sam's ears. He recognized it as a Dutch oven lid being dropped into place.

"You didn't lie this time, Gid. You can untie that rope now."

With nervous fingers Bowman slipped off the rope. Then he looked up at Sam Kirk. His eyes suddenly widened, and his mouth dropped open. His startled cry broke short as Sam swung his gun barrel down and took Bowman behind the ear.

Bowman sprawled out and lay limp on the grass. Kirk looked down at the unconscious man without pity. "Just for safety, Gid," he breathed.

Sam tied his horse and moved toward the sound he had heard. More camp noise reached him as he went ahead—the clatter of tin plates, the lift of conversation, the stamping of hoofs, and the occasional bawling of a cow or calf.

In the edge of the brush he lay flat on his belly to study the camp in the waning daylight. He could count half a dozen men eating supper around a campfire. Cut into a bank nearby was a dugout, and close beside it was an aging corral of rocks and brush. An old abandoned buffalo hunters' camp, most likely.

In vain he sought Quirt Wolford. The only man he knew there was Claude Hatch. Sam's teeth clenched momentarily as he watched the one-time Figure 4 cowboy, sitting apart from the others, picking disconsolately at a meal that seemed to have no taste for him.

I hope it chokes you, Sam thought bitterly.

Then Sam's heartbeat quickened as Quirt Wolford stepped out of the dugout. From the way the men all stopped eating to look at him, Sam sensed that they were afraid of him. Even at that distance, he could feel the dread that followed the outlaw as he walked toward the cookfire.

Another man came out behind Wolford. He was

much the same size and of much the same bearing. He spoke carelessly to Wolford, as an equal. Sam sensed that here was the only man in camp who was not in fear of the band's leader. He was a gunman, that was plain from the way he wore a double set of .45s, low and tied to his legs.

Carefully Sam raised his gun and rested it in the low fork of a mesquite tree. His heart hammering dully, he licked his lips and drew a careful bead on Wolford as the big man leaned over a Dutch oven, then straightened with two biscuits in his hand. For two long seconds Sam squeezed on the trigger.

Then, scowling, his finger released the pressure. Too far. He wished he had brought a rifle.

He had to get closer. For a time he scanned the camp, looking for a way to get closer without being seen. He thought he saw it. By backing into the brush and skirting around a deep, flood-cut arroyo, he could get behind the dugout and creep in by the old rock corral.

Five minutes later he was crouched behind the piled-up rocks, carefully searching for Wolford.

Excitement burned within him like tall grass afire. He had to be quick. Gid Bowman was likely to come out of it any minute, and he would come out yelling.

But Sam held back, trying to make his plan. He had only a half-formed one in his mind. Main thing was to kill Wolford. After that, he'd take care of himself the best way he could. Maybe the men wouldn't put up much of a fight. He was hoping for that. But if they did, and luck stayed with him, maybe he could hold them off until darkness gave him a chance to get away.

Wolford sat cross-legged on the ground, eating out of a tin plate. At this angle, sitting sideways to Sam, he made a poor target. A bullet fired from here would strike him in the arm. It wasn't likely to be fatal. Sam had to inch around for a better position. Anxiety began to beat at him like a club beating a rug on a line.

At last Wolford stood up. Sam's breath caught. He leveled the gun across the top of the rock fence, waiting for Wolford to turn.

Then it happened. From across the campfire, in the brush, an excited voice called, "Quirt, look out! Kirk's there somewhere, and he's trying to kill you!"

It was Gid Bowman's voice. In desperation Sam squeezed the trigger and missed. Wolford broke into a run, whipping out his gun and firing back as he sped for cover.

Some of the rustlers were caught without their guns. But enough of them were armed that the fence instantly became a beehive of snarling bullets, smashing into the rocks or striking them at an angle and whining away into the dusk.

In bitter disappointment Sam crouched low and tried to reach better cover. But bullets kicked up dust around him and drove him back. He was hemmed in. All he had was the fence, and a steep bank behind it.

His heart sank in despair. He had had his chance, and it had slipped through his fingers like water. Maybe he could get out of here, maybe he couldn't. Whether he did or not, Quirt Wolford was still alive. Sam knew he wouldn't get another chance at him.

He crawled back into a corner where they would have less chance of getting at him from behind. And there he waited, firing only when he saw something to fire at, trying to watch in front of him and behind him at the same time. He watched the dusky blue of the skies deepen into the black of night. It seemed that it was taking forever.

Then they rushed him. Above the hammering of gunfire he heard Quirt Wolford urging the men on, heard him hollering something about getting Sam before dark.

Sweat cold and clammy on his face and on his hands, Sam used both guns, the one he always carried in his holster and a second one he had jammed into his waistband before he rode away from the Figure 4. He fired as fast as he could pull the triggers, so fast that he could not aim with accuracy at the blurred figures which rushed toward him.

But the desperate hail of fire from his guns stopped the rush. The outlaws dropped back, and he saw one of them being carried. He slumped wearily, his heart pounding, his lungs pinching painfully because he had held his breath so long. With trembling fingers he reloaded the two guns and counted his cartridges.

Then he settled back and waited. Next time, they would get him.

Espy Norwood and Arch McCavitt rode side by side, Espy studying the soft tracks which they followed while Arch looked ahead, watching for sign of riders.

Espy swung down to check something on the ground. "Freshest sign we've seen, Arch," he said. "They're not far ahead of us now."

Arch frowned, jerking his head toward the west. "We better catch them pretty quick, or we're in for another night's camp, and a hungry one at that. It'll be dark in a little while."

Remounting, Espy nodded. "Yeah, and chances are Sam'll keep riding, like he did last night. Bet he knew we'd come after him. And he knew we'd figure that he was headed for Bowman's. So he didn't stay there long."

Arch grinned. "Well, I hope *I* never have to spend another night there. That place smells like somebody's hog pen."

The sun went down in a blaze of red and gold. Dusk closed over the two men like a fog.

Worriedly Arch asked, "You reckon we're ever going to find them?"

A sudden burst of gunfire exploded somewhere ahead of them. Espy glanced at Arch and caught the excitement in the redhead's eyes.

"We've just found them," Arch declared. They raked rowels along their horses' sides and sprang into a full run.

At the edge of the brush they reined up in a shower of sand. They stared hard into the darkness that gathered about the outlaw camp, trying to find where Sam was. Someone down there moved, and instantly a bullet sought after him.

"Sam's still in the game," Arch said in relief.

"Yeah, but we'd better get him out in a hurry. You ready?"

Arch nodded. "Ready."

Side by side they spurred out of the brush and into the outlaw camp. Arch's horse almost ran one man down. Caught by surprise, the rustlers put up no resistance for a moment.

"It's us, Sam," Espy called out. "Get up here behind me."

Sam wasted no time. Espy kicked his left foot free of the stirrup. Sam used the stirrup to swing up behind Espy's saddle. An outlaw came running, his gun blazing. Arch McCavitt cut him down.

"Let's go, Arch!" Espy shouted.

In the space of five seconds they had ridden down into the camp and were spurring out again. The surprise was gone. Now Quirt Wolford was cursing and yelling for his men to rally.

"Get them! If they get away they'll hang us all!"

Guns began to talk. Bullets whispered over Espy's head. He bent low in the saddle and kept spurring. Then Quirt Wolford loomed ahead of him. Wolford's gun belched fire. Arch McCavitt jerked, then pitched forward in the saddle. Espy leveled one shot at Wolford and saw the man reel, grabbing his left arm, high against the shoulder.

Then Espy was busy grabbing at Arch, holding him in the saddle. His heart was one huge chunk of ice. "Hold on, cowboy," he gritted. "We're getting out of here."

Sam guided Espy to the point where he had left his horse. He mounted. Then the two of them held onto Arch and kept spurring, trying to outrun the pursuing horsemen they could hear smashing through the brush behind them.

Quirt Wolford's arm burned as if a hot iron were driven into it. The blazing agony fed his fury.

"Get after them!" he bawled to his men who were swinging into their saddles. "Damn your cowardly souls, get them! Don't come back till they're all dead, do you hear?"

He choked on the dust that swirled from the horses' hoofs. He coughed it away and cursed the fire that ate at his arm.

Matt Ollinger caught him by his good shoulder and looked at the wound. "Looks bad, Quirt. You better do something about it. Or let me do it."

Ollinger led him into the dugout and lighted a lantern. He held a cloth to the torn flesh to slow the bleeding, lifting it occasionally to study the wound.

"Bullet's still in there, Quirt. We'll have to dig for it."

He reached upon a shelf and brought down a bottle. "Better take a good long drink, Quirt. This ain't gonna be fun."

Wolford gulped down some of the whisky, and Ollinger made him drink some more. Wolford's face, which had paled from shock, now began to flush with color again. He stretched out upon his bedroll on the dirt floor. Ollinger opened the long blade of his pocket knife and held it in the flame of the lantern until its edge began to glow. He let it cool, then began to probe at the wound.

Wolford cried out.

"Easy, Quirt," Ollinger said. "You better take another drink."

He went at it again. This time Wolford held on as long as he could. Then his cry turned into a scream. The outlaw jumped up from the bedroll and shoved Ollinger aside in a roaring fury. Grabbing his bleeding arm, he lurched out the door and into the night.

Ollinger picked himself up from the dirt floor and hurried out after him. "Quirt," he said, "we've got to get that bullet out."

Wolford violently shook his head. He swayed drunkenly, half from the whisky and half from pain.

Ollinger argued, "You're liable to develop gangrene with that slug in there."

"No, I tell you!" Wolford's voice raged high and wild. "We'll leave it alone!"

After a while the men began straggling in. They shrank back from Wolford's blistering fury.

"It was just too dark, Quirt," Jake Claymore said.

Reeling as he walked, Wolford cursed them all, one at a time. Most especially he cursed Gid Bowman. When the rage was worked out of him, he sat down heavily.

The game was over, he knew that. It wouldn't be long now until the Figure 4 would sweep down here for vengeance. And Wolford's band wouldn't stand a chance against them. If only there were some way to stop the Figure 4 . . .

And suddenly, in his desperation, he thought he saw the way. Matt Ollinger! And Espy Norwood's kid!

"Ollinger," he called out, "come over here. And Jake, you and Hatch too."

Matt Ollinger sauntered over. Claymore and Hatch followed him, keeping their distance.

"Matt," Wolford said, "you're going to get Norwood's kid, all right, just the way we were talking about. Reckon that woman's in town by now?"

Ollinger nodded. "She ought to be."

"Then go find her. Tell her we'll have that youngster for her by tomorrow night. After dark, you take her to the old Brewster shack just outside of town. We'll bring the kid."

Wolford turned to Hatch and Claymore. "It's up to you two to steal Norwood's kid and get him to Mobeetie by tomorrow night. You'll have to move plenty fast."

Hatch stood defiantly. "Not me, Quirt. I've had enough. You got me drunk and got me to stealing cattle. That's bad enough. But then murder, and now kidnaping. I won't have any part of it."

Wolford slapped Hatch across the mouth with the back of his powerful hand. Hatch was big enough to put up a fight. But instead he backed off a step.

"Yes, you will," Wolford said. "Getting our hands on that kid is the only thing that'll keep the Figure 4 off of us now. And you'll know where to find him. You'll help, Hatch. You'll help or I'll kill you!"

A few minutes later Hatch and Claymore rode out, toward the Figure 4. And Ollinger was on his way to Mobeetie.

Gripping his aching, burning arm, Wolford whirled upon his other men. "Don't just stand around there. Mount up. We're getting out of the Panhandle. And we're taking the Arrowhead herd with us!"

17

Espy Norwood kept his horse close beside that of Arch McCavitt. His supporting arm was around Arch's shoulder, and Arch's weight was heavy against him. He held the horses still in a black pool of shadow, while Sam Kirk walked out into the starlight to listen, away from the horses and the creak of saddles. Presently Sam came back.

"I don't hear anything, Espy," he said. "I reckon they've turned back."

"It's a good thing. We've got to get Arch to town the quickest way we can."

Voice heavy with worry, Sam said, "I know a ranch west of Gid's place where we can get a wagon. But it's a long ride. Reckon Arch can make it?"

Espy shook his head. His throat was so tight it hurt him. "We've got to try. I've stopped his bleeding, but he's in a bad way."

Espy sighted on the stars, and they rode out. They tried a jog trot but had to give it up. It was too hard on Arch. So they settled down to a walk, slow as it was. Espy held Arch a while, then Sam took a turn.

After an hour of riding in silence, Espy said, "Sam, there's a lot here that I don't know. And I think it's time somebody told me."

Sam was a long while in answering. "Yes, Espy, I suppose so. After all this, you're going to find out anyway. I'd rather you found out from me, so you'll know just the way everything was.

"Frank Bowman was a good man, Espy. I want you to know that right at the start. He did what he did because he thought he was justified. When he found out he was wrong, it was too late for him to back out.

"He was a farsighted man, Mr. Frank was. The Figure 4 had always been a profitable outfit. But he could see another day coming. He knew the free range wasn't going to last many more years. Settlers were already beginning to show up, buying state land they hadn't ever seen and coming to take it, even if it was in the middle of somebody's ranch.

"Some outfits fought them. But not Mr. Frank. The way he saw it, they had the deeds and the land was theirs. So instead of fighting, he tried to buy up or lease up the land he had built the Figure 4 on. He had just as well have butted his head against an adobe wall.

"Turned out the land certificates were in the hands of a bunch of speculators in Austin. They found that Mr. Frank had a big investment in improvements already and wanted the place mighty bad. So they shoved the price up sky-high. He just couldn't go it."

Espy nodded. He could understand that. He knew that Texas was one of the most unusual of all the states in that it owned all its land. In most states the land originally belonged to the federal government.

But Texas, bargaining as an independent republic, had retained title to its land. Later, as a young state, it had made good use of land in place of currency. Certificates for millions of acres floated around all over the state. And many of the holders had never even seen their own land.

Sam said, "Mr. Frank got to looking around and found a man who had certificates on land west of here. Not as good as the Figure 4, mind you, and not near as much of it. But it was a nice place, anyway. Mr. Frank paid him all he could on it and promised him the rest soon.

"So, to raise the rest of the money he needed, he sold a half interest in the Figure 4 operation to the syndicate you're working for. He knew it wouldn't be many years before he'd have to give up the Figure 4 range anyway, so he didn't figure the partnership could last too long. He let the syndicate write in some mighty strong terms, just so he could get the money.

"That's the reason the syndicate had the right to name its own manager after he died. It just never entered Mr. Frank's head that he wouldn't outlive the partnership."

Sam scowled. "Well, Espy, you know the history of the syndicate, and the kind of trash they sent out here. Drunkards and arrogant asses that somebody wanted to get rid of for a while. First thing we knew they were running the place to suit themselves, or at least were trying to. Mr. Frank was a patient man, and he stood it a long time. But finally he turned bitter about it too.

"Worst thing was that to show how important they were, they started accusing him of first one thing, then another. They'd get peeved over some little thing and start threatening to sue him, to take over his share of the partnership. He was scared, Espy. He was afraid they could do it, if the thing ever went to a high court. He didn't think a little man like him could whip a big outfit like the syndicate.

"Then his brother Gid got to working on him. 'Bite them before they bite you,' he kept telling Mr. Frank. 'They're going to get you sooner or later. You better take all you can from them before they do.'

"Mr. Frank was no thief, Espy. But it looked to him like the syndicate was out to swindle him. How was he to know that these blowhards didn't speak for the whole bunch?

"In self-protection he let Gid take a few Figure 4 cattle, change the brands over into an Arrowhead, and drive them to the new ranch farther west. Somehow or other Quirt Wolford threw in with Gid. They didn't stop with a few cattle, they took a lot. And a good many of them never got to Mr. Frank's other ranch.

"I started missing cattle. One day a couple of the boys and I trailed a bunch and ran into Wolford and some of his men. One of the Figure 4 punchers got shot in the arm. After that, Mr. Frank told me what he'd done.

"I tried to talk to him, to make him see what he was getting into. But by this time the thing was plumb out of hand. Mr. Frank saw he'd done wrong. But it was like starting a big rock to rolling down a hill and not being able to stop it. He couldn't make Wolford and Gid quit. They'd gotten the taste, and they liked it too well. Mr. Frank was in too deep himself to go to the law. There was only one way. But Gid Bowman was his brother, and Mr. Frank wouldn't do it.

"So the thing went on, and got worse all the time. Some of the cattle got to the Arrowhead, but a lot of them didn't. Some of the cowboys began to figure it out. They didn't want to get mixed up in it, so they started leaving. That's why Mr. Frank took to hiring the slowest, sorriest men that came around. He didn't think they were apt to get wise.

"It was showing up in the cattle counts, bad. So I started doctoring up the tallies to help Mr. Frank, hoping all the time that something would happen, and we could straighten out. Before long I had myself stuck to it and couldn't turn aloose.

"Mr. Frank's health wasn't any too good anyway. The worry just about finished him. Then the syndicate sent Geoffrey Spence out here. He was as different from the others as daylight from dark. And smart ... He began adding things up for himself. So one day Mr. Frank squared his shoulders and told him the whole story, with me sitting there listening.

"But Quirt Wolford got his hands on the message Spence sent to headquarters in Kansas City. A couple of days later, Spence was killed in a 'hunting accident.'

"Mr. Frank knew it was murder. It was more than he could take. His heart just gave out on him."

Sam Kirk's voice was taut with hatred. "Quirt Wolford killed him, Espy. He killed Frank Bowman just as sure as he killed Spence and Cotton.

"After Mr. Frank was buried, I sat down and wrote a letter to the syndicate. I told them the story. Three nights later, Quirt Wolford brought it back. He had stolen it out of the post office, the way he was stealing any other Figure 4 mail that looked important— the way he'd gotten his hands on Spence's report.

"Wolford warned me not to try anything like that again. He said that if the syndicate caught up with him, he'd implicate me in Spence's murder. It wouldn't be hard to do, because I'd been with Spence a good part of the day he was killed. And what I had done to the tallies would make it look even worse.

"Nobody else knew the story, nobody but Arch McCavitt. He'd figured most of it out, and I'd admitted the rest to him. Not even Mary Bowman had any idea what had been taking place the last three years. So I was stuck, Espy.

"Then you came along. The first time I saw you, I knew you were the kind of man who wouldn't stop digging till you had the truth. That's why I tried to block you. Now you know it all. You can do what you want to about it."

Espy nodded grimly. "I'm glad you told me, Sam. It ties up a lot of loose strings that've been dangling. And whatever happens now, I'll see that you're in the clear."

He was thinking of one thing in particular, a letter he had found in Gid Bowman's dugout, and his resulting accusation of Mary Bowman. He had been wrong, he could see that now.

But Sam's story wasn't going to help Colonel Judkins's position against the syndicate directors when they got here. If anything, it would make the situation even more hopeless. They would break the colonel. There wouldn't be a thing Espy could do to help him.

When daylight came and they struck a trail that was familiar to Sam, they eased Arch to the ground under the shade of a chinaberry. Sam loped ahead. Much later he came back in a wagon, his horse tied on behind. A cowboy from the other ranch was with him.

Arch had lapsed into complete unconsciousness, his breathing labored. Espy and Sam carefully placed him on a mattress that had been put in the back of the wagon. Re-examining Arch's wound, Espy said, "What do you think Quirt Wolford will do now, Sam? He'll know it won't be long till we'll be back to get him."

Worriedly Sam said, "I expect he'll try to get out of the country. And knowing Wolford, I don't think he'll go out empty-handed."

"What do you mean?"

"I mean that it's not extra far from the Arrowhead to the New Mexico line. Wolford's got a greedy streak in him a foot wide. Those cattle in the Arrowhead brand belong to Mary and the syndicate. But I'd bet you a hundred dollars Wolford tries to take them with him, if he thinks he's got any chance at all."

Espy rubbed the back of his neck. It made sense. "Then you go back to the ranch, Sam. Round up the men. I can get Arch to Mobeetie with your friend's help.

"Get the Figure 4 outfit to town as quick as you can, and I'll go with you from there. If Wolford tries to take the Arrowhead herd, we'll stop him. And this time, he won't get away."

Margaret Tellison sat in her hotel room, nervously fanning herself with a folded sheet of paper and wishing it weren't so miserably hot. Her window was up, but she didn't dare sit near it. The door was closed and the lock bar fitted firmly in place.

Her heartbeat still quickened every time she remembered the narrow escape she had had this morning. For two days she had stayed close to her hotel room, answering to the name of Jones and awaiting some word from that disreputable man, Ollinger. This morning, unable to hold herself in any longer, she had gone out for a stroll. And on the plank sidewalk in front of a long frame saloon building, she had almost come face to face with Espy Norwood.

She had seen him just in time, helping lift an unconscious man out of a wagon and carry him inside. Margaret Tellison had shrunk back into the recessed doorway of an adobe building and waited there with ashen face, her heart driving like a pump handle. Only when Espy no longer was in sight did she realize she was in the entrance of a saloon, and half a dozen men were staring. She had whirled around, hurried back to her room, and locked herself in.

Later, when someone had knocked on her door, she had shrunk against the wall, afraid to answer, mortally fearful that it was Espy Norwood, that he had seen her after all.

Only when Matt Ollinger called his name had she opened the door.

"Be ready when dark comes," he told her. "A friend of mine will bring the boy."

Ollinger had hesitated a moment before adding, "And by the way, don't say anything about your agreement with me, about the money you're to pay me. I'd rather my friend didn't know our arrangements."

The hotel manager had told her about Espy Norwood and Arch McCavitt later, when he brought her meal to her room.

"Arch is laid up in the back room of his place," the gray-mustached man said worriedly. "Can't tell yet whether he's going to pull through or not. Looks mighty bad. Doctor told me he hasn't been conscious since Norwood brought him in."

Margaret remembered Arch McCavitt from a long

time ago. A red-haired cowboy, wild, uncouth. She had always known he would come to no good end.

A sudden thought struck her and brought a clutch of fear to her throat. What if it hadn't been Arch? What if Espy had been shot instead?

When darkness came, she was pacing the floor of the tiny room, excitement prickling her skin like needles. Her imagination ran wild. What if something went wrong? What if they let something happen to Kenny, those impossible ruffians? What if Espy caught up with her before she could get Kenny back to the protection of Kansas City?

Her nerves stretched taut as a fiddlestring. Frightened tears were burning her eyes when Ollinger's knock finally sounded on the wooden door.

"Ready, Mrs. Tellison?"

He had rented a buggy in the name of Mrs. Jones, and it was waiting in back of the hotel. Silently he flipped the reins, and they pulled away into the night. The nearness of this rough man, sitting close beside her on the buggy seat, set her heart to beating in fear. She shrank away from the smell of sweat and tobacco which clung heavily to him. She hoped to heaven that never again would she be forced to deal with men of this kind.

It took half an hour to reach the shack. Before they got there, Ollinger stopped the team. "I'll take my money now, before we go on in."

Stiffly she said, "The agreement was that I pay you when I get Kenny."

"He's there. And you'll pay me now!"

She hesitated, but her pounding heart got the best of her. The money was rolled and tied in her purse. He hefted it, then shoved it in his pocket without counting it. "It'd better all be there," he said. "Remember, I know where *you* live."

Yellow lamplight reached out from the shack's tiny windows. Ollinger helped her down. In her excitement she hurried to the shack and reached for the door. Ollinger grabbed her arm and jerked her back.

"You want to get shot? We better sing out before we start in there."

He called, "It's me . . . Ollinger!" The door swung inward.

Margaret rushed inside. Kenny's eyes widened, then he hurried into her arms. "Aunt Margaret," he cried, "what're you doing here?"

She hugged him tightly, then held him off for a look. "You poor darling. You've been frightened to death."

He drew back. "No, I'm not. I'm not scared, not a bit." His voice was a little wavery, but he was putting up a game show. "Are you going to take me back to Daddy?"

The eagerness of his question set Margaret aback. She didn't know quite what to say. It hadn't once entered her mind that he might want to go back to his father.

She looked for the first time at the men around her. Two had the appearance of common cowboys. But the third one made her take an involuntary step backward. She tried hard to keep the blood from draining out of her face. He was big and broad-shouldered, with a black beard and fevered black eyes. His left sleeve was torn away and the arm bound tightly by a dirty cloth, which had been soaked through with blood, now dried a wine red and turned to hard crust.

She feared him instinctively, the same way she knew and feared a mean dog even before it showed its teeth.

His burning eyes glared at her. He swayed drunkenly. But he wasn't drunk. He was sick.

His voice was drawn up tightly, as if in pain. "You've got your boy, Mrs. Tellison. Now how about the money?"

She saw the sudden worry waft into Ollinger's washed-out eyes.

"I don't know what you mean," she told Quirt Wolford.

He snarled, "You take me for a fool, woman? You think I'm stupid enough to believe a man like Matt Ollinger would agree to kidnap this boy for you just because he hates Espy Norwood? How much have you paid him?"

Hesitantly she said, "Five hundred dollars."

"Give it to me, Matt."

Ollinger reached for his gun. But sick though he was, Wolford beat him. Ollinger let his gun slip back into the holster, his black-whiskered face a shade whiter.

"I said give it to me, Matt."

Smoldering, Ollinger pulled out the roll. "Take it, Jake," Wolford ordered. "Count it."

Jake Claymore quickly ran through it. "It's all here."

"Give half of it back to Ollinger."

Scowling, Matt Ollinger snatched his share.

Wolford's lips formed a hard smile. "Next time, Matt Ollinger, you'll not try to cheat me. You thought we'd take the risk and you'd take the money. They don't do that to Quirt Wolford. Not but once."

Wolford's feverish eyes flicked back to Margaret Tellison. "How much more you got in that purse?"

Defensively she held it tight against her bosom.

"Get it, Jake." Claymore wrested it from her hands,

took the remaining money out of it, and thrust the empty purse back at her.

Choking down her rage, she drew Kenny to her. But he pulled away, his eyes accusing her. "Did you do what the man said, Aunt Margaret? Did you have them steal me away from my daddy?"

The hurt in his voice brought burning tears to her eyes. "Kenny, *I* didn't steal you—your father did. He stole you from me."

The boy pulled away from her. "I want to go back to him."

"Kenny, I'm taking you to Kansas City."

"No! I don't want to go back there. I want to go to Daddy."

Quirt Wolford made a signal, and Jake Claymore caught hold of the boy.

Wolford said roughly, "He's not going anywhere with you, and he's not going to his dad either. He's going with *us*."

She raised her hands to her face, wanting to cry out but unable to do it.

"You take a message to Espy Norwood for me," Wolford said. "Tell him we've got his boy. And tell him that if he wants to see this kid alive again, he'd better leave us alone. Tell him we're getting out of Texas and we're taking the Arrowhead herd with us. If he makes a move to stop us, this kid'll die!"

Margaret Tellison fell to her knees, sobbing uncontrollably. She reached out a hand toward Kenny and touched nothing.

Wolford looked contemptuously at Matt Ollinger.

"You coming with us?"

The outlaw hesitated a moment, his pale eyes ruefully observing the empty purse that lay open at his feet. "Yeah," he gritted. "Guess I'd just as well."

They walked out into the darkness, and in a moment the hoofbeats had faded out of hearing. The only sound left was the desperate sobbing of the woman who lay face down upon the floor.

a we walked quietly . . . you should act naturally, you
know. But I don't like leaving you here alone, Doc.
Are you sure you won't . . ."

"Go along now, and let me . . . guard your patient for
you. Nothing will happen, Matt."

18

Espy's sleepless eyes burned as if there were sand in
them. He had dozed a little, off and on through
the day, but that was all the sleep he had had. Now,
under the restful glow of lamplight, he leaned his
straight chair backward on two legs, resting his head
wearily against the flowered wallpaper.

The girl Lilybelle had hardly moved from her chair
at Arch's bedside. When Arch showed signs of stirring, she arose quickly, hopefully, tenderly touching his face or his hand with her fingers. And when
Arch lapsed back into stillness, she would slowly sink
down again, the silent tears glistening on her cheeks.

No paint and powder now hid the grave beauty of
her face. Her dress was a plain, simple one. A small
gold cross hung over her breast. Several times Espy
had seen her clutch the cross, her head bowed, her
eyes closed.

Heavyhearted, Espy closed his own eyes. He tried
to doze, bending his head forward so that his stubbled chin almost touched his chest. Through his mind

ran tortured thoughts of Arch McCavitt, and Quirt Wolford, of Mary Bowman, who now must learn that her father had been stealing his own partnership cattle, of Colonel Judkins, who soon was about to lose everything he owned. Any day now, that attorney Slagel was due here with some of the syndicate directors. The fur was bound to fly.

Espy dozed. A hard, urgent rapping on the door jerked him upright, blinking in sleepy-eyed surprise.

"Espy!" a woman cried. Espy hurried to the door, thinking of Mary Bowman. But it wasn't Mary Bowman. He stepped back, astonished.

Margaret Tellison's hair was in disarray, her eyes red from crying, her lips pinched and pale. "Espy," she sobbed, "those horrible men—they've taken Kenny."

For a moment he was speechless, completely dumbfounded by her presence here. "What men, Margaret?"

She broke hysterically. "They'll kill him, they'll kill him!"

In sudden desperation Espy grabbed her shoulders and shook her violently. "*Who*, Margaret? Who's got Kenny?"

Somehow she managed to blurt out the whole story. A helpless weakness washed through Espy. He sank into the chair, his head in his hands.

"Why did you do it, Margaret?" he asked, hardly above a whisper. "Do you hate me so much?"

He was totally unprepared for what she did then. She knelt before him and took his hands. "No, Espy. I don't hate you. I *never* hated you. I've loved you almost since the first time we met."

He stared at her, not able to believe. Her voice was set hard in an effort to keep it from breaking.

"I tried to fight myself, Espy, and when I couldn't

do that, I fought you. Ever since I've been old enough to think for myself, I had my mind made up. I was sick of small-town life, of small-town poverty. I was going to marry a man who could take me away from that. I had it all planned.

"Then you came along. I did everything I could to rid myself of my love for you. It didn't work, not even after Jeannie married you. I thought after I married Edgar Tellison it would be different. But it wasn't, Espy. I was still in love with you.

"That's why I wanted Kenny, I guess. If I couldn't have you, then I wanted your son. Can't you see, Espy? Can't you understand how it was?"

Her shoulders shook, and she bowed her head so he could not see her face. "Espy, can you ever forgive me?"

He pulled his hands away and turned his back. For a long time he stood there thinking, his face heavy with despair. Finally he turned back and looked down at her. "I forgive you, Margaret. But I want you to leave. I never want to see you again."

He added then, "I'm sorry for you, Margaret."

She begged, "Is sympathy all you feel for me, Espy?"

He nodded. "That's all. That's all there'll ever be."

She stood up slowly, her back set rigid in resignation. "Good-bye, Espy."

"Good-bye," he told her. And she was gone.

In black misery, he sank into his chair. Lilybelle had watched and listened without a word. Now she arose and walked to him. With a compassionate hand on his shoulder, she said, "Your son?"

He nodded, unable to speak.

Her voice was bitter as she looked toward Arch. "So Quirt Wolford gets away. But someday, somewhere, I may see him again. And if I do, Espy, I promise you I'll *kill* him!"

Unable to bear the cramped little room, Espy shoved through the door and walked out into the saloon itself. There was little trade tonight, and what customers were there kept their voices subdued. Everyone knew about Arch.

Espy pulled out a chair and sat down at a table alone. With his knotted fist he struck the tabletop so hard that the sardine-can ash tray bounced off and clattered on the floor.

He sat there a while, not seeing, not hearing. Then he signaled the bartender. "Whisky," he said.

The strong smell of it pinched his face as he poured the tall glass half full. Something within him cried out a warning. But one wouldn't hurt him. He *had* to have something.

He took it all in one long gulp and strained for breath as its fire burned down his throat. He felt the warmth of it spread through his body and into his brain. The first he'd had in more than a year. A terrible craving began to eat at him. He wanted more. The voice within cried out again, and yet another time. But Espy Norwood no longer heard. He never stopped until the bottle was empty, and he slumped senseless upon the table.

A strong hand shook his shoulder. He stirred resentfully, his head exploding in pain, his eyes aching unmercifully against the bright glare of daylight. He shut them tightly.

"Espy," a girl's voice said. "Espy, come out of it."

He turned over and almost fell to the floor. He realized dully that he was lying on a steel cot. He let his feet fall heavily over the side. He sat up on the edge of the cot, both hands pressed hard against his head. He could hear Mary Bowman's voice, but was still unable to see her.

"Espy, please, get hold of yourself."

When finally he could see again, he found that he was in Arch's room. Somebody had set up a folding steel cot and placed him upon it. Lilybelle still sat where she had been. Her face was drawn and her eyes ringed with gray. She still hadn't slept. And Arch hadn't awakened.

Mary Bowman stood in front of Espy, her hand on his shoulder. Sam Kirk waited behind her.

"Espy," Mary insisted, "you've got to come around. The Figure 4 directors got to town last night. The man Slagel has heard everything. He's bringing them here right now."

Espy heard the words, but he had a hard time getting them through his head. "Mary," he said, "when did you get here?"

"We got in a little bit ago. We rode through the night. The whole Figure 4 is here."

Espy shook his head. It seemed to be getting clearer. He looked past Mary, to Sam. "Sam, did you tell her?"

Mary answered for him. Tight-lipped, she said, "Yes, Espy, he told me everything. Now, get up, quickly. You've got to get straightened out before Slagel gets here."

Espy stood up uncertainly. The room reeled about him. His head was still splitting. Mary caught hold of him, steadying him.

"I'm sorry, Mary," he said. Shame kindled hotly within him. "I've made a big fool of myself. For more than a year, I held myself back. And last night I just let everything go."

She smiled tightly, her voice sympathetic. "I understand, Espy. You don't have to apologize to me."

"I won't ever do it again, Mary," he insisted. "I promise you."

"I'm glad, Espy. But hurry. You've got to get cleaned up."

A water pitcher and washbasin sat on a small stand against the wall. Espy poured the basin full of water, glancing at himself in the mirror above the stand. He looked like a bear coming out of hibernation, his hair atangle, his eyes still red, his face whiskery.

The cold water against his face braced him some, but he was still wobbly on his feet. He ran a comb through his tangled hair, wincing at the way it pulled.

He heard a commotion outside the room, in the saloon, and he heard a voice say, "He's in here, gentlemen."

Opening the door, Espy walked unsteadily out into the saloon. The tall, spidery lawyer confronted him triumphantly. Slagel turned back to the half dozen men who accompanied him.

"There, gentlemen. Now you see the kind of man to whom Colonel Judkins has entrusted our huge investment."

He shook his cane in Espy's face. "You're a disgrace, Norwood. Is it any wonder that with men like you running our affairs out here, Colonel Judkins has allowed our partner to steal us blind?"

Espy stiffened, a ripple of heat working under his skin.

Slagel went on. "A drunken lout. That's the kind of man you sent out here, Colonel."

Espy's chin dropped. Colonel Judkins was here! The old man slowly stepped out from among the directors. He stared unbelievingly at Espy, his dark brown eyes pinched with pain, his weathered face long and grave.

Voice bitter with disappointment, he said, "Espy, I wish I hadn't come."

The colonel might have believed him. But Slagel never gave him time to answer.

"Perhaps you sent this kind of man here on purpose, Colonel. Perhaps you were stealing from us just the way Frank Bowman was."

Espy exploded. His fist came up like a rock from a slingshot. Slagel's head jerked violently. The lawyer reeled backward, striking a table and knocking it over, sprawling ignominiously on the floor. He lay there a minute, shaking his head, half senseless.

Espy saw the color leave the colonel's face. Suddenly Judkins was an old, old man, the spirit and the will completely gone. The colonel sank into a handy chair, his face a gray mask of hopelessness.

This finished it. He was ruined now.

Espy's shoulders slumped. Shame spilled over him. His head hanging, he said, "I'm sorry, sir."

Judkins answered weakly, "No need to apologize, Espy. *I'm* the one at fault, not you. You didn't want the job, and I all but forced it on you. I'm the one who should've known better."

The half dozen directors had all stood in shocked silence, not one of them speaking. Mary Bowman suddenly spoke up, her voice strong and determined.

"Just a moment, gentlemen," she said, "before you condemn Espy Norwood, or Colonel Judkins. Neither of them has done any wrong, and Slagel knows it. He has lied to you.

"Yes, you've lost cattle, a lot of cattle. I won't deny that. But I promise you that I'll make up your losses.

"I don't expect any of you gentlemen to understand what made my father do what he did. But *I* understand, and I know he was wrong. I don't want anything that doesn't belong to me. We'll round up the Figure 4 cattle. If there aren't as many left as the syndicate is entitled to, I'll make it up out of the Arrowhead herd. You won't lose a thing, gentlemen. That's a promise."

Staring at the girl, Espy felt the stir of admiration, of deepest pride. When this was over, she wouldn't have enough cattle left to stock a nester spread. She must know that. And yet, to save him, and to save Colonel Judkins, she was giving up all she owned.

The colonel looked at her in disbelief, his square beard trembling. One of the directors grinned. "By Jove, gentlemen, I'm for it."

Another chimed in, an American voice. "Sounds square to me."

Espy breathed easier, and some of the weight slid from his shoulders. But a chilling thought came back to him. Sam Kirk voiced it for him.

"There won't be any Arrowhead herd, Mary, if we don't stop Quirt Wolford. And we can't do that. He has Kenny Norwood in his hands."

Espy Norwood felt all eyes turn toward him. And now came the bitterest decision he had ever made in his life. He walked to the open door and looked out upon the dirt street of Mobeetie. He thought of Frank and Mary Bowman, of Geoffrey Spence, of Cotton Dulaney and Arch McCavitt—of all those who had suffered because of Quirt Wolford. Most of all he thought of Kenny.

Three men had already died for the Figure 4. Another lay in the back room there, hovering on the dark brink between life and death. Were it his own life in the balance, Espy would know what to do. But it *wasn't* his life.

Espy shut his eyes tight, trying to hold back the burning in them.

The answer came to him, plain and inescapable. Kenny was yet a boy, but he was game. His fight with Joe Kirk had been ample proof of that. Old Jess Cooley had told Espy the story. In only a few years Kenny would be a man. And were he a man, what would be his decision?

Espy knew, for it would be the same as his own.

He turned back toward the waiting group, his eyes bleak.

"If we're going to catch Wolford, we'd better be a-riding."

19

A lazy film of dust followed the strung-out Arrow-head herd, slowly dissolving in the easy warmth of a summer wind. The pace was brisk, for Quirt Wolford's men were pushing hard, yelling, swinging their ropes, crowding, shoving.

And up and down both sides of the herd, Quirt Wolford rode endlessly, shouting and cursing, punishing his horse, punishing his men, punishing himself.

The smaller calves and the older cows had dropped back farther and farther until now they were in the drags.

Gid Bowman rode there, heavy and lifeless in his saddle. Claude Hatch was there, too, with the boy Kenny Norwood, shoving the tail end of the herd. Face masked by sweat-streaked dust, Hatch rode out to meet Wolford.

"Quirt," he protested, "we're driving too fast. Calves back here can't keep up."

Wolford scowled at him. His left arm hung limp. His black eyes were ablaze with fever. Half the time he stayed in the saddle only because of the tight grip his right hand held on the horn. He swayed, his face slack in a sick, pasty pallor.

"Leave them, then," he growled. "We got no time to worry about the slow ones."

He jerked his square chin toward Bowman and the kid. "Is Gid still drinking back there?"

Hatch nodded. Wolford said something under his breath, then, "Tell him, by God, that if he gets too drunk to ride, we'll just leave him afoot. He's been on that bottle ever since they shot up our camp.

"Now keep these drags moving, Hatch. I'll shoot the man who lags!"

Cruelly he jerked his horse around and headed once more toward the point to keep them moving.

About midway, Matt Ollinger reined in his horse a moment, catching his breath and looking back toward the dusty drags. He saw Wolford coming, and hatred crept into Ollinger's dust-burned eyes. He asked himself why he had stayed. But he knew. Wolford was riding for a fall. And maybe Ollinger could pick up the pieces.

They had made a swift drag over the Arrowhead range. There hadn't been time enough or men enough for a thorough sweep. But they had gotten away with a big part of the herd. He guessed there were a thousand head or so here.

Wolford furiously reined in beside him. "Keep moving, Ollinger. Nobody's slacking up on this drive. Nobody!"

Ollinger's pale eyes narrowed dangerously. "Hold on, Wolford. You don't talk to me like that. Nobody does. I came along because I wanted to. I don't take orders, I do what I choose."

Wolford's right hand slid off the saddle horn and

onto the butt of his gun. "You'll do as I say! Shove cattle or I'll shoot you right where you stand!"

Ollinger bristled, but he could see the rattlesnake fury behind Wolford's black eyes. He weighed his chances and knew they were slim.

Ollinger rode off, yelling at some lagging cows, forcing them to break into a stiff trot. Wolford stayed back, too cagey even in his fever to ride ahead and risk a bullet in his back.

Ollinger's cheeks were rigid. A storm brewed in his sky-pale eyes. When he was far enough ahead of Wolford, he dropped back to the man behind him, a gangling, scar-faced outlaw they all called Mose.

Jerking his head Wolford's way, Ollinger said, "He been chewing on you too?"

Mose scowled, deepening the long scar that ran down his cheek. "Who ain't he been chewing on?"

"How long are we going to take it, Mose?"

The tall rider's eyebrows lifted. "What're you getting at?"

Ollinger said, "He's going crazy with pain and fever. That bullet's still in his arm, and it's going to kill him. But he's going to kill some of us first, the way he's going. Are we just going to wait around for it to happen?"

Mose frowned. "I don't know what we can do about it."

"We'll wait for our chance and get his guns. Then we can set him afoot and take the herd for ourselves."

"That's pretty rank, Ollinger."

"Is it any worse than he deserves, Mose? Haven't you had a bellyful of him cursing you and driving you, and taking a lion's share of everything? And if it's a fight you're a-scared of, don't be. In his shape, without his gun, he'll be like a rattler with his fangs pulled out."

Mose pondered a moment. "Reckon you're right, Ollinger. He's had it coming. Holler when you're ready."

Ollinger rode on ahead, to talk to the next man, and start the word passing around the herd.

Wolford rode toward the drags again. The smell of his horse's sweat was strong and sour. The animal was giving out, and it was a long way to the New Mexico line, even yet. Wolford hunched over the horn, his arm throbbing unmercifully, a deep throbbing agony that reached all the way to his brain. A swimmy red haze was beginning to obscure his sight.

He pulled up beside Claude Hatch and the kid. "Get off that horse, button. I'm taking it."

Defiantly Kenny sat still. Wolford caught his thin shoulder and hurled him down. Laboriously Wolford eased to the ground. Kenny Norwood had gotten up and was dusting off his clothes. He scooped up a rock and hurled it at Wolford. The outlaw twisted away from it, but it struck his wounded arm. He cried out against the blinding surge of pain. He grabbed the boy and flung him to the ground again.

Claude Hatch dismounted and caught the boy. He shoved Kenny behind him. "That's enough, Quirt. He's just a kid."

His voice trembled with anger. Ever since last night, he had watched in silent rage while Wolford mishandled the boy, flinging him around, striking him, cursing him. Now it was time to stop being silent.

Wolford calmed a little. "His horse is fresher. I want him. Change my saddle over, Hatch. The kid can take my horse. And he'd better make him keep up."

Hatch changed the saddles. The herd was drifting

on away, with Bowman slacked drunkenly behind the drags.

Worriedly Hatch asked, "What do you figure on doing with the kid, Quirt, when we get to safety?"

"What do you care?" was Wolford's bitter reply. "You hate Espy Norwood same as the rest of us do."

Fear weakened Hatch's voice. "That don't call for killing kids."

"I won't leave him to talk. You don't have to watch it, Hatch. Now get back to the herd, and make that kid work."

Wolford struggled back into the saddle, his face purpling with pain.

Hatch flung the boy's saddle onto Wolford's tired mount, watching in fear and black hatred as the big outlaw rode away. Wolford's back made a broad target. For a moment Hatch's hand rested on his gun. It would be easy, from here. He even went so far as to draw the gun half out of the holster. But his hand shook, and his heart rose high in his throat. He dropped the gun back where it belonged, cursing himself for a coward.

When the horse was saddled, Hatch looked down at the boy. For several hours a half-formed idea had been running through his desperate mind. Now was the time, if he was ever going to do it.

"Wolford aims to kill you, boy," he said bluntly. "Our only chance is to run. It's a poor chance, but the only one we've got. Are you game?"

His tanning face drawn up grimly, Kenny nodded. "I'm game."

Wolford had disappeared over a rise. Bowman had his bottle lifted high. Half a dozen cows had dropped back behind the drunken man. He hadn't seen them. He wasn't seeing anything.

"Let's go," Hatch said.

They spurred into a lope, heading straight east. A little to the right ran a green, brushy draw. Hatch pulled toward it, hoping it would hide them, hoping desperately that no one would see them riding away.

Gaining the safety of the draw, he pulled up a moment and looked back. No one was coming. Maybe they could get a long start before they were missed.

"We're going to have to push, Kenny. I don't know how long your horse will hold out, but we'll have to run him for all he's got. And when he's gone, we'll double up on mine. Let's ride."

They spurred out again, both too busy now to be looking back.

Wolford never missed them until he made another inspection of the drags. He jerked erect in the saddle as he realized that Gid Bowman was alone.

Cursing darkly, he spurred to Bowman's side. "Where's Hatch?" he demanded. "Where's that kid?"

Reeking of whisky, Bowman stared at him bleary-eyed. He mumbled something unintelligible and hunched lower in the saddle.

Wolford looked back to the cattle that had strung out behind the sodden ranchman. The rest of the story was glaringly clear.

A choking rage swept Quirt Wolford. His right hand moved with a blur. The first shot rocked Gid Bowman back. The second knocked him spinning from the saddle. Bowman's horse squealed in terror and whirled away, loping pell-mell around the herd, reins trailing. Wolford leaned over Bowman's body and emptied his gun in a blind red spasm of fury.

The sudden violence drew the other men quickly. They gathered in a circle around Wolford, their eyes first on him, then on the torn body of Gid Bowman, whose lifeless fingers still choked the neck of a bottle while the last of the red liquid drained out and was swallowed up by the thirsty sand.

"Ollinger! Mose!" Wolford shouted. "He let Hatch and the kid get away. Go after them! Bring them back!"

Ollinger glanced over the other men and saw grim agreement in their eyes. Now was the time.

"No, Quirt," he answered. "You've given your last order."

Wolford's face was ablaze. He brought up the gun. But it was empty. He stared unbelievingly at his riders who now ringed him, faces sullen and defiant.

"What is this?" he demanded. "What does this mean?"

Ollinger answered curtly. "It means you're through, Quirt. We're taking your guns and we're taking your herd!"

Realization was a long time soaking in. And when it did, Wolford slumped, a sick man, a desperate man.

"But why? Why?"

"Because you're not a man anymore, you're a hydrophobia wolf. That wounded arm has driven you out of your head, and we've had to suffer for it. But now it's just you, Quirt. We're going on without you."

Ollinger was in favor of leaving him afoot and helpless, to die on the prairie. But a couple of the men held out against that.

"All right, then," Ollinger said finally, "we'll let you keep your horse. But no guns. And stay away from us. If you show up near the herd, we'll kill you on sight!"

So Quirt Wolford was cast adrift. He rode off alone, hunched low over his saddle horn, his swollen, throbbing arm hanging useless at his side.

"He won't last a day," somebody said.

Now Matt Ollinger was the boss, and he was quick to show it. "Wolford was right about one thing," he said. "Without that boy for a hostage, we haven't got a chance. You men keep the herd moving, fast. Mose, you go with me. We're going to get that kid!"

Kenny Norwood's horse was flagging fast. He'd gotten a good run out of him that first mile. But now he was slowing down.

"Keep him coming, kid," Claude Hatch said desperately. "We've got to make all the miles we can."

A rider can sense when an animal beneath him has to labor harder and harder to keep up his speed.

Kenny got another mile out of him. But now it was over.

Claude Hatch got down and unsaddled the worn-out animal. Slipping the bridle off and dropping it to the ground, he waited for the horse to move. It didn't. It stood heaving, the sweat dripping.

Hatch mounted first, then gave Kenny a lift up behind the saddle. They set out again at a slower pace, saving strength.

They had gained another three or four miles when Kenny looked over his shoulder. "They're coming," he shouted. "Two of them."

Hatch glanced back once to see how much of a lead he had. Then he touched spurs to his sorrel and called up the speed he had saved. With no stirrups, Kenny began to bounce. He hugged up against Hatch and held onto him like a burr. Hatch kept his spurs raking. For a long time he maintained the lead. But slowly he began to lose it. The two riders were catching up.

Desperately he looked for some sign of help, a house or a shack or a dugout. But he saw none, and he knew there wouldn't be one. There was nothing to do but run as long as he could, then stop and fight.

Ahead of him, cradled between a double row of cottonwoods and cedar, he saw a crooked creek bed. He made for it, spurring hard. When he reached it, he pulled to a quick stop, swung his right leg over the horse's neck, and dropped off on the left side. He lifted Kenny forward into the saddle.

"Move out, kid," he said quickly. "Head for Mobeetie. Follow the creek till you're out of sight. It's you they want, and maybe I can fool them here for a while."

Before Kenny could say a word, Hatch slapped the horse across the rump and sent him running.

Hatch bellied down behind a flood-cut bank, gun in hand. He took off his gunbelt and laid it out beside him, where he could reach the cartridges easier. When the riders were two hundred yards away, he fired the first shot. That would slow them down. They would be a long time closing in.

Not one hour had passed since he had joined Quirt Wolford that he had not cursed himself for a fool, and flinched under the cruel whip of conscience. The big dreams he had dreamed were gone like the smoke from yesterday's fire. There had been a time, once, when he might have made them a reality. But not now. He had smashed them. No one else could be blamed for it, really. He had done it himself. Mary might forgive, but she could never forget.

So he let the dreams go. They no longer mattered. All that mattered now was redemption. And here, perhaps, was the place to win it.

The sweat crept from under Hatch's hat and trickled

down his face, burning his eyes, carrying the taste of salt to his lips. The sand was stove-lid hot against his skin.

But his conscience was still. And Claude Hatch was smiling.

Espy Norwood had spoken few words since they had left Mobeetie, and none since they had found the first sign of the Arrowhead herd being driven westward. His face was rigid as stone.

Beside him rode the sheriff and Sam Kirk, and behind him a dozen Figure 4 cowboys, as well as several townsmen and friends of Arch McCavitt who had declared themselves in. Altogether there were twenty men.

Espy rode like a man in a trance, a wall built around himself. He heard nothing, felt nothing, saw nothing. He had driven himself without mercy, trying hard not to think, knowing that if he *did* think, he couldn't go through with it.

Sam Kirk jerked his horse to a halt. "Did you hear that?"

Espy had heard nothing. But now he did hear it. Distant gunfire.

Then the sheriff pointed. "Look yonder. Somebody's coming on horseback, and in a hurry too."

The lone rider evidently saw the group of horsemen. He immediately swung their way. Watching him, Espy realized it wasn't a man. Too small.

Suddenly his breath stopped. Could it be . . .

Yes! By George, it *was*—Kenny!

Espy jabbed spurs to the horse's sides. He was fifty yards in the lead when he reached the boy, slid to a stop, and jumped to the ground. He grabbed Kenny out of the saddle and crushed the boy to him, closing his eyes against the sudden burning. He tried to say something to his son, but his throat was choked tight. He just held him a long moment, making no further effort to speak.

In high excitement, Kenny blurted his story. From far across the hill an occasional shot still echoed.

"Come on," Espy said, "let's try to help Hatch."

But the gunfire stopped before they reached the creek. Espy exchanged glances with Sam Kirk. They knew.

Two riders pulled up out of the creek bed. They stopped and stared in consternation at the twenty horsemen. Then they turned and dropped back out of sight.

The sheriff made a sweeping motion with his arm. The posse spread out in a wide fan-shaped movement and closed in upon the creek. Espy stayed in the center. When a bullet picked up dust in front of his horse, he touched spurs and made a dash for cover.

His mount hit the bank and slid down. Espy caught a glimpse of a tall man with a scar face and triggered a shot at him. The tall man broke into a hard run down the dry creek bed, where one of the other possemen was sure to get him.

Another bullet thumped into the dried bank beside Espy, sending a shower of sand into Espy's face. He jumped free of the saddle, turning the horse loose and diving belly-down beneath a cedar. The gunman was behind a cottonwood on the other side of the gravelly bed. Espy fired once. His shot was quickly answered. The man was a good marksman, for the bullet sliced through cedar leaves just above Espy's head.

There was only one way to get him. Espy had to reach the other side—get to the top of the bank.

He fired once more at the cottonwood, then sprang up and pelted across the gravel. He felt something tug at his pants leg and burn his skin. He dived headlong behind a smaller cottonwood and lay there a moment, getting his breath back. He looked above him. The bank wouldn't be hard to scale, but he would be exposed to fire while he was climbing.

He took a deep breath and jumped for it. He heard one shot . . . two. Then he was on the bank.

Crouching, he ran toward the cottonwood behind which the gunman had hidden. For a second, as he looked down over the bank, he saw nothing. Then the gunman raised up. They saw each other at the same instant. Both men's guns swung around, and two gunshots echoed down the creek bed, one a split second ahead.

Espy gripped his gun for another shot. But it was unnecessary. Matt Ollinger stumbled down the steep bank and pitched forward. He rolled over once and lay still.

In a few minutes the possemen had all gathered. With them was the tall outlaw, his hands tied to his saddle horn. Solemnly Sam Kirk motioned to Espy.

"I've found Claude Hatch," he said. "He's over here."

Hatch lay on his stomach behind a cut section of bank where he had made his stand. His cartridge belt lay before him, the loops empty. Espy lifted the gun from his limp hand and checked the cylinder. He shook his head.

"Not a single one left, Sam. He stayed with it right to the last."

Sam nodded gravely. "He always wanted to be somebody big. But he just didn't have the stuff."

Espy said, "You're wrong, Sam. He had the stuff. This is the biggest thing a man could do."

20

Far off on the right flank, Quirt Wolford had followed the Arrowhead herd, vengeance-lust burning relentlessly in him. A hundred times his right hand had felt for the gun that ought to be on his hip. His fist would knot, and a dry curse would well up. They wouldn't get away with it. He'd get a gun somewhere, and he'd get his chance. He'd see Matt Ollinger and the rest over the sights of it before he was done.

If only it wasn't for this damned left arm, this swollen, blackening arm that raged with the fires of hell.

Wolford's lips were dry and cracked with fever. A sickening red haze obscured whatever he looked at, and it was getting worse. He was starving for water—he'd trade half that herd for a full canteen. And this aching, this godawful throb that jarred his whole body—he'd sell his soul to rid himself of it before it drove him out of his mind.

He watched the approaching riders for a full minute before the meaning of what he saw hammered through to his fevered brain. He saw confusion strike the outlaws at the herd. One of them fired at the posse before it was within range. The rest of them waited no longer. They abandoned the cattle and ran.

Wolford reined up in a low swale and watched. He saw the posse gradually eat up the distance and take in the rustlers one by one. There was no shooting. Not a man put up any resistance when he saw he was caught.

Wolford watched, and he began to laugh. It was a wild, high, wheezing laugh born of a fever-crazed mind.

Laughing, he leaned over too far. He made a grab at the saddle horn—too late. The ground rushed up toward him. He landed with full weight on the poisoned, rotting arm. A cry of anguish tore from deep within him, and a spinning pool of darkness swam up to meet him.

With a supreme effort he managed to raise up onto his knees, and finally to his feet. He swayed like a drunken man. A searing lance thrust through his body, again and again and again. He stumbled forward, toward his horse. The animal shied, pricking its ears at him, but it didn't run. Catching the reins, he tried twice to shove his foot into the stirrup before he finally made it. It took all the courage he could muster to pull himself into the saddle. He took a tight grip on the horn this time. The world was spinning crazily.

Fear began to take hold of him. If he ever fell off again, he knew, he could never get back into the saddle. He'd walk and stumble and fall down and die.

The agony of the arm was getting worse. A doctor! He had to have a doctor. What good was freedom if a man was dead? He had to do something about that arm.

His vision was failing him, but he still knew directions. He reined the horse around and headed him back. He'd find Mobeetie. He *had* to get to Mobeetie.

How he finally got there, he didn't know. Part of the time he'd been out of his head, his fever-racked body leaning heavily over the horn. How many hours or days he'd been, he could not know. But one thing he did know. That was Mobeetie ahead.

The sight of it cleared his head. Caution. He had to use caution.

He knew where the doctor lived, in a two-room adobe house. Wolford picked it out and guided the horse toward it. Warily he watched for sign of people. They wouldn't take him. He wouldn't let them take him.

He saw the water barrel at the back door. Thirst was a living devil in his parched throat, driving him wild. He eased down from the saddle, groaning at the knifing pain. He stumbled toward the barrel—shoved his face into it. The cool taste of the water almost made him fall unconscious again. He straightened, holding the edge of the barrel until he had steadied. Then he leaned over and drank slowly.

The effect of the water was almost miraculous. His vision cleared. He could stand now and not sway so much. He could walk without stumbling.

But that arm still throbbed, a steady, driving, crazing pain.

He walked around the house and pounded on the door. A Mexican boy with a broom in his hand finally opened it.

"Doctor . . ." Wolford said, ". . . got to see the doctor."

The boy's brown eyes widened qualmishly at the sight of Wolford's swollen, blackened arm. "*No está—no está.*"

"Where is he?" Wolford grabbed the kid desperately and shook him with his good hand. "Where is he?"

The frightened youngster pointed toward the back end of a frame saloon a hundred yards away—McCavitt's saloon. "*Es con Señor McCavitt. En la cantina.*"

Through the open door Wolford saw a gun belt hanging on the wall. He shoved inside, grabbed the belt and yanked it down from the peg. The boy, boogered like a jackrabbit, darted past him and out the door. Wolford yelled, but he couldn't catch him.

He lurched through the door and back outside. He moved heavily toward the saloon.

At the rear of the building he paused uncertainly, wondering which of the two doors to try. There was a window. He squinted painfully, trying to see outside.

He saw a man lying on a bed, still and quiet, as if asleep. A girl sat watching. A second man was cutting white cloth with a big pair of scissors. Wolford got it through his brain that this man was cutting a bandage. He must be the doctor.

Wolford tested the doorknob. Shoving the door open, he drew the gun and stumbled inside.

The doctor and the girl stared in surprise. The girl started to stand up. Wolford waved the gun at her. "Keep still."

The doctor's eyes dropped to Wolford's bad arm. In shock, his lips moved with words unsaid.

"You're coming with me, Doc," Wolford said. His voice was labored and thick. "My arm . . . you got to treat my arm."

The doctor laid the scissors on the edge of the bed and moved cautiously toward Wolford. "My God, man," he said quietly, "that arm . . . You can't go anywhere."

"Got to get away. Go west. You'll go with me. Take care of my arm."

The doctor nodded toward Arch McCavitt, who lay pale and still on the bed. "I can't leave here. This man needs me, just as you do. If I leave, he may die."

Wolford exploded. "To hell with him. You got to go!"

He waved the gun. The doctor paled.

The girl stood up with hatred in her eyes. "If you take the doctor, you'll surely kill Arch. And if you do that, I'll kill *you*, Wolford."

He ignored her. "You coming, Doc?"

The doctor nodded hopelessly. "Very well."

Suddenly he tensed. The clatter of hoofs sounded on the street out front. There was a shuffle of feet in the saloon.

"What's that?" Wolford demanded.

The girl listened a moment, then smiled triumphantly. "The posse," she said. "It's come back."

Wolford heard the clump of boots and the jingle of spurs on the wooden sidewalk out front. They came through the front door. He heard someone say, "Howdy, Norwood. Any luck?"

The footsteps kept coming toward the door.

Wolford stiffened. Norwood! Gone now was his desperate desire for escape. It was swallowed up in a blinding surge of hatred. Norwood! It was Norwood who had ruined him, who had destroyed all Wolford had built. Now Norwood was coming, and Wolford was waiting for him. His hand tightened on his gun. He edged carefully to the back wall, where he could face the door, where he could get a clear shot. He waited there, his lips flat against his teeth, his eyes aflame.

"Don't move, either one of you," he gritted. "Do and I'll kill you."

The door opened, and he squeezed the trigger.

Disappointment had a bitter taste for Espy Norwood, riding back to town with part of the posse. Sure, the race was over and the fight was won. Even now, some of the Figure 4 cowboys were driving the Arrowhead herd back to its home range. And Quirt Wolford's men rode with the posse, hands tied to their saddle horns.

Best of all, Kenny Norwood rode beside his father. Kenny hadn't been hurt, so far as Espy could see. Mistreated, yes, but not hurt.

Even so, disappointment's keen edge cut at Espy. Quirt Wolford had gotten away.

He wouldn't get far. That's what his own men had said. Might even be dead already. But that wasn't the way Espy had wanted it. Not the way at all.

As the posse rode into Mobeetie, people gathered to watch. Down the crooked street, Espy could see a crowd in front of the hotel.

Sam Kirk pulled in beside him. "Mary's down there, and the directors too. Want to go on and give them the whole report?"

Espy shook his head. "You go, Sam. You tell them. You'd better tell Mary about her uncle, too."

"What're you going to do, Espy?"

"I'll be down after a bit. I want to stop off and see about Arch."

Kenny reined up with him. Espy said, "You go on

with Sam, son. Saloon's no place for you. Not even Arch's."

He tied his horse to the hitchrack. He paused at the open door to take off his hat and sleeve the sweat from his face. Thunder, but he was dirty. Three days' beard, three days' dust. And tired—he could sleep a week.

"Howdy, Norwood," the bartender spoke. "Any luck?"

Espy nodded wearily. He walked on back toward Arch's room. The saloon was quiet, for its few customers stood outside, watching the posse move on down the dusty street. He shoved open the door.

The porcelain knob shattered under his hand.

Espy stumbled backward as the roar of gunfire shook the walls. He glimpsed the man who faced him. Then he leaped aside as Wolford fired again. Espy's hand went down and came up with a gun.

"Norwood!" There was no mistaking Wolford's voice, even though it sounded tight with pain. "Norwood, throw your gun in here."

Espy did not.

"Throw it in here," Wolford gritted again, "or I'll shoot the man on the bed."

Espy pitched the gun into the room. He knew what was coming now.

"Now walk on in here!"

Espy's stomach went weak. A long time since he had known fear like this, fear for himself. But it was here now, his heart hammering, his breath short and painful. He wondered if any man could ever walk into the jaws of death and not feel the awful squeeze of fear.

With short, halting steps, Espy walked through the door. He faced Quirt Wolford, and he was not ready for what he saw. Wolford was a crazy man. His fevered black eyes tried hard to focus on Espy. His right hand was shaky on the gun. And his left . . .

Espy went sick at the sight of it, the smell of it.

Wolford laughed crazily. His hand steadied, tightening on the gun. Espy's breath stopped. He braced himself.

Lilybelle moved so swiftly that Espy barely saw her. Her slender right hand darted downward. The long steel scissors flashed silver as she brought them up.

Wolford screamed.

The gun slanted toward the girl. Wolford's lips tightened as he tried hard to level it at Lilybelle.

Espy dived for his own gun, on the floor. He scooped it up and shot fast.

The muzzle of Wolford's weapon tipped downward. It slipped from his fingers and fell to the floor. Wolford sighed, swayed forward, and rolled over on his face.

Lilybelle's cheeks drained white in horror. She whirled away, falling across Arch and weeping bitterly.

Espy began to get his breath again. He wiped the cold sweat from his face and walked shakily to the girl. He placed his hands on her heaving shoulders.

"It's all right now," he whispered. "It's all right. You gave me the break I needed. Everything's all right."

She sobbed. "It was terrible . . . terrible."

"Sure," Espy said. "But it's over. All over."

Abruptly she stopped crying. She raised up, her eyes wide. "Espy! Doctor! Come look!"

Arch was beginning to stir. His eyelids fluttered.

The gunfire. It had shaken him out of his coma, Espy knew.

Painfully, a little at a time, Arch opened his eyes. It

took him a minute to begin to see. By that time the room was full of people who had crowded in to find out what the shooting was about. But the only thing Arch saw was Lilybelle, standing over him, her white fingers gripping his hand. Arch's face creased with a smile.

"I sure never figured I'd get to heaven." His voice was weak, but the life was there.

Lilybelle squeezed his red-whiskered face between her hands and kissed him softly. She was sobbing again, but this time it was different.

When he could, Espy told him, "She hasn't left you two minutes since we brought you in here, Arch. You better marry that girl."

Arch looked softly at her. Weakly he raised his hand and touched her honey-colored hair.

"I'm figuring on it," he said.

The best place the syndicate directors could find for a board meeting room was the dining room of the hotel. They used it.

Determinedly Mary Bowman stood before them and restated her promise. "We'll start a roundup immediately. We'll get a full and accurate count. If the syndicate's share isn't there, I'll turn back as many of the Arrowhead cattle as I have to. I'll make the count good."

They had asked her to leave them then, so they could discuss the matter freely.

Now she was at the Lee & Reynolds store, making provision for the supplies the Figure 4 would need in its roundup. Espy and Sam helped her.

Sam said, "Don't you worry, Mary. We'll build the Figure 4 back to what it was. You just wait and see."

Mary shook her head. "Not *we,* Sam. I'm leaving

the Figure 4 as soon as the count is done and we've squared things up."

Sam was incredulous. "Leaving?"

Her voice was pinched with sadness. "I couldn't go on living there, Sam. Not after all that's happened. I'll move to the Arrowhead. It's not big, but it's mine. I'll make a ranch out of it someway."

Worriedly Sam said, "I'm afraid, Mary, that you're going to have to cut the Arrowhead herd plenty deep if you make your promise good. Fact is, there won't be much left of it."

Her lips were tight. "Then I'll do the best I can with what I *do* have. I'd rather have a ranch with no cattle on it than to keep what isn't mine."

Espy was standing outside the hotel, waiting, when the directors finally broke up their session. The lawyer Slagel came out scowling. His jaw was swollen. He caught Espy glancing at him, and he glowered darkly. He strode away, fiercely swinging his cane.

The colonel slapped a heavy hand to Espy's shoulder. He was grinning broadly, the way he had used to do.

"Well, Espy," he said, "we won. We whipped Slagel's ears down. The syndicate's keeping its money in the Figure 4. In fact, we've decided to see what we can do about buying or leasing the land."

Espy grinned. "Congratulations, Colonel."

The old man's brown eyes danced in triumph. "It was Mary Bowman that did it, Espy. She had them eating right out of her hand. She's a little princess, that girl is."

Then he said, "They left me in full charge, Espy. I'm going to need a permanent manager on the Figure 4. What do you say?"

Espy shook his head. "Thanks, Colonel. But I can't take it."

Judkins's thick eyebrows arched. "What's the matter? Have you got another job lined up?"

"You might call it that, I guess. But don't you worry about a manager. Go talk to Sam Kirk, Colonel. You won't find a better man."

The colonel nodded thoughtfully. "I'll talk to him, Espy. But what are you going to do?"

Espy grinned. "I'm going to try to marry a princess."

The afternoon sun was a bright gold memory, and the fiery red was slowly bleeding out of the clouds that hovered low over the hills to the west. Mary Bowman and Espy Norwood walked arm in arm out past the Figure 4 saddle shed. They stopped to watch while Jess Cooley bolted a chuckbox to a wagon bed and tried at the same time to tell Kenny Norwood how to hold a rope.

Joe Kirk cast a quick loop at a cow skull nailed to a wooden keg. He caught it. Kenny tried and missed.

Jess called, "Now, Kenny, do like I told you. Don't hold the rope so close to the loop. Back your hand up a little. That's it. Now swing it over your head till it feels right, then throw it just like you'd throw a rock."

Kenny did. And this time he caught. Jess hollered. "That's the ticket. By the time this roundup is over, I'll have you almost as good a roper as I am. *Almost*."

Espy chuckled, and Mary Bowman smiled. They walked on up the slope.

Mary said, "Kenny's doing fine. I was afraid what

he's been through might hurt him. But it doesn't seem to have bothered him much."

Espy shook his head.

Mary said, "The cowboys have all taken a liking to him. He'll have a lot of good teachers."

Espy nodded seriously. "Yes. But he needs a mother."

Her eyes lifted questioningly. Espy tried to go on with what he wanted to say. It wouldn't come out. They stood together in silence by Frank Bowman's spring, watching the water gush out and splash down the hillside.

"In a way, Espy," Mary said, "I'm going to hate to leave all this. It's been a part of me, and I've been a part of it for so long. It's always hard to break away from the things that bind you to the past."

Espy knew. He'd been through it. It had taken years for him to break away. But he had done it. And now he was free.

"Mary," he told her, "the colonel offered me the managership if I'd stay. I turned him down."

She looked at him in surprise. "Why?"

"You're starting a new ranch, Mary. You'll need a manager."

Her hand tightened on his. "Thanks, Espy. But what good is a manager when I don't have any cattle?"

Espy said, "Mary, I've been saving money for a long time. I've got a good-sized account stashed away in a Kansas City bank. And the colonel has promised to get me as much more as I need.

"I'd like to stock that ranch for you. I'll furnish the cattle, you furnish the land. We can work out a partnership. What do you say?"

She said what he had wanted to say, when he didn't

have the words. "I'll do it on one condition, Espy. This will have to be a lifetime partnership—all the way!"

He reached for her. She came with face upturned, and they sealed the contract.

THE TIME
IT NEVER
RAINED

In a broad sense this book is dedicated to the old-time Western ranchman, whose lifestyle gave him an inkling of Heaven and more than his proper share of Hell.

In particular it is dedicated to my father, Buck Kelton . . . one of them.

INTRODUCTION

During the long Texas drouth of the 1950s a joke—probably already as old as the state—was told again and again about a man who bet several of his friends that it never would rain again, and collected from two of them.

Indeed, it seemed the rain *was* gone forever. For parts of West Texas the ordeal lasted a full seven years. Though some would argue that it was not the most devastating drouth they had ever seen, it was by all odds the *longest* in memory.

Each new generation tends to forget—until it confronts the sobering reality—that dryness has always been the normal condition in the western half of the state. Wet years have been the exceptions. Walter Prescott Webb, in his classic *The Great Plains*, noted how the land changes west of the 98th meridian, and how this has affected the people who live there, etching its marks upon their characters and impacting upon their culture. Traditionally it has taken a strong-willed, individualistic breed to live west of that line, especially when that living is tied closely to the soil, as is the case with the rancher and the farmer. Those not strong enough either did not cross the line or retreated after being bruised by the demands of that uncompromising land. Those who remained became tough, resilient, and almost militantly independent. As a group they have been like the old rancher who declared, "I don't want anybody giving me anything, and I don't want anybody telling me what to do; I just want to be left the hell alone!"

This fierce protectiveness for one's own prerogatives has been compromised to some degree in the last generation or so, but enough remains to be a potent political factor. Resistance to regulation may be stronger in drouth-prone West Texas than anywhere. This trait remains a puzzle to people in other areas, willing to trade their freedoms piecemeal for what appears to be a guarantee of security. They, perhaps, do not have this heritage of recurring struggle for survival which every succeeding generation of West Texans has had to face, each in its own time.

My father's family has been west of the 98th meridian more than a century, and not one generation has been spared this cycle of drouth and hardship. When Dad was about seventy-five, I asked him how many really wet years he had seen.

"Four," he replied. "They were 1906, 1919, 1941 and 1957." That was little more than one out of twenty. He had seen twice that many dry spells severe enough to be termed drouths. The rest of the time varied between "pretty good" and "pretty dry."

Drouth by Texas definition is a period of severely deficient moisture that laps over from one year into another. Often it is of two to three years' duration.

Anything shorter, though it may be serious, is termed a *dry spell*, as if more annoyance than hardship.

In the mid 1950s I asked a Kansas lamb buyer about conditions in his area. He said they were tough; he had suffered through three drouths that summer. I did not totally relate to his terminology. I told him we were already in the third summer of the same drouth. As it turned out, we had three more to go.

Drouth by Texas standards does not necessarily mean a total absence of rainfall. Rains may indeed come, occasionally, but they are usually light, and moisture from one seldom remains until the next. Natural selection has long since eliminated those native plants which cannot endure extended dry conditions, but the plants which remain tend to go dormant. They retain life only in their root systems, not above the ground for livestock to graze. Introduced crops and "improved" grasses seldom survive the more cruel of these tests.

In earlier times, livestock on such drouthy ranges would literally starve. By the 1950s, good transportation had made it possible for stockmen to haul in feed or to ship livestock to market before they declined to such a desperate condition. This did not prevent the economic collapse of a substantial percentage of ranchmen, however.

Their plight led to a number of federal aid programs supposed to keep them on the land. Many of these programs compounded the problem instead of presenting a solution. They were initiated hurriedly with few ground rules by politicians who coveted favorable publicity. When rules finally were completed months later, they were enforced retroactively, placing extra hardship upon many of the early participants. In the main the programs were inadequately planned and motivated more by political consider-ations than by sound appraisal of actual needs. Many ranchmen, like my character, Charlie Flagg, elected to shun them but suffered nevertheless because the pro-grams' inflationary impact nullified the benefits for those who participated and added to the economic misery of those who did not.

The Time It Never Rained as you read it here is my third version. I began writing the first shortly after the drouth was broken. It failed to find a publisher, as did a second version in the early 1960s. I set the novel aside for about ten years. After critical acceptance of *The Day the Cowboys Quit* in 1971 I decided to try again, completely rewriting it. Perhaps I had become a better writer after ten years, and perhaps editors were more prepared to accept the premise that all which comes out of Washington is not necessarily golden.

By this later time I was able also to treat racial problems more frankly, particularly the relationships between ranch workers of Mexican heritage and the Anglos who employed them.

During the 1950s I was a farm and ranch reporter for the San Angelo *Standard-Times* and covered the drouth story day after day, month after month, year after year. Most of my friends and many of my relatives were fighting the battle at ground zero. I watched them, and I bled with them, inside.

I hoped the novel would give urban people a better understanding of hazards the rancher and the farmer face in trying to feed and clothe them. The heaviest readership, however, was west of the Mississippi. In effect, I found myself preaching to the choir.

Many people over the years have asked me if I based Charlie Flagg on their fathers. My mother was convinced that I wrote it about *my* father. The truth is, I did, in part. I wrote it about him and about many, many others I knew, people who still retained an old frontier heritage of fighting their own fight, testing one strategy and when it failed trying another, but above all simply enduring, and enduring.

They are not the traditional Western fictional heroes, standing up to a villain for one splendid moment of glory. They are quiet but determined men and women who stand their ground year after year in a fight they can never finally win, against an unforgiving enemy they know will return to challenge them again and again so long as they live.

They are the *true* heroes.

ELMER KELTON
San Angelo, Texas

PROLOGUE

It crept up out of Mexico, touching first along the brackish Pecos and spreading then in all directions, a cancerous blight burning a scar upon the land.

Just another dry spell, men said at first. Ranchers watched waterholes recede to brown puddles of mud that their livestock would not touch. They watched the rank weeds shrivel as the west wind relentlessly sought them out and smothered them with its hot breath. They watched the grass slowly lose its green, then curl and fire up like dying cornstalks.

Farmers watched their cotton make an early bloom in its stunted top, produce a few half-hearted bolls and then wither.

Men grumbled, but you learned to live with the dry spells if you stayed in West Texas; there were more dry spells than wet ones. No one expected another drouth like that of '33. And the really big dries like 1918 came once in a lifetime.

Why worry? they said. It would rain this fall. It always had.

But it didn't. And many a boy would become a man before the land was green again.

1

Rio Seco was too small to afford a professional manager for its one-room Chamber of Commerce. The part-time volunteer, elected because no one else wanted the job, made his living selling an independent brand of gasoline two cents under the majors though he bought it from the same tank truck that serviced half the stations in town. A man of wit, some people thought, he had erected a big red-and-white sign on the highway at the city limits:

WELCOME TO RIO SECO
HOME OF 3,000 FRIENDLY PEOPLE—
AND THREE OLD CRANKS!

Farther inside the city limits, half-hidden between a Ford billboard and one for Pepsi-Cola, he had placed another sign:

THIS IS GOD'S COUNTRY
DON'T DRIVE THROUGH IT LIKE HELL

This cattle, sheep, and farming town was much the same as fifty others dotted along the interminable east-west highways which speed traffic across the great monotonous stretches of western Texas ranch country. To an impatient motorist hunting a cooler place to light before dark, these dusty little towns are all cut from the same tiresome pattern and, despite the signboard, a long way from heaven.

Like most of them, Rio Seco had old roots. It had been born out of necessity, a trading place for sprawling cow outfits, for scattered sheep camps and industrious German dryland farmers who had come west with their wagons, their plows, and a compulsive will to build something. The town long ago had made its growth and found its natural level. Now it held steady, gaining no ground but losing none. Oil companies had come and punched their holes and found them dry. They had gone again, leaving dreams of quick riches to drift away on the arid wind like the cotton-white clouds that promised rain and failed to deliver.

Life still depended on two fundamentals: crops planted by the hand of man and grass planted by the hand of God.

Give us rain, they said at Rio Seco, *and it makes no difference who is in the White House.*

If one thing set the town apart, it was probably the trees—pale-green mesquites and massive, gnarled live oaks, rustling cottonwoods and shady pecans, watered by a hundred windmills whose towers stood tall above a timid skyline. Modern municipal mains provided purer water for drinking and cooking, but most of the older generation clung to wells for yards and gardens and trees. For a man who has often turned his face to the hot breath of drouth, the sight of a windmill tower—its big steel fan clanking patiently and pumping up water clear and cool—somehow reaches deep and touches something in his soul.

The town had three cultures—Anglo, German, and Mexican. The first two had largely merged through the years—beef and beans and apple strudel. The third remained unassimilated, except perhaps in Rio Seco's unhurried pace of living. Most of the Anglos were addicted to Mexican food, and most of the Mexicans loved football, but these were superficial things.

Many of the older rock homes had a no-nonsense squared-off solidity the Germans had brought from their original settlements in the Pedernales River section of the hill country. Across the railroad tracks, beyond roads dusty from passage of livestock trucks on their way to the shipping pens, lay the Mexican part of town—ageless adobes and small frame shacks, and a fair number of modern GI houses built since the war. The old and the new stood side by side in sharp contrast: a wrinkled, ancient Mexican working up adobe bricks out of straw and mud in a barefoot method known to the fathers of his grandfathers, while next door a three-man crew with electric saws cut raw lumber for a new frame house. Two small brown-faced boys sat on a forebearing Mexican burro, their black eyes alive with curiosity as they watched an older brother tuning the motor of a hotrod.

For the ranchman, business centered around Emmett Rodale's old stone bank and Jim Sweet's feedstore-wool warehouse, a long, cool, cavernous building of concrete tile. There in round, well-packed jute bags wedged between steel poles and stacked nearly to the high ceiling lay stored the gray-white

fleeces that for three generations had been a corner-
stone of Rio Seco's economy.

For the farmer, business focused on the same bank,
the cotton gin and a small grain elevator with twin
steel tubes that stood taller than anything else in
town except the sun-catching silver water tower em-
blazoned with crudely painted red letters: SRS '51.

In the second floor of the rock-fronted courthouse
was a room which in recent years had emerged as another important economic fact of life: the county office of the federal PMA. Next to rain, perhaps, it had
become the *most* important fact. Here the man of the
land came to declare his crop acreage, his past year's
plantings. Here he was told how much land he would
be allowed to seed in cotton, in grain sorghums, in
whatever other crops might be under federal control.
Here he came for price support and to receive checks
to help him pay for terraces and water-spreading, for
water wells and surface tanks, for battling back the
prickly pear and thorny mesquite.

Here he sold his freedom bit by bit, and was paid
for it on the installment plan.

March Nicholson, the county PMA officer, stood
at the open window, looking down on the freshly
mowed courthouse lawn, the buried sprinkler system
showering green bermuda grass dotted by patches
of dying winter rye. It always irritated him the way
people parked haphazardly around the courthouse
curb, ignoring the town ordinances, if indeed there
were any. Across the street under a live-oak tree, half
blocking the driveway to Nicholson's rented home,
stood a pickup truck with a Hereford cow tied in
the sideboarded bed and a saddled horse in an open-
topped trailer hitched behind it. Horse droppings

had tumbled over the tailgate and onto the ground; Nicholson would have to use his shovel tonight. He cursed under his breath. In the back of another pickup waited two Border Collie sheepdogs, resting but alert-eyed, watching a farmer pull up in a bobtail truck with two big tractor tires and several sacks of planting seed.

Nicholson's baleful eye was pulled away from the horse droppings by a brush-scarred green pickup pulling into an open parking space.

"Well, I'll be damned. I wish you'd look who's come to the meeting."

His district supervisor pushed to his feet from a chair in the courtroom's jury box where he had slouched to read a copy of the morning San Angelo paper. He watched a heavy, graying ranchman step out of the pickup and limp up the concrete sidewalk toward the front steps of the courthouse. He saw nothing which made that man look different from the couple of dozen stockmen and farmers already gossiping in the courtroom.

"I don't know him. Is he somebody special?"

"He's Charlie Flagg."

The name meant nothing to the supervisor. "One of the rich ones?" he guessed. In this part of the country it was often hard to tell the rich man from the poor one by looking at him. The rich man was as likely to be wearing patched trousers and runover boots as the most destitute Mexican cowboy in town. One could not afford to put up a front and the other did not have to.

Nicholson shook his head. "No, not rich. Charlie Flagg is one of those operators in the middle ground . . . smaller than a lot of them. You've seen that sign on the edge of town, the one about the three old cranks? Charlie Flagg is Crank Number One."

The supervisor watched the ranchman pause on the front steps to swap howdies with a deputy sheriff. The deputy, who probably did not swing a leg across a horse's back twice a year, was dressed in a neatly tailored Western shirt and tight-legged cowboy pants, shiny high-heeled boots and a nicely creased Stetson hat. The rancher, probably on horseback half his waking hours, wore a nondescript straw hat beaten badly out of shape and a pair of old black boots, his baggy khaki trousers stuffed carelessly into their tops. There was a lesson in this somewhere, the supervisor thought; someday he was going to reason it out.

"Gives you trouble, does he, March?"

"No trouble . . . or anything else. Never sticks his hard head into my office. He's one of those old moss-horns who thinks he made it all by himself and he doesn't need anybody. I've tried to get him to go into some of our programs. You ought to hear him snort. Says the government didn't help him when he was getting started and he doesn't need it now."

"Then I'd simply forget about him if I were you. Some people you can't change; you just have to out-live them."

"Charlie Flagg is too contrary to die; he'll outlive us all."

Nicholson's face twisted as he looked at the men who sat in little groups scattered around the big courtroom, talking weather and crops and prices. He had sent out five hundred postcards announcing the meeting; this looked like about all the crowd he was going to get.

"It's frustrating," he complained. "A man devotes

his life to service, and this is the response they give him. Sometimes I wish I was selling cars in San Antonio."

The supervisor said, "The rest'll come in when it's time to get their checks."

Nicholson walked down the aisle and out into the hallway to see if there were any laggards. He saw Charlie Flagg come up the steps, laboring a little because of a slightly game leg. Part of a postcard stuck out of one shirt pocket. Nicholson shoved his hand forward. "Mister Flagg, when I sent you that card I had no hope you would actually come to the meeting."

Flagg gripped Nicholson's hand hard enough to bring a stab of pain, but he looked puzzled. "Meetin'? What meetin'?"

"The meeting to explain the changes in the farm program."

Flagg shrugged his heavy shoulders. "They change the farm program the way I change socks. Before you can get your meetin' over with, they'll be callin' you from Washington to tell you it's all different."

Nicholson sagged a little. "You didn't come for the meeting, then?"

Flagg shook his head. "I come up huntin' the judge. They sent me a call for jury duty and I got a shearin' crew comin' tomorrow. Court can wait, but a shearin' crew won't."

Nicholson saw that the postcard in Flagg's pocket was not the one he had mailed. "Well, I still say you'll be in to see me someday, Mister Flagg."

Flagg's gaze was steady and without compromise. "What I can't do for myself, I'll do without."

A short, stocky ranchman came up the stairs in time to catch the last of it. He paused to spit a long stream of brown tobacco juice at a hallway cuspidor, getting most of it in. "You're preachin' again, Charlie," he grinned, "and this ain't even church."

Charlie Flagg turned, a little embarrassed. "Hello, Rounder. I didn't go to preach, but he asked me and I told him."

Rounder Pike laid a rough hand on Flagg's shoulder. "You're fartin' against the wind, Charlie. We've got used to government money like a kid gets used to candy. Most people wouldn't quit takin' it now. Them as did would go right on payin' the same old taxes and not get nothin' back. We're like a woman that's been talked into a little taste of sin and found out she likes it. You'd just as well join the crowd. You're payin' the freight anyway."

"Never."

"*Never* is an awful long time." Pike gripped Flagg's shoulder, then walked on into the courtroom.

Nicholson motioned toward the door. "There's plenty of room, Mister Flagg."

Flagg started to turn away. "You'll find, Mister Nicholson, that ranchers are contrary people. And *old* ranchers are *awful* contrary." He limped down the hall toward the office of the county judge.

Nicholson's supervisor had come out into the hallway to listen. He said, "One of those *rugged individualists,* isn't he?"

"Someday he'll just be a *ragged* individualist. He's standing still while time goes on by. But he'll be in to see me one of these days. He'll come in like all the rest."

The supervisor frowned, watching the rancher go through an open door. "Somehow, I hope he never does."

Nicholson's eyebrows went up.

The supervisor said, "He's gone out of style, but

the world will be a poorer place when it loses the last of his kind."

"You sympathize with him?"

"I pity him, a little. A man can get awfully lonesome standing out there all by himself."

2

It was not yet midmorning, but already the southwest wind touched warm against Charlie Flagg's stubbled face as he climbed the narrow ladder up the steel tower of the windmill to look beyond the empty livestock pens and across the big pasture. He could see the sheep half a mile away in a drift of gray dust. He cocked his head to listen, but he couldn't hear them over the racket of Teofilo Garcia's shearing crew setting up equipment in a corral.

Beneath him, gentle whiteface cows drank cool water from a long concrete trough. They paid him no attention. A steer calf touched its nose curiously to a plastic bottle which Charlie had wired on as a no-cost float to save six dollars. Charlie's spur jingled, and the calf jerked its head up, startled, water dripping from its hairy chin. "Don't worry, pardner," the ranchman spoke quietly. "We already done our job on you. This is the day for the sheep."

Charlie Flagg was far past fifty now, a broad-shouldered man who still toted his own feed sacks, dug his own post-holes, flanked his own calves. The scorch of summer sun and wind had burned him deep. His face was so brown he might have passed for a Mexican shearer, had his eyes not been the deep blue of a troubled sky.

His Western straw hat was bought new in April but now in May was already spotted with sweat stain, the brim curled higher on the right side than on the left because the right hand was the one he used to grip it. He wore it for service; at his age he had no interest in show. His khaki pants fitted low and loose on broad hips. He had been letting his belt out gradually, and a little of soft belly pushed against the silver buckle. He used to depend upon hard work and hot summer to take that softness away. The last few years, October found most of it still there.

He hooked an arm over an angle-iron rung and leaned out, sun-grinning against the glare. He surveyed the band of sheep and counted six riders beside or behind them. Satisfied, he turned away and let his gaze drift leisurely over the ranch while the steel fan clanked and groaned above him, and the sucker-rod bumped against the standpipe as it pumped up and down. It always hurt his leg a little to climb this ladder, but the view pleasured him enough to be worth the pain.

It was a comforting sight, this country. It was an ageless land where the past was still a living thing and old voices still whispered, where the freshness of the pioneer time had not yet all faded, where a few of the old dreams were not yet dark with tarnish. It had not been so long, really, since feathered Comanches had roamed these hills a horseback seeking after game, or occasionally in warpaint seeking honor and booty and blood. Eighty years . . . one man's lifetime. Across Warrior Hill and down along a creekbed where a wet-weather spring seeped during the good years, a person with sharp eyes and lots of time might still turn up arrowheads as perfect as the day skillful brown fingers had shaped them from brittle flint.

Old August Schmidt had told Charlie once that in his youth he could still see the smokestains of Indian campfires beneath a ledge of limestone ancient beyond imagination, relic of some primeval sea; and once in that deep swale below where the house now stood, he had ridden unexpectedly upon a shaggy buffalo bull, last remnant of the vanished herds.

When August had been an old man he had shown Charlie the slumped remains of a Mexican mustanger's dugout, a primitive camp used as headquarters for a winter—maybe as much as a winter and a spring—while the raw-hider ran down the last of the wild horses.

It was in the mustanger's time that Warrior Hill had earned its name. An aging Comanche—alone, so far as anyone knew—had made his way back from the reservation in Indian Territory far to the north, perhaps for one final hunt on ancestral grounds, perhaps simply to die where his grandfathers had died. The mustanger saw him and found two Rangers tracking him. Together they gave chase and ran the old warrior and his gotch-eared pony to ground. On top of the hill the Comanche jumped down from his lathered and droop-headed horse, raised his arms toward the sky and sang a chant that made the mustanger's blood run cold. Then he turned with bow in hand and charged the guns, shouting defiance into the face of certain death.

His bones were still scattered on that hilltop when

August Schmidt had bought the land. The old German settlers, more than any others of early Texas, had somehow understood the Indian and had made their own treaties with him. August Schmidt had loved this country on sight; he thought he knew why the old warrior had come home to it. He gathered the bones and carefully covered them with a cairn of stones on top of the hill. The rest of his life he tended the cairn, keeping it as neat as it had been that first day. The hill was a place he could go when he needed solitude to think. It was a place that always seemed to give him strength when he faltered in the trying years, for there he had buried a man strong beyond measure.

Each of these men had had his own time—the Indian, the mustang hunter, the pioneer rancher—and each had passed from the scene. For more than twenty years now it had been Charlie's turn to use this land, to shape it in his own way and to be shaped by it. To a degree he never knew, he had been shaped by all those who had gone before him.

He called his ranch Brushy Top, after the brushy Concho divide which ran along the edge of it. It was not so large that he could not see beyond it from here. North and west it was his to the edge of the cotton farms on Coyote Flat. To the south and east lay Page Mauldin's vast expanse of live-oak hills. Charlie had fifteen sections of rangeland in all—three deeded, the rest under lease. Almost ten thousand acres, the way people figured it in town, but Charlie tallied it easier in sections. It took fully four acres in this country to feed a sheep, twenty for a cow. Charlie's was not large as Texas outfits went—not large enough that the worry of it followed him to bed at night the way Page Mauldin's far-flung ranch operations did. But it was enough that Charlie had brought up a son on it and sent him to all the school he would take, and he had never missed paying Lupe Flores his monthly wage.

West of the corrals and away from their hoof-churned dust, two houses sat protected by the deep shade of long-reaching old live-oak trees. One was a white-painted frame with rubboard siding and a porch. Charlie had built it good and solid, hoping it would content his help and make them want to stay. Lupe and Rosa Flores had lived in it seventeen years. The house had been expanded gradually as their five children came along.

At fifteen, Manuel Flores was out on horseback doing a man's part as ranch boys were expected to do, helping round up and drive the sheep. Charlie could see little Juan, the youngest, playing cowboy on a stick horse in the broom-swept front yard. The girls Anita and Luisa were likely in the house helping their mother with the cleaning and the cooking. Candelario, seven, was hanging onto the shearing-pen fence, large brown eyes a-sparkle as he watched the transient Mexican hands sharpen their shearing heads and stretch a greasy shade tarp from each side of the rig for the job that was soon to begin. Candelario was learning some new words down there from Garcia's crew. If he took any of them home, Rosa would blister his bottom with a willow switch.

Charlie's own house had stood for most of seventy years. Its square lines bore the strong flavor of hill-country German, for when August Schmidt had become able to afford it he had brought an immigrant rockmason from Fredericksburg to help him, and with his own hands he had built this house to stand forever. The limestone blocks had been chiseled one at a time into straight lines that would butt together without a flaw. Age and weather had darkened the stone, but the building seemed as sturdy now as it had ever been.

August Schmidt had grown old here before he sold the place to Charlie. Now Charlie would grow old in this house, and someday, perhaps, his son.

Charlie watched his wife, Mary, wearing a floppy old straw hat with a brim wide as a Mexican sombrero, move through the front gate into their yard. When Tom had first learned to walk, Charlie had found him one day at the barn, toddling dangerously around the horses' feet. That was when Charlie built the white picket fence, with the gate latch high and on the outside.

Tom had been a fool about horses even then. At twenty-two, he hadn't changed much.

Mary started work in her flower beds, trying to do some trimming before the day turned hot and she had to start dinner. Those damn flower beds! Years ago Charlie had to hammer and chip them out of caliche and solid rock for her, then haul good soil from way over on the Flat with a team of mules and a wagon. It took a dozen trips. For such a little woman, she had a streak of stubbornness broad as a saddleblanket. The German blood showing out, he figured. After traveling across the Atlantic to fight Germans in World War I, he should have known better than to marry one here at home.

The garden was Mary's red flag of defiance against the dry nature and plainness of this rolling range country. Charlie raised hell about the water it took, especially when he was obliged to drill another well and put up a new steel windmill behind the house. But no matter, she raised her flowers anyway—petunias and pinks, roses and larkspur, zinnias and phlox.

Charlie would have been content with the flowers
Nature chose to put there; they were many and colorful when the season was wet. But he guessed a man
had to tolerate a few things. The world had known
but one perfect man, and no perfect woman whatever.

He climbed slowly down from the mill, careful not
to let a foot slip on the thin, slick angle-iron. He favored his left leg a little; it had been broken in a horse
fall years ago. Few were the old-time cowboys who
didn't have a bad leg or a crooked arm or some other
mark of the trade. On the ground he moved toward
the shearing pens, stopping at the netwire fence to
run his big hand playfully through Candelario's
coarse black hair.

"*Qué dice, muchacho?*" ("What do you say,
boy?")

The boy was momentarily startled. He had been so
interested in watching the shearers that he had not
heard Charlie coming. His brown face turned all grin
and dark eyes. It pleased Candelario that Charlie often spoke Spanish with him, though Charlie's Spanish was typically *gringo* and often caused the kids to
giggle behind their hands. Rosa Flores spoke only English in her house and demanded that her children
learn to speak it with less accent even than hers. She
said too many Spanish children—she always spoke of
them as Spanish rather than Mexican—knew no English when they started to school. Through this fault
of their parents and not of their own, they fell hopelessly behind from the start. Most would stay behind
as long as they lived.

But Lupe spoke Spanish with his children. He was
more orthodox than Rosa and had less schooling.
Hence in Candelario's boyish reasoning, Spanish was

a man's language and English was for women—and Anglos. He liked to hang out with the shearers, marveling at the profane glories of border Mexican.

Charlie heard a startled shout and turned quickly, in time to see a boy lose his footing and fall from a sacking frame. The lad grabbed at a wooden brace and broke his fall, landing on a pile of empty wool sacks. He got up shame-faced, dusting himself. From the shearing pen came derisive laughter and some whistling.

Charlie heard a girl laugh. Anita Flores stood at an outside corner of the pen, watching. She wore an old cotton dress and stood in bare feet, a wisp of a girl just coming to flower. Her olive face was freshly scrubbed, her skin smooth as cameo. At sixteen, she would not be long in becoming a woman.

She was laughing at the embarrassment of the young wool tromper, who climbed back up on the frame. Anita Flores was always seeing something to laugh about.

Charlie noticed then that some of the shearers had not resumed work; they were staring at Anita. They saw the woman, not the girl.

"Anita," he said sternly, "you oughtn't to be out here."

Laughter still bubbled in her brown and innocent eyes. Her voice carried a soft suggestion of Spanish accent. "Mama didn't need me. I came out to watch for a little while."

"Rosa wouldn't like seein' you at the shearin' pens."

"She has always let me, Mister Charlie."

"Things change." The wind lifted her cotton skirt a little, and Charlie knew damned well why Chuy Garcia had tumbled from that sacking frame. He dug the pointed toe of his boot into the sand. He had no daughter of his own. He and Mary had buried one long ago, an infant. In some measure Anita had substituted for the one they had lost. Still, she wasn't his own. How could he tell her the facts of life? That was for her mother to do.

"The men are all lookin' at you," he said. "They ain't lookin' at you like some little girl."

Anita glanced at the idle shearers, and she blushed.

Charlie said, "They don't mean you no harm. They just been out in the shearin' camps awhile. But they might take a wrong notion—might think you was offerin' somethin' that you're not."

Damn, he thought, *that was a left-handed way to put it. But how do you tell a girl what she ought to know unless you say things straight out?* Charlie Flagg had never been of a devious nature. He had always been a man to say what he thought and let the chips fall.

Her cheeks coloring, she said quietly, "I'll go, Mister Charlie." But a twinkle of laughter lingered in her eyes. "It *was* funny, the way Chuy fell. He always thinks so much of himself . . ."

"Wouldn't of been funny if he'd broken a leg."

This kind of male interest was probably new to her, Charlie mused as she walked away, but she'd damn well better get used to it. She was ripening in a hurry. *Rosa and Lupe and us, we'll have to watch her if we don't want somebody to pick her green.*

Teofilo Garcia's teenage tie-boys went back to sweeping the wooden shearing floors as Charlie walked through the gate. These boys would roll and tie the fleeces when each shearer finished a sheep, then pass them up to young Chuy Garcia to be tromped tightly into the bags. In slack moments they would sweep the floors again and again to keep the wool from picking up trash and dirt.

To the shearing captain, Charlie said, "Sheep comin', Teofilo."

"Ready, Mister Charlie." Teofilo Garcia rubbed excess engine oil onto his already greasy trousers and glanced at the departing girl with a measure of relief. "Old engine of mine, she's give a little trouble. Temperamental, you know, like a woman. You got to treat her like a woman, with patience and kindness." He hit the starter. The engine turned over once and sputtered out. It did the same a second time. Cursing with conviction, Teofilo kicked the machine and tried again. This time it caught. "Also, you got to be firm."

Teofilo was about Charlie's age, weighing two hundred and fifty or sixty pounds but bull-stout, even with his large belly. He didn't have to shear sheep himself any more; he was *capitán*. He was the entrepreneur, owning the truck and the shearing machine. He contracted the jobs, furnished equipment, tie-boys, cook and grub, and he took the first share of the gross receipts. The shearers furnished their muscle, skill, and the shearing heads they attached to the eight long-armed "drops" of Teofilo's smelly machine. It was a man-bending job—hot, heavy, numbing of muscle and mind. Little wonder that many a shearer came to hate the sheep and love the bottle that dimmed the everlasting bleating which echoed in his ears after the sheep were gone.

Teofilo cut off the machine and nodded in satisfaction. Charlie said, "If everything's fixed, I reckon I'll ride out and help the boys bring the sheep in."

Teofilo wiped a sleeve across his sweat-beaded forehead. "Bad day to be out in the sun, Mister Charlie. Too hot and dry."

"Cooler out there than in these pens. As for dry, we generally get some rain in May."

Teofilo shook his head. "Not this time. Yesterday this whirlwind came across the road and hit my truck. It was turnin' backwards. That's one bad sign, Mister Charlie. I think it won't rain now for a very long time."

Charlie smiled tolerantly. Most Mexicans he knew put lots of faith in signs. "It always rains when I got sheep to shear and need it to be dry."

His red-roan horse, Wander, stood hipshot at the far end of the pen, switching his tail to scatter the flies that had found him. Charlie lifted the leather reins from the fence where he had looped them, swung into the saddle and angled the horse between the tall upright cedar posts that marked the gate, ducking needlessly to pass under the taut twisted wires that braced the posts one against the other. The roan's hoofs lifted puffs of dust as he trotted away from the corrals. Out here by the salt troughs, where a dozen ribbon-like sheep trails converged and the animals congregated after watering, there never were any weeds or grass to hold the soil down. Even so, it seemed to Charlie that the ground was dustier than usual. Sure needed a rain to pack it.

The Hereford cattle that had been up to water were drifting out toward the waiting shade of live-oak trees. Charlie rode behind them and gave a loud holler, wanting them well out of the way when the sheep came in. Sheep had a way of always looking for a booger. The cattle moved into an easy trot, but as quickly as Charlie stopped pushing, they slowed down. One cow stopped and looked back to see if he was still coming. Tame as town dogs, Charlie thought. A man could almost walk up to them afoot in the pasture. They were far different from the wild brush cattle he had worked in the Pecos country during his youth. With those highheaded old sisters of fond memory, a cowboy did well to catch one glimpse of their hoisted tails as they clattered off into the thickets. A man took little pride in cattle like those old snuffies—only in his ability to be as wild as they were and to handle them. It had always seemed a game of sorts to Charlie, though a rough one. There had been exhilaration in the chase, the spurring and yelling and smashing through brush, the swinging of the rope and bringing those wild cattle crashing to earth. He had not had to concern himself with the economics of the thing; he was simply working for wages then, and the wages never went up. But later when he went into ranching for himself he quickly found it was difficult to show much profit on that kind of cattle or that kind of operation. These blooded Herefords were poor sport but far more negotiable at the bank.

Eventually he had matured to a point that he took pleasure in looking at these cattle, in knowing they were his, even if sometimes the market went down and they didn't pay their way, and it took what the sheep made to cover the cattle's loss. He would never want to be without some good cattle around.

He watched a roadrunner as it darted from under a clump of prickly pear and trotted along a dusty cowtrail, its long black, white-tipped tail stretched out, its spindle legs carrying it at an incredible speed. *Paisano,* the Mexicans called it; chaparral was the name the Anglos gave. It suddenly raised its tail like a rudder and stopped short. It jumped and came back around facing Charlie, watching him for sign of treachery. Plainly not liking his looks, the lean bird made a brief run for momentum, soared up and glided across the low brush. Charlie watched it as long as it was in sight. He could not imagine this country without the roadrunner, any more than he could imagine it without the prickly pear and the live oaks, the jackrabbit and the horned toad. They were all an integral part of it, biding their time to take it back if man ever relaxed his hold.

He had often thought that if man were to disappear, the domesticated livestock would not long survive. Fences would sag and rust away. The artificial watering places would go to dust, forcing livestock to the natural creeks and rivers. There, in time, the sheep and goats would fall to the bobcats and coyotes, which thrived despite man's most diligent efforts to bring them under control. Perhaps even the lean gray wolf—so long gone from here—would return to hunt and howl at the moon. The gentle cattle would fall to drouth and to the wolves. The land would go back to those creatures which impartial Nature had found fittest by ruthless selection and survival through ages past all reckoning.

Charlie met the sheep a quarter mile out from the corrals. In this West Texas range country the old method of herding sheep had gone out years ago. Coyotes had been thinned enough that ranchmen built sheepproof fences and turned their flocks loose to range free over the pastures just as their cows did. The word *cowboy*, once guarded with a vigilant jealousy, had come to apply as much to the handlers of sheep as to handlers of cattle. The average ranchhand was likely to be some of both. The hard knuckles of economics had driven most West Texas cowmen to discard their prejudice and turn to sheep. They found to their consternation that the two species mixed well, a proposition once considered akin to heresy. Now they raised cattle for respectability and sheep for a living.

A fat old ewe plodded along head-down in the lead, using a deep-worn trail and taking all its unnecessary jogs and turns, wearing the trail a little deeper and assuring that her descendants forty years from now would follow exactly in her tracks. The rest of the band strung out complacently behind, giving unquestioning trust to those up front. There was a constant din of blatting lambs and anxious mothers, looking back for offspring lost in the shuffle. Nothing could be so anxious, and so ineffective in its anxiety, as a sheep.

Tom Flagg rode near the lead, keeping his horse reined to one side out of the dust. At twenty-two, Tom fitted Charlie's image of what a cowboy was supposed to be—the image Charlie had tried for at Tom's age but had been too busy or too broke to perfect. Tom sat his horse with the pride and easy grace—even the arrogance—of one born to the leather. He rode with back straight, shoulders squared. He wore his straw hat low over his eyes and cocked a little to one side in a go-to-hell attitude, the brim flared and the crown carefully dented fore and aft. Instead of some old blue work shirt, he wore a Western-cut shirt with imitation pearl snaps, a shirt he had ripped at a rodeo and couldn't wear for show any more. His square silver belt buckle glinted in the sun, a buckle he had won roping calves in Pecos on a Fourth of July.

Charlie had heard Mary say Tom fancied himself too much, but Charlie didn't put stock in that. Tom had something to fancy himself for. There was little worth doing that he couldn't do on horseback

except perhaps make love. Tom had learned all his
father could teach him about cowboying, and more
besides. He could do things with a rope that Charlie
had never attempted in his best time. If he was a little
on the wild side, as some people said, it didn't worry
Charlie. He had scattered a fair crop of oats himself
before the muddy trenches of France stole the exuberance from him. Whiskey was better if it was slow
to age; maybe a man was the same way.

Charlie said, "Everything go all right?"

Tom shrugged. "You put *me* in charge, didn't you?"

Charlie had given his son the responsibility, though
tacitly Lupe Flores was head man when Charlie was
not around. Lupe was a patient, unassuming teacher
and something of an insurance policy. Many a time
he had pulled Tom Flagg out of a jackpot so easily
that Tom never realized he had even been in trouble.

Charlie held his ground and let the sheep slowly
pass him. He nodded to a dark-skinned Mexican of
forty or more who worked for Page Mauldin and had
come over as swap-out neighbor help, a custom as
old as the ranching industry. "How's it goin', Diego?"

"*Bueno*, Mister Charlie . . ."

Diego Escamillo might speak to Charlie's son as
"Tom," but he would address the older generation
only as "Mister Charlie" or "Mister Page," a waning
relic of deference lingering from an ancient pattern of
racial relationships. Charlie recognized it as a dying
custom and did not particularly mourn it, but he was
still taken by surprise sometimes when some young
Mexican called him by his first name without the
"Mister." Archaic or not, he sort of liked it.

Manuel Flores, fifteen, rode along on the outside of
the "drags." He sat his brown horse with the careless
grace of a brush-country *vaquero* born to the saddle,

which indeed he had been. His ancestors had worked cattle and sheep for generations before the Alamo. He could be one hell of a cowboy, Charlie figured, if he lived on a ranch large enough to give him a challenge.

Manuel carried a young lamb stretched belly-down across his brush-scarred old hand-me-down saddle. Charlie asked him, "What's the matter with that *cordero*?"

"Lame in one leg, Mister Charlie. He can't keep up."

"You'd just as well of left him. His mammy would find him again soon as we turned her loose."

Manuel frowned. "A cow might, but a ewe isn't too smart. I'll do what you think is best, Mister Charlie."

Charlie knew Manuel wanted to find out what was the matter with the lamb's leg. He had always been like that, keeping a penful of cripples and dogies around. From the time he had been five or six years old Manuel had gotten more pleasure from feeding some dogie lamb than from feeding himself.

Manuel said, "I know his mother when I see her. I can get them together again."

Charlie had always been able to identify every cow he owned, and to match her with her calf, but he had never reached a point that most sheep did not look the same to him. Manuel had an eye for them, though. If Manuel said he could find that ewe in this bunch, he could do it.

"All right, *muchacho*, take the lamb and find some pocket to put it in. And you'd better chalk that ewe's nose before they shear her because she won't look the same with the wool off."

Lupe Flores walked next to the netwire fence, leading his horse and pushing up the drags, punching lazy ewes into movement, keeping tired lambs on the go.

There was an old and remarkable affinity between Mexican and sheep, an affinity the Anglo rarely attained, a thing that went back perhaps to the *pastores* of old Spain. Lupe talked quietly and gently to them most of the time, but an old-time muleskinner would have marveled at Lupe when the lid blew off. Using the worst of two languages, he could singe the bark from a cedar post at twenty paces on those rare occasions. Seven or eight years younger than Charlie, Lupe outweighed him by twenty pounds. The extra weight caused him to sweat heavily as he walked behind the sheep. His dark, round face was caked with dust, ribboned by sweat.

"*Hace calor*," said Charlie. ("It's hot.")

Lupe whistled agreement under his breath, his face as affable as a Collie dog's. He had always been this way, agreeable to anything Charlie said, dependable but never self-asserting. Some Mexicans—especially the younger ones—gave Charlie an uncomfortable feeling that they were saying one thing in agreeing with him while something altogether different was going on behind those black eyes. He had latched onto Lupe years ago because he had not seen that quality of resistance in him. Whatever Charlie wanted always seemed to suit him fine; there was never any argument or sign that Lupe even considered one. He was comfortably subservient, every ranch owner's ideal for a hired man.

Charlie said, "Teofilo tells me it's not goin' to rain. Says he seen a whirlwind turnin' the wrong way."

Lupe's face twisted in disdain. "That Teofilo, he's always got some superstition."

Charlie smiled at the boy Manuel. "What do you think about it, *muchacho?*"

Manuel shrugged. "My science teacher, she says

these old superstitions are left from the Dark Ages. She says if you want to know about the weather, call the Weather Bureau."

Charlie grunted. He had long since decided that when the Weather Bureau predicted rain a man had better wear his sunglasses.

Lupe Flores halted in midstride. "Rattlesnake!" He handed his bridle reins to Charlie, grabbed up a dead mesquite branch and climbed over the netwire fence where it was tightest against a cedar post. Charlie saw the snake slithering away through the short dry grass. As Lupe caught up it whipped its body into coils, its ugly head lifted high, its beady eyes fixed on Lupe, its forked tongue darting. The rattles set up a song that made Charlie's roan horse shy quickly to one side, almost jerking Lupe's bridle reins from Charlie's hand.

A frenzy came over Lupe. Range men, like range animals, have an instinctive fear and hatred for snakes. A deer or a roadrunner will kill one when they have the chance. Lupe swung the stick, catching the snake behind the head and bursting its lead-gray skin. He swung again and again, cursing all the while, keeping it up long after the snake was beyond recovery. He stood with shoulders heaving and looked at the long body battered and torn but still convulsing. He cast aside the big stick and picked up a smaller one, whittling a sharp point onto it. He forced it through just behind the snake's head. He raised the stick, allowing the snake to hang free. The tail twitched, still rattling a little. Lupe cut the rattles off, then draped the snake over a nearby limb, its white belly up.

"There," he said, returning to the fence with hat in his hand, wiping sweat from his dusty face onto his sleeve. "Leave him that way, it brings rain."

Charlie couldn't hold back a smile. "*Now* who's superstitious?"

Lupe climbed back over the fence and dropped heavily, reaching up for his reins. "That's no superstition, Mister Charlie. It really works."

Charlie glanced at Manuel. The boy looked away, hiding a grin that would not set well with his father.

As the sheep approached the corrals, Tom Flagg edged his horse forward. The ewe in the lead halted and looked distrustfully at the open gate. She held her ground and thought things over while the rest of the band bunched uncertainly behind her. If anybody made the wrong move, she would dart back into the bunch, starting a general rush of sheep away from the gate. But Tom squalled at the proper place and the proper moment. She broke for the opening. The rest of the sheep strung along behind her. One jumped over the shadow of the cross wires, and the next half dozen dutifully jumped just as she had, though probably none had any idea what they were jumping for. It was simply the thing to do.

Halfway across the pen the lead ewe stopped to look around again, squatting to deposit some pills. Once more the sheep balled up behind her, and movement through the gate was halted. The riders outside yelled and swore. Charlie made some crackling comment to the effect that he would sell her to a San Antonio packer for baby food.

One of Garcia's shearers skirted along the fence until he got behind the ewe. He held a noise-maker, a heavy wire loop with empty tin cans strung on it like loose beads. He shouted a Spanish oath that defied translation and rattled the loop, then tossed it at the ground behind the ewe. She dashed wildly against the fence on the far side. The jam melted. In a minute all the sheep were inside the gate except one big breakaway lamb. Afoot, Lupe hemmed it in a corner, grabbed and lifted it bodily over the fence. He turned the thrashing lamb loose unceremoniously. It landed on its feet almost like a cat, dropped to one knee, then got up and trotted highheaded toward the other sheep, bleating for its mother.

As Charlie expected, Manuel carried his crippled lamb to a small set of pine-panel pens nearby and eased it to the ground. The lamb circled the tiny enclosure limping, bleating, looking for a way out.

When the boy came back Charlie said, "You see after that lamb soon as you have time. Be sure he's turned back out with his mammy when we finish shearin'."

"I will, Mister Charlie."

"There's no need in bottle-feedin' him long's he's got a mammy." Bottle-feeding or carrying grain to a bunch of whippoorwill-poor dogie lambs didn't suit Charlie in the least. He always said fiddling with a few head that way took more time and trouble than it was worth. Sheep were all right in a bunch, but he had little use for them singly.

He watched Manuel hunt for and find a piece of blue chalk that had been lodged under a nail on a cedar post ever since last shearing; there hadn't been enough rain to dissolve it. Manuel worked his way through the ewes and in a few minutes spotted his quarry. He made a rush and grabbed her by a hind foot, then got hold of her head, pulling her up tightly against his legs while he made two or three chalk rings around her nose and mouth, where the shearers wouldn't take them off with their clippers.

How he could pick that ewe out of the bunch was a mystery to Charlie. But he would wager a fifth of

Jack Daniel's that when the shearing was over and this ewe turned with that limping lamb, they would claim each other as mother and child.

Charlie customarily did most of his ewe culling in the fall, when it was time to wean and ship the lambs. But now while Lupe and the others pushed some of the sheep into a smaller pen close to Teofilo's shearing machine, Charlie stood at the gate, watching closely. He grabbed ewes whose bags had fevered and spoiled; he marked their noses with blue chalk, making straight lines that would not invite confusion with the ewe Manuel had chalked. He found one broken-legged ewe and marked her too. When shearing was done and the lambs remated, Charlie would pull out these chalked ewes, put them into a trailer and haul them to the auction sale in San Angelo. He had no patience with free boarders which ate grass but didn't pay their keep. Their lambs were either dead or do-gied anyway.

The men drove a sizable bunch of ewes into the pen where the shearing machine was roaring and popping. While the shearers stepped back under the stained tarp out of the way, Tom took off the leather chaps he had worn for protection against the clutching mesquite thorns. He flapped them and hollered. "*Hu*-cha! *Hu*-cha!" He split half the sheep onto one side of the machine, half on the other. He pulled a plank panel into place, securing it with a piece of rusty baling wire to prevent them from running back and forth from one side of the machine to the other and creating havoc during the shearing. He paused a moment with the chaps draped over one shoulder, sweat making large spots in the Western shirt under the arms and down the middle of his back. He cast a hopeful glance toward the barn.

Charlie asked, "You lookin' for somethin'?"

Tom shook his head. "What would I be lookin' for?" But Charlie saw letdown in his son's face. Tom said loudly, over the clatter of the machine, "This ought to keep Teofilo busy awhile. We'll go back and scout that pasture before dinner." He moved on toward the horses, pausing to buckle the chaps around his waist and hook the snaps around his legs. Charlie saw him glance once more toward the barn, then out along the town road.

Four shearers were stationed on each side of Teofilo's machine, one for each of the "drops." They walked out among the sheep, each man searching for one he wanted to start with. It was said—with justification—that if a ranchman wanted to cull his poorest-shearing sheep, he had only to follow the shearers and mark out the ones they picked to shear first. Invariably they sought the easiest, those with the shortest wool. The animal with the longest and the best wool was the hardest and the slowest to shear; therefore it was usually the last to be flopped down on the shearing board. After all, the quicker a man sheared a sheep, the more money he made. That the shearer's convenience and the rancher's selection program worked at cross purposes was of little concern to either man.

As each shearer found a sheep that suited him, he grabbed it by a hind leg and dragged the animal back toward the noisy machine. The frightened sheep would struggle and pull away on the other three legs. Along the front edge of the ground-level shearing platform was a one-by-two-inch trip board, nailed down to help the shearer throw the sheep with less effort. It also helped keep dirt from being kicked onto the shearing board where it would work into the wool.

Planting his knee on the sheep's side, the shearer would start the clipper with its metallic *shir-r-r*. He would trim the fragile legs, then make the first parting of the fleece down the belly. His hands moved fast and sure in long, bold strokes.

After all these years the skill of the Mexicans still held fascination for Charlie. There was something hypnotic in the rhythmic movement of the clippers, the quick wrist-flick at the end of each stroke that righted the combs for the next cut. Charlie liked to watch the fleece fold away from the animal's body and expose the bright cream color of the inner wool, a sharp contrast to the dirty-gray outer tip. The legs and belly finished, the shearer would pull a greasy leather string from his waistband and tie the legs, then proceed to slice away the wool on sides and back. Nearing completion, he would signal the tie-boy. The boy would step in and begin to roll the fleece, keeping the rich, clean side outward and rolling the dirty side under where it wouldn't show. The idea was to make a good impression on the Boston wool buyers, who, of course, knew better. When the shearer stepped away, the tie-boy would hand him a small metal disc to show that he had finished a sheep. At the end of the day each shearer would tally his "checks" with the *capitán*, for his pay was based on the number of sheep he turned out. A shearer who couldn't attain speed didn't earn enough to justify the *capitán* in feeding him. If he was not an in-law it would sooner or later be pointedly suggested that he try some new occupation, such as fixing flats in a Texaco filling station.

There was not much for Charlie to do except stand around and keep an eye on the shearers. He was convinced they did a better job when the flock owner was on hand; they hacked up less wool and cut fewer sheep. Not that he ever had much difficulty with Teofilo's men. To Teofilo, Charlie was an old and dependable client who must constantly be cultivated. When the winter was long, in-laws grasping and rations short, Charlie was one of the several ranchmen Teofilo could always approach for a *renganche*, more commonly called *regancho*, an advance on the next shearing. An old paternalism still persisted in sheep shearing, the *capitán* to the shearer and the rancher to the *capitán*.

Charlie especially watched the tying table where the tie-boys wrapped paper twine around each fleece and pitched it up to Teofilo's son, Chuy, the sacker. The long sacks hung suspended inside a wooden sacking frame, tall enough that the bottom of the sack was clear of the ground. The sacker simply dropped the fleeces in and packed them down tightly with his feet until the seams of the wool bag seemed ready to split.

When an occasional spot of black wool showed up in a fleece, Charlie would tear that part out with his hands, dropping it into a small towsack hanging on the fence. He tried to keep that kind of sheep culled out, but a few always cropped up, a throwback to some ancient *churro* which had grazed the Southwestern deserts when herders still carried rifles and slept with an eye open for prowling Indians. It was a strong strain, one which many generations of more refined blood had not completely obliterated.

Little Candelario Flores stood hungrily looking for something to do that he might join the men. When the first pen of sheep was finished, Charlie turned them into a long narrow alleyway and let some unshorn sheep in to replace them.

He studied Candelario a moment. "Want to help me, Candy?"

"Sure, you bet." The boy was halfway over the fence before he finished answering. Charlie said, "Now, it's a responsible job that I wouldn't give to just *anybody*. It's a job for a real top hand that knows how to watch out what he's doin'."

"I'm a top hand, Mister Charlie."

"Sure. Soon's your legs grow out a little, you'll lay ol' Manuel in the shade." Charlie handed the boy a can of black medicine and a paint brush. He pointed to the freshly shorn sheep. "You just work through yonder and dab a little *tecole* on all the fresh cuts you can find. Then maybe me and your daddy won't have so many screwworm cases to doctor this summer."

It was the first time the boy had ever been handed such an awesome responsibility. He splashed the black *tecole* like water, getting as much on himself as on the sheep.

Rosa will be real put out when he gets home, Charlie thought, looking at the spotted clothes. *But a boy don't get to be a man with clean britches on.*

Charlie poured red branding paint into a coffee can and got his sheep-branding iron from inside a shed. It somewhat resembled the irons he used to burn his C Bar onto the cattle except that it was short, with a wooden handle, and it was not meant ever to be heated. Because of the wool there was no practical way to fire-brand a sheep except perhaps across the nose, something Charlie would not consider. He dipped the end of the iron into the paint, then touched it to the sheep's backs, leaving the C Bar just above the tailbone. A year's weathering might bleach it considerably, but it would still be legible when the sheep came back for another shearing.

Just at noon the riders brought in a few ewes they had missed on their first sweep of the pasture. One by one the shearers began to walk away from the hot machine, pausing to quench their thirst from a water can, some splashing water over their faces from a faucet. Teofilo watched for the last shearer to finish, then cut off the machine to avoid wasting gasoline. It ran 27.9 cents a gallon. The old motor continued to smoke and crackle as the heat slowly left it.

Candelario was *tecole*-spattered from head to foot, worse than Charlie had expected. He was glad *he* didn't have to go over to Rosa's house and hear what she said. He put a heavy hand on the boy's shoulder. "You done real good, Candy. If your ol' daddy ever gets stove up to where he can't work, maybe I'll let you take his place."

Candelario accepted that as pure fact. "I wouldn't want my papa's job. Maybe you can find a job for two men."

"Maybeso."

The shearers straggled out to their camp, where a gray-bearded Mexican cook was finishing dinner in Dutch ovens over an open fire. He had a pickup backed into the dark shade of green live-oak trees, a chuckbox mounted on the rear of it. There were times, working away from headquarters, when Charlie ate with the shearing crew and liked it. But a little bit of shearing-camp grub went a long way. Charlie liked chili pepper in moderation, but there was a stopping place. This old cook of Teofilo's had never heard of it.

Charlie waited until the riders unsaddled and turned their horses loose in the waterlot. He poured oats into a long wooden trough while the horses crowded around him. He placed Wander in a pen by himself because the roan was a tyrant and would fight the other horses away from the feed until he got all he wanted. Greed and despotism were not traits of man alone.

By habit the men waited for Charlie to take the lead, then strung out behind him toward the houses. Lupe came first, then Diego Escamillo of the Page Mauldin ranch, then Manuel and Candelario. Tom held back, a rope in his hands. He swung the loop and picked up both of Candelario's feet, jerking up the slack but taking care not to trip the boy and make him fall. Candelario looked back in surprise, then grinned when he saw it was not his brother who had done him in.

Tom said, "I'm sorry, Candy. Thought you was an Appaloosa horse . . . all them spots."

Lupe said, "His mama will make him eat outside, like a horse."

Charlie winked at Lupe and said protectively, "Don't you-all be puttin' off on my helper. He's workin' for *me*."

Candelario was as pleased as when Charlie had handed him a fifty-cent piece for the *tecole* job.

The Mexicans turned off toward the frame house with the swept yard. Charlie and Tom went on to the big rock house but did not go directly in, for that might have caused a minor uprising. Mary's rules were well understood and scrupulously obeyed. Charlie walked around to a small rock house in back, where a narrow trough was full of cold running water. It flowed through here on its way from windmill to an open stock tank. August Schmidt had built this for cooling milk decades before the ranch acquired electricity. Now Mary had a refrigerator big enough to chill a grown horse, but the milk house was still a handy place to wash up and avoid confrontation with her at the door.

Charlie flopped in his favorite living-room rocking chair where he could feel a breeze moving through the deep windows off the porch. He had never considered an air-conditioner. The thick stone walls, the high ceilings and windows almost to the floor kept the house comfortable through summer.

Above his chair was an old framed print of a Frederic Remington painting. It showed an Indian warrior, his horse run to ground by pursuers. The lone brave stood afoot on a small knoll facing his enemies, defiant against inevitable death. Charlie had bought it and placed it there years ago because it seemed to fit the story of his own Warrior Hill as August Schmidt had told it to him.

Mary was banging around in the kitchen, rattling cookware and dishes. She stepped into the dining-room doorway, rubbing her hands in an apron. "Don't you-all get too comfortable. Dinner's about ready."

A niece of August Schmidt, Mary was about ten years younger than Charlie. He had been on the sundown side of his twenties when he had met her, worrying that he might face the rest of his life as an old bachelor like so many graying cowboys he had known, sleeping cold on long winter nights in some far-off and lonely cowcamp. He had begun thinking regretfully about the pretty girls he had met and hadn't asked. Mary was from over on the Pedernales, barely twenty then, tiny as a hummingbird and looking just as delicate.

Charlie had had no idea how strong a hummingbird really was. After all these years it sometimes surprised and disconcerted him to see how much hard-steel strength could be wrapped up in a small package.

She was not much larger now than when he had first met her; she had broadened a little in the hips but was never inclined toward fat. Her face showed lines, and when the light fell right it picked up silver strands in her brown hair. A pity, Charlie thought sometimes, remembering, wishing he could have put her in a picture frame and kept her just the way she was when he had married her. In temperament as well as in looks.

In the beginning Charlie had thought Mary's hill-country German mother had bequeathed her nothing except her considerable cooking skills. But he had gradually found there was more; Mary had her mother's square-headed determination and stubbornness as well.

The big kitchen always teased Charlie with a rich aroma of baked biscuits, chili beans, cooling cake, sugar-crusted apple pie. The hell of it was that she would cook up a tableful of strong ranch staples and rich German *Mehlspeisen*, then talk her damnedest to keep Charlie from eating it. She never stopped guying him about his weight.

Mary called, "Chuck!" Charlie got up from the comfortable chair and walked heavily in to the big table. She had baked half of a fat kid. Kid goat was food for a man who worked hard—solid and filling, yet easily digested. Shearing crews preferred it to beef or mutton; it did not lie heavy on their stomachs as they went back to hard, hot labor. Mary had a platterful of brown biscuits, a bowl of fresh red chili beans and glasses of iced tea so cold the condensation was running down the sides.

There was a small platter of French-fried potatoes,

too, but when Charlie reached for them Mary quickly moved the platter next to Tom's plate. "Charlie, you'd better leave the potatoes alone."

"What did you fix them for if I can't eat them?"

"I fixed *you* something else." She pushed a bowl of turnip greens in front of him. If there was one thing he couldn't stand to see on his plate, it was turnip greens. He growled a few words in Spanish and made up for the potatoes by eating more baked kid, biscuits, and beans. When he pushed back from the table the greens were still untouched.

Ranch custom dictated that each man carry his own plate, glass, and utensils to the kitchen sink; this was a throwback to chuckwagon days on the open range when every wagon had a washtub into which the cowboys dropped their tinware. The cowboy who failed to do so faced corporal punishment at the unmerciful hands of an outraged cook. Scraping well-cleaned goat ribs into a big brown grocery sack, Charlie saw Tom peer intently out the window.

"You been lookin' for somethin' all mornin'," he challenged.

"Been expectin' some company." Tom turned with relief in his face. "It's drivin' up right now."

Charlie growled. Last thing a man needed at shearing time was a lot of company. He saw a pickup stop in front of the white picket fence, the dust drifting past it and spreading across the yard. He saw a two-horse trailer with just one horse in it. That alone was enough to make him suspicious.

Tom stepped onto the porch and waved. "You-all get out and come in!" Two young cowboys slammed the pickup doors and stopped to stretch their arms and legs. They had evidently traveled some distance. Saddles and suitcases were piled in the bed of the pickup. They hadn't come out of a sheep pen, that much was plain. They wore rodeo clothes, bright shirts, and new Levi's tucked into fancy-stitched Leddy boots.

High on the hog, Charlie thought darkly, looking at them. When he was their age and working for cowboy wages, he could not afford to dress like that. Now he could afford it and no longer had the inclination.

Eagerness lighted Tom's face. "Dad, I reckon you know the boys, Shorty Magee and Chuck Dunn."

Still suspicious but bound by the tradition of hospitality, Charlie thrust out his hand. "I've won a dollar or two, bettin' on you boys at the ropin's."

"Lost a little too, I expect," grinned Shorty Magee. He was as his name implied: short, heavy-set but strong as a little brown bear. When he went down the rope to flank a calf, the calf had as well give up and lie down; it didn't have a chance.

Shorty said, "You'd win a right smart more bettin' on Tom."

Chuck Dunn was six feet tall and wouldn't weigh a hundred and twenty pounds soaked in salt water. They made a contrasty pair, these two, the long and short of it. Chuck said, "Pleased to meet you, Mister Flagg." They looked out toward the corrals, where the sheep still bleated as much as when first brought in. "Looks like you're smack in the middle of shearin'. Tom didn't tell us . . ."

Tom broke in quickly, "You-all had dinner? There's aplenty left."

"Sure is," said Charlie. "You-all like turnip greens?"

Shorty said, "We et in town. Tom, you ready to go?"

Charlie's suspicions were confirmed. He looked severely at Tom. "Go? Go where?"

Uneasily Tom shifted his feet. "Look, Dad, I got a chance to make a killin'. There's a rodeo over in the hill country, and a bunch of the boys has matched me in a ropin' against ol' Gordy Hansel. They got a good pot raised."

In deference to the company Charlie tried to cover his irritation. "Dammit, Tom, if it was some other day . . . but we got shearin' to do. Shearin' time, a man can't run off someplace to a rodeo. He's got to stay home and attend to business."

"But this *is* business to me. I can pick up several hundred easy."

Even if you did, Charlie thought, *you wouldn't get home with any of it.* "I've seen Gordy rope. Flies don't light on him."

"He's had five thumbs on each hand lately. I'll beat him."

"Some people must not think so or they wouldn't of put up money on him."

"Ain't my fault they don't know better. Dad, it's been set up for two weeks."

Stiffly, Charlie said, "You ought to've told me."

"I meant to, only you had this shearin' date, and . . ." He frowned. "Look, Dad, you won't miss me. You got all the sheep up that Teofilo can shear the rest of the day. All I'm doin' is sittin' around on a horse anyway. I can find somebody in town who'll do that for me for eight dollars a day and I'll pay him myself."

Charlie was about to turn him down when Mary started in. "Tom, you've got to learn that when there's work to be done around here, that comes first. Your father's not going to let you go, and that's all there is to it." A touch of German accent always came out when she was provoked.

Her intervention rubbed Charlie the wrong way. *Damn woman, always trying to tell me what to do.*

Perversely Charlie said, "All right, just this once. But don't you pull this again."

Mary turned away, anger sharp in her eyes. It bothered him little. He didn't try to analyze how his annoyance at Tom so easily transferred to Mary and left Tom clear. Charlie could never remain angry at Tom very long; that anger slipped through his fingers like dry sand. Tom was too much a copy of Charlie himself; he knew what he could do, and he never looked behind him. No doubt or hesitation. Charlie said, "We'll make do. But don't you forget that this ranch is the main thing we got to think about. Me and you'll be pardners in it someday."

Tom breathed easier. "Just what I was thinkin' myself. I got to get all my runnin' done and my pile made. Plenty of time later to be stuck on the ranch when I'm too old to do anything else."

Charlie growled. He knew where that put *him*.

Tom was back from his room in three minutes wearing clean clothes and carrying his black metal suitcase. Plainly enough, he had already had it packed. He leaned way down to kiss his mother's cheek. "Bye, Mom. I'll bring you a pretty."

Mary didn't look at Tom; she looked at Charlie, and her eyes told him he was going to hear more about this later, when no one else was around. Inwardly Charlie began bracing himself. She said tightly, "Don't you boys drive too fast or get into any trouble."

Charlie walked out on the front porch with Shorty

Magee and Chuck Dunn. Brow furrowed, he asked, "You right sure he'll beat Gordy?"

"He could beat Gordy with a cotton rope," Shorty answered confidently.

Charlie glanced through the open door to be sure Mary wasn't watching. He pulled out his wallet and slipped a ten-dollar bill into Shorty's hand. "If any of that Hansel bettin' money comes floatin' around, cover this much of it for me."

The boys walked to the barn to get Tom's roping horse and his saddle. Manuel came out of the Flores house and trotted down to the barn to catch up. Since he had been able to walk he had been tagging along in Tom's footsteps, watching, trying to learn to do everything Tom did. He was good, but he would never be as good with a rope as Tom was. That was fine with Charlie; one hot-shot roper at a time was all this ranch needed anyway.

Candelario came out moments later, running hard. He wore fresh clothes without the *tecole* spots. Charlie would have to get along without Candelario's help in the crowding alley this afternoon; Rosa's message was loud and clear.

Presently the three cowboys came back to the house, leading Tom's gray roping horse, Prairie Dog, saddled and ready for business. Manuel and Candelario walked along beside Tom, Manuel taking long strides and Candelario trotting to stay up. Tom opened the trailer gate; the gray stepped up onto the wooden floor like an old trouper.

Something occurred to Charlie, and he walked down to the trailer as Tom tied the reins and closed the gate. "Seems to me I heard you tell Bess Winfield on the phone that you was takin' her to a dance."

Tom snapped his fingers. "Plumb forgot. How

about you callin' her for me and tellin' her I can't go? Tell her I'll bring her a pretty."

"That's no job to put off on your ol' daddy. *You* tell her."

Tom double-checked the latch. "Well, when I don't show up, she'll know I ain't comin'."

"One of these days you'll come home and find out she didn't wait."

Tom smiled. "When I tell them to wait, they wait."

Charlie shook his head. *Boy, have you got a lot to learn!*

The three drove away in a hurry, leaving a trail of dust thick as a Gulf Coast fog.

Mary set in on Charlie. "You don't know those boys; you don't know if they're reckless drivers or not. You don't know but what they'll be in the ditch before they get twenty miles."

Charlie gave her no rise, and she went on. "Tom is twenty-two years old, but he's not a man yet. He won't be a man till he learns to be responsible."

Charlie didn't look at her or argue with her. He pulled his hat down tight and walked to the shearing pens.

3

The working crew saddled fresh horses and rode into a new pasture to gather sheep for the next day's shearing. Those sheep would spend the night in a small fifty-acre enclosure known as a "trap." Its grass was purposely conserved for such overnight grazing or for a handful of hospital animals. Charlie remained in the pens, chalking out cull sheep to be sold, watching the putting-up of the wool.

When the riders returned at midafternoon to crowd their sheep through the trap gate, Manuel pulled away and rode toward the pens. Charlie sensed that the boy wanted to talk to him. He tilted a large metal can, poured ice water into the wide lid and handed it across the netwire fence. "Dry?"

"Awful dry," Manuel said, dismounting to take the water. He drank thirstily, pausing to slosh some around in his mouth and wash the dust down. He wiped his face on a half-rolled sleeve, leaving a streak where dust had turned to mud.

Charlie thought idly that he never used to see

old-time cowboys roll their sleeves up. They believed in buttoning the sun out. But this was a new generation.

"Mister Charlie," Manuel said, "I rode up on three wetbacks hidin' out yonder in the brush."

"There's wetbacks passin' through here all the time."

"These sure do look hungry."

"Why don't they come on in? Ain't nobody goin' to hurt them."

"Too many people here. They're scared of the border patrol. Asked me if I thought you might have a few days' work for them. I told them you don't hardly ever hire a wetback."

Charlie nodded. "Once the border patrol catches you givin' them work, they'll rag you from then on. I got enough problems to put up with; I don't need the border patrol."

"That's what I told them." Manuel's eyes were concerned. "They're still awful hungry."

Charlie stared at the boy, irritated by his persistence. "You're the damnedest kid I ever saw to be pickin' up dogies all the time!"

Manuel ducked his head. Charlie was instantly remorseful for having spoken sharply. He considered a moment and said, "But hell, it shows there's a streak of kindness in you, *muchacho*, and kindness is one thing this world is short of. Think you could find them again?"

Manuel straightened. "They're right yonder." He pointed to a mesquite thicket.

"Tell them to come in and see me. I don't want nobody to leave this place hungry, Mexican or white." He put his hand on top of Manuel's old hat and affectionately pressed the crown down flat against the boy's head. "You doggoned dogie-hunter!"

Manuel smiled. "Thank you, Mister Charlie." He pulled the horse around and rode away faster than he had come.

Soon Charlie saw three men moving timidly toward the shearing pens from the cover of the brush. He watched, frowning, finally climbing over the fence to wait for them.

For generations the Mexican people on both sides of the Rio Grande had moved freely back and forth across the river to work and to live. International boundaries were fiction to them. They considered everything south of the Nueces River their own open and natural range. In recent times the United States government had tried to close the border. But old habits of a slow-changing people are not altered overnight by words on paper—words many could not even read.

These were from across the river; a man who knew Mexicans could tell that as far as he could see them. They carried the wetback's typical cloth satchels with colored stripes, and Charlie could see that the satchels were empty. If they had any food when they came across the river, it was long gone. Many came with no food at all, certain that as soon as they reached the north side of the Rio they would be in a bountiful land of milk and honey where no man was ever hungry, no pocket ever empty. These men's clothing had been patched until little was left for patches to cling to. Two wore leather *huaraches* which covered nothing more than the crusted soles of their brown feet. One wore an old pair of worn-out brogan shoes not as good, even, as the *huaraches*. A little in the lead came an old man with gray-salted hair and heavy gray mustache. The others were younger, one only fourteen or fifteen. A father and two sons, Charlie judged. Pity stirred him, and he knew why Manuel had been so touched. The old man was more than merely hungry. By his eyes, Charlie knew he was sick.

Thank God, he thought, *I was born north of the river.*

The old man removed his tattered straw hat, bowed stiffly as *peones* in Mexico had done for untold generations, and spoke in border Spanish: "*Mi patrón,* we are much indebted."

They were always courtly, no matter how bleak the circumstances. It was a trait of the humblest.

Charlie extended a pack of cigarettes to the old man. Mumbling his *gracias,* the *viejo* took a cigarette and passed the rest to the oldest son. The youngest came last, as was considered proper. He removed a cigarette and held the pack while Charlie lighted the old-timer's smoke, then the eldest son's. Charlie struck a fresh match for the boy, but the youngster shook his head and handed the pack to Charlie. He glanced at his father and put the cigarette in his shirt pocket. "I save it for later, *patrón.*"

Keeping it for his father, Charlie knew. He started to put the pack back into his pocket, reconsidered and gave it to the old man. "Keep it," he said in *gringo* Spanish. "I have more."

The *viejo* thanked him again. He drew upon the cigarette with a deep and terrible hunger. He closed his eyes, losing himself in the luxury of the moment. He told his story then. To Charlie it was an old one he had heard a hundred times, always the same except for minor individual variations. They had come upon evil days in the country south of Ciudad Acuna, the Mexican said sadly. For a long while now the good *Dios* had not chosen to send rain down on the state of Coahuila, and in truth, nowhere else along the

border. The fields had fallen barren. Buckets dropped
in the wells came up with mud, and finally only sand.
The people's own little lands knew only poverty, and
their patrón —hard hit like the rest—had work now
for no more than a few. The old man and his sons, as
so many thousands like them, had come to "the other
side" to find employment, to send money home to
buy food and clothing for those of their family who
must stay behind—the women, the little children.

"We do not beg, *señor*, or ask you to give us something we do not earn. We ask for a chance to work.
We are hard workers, my sons and I."

Charlie rubbed the palms of his hands on his dirty
khakis. There were so many of these people, so damn
many of them, and always so hungry . . . He glanced
into the old man's muddy eyes and looked away. For
a moment he felt a twinge of guilt that these people
were hungry and he was not, and then a brief resentment against them for arousing that guilt. Both
passed quickly, the guilt and the resentment. "I am
sorry, *amigo*. You know the laws of my country. You
swam the river without papers, and it is prohibited
that I hire you. Like you, I believe this law is unjust,
but no matter, it is still the law. If the *chotas* catch
you they will take you back across the river and make
you walk home hungry. If they catch you *here*, they
will also be angry with me."

"*Señor*, they can hurt us but little, for we are already hungry. And we do not intend to be caught."

"No one escapes the *chotas* forever. They have eyes
that see in the dark. They will find you."

The old man's face began to fall. He repeated desperately, "We do not beg. We ask only to work."

Charlie shook his head. "I have no work for you.
But you will not leave here hungry. Follow me."

He thought at first about taking them to Teofilo's camp. But except for the goat kids Charlie had furnished, the food there was Teofilo's. Garcia had bought and paid for it. Texas-born Mexicans—themselves often only one generation away from the river—often harbored resentment against the wetbacks. Despite their blood ties they considered them interlopers, a threat to their own jobs and security.

"We have food left at the big house. I will take you to *la madama*. She will feed you and give you food to carry along. Then you had better be on your way. If the *chotas* hear we are shearing today, they will probably come out to look us over. You will not wish to be here."

The old man said gratefully, "These are hard times that we must come to you this way. If ever the fates turn around, we shall do the same someday for you."

I hope to God not, Charlie thought.

He escorted them to the house and called Mary. He saw the pity in her eyes, and he tried to cover his own. Gruffly he said, "Some dogies Manuel found. Feed them." He glanced at the town road, looking for dust which might mean a border patrol car. The three Mexicans sat in the shade of the big live-oak trees and began to wolf down what was left of Mary's baked kid. Charlie was gratified when the young one took a big helping of the turnip greens. *I hope he eats them all.*

He thought about the apple pie from which Mary had given Tom a slice, then put the rest back up in the cabinet. Charlie had thought he would slip a slice of that tonight when she wasn't looking. He knew now it would probably go to the Mexicans along with everything else. She was generous to everyone but him.

He waited until Mary was in the house before he allowed his voice to soften. "When you are through, I would advise that you go on north. Perhaps you will find work farther away from the border."

"*Buena suerte, patrón.* May the dry time never fall upon you."

In the hurry of the hot and dusty shearing pens, Charlie's mind soon drifted away from the three Mexicans. He heard nothing over the din of bleating sheep, the clattering protest of the cranky old shearing machine that seemed to have a malevolent will of its own. He stood at the tying table, critically examining a breaky fleece, result of a sheep that had sickened sometime last winter, leaving a weak spot at that point of growth in the fiber. He was grumbling to himself, knowing he must sack this fleece apart from the good ones or risk its being found by a sharp-eyed wool buyer who then might dock his entire clip; they were always looking for an excuse to trim a man, he thought.

Charlie turned as an automobile's side window flashed a reflection across the tying table. He recognized the green government car, the round symbol on its door. Border patrol!

Damn chotas, always slipping up on you!

His first impulse was to look toward the house, but he managed not to. Maybe the three wetbacks had eaten and left. He got a grip on himself and moved through the shorn and unshorn sheep, shoving ewes and lambs aside with his knees. Two green-clad patrolmen climbed out of the car.

"Mister Flagg?"

Charlie nodded, and one patrolman extended his

hand. The grip was firm and friendly. "Parker's my name. And this is Oliver Nance." Nance's face was cold and without cordiality, but Parker's easy drawl put Charlie partly at ease. Texas, he figured, or perhaps Oklahoma. He couldn't be *all* bad. The patrolman said, "We heard you were shearing, and we thought we'd like to watch a little. Oliver is new to this part of the country. He hasn't seen much shearing done."

Nance had no patience with pretense. "We came to see if you're working any wetbacks."

Charlie cast him a hard glance. The man was honest, anyway.

Parker frowned but said nothing.

Charlie said, "I don't work wetbacks."

Nance didn't ask a question; he made a statement. "Then you won't mind if we look around a little."

Too much honesty could get a man disliked. Tightly Charlie said, "Help yourself." He said more than that, under his breath. *Damnyankee! You could tell it as quick as he opened his mouth. Damnyankees always coming down here on us like locusts, thinking they're two notches better than Jesus Christ!* He had an old-Texan aversion to Northerners. His heritage from a Confederate grandfather made it automatic that he class them all as damnyankees until they had proven to his satisfaction they were all right. That sometimes took a right smart of proving.

Nance studied Teofilo's shearing crew and started to climb over the fence into the pens. Parker said, "Those are all local Mexicans. You won't find any wetbacks in there."

"How do you know till you look?" Nance climbed over and shoved his way through the sheep, his eyes on the shearers.

Stupid as *well* as arrogant, Charlie thought irritably. This would be a slap in the face to Teofilo's men; to be mistaken for a wetback was considered no compliment. Maybe they would bounce Nance out of there on his butt. On reflection Charlie knew they wouldn't do that. They would simply turn on a cold contempt and mock him with their eyes. Generations of living in this country as a minority group had honed to a fine edge this ability of the Mexican people to put a *gringo* in his place without speaking a word or making any overt move that might invite stern reprisal. Charlie thought, *You've never been insulted, Yankee boy, till you've been insulted in silence by a Mexican who knows how to give you the treatment.*

Parker's jaw ridged. "I'll apologize for him, Mister Flagg. Occasionally they send us one of these new boys who already knows it all."

One of the shearers snickered, and the others followed suit. Even the tie-boys took it up.

People who lived long in the border country usually could tell at a glance whether a man was native-born or if he had recently arrived with muddy water dripping from his clothes. It showed in details hard to explain but easy to recognize—the clothing, the haircut, the general manner. To one who knew Spanish, a wetback was betrayed by his speech. Even a Yankee *chota* soon learned to know.

Motioning broadly with his big hands, Teofilo Garcia assured Nance that his shearers were all right. "Every man here is *puro* American, and votes Democrat."

Nance's face darkened in anger as the men quietly mocked him. He turned on his heel and pushed roughly back through the sheep.

With mild rebuke, Parker said, "I told you. If you get the locals mad at us, who's going to tip us off about the wets?"

Nance stiffly rejected any reproach. "I didn't like their attitude."

Charlie felt a glow of quiet triumph. He did not dislike border patrolmen, exactly; he realized they had a duty to perform. It was that duty which he disliked. In his view the wetback was no criminal; he was a hungry man desperately seeking work, and it took a lot of guts to set out across uncounted miles of unknown country in hopes of bettering oneself. Charlie identified because of his pioneer heritage. This guttiness, he felt, was a character strength which was disappearing from American life. He was glad they still had it in Mexico.

He glanced in the direction of his house, and the breath went out of him. The three Mexicans were walking toward the pens, swinging those telltale cotton satchels. The satchels were full now, for Mary had been to the pantry.

Ay, Chihuahua! Didn't those innocents know what a *chota* looked like?

Parker saw them about the time Charlie did, and he glanced at Charlie in disappointment. Charlie was tempted to wave the three away, to shout for them to run. But that could get him sent to jail, or at least heavily fined. A ranchman could feed a wetback or even hire him to work without actually being liable to prosecution; no penalty had been provided. But the minute he advised him to run, he became an accessory to unlawful flight. So Charlie watched, numb, as the three Mexicans halted, realization striking them like a club.

"*Alto!*" Parker shouted. "*Alto!*"

The three took out for the brush as hard as they could run. The boy was far in the lead. The oldest son was hanging back, looking over his shoulder at the faltering old man.

Nance hurried to the green car, reached into the glove compartment and pulled out a pistol. Charlie's blood went cold. He wanted to shout, but no words came. He was sure Nance would fire at the fugitives. But Nance fired harmlessly into the air, causing a tied horse at the fence to lunge against the reins and snap them in two. The horse went trotting off in fear and confusion, stepping on one broken rein and jerking its head down. The old man stopped and raised his hands. The oldest son, seeing his father halt, turned and came back to stand dejectedly beside him. Only the boy kept running.

Parker waved for Nance to go after the young Mexican. Nance shouted something at the halted pair as he passed them on the run. He disappeared into the green tangle of mesquite. Parker walked out and brought the pair back. He allowed them to stop and pick up the satchels they had dropped when they started to run. The boy had held onto his. The old Mexican's eyes swam in tears of frustration. The younger man stood silent, defiant. Parker brought handcuffs out of the car. In Spanish he said, "I would not use these if you had not run."

The *viejo* said in a thin voice, "A man tries."

Charlie stood where he was until the pair were near him. Shaken, he said to the old man, "I am sorry. Why did you come back?"

"I would not go without thanking the *patrón* again. We had nothing to give you but our thanks."

And that, thought Charlie, came at a hell of a price.

While they waited for Nance, Charlie asked Parker, "What you goin' to do with them?"

"Jail a day or two. Then we'll ship them back across the river."

"They came here because they was hungry. They'll still be hungry when you send them back."

Parker flared. "Do you think you're telling me something new? What am I supposed to do about it? You know the law."

"I know the law is as blind as a one-eyed mule in a root cellar. Don't it ever bother you to take them back across?"

Parker studied the forlorn Mexican, and Charlie saw pity come into the patrolman's face. "I wake up nights . . . But hell, I don't pass the laws, I just carry them out. If it wasn't me, somebody else would do it. At least I try to treat them human. Some people wouldn't."

He glanced toward his partner. Nance trudged back, breathing heavily. His uniform was spotted with sweat, his face flushed with heat and anger. "Got away in the brush. Damn kid ran like a deer." He opened the rear door of the car and gave the old Mexican a shove. "Get in there!"

Sharply, Charlie said, "Take it easy. He's just a sick old man."

Nance whirled. "Don't you tell me what to do. You lied to us."

"I didn't lie. You asked if I was *workin'* any wets. These was passin' through and I fed them, that's all."

"If you ranchers would stop feeding them they'd quit coming. There are laws about that."

"And have a man starve to death in one of my

pastures? There's a law about that too, a damn sight older than *yours*."

Parker tugged at Nance's sleeve. "Come on, Oliver."

Nance backed toward the car, eyes still hostile. "You ranchers think you're above the law, but you're not. I'll be watching you, Flagg."

Parker took Nance's arm. "Come on, I said. Let's go."

Nance slid into the driver's seat and slammed the door. Parker entered the other side where he could turn and watch the two wetbacks. The border patrol had not yet begun providing a grill between the back seat and the front in all of its vehicles. The pair seated behind the patrolmen could grab them and take over the car if the patrolmen's vigilance lapsed. But Charlie knew that was not the nature of the average man who came from across the river. Few criminals ventured deep into the ranch country, for travel was long and hard, and that kind gravitated more to the cities where pickings were varied and easy. These were humble men whose crime was that they refused to submit to hunger. Wetbacks might run or hide to elude capture, but once caught they were usually docile. In Mexico the ancient law of *ley fuga* was deeply ingrained, etched in blood. Even a common pickpocket might be killed for breaking away.

The pistol shots had brought an abrupt end to the shearing. Every shearer was standing against the fence, and the tie-boys had climbed up onto the sacking frame to watch. Some approved of the capture, some had been rooting for the wetbacks. Grumbling. Teofilo Garcia began trying to shoo the men back to work. The machine was using up gasoline. It took awhile; they had to discuss the incident in all its details first. When finally all were in their places and the wool was peeling again, Teofilo lumbered to the fence and leaned his considerable bulk against a cedar post, his shirttail hanging out, the knees of his old khaki trousers crusted with wool grease.

"Nothing here was your fault, Mister Charlie. Wetbacks like those, they get caught every day."

"They're so goddamn hungry . . ."

Garcia shrugged. "Half the world is hungry. A man can't cry for all of them." Teofilo watched the dust trail spread along the town road. "Damn smart-aleck *chota* . . . damn *boludo* . . ."

Page Mauldin drove a black Cadillac. It was seldom washed because Page might have to wait, and he seldom sat still that long. Its sides bore long scratches from limbs and thorns. Whenever Page saw cattle or sheep in a pasture and took a notion he wanted a better look, he wheeled off the road, across the bar ditch and headlong out through the brush.

He had spent more of his life in a saddle than in a car. When he paid good money for an automobile he figured it should do at least as much as a fifty-dollar horse. He did not buy Cadillacs for show; he didn't give two whoops and a holler about appearance. He simply reasoned that it took a car of high caliber to stand up to the fifty or sixty thousand miles of willful abuse he would give it in a year. On an open highway, especially the long straight stretches across the ranching country west of San Angelo, his cruising speed was eighty miles an hour, if he was in no particular hurry. On rough country trips—rubboard graded roads and ranch two-rutters—he dampered his impatience and held to sixty or so.

A lesser car would shake down to scrap iron.

Page Mauldin braked to a stop at Charlie's shearing pens. A gray billow of dust fogged over the car and into the crowded sheep. Page stepped out, chewing an unlighted cigar. He was a tall, angular man with nervous hands that never stopped flexing except when gripped to a steering wheel. He chewed down a cigar faster than most men could smoke it, working off a feverish energy. He was ten years older than Charlie Flagg and looked twice that. His eyes were recessed into dark-patch hollows, for he never took enough rest. He had a way of stepping in, sizing up a situation, doing whatever his snap judgment dictated, then leaving before the dust settled. Buy, sell, hire, or fire . . . it never took long. With ranches scattered all over West Texas, he always needed to be somewhere else.

Page walked to the corral fence and peered critically at the sheep, mentally setting a price on them. His rumpled gray suit looked as though it had been slept in, and probably had. His felt hat was flat-brimmed except for a small flare on the right side. The left side was drawn down almost to the point of covering his dark, worried eyes. Page's only vanity was that he tucked his trouser cuffs into the tops of his black boots. One had worked out while he drove. He shoved it into place.

Momentary humor flickered in the old ranchman's eyes. "You don't look much like Bo-Peep."

Charlie was too tired to think of a peppy answer. He climbed across a wooden sheep panel and shook Page's hand. "Let's go to Teofilo's camp and get us some coffee."

Page looked impatiently at his watch. "I ain't got time."

"You had time to drive this far. You got time for coffee."

Charlie noticed a young girl sitting in the Cadillac. He beckoned her with a broad sweep of his hand. "Kathy, you'd just as well get out of the car. Me and your daddy are fixin' to have some coffee."

She pushed the door open and slid out, both of her booted feet hitting the ground at the same time. She slammed the door then paused to push her blue jean cuffs into her boottops like her father. Kathy Mauldin was fourteen, best Charlie could remember. It had been a disappointment to Page that she was not a boy; he had been trying with some success ever since to make a boy of her.

"You want some coffee with us?" Charlie asked her.

She shook her head. "I'll watch the shearin'. Or if you got anything you need me to do, I could ride your horse." The offer was made hopefully.

Charlie pointed. "I got some riders out yonder scoutin' for whatever they missed earlier. You can take the roan out and find them if you're a mind to."

Page frowned. "Kathy, we ain't stayin' long."

Kathy said, "You could go on. I could ride home tonight with Diego when he's finished here." She glanced at the car. "Anyway, I'd like to show Manuel my new .22."

Charlie said, "Let her stay, Page. Hell, I've paid wages to grown men that wasn't half as much help."

Page seemed about to turn them down until a thought struck him. "That'd save me goin' back to take her home. I could go from here straight to San Angelo."

The matter was settled. Kathy opened the rear door and dragged out a shiny new rifle, which she proudly showed to Charlie. He dutifully made some fuss over it, though guns had never particularly interested him since his Army days in World War I. A gun, to him, was nothing more than a tool, on about a par with a Stillson wrench except more dangerous. He made it a point to leave the bolt open when he handed it back to Kathy, and he locked the safety. He didn't have to mention it; she got the message.

"I might load it up later," she said, "and go shoot a rabbit."

"That'd be fine," Charlie replied. "Later."

He watched her carry it out to a barn to leave until she was ready to use it. Then she trotted eagerly to his roan horse, tied down the fence away from the sheep. The stirrups were too long for her, but that was of no consequence; she could ride like the Indians who used to hunt over these hills. Charlie had once remarked that she must have been weaned on mare's milk; he remembered how Mary had taken affront at that. He watched her kick the roan into a trot with her bare-heeled boots and ride into the pasture.

He asked Page, "What's she goin' to do when she wakes up someday and finds out she's a girl?"

"You tryin' to tell me I ain't done my duty by her?"

"I'll let *Mary* tell you that; she's said it often enough."

Page said soberly, "Your Mary is always tellin' me I ought to get married again and have a woman in the house to set an example. But I've got old Elvira Escamillo, the housekeeper. She's a woman."

"Diego's mother? Hell, she's too old to keep up with Kathy, and so deaf she can't hear thunder."

"Kathy's all right." Page made it clear the subject was closed. "You said somethin' about coffee."

The Mexican cook was peeling potatoes beneath the long, crooked arms of a huge live-oak tree, a sun-bleached straw hat set far back on his head. Seeing

Charlie and Page, he stood up and set the pan of potatoes on his chuckbox lid. He took out two tin cups
and moved to the coffeepot suspended from a steel
rod over a smoldering campfire for convenience of
the shearers as they periodically took a rest, one or
two at a time. Years ago he would have removed his
hat in deference to the *guero* ranchmen; he extended
the two cups in a gesture which paid service to tradition but did not compromise his dignity. His smile
showed a strong set of white teeth some younger men
would give a fortune for. "Coffee?"

Charlie had misgivings about the sanitary condition of the cups, but camp coffee was usually strong
enough to kill almost anything. "Thanks, Mike." The
cook bent and poured and made some idle comment
about the pretty day, to which both Charlie and Page
made an equally idle response.

Charlie blew the steaming black coffee awhile,
then tentatively touched the rim of the cup to his lips.
His eyes brightened at the sweetness. Mexican camp
cooks usually boiled coffee and sugar together. That
saved expense. If a *capitán* let his shearers use all the
sugar they wanted, he would have to buy a barrel a
week.

Charlie studied Page's face. Page looked weary,
though he would not stop until he dropped. "You
look like twelve miles of corduroy road. You ever
sleep any more?"

Page grunted but gave no other answer. Charlie
wished he could lure him away to a fishing trip on Devil's River this fall—anything to make Page relax. But it
would be useless. He had tried once. Page brooded
so much over business that Charlie had to take him
home the second day.

It had not always been like this. They had worked

together when Charlie was a big button and Page a cowboy in his twenties. They had ridden broncs together for twenty dollars a month and roped wild cattle out of the thickets and slept on the same blanket under the prairie stars, at a time when the buffalo-grass turf still knew the bite of wagonwheels more than the crush of pneumatic tires. Those had been the good days, the young days, when five dollars in his pocket made a cowboy feel rich as a packinghouse owner. But a change had gradually come over Page. What seemed at first a healthy ambition developed into a cancerous growth, relentlessly twisting him into a driven slave.

Charlie had once heard a cowboy say that most men get drunk on whiskey, but Page Mauldin got drunk on business.

Page said, "Met the *chotas* comin' out of your place. Picked up some of your *hombres*, I reckon."

"I didn't have no *hombres*. They *did* catch a couple that stopped here to get somethin' to eat."

"Damn Immigration, they're thicker'n screwworm flies. I had a crew of *mojados* buildin' fence on my Brewster County place. Immigration suspicioned they was out there but they never could find them; those boys could hide under a bush too small for a rabbit. Finally, the day the boys finished the job, they all went down to a windmill to take theirselves a bath in the tank. Immigration slipped up on them while they was in the water. You never seen such a scatteration of naked men in all your life . . . runnin' ever whichaway through the brush with them *chotas* after them like huntin' dogs. They never caught a one of them boys. After the Immigration give up and left, the boys come driftin' back to pick up their clothes. All but one. Last time I was out there his clothes was still hangin' on the fence where he left them. I expect there's still some poor lonesome Mexican boy out yonder prowlin' the thickets, naked as the day he was born . . . ashamed to show his face . . . or anything else."

Page looked dourly at his cup. "Damn if I know why I'm sittin' here wastin' time. I got a dozen places to be."

"If you don't slow down you'll take a heart seizure one of these days, and then we'll always know where you're at."

"A man'll rust out before he wears out." Page stared across the steaming cup toward the ewes in the shearing pens. He changed the subject. "I can't tell that the dry spell has hurt your sheep much."

"Sheep's a dry-weather animal by nature, as long as you don't overdo it."

"I tell you, Charlie, they got an old-timey drouth out west of the Pecos. Remember 1918? Country's got a scorched smell to it, like there'd been a prairie fire over it, only there ain't been nothin' to burn." He grimaced. "I seen that your surface tank has gone dry over in the Red Mill pasture. Why don't you drill a well there and be done with the worry?"

"It's a long ways down to water, and it'd cost a right smart. I might need the money later to buy feed with."

"If you'd swallow that hard-headed pride and go to the PMA office, the government would pay half the cost of a well for you."

"I'll spend my own money if I spend any atall."

"Damned if I understand you, Charlie. *Everybody* takes money one way or the other, directly or otherwise. The railroads get it . . . and the airlines . . . and the schoolteachers. Half the people that go around talkin' about independence and free enterprise have got their own pipeline to the government money. They each got a different name for it, is all. Them livestock of yours, they won't give a damn whether you pay for a well with your money or Uncle Sam's. The water will taste the same."

Charlie squeezed the tin cup so hard he bent it a little. "Anything I've ever done on this ranch, I've done because I thought it was worth somethin' to me. If it's worth buildin', I'll do it myself. If it's not worth enough for me to spend my own money on it, it's not right to expect somebody else to do it, maybe some New York ribbon clerk that's havin' a hard-enough time feedin' his own."

"That ribbon clerk has got *his*. He's got a minimum wage, and unemployment pay if his job gives out; that's somethin' me and you ain't got. His kids get cheap lunches in school because the government gives food away. He rides to work on a subsidized bus or in a subway that don't charge him what it really costs to run. If he's bought him a house, he's probably got a government loan at interest a lot cheaper than me and you can get. We ain't paupers, Charlie; that ain't the point. Most of the people who get government money ain't paupers. It ain't given to us because we need it; it's given to us because somebody needs *us* . . . they need our vote. So everybody's gettin' it, and you're payin' your tax money for it. Only way you'll ever get any of that back is to claim what's comin' to you. If you don't, somebody else will."

Stubbornly Charlie said, "That ain't the way I was brought up, or you either. We was taught that every man starts with an even chance. We was taught to believe in a man rustlin' for himself as long as he's able. If you get to dependin' on the government, the day'll come when the damn *federales* will dictate everything you do. Some desk clerk in Washington will decide where you live and where you work and what color toilet paper you wipe yourself with. And you'll be scared to say anything because they might cut you off of the tit."

"Government's done some good things for us, Charlie. You think the electric companies would've ever got off of their lard butt and built lines out to these farm and ranch houses if it hadn't been for the REA? They don't tackle *nothin'* they don't see a profit in. We'd still be lightin' a kerosene lamp when the sun goes down."

"But that was a loan; it's bein' paid back. Nobody got it free. I got no quarrel either with the educational things like the county agent comin' out here and teachin' these Flores kids how to feed a lamb or how to tell one grass from another, and the Soil Conservation Service showin' us how to kill brush and hold the grass and turf together. But the things we can do for ourselves, we ought to do without holdin' out a tin cup."

Charlie looked across the pasture, remembering. "You never did know my ol' granddaddy; he died when I was still a boy. He come to this country when the Comanches still carried the only deed. Granddad, he kept his powder dry and didn't look to the government to hold his hand. He went through cruel hard times when there was others takin' a pauper's oath so they could get money and food and free seed, but he never would take that oath. He come within an inch of starvin' to death, and he died a poor man. But he never owed any man a debt he didn't pay, and he never taken a thing off the government."

"He's been dead a long time, Charlie."

"Not long enough that I've forgot what he taught me. I've always paid for what I wanted, or I've done without."

Page Mauldin emptied his cup. "That's the difference between us, Charlie. You don't believe in this stuff and you stand by your convictions. I don't believe in it either, but I take it because it's easy money and because everybody else does. You'll shove your feet under a poor man's table as long as you live."

Three hundred yards out from the corrals a little bunch of sheep was being driven along the netwire pasture fence. Two riders broke away and came loping in to open a gate. Kathy Mauldin and Manuel Flores were racing each other. Charlie frowned, hoping Kathy wouldn't hurt that roan.

Both youngsters jumped down, hitting the ground running. At the gate they wrestled playfully to see which would grab the latch first. At the distance and over the bleating of the sheep, Charlie could not hear what they said to each other, but he could tell they were laughing.

"I wisht you'd look at that," Page said darkly. "These kids nowadays, they can't tell one color from another. I wonder sometimes what this world's comin' to."

Charlie shrugged. "It'll be them that has to live in it, not us. We're already over the hill."

Manuel swung the gate open, jumped back into his saddle and turned toward the little bunch of sheep. By his gestures Charlie surmised he was telling Kathy where to position herself and the roan horse to help put the sheep through the gate. It was a waste of time, for Kathy already knew more about sheep than Manuel could tell her.

Page watched, still frowning. "You're raisin' yourself a good cowhand there, Charlie. I wish Diego had raised one or two like that."

"Manuel? He's a good boy, as willin' a kid as you'll ever see."

"Too bad he's a Mexican."

Charlie glanced sharply at Page. "What do you mean by that?"

"I mean if he wasn't, he could make himself into just about anything he wanted to be—doctor, lawyer—even a banker if he's got a mean streak in him."

"A doctor would be my bet. You ought to watch him with animals." Charlie pondered. "I reckon he could still be any of them things if he was of a mind to. Everybody gets his chance in this country."

"Not everybody, Charlie. Damn shame he wasn't born white. But I reckon the country'll need good cowboys, too, for a while yet. I know I will. I'm leasin' me another outfit."

Charlie looked thoughtfully toward the black Cadillac. More hard miles ahead. "You ever goin' to be satisfied, Page?"

Not many men in West Texas spoke reproachfully to Page Mauldin. Not many dared. There was a widely circulated story about him—untrue but illustrative of the view most people had. Page was supposed to have made a large purchase in a town far from home. When the clerk asked what bank he wanted to draw on, Page was reported to have said, "It don't matter; I got money in all of them."

Even the Boston wool buyers, ordinarily as independent as a hog on ice, spoke with some deference to and about Page Mauldin. His wool clip was scattered in half a dozen warehouses, and it was among the biggest in every one.

Page said, "Charlie, I come over to offer you a chance to go into this deal with me. It's a chance for you to make somethin'."

"I already got somethin'."

"This little greasy-sack outfit? It ain't big enough to cuss a cat on."

"Big enough to suit me."

"I been tellin' you for years—if you ain't there when the balloon goes up, they make the flight without you. You don't have to sit here on a poor-boy spread all your life."

"It's made a good livin' for two families—mine and Lupe's. It's paid for. A man can have a little bit and feel rich, or he can have a lot and feel poor. Sometimes, Page, I feel like you'll be poor all your life."

"A man's got to build somethin' he can leave for his daughter."

"You'll leave it a lot sooner than you think if you don't take to slowin' down."

The sun had set, but daylight lingered as Manuel Flores walked from his house down toward the barn where Kathy had told him she had left her new .22. He carried his own ancient singleshot, the stock dull and scratched, the original front sight long since replaced by a dime, fitted and filed down. He didn't see Kathy at the barn, where she said she would meet him; he guessed she was still up at the Flagg house eating supper.

A boy of about his own age walked out toward him from the shearers' camp, stopping to regard the rifle in Manuel's hand. "Going to shoot an elephant?"

Manuel nodded at Chuy Garcia, the *capitán's* son. They had been schoolmates ever since the first grade.

Chuy usually spoke Spanish when he could, so Manuel answered him in kind. "Just a jackrabbit or two. Kathy Mauldin has a new rifle she wants to try out."

"That rich little *guera*? She has a new *everything*. With all that money, all she has to do is snap her finger."

Manuel studied Chuy uncomfortably. Chuy never had much tolerance for *gringos* in general and rich ones in particular. In school he was everlastingly plotting some minor form of rebellion to demonstrate that he needed nothing they had to offer.

"Kathy is all right," Manuel said defensively.

"Because she never makes you take off your hat and bow to her, and say *'Yes, madama'*, and *'No, madama'*? You think she sees you as an equal? You are a fool, Manuel. She is laughing at you all the time."

Manuel began to be flustered. "You are mistaken, Chuy."

Chuy snorted. "Why do you think she wants you to go hunting with her? It is so she can show off her new rifle and be better than you are because you have only that old relic."

Manuel rubbed his hand along the worn stock. "It is a good rifle."

"But old. Where did you get it?"

"Mister Charlie gave it to me. It is one he used a long time ago."

"*Mister* Charlie! Always *Mister* Charlie! Generous, isn't he, giving you something so old and worn out that he no longer wants it? I suppose you bowed and told him how grateful you were?"

"I said 'Thank you,' the way my father told me to. I did not bow."

"It was probably your father who bowed, then. They are great ones to bow and speak softly, these old men. They are all afraid some *gabacho* will not like them."

"I do not like you to talk about my father that way. I do not see *your* father talk up to the ranchers, either."

"Because he is afraid like all the rest of them. He is too old to change his ways. He has been under the *gabacho* paternalism so long he would not know how to live without it."

Manuel mulled over the word. "What do you mean, paternalism?"

"The way the rancher pats you on the head and treats you like some pet dog, the way I saw old Charlie Flagg do to you this afternoon."

Manuel thought back, puzzling until he remembered how Charlie had pushed Manuel's hat down. "He meant no harm by that . . . it is just his way of playing."

"A man plays with a dog, too."

Manuel's face twisted. The *capitán's* son always made him uncomfortable, made him feel somehow disloyal to his blood. Yet in some disquieting way he was always drawn to listen, to consider. Chuy usually left him a lingering and troubled suspicion that there was truth in what he said.

He wished sometimes that Chuy Garcia would move from Rio Seco. Manuel did not like this uneasiness that Chuy aroused in him.

Kathy Mauldin came whistling down from the big rock house. Chuy said, "Listen to her. I bet she had a better supper than you and me."

Kathy was oblivious to Chuy's contempt for her. "Hi, Chuy," she said cheerfully. "Want to go shoot a few rabbits with us?"

Chuy looked Manuel in the eye as he coldly replied

to Kathy, "I have more important things to do." He walked back to the shearers' camp.

If he had meant to offend her with his tone, he failed. Kathy skipped on to the barn and came back with the new .22 in her hands. "Okay, Manuel, let's go. I bet I can outshoot you."

Manuel cut a quick glance at her. Chuy had aroused a nagging suspicion. "We'll see," he said with a sudden reserve.

This had been a moderately good jackrabbit year, although Manuel thought dry weather was causing some drop-off in numbers. They were not overrunning the country as in the occasional lush years of tall grass and plentiful weeds. He remembered what Charlie Flagg had told him once:

"Nature has a way of protectin' the wild creatures, like the jackrabbits and the cottontail. You take a good year, when there's plenty to eat and the rabbits are healthy, they just naturally breed up better. They have bigger litters, and more litters in a year's time. Seems like when the year is good, God likes to see more creatures alive to enjoy it. You take another year when it's dry and the animals have a hard time, Nature cuts the numbers to fit the feed. She ain't sentimental. Some starve to death, and maybe some disease like rabbit fever sweeps the country. But mainly there's just less rabbits born. There's not as many litters, and not as many babies to the litter. He knows how much feed there's goin' to be, and He fits the creatures to it."

Manuel had always liked to hunt jackrabbits, ever since Lupe had decided he was old enough for Charlie's .22. For justification he often reminded himself that it didn't take many jackrabbits to eat as much as a sheep, and that if the jackrabbits became numerous enough they might conceivably starve out the sheep and cattle. That was one reason many ranchers were liberal in their tolerance for responsible rabbit hunters who would not be reckless and bring down a bigger animal. But Manuel knew this, on his part, was only an excuse. The simple truth was that he liked to hunt. And about the only thing in open season the year around was the jackrabbit.

A hundred feet away a gray jackrabbit popped out of a mesquite and began to gallop along slowly, long black-tipped ears working back and forth while he tried to decide if he was in any danger.

Manuel said, "Let's see how that new gun shoots."

Kathy Mauldin shook her head to fling her long braid back over her shoulder and out of her way. She closed the bolt and raised her rifle. She whistled softly, gambling whether the rabbit would stop out of curiosity or be startled into flattening its ears back and streaking away. The rabbit stopped and sat on its haunches, its sensitive ears working. The rifle cracked. The rabbit took one long jump and fell.

Another jackrabbit, flushed by the shot, darted out from nearly. Kathy feverishly worked the bolt back and tried to ram another cartridge into the breech. Manuel fired. The rabbit rolled, its white belly flashing.

Kathy whistled. "Hit him on the run. I couldn't of done that, even with this semiautomatic."

Manuel straightened a little, allowing himself a moment of pride. "With a singleshot you have to learn to shoot straight. You just get one chance."

The girl sniffed. "You're braggin'. Bet you can't do it again."

A cottontail rabbit broke from beneath a prickly pear clump. Manuel brought his rifle up in reflex, then lowered it.

"Aren't you goin' to shoot?"

He shook his head. "I never did like to kill a cottontail."

He didn't know exactly why. The jackrabbit with its lanky body and gangly legs was not a pretty creature, not one to arouse any protective feeling. Besides, its speed and wily trait of zigzagging gave it a good chance, made it fairer game. But the little cottontail with its soft furry body and its large brown eyes seemed pathetically helpless. Manuel felt the same emotion toward the cottontail that he felt for dogie lambs and calves.

Kathy raised her rifle but did not fire. The rabbit darted beneath another prickly pear, its cotton-puff tail bobbing.

She turned to look at Manuel, and there seemed to be laughter in her eyes. "You've got a soft streak in you."

He shrugged, ill at ease, defenseless against a girl's laughter. "They always make me think of a little girl in a fur coat."

"And you wouldn't shoot a little girl in a fur coat?"

He frowned. "Not unless she laughed at me."

"I'm not laughin' at you, Manuel. But I know lots of boys who'd of shot that rabbit."

"If you want to, go hunt with them, not with me."

She looked at him quizzically. "I always hear people say that Mexicans are supposed to be cruel."

That angered him. "And *gringos* always show off their money."

Her eyes shifted to the new rifle in her hands. Any hint of laughter was gone from them now; she looked hurt. "I didn't think of it like that. I didn't bring this rifle out to brag; I just thought you'd like to see it." She held it forward. "Here. I'll trade you for a while."

He took a tighter grip on the singleshot. "This old one is all right for me. It hits what I aim at."

Uneasily she lowered the new rifle to arm's length. "I didn't intend to make you mad, Manuel, and I didn't come here to show off."

He felt ashamed for flaring at her, and he wouldn't look into her face. Staring into the dusk he said, "I didn't mean you, Kathy. I didn't mean anybody in particular. I know a lot of *gringos* who don't show off their money. I know some who don't even *have* any."

He found she was looking at him. He turned quickly away.

She said, "And I know a lot of kind Mexicans. Most of them I know *are* kind. Especially when they won't shoot a cottontail rabbit, or a girl who talks when she ought to listen." She extended the rifle to him again. "Now, you want to trade?"

He shrugged, bringing himself to look at her. "I guess." He gave her the singleshot and took the repeater, turning it carefully to look it over. It was a beautiful thing, heavy in his hands and still smelling of new oil.

Kathy pointed. "Yonder's another jackrabbit. Try a shot."

Manuel did, but the slug picked up dust. The rabbit abruptly changed course. Manuel pumped another cartridge into the breech and threw the rifle to his shoulder again.

He heard a startled cry from inside a mesquite thicket, near where his first bullet had missed. A man jumped up, hands in the air. *"No me mate!"*

Manuel froze. He heard Kathy gasp. For a moment he had a wild fear that he had shot someone.

"No me mate!" the voice pleaded again. *"Me rindo."* ("Don't kill me! I surrender.")

Manuel almost dropped the rifle. He found the safety catch and set it. In shaky Spanish he said, "We did not know you were there."

He moved closer. Kathy followed a little behind him, frightened. The Mexican stood with hands in the air. In the dusk Manuel saw this was not really a man; this was little more than a boy. He said in English, "Kathy, it's a wetback I found this afternoon. This is the one that got away from the border patrol."

The youngster trembled. Manuel began to regain his wits.

"*No tenga miedo,*" he said quietly, motioning for the Mexican to put his hands down. "Don't be afraid. We won't hurt you."

"I thought you were *chotas.*"

"Even a *chota* would not shoot you. We are your friends."

The boy dropped to his knees. His hands shook beyond any control.

Manuel was acutely aware of the rifle in his hands and the fear the young Mexican had of it. He wished he didn't have it. "Don't be afraid," he said again, knowing the advice was wasted. "There is no Immigration here now."

The Mexican raised his gaze to Manuel's eyes. "The *chotas* . . . they took my father and brother away?"

Manuel nodded.

Hopelessly the wetback said, "I had thought perhaps they would somehow escape, that they might come back to me."

"They took them to jail. You're alone now. What are you going to do?"

The boy shrugged. "What we had all intended to do, I suppose. Go and find work. We came because our family is hungry. Now it is up to me to send them money."

"How old are you?"

"Fourteen."

It surprised Manuel that the boy was even younger than himself; he looked older. "You are too young. No one will hire you."

"Someone will."

"You would be better off to go back to Mexico. Come to the house with us. My mother will feed you, and you can start home tomorrow."

The boy shook his head. "I will not return home."

"You'll go hungry."

"I have food in the bag, food your *patrona* gave me."

"It will not last long."

"It will last until I have work."

Manuel glanced at Kathy in frustration. He knew she understood all of it; old Elvira, the Mauldin housekeeper, spoke little but Spanish. "They all think the money's just lyin' on the ground over here," he told her in English. "They think you pick it up like you'd pick flowers."

Kathy replied, "The faith of the mustard seed."

Manuel dug into his pocket but came up with only a dime. "You got any money with you, Kathy?"

She shook her head.

"I thought your daddy was rich."

"We just *owe* money; we don't ever *have* any."

"Well, I guess it wouldn't help him much anyway. He can't afford to go anywhere that he could spend it." He looked at the girl. "It's fixin' to get dark. We better go back."

She nodded. "Diego's probably itchy to get home." She pointed her chin at the wetback. "But what about him?"

"What *about* him? We haven't got anything to give him, or any way to help him. He'll go on his way, and sooner or later the Immigration will get him. Maybe he'll have a chance to earn a little money first and maybe he won't. Probably he won't."

To the young Mexican he said, *"Buena suerte."* ("Good luck.")

"Gracias. Mil gracias."

Manuel started for the house, Kathy trotting to keep up with him. She protested that he was going too fast and he slowed a little, but not enough.

She demanded, "What're you mad about now?"

"Who's mad?"

"You are. I didn't do anything."

He slowed more. "It's just these dumb wetbacks, comin' over here thinkin' everything's goin' to be like lickin' up ice cream. There's nothin' you can do for them."

Kathy said, "Then there's not much point worryin' about it, is there? It's not our problem."

Manuel shook his head. "No, it's not our problem."

Directly Kathy saw another jackrabbit and pointed. Manuel felt no inclination to raise the rifle to his shoulder. He gave the rifle to her and held out his left hand for his singleshot. "It's a nice gun, Kathy, but I guess I've shot all I want to with it."

Charlie Flagg sat in darkness on his screened-in porch, his rawhide chair leaned back against the rock wall. He still had his spurs on, his boots propped up on an old iron milking stool that had been kicked around the place for years, a relic left over from the time of August Schmidt. A south breeze flowed past him, cooling to his skin after the long day's heat.

The newly shorn ewes and their lambs had been turned out to graze. Charlie had scattered alfalfa hay in front of the gates to hold the ewes until they had paired with the lambs. The only bleating he could hear now came from two orphan lambs. Their mothers had died on the board because of the weight of a shearer's knee on their water-filled bellies. The heat had almost killed a couple of others, but Charlie had saved them by pouring water over their heads until they revived and staggered off to a far corner of the pens, there poking their heads under each other's bellies for what shade they could get.

Only two lost out of a full shearing day; that wasn't bad. Charlie had the fleeces, and that was a major part of an older ewe's value anyway. He wasn't keen on seeing two more orphan lambs in the dogie pen, but he knew Manuel would take care of them; that boy had a knack.

From over in the Flores house Charlie could hear the protests of the younger children as Rosa sent them off to bed. He liked to listen to her heavily accented English. It was a wonder to him that her children spoke it so easily, and with so little accent. A stranger, listening to them with his back turned, would have to perk his ears up to tell whether they were Mexican or Anglo.

Lupe Flores would be down at the shearing camp, swapping windies with Teofilo. Charlie could see the flicker of the campfire. Some of the shearers would be gambling with the metal checks they had earned that day, and Teofilo would be keeping one eye on them. A *capitán* had to leave the reins loose enough that his men could have some fun, but he could not allow anyone to win so much that it stirred bad blood. Intermittently Charlie heard the strum of a guitar and voices lifting in the ancient Mexican *canciones de muerte y amor* (the plaintive songs of death and love).

In a way Charlie wished he could go down there and share the company. He was vaguely lonesome. But an old reserve held him back. As the ranch owner— and more to the point, as an Anglo—he wouldn't fit in. With one or two or three individually it would be fine, but not with the crowd. He wouldn't be comfortable, and neither would they. His presence would be an inhibiting factor in the camp.

Charlie never tried to analyze or rationalize his feelings toward Mexican people; he would never have thought of apologizing to anyone for them. He did not dislike Mexicans; on the contrary he liked most of the ones he personally knew and respected them. Yet he tended to distrust the strangers among them. It was an inherited attitude going back through generations of forebears whose names he did not even know. It was deeply grounded in history, in wars won and lost, in the Texas revolution, and the bitter decades of border strife that followed, when each side feared and halted the other with equal blindness and ferocity, when one was *gringo* and one was *greaser*, when blood spilled on both sides of the river and no one was innocent.

Charlie's philosophy, though he did not fully realize he had one, was simply "live and let live." He took it as unquestioned fact that Mexican people in general possessed a different outlook, a different set of values. They were of a culture most Anglos never understood or seriously tried to understand. The most common charge was that Mexicans were improvident, that they lacked the Anglo's drive for success. Yet often Charlie envied the Mexican for not always being caught up in a constant blind rush, for placing less value upon accumulated dollars than upon the enjoyment of life's simple pleasures, for not wasting today worrying about tomorrow and more accumulation. Pinned down, Charlie would not have said this was inferiority. For all he knew or gave a damn, they were right.

Like most Anglos he knew many Mexicans who did not fit the blanket assessment he casually set upon the group. In Charlie's earliest years old Juan Nieto probably had as much influence on him as his own father. Juan had never learned to read or write, and his knowledge of the Bible was restricted to his sometimes distorted but always elemental interpretations of what he had learned from the priests. Nevertheless he had absorbed Nature's lessons with a keen eye and questioning mind. He had taught Charlie about the earth and the creatures, the way the various species interdepended upon one another, the way the Indians and the early Mexicans lived with nature instead of working at cross purposes with her. Juan had taught Charlie the fine points about riding and roping, the details about horses and cattle and sheep that the Mexican eye often sees and the Anglo overlooks.

Then there were Lupe and Rosa Flores. Rarely did Charlie think of them in terms of their race. They were simply people to him—good people. He took pride in their loyalty to the ranch, their honesty, their hope that their children might grow up to a better life than their own. If some of his liking was based on the fact that they simply never gave him any argument, any resistance, he did not realize it.

And Teofilo Garcia. Teofilo was a businessman. As

such he stood in the top order of the caste system which developed within most Mexican communities. Shy on formal education, he nevertheless had an aptitude for both figures and mechanics. His principal fiscal shortcoming as Charlie saw it was an easy tolerance for less ambitious relatives and in-laws who worked far less than he did and swarmed around him like an invasion of locusts as their winter rations ran thin. The result was that Teofilo usually had to visit his spring customers for an advance to get his shearing outfit in working order.

Mary Flagg stepped out onto the porch and eased into her rocking chair, disturbing the aimless drift of Charlie's thoughts. She had been in the kitchen picking rocks out of beans for next day's dinner. Charlie glanced at her small outline in the darkness. She had been cool since he had let Tom go to the roping. He figured she was going to bring up the subject again, so he tried to head her off.

"Listen to the music over in the shearin' camp. Funny thing to me why other people can't put their hearts into music that way. When a Mexican sings a cryin' song, he cries all over, and he makes you cry with him."

"You shouldn't have let Tom go. His place is *here*. But every time he asks for something, you let him have it."

Charlie gritted his teeth and decided against arguing with her. He never could get the last word, and there was no use raking an old bed of coals. What was the harm in letting the boy do what pleased him now and again? The years ahead held time enough for him to shoulder the burden of manhood.

Mary began to rock her chair gently. The creak of

it was vaguely irritating to Charlie, for it overrode the music from the camp.

Why is it we seem to rub each other the wrong way any more? he wondered. It didn't use to be like that. If this is part of growing old, the hell with it!

Sometimes it was restful to let his mind reach back to those early years. The past was a warm and secure refuge from an uneasy present and an uncertain future. It was unchanging, dependable, an anchor post he could tie to. It was not that times had ever been easy. He and Mary had struggled along in the beginning on a rocky, water-shy bit of leased range farther west, living in a drafty old two-room shack with a smoky woodstove and a single coal-oil lamp. But Charlie could remember the pride they had in it, for it was their own. There had been a warm sense of sharing, even when there was so little to share. There had been a closeness then, and an eager physical love that held them together like two strong and opposite magnets. This had been a bridge for them over those first years of hardship, a source of strength when they clung together and watched the lowering of a tiny casket into a rocky grave. They had observed older couples pulling apart, slipping the bonds that had originally tied them. They had discussed it many times and assured themselves that it would never happen to them.

But it had. Somehow, dammit, it had. They had not sensed it fully at the time, and neither had ever verbally admitted it to the other. Thinking back on it, Charlie was fairly sure it had begun when Tom was born. Before, there had been only the two of them, and they had held to each other. Now there was someone else to take Mary's attention, and this ranch to take Charlie's. More and more, Mary became absorbed in the keeping of the rock house and the garden and the raising of the boy, while Charlie was busy with horses and cattle and sheep, with building fences and putting up windmills.

It was ironic now, when he thought of it, that their best time together had been those years of hardship. When life had eased and their financial condition became more secure, they had drifted into diverse paths. They seldom sat and talked as they used to. They slept in separate rooms, and Charlie seldom fumbled his way to Mary's bed any more. Even when he did, she was likely to drop off to sleep and leave him feeling like a damn fool.

He felt a need now to make conversation, to get her mind away from Tom. He told her about Teofilo Garcia's wrong-way whirlwind and Lupe Flores hanging a rattlesnake belly-up on a bush. "Rain sign . . . dry-weather sign. They're great ones for superstition, these Mexicans."

He could sense worry in Mary's voice. "Charlie, do you think Teofilo could be right?"

"It's just a foolish superstition."

"It *has* been a long time since it rained. Somehow I have a bad feeling."

Charlie shifted his boots on the stool, his spurs jingling a little. "You're turnin' as spooky as them Mexicans."

He sat silently a while, breathing the good cool air. He began to notice the dry smell of dust in it. Sheep had stirred a lot of ground today; now the wind was picking it up.

Well, a shower would fix that. They ought to be due a shower any day now.

He happened to glance up at the black sky. "Looky there, will you, at that quarter moon! It's standin' on end to let the water run out. I tell you, woman, that's a sure sign of rain."

4

Charlie never knew for sure how some of the rocks would roll down off that cairn on top of Warrior Hill. There hadn't been any rain to wash them down. He reasoned that livestock walking this way probably dislodged them from time to time. He had considered putting up a little protective fence, but somehow the idea of a fence didn't seem to fit for an Indian who had spent his life free and unfettered. Fences were an invention of the white man, built to keep other people out but at the same time locking himself in.

Charlie picked up the fallen rocks and carefully put them back into their proper places. He had promised old August Schmidt that he would keep up this grave just as August had kept it. At first it had given him a queasy feeling, but in time he had come to enjoy an occasional climb up here. From on top of this hill he could see every part of his ranch, and far beyond it. Gradually, as he had come to love this land the way August had loved it, he began also to feel a kinship to this Indian, who must have loved it more than either of them.

"Been awful dry, Old Warrior," Charlie said when he finished with the rocks. "I'm afraid you might not be so proud of it if you could see it the way it is now."

Other places might have several drouths in a single summer. Texas was more likely to have several summers in a single drouth. Drouth here did not mean a complete absence of rain. It meant extended periods of deficient rainfall, when the effects of one rain wore off long before the next one came so that there was no carryover of benefits, no continuity.

Charlie Flagg's rain signs failed him; the summer was dry. He had been away to war during the famous old drouth of 1918, so he had not seen that one with his own eyes. He remembered none like this except perhaps '33. All this summer it had showered but three times. Each time, the sun broke out from behind the paltry clouds and the west wind swept in furnace-hot, stealing the scant moisture before the grass had time to taste the life the brief rainfall had falsely promised.

Charlie watched the grass burn a golden brown, then saw the gold fade to dusty gray as life retreated into the roots beneath the baking ground. He saw even this dead mat of grass dwindle as the animals continued to graze it. The ewes remained in good flesh, and their bags were rich with the milk flow for the normal term; the lambs should go out acceptably heavy this fall. Sheep always did well in dry times, so long as there was feed. Their ancestors had endured for untold centuries in the Pyrenees and on the open deserts of Spain, and before that perhaps on the hot sands of Morocco long before the first woolly Merino timidly set a cloven hoof upon the alien soil of the New World.

It was the cattle that suffered first; they were bred for the green midlands of England. The calves had no bloom, and Charlie was sure they would come up thirty or forty pounds light this fall.

Now in September the days were still hot but the nights cooled quickly, and the early mornings made a man hunt for a light jacket. Charlie knew he could no longer put off his annual prewinter visit to the bank.

He told Mary only that he was going to town, but instinctively she knew the rest of it. Her intuition always made him uneasy; it gave him an uncomfortable feeling that if ever he had some dark secret she would sense it immediately and discern all its sordid details. That, more than morality *per se*, had kept him from yielding to temptation on occasions through the years when pretty eyes had offered invitation.

She said, "You tell Emmett Rodale it's been a long time since he's been by for dinner. Tell him I'll fix him one of those apple strudels he always likes."

"Bein' nice to Big Emmett won't make him charge us any lower interest. Friendship stops at the door of the bank."

"An old bachelor never eats right; he never saw fit to marry some good deserving woman who would take care of him."

"I never heard him complain about it. I'll bet Big weighs three hundred and fifty pounds. I'd be rich if I could raise cattle that had his fleshin' qualities."

Driving his green pickup toward town, Charlie skirted the edge of Coyote Flat, the dust rising behind him like a white fog. On one side of the parched caliche road lay a drouth-stunted cottonfield that belonged to farmer Emil Deutscher. A pickup sat in

THE TIME IT NEVER RAINED 337

the edge of the rows, one door standing open, the back glass broken out. Emil stood in the short cotton, his big hands on his hips as he surveyed in droop-shouldered discouragement the thin scattering of open white bolls.

Charlie braked to a gradual stop, waited for the dust to drift away, then backed up, looking over his shoulder so he wouldn't run into the ditch. By tradition there should have been little common ground between Charlie Flagg and Emil Deutscher. One was a ranchman, a man of the saddle whose only interest in farming was a small-grain patch he kept for winter grazing, more or less against his will, and in which he always hired someone else to do the plowing. He didn't own a tractor and never intended to. Emil, on the other hand, was strictly a farmer. In the beginning Charlie had laughed about Emil's heavy German accent and his plows and his pigs. But gradually he had found that when the work was done they thought much alike. They enjoyed the same things—a good tight house, a comfortable chair, a game of forty-two, a hot, heavy, fresh-cooked meal. The man in boots and the man with the lace-up brogan shoes had come first to mutual respect, then eventually to friendship. Their wives, especially, had much in common. Sometimes Charlie thought Hildy Deutscher spent as much time in Mary Flagg's kitchen as in her own; she burned more gasoline in her car driving over here almost every day than Emil burned in his tractor getting the fields properly worked up. The two women rattled incessantly in the half-German, half-English mixture both had brought from the old country settlements. Charlie seldom had any real idea what they were talking about.

He halted at the edge of the road, leaving room

for the yellow school bus he knew would be here shortly to pick up the Flores children and others who lived along this route. He struggled over the fence, supporting himself on a cedar post and grunting as he brought his leg across and dropped to the soft ground. His weight had stretched the wire.

Emil walked toward him, halting in the edge of the cotton. Near Charlie's age, he was medium-tall, a blocky man in grayed-out denim overalls that once had been blue. His square, friendly face was ruddy, blistered by harsh sun and constant wind. His blond-haired, fair-skinned Nordic ancestors had not bequeathed him proper protection for the severity of the climate he faced. The burn of the sun left tiny blotches in his skin, blisters that might turn to cancer if not periodically treated. It was a price a man paid to stay here.

They howdied and shook and talked about how uncommonly hot the days were. Charlie said, "Your cotton looks about like my grass. Ain't makin' much, is it?"

Emil Deutscher soberly shook his head. His German parentage showed strongly in the way he put his words together. "I will gather many acres before I have a bale. Those Mexican picking crews, they have been here to see. They take one look and then go on to the plains. They say the picking is always better at Lamesa."

Charlie nodded. He had seen a lot of transient family groups from down in the Lower Valley, going along the roads in their tarp-covered trucks. He hadn't seen many stop for anything but gas. "Maybe next year."

"Sure, next year. It's a great next-year country."

Emil knelt and scooped up a handful of dry earth. He let the dark soil run slowly through his fingers, the thinnest of it drifting away like a silken veil in the west wind. "Look at that, Charlie. Best soil in the world."

"With rain it'll grow anything. Without rain it ain't worth a damn."

"The rain will come. We'll make a crop of winter oats and wheat." Emil picked up another handful of soil and stirred it with a grimy finger. "As you say, it will grow anything in the world, when God sees fit to give it moisture."

"I'd settle just to grow some fresh grass. You can keep your farmin'."

"Everybody is at heart a little of a farmer, Charlie. Even you, I would bet."

Charlie shook his head. "Not me. And can you see one of them Houston oil men out here with a plow-handle in each hand?"

"Even the city people, Charlie, they like to plant things and see them grow. When you are in the city, look up high in the windows of the tall buildings and you will see little flower beds there, little flowerboxes. When you look at the big buildings, you see nothing except man. When you look in the tiny flower-box, you see a little bit of God. We are all tied to the Mother Earth. Deep inside, everybody wants to go back to it. Me and you, Charlie, we are the lucky ones. We never left it."

Charlie looked at the poor cotton. "Not so damn lucky, maybe."

"Next year, Charlie." Emil stared at the dirt in his hand. "It takes away from us sometimes, but later it ᴋ back more than it took. Next year . . ."

* * *

Charlie parked his pickup across the street from the bank and stood on the corner, waiting. The traffic light seemed a long time in changing. He turned his back to the wind and watched the noisy passage of a livestock truck carrying a double-deck load of ewes, probably to market. Many stockmen were selling off part of their older animals to lighten the grazing load on suffering pastures.

Bad weather's got a lot of the boys boogered, he thought. *But if a man sells off the mother stuff, where'll the lambs and calves come from? You can't produce without a factory.*

Charlie glanced without enthusiasm toward Big Emmett Rodale's bank. He took out his old railroad-type watch. Early yet. It always paid to let Big have his morning bowel movement before you went to talk business with him; his humor was better. Charlie walked down to the coffee shop and pushed the door open. The thick aroma of soapy steam, frying grease, and reheated doughnuts wrapped around him like a soggy blanket. He had only pity for a man obliged to take his meals in a place like this.

The shop was half full of merchants and store clerks with white shirts and dark ties, ranchmen and farmers in greasy hats and Levi's and khakis, all drinking coffee together and swapping gossip like idle wives. Some of the ranchmen who lived in town could be found here about this time any day. It amazed him that they could run a ranch from the coffee shop, but they seemed to manage. For all his hard work, he couldn't discern that he made any more money than they did.

Rio Seco was one of those West Texas towns where time and circumstance line once drawn between townsmen and country people. Many ranchmen lived in town, and many businessmen owned acreage in the country. Hardly a farm or ranchhouse was so far beyond the forks of the creek that it did not have electricity. Nearly every country home had butane gas, hauled by truck and pumped into underground steel tanks. Woodchopping had gone out like the freighter's mule. Many a salaried employee locked up at 5:30 and drove a few miles to some small place he owned or leased and had stocked with cattle or sheep. Prices had trended steadily upward the last several years. Townsmen had eagerly invested their money in the land for its green promise of abundant profit. Rio Seco had hardly a barber or lawyer or storekeeper who did not boast ownership of a few cattle. Cattle were easier than sheep for the part-time operator because they needed less attention. These days you did not need a lifetime background in livestock to make money out of cattle. All you had to do was buy them and turn them loose. Any fool could show a profit on an up market.

Many townspeople were asking themselves why they had not stumbled onto this bonanza twenty years ago. They looked with suspicion on the traditional ranchmen who had been in the business thirty or forty years but drove old cars and lived in clapboard houses so aged that there was still gingerbread latticework across the front porch and oval glass in the front door. *They've got it made, all right,* most folks agreed. *You couldn't stay in the livestock game that long and not be rich.*

In Texas, nothing gave a man status like ownership of cattle. Now there was status enough for everybody. The goose was hanging high, and they had the world by the tail on a downhill pull.

Charlie knew most of the men here by their first names, so it took him a while to shake hands all around. It tickled him to see people like druggist Prentice Harpe wearing their suit pants tucked into the tops of shiny cowboy boots. Four or five years ago Prentice had bought a load of speculation cattle and his first pair of boots, all the same day. The cattle had made money. Nowadays he wore boots to church.

A couple of men squeezed up in a booth to make room for Charlie.

"Coffee, Mister Charlie?" He looked up at the waitress, a tall, slender young woman whose mouth smiled but whose eyes were tired and sad.

"Coffee'd suit me fine, Bess."

Harpe said, "You better try a slice of this boggy-top pie, Charlie. It's mighty good."

Charlie liked the looks of it, but because the others were eating it he ordered a doughnut instead. He always had to be different.

Bess Winfield spilled a little of the coffee in Charlie's saucer and leaned over to put a paper napkin under the cup to keep it from dripping. Charlie protested, "No need, Bess, I can do it myself."

But she fixed it anyway while Charlie fidgeted. He wondered if he would ever be old enough that it did not make him uneasy to have an attractive young woman this close to him. Bess's white uniform fit snugly over full breasts that held his attention even though he felt guilty. Just because the fire had died out at home didn't mean a man's mind didn't still stray in that direction sometimes. He hoped no one else noticed. He decided they were probably looking at Bess too, not at him.

The crowd talked dry weather and cattle prices

awhile, and football and the ungodly high cost of labor. Gradually the men began getting up and leaving, one at a time, until Charlie was left by himself, sipping a third cup of weak coffee without enthusiasm, staying here only because he had rather drink bad coffee than go sit down across the desk from Emmett Rodale and ask him please to set him up a line of credit for the feed he would need this winter. No, Charlie might imply the word *please,* but he wouldn't say it out loud. A team of Percheron draft horses couldn't have pulled that out of him.

Bess came around with the glass pot half full of coffee. Charlie placed his hand over his cup as a sign he had had enough. In truth, he had had enough after half of the first cup.

He said, "You look tired, Bess. Busy mornin', I suppose."

"No worse than any other."

"Maybe you and Tom danced too much last night."

"We didn't dance atall."

Surprised, Charlie said, "Tom told us you-all had a date."

"We did, but some of the boys got up a roping down at the arena. I sat out there in my dancing dress on the hard boards of that grandstand and watched them rope till past midnight."

Charlie scowled. "If I was a young man again, be damned if I'd leave a pretty woman sittin' by herself while I was off with a bunch of ugly cowboys."

He remembered it hadn't been that way with him and Mary—not in the early years, anyway.

She said, "I wish sometimes you *were* a young man, Mister Charlie."

Bess Winfield's parents had come to Rio Seco as tenant cotton farmers years ago. Her father had been

allergic to calluses on his hands, though it was generally supposed he had them on his rump. Bess was a
pretty girl, as girls went in a small town like Rio Seco.
Charlie thought she deserved better than working in a
sweat kitchen, and she could have had it. He knew she
had received several proposals, most of them honorable. She had declined them all to wait for Tom Flagg.

It had been a long wait.

"I'll talk to him," Charlie said.

She shook her head. "No, don't. If he ever
changes—and maybe he will—let it be on his own."

The Ranchers & Farmers Bank was about the oldest institution in town. It dominated a corner, its
thick limestone walls and age-yellowed mortar showing the sturdy German influence which had come
here in the early times from the old Pedernales River
settlements. Long years had stained the stone, but the
building stood solidly, a living tie to a pioneer period
that had passed into the fading shadows of old men's
memories.

Inside, the buzz and clatter of electric calculators
and the insistent ringing of an upstart telephone did
not dispel the bank's elusive flavor of a bygone era.
It still had its high ceiling with elaborate metalwork
painted white, the electrical wires running across the
surface in metal conduits instead of being hidden inside the walls. The old walnut counters still stood
with their delicate lathework and marble tops, worn
down by generations of arms and elbows. Occasionally someone would suggest that the place was dingy
and needed a complete redecoration to brighten it. Big
Emmett would hump his back like an angry bulldog.

"It was plenty fine for your ol' daddy," he would snort. "You figure you're better than your ol' daddy?"

Someone had suggested that a complete modernization might appeal to the ladies and draw more of them into the bank. Bachelor Big had risen to heights of profanity that would have done Sam Houston proud. "This is a bankin' institution, not a powder room! Women run everything else in the country today. Be goddam if they're gettin' this bank!"

Other institutions might go cosmopolitan and turn their backs on the ladder by which they had climbed. Emmett Rodale's was still plainly an agricultural bank. Across the big walls hung old ranch pictures— the Sugg Ranch remuda of horses watering in the Concho River, the last delivery of big Longhorn steers out of Crockett County, a string of freight wagons drawn by mules hauling wool to San Angelo. There was a picture of Emmett Rodale himself at twenty, a cowboy on the old Bar S. A big, dusty pile of *Sheep and Goat Raiser* magazines sat atop a small table in a vacant corner, and last year's dried-out maize stalks leaned against a windowsill.

The bald, portly banker rocked back in his outsized chair when Charlie Flagg stepped into the building. Rodale wore a necktie in concession to propriety but left it at half mast in protest against total conformity. His reading glasses were perched halfway down his nose, for he had been reading the new issue of *West Texas Livestock Weekly*. He frowned at Charlie over the rims.

Beside the front door stood a free scale. By habit, Charlie always paused to weigh himself. That is, he always stepped onto the scale. He never looked any more where the pointer stopped; he didn't care to know.

Big's voice could peel the scales from an armadillo. "What're you doin' here, Flagg? You're supposed to be out yonder workin'."

Half the people in town were afraid of Emmett Rodale. The rest knew the way to get along with him was to answer him as roughly as he talked. He had a loud bark but no teeth.

Charlie nodded toward the scale. "You ought to use that thing yourself once in a while. You're gettin' as fat as a pet coon."

Big grunted and laid the paper down. "Pot callin' the kettle black. Tell me what you come to ask for so I can say *no* and get you out of my hair."

Charlie looked at Rodale's bald head. "Out of what?"

A secretary tittered. Rodale frowned. He took off his reading glasses and wiped them on his necktie. "Set down, Charlie. You're the only man in Rio Seco who's got a meaner mind than I have. I'm glad to have you in here where I can be watchin' you."

Charlie kept his feet. "Ain't any use me sittin' down till I find out if you're goin' to do it. If you ain't, I'd just as soon head for San Angelo and find a banker that will."

"Do what?"

"Set me up a line of credit so I can buy feed this winter."

"For you or for them livestock? *You* could do without."

"Do I get it or not?"

"You get it. Set down!"

Charlie pulled the straight-backed chair out and seated himself. They talked awhile about the weather and the short grass and the fact that winter was staring them in the face. Charlie passed on Mary's invitation to dinner, and Emmett said he would be out the first chance he got. Charlie knew he would, too, for Big dearly loved home cooking. And all other forms of cooking.

Charlie asked, "Seen Suds O'Barr this mornin'?"

The banker shook his head. "Nobody ever sees Suds till afternoon."

"He's supposed to meet me here. My lease is runnin' out. We're fixin' to talk terms on a new one."

"How much does he figure on raisin' the price this time?"

"Been a spell since I've talked to him, but I know he was out the other day, lookin' to see if my sheep were in good flesh. Lease year is a bad time for sheep to look good. Makes the landlord greedy."

Sam O'Barr was the real name, but he was better known—out of earshot—as Suds. His father had been a rancher here in the early times, a hard-working builder and shrewd investor. He had wanted to be sure his son didn't have to work and sweat the way he did. He had succeeded, for the heaviest thing Sam had lifted in twenty years was a case of beer. Realizing his mistake almost too late, the old man had so arranged his will that Sam could never sell the land. He could only lease it out and live from the income, unless he chose to work the land himself, an unlikely proposition.

The last time Charlie had seen him, Suds O'Barr had come walking unsteadily down the town road toward Charlie's barn. His breath like the south wind off a brewery, he explained that he had been out driving around, looking at his land, and had let his car run off into the ditch. He had been unable to get it out. "You know," Suds had said with a surge of pride, "I had just six cans of beer left in the ice chest. I put them in a paper sack and brought them with me. I figured it was two miles to your house, so I divided two by six to see how long to make each can last me. I just missed it by two hundred yards."

Charlie never knew whether to feel contempt or pity for Suds. Mostly he just avoided him. Once Suds had had all the money a man could reasonably want, pretty women running after him, ready, eager, and willing—everything the average man thinks would be required to provide him the good life. But Charlie figured the most poverty-stricken Mexican in Rio Seco was better off than Suds.

"Big," Charlie mused, "lots of folks cuss a man who throws his money around the way Suds did when he had it. But the same folks will cuss the miser. Who knows what it takes to suit people?"

Sam O'Barr was trailed by a wispy little man who strained to shut the heavy door behind him. Sam's step was straight, but his face and hands were nervous. Plainly, he needed a drink. He had probably denied himself for the business conference.

"Mornin', Charlie." He extended his hand, which felt cold and had no grip at all. "You-all know my attorney, Gerald Aronson?"

Aronson had been Doc O'Barr's attorney in happier days. In recent years he had had the unpleasant duty of defending Sam O'Barr in divorce suits, a paternity case and the like, fighting a losing battle to hold together the tattered remnants of the O'Barr inheritance. It was over now. Little was left that anyone could take from Sam.

O'Barr glanced around nervously. "Well, I got

things to do, so let's get her uncorked. Where would you like to go to talk, Charlie?"

Charlie looked at Big Emmett. "If Big can spare the time, I'd like to do it right here with him sittin' in. He's my banker."

Big shrugged. "I got nothin' to do but work. Set down, fellers."

Sam and Aronson seated themselves and glanced nervously at each other. Sam turned to Charlie. "Ought not to take but a few minutes. Gerald got the new lease agreement typed up last night."

Aronson pulled a set of blue-backed contracts out of his briefcase. Charlie fished his spectacles from his shirt pocket and began to scan the papers.

Too quickly, Sam said, "It's the same contract as last time."

Charlie frowned. "It would appear to be, except . . ."

"We adjusted one or two little details."

Charlie grunted. "I already found one of them . . . the price."

O'Barr flushed and looked away, his hands shakier. He pulled a silver flask from his coat pocket. "Anybody mind?"

Big's sharp eyes appraised O'Barr but betrayed no judgment. "Go ahead." O'Barr turned the flask up and swallowed twice. He coughed, then screwed the cap back into place and looked around furtively to see if any of the women employees had been watching him. "Held off all mornin'," he said defensively, "but there's a limit to how long a man can run on the rim. Anybody else care to strike a blow for liberty?"

Nobody did. Charlie said, "We was fixin' to talk price. Everything in the contract suits me but that.

You're askin' too much." He handed the contract to Big for the banker to read, which he did with a frown that would worry even a bank examiner.

The drink relaxed O'Barr a little. "Five years now we been on the old price, Charlie, a dollar an acre. Things was different when we signed that. Livestock prices have gone up, and you've had some good years. You've done right fine, and all the time I been gettin' the same old price."

Evenly Charlie reminded him, "Other times it's run the opposite. We've done a contract when things was good, and I was stuck with a high price when livestock went down."

"It's never broke you, Charlie. That old country of mine has been right good to you through the years."

It struck Charlie funny, O'Barr calling it *that old country of mine*, as if he felt some affection for it. All it ever meant to Sam was the lease money. Some men like Charlie Flagg and Emil Deutscher derived a strong sense of pride from standing on their land, crumbling the soil through their fingers, smelling the new grass, feeling the ebb and flow of life in the earth as the seasons came and went. Other men like Sam O'Barr regarded land with no more passion than they would figure a rent building or a set of coupons in a safety box at the bank, waiting to be clipped. It was simply a commodity to be used, traded, or sold.

Charlie said, "A dollar and a half an acre is way too much."

O'Barr shrugged. "Cost of livin' is goin' up. If you don't want to pay it, I got a man who's spoken for it and said he'd give me that much. Naturally for old times' sake I'd give you first refusal."

Momentary alarm brought prickling to Charlie's skin, an alarm which slowly changed into anger. He stared at Sam O'Barr's eyes, and Sam looked down at the floor. He suspected Sam was bluffing, but he couldn't tell by looking; Sam always had this guilty air about him. The way things were today, a vacated lease didn't go begging for long. Some townsman was always willing to pay more than it was worth, certain he could make a killing in the cow business.

Charlie saw that Big was disturbed by the price. Charlie said, "Sam, I'd sort of expected a little increase—a dime, maybe—but nothin' like this. Dry as the country is, I can't pay this price." He continued to study O'Barr's face, wishing for a sign whether Suds was "loading" him. Recklessly he decided to see O'Barr's cards. "If you got a man who can, maybe you better go see him."

O'Barr stiffened. "You mean you don't want the lease?"

"Sure I want it, but not bad enough to commit suicide for it."

O'Barr began to tap his fingers. He cut his rheumy eyes to the attorney. Aronson said nothing; he obviously had no pride in his mission. O'Barr said, "Charlie, you've had that place a good many years. I'd hate to see you give it up. What would you do with the stock you've got on it?"

"There's other land I can lease. Or I might just sell them and put the money on storage in Big's bank. Sometimes I wonder what a man wants to beat himself to a nub fightin' a big ranch for anyway. Nine times out of ten his money would earn him more in a savin's account drawin' interest, and not take any sweat, worry, or gamble. As a way of makin' money, ranchin' is awful highly overrated."

O'Barr's hand slid to the pocket where the flask was. He drew the flask half out, changed his mind and let it slide back. "Look, Charlie, just because I like you . . . just for the sake of old times and your friendship with my good ol' daddy . . . I'll whittle the price a little." Charlie could see him painfully running the totals through his fogged mind, figuring how much a reduction was going to cost him. O'Barr said, "How about a dollar-forty?"

Charlie glanced at the banker. Big winked without otherwise letting his expression change. Charlie had broken O'Barr's bluff. They would wrangle, but Charlie would wind up getting the place for a dollar-and-a-quarter.

"Sam," Charlie said, "did you ever stop to figure what would happen to the land if you ever hung a man on it at a price he couldn't afford to pay?"

"He'd pay if he signed the contract. He'd have to."

"He'd be forced to take it out of the land. He'd keep pilin' in more and more cattle and sheep to squeeze out more money to pay the lease."

O'Barr shrugged. "That's what the land is for."

"There's a limit to what you can take out of it. Treat the land right and it'll take care of you. Overgraze it . . . abuse it . . . and in twenty years it'll look like the Sahara Desert."

O'Barr shrugged again and looked out the window, his hand in his coat pocket, impatiently rubbing the flask. He said with total indifference, "Twenty years from now I'll be dead!"

Charlie parked his pickup at the curb in front of the big rambling wool warehouse. The little front door had been a waste of money, for few people used it. By habit Charlie walked around the side to climb up onto the concrete loading dock and enter by the huge roll-up door through which the wool went in and out. It was like stepping into a half-dark cavern, the air cool and heavy with the pleasant odor of raw wool, packed tightly in jute bags and stacked halfway to the ceiling.

He lifted his hand in greeting to half a dozen loungers loafing on wool and feed sacks. Some were the same men he had seen earlier in the coffee shop; they hadn't gotten any closer to their ranches. They were sitting around discussing solutions to all the world's problems and wondering why nobody at the top was smart enough to see things the same way. Charlie paused for a look at a stuffed coyote that bore a pained expression. Some wag had lately added a sign: *Bitten by a Boston wool buyer.*

Warehouseman Jim Sweet pushed to his feet and moved leisurely to meet the ranchman. "Mornin', Charlie. What can I do for you?"

Charlie said, "Need some wheat seed. Thought I'd get Emil's oldest boy to dry-plant it for me in that little grain patch of mine. If it comes a rain I'll have green grazin' this winter for some cows and calves."

Jim Sweet lost his grin. "Sure, Charlie. Only, it's been a long time since I remember sellin' you any wheat seed."

"Been usin' oats. Thought this time I'd try wheat and see if it stands the winter better."

Uncomfortable, Sweet rubbed the back of his neck. "I can sell you all the seed you want, Charlie, but I'm not sure you can plant it. There's government regulations on it now. You can't grow wheat without you got an allotment. On account of the surplus, you know."

"I just want to graze it. I don't figure on turnin' none of it over to the government."

"Ain't my doin', Charlie. Me, I'd as soon cut the whole thing wild aloose and see where it lights. But they got the regulations, and they'll bear down on you. It just happens that the PMA man is in my office right now, lookin' up some figures. I'll get him to tell you what you can do and what you can't."

·Charlie protested, "I ain't goin' to ask nobody . . ." But the warehouseman was already gone. In a minute he was back with the official.

March Nicholson nodded at Charlie, his eyes neither friendly nor unfriendly. "Morning, Mister Flagg. What is it you want to know?"

Charlie had a fleeting sense of being trapped, and he was angry at the warehouseman. "I didn't go to make a federal case out of it. I just wanted to plant a little wheat, is all."

"For grazing?"

"Sure. I'm not a farmer."

"It's all right if you just graze it. But once it starts to head out you'll have to plow it under. You're not allowed to cut it without an allotment."

Charlie felt his face turning red. Nothing nettled him quite so much as for someone to tell him what he could not do. "Supposin' it was doin' real good and I decided I wanted to cut some and put it up for feed?"

"We couldn't allow that. Next spring I'll come out or send an inspector to be sure it's plowed under."

"And what if it isn't?"

"We'd have to file a complaint against you."

Charlie swore under his breath. "I been more than twenty years workin' out that land and payin' for it. Now it's mine. If I want to grow wheat on it to feed to my own sheep or cattle, I don't see where anybody else has got any business pokin' into it."

"There is a certain logic, Mister Flagg, if you'll

think about it. If you weren't allowed to grow that feed for yourself, you'd buy it from somebody who *did* have an allotment. That would help keep down the surplus."

"Hell's fire, if I decide to grow oats or barley and harvest *them*, I ain't breakin' no law, am I?" When Nicholson said no, Charlie went on heatedly, "I'd still be raisin' my own feed, and I wouldn't be buyin' that man's wheat. So if I'm not goin' to buy from him anyway, it oughtn't to make any difference what kind of feed I grow."

Nicholson's mouth tightened. "The law is specific. It says you can't harvest wheat. My job is to carry out the law, not to question it."

"It's my land!"

"But harvest wheat from it without an allotment and you'll pay a fine or go to jail! If you don't like laws, Mister Flagg, perhaps you should move to some country where they don't have any."

"I liked *this* country before it was saddled down with so many of them."

Nicholson gave up the argument and stamped away. Charlie's jaw jutted out as he watched the young man leave the building. "Damn *federales*, they're gettin' worse than the smallpox."

Jim Sweet mused, "He tried to be civil to you, Charlie. But you got him so stirred up now that he's gone off and left all his papers in my office. He'll be back directly and *I'll* have to listen to him." He looked around and saw that the crowd of loafers was supporting Charlie. "You're no farmer, Charlie, so why raise all the fuss? You wouldn't cut that wheat. A Russian firin' squad couldn't make you cut it."

"Hell no, I wouldn't of cut it. But I didn't want *him* tellin' me so. It wasn't them *federales* that worked

and did without so I could pay for that land. It wasn't
them that drilled the wells and dug the tanks and
fought the brush. They've taken aplenty from me in
taxes, but they ain't contributed a damn thing, and
I don't *want* them to." He turned stiffly toward the
seed sacks. "Give me some oat seed."

"Change your mind about the wheat?"

Charlie nodded grimly. "If I can't work my own
land without some white-collar bureaucrat lookin'
over my shoulder, the hell with it!"

Tom Flagg switched off the headlights and stepped
out of his pickup in front of Bess Winfield's small
house, carrying a box of candy he had bought at the
drugstore. The front of the place was dark, but he
could see a light somewhere in the back.

The Winfields—Bess and her mother—lived in an
old frame house at the edge of the Anglo section. A
man could throw a rock from here to *Little Mexico*
without straining his arm. That helped make the
rent cheap. The front steps were of concrete, but the
boards on the skimpy front porch were warped and
slightly loose beneath Tom's feet. He tucked the candy
under his arm and knocked firmly on the screen door.

Waiting, he wondered what had been eating his father. Charlie had stomped in from town like an old
bull on the prod, hooking at everything that moved.
Charlie had chewed Tom up one side and down the
other about half a dozen things. Not the least of them
had been Bess Winfield. "You go see that girl!" he had
demanded. "You go see her tonight. And if you don't
tell her you're sorry, I'll *make* you sorry." Usually
Tom could smooth Charlie's ruffled feathers without

much difficulty, but this time he thought he'd leave well enough alone. He had intended to see Bess anyway. He had been working hard. His hands itched for the touch of silk, and the soft skin beneath it.

Through the dim light that came from the back, Tom saw Bess walk out of her bedroom. She wore a faded cotton dress. A wisp of hair hung down in a loose curl on her forehead. Her face looked tired. Tom caught the burned odor of fresh-pressed clothing. He could see the ironing board in the bedroom, a half-finished dress draped across it, the hem moving gently in the good breeze that drew through the bedroom. He had found some time ago that it was the coolest room in the house.

Bess snapped on the living-room light and recognized Tom. She stood uncertainly inside the screen, saying nothing.

Tom spoke first. "Aren't you even goin' to say howdy-do?"

Coolly she asked, "Isn't anybody roping down at the arena tonight?"

"I didn't go by. Just came to see you, Bess." She continued to stare at him. He held up the candy. "They tell me if pretty talk don't do the job, try bribery."

Usually it didn't take much to bring a glow to Bess's eyes. The ice was never so thick that he could not melt it with a smile.

Bess pushed the screen open. "It isn't locked." Her eyes were brittle. Tom caught her chin and started to kiss her. She stepped backward and nodded gravely toward the open front door. "Tom, the neighbors."

"What do we care about the neighbors?"

"What do *you* care about *anybody?*"

Tom's eyes narrowed. Going to be one of *those*

nights, looked like. Good thing he had brought the candy. He pushed it forward. "Where do you want me to put this?"

Bess shook her head resentfully. "Eat it yourself, or pass it out among your calf-roper friends."

"I'll bet your mother'll eat it. Where is she?"

"Had to make a trip to San Angelo. She won't be back till late."

Late. That was fine, provided he could weather the chill. "Look, Bess, I'm sorry about last night. If I'd known the dance meant that much to you . . ."

"It wasn't the dance. It's just that you never even asked me. You took me out to that arena and left me sitting there by myself. You never came over and said as much as hello all night. Not till you got through playing that game. Then you thought I ought to be ready and eager to play *another* game, to finish up a fine evening for *you*. I don't mean any more to you than that gray horse of yours. Use me, feed me a few oats, and turn me into the corral."

Tom said, "Look, Bess, I came to apologize. Now, what more can I say?"

She had no answer. She simply bit her lip.

In the bedroom, the unplugged iron was crackling as the heat drew out of it. Tom glanced in that direction, speculating. *Putting the squeeze on me, that's what she's doing. Well, I'll call her on it.* He stared at her, wanting her but not wanting to put himself in the position of giving in to her. He set the candy on a bookshelf and turned back toward the door. "I'm sorry it's this way, Bess. Good night." He pushed the screen door open and started out, slowly and deliberately. Bess watched, her hands lifting and clasping above her breasts. "Tom, where are you going?"

He shrugged. "It doesn't make much difference. I'm not wanted here."

She took a long breath and crushed her hands together, color rising in her face, a tremor in her throat. "Tom," she spoke thickly, "come back here."

5

Nothing more than an occasional teasing rain-shower found Charlie Flagg's Brushy Top ranch, hardly enough to wet a man in his shirtsleeves. The sun would steal the scant moisture almost before Charlie could ride out to see how deeply it had penetrated in the pastures, probing with a pocketknife blade the way he would plug a watermelon.

Sometime late that fall the coyotes came in. Best anyone could tell by their sign they were a pair—a male and a female. Sheepmen had cleared this region of coyotes long ago, but always they continued to breed up on the fringes of sheep country, on the big open cow ranches to the west and north. Coyotes seldom bothered cattle except occasionally a small calf. The straight cowman paid little attention unless they depredated his chicken-house; *that* got him sore. The coyote was in no danger of extinction or even serious depletion, for he mated joyously and reproduced in bountiful numbers outside the netwire boundaries that marked the sheep lands. And he was always pacing those perimeter fences, pressing tirelessly for entrance, digging under, climbing over, a powerful instinct drawing him to ancestral denning grounds.

To a sheepman, the presence of a coyote is like a sliver of ice pressed against his spine. Uncommonly intelligent, the coyote is often hard to kill. Some of the wiser ones range over a given area for years, slaughtering sheep with impunity and cleverly eluding everything from traps and cyanide to airborne hunters sent against them in desperation. In time a coyote's slashing teeth can run up a staggering death toll, his ravenous appetite driving the marginal operator to the brink of bankruptcy. A killer coyote preys mercilessly on a sheepman's mind, ruins his sleep, and makes him a hard man to live with.

Lupe found the first dead ewe. "The government's got trappers, Mister Charlie," he said. "Maybeso we better call the government."

Charlie said, "They're *my* sheep."

He telephoned an old trapper he knew. In the three days before the man got there, Charlie and Lupe found more dead animals. Gravely studying the dried-crimson sign, the trapper said, "You're right, it's coyotes. See yonder? They bit through the jugular vein and licked up the blood. Then they tore into the flank and ate the fat out from around the kidneys. Sheep probably wasn't plumb dead yet. Male and a bitch, I'd call it. Could be passin' through, and again they might be lookin' for a likely place to den up this winter. Liable to be hell to catch, Charlie. See that track? The old male's got a bad limp. Missin' part of his right forefoot. Lost it in a trap, would be my guess. He'll be trap-wise now."

Charlie ground his teeth together in useless anger as he stared at the torn body and glazed eye of what had been a good yearling ewe. "Why should they come in on us now? Been years since I had any coyote trouble."

The old trapper, who hadn't shaved in a week, shrugged his shoulders. It was a warm afternoon, and he unbuttoned his coat. Soon as he did, Charlie knew he hadn't bathed in a week either. "Who knows why a coyote travels? Maybe he's smarter than people. Maybe he knows it's a hard winter comin' and he's lookin' for a place where they'll find enough to eat. Animals has got an instinct about such things. People don't. All people know is what they see in the papers, and half of that is damn lies."

Charlie rubbed his fist. "Do whatever you have to. I want them two varmints caught or run off."

"I'll do the best I can. But you better be ready to catch a little hell over it."

Charlie stared at him in wonder. "What kind of hell?"

"People get funny notions. The other day I had a woman walk up to me on the street and call me a murderer. Damn near swallowed my tobacco, it surprised me so. She said I was a murderer, catchin' and poisonin' coyotes like I do. I tried to tell her about the way they kill sheep and chickens and calves and such, but she wasn't interested in none of that. She said it was murder to trap and kill a coyote. I asked her if she ever set a mousetrap or sprayed flies, but she said I was just tryin' to change the subject on her. I wonder what makes people act that way?"

Charlie shrugged. "Coyote's a romantic animal, I reckon, if you ain't had to contend with it. There's lovable animals, and there's *un*lovable animals. Hell, I always liked a coyote myself, in his proper place.

But his proper place ain't in my sheep pasture. People that never saw one of their own lambs with its guts ripped out don't know how unlovable a coyote can be. I guess everybody sees what he wants to and overlooks what he don't care to see. Other people look at the dead coyote and pity him. Me, *I* look at the dead sheep."

Through the next weeks the trapper tried everything in that unwritten book of tricks the old-time varmint man keeps in the back of his head. He used it all, from steel traps to the new cyanide guns with a .45-caliber poison pellet that fires into the coyote's throat as he opens his mouth to take the bait. All these guns ever killed for Charlie was time and a pair of stray dogs that had no business in a sheep pasture anyway. The wily coyotes seemed to know the lures for what they were and go out of their way to leave them alone.

One day the trapper came to Charlie's house, the staggering odor of spoiled meat and coyote-urine bait clinging to him like some foul old coat.

"Charlie, I got somethin' to show you. It happened to me once before, years ago. If I was to tell you, you wouldn't believe it."

The trapper's pickup had an air that was overwhelming. Charlie sat near the door, the window rolled down all the way as the trapper drove him out to a trapline he had laid near a brushy watering place. The sign was plain. Tracks showed where the limping male had walked down the line, pausing to sniff suspiciously at each bait, then moving on without touching it. Finally at the last trap the coyote had stopped long enough to leave the unmistakable testament of his contempt on top of the bait.

In spite of himself, Charlie grinned. He felt a momentary admiration for the wise old killer, much as he wanted to see him dead.

The trapper asked, "You ever see a coyote laugh?"

"Can't say as I ever did."

"Bet you a hundred dollars to a Mexican peso this one was laughin' to bust his ribs."

Charlie's sheep kept dying by ones and twos and threes. Traps and poisons wouldn't get these coyotes. He knew he had to try something else.

Chewing warmed-over mutton at the supper table, he stared vacantly across the room and out the open windows where wind was kicking up dust in the ranch yard. At length he mused aloud to Mary and Tom, "Some people say we ought to let the coyote alone, that we got to have them for the balance of Nature. But most of those people live in the cities, where they threw Nature out years ago. They ain't goin' to give up their automobiles and paved streets and sewer systems to get Nature back, but they're damn sure free with advice on what the *other* man ought to do." He looked around for response and received none. "I say *man* has got to be considered a part of Nature's balance, too. You can't raise coyotes and sheep together any more than you can have paved streets and coyotes together. You can't eat a coyote or wear his fur.

"I been thinkin' what to do, and I've decided we'll throw an old-fashioned wolf drive—call all our friends and neighbors in. We'll show them a good time—give the boys somethin' to think about besides dry weather. And we might catch them coyotes."

Actually, a coyote was not the same thing as a wolf, but the Texas sheepman customarily called him that anyway. It was a natural shortening of the old term "prairie wolf." This part of the country hadn't seen a real wolf in fifty years.

Wolf drives had been one of the means used to clear the region of coyotes a long time ago.

Looking across the table at Tom, Charlie saw anticipation kindling in his son's eyes. This was a thing that would appeal to Tom's cowboy instincts. A wolf drive could be *muy bravo*—horsemen, pickups, and jeeps strung out in a ragged line, moving across the pasture like African beaters in a lion hunt. Once a coyote jumped up, everybody took after him hellbent for leather. Many a tough cowboy had tried one such drive and had sworn off for life.

The first thing Charlie did was to telephone Page Mauldin and invite him. Page was silent so long that Charlie thought the connection had been broken. He started to hang up and ring Central, but Page spoke.

"I'm gettin' old for that sort of thing, Charlie. So are *you*, for that matter."

"It could be a right smart of fun."

"I remember that kind of fun all too well. I remember settin' ol' Jase Ivy's leg in camp and tyin' a splint to it after a horse fell on him in '32. There's folks that think a sheepman is a quiet, timid soul, but they've never seen him chase a coyote. The wildest old-time cowpuncher—drunk or sober—never rode like a sheepman does when he spies a wolf. He'll tear through mottes and thickets, over fences, across a prairie-dog town—it don't make a particle of difference. I've seen a sheepman go off the bank of a washout, spurrin' all the way down."

"Then you ain't comin'?"

"I didn't say that. I'll be there."

Page volunteered to share the cost with Charlie to hire a flying hunter from out west at Fort Stockton.

Rounder Pike and a couple of other neighbors did likewise. The flyer would increase the odds. The neighbors knew that if the two marauders should move away from Charlie an adjoining ranch's sheep had to be the next to suffer.

A simple thing in its first conception, the drive grew into something far larger than Charlie anticipated. Fall shearing season was over, so he hunted up Teofilo Garcia's old camp cook, Mike Noriega, and hired him to be in charge of the fixings. The day before the drive they set up a chuckbox in the customary live-oak thicket and dug pits for the barbecue. Lupe Flores and the cook slaughtered several Spanish kid goats while Charlie cranked the telephone and reminded his friends what he had in store for them—a big feed and a chance to run a wolf.

Tom brought out his two *compadres* of the rodeo circuit, chunky Shorty Magee and lean Chuck Dunn. At the supper table Charlie couldn't get a word in edgewise. The boys kept talking of rodeos they had been to, especially the ones where they had won big money. Charlie noticed these were mostly a safe distance from home, where no one was likely to check on their stories. After supper he stretched in his easy chair and propped up his sock feet. The boys started playing some of his dusty 1920s records on the old windup phonograph that still held a place in the corner of the living room, though it was seldom used any more. They played the blue yodels of the original Jimmie Rodgers and sentimental old country tunes by Vernon Dalhart, songs like "The Death of Floyd Collins," "The Dream of a Miner's Child," and "A Handful of Earth from Mother's Grave."

Shorty was a fair hand with a harmonica, and Tom fetched his guitar. The boys played and sang along with the records while Charlie leaned back and enjoyed it, his eyes closed, his toes twitching to the rhythm. It took him a while to realize the boys were poking fun at the sobbing old songs.

Sourly Charlie arose, picked up his boots and tromped off to bed, muttering to himself. Buttons these days, they never listened to anything but honky-tonk stuff. They didn't know what good music was.

Garcia's cook crawled out of the blankets in the dark hours after midnight to start the barbecue. He burned big piles of live-oak wood down to coals, then set the goat meat above them on wire grills to cook slowly in the rising heat. Periodically he swabbed the meat with a sauce he claimed was an old Noriega family secret. Charlie knew it was made up mainly of a commercial mixture from the grocery store, plus some ground-up *jalapenos* and other Mexican peppers to give it authority.

Before good daylight, fifty or sixty horsemen and a dozen or more pickups and jeeps stood ready at Charlie's barn. Some of the horsemen paced restlessly, eager to be on the go. Others filled plates with scrambled eggs and bacon or steak, gravy and hot Dutch-oven biscuits, then squatted near the pleasant warmth of the campfire or the barbecue pits, laughing and talking. Charlie had told Mary to stay in bed—he would eat with the company at the chuckbox—but he had clomped around and made so much noise that she had gotten up anyway. She did not go outside, where the presence of a woman might inhibit the conversation. Charlie stood with plate in hand, savoring the aroma of outdoor food, enjoying the drift of good-natured talk. It was reminiscent of old times out on the Pecos River, when he had followed a roundup wagon on a cow outfit, times whose pleasures he fondly remembered and whose hardships he had conveniently chosen to forget.

The air was crisp, the sky open and turning orange with dawn. This, he felt, was going to be a great day, the weather perfect, the crowd cheerful. Some sheepmen had come from as far away as the next county. There was more to it than simply the pleasure of a chase. If the coyotes should leave Brushy Top, who could say where they might take a notion to locate next?

It was well that Mary had arisen, for a few men brought their womenfolks, and more women would arrive as the day wore along. Charlie thought Mary ought to hear enough gossip today to spend a month digesting it all, the way a cow coughs up a cud to chew and digest it in her leisure.

Page Mauldin was there early, bringing Diego Escamillo and three other Mexican ranchhands to help. He said sternly, "I reckon you know, Charlie, I ought to be in Fort Worth today for a bank meetin'. It's costin' me a right smart to be here."

"Then go on," Charlie replied, trying to sound just as stern. "But leave Diego. He's a better hand than you ever was."

Charlie meant well, but Diego grinned self-consciously, embarrassed at being placed in the middle.

Page shook his head. "I better stay. You're apt to need a keen mind before the day is over to get you-all out of trouble."

Charlie nodded. "That's why I'm tickled that you brought Diego."

Diego turned away to see after the horses.

Halfway across the yard Charlie could hear the loud, happy laugh of little Rounder Pike. Rounder had a chuckling crowd gathered around him—he usually did—and was spinning them a windy. "So the boss phones up ol' Son one day and says, 'Them coyotes botherin' you any, Son?' and ol' Son he says, 'No sir, they ain't botherin' *me* none, but they're sure givin' your sheep hell!'"

Nearer at hand, Yancy Pike was frowning. They were brothers—Rounder and Yancy—but different as molasses and vinegar. If you wanted hard-headed business advice with a Puritan conservatism, you went to Yancy. If you wanted pleasant company for a fishing trip or a buck-buying junket, Rounder was your man. Yancy Pike was tied to his ranch like a miser to his gold. He never came to town except when groceries ran low or there was business to transact. He had a hard time keeping hired help because he didn't believe in wearing out bedding by overuse or paying a wage that would put too much money in a working man's pockets and perhaps endanger his morals. He didn't believe in letting grass "go to waste"; he stocked his land to the hilt. When a sprig of grass came up, a sheep was standing over it waiting to nip it off. This conservation crap was all right for a *rich* rancher, he claimed, but a poor man couldn't afford it.

Rounder Pike was a little man with a big voice, a cud of chewing tobacco and a deep-creased face split by a perpetual sly grin that made him look as if he had just heard a dirty joke, or told one; likely as not, he had. When you wanted to talk to Rounder you never phoned his ranch except in last resort, for you probably wouldn't find him there anyway. You tried a dozen places in town first—the domino hall, the drugstore, the coffee shop, the wool warehouse. While Yancy made work a fetish, Rounder did not believe in doing it to excess. He was not afraid of work, however. When he had to he would dig in and labor like a Trojan, taking solace in the knowledge that when he finished there would be a six-pack of cold Bud waiting in the icebox.

Rounder was telling his audience: "There was this drouthed-out rancher who died and went up to the Pearly Gates. St. Peter met him outside and asked him what his name was. 'I'm Jasper Mulligan from Pecos County,' the rancher says. St. Peter looks him up in the book. He starts to read and says, 'Oh my,' and the farther he reads the worse it gets. Finally he looks up real sad and says, 'I'm awful sorry, but with a record like this I can't let you in these gates. I'll have to send you down to Hell.' The rancher shrugs his shoulders and says, 'Well, at least that's *some* improvement.'"

Yancy Pike glowered over a cup of steaming coffee he held in both hands, warming his fingers. To Charlie he grumbled, "Listen to that brother of mine. To hear him clownin' you wouldn't know there's a dry spell on, that there's men here sick from worry. Some things just ain't to be joked about."

Charlie observed, "When a man's sick with worry, a laugh or two can be good medicine. The way Rounder looks at it, the world is a big pile of barbecue and beans."

"He'll stop laughin' one of these days. You watch when he really feels the pinch. Like in the big Depression. He was off ridin' freight trains and bummin' around havin' hisself a high old time. I stayed with Daddy on the ranch and worked my fool head off. And when the time come, Daddy left him as much of the ranch as he left me."

"Rounder was sendin' money home when he had it, wasn't he?"

"But he could of been here where he belonged. We could of used him."

That was exactly why Rounder hadn't stayed, Charlie had always figured. Rounder thought a lot of his brother but liked him best when he could wave at him from a distance.

Yancy said tightly, "You just watch; he ain't got the guts for a real pinch. He'll fold up like a wet rag. He won't be laughin' then."

Some said Yancy was envious because it seemed Rounder could make as much money running his ranch from the hotel lobby as Yancy could by laboring from sunup to dark and then turning on the lights. Rounder ran fewer sheep, fewer cattle, but his lambs and calves always weighed more than Yancy's at delivery time, so they grossed out much the same. Rounder said this was because he took care of his grass, but Yancy claimed it was just luck. Their ranches lay side by side, sharing fences. Yancy's was always bare-looking and dry when Rounder's was still half green. Anybody could see that Rounder received more rain, Yancy declared. Some dark alignment with Satan, if the truth be known.

As the sun spilled over the tops of the live oaks to take up the chill of fall air, Tom Flagg rode in from the foot-trap, driving the horses. Charlie saddled his roan, Wander. Lupe Flores and his oldest son Manuel caught their mounts. Because Manuel was sixteen, Lupe had let him stay home from school today. But little Candelario wasn't being allowed to make the wolf drive. Candelario watched the others saddle up. His eyes begged.

"Mister Charlie, I don't *have* to go to school today. I can make it up."

Charlie hated to tell him no, though he considered Candelario too young for the risk. "You'd have to go ask your mother," he said. That was an easy way out, because Rosa would not let the children miss school for anything less than a broken leg or a funeral. She had raised hell even about Manuel.

Candelario argued. "I've got better eyes than Manuel. I bet I could see those coyotes before anybody else."

Charlie said sympathetically, "I sure wish I'd thought about this bein' a school day." In truth, he *had* thought about it. He had purposely chosen a school day to prevent having a lot of youngsters around to worry about. "But I tell you what, Candy: if we get those coyotes, we'll bring them home for you to see."

Candelario was not satisfied, but he knew this was all he was going to get. "Okay, Mister Charlie," he murmured, turning away with his shoulders in a slump. He wouldn't be worth a lead nickel in school today. He would sit dreamy-eyed, picturing the great ride he was missing, envisioning the horsemen chasing a coyote across the school yard just in time that he could step out and kill it with a well-aimed rock and be the hero of the day.

Manuel stayed as much out of sight as he could, not pressing his luck.

Charlie's smile left him as he saw a couple of teen-age boys with shotguns in their hands. Right then he began to have an inkling that he might have bitten off a chunk too big to chew. It hadn't crossed his mind that some kids might cut school. But here they were, their fathers friends of his. Tact had never been one of Charlie's better traits, but he wished he had a little more of it now. He began noticing how many other

guns there were. The place bristled with them. Somehow he had not counted on it being this way. He had
figured on only a few firearms, and these in the hands
of coolheaded men.

A clammy feeling sank way down to the bottom of
his stomach and lay there cold as yesterday's clabber.
He remembered a time in the late '30s that he had
been called out to help on a posse that was trying
to run down a pair of car thieves. They had broken
jail in Rio Seco, stolen guns and set out afoot across
the Page Mauldin ranch. Charlie hadn't been half so
scared of the armed fugitives as of his fellow possemen toting guns.

He saw one of the boys break open his shotgun
and shove a shell into the breech.

Charlie warned, "I wouldn't go loadin' it yet, boy.
Plenty of time when you see the coyote."

The youngster showed him a square-shouldered
confidence. "You don't need to worry about me, Mister Flagg. I been handlin' guns since I was a kid."

His finger accidentally touched the trigger. Flame
belched and buckshot thudded into the ground. The
loosely held stock recoiled against the boy's ribs.
Horses squealed in panic, some starting to pitch. A
rider caught off guard hit the ground so hard that
Charlie heard the breath gust out of him. All over the
place, men were grabbing at horses. Charlie's roan
jerked away, Lupe spurring after him.

Hunched over and rubbing his bruised ribs, the
boy forced a crow-eating grin. "I believe maybe I'll
just leave this thing here."

"That," Charlie said firmly, "would suit me to a T."

Lupe brought the roan back. Charlie swung into
the saddle, his legs stiff from the cold. His good humor had deserted him like a fair-weather friend. It

would be the eighth wonder of the world if somebody didn't get shot today, he thought darkly.

"We'll take the lamb pasture first," he said to
those close enough to hear him. "Ain't much brush
or rough country in it. It'll give us a chance to shake
down."

The vehicles would be the biggest problem. Lots
of places in Charlie's pastures they wouldn't be able
to move in a straight line, or couldn't move at all.
In areas of heavy brush and rock outcrops or wash-
outs they would have to break formation and go
around the best way they could find. It would be up
to the horseback riders to fill in the gaps. It was the
horsemen—and the airplane pilot—who would make
or break a coyote drive in rough country.

Yancy Pike had little to do with his brother Rounder
except when he could use him. Now he walked up to
Rounder and said, "You takin' your pickup?" Rounder
nodded. Yancy said, "If you don't mind, then, I reckon
I'll just ride with you. I'm afraid mine won't make it."

Yancy's was the same model as Rounder's. But why
subject two pickups to the wear and tear if Rounder
was going anyway?

In the pasture Charlie started down the netwire
fence, dropping off jeeps and pickups at regular intervals, spacing riders between them like teeth in a
comb. On signal, the group began to move forward.
Going was slow for the vehicles because they could
not afford to outpace the horses. Before long the situation would probably be reversed. The group had
not gone a quarter mile before one of the lower-built
pickups snagged *whum-m-m-p!* on a high center. It
took three horses and some crackling language to
pull it free.

Charlie muttered to Lupe, "Those chuckle-heads in

Detroit must think we got nothin' but paved roads out here."

By the time the group reached the back fence it had scared out nothing but sheep and jackrabbits. However, it had a chance to warm up and begin to feel a growing excitement. A couple of drivers decided their vehicles weren't made for this terrain. They parked them on a two-rut fence road and doubled up with other drivers still determined to go ahead.

In the second pasture Charlie separated a couple of boys who became so wrapped up in talk that they kept straying out ahead of the bunch. This pasture was cleared with little difficulty and without finding the coyotes.

Overhead, the flyer slowly made passes back and forth in front of the line, watching for the flash of brown that would mean a coyote had broken out of hiding.

The third pasture would be the last until after noon. Worry nagged at Charlie. He wondered if they would actually ever jump the coyotes. While none of the men talked of leaving—they wouldn't go until they ate the barbecue—he knew some were growing restless. All this riding without any action . . .

Halfway across the pasture Charlie heard a shout from down the line. Horns honked. A cloud of dust began to rise, horsemen and pickups rushing in. Edging toward them, Charlie could hear shouting and the brittle protest of mesquite brush as heavy vehicles plowed recklessly through it.

Lupe came loping up, excited. "Coyote, Mister Charlie?"

"I reckon. Everybody's roused up."

The parade was sweeping toward Charlie, dust boiling in thick clouds. Shotguns boomed. He saw the little animal then, darting back and forth in front of the pursuers, dust puffing around him as the shots missed.

Charlie pulled up in exasperation. "That's no coyote, it's just a damn fox. And somebody's fixin' to get his neck broke."

He heard brakes squeal as a pickup and a jeep almost sideswiped each other. Gunfire crackled. The riders bore down on Charlie, yelping happily after their elusive quarry. Charlie sat his ground. At least now maybe they would stay with him after dinner.

The flyer came over low, the plane's wheels almost touching the tops of the frost-denuded mesquite trees. He pulled up quickly when he saw what they were chasing.

Charlie sent Lupe forward with orders to let the fox go.

When the hunters returned to headquarters at noon they found that women had brought cakes, pies, and fruit salad. Charlie swore a little at sight of two washtubs filled with iced-down beer. He started to call Mary and demand to know who in the hell had ordered *that*. Then he saw Suds O'Barr, and he knew. No telling what a few cans of beer might do to somebody's nervous trigger finger. But this was supposed to be a party, after a fashion. He didn't want to throw a wet blanket over it.

He had invited a minister out to say grace before the meal. Charlie seldom went in to hear his sermon; always too busy, seemed like. But Mary usually went, hoping to pick up enough religion that some would rub off on her reluctant spouse. Failing that, maybe she would develop enough influence Up Yonder to get him into Heaven anyway. Charlie saw the minister staring disapprovingly at him over the tubs of beer. Charlie shrugged in innocence and retreated.

He noted that the minister in his blessing said nothing about the reason for this gathering today, to kill coyotes. He suspected the minister's sympathies were more with the coyotes than with the men; they weren't raiding *his* flock. But no matter, Charlie fed him anyway.

The meal done, the live-oak motte looked as if a tornado had swept it. The men sat around rubbing their bellies, smoking, drinking up the last of the beer. They talked about dry weather, horses, sheep, cattle, and women, more or less in that order, though Charlie observed that Tom and the younger set tended to put women first, even ahead of horses.

Weather warmed considerably after dinner. The afternoon sun caused most horsemen to peel their coats and tie them behind their cantles. The pickup riders rolled their windows down. They found nothing in the first pasture. They worked the second, and still no luck.

Late in the afternoon Charlie worriedly let down a wire gate and motioned the hunters into the final pasture. By now he had lost a large percentage of the crowd. As the remaining men gathered around him he said, "We've cleaned this place like a fine-tooth comb. If they're not in this pasture they've drifted plumb out of the country."

The flying hunter had had to go to town to land for a tank of gasoline. Now he had returned to finish the drive. Leisurely he worked back and forth, the rough roar of the motor causing Charlie's roan to shy every time the plane passed over. Charlie glanced up and thought how low that contraption would have to dip for the flyer to shoot a coyote on the ground, low enough to get mesquite thorns in the gas tank. Charlie wouldn't ride with him in that kite for all the wool in Boston.

The line ragged out. Charlie felt the same disappointment that slumped the shoulders of the other riders. The pair of coyotes must have drifted away. Looking for fresher game, perhaps. But that probably wouldn't be the end of it. Chances were they would come back. When a coyote developed a liking for your place, he was loyal to it. You never counted yourself rid of him until you saw him dead.

The racket started abruptly. To Charlie's right a horn honked. Someone shouted. A shotgun blasted and the race was on. He could see horses running, pickups and jeeps pulling in. He caught a blurred glimpse of tannish color.

Coyote!

It had jumped up ahead of the hunters and had tried to hit the fence. The wing men headed it off and turned it back toward the center. Now it was running like a deer, dodging in and out of the brush. The warwhoops came to Charlie as the riders pressed in. There was a gunshot, another and another.

Motors roared. From all over the pasture, drivers floor-boarded their pickups and jeeps to be in on the kill. Autumn-hardened mesquite splintered under the impact of speeding vehicles, branches flying like chaff from wheat. Charlie heard a windshield smashed by a heavy limb, but the pickup never slowed. He heard a loud bump and saw a pickup leap into the air, then plump down hard. It was Rounder Pike's. His brother Yancy gripped the door and seat and looked pale enough to die. Rounder was grinning like a monkey eating bananas, never missing a stroke on his cud of chewing tobacco.

The horsemen had the coyote hemmed in—or thought they had. Some were swinging ropes, trying to get a throw. But they were casting their loops too quickly and spoiling their chances. The coyote doubled back between a horse's legs, and the horse set in to pitching. The rider dropped a shotgun. The horse stepped on it, snapping the stock.

The flyer circled once for a look. He couldn't get a shot because of the riders.

Tom Flagg and his rodeo friends Shorty and Chuck went spurring by Charlie as if he were standing still. Tom and Shorty were shaking down their ropes, building loops. Chuck carried a shotgun. Tom let out a jubilant yell and cast a quick throw as the coyote barreled past him. The loop missed and caught instead around a mesquite stump. Riding full tilt, Tom hit the end of the rope before he could pull up. The impact set the mount back on its haunches. The rope snapped. Tom slid over the gray's shoulders and rolled in the dry grass. He jumped up, grabbed his hat, then caught the reins before the horse could break away. Tom was back in the saddle before the dust cleared.

Now two pickups were in full chase. One was an old model with a running board. A cowboy stood on it, his right arm hooked over the rear-view mirror for a hold while he kept a two-handed death grip on a shotgun. He trained the barrel on the coyote just as the pickup lurched and a thorny mesquite limb raked him, taking half his shirt. The buckshot blasted through the front fender and blew the tire.

The other pickup was almost upon the coyote, the driver trying to run the animal down. The coyote

swerved abruptly and changed direction. The driver
wheeled about in a vain effort to keep up. His front
wheels dropped into a hole and stopped him dead in
the path of the other pickup, which was still rolling.
Brakes squealed. Men shouted. The pickups bumped
with a crunch of metal and glass. The cowboy on the
running board slid belly down in the dirt, the rest of
his shirt strung out behind him.

Charlie reined up and let the chase go. In disgust
he slapped his felt hat against his leather chaps. He
shouted, "Hell's bells and damnation!"

Tom Flagg made a quick splice. He and Shorty
were still in the chase, swinging their ropes. Shorty
missed. Tom's loop went around the coyote, but the
animal was through it and gone before Tom could
jerk up the slack.

Shotgun in hand, Chuck Dunn shouted excitedly,
"He's comin' at me. I got him, boys!"

He raised the gun and squeezed the trigger just as
his horse made a jump. The muzzle flew up. Out of
killing range but close enough for a burn, Shorty Magee's mount caught the force of the pellets across the
rump. The horse bawled and went straight up. Shorty
squalled once, grabbed at the saddlehorn and missed
it. The horse came down without him.

Page Mauldin, old as he was, had caught the fever.
He spurred after the coyote, rope in his hands.

Charlie shouted after him, "Page, you watch yourself!" He had as well have been talking to his own
roan horse. Page had reverted, for the moment at
least, to his wild old cowboy days. Charlie could hear
him yelling in delight, closing in on the coyote. Manuel Flores spurred after him, close behind.

Charlie didn't see what Page ran over, but he saw
the horse spill, saw Page's hat go sailing as if the old

ranchman had thrown it. In a swirl of dust he saw the
horse staggering to its feet, Page hung to the stirrup.
Frightened, the horse began to run.

Charlie swallowed, his heart almost stopping. "Oh
my God!"

But Manuel Flores was there in seconds, grabbing
the loose reins, wrapping them quickly around his
saddlehorn, bringing Page's horse to a stop. Before
Charlie could get there, Page had kicked his foot
free of the stirrup. He lay on his right hip, propped
upon his elbow. Page shook his head, looking around
wildly for a moment, afraid of being kicked by the
horse. But Manuel had led the animal off twelve or
fifteen feet, out of the danger range.

Charlie swung heavily to the ground and found Diego Escamillo had beaten him there. Diego bent down
over his employer, his black eyes wide with concern.
"I'm all right," Page said. He was feeling foolish and
showed it. "Dammit, Charlie, did I do that?"

"You sure as hell did. I thought for a minute you
was one of them kids."

"I reckon I got carried away. But I like to've caught
him."

"And like to've killed yourself. If it hadn't of been
for Manuel, you'd of had your tail in a crack."

Page turned his eyes to Diego. "Get me up from
here. Let's see if there's anything broke."

Diego carefully helped him to his feet. Page took
two or three short, cautious steps. He was shaken but
otherwise all right.

Charlie said, "Hell of a note, the richest man in Rio
Seco brought down by a coyote."

Page Mauldin jerked his chin at Manuel, and Manuel brought him his horse. Diego tried to help Page
back into the saddle, but Page impatiently waved him

away. He mounted stiffly and slow, reaching down to pat the nervous animal on the shoulder. "Be gentle now," he said quietly to the horse. "Wasn't your fault, it was mine." Page turned then to young Manuel.

"Boy, I owe you."

Manuel shrugged, self-conscious at the attention. "It was easy."

"Not from where I was. I'll pay you, boy."

"You don't owe me nothin', Mister Mauldin."

"You got a horse of your own, *muchacho*?"

Manuel glanced at Charlie. He had the exclusive use of a couple, but they really belonged to Charlie; everything on the ranch did. "No, sir."

"You'll have one. I'll give you a colt to raise and break for yourself."

Manuel glanced again at Charlie, his eyes asking if it was all right. Charlie said, "Page, I'll hold you to that. He could use a good horse."

In the dust and confusion the coyote would have been lost had it not been for the flyer. He got the animal lined out, swooped down like an eagle after a baby lamb and sent it rolling with a single shot.

Charlie rode up to the red-faced Chuck Dunn and pointed with his chin. "You better take that gun and go finish the coyote off." But Chuck had lost interest in shooting. Charlie went ahead and gave the animal a *coup de grâce* with his own .12-gauge.

Charlie sat at the supper table with Mary, munching leftover kid from the noon barbecue, eagerly looking at the variety of pies and cakes brought by the women who had spent the day here. He knew he had better eat his fill tonight, for Mary would give them all to the Flores family to prevent his having the plea-

sure of them. Tomorrow there would be nothing for
him but turnip greens.

He had used some salty language in the heat of
frustration this afternoon, but now he chuckled as
the memories came back to him in the comfort and
quiet of the kitchen. Mary demanded, "You going to
tell me, Charlie Flagg, or are you going to sit there
and laugh to yourself all night?"

Charlie shook his head. He doubted it would be
funny to her, but he told the whole story the best he
could. Only a time or two did he catch the flicker of
humor in her eyes. He said, "It was worse than the
wreck of the old 97. Most of them took it in good
humor, though, except Shorty Magee. He was lookin'
for somebody to fight. Tom had to leave the bunch
and take him to town."

"You never did see anything of the second coyote?"

"Not a hair. The one we got was the bitch. I reckon
that old dog-wolf has strayed out of the country."

"Without his mate? That doesn't sound natural to
me. Anytime you find a female, there's usually a male
nearby."

Charlie took that to cover more than just the coyotes; he took it for pride in her sex. He shrugged.
"Comes a time a man just has to get away to himself."

Mary was not impressed. "I'll bet you just missed
him."

"Not hardly. The way we screened them pastures,
not even a jackrabbit could've got by without us
seein' him."

She said indulgently, "Maybe you're overrating
yourselves."

"No-siree. I tell you, we didn't miss a thing."

The telephone rang. Charlie set down his coffee

cup and walked stiffly over to answer it. It was still the same old crank-up wall set August Schmidt had turned over to him years ago. "Hello!" He always shouted as if he were afraid the phone wouldn't work and he wanted them to hear him anyway. "Who is this? . . . Oh, hello, Tom . . . What's that? Doctor's just got through workin' on Shorty? I didn't know Shorty caught any of that buckshot . . . Oh, I see."

He cupped his hand over the mouthpiece and explained to Mary, "Wasn't buckshot, it was prickly pear thorns. When Shorty fell off, he landed square in the pear."

He turned back to the telephone. "What's that you say? You just saw Rounder Pike?" Charlie's eyes widened a bit. "No! That old liar is just hoorawin' you . . . What? He really did? . . . They really did?"

His face gradually fell. He pursed his lips, then drew them back against his teeth, sneaking a quick look at Mary and turning sheepishly away. Charlie finally shrugged. "Okay, son, that's the way it goes sometimes. You can't win them all."

He put the receiver on the wishbone hook and gave the handle a quick turn to signal Central he was through.

Mary waited for him to volunteer the information, but he didn't. She said, "You'd just as well tell me. I'll find out anyway."

Reluctantly Charlie told her, "Couple of wetback Mexicans walked up to Rounder's ranchhouse a little while ago, hungry and awful scared. Seems they was crossin' our west pasture afoot this afternoon. All of a sudden those pickups and jeeps were comin' right at them, and men on horseback and that airplane overhead. They thought every border patrolman in Texas was after them. They took to the brush and hid. Our drive went right over them. They could've raised up their heads and spit on a man. The drive went right on by, but them wetbacks just laid there scared to death.

"And then that old dog-wolf got up out of the same brush and came a-limpin' by them sassy as you please!"

6

Page Mauldin didn't forget his promise to Manuel about giving him a colt. He phoned Charlie one day at noon and told him to bring the boy over after school. Page had a penful of colts up for working; Manuel could take his pick.

Charlie was waiting when Manuel and the other Flores youngsters got home. "We'll go hook the trailer to my green pickup," he told him. Manuel ran to the barn so fast that by the time Charlie got there in his limping gait, the trailer was already hitched up and the pickup motor was running, ready to go. Charlie pointed out that the Flores family cow had not been milked yet.

Lupe smiled warmly at the eagerness in his son's face. "You go on with him, Mister Charlie. I'll milk tonight."

Charlie had always had an eye for horses; he spotted the colts in the pen while he was still two hundred yards away. He drove by Page's rambling old frame house, pulling up beside the corral. Manuel slid out and scrambled up on the fence to look down upon the colts.

Page Mauldin walked out of the saddle shed, followed by Diego and Kathy. Charlie frowned as he saw the girl. She was dressed like a hard-working boy in an old blue work shirt, faded jeans, and a pair of old run-over boots. Capping it all was a cowboy hat that looked as if horses had run over it. Knowing Kathy, Charlie would bet they probably had.

If Mary saw her, she would go out through the roof, Charlie thought.

Page Mauldin shook hands with Charlie and then walked up beneath Manuel, who was most of the way up the fence, bracing his legs against the planks, splintered where horses had chewed on them. "*Muchacho*, you a pretty good judge of horseflesh?"

Manuel shrugged. "I don't know . . . not real good, I guess."

"You can have your pick out of that pen. Whichever one suits you the best."

Charlie had no intention of climbing that fence when he didn't have to. His bad leg didn't need that. He leaned against the boards and peered between them, studying the colts with a practiced eye. In a minute he thought he had located the best pony in the pen, a bay.

Manuel asked, "What do you think, Mister Charlie?"

Charlie wanted to help him, but on the other hand he didn't want to put his oar in. The boy needed to learn to take his own responsibility. Charlie sidestepped. "There's a bunch of good ones, *muchacho*."

"That's the trouble; there's too many good ones."

Charlie glanced at Page to see if the old rancher was going to make some suggestion. But Mauldin just stood there, smiling.

Kathy climbed up on the fence beside Manuel. "How about lettin' me pick him for you?"

Manuel studied her dubiously. "I don't know . . ."

"I've been watchin' these colts ever since they were foaled. I bet you I can place them in one-two-three order, just like a horse show."

Page said, "Now, girl, you let him alone. You let him pick for himself."

Charlie gave Page a moment's study, wondering if the ranchman hoped Manuel *wouldn't* pick the best colt in the pen. Rich men were like that most of the time—tight.

Manuel looked at the horses, then at Kathy, then back at the horses. He said cautiously, "Which one do you think is the best?"

Kathy didn't hesitate. "That bay yonder."

Manuel observed the colt closely. Charlie suspected the boy hadn't really looked at him before; he had been confused by having to choose from so many. Manuel said, "Funny, that's the same one I'd about decided to pick."

Kathy said, "Then you picked real good."

Diego Escamillo glanced at Page, and the rancher nodded. Diego climbed over the fence, rope in his hand, and dropped down inside the corral. He shook out a horse loop, moved carefully toward the colts, swung the rope in a quick figure eight and caught the bay around the neck. Kathy and Manuel jumped down inside the corral and trotted up to Diego. The colt reared back a little against the rope and rolled its nose in alarm. But in a minute the boy and girl both had their arms around its neck and were talking to it as if it were a pet dog.

Diego stood holding the rope and smiling at the two youngsters. He had no family of his own, except his mother who kept house for Page. Long years ago Diego had married a frail little Spanish girl from Del Rio. When time came for the first baby to arrive, he had set out with her for town and had hopelessly stuck his car in a deep hole of mud miles from the ranchhouse, miles from town. The baby had been born right there in the car, a little girl who took a few halting breaths and died. The mother survived it only a couple of days. Diego had never had the heart to marry again. He had helped raise Kathy, watching over her like a mother hen in the absence of a father who was always on the go.

Page ruefully shook his head. "I didn't count on him pickin' the best colt I've raised on this ranch in the last two years."

Charlie grinned. "Then you oughtn't to've had that colt in the pen. You know these Mexican boys . . . they got an eye for good horses."

"Wasn't the boy, it was the girl. My own daughter, she done me in."

"If you'd trained her in the kitchen where she belongs, she wouldn't of done it."

Winter's first norther swept raw and mean out of a clear sky that almost purpled, then turned a dirty brown as the wind howled in. Dust—choking, eye-burning dust—melded sky and horizon line so that Charlie could not tell where one ended and one began. Christmas came and went, but few clouds ever did. The winter rodeo season moved into full swing and Tom Flagg was gone too. He never asked any more; he just went.

As each dry norther came, Charlie marked the date of it on the big feed-store calendar in the kitchen, the one with the picture of the fine whitefaced cows in tall green grass, obviously made a long way from Texas. The only moisture he recorded was a couple of light showers that gave him the taste but none of the substance, and one sleet storm he didn't want at all.

This morning he left the warmth of the big kitchen to step out onto the porch. He turned up the collar of his coat against the frigid blast of a new dry norther and shoved his cold-chapped hands into the flannel-lined pockets. He limped in the direction of the barn, blinking at the bite of the dust. Chunky Lupe Flores had been watching for him; he angled across to join Charlie, shivering a little and glancing toward the dust pall that lay crescent-shaped in the north.

"*Muy frio*," Lupe said. ("Mighty cold.")

Charlie nodded. "Seems like once these northers set a dry pattern, they just won't change."

Lupe made an effort at a joke. "The time old Noah built his Ark, we don't get but a quarter-inch here at Rio Seco."

Charlie had laughed at that joke when he was ten years old. He only grunted now. "If this was meant to be a desert, the Lord would've stocked it with camels."

Lupe stood to one side and made hand signals while Charlie backed the green pickup toward the open barn door. Charlie had done this so much lately he felt he could back into place without even looking behind him. The two men walked into the barn where tall stacks of sacked feed lined each wall. Charlie grabbed the string-tied ears of a sack; Lupe grasped the bottom corners. Together they swung the sack and let it slide across the bed of the pickup, slamming against the steel headache rack that protected the cab. They worked in rhythm, but after a few sacks both men grunted heavily from the exertion. When Charlie had counted ten he waved quit and leaned against a stack to catch his breath. He rubbed his shoulder. Damn rheumatism was bothering him a little there, and in his weak leg as well. The norther, he thought; he was getting to be a better weather prophet than the Weather Bureau. Loading these hundred-pound sacks didn't help, either.

"Wish Tom was here. I'd let *him* handle this little chore."

"Me and you, Mister Charlie, we're gettin' too old."

"Speak for yourself; don't go tryin' to make an old man out of *me*. I can work as hard as I ever did; I just don't like it as much as I used to. That's what I got a husky son for, if he wasn't always off rodeoin'."

"And winnin'," Lupe pointed out with a smile. He was as proud of Tom's rodeo success as Charlie was, for Lupe had helped teach him.

Charlie admitted, "Maybe he's the smart one. Anything beats haulin' feed to a bunch of bawlin' cows and bleatin' old nellies. Just wisht he was home a little more, is all."

The load of feed weighed down heavily on the pickup's springs as they drove into the pasture. Charlie had started feeding earlier than usual this winter. He had been disappointed in his calves' weaning weights last fall, and the prices hadn't been as good as they needed to be for the cost he had put into the cattle. Seemed that in a good year the calves always came up too heavy to suit the buyers and were penalized for being overweight. In a dry year the buyers perversely sought after heavy calves and docked the light ones. It was a hard game to win. At any rate Charlie had put his cattle on feed ahead of schedule to be sure the cows gave milk enough not to stunt their calves from the start. Sheep being better rustlers on short range, he had not intended to feed them at all except for a short spell before lambing time, to build up the milk. But the grass was poor and dry with scant life in it, so all his ewes were on feed before Christmas.

Seeing a little band of sheep, Charlie wheeled the pickup off the two-rut road and bounced out across the pasture toward them. A few cattle came trotting in, their hoofs raising dust in bare spots where the grass was supposed to be. Charlie tried to feed each pasture at as nearly the same hour every day as he could; Nature gave animals a strong sense of time. After a while the livestock knew when to be waiting, and where.

Charlie stopped, idling the engine while Lupe climbed into the bed of the pickup and cut the string on a sack. Then, as Charlie slowly drove in a broad circle, Lupe balanced the sack over the tailgate and dribbled cubes out onto the ground.

A contrary old cow slung her head, belligerently horning all the others out of the way despite the fact that there was a long line of feed and plenty for all. Cows lower down on the pecking order yielded her room and went back to eating. The sheep flocked around indiscriminately, mixing with the cattle, eagerly picking up the small cubes. They would not let any go to waste; they would nose out any the cattle's hoofs pressed into the dirt.

Lupe crawled into the pickup cab again, the cold wind drawing a chilling breath through as he held the door open. Slamming it, he twisted his shoulders to look out the rear window.

"You know somethin', Mister Charlie? It makes me feel good to see stock eat."

"Me too, if I'm not havin' to pay for it. But every time we haul out a pickup load of feed, that's forty dollars shot to hell."

As they approached each bunch of cattle or sheep, Charlie would pause long enough to look at them all, to assess their condition. Occasionally he would lean out the window and call to Lupe: "Let's feed this bunch a little more; appears they're goin' downhill a mite." Or again: "Taper off a shade; these are doin' fine."

In almost every string of sheep he saw some older ewes he wished he had sold last fall when the market was still decent. It wouldn't do to ship them now, for the midwinter market was draggy; nobody bought ewes in the wintertime except the packers. Last fall Charlie had decided to hold his older ewes and gamble that it would rain. So many people were selling their flocks short, he figured a good rain would mean a spirited demand by people trying to restock. The man who plugged along and kept his ewes stood a nice chance to turn a profit. But now he could see that a fair percentage of his older ewes weren't going to lamb at all. There hadn't been enough green feed last fall to bring them into heat, and all they had received from the bucks was companionship. If Charlie was not careful he might put more feed into them than their wool next spring would pay for, and not have lambs to sell either. A poker player was not half the gambler that a man in the ranch business was.

Now Charlie was hoping for an early-spring rain to bail him out, to help him stop feeding before long.

When the last of the feed was poured, the two men spent the rest of the morning working on a windmill which Charlie had named Pee Wee because it afforded only a small stream of water. Lately it hadn't pumped at all. Even in wintertime, livestock needed plenty of water.

It was noon when they drove into the ranch yard. Even cold and hungry, Charlie didn't look forward to mealtime with much anticipation. When he and Mary were alone in the big house there was a cold emptiness Charlie couldn't get used to. It was a cavernous old place with big, lonely rooms and a deadly quiet. They seemed to have little to talk about; he had wearied of discussing dry weather, and Mary had wearied of hearing about it. Often as not, the loneliness drove Charlie to the refuge of the barn and corrals, or across the yard to sit awhile with the Flores family and listen to the shouts and laughter and happy thumping of bare brown feet. Mary had turned more and more to visiting friends in town and to a bridge club she had joined years ago but never used to find time for.

Winter wore on relentlessly with a constant series of cold, dry winds that droned a dusty dirge across the hills and prairies, robbing strength from thinning livestock, seeking out and stealing any vestige of moisture that might still cling in hidden places. Out of necessity, feeding became heavier; it took fifteen sacks of cake a day rather than ten to keep the cattle from showing their ribs. It took longer now to circle the pastures and see that the sheep and cattle received extra protein to supplement the meager dry feed they still managed to rustle on the range. Charlie and Lupe each went in their separate pickups now, splitting the work because there was so much of it.

Charlie's eyes narrowed grimly as he watched the feed trucks drive in periodically to replenish the diminishing stacks in the barn. He read the bills and wrote the checks and was thankful he had always been of a saving nature.

Still, whenever a man got to feeling sorry for himself in this part of the country he had only to look to Mexico to see someone in worse condition. Drouth had become a crippling plague down there—starving the fields, starving the livestock, starving the people. The migration of Mexican wetbacks swelled steadily. More and more of them stopped by the ranch, hats in hand, to ask for a job or for something to eat. Desperation lay dark in hungry eyes. More often than not, the *hombres* wore ragged clothes which no longer fit them. Sometimes their trousers were tied with a length of cord to keep them from falling. Charlie would watch a Mexican hungrily eat raw lard or bacon grease straight out of a can to satisfy some awful craving, and he would feel his stomach turn over.

Occasionally he came across a wetback far out in the pasture, heading north afoot. Often they scurried for cover, fearing he might be a border patrolman. Once an old Mexican walked to him with his trembling hands in the air, expecting Charlie to clamp steel cuffs on him and take him to jail. Instead, Charlie took him to the house and filled his belly, then pointed him north, into the raw wind. There was more work to the north, and fewer *chotas*.

When his back ached from lifting feed sacks, Charlie was sorely tempted to hire one of these men for however long he might be able to keep him. It was not the law which stopped him; Charlie shared the Mexican's dim view of hard and fast boundary lines. He considered the law to have been passed in ignorance by people a thousand miles away who would not accept the jobs themselves and knew no one who would. The same people who cried to keep foreign workers out were happy to bring foreign wool in so they could buy it cheaper. That way they hanged the rancher on two scaffolds at the same time.

"No," he told Lupe Flores, "I got a reputation among the *chotas* as bein' a rancher that don't hire wetbacks. They don't bother me. If I ever get to the point that I *have* to hire one, maybe I'll be able to get away with it awhile."

Wherever the coyote had been, he came back. Charlie's fresh lamb crop was too much temptation. Charlie looked at the chewed-up remains of the first baby lamb and felt his stomach sinking. Before many days there were more. That same old crippled wolf, the tracks showed. And the trapper's results were as negative as before.

A wolf drive was out of the question now. Horsemen would stir up the sheep too much for the safety of the new lambs. A cow separated from her calf would hunt until she found it. A ewe lost from her lamb did not concern herself long; the lamb was abandoned, while for the ewe life went on as always. Much as Charlie hated the thought of the bloody sacrifice, he knew it was better to lose lambs on the installment plan than to risk wholesale starvation by cutting them off from their mothers.

One cold, miserable day Charlie—by pure accident— came upon the old coyote in the middle of a pasture far from headquarters. Charlie was riding an owl-headed brown horse that cow trader Tooter Thomas had palmed off on him, one Charlie had been trying unsuccessfully to trade to someone equally unwary. It had been years since he had owned a horse he considered to be in the same class with Wander, but he could not afford to ride the roan to death. Sometimes he had to accept second best.

A cold rain set in after Charlie left the barn. It was not enough to put usable moisture in the ground—just enough to soak his clothing and chill him through.

Only time it's rained this winter and it catches me six miles from the house, he thought irritably. On a day like this it was easy to be irritable. If there had been enough rain to grow some grass or weeds, he would be happy to get wet.

Another damn teaser. I'd as soon have the sunshine.

His sudden confrontation with the coyote was as much a surprise to one as to the other. Without warning Charlie was hauling up on the reins and looking into the amber eyes of the predator which had just walked out of the mesquite not twenty feet away. It was a pitifully old coyote with blackish-brown coat ragged from uneven winter growth. His flanks were lean. Probably his hearing and his eyes had begun to go bad on him. His crippled forefoot, which he held up in front of him, was another handicap he was too old to overcome. Chances were he subsisted mostly on rats and such—and sheep. A rabbit had sense enough to run. A sheep, likely as not, would stand and stamp its foot until it was too late to get away. And even if it ran, it would soon stop to see if the coyote was still coming.

A sheep perpetually courted disaster just by being a sheep.

For a moment Charlie and the coyote held their ground and stared at each other, dumfounded. Then the coyote whipped back and sprinted away on its three good legs. Charlie yanked the hornstring loose and grabbed up his rope. He tied it to the horn, shook out a loop and went spurring.

As a young man in coyote country along the Pecos, Charlie had tried several times to rope a coyote. Only once had he ever made a catch. He saw little chance of doing it now. But here he was, and there was that sheep-killer, and the rope was the only weapon he had.

For a fleeting second Charlie thought he saw a man watching from the brush, and the sight gave him a start. But there was no time for speculation. The coyote was getting away.

The lazy brown horse lagged. Cursing, Charlie swung the loop back over his shoulder and lashed the animal's rump. The brown leaped forward, his hind end momentarily seeming about to overtake the fore part.

Sensing the horse was closing, the coyote darted to one side. Charlie's left hand drew hard on the rein, and the horse followed. Charlie kept touching spurs to the brown's hide, not jabbing him but simply reminding him who the boss was. Once more the coyote turned back, this time almost under the horse.

Charlie flipped out a small, fast loop, the kind he had learned on the Pecos and had taught to Tom. He saw it drop around the coyote. "Now, you sheep-killin' devil . . ." He sucked a sharp breath between his teeth and yanked the slack up tight like a fisherman setting a hook. The loop fitted around the coyote's neck and the bad foreleg. Charlie hauled back on the reins, sliding the brown to a stop. The coyote flipped over backward, yelping. Instantly it was up and darted between the horse's legs. In panic the brown snorted and jumped. The coyote went under, trailing the rope. As the horse came down, one hind leg caught in the tangle of lariat.

"*Whoa-a-a*, you jugheaded idiot!"

Caught off balance, Charlie lost a stirrup. The brown bawled in fear and began to pitch, entangling itself more. The loose stirrup flopped up and down while Charlie grabbed for the horn. His rump hit the saddle, hard, then he was up again, this time far out to one side.

"*Whoa-a-a* there, I'll . . ."

That was all he managed to say. He bumped behind the cantle, and he knew he was gone. Instinctively he kicked the other foot out of the stirrup to keep from being hung to the saddle. One more jump and he sailed clear. He landed on his feet, but his weak left leg caved under him with a pain like the hard thrust of a beef-carving knife.

Busted her again, goddammit! he thought as the muddy ground flew up and slammed the wind out of him.

He lay struggling for breath, pain flashes darting wildly before his eyes. The brown horse took out as fast as it could run. Caught helpless in the rope, the coyote bounced up and down like a matchbox behind a freight train.

There wouldn't be enough left of him for bait. Charlie would have felt a little sorry for him if he hadn't seen so many dead sheep.

Slowly getting his breath back, Charlie pushed up onto his hands and knees, then managed to stretch the aching leg out in front of him. He wiped mud from his hands onto his khaki pants and gingerly felt of the leg. Pain popped cold sweat onto his face. Presently he was sure of one thing: the leg had not rebroken.

He pushed to his feet, but pain pierced him so fiercely that he eased to the ground again. Sprained ankle, that's what it was. He couldn't walk on it. Yet, he couldn't stay here, and it was a cinch that brown horse wasn't coming back to fetch him.

If he had been in a pasture closer to home, the horse probably would return to the barn sooner or later. Someone would see it and know there was trouble. But out here too many fences separated him from headquarters. The brown would wander aimlessly over the pasture, finally finding a windmill somewhere and going to water. He couldn't go home until somebody took him.

It was worth it, Charlie thought, getting rid of that damn coyote. But this is one hell of a mess.

He wouldn't be missed until night, when he failed to show up for supper. By then it would be dark, and he would stand about as much chance of being found in the dark as a snowball stands in hell. Best he could hope for was to sit here until tomorrow. He was already wet and cold, and before long he would probably be hungry. There was no dry wood with which to start a fire, and damn few matches in his pocket. By tomorrow morning he would probably be coughing his lungs out with pneumonia.

Looks like, Brother Wolf, we got each other.

He made another painful try to get to his feet. He found he could stand, but he could not put enough weight on the left leg to walk. He looked about for something that might serve as a crutch. And he saw the man.

A Mexican, afoot, moved uncertainly toward Charlie, halting at intervals as if undecided whether to come ahead or to cut and run. For a moment, before he collected his wits, Charlie felt the same way.

He shivered. It was spooky, seeing somebody out here like this, unexpectedly, so far from anywhere. Given a moment to think, he knew what the man was—a wetback crossing the country.

"*Está bueno*," Charlie called. "*No tenga miedo*." ("It's all right. Don't be scared.")

It would be raw irony now for the Mexican to panic and run away when Charlie needed him so badly. For a moment or two it appeared he would. The Mexican *was* scared, but he came on, a few feet at a time. A dozen paces from Charlie he stopped, wary as a young bronc. "You are not a patrolman?" he asked in Spanish.

"No. *Soy ranchero*."

The Mexican was young, around twenty or twenty-one, best Charlie could judge. He had several days' growth of whiskers that had not yet lost a youthful softness. His face was thin. An unhealthy pallor lay dull where the strong brown color should have been. His clothes were too large, though Charlie figured they probably had fit him once. The boy coughed. This cold rain, and the kid had only a worn-out cotton jacket that turned neither water nor wind.

The boy got his throat clear. "You put on a fine show, *señor*."

Charlie grunted and replied in the boy's language. "It was not meant for a show." He stared at the young wetback, and a tug of ancient prejudice came unbidden. For a moment he felt a stir of resentment for his dependence upon this stray Mexican. He felt somehow belittled. But the moment passed, and he was grateful for whatever quirk of chance had placed this boy here.

"My leg is hurt. Will you help me, *muchacho*?"

"Whatever I can do, *patrón*."

"I cannot walk on this leg, and I cannot sit out here all night in the cold, waiting for help."

The boy looked him over. "I cannot carry you. But perhaps I could help you walk."

"That is the best we can do."

The foot was swelling. The boot was already much too tight to slip off. Charlie looked regretfully a moment at the good Leddy boot, wishing he could save it. But he could buy more boots; this was the only left foot the good Lord was ever going to give him. He took out his sharp pocketknife and cut a long slit in the leather to ease the pressure.

"A shame," said the boy.

Charlie shrugged agreeing. Those boots had cost him forty-five dollars new. He pointed his chin at the floppy-sole pair the young man wore. "You are a cowboy?"

"*Sí.*"

Charlie wondered about that. He had seen many a man—Mexican and Anglo—who claimed to be a cowboy but couldn't pour water out of a boot if the directions were printed on the heel. "Have you ever worked on a ranch?"

"*Sí,* all my life I have lived on one ranch. My father was born there before me."

Charlie knew, but he asked anyway. "Why are you here, then?"

"The cattle die because there is no grass. There is nowhere to sell them. Our *patrón* can no longer keep us all."

Charlie wished he had a dollar for every time he had heard substantially the same story, and always true. The thought crossed his mind that this boy, with ranch experience, might be good help around the place.

"Let's try it now." He put his left arm around the

boy's shoulder. They began a slow, tortured movement in the direction of the house. Charlie found he could not lean heavily on the boy; the Mexican was not strong enough to support him. Even with help, Charlie had to put weight on the injured left foot. He would take ten or twelve steps, then stop, his teeth clenched. It was like stepping into a bank of live coals without a boot on.

They stopped often to rest. After what seemed an hour, Charlie looked back. He could still see where he had roped the coyote.

"A turtle could outrun us," he gritted.

"A turtle would have four good legs. We have only three."

Once while they rested the boy pondered, "Perhaps I could find the horse."

"You couldn't catch him, not afoot."

An hour of painful limping brought them at last to the two-rut windmill road. Charlie sank to the ground, breathing hard. "This is as far as I can go, *muchacho*."

The boy was nearly exhausted too from supporting so much of Charlie's weight. "Is it still a long way from the house?"

"A long way." Charlie rubbed his foot, grimacing at the throbbing, searing pain. It had swollen so that he knew he would have to finish cutting that boot off when he got home . . . *if* he got home.

The boy began to cough. They were booming coughs that came from down deep and doubled him over. *He's in worse shape than I am,* Charlie thought. *But at least he can still walk.*

"*Muchacho,* would you go on to the house and get help? You can find it easily now. Just follow this road."

The boy was dubious. "What of the *chotas*?"

"We never see *chotas*." Well, almost never.

The Mexican looked uneasily down the road.

Charlie said, "There is medicine for you at the house. And money."

The boy took a step or two and stopped. "I need work, *señor*."

"I have no work for you, but I will pay you to bring help. You will be fed and given a bed."

The boy broke into a fit of coughing. Reluctantly he said, "*Bueno*, I will go." He started down the road.

Charlie called after him. "I never did ask you your name."

The boy turned. "José. José Rivera."

"Come back for me, José."

"I will be back, *señor*."

Charlie sat in the middle of the road and watched the boy as long as he could see him. He lost sight of him where the old road made a bend around a live-oak motte. Trembling with cold, his clothes still wet, Charlie broke up a dead mesquite limb and whittled away the wet bark with his knife. He pared off a pile of dry shavings. Then he began trying to build a fire. But the chilly west wind blew out each match before he could get the shavings to blaze up. In a few minutes his last match was gone.

"Son of a bitch," he muttered, shivering. He sat on the damp ground, staring helplessly at the pile of shavings and the scattering of dead matches. He thought dismally of the thousands of times he could have built a fire and didn't.

A dark loneliness settled over him. The boy had said he would be back, but Charlie was not sure. An old Anglo feeling took hold of him: *you never can depend on a Mexican.* But he couldn't blame the boy much if he didn't come back. Chances were this was Rivera's first time across the river. He was skittish as a bobwhite quail. In his mind the border patrol was trailing him, and he was scared. When he reached the ranch headquarters he would circle it as warily as a coyote stalking a henhouse, watching for a booger. At the first sign of anything suspicious he would break and run for the brush.

And Charlie Flagg would sit out here all night, soaked through and chilled to the bone.

Trembling, Charlie looked at his pocketwatch again and again. Wouldn't be long now till dark, and then he'd be in a fix sure enough. That's what a man got for setting his hopes too high. That's what a man got for putting all his hopes on a damn Mexican kid. He knew sure as hell he would never again see or hear anything of that ragged *mojado.*

The west wind was whistling through the mesquites with a breath bitter and icy, and it was a long way from spring.

Charlie heard the rattle of Lupe's blue pickup before it came around the live-oak trees and into view, an empty horse-trailer bouncing behind it. For a moment he did not believe what he saw. He shouted involuntarily. He pushed to his feet and hopped to the edge of the road, a happy grin breaking across his cold-purpled face despite the pain in his leg.

Lupe braked the pickup to a fast stop and jumped out, his eyes wide with concern. "You hurt bad, Mister Charlie?"

Charlie was so glad to see him he pumped his

hand. "Not now, but I was by way of givin' up. You and this old pickup are the prettiest damn things I've seen all day."

Lupe took Charlie's arm around his shoulder and gave him support. "I got the heater goin'. Pretty soon now you get warm."

Charlie hobbled the few steps with Lupe's help and grabbed onto the door handle. He glanced at the trailer. Lupe said, "I brought Manuel and his horse. I let him out at the gate, and I told him, 'You go see if you find Mister Charlie his brown horse, else he tear up a good saddle.'"

Lupe raised the pickup seat and lifted out a bundle wrapped in a gunny sack. It was a half-empty bottle of whiskey. "This," he said, handing it to Charlie, "I keep here just for sometime like now."

Charlie had long suspected it, but he had never seen Lupe with a bottle. What little Lupe had ever drunk had not been enough to impair him in his work. Under the circumstances Charlie had no inclination to reprimand him. Next chance he got he would buy Lupe another bottle. He wondered why *he* hadn't thought of this for the cold days, a survival kit under the seat of his own pickup.

He slid in, careful not to bump the injured ankle against the door. The warmth of the noisy old heater brought one shivering spasm of chills to him, then he began warming. He took a long pull on the bottle and handed it back. "Lupe, you're worth a million dollars. Only, don't ever ask me for it."

"Mister Charlie, you look like you catch the double pneumonia. We better get you to bed."

"I'll make it now. I ain't nobody's baby."

"That's what the trouble is: it is too long since you *was* a baby."

Charlie grumbled, "You know what it is that makes a man get old? It's people tellin' him so all the time till he gets to believin' it." He thought of José. "That wetback kid . . . he got in all right, did he?"

Lupe nodded and started the pickup moving. In low gear it sounded like a coffee grinder. He made a wide circle, heedlessly smashing down the winter-brittle brush, and bounced back into the road, heading toward the house. "Yep, Mister Charlie. Without that boy, I don't know where to look for you."

Charlie frowned. "He's got an apology comin' to him. I wouldn't of given a plugged nickel for the chance that he would go in."

"He's one pretty sick boy. Rosa, she's make him take a hot bath, then she's move Candelario and Juan and Manuel out of their room and put that boy in it. He has the double pneumonia, I think."

Lupe had had double pneumonia himself once, fifteen years ago. Now when someone came up with a runny nose, he immediately predicted double pneumonia. It was a thing he had personally come to grips with, and learned to respect.

"Did you call a doctor?"

Lupe shook his head. "This boy, he is a wetback. Maybe the doctor, he tells the *chotas*."

"I'll call Doc Fancher. He's higher than a sycamore tree, but he minds his own business."

"You think he would come out here for a wetback?"

"He's a doctor. He reads symptoms, not pedigrees."

Lupe drove Charlie up to the main house. Getting out first, he hurried around the pickup and gave Charlie help up the steps. Mary's eyes showed anxiety for a moment, but she quickly covered it up. Holding the screen door open, she said with just a touch of sarcasm, "Fell off, did you?" She didn't believe in giving a man sympathy; it went to his head.

"Throwed off. *Throwed* off, woman. There's a difference."

"*Fell* off. A man your age tryin' to rope a coyote like some twelve-year-old button . . . you *should* have fallen off."

"I caught him, though. Damn horse . . . when I can get to it I'm goin' to sell him to a buyer for a soap factory, and I'm goin' to buy me a whole case of that soap, and then I'm goin' to . . ." He ran out of steam. He didn't know what he *was* going to do, except sit down as soon as he could. He demanded of Mary, "You been over to Rosa's to see about that boy?"

"I went. He's pretty sick."

"We better call the doctor, then. Lupe, help me to the phone."

Charlie leaned his shoulder against the wall and turned the crank. "Hello, Central?" he yelled. "Get me Doc Fancher." A long pause. "Is Doc Fancher there? . . . Sure, I want to talk to him. Why else would I of called? . . . Well, tell him he can eat supper later. I ain't had mine either." Another long pause. "Doc, Charlie Flagg. We got a sick boy out here, and I want you to come to see after him . . . No, I can't bring him in . . . Why? Because the Immigration would fine me so much I couldn't pay your damned exorbitant fee, that's why . . . Yeah, he's one of *them,* but if it hadn't of been for him you'd probably have to treat me for the double pneumonia." He started to hang up but added: "And while you're out here I'll let you look at my ankle. I got it sprained . . . No, I won't tell you how; that's *my* business. You just get your lard butt out here!"

He hung up the receiver and gave the crank a short twist. "One thing I learned a long time ago about them city people . . . you got to talk to them in language they understand."

The doctor was a short, chunky man built something like banker Rodale, for comfort rather than speed. In a grave voice he could prescribe sugared water for a hypochondriac, then hint that it might be well if the patient settled all his bills quickly, "just in case." There was a streak of mean in him. He rubbed Charlie's swollen foot firmly while Charlie went three shades of white. "Hurts, doesn't it?" said the doctor.

"I didn't have to pay you to find that out," Charlie answered tightly.

"But you *will*. You know I missed supper on account of your little cowboy stunt."

Charlie glowered at him through half-closed eyes. "I been wonderin' who the third one was. Now I know."

"The third what?"

"That sign at the edge of town, the one that tells about the three old cranks. I figured me and Big Emmett was two. It's bothered me a right smart tryin' to decide who the third one was. Now I won't have to worry about it any more."

The doctor's sensitive fingers explored the ankle while Charlie muttered under his breath and twisted one of Mary's fancy doilies to the point of ruin. "I don't suppose I could get you to come to town for an X ray?" Charlie shook his head, and the doctor said, "I didn't think I could. I'm sure you didn't do any lasting damage except to your pride, and you've got an excess of that anyway. You keep your weight off of that foot after I wrap it."

"I got a ranch to run. I can't stay off of this foot."

Fancher said, "It's always been a mystery to me why people will go to great expense to get a doctor's advice, then ignore it."

Charlie's brow wrinkled. "What do you mean, great expense?"

"You'll know when you get my bill."

The doctor stayed for supper; Mary wouldn't have it any other way. Now that Charlie was over his chill he found he was ravenously hungry. "What about that Mexican boy, Doc?"

"I gave him a shot of penicillin and left some medicine with Mrs. Flores. Maybe she'll give it to him and maybe she won't. You know how Mexicans are. If he doesn't come along, call me and I'll be back."

"Thanks, Doc." Charlie frowned awhile in silence, busying himself eating his supper, even a few turnip greens. "I'd as soon you didn't mention this to anybody. After what that boy done for me, I'd hate to see the *chotas* pick him up."

"I have a territorial agreement with the border patrol. I don't look for wetbacks and they don't practice medicine."

Rosa Flores shushed her playing children. "Don't you remember there's a sick man in yonder?" She sniffed suspiciously at the bottle of pink medicine the doctor had left. Facing Lupe, she shook her head with disapproval. "It doesn't smell as if it had any life in it." She had switched to Spanish now, for this was a thing that did not concern the children. They understood Spanish perfectly, of course, but when Rosa spoke in Spanish to Lupe it was a sign that it was none of their business. They quieted down so they could hear better.

Lupe held the bottle under his nose, unimpressed. "What is it?"

"Sulfa-something, the doctor said. Supposed to help break the fever. But the way to break a fever is to burn it out; everybody knows that. Bring me the bottle of whiskey you keep hidden under the seat of the pickup."

Lupe blinked. "Shame, woman, to accuse me so."

"I do not accuse you; I simply know it is there. Bring it!"

Lupe shrugged and wondered why, of all the women in the world, it befell his lot to marry one so crafty. She was a good wife in most of the marriage arts, but a man did not always want a wife to know so much. It seemed to him sometimes that Charlie Flagg had the same kind of trouble. Why *they*, of all men? He walked out to fetch the whiskey.

On the butane stove Rosa was brewing a strong cup of tea. When its color was dark enough to suit her, she poured a healthy portion into the cup, considered, and added a little more. She held the bottle up to the light, noting that it was not far from empty.

"It has been a long winter," Lupe shrugged, turning away to roll a brown-paper cigarette and avoiding her prying eyes.

In the boys' room, seventeen-year-old Anita Flores stood by the wall, staring in curiosity at the young man who lay on the bed, his face and beard dark against the white pillowcase and sheet. Sweat glistened on his forehead.

Anita looked up as her mother came in with the tea.

"I don't think he's really asleep," she whispered. "His eyes are closed, but he is restless and keeps turning."

"All right, you go on about your business." Rosa shook the boy's shoulder. "Can you raise up?"

He opened his eyes and blinked, his gaze finally fastening on her. "I think so," he said, and pushed up on his elbow.

"Drink this." Rosa held the cup to his lips. He took a long swallow and coughed violently. Rosa held the cup until he became settled again, then once more put it to his lips. "Drink it all now. It will do you much good." She watched the boy struggle to force it down. "Men," she said loudly enough that Lupe could hear her in the other room. "When it is for fun they will drink like a fish. But when it is for their own good they fight it."

The cup empty, José Rivera sank back onto the pillow. Anita Flores stepped up with a damp cloth and touched it carefully to his brow, pity in her dark eyes. "Mama, is the doctor sure he's going to be all right?"

"Nothing is ever sure except debt and death. But he should be all right when he sweats the fever away. We'll put on more blankets."

"He's very young, isn't he?"

Rosa's brow furrowed. She took the damp cloth from her daughter. "And he is a *mojado*, too, remember that." She pointed to the door. "You go make down pallets on the living-room floor so the boys can get to sleep."

Anita stood with her hands behind her back and stared at the boy. "I wonder what he will look like with all those whiskers shaved away?"

"He will still look like a *mojado*. Go on, do what I tell you."

The girl stopped at the door and looked back. "I'll bet he is handsome."

If there was anything good to be said for a duster, it was that once the storm was over the land seemed reborn. Perhaps it was only the contrast, but the sand-scoured air smelled clean, with almost a rain-washed freshness, when the dust had settled. One welcomed the calming of the wind as a soldier welcomes the stilling of the guns.

Crutch under his arm, Charlie hobbled onto the screened front porch. The winter sharpness was gone today; the sun's warmth was gentle and kind to a man's nagging rheumatism. He called to Mary, "Sure is a pretty day. Makes me want to go back to work."

She came out to look critically at him, and across the still yard. "Well, you're not going to. It won't break Lupe's back to struggle along without you another day or two. There's no school today, and he's got Manuel to help him."

Charlie grumbled. "What if I didn't have Lupe? I'd *have* to work."

"The point is, you *do* have him. If you feel like you have to work, you can help me pick the rocks out of some beans."

He let his voice go sour. "And hold your knittin' for you, I suppose?" He turned and moved past her, back into the house, swinging along and cursing this unwieldy, galling, devilish crutch. He had hated crutches since the time he had broken his left leg. The doctor had told him later he would not have so much of a limp today if he had not put the crutches away too soon. Charlie found his closet door ajar and used the end of the crutch to push it wide open. Leaning his shoulder against the jamb, he began poking through the clothes. The crutch slid to the floor with a bang.

Mary demanded, "What're you looking for? I'll get it for you if you'll stop tearing everything up."

"Lookin' for the cane I used to have in this closet. I've had me a gutful of that crutch."

"Just the same, you'll stay on it. You know what Doc Fancher said."

"That quack? What does he know?"

She bent and picked up the crutch. "Enough that people pay him for his advice. When was the last time anybody paid you for yours?" She pushed the crutch at him. "Here!"

Charlie muttered, but he took it. Mary firmly closed the closet door, punctuating the end of an argument that had not properly even started.

He said, "Anybody was to drop in, they'd get the idea you think I'm a ten-year-old boy."

She nodded stiffly. "Yes, they might."

Charlie turned away on the crutch. *Anybody ever marries one of them squareheaded Dutch women, he'd better figure on catching hell.* He bumped across the living-room floor and picked up his grease-spotted hat.

She said, "I told you, Charlie, I don't think you ought to go out."

"I heard you." He put the hat on his head and pulled it down firmly. He slipped his khaki jacket on and had a hand on the doorknob when he turned to ask, "You been over and talked to Rosa this mornin'?"

"I was there."

"How's the patient?"

"He was up and around the house all day yesterday, working on leather for the boys. While ago I saw him go to the barn."

"Good. I need to talk to him. Soon's he looks fit to travel, I'll slip him a little money and help him be on his way."

Mary frowned. "Charlie . . . ?" Her voice was softer. "Do you have to? I mean, with that game ankle you could use some help. Lupe and Rosa are kind of taken with this boy."

"He's a wetback. Border patrol ever hears about him, they'll grab him up. Best favor we can do him is to send him north. Once he gets above San Angelo he's got a chance."

"It seems a shame. But I reckon you'll do what you think is best."

I always do, he thought, *once I get out of this house.* "I don't make the laws. I wisht sometimes I *could.*"

He started across the yard, cursing the clumsy crutch. A little black dog that Candelario had brought home from school came trotting out from the barn to meet him. It wagged its tail so hard it seemed to lift up its hind quarters in the effort. Charlie had seen Arkansas-type oak-motte hogs that appeared to be all head; this dog seemed all tail. "*Andele, perro,*" Charlie growled. "Git out of the way." But the dog stayed with him, its tail striking his crutch. As a sheepman, Charlie's first impulse was to dislike the dog; any dog was a potential sheep killer if it ever got the taste of blood. But this nondescript black pup had attached itself to Charlie with a blind affection that hadn't been asked for. Charlie was stuck with it, like it or not. "*Bueno, bueno,* don't knock the crutch out from under me!" The dog ran ahead, then wheeled back and barked happily, tail jerking its whole body. "Silly mutt," Charlie said, "I can't run with you."

Candelario popped his head out the barn door, then disappeared back inside. Charlie heard him say, "*Está bueno. Es el patrón.*" ("It's all right. It's the boss.")

Candelario and José sat spraddle-legged on the wooden floor of the saddle shed, long leather straps spread out before them. José was using a set of leather-stamping tools Tom Flagg had once begged for until Charlie bought them. Tom had soon wearied of leather work, as he wearied of almost anything he could not do on horseback.

"*Qué tál?*" Charlie said. "*Como está?*"

"Okay," the young man grinned self-consciously. "Much okay." He reverted to Spanish. "Candelario is teaching me English."

Candelario pointed happily, "José is making something pretty out of my old bridle. Just looky there, Mister Charlie."

José was putting a flower design on a plain leather headstall Charlie had bought once for Candelario. It was as neat a job as Charlie had ever seen in a professional saddle shop. "That is good. How did you learn?"

"One must learn something if one is not to be a cowboy all his life. But I found a saddlemaker can become hungry too, when no one can buy a saddle. I went back to being a cowboy."

"Bad luck."

"*No le importa,*" José shrugged. "My father was a cowboy. A man is what his father was. If his father was poor, *he* will be poor. It has always been so. He has little chance to get away unless he can become a politician and steal. I have not the head for politics."

Charlie had long observed the Mexican people's

stoic acceptance of fate, but he had never quite approved of it. He had no patience with anything that put an arbitrary limit on a man, that held him back from doing the best he was capable of and being rewarded for it to whatever extent the market would bear.

"Feeling better, José?"

"Much better. I could ride a horse now. I could work if you would let me."

Charlie leaned against a saddle rack, sticking the crutch out in front of him as a prop. His eyes narrowed. "As I told you before, I do not need any extra help."

José pointed his chin at the crutch. "With that, there are many things you cannot do. I can do them for you."

"I know, boy, but . . ."

Candelario piped up, "Let's keep him, Mister Charlie. I'll help you pay him."

Charlie glanced quizzically at the boy. "With what?"

"I get a nickel every schoolday to buy a bar of candy to go with my lunch. I don't need any candy."

"Every boy needs candy, son; the sugar helps make you run fast."

José pushed to his feet. "Look, *patrón*, I can ride any horse. I have always been a good bronc rider."

"We have no broncs here. I buy my horses already broken."

"What about that horse that threw you?"

"He is not a bronc. He is just a jughead."

"Then I will ride your jugheads for you."

Charlie shook his head. This *majado* must have been something to listen to when he was trying to sell someone a saddle.

"Look, *señor,* see how I can rope." José took a rope down from Charlie's racked saddle. He stepped into the sunshine and shook out a loop. "Candelario, run away from me."

Candelario ran. The black pup ran with him, barking in foolish excitement. José swung the loop, threw it, and jerked up the slack around Candelario's belly.

Candelario laughed as he loosened the loop and dropped it to the ground, stepping out of it. "Just like Tom, Mister Charlie."

Tom. That only served to remind Charlie that he hadn't heard from his son in two or three weeks; he was off chasing the rodeo circuit from Cape Cod to Hickory Bend. *We already got one roper too many around here,* he thought. *But this Mexican knows what he's doing, and that's the truth.*

The young man's eyes pleaded. "Please, *patrón,* there are many other things I can do, things I have not shown you. I will work hard, and I will never complain."

Charlie had it on his tongue to say *no* again, but he couldn't get it said. If Tom were here, pulling his weight, it might be different. Charlie looked at José, then at Candelario. The little boy's eyes pleaded even more than José's. Charlie reached down and picked up the headstall from the floor.

"That brown horse rubbed my bridle off somewhere the other day. It's lost out in the pasture. Could you make *me* one like that?"

He found Mary seated at the kitchen table, dry pinto beans spread out in front of her. She was carefully picking out the scattered few rocks, raking the clean beans noisily into an aluminum pan. Pushing down the reading glasses she used any more for close work, she looked up at Charlie. "Well, did you tell him?"

Charlie shrugged and went poking through a stack of newspapers for the latest issue of the *West Texas Livestock Weekly.* "What are you so all-fired anxious to have him leave here for?"

7

Though it was April, Manuel Flores's bay colt was still shaggy; he had not shed off his winter coat and slicked down for the spring. He was getting more nourishment out of a feed trough than he was finding in the pasture.

Manuel hung his milk bucket on a fence post and went through the corral gate to pet the horse a little; the milk cow could wait. The colt walked up and nuzzled him, looking for the sugar or the carrot or the piece of apple Manuel usually brought him every afternoon as soon as the Flores youngsters came home from school.

The north wind scooped up dust from the pen and flung it into Manuel's eyes. He ran his tongue over his teeth to remove the grit. At the barn he watched his father and José Rivera swing sacks of cottonseed cake onto the two ranch pickups for the next day's feeding. Charlie Flagg stood by a fender, silently supervising. It was a job that did not require much instruction. Manuel knew the feeding should have ended much earlier than this. He knew it was like no spring he had known on Brushy Top.

He had been born in the white frame house, and he had slept few nights away from it in his life. As a small boy his senses had come fully alive only when he was outdoors, and this feeling for the open remained unchanged. He responded instinctively to the sun and the wind and to the animals which fed on this land. He sensed the seasonal ebb and flow of life in the ground beneath his feet. He sensed birth and death and rebirth, as generations of his forebears had sensed it living tied to the earth.

Where in other years he had enjoyed the cool freshness of April rain, the smell of green grass and the splash of wild flowers spread like an Indian blanket across the valleys, he found now the parched smell of dust. Spring weeds made a try, then seemed to draw back into the ground like some wild animal too early out of hibernation. Old grass left from last year showed a touch of green at its base, but the color could climb no higher and would shortly retreat again. Only the brush—the mesquites and live oaks and cedars—produced any solid green. Their roots went deep, where water still hid from the sun. He heard grizzled *viejos* say there had been a drouth far back in the past when even these had died.

He noted that when men met, whether Anglo or Mexican, the first subject to come up was usually rain. The parting words were almost invariably something like, "Maybe we'll get a rain pretty soon," stated hopefully but with little conviction, as if fishing for some supporting comment from the other party, a leaning together for strength. Manuel found it an empty and tiresome ritual, but he understood it. Drouth had become the overriding concern not only of the Anglo ranchers but for the Anglo and Mexican hands who worked for them, as his own father worked for Charlie Flagg. Their survival was tied to that of the ranchers, inseparable and increasingly precarious.

Candelario had tagged along half a dozen paces behind Manuel, near enough to watch everything but far enough that he could turn back if he saw unpleasant work ahead. "Manuel," he said from outside the corral, "Mister Charlie is coming."

Charlie Flagg limped up to the fence, catching a tuft of Candelario's coarse black hair and giving it a playful tug. "You learnin' anything in school, Candy?"

"I'm learnin' to get tired of it."

"You got a long ways to go, boy, if you don't want to grow up ignorant like me and your old daddy."

"That's better than bein' smart like some of those teachers."

"Those teachers ain't feedin' cattle and snotty-nosed sheep halfway into the summer." Charlie looked through the fence at Manuel, who had his arm around the colt's neck. "Manuel, you got anything to do besides milk your cow?"

Manuel shook his head. "Not till tonight." He straightened with interest, hoping Charlie had a horseback job for him. If so, Candelario might be given the pleasure of milking that brindle cow.

Charlie said, "It's gettin' time we cut that colt of yours; that's why I shut the gate on him. Thought since he's yours, you ought to be here to see how it's done."

Manuel tightened his arm around the young horse's neck. Regret colored his voice. "Do we have to, Mister Charlie?"

"We have to. If we leave him as a stud he won't be

much 'count for you to ride. If we geld him you can make a good usin'-horse out of him."

Manuel had been brought up not to doubt Charlie Flagg's word; Lupe always said Charlie was one *guero* who never lied to him. "Couldn't we wait awhile, Mister Charlie?" Maybe if they waited awhile, everybody would forget it.

"He's already a yearlin'-past; it's time. I like to do this job in April, after it's through bein' cold and before it gets hot, or in October. By October he'll have growed more. Almanac says the signs are right. Best we get it over with, *muchacho.*"

Tears burned Manuel's eyes; he thought of the pain for his pony, and the humiliation. Through the fence he saw that his father had walked up and that Lupe agreed with Charlie Flagg. José Rivera only looked on, not knowing except in a general way what they were talking about. He hadn't learned much English.

Charlie came through the gate and left it for Lupe or Jose to close. He put his hand gently on the horse's withers. "It's got to be done one time in his life. The longer we put it off the worse it'll hurt him."

Manuel hugged his pony's neck, keeping his face turned away so nobody could see the tears he was trying to rub off onto the shoulder of his shirt. "All right. But he may not ever like me any more."

Charlie moved his big hand from the horse's withers up to Manuel's shoulder. "A horse don't hold a grudge, son. He's not like people."

Charlie sent Candelario running to his house to fetch some warm water in a bucket. Then he told José in Spanish to rope both the colt's forefeet. José swung the loop and laid it easily around the feet as Manuel stepped back and the colt moved forward. The young bay plunged and kicked, frightened by the unaccustomed bite around its ankles. José jerked, and the colt went to its knees. Charlie Flagg gave its shoulder a hard push; it went down heavily on its side. José pulled the forefeet back and took a wrap around the left hind leg, pulling it and the forefeet tightly together. He took a couple more wraps, these around all three legs, and made a tie.

"*Bueno*," Charlie said, "we'll tie that right leg up." José did not know Charlie's method, so Charlie did it himself. He tied a second rope around the heavy part of the colt's neck, then looped part of the rope over the right hind leg, pulling it as far forward as he could with José and Lupe both helping him. This left the scrotum exposed.

The colt thrashed, lifting its head and slamming it to the ground in fright. Charlie said, "Pet him, Manuel. Talk to him so he won't hurt himself."

Manuel patted the colt's neck and gently rubbed its nose, speaking softly in Spanish, the language he always used with animals. The colt still kicked a little, struggling vainly against the unaccustomed ropes. "He's goin' to be mad at me," he worried aloud.

Charlie Flagg limped off to the barn. He came back with a syringe and serum and a brown bottle of Lysol. By this time Candelario came running, swinging the bucket and spilling water with every step. Lupe reached across the weathered plank fence and took the bail as Candelario lifted the bucket with both hands. Charlie poured some of the Lysol into the warm water, mixing it with both of his hands. He opened his big pocketknife to the fleshing blade and dropped it into the bucket. He sloshed the syringe around in the water a moment, wiped the needle dry with his fingers and jabbed it through the rubber top of the serum bottle. "We'll give him about 10 c.c. of penicillin. That's more than most of my horses ever got."

Manuel patted the pony's neck faster as Charlie made the injection. The skin rippled a little where the needle went in, but the colt made little other sign that it felt anything.

Charlie carried the bucket of water behind the colt, knelt, and splashed some around the region that was to feel the knife, washing it with his hands and rinsing with more Lysol water. He fished his knife out and motioned for Lupe to take the bucket away. "Watch his hoofs now, Manuel. Even tied, he'll kick a little."

Manuel lifted the pony's head and cradled it in his arms as he watched Charlie split the scrotum. The horse flinched as the seed popped out. Charlie used an emasculator to pinch it off and crimp the cord to minimize the bleeding. The colt groaned, partly from pain, partly from fright. Charlie talked to it as he worked. "Easy now, son. Be gentle now, *potro*."

Charlie was talking English to him, Manuel was speaking Spanish. Manuel told himself it was no wonder the pony was confused.

When the second seed was out, lying in the sand, Charlie wiped his sweating face on his sleeve. Manuel realized how much strain this had been on the ranchman, and how much Charlie disliked this job.

Charlie dropped his knife in the bucket and said, "Where's that salted bacon grease, Lupe?"

Manuel's father handed Charlie a coffee can. Charlie dipped in and brought out a handful, which he smeared liberally over the fresh wound. "Ain't bleedin' much. That's a good sign."

That might be true, but it was enough to make Manuel's stomach queasy. He patted the pony's neck faster and realized he had quit talking. He began speaking softly again, telling lies. "That didn't hurt much; you won't even know it when you get up." The tears had quit flowing, but inside he was still crying a little.

Charlie said, "Let's untie him easy and let him up slow. We don't want him to strain himself and come up with a rupture."

The ropes came off. Manuel eyed the hoofs warily, knowing one could knock him senseless if it hit him right, but he kept a careful hold on the pony's neck. As the colt became aware that it was free, it struggled to get its feet on the ground. It got up front-end first, the hind legs shaky and weak from shock and the ropes' cut-off of blood circulation.

Lupe knelt and looked between the hind legs, from far enough that he would not get kicked. "Don't look like he'll bleed much."

Charlie nodded in satisfaction. "I been watchin' the almanac. The signs are in the legs. Cut a colt when the signs are in the legs, he don't generally have much trouble."

Manuel still had his arms around the pony's neck. Charlie washed the blood from his hands in the Lysol water, dried them on the legs of his khaki pants, then came up and patted Manuel on the shoulder. "I didn't check signs on *you*, boy. You all right?"

"Sure, Mister Charlie. I'm glad it's over."

"It ain't all over; he'll bear a little watchin'."

Manuel said, "I'll come out and sleep in the barn tonight; I'll watch him." Then he raised his head and blinked. "But I forgot. I'm supposed to take Anita in for the dance at school tonight. If I don't go with her, Mama won't let her go."

Charlie said, "The colt don't have to be watched that close. José'll take a look at him once in a while."

He began to smile. "Thought you didn't have any use for dances."

"Tonight's is for Buddy Thompson. The Thompsons are leavin', you know."

Charlie nodded, for through him had come Manuel's first knowledge of the fact that the Thompson ranch had gone under. Batch Thompson operated leased land which touched against part of Charlie Flagg's netwire perimeter fence. The story as Manuel heard it was that Thompson was paying a lease price pegged too high for the realities of this hard time, and the distant landowners refused any adjustment to compensate. He had been forced to throw in the cards.

Manuel had been over to Batch Thompson's ranch several times as neighbor help with his father. He had found Thompson fussy for his taste, and prone to the use of sorry horses. Manuel had picked up his father's and Charlie Flagg's tendency to judge a ranch by its horses. But whatever his feelings about the ranchman, Manuel had always liked Thompson's son Buddy, a year or so ahead of him in school. Moreover, as the Thompsons moved away the Rodriguez family who worked for them were left at loose ends and had to leave too. The school would be a duller place without dumb old Paco Rodriguez jamming his foot into a wastebasket or spilling books out of his messy locker every time he opened the door.

The drouth's unpleasant changes were crowding into Manuel's world; he could no longer ignore them.

It had always been a mystery to Manuel why there was a rule against any footwear except tennis shoes on the gymnasium floor during school time, while all shoes were acceptable at a dance. For these occasions an old jukebox was rolled out from a storeroom. It was rigged to operate without coins, though half the time it played a different number than had been punched for. Most of the records were out of date because nobody in authority took the time, trouble, or expense to change them. But the music was free, and that made up for a lot of shortcomings.

The dance was not officially dedicated to Buddy Thompson and the Rodriguez youngsters, but informally it worked out that way. It was a time for saying goodbye, for building a good memory to last after friends had gone.

Manuel had not yet learned to dance. He spent most of his time in the concession stand helping sell Cokes and 7-Ups, peanuts and chewing gum for the class treasury. If they ever saved up enough money, the class hoped to make a trip to the Yellowstone. Covertly Manuel watched the swirling skirts. He felt his evening justified when he caught a quick glimpse of a well-shaped thigh; they were *all* well-shaped that far up. The last few times he had brought Anita here he had begun building his nerve to lead some giggling girl out onto the floor. He had considered asking his sister to teach him a few basic steps, but once she got to one of these affairs there never was time. The boys clustered around her like flies after sugar. He had heard it said she was the best-looking girl in Rio Seco, but being a brother he could not take an objective view. There were several he would place higher, some he had never seen barefoot and in an old blue shirt and Levi's.

He tried always to keep track of Anita. Rosa had admonished him to be watchful that she was never persuaded to go outside with a boy. "Your sister is a good girl," Rosa told him, "but even a good girl likes to hear a boy make pretty talk. You will do it yourself one of these days; there is no boy that remains a saint."

Manuel was worried about only one: Danny Ortiz. He always frowned when he saw Danny on the dancefloor with Anita, and it seemed he was out there more than any other boy. None of the others liked to arouse Danny's anger by pressing too hard for Anita's notice when Danny made it plain he wanted her for himself. Danny was the son of a well-to-do businessman and money lender, a man of high finance and low repute. Hated and even feared, Old Man Ortiz was a power among his people though most privately condemned him as a *coyote*, a flesh-peddling profiteer and *mordeleon*. They waited with patience and a serene confidence for that day of retribution when God would strike him down. God, the people said, always found a way to make a man's sins become their own punishment. Old Man Ortiz had much retribution ahead of him.

Danny, Manuel thought, was cut from the same cloth. He had a predatory eye, like a chicken-thieving coyote except that Danny was not interested in chickens. Manuel's stomach always drew into a resentful knot when he saw Danny looking at his sister, arrogantly flaunting the thought that lay behind those coyote eyes. When Danny danced with Anita he held her close and cheek to cheek, something none of the other boys had nerve to do. Manuel sensed that it was part physical gratification with him, part exhibitionism. Danny Ortiz would always have the most money, the reddest car, the finest clothes, the prettiest girl.

Manuel tried not to look at Danny and Anita. He

switched his attention to Paco Rodriguez, bumbling his way around the dancefloor with Flora Garcia. He felt almost an envy of Paco; he might be clumsy, but at least he was out there. Manuel had not summoned that much nerve.

Buddy Thompson came to the concession stand, breathing heavily from the dancing. He stepped up in front of Manuel and looked him calmly in the eyes. "Hi, Meskin."

Manuel returned the level gaze. "What do you want, *gringo*?"

The words would have sent Manuel's parents into a silent fury, or left Buddy's father red-faced and stomping. But between these two young men they meant nothing; by using them they were somehow making fun of the prejudices held by an older generation. Buddy broke into a lazy grin. He slapped a quarter down on the wooden counter with the palm of his hand. "A Coke. Take somethin' out for yourself, too. I'm buyin' you one more drink before we pull up and leave here."

Manuel smiled. "Finally goin' to spend a little of it, are you? Damn, but you *gabachos* are tight." He stuck two bottles under a pair of openers and popped off two tops at one time. He shoved one bottle at Buddy Thompson, then rubbed the heel of his hand over the mouth of his own before he turned it up for a long swallow. "I never saw you breathe that hard from *workin'*."

"Workin' never was worth it. Dancin' is. You ought to try it."

Manuel pointed his chin. "Paco's dancin' enough for both of us."

Buddy chuckled. "Paco's heart is in the right place; it's just his feet that sometimes don't work right. I'll miss that clown." His smile died. "I'll even miss you, Manuel. We had some good times."

They looked at each other, little of the barrier between them that stood between their fathers. Manuel said, "Looks like your dad could've found him *some*-place around here cheap enough to lease. Looks like there ought to've been somethin' . . ."

"He tried. There just wasn't nothin'. So he's got him a job with a feed company, travelin' out of San Angelo. Times like this, there's one thing that's bound to sell good, and that's feed."

Manuel grimaced. "Big place, San Angelo. I bet they got forty–fifty thousand people over there. It'll be like movin' to New York."

Buddy shrugged sadly. "Dad says we got to live where there's a livin'. There's no livin' here." He looked around the gym, slowly studying the people he knew. Most of them he had known all his life. "We may be just the startin' of it; there's liable to be a lot more leave here if things don't pick up." His gaze came back to Manuel. "Who knows? *You* may even wind up in Angelo."

It was not a new idea to Manuel, but cold dread came whenever the thought intruded. "I hope not. I don't know how I could ever stand to leave Rio Seco. This has always been a good town."

"Everything dies someday."

"It's hard to say goodbye to people. I don't think I could do it." His eyes narrowed as he sought out his sister, on the dancefloor with Danny Ortiz again. "There's one I'd like to say goodbye to."

Buddy followed Manuel's gaze. "Danny? Don't you let him worry you. He puts on the dog, but he's a nothin', a great big nothin'." His eyes narrowed. "You don't suppose *she* takes him serious, do you?"

Manuel shrugged. "Just because she's my sister doesn't mean she's smart."

"She *is* smart, Manuel. Anita's about the smartest one girl I ever knew. Prettiest one, too." Buddy watched the couple dancing.

Manuel saw something in Buddy's eyes he hadn't seen before, a wish that was plain to read. "She doesn't really like Danny much; she's told me that. He scares her a little, even."

He thought he saw relief in Buddy's face. Buddy said, "She's a real good girl. I always kind of wished . . ." He let the statement drop.

Manuel frowned at his Coke. He thought he could finish the rest of the sentence: *wish she wasn't a Mexican.* From someone he didn't like so much, Manuel would have taken offense. With Buddy it was a natural consequence of his upbringing; it was a reflection of his father's teaching. Manuel thought it wasn't Buddy's fault, not in the main; he couldn't help the way he had been conditioned.

The tune on the jukebox was almost over. Buddy was still watching Anita. "Manuel, you reckon she'd mind?"

"Mind what?"

"Mind if I asked for a dance, just this once, this bein' my last time here and all . . ."

"One way to find out. Ask her."

Buddy hesitated. "You don't think she'd take it wrong, do you? I never asked her before. I was always afraid she might think . . ."

Manuel knew the rest of *that,* too, though Buddy couldn't or wouldn't bring it out in words. Some of the Anglo boys regarded the Mexican girls as easy, fair game for anything they wanted to try. An Anglo boy's motives were in question if they encouraged that attention.

Manuel pointed out, "Johnny Willis was dancin' with her while ago, and Bill Jones. They weren't afraid to ask her."

Buddy's courage came up. "I'll tell her you said it was okay."

"You better leave me out of it. She won't figure I've got any business sayin' one way or the other."

The tune ended. Buddy handed Manuel his wet, empty bottle, wiped his hand on the leg of his trousers and walked hurriedly to the edge of the floor to catch Anita before anyone else could. Manuel saw with satisfaction that she seemed pleased. He also saw the knife-edge glare Danny gave Buddy.

As the music started, Danny came by the refreshment stand, eyes half closed in anger. Manuel said, "How about a Coke, Danny?"

Danny blinked at him, his mind still elsewhere.

Manuel said, "It'll do you good, Danny. It'll help cool you off. From the dancin'." He supposed the malice showed in his eyes, for Danny flared perceptibly, mumbled something that didn't carry above the sound of the jukebox and walked off to the chairs spaced along the wall. In a little while Danny was reaching behind the chair and pinching one of the Torres girls on her broad rump. That was something Manuel had long wished he had the nerve to do. But he could tell that Danny hardly took his eyes from the couple on the dancefloor; he had an idea Danny was mentally transferring the favor from Luz Torres to Anita.

Manuel scowled, making up his mind that he and Anita had something serious to talk about on the way home.

A girl spoke behind him. "Manuel, did you come here to sell soda pop or to dance?"

Turning, he saw Kathy Mauldin. His eyes widened in surprise. He had never counted her as a pretty girl and still didn't, but he was not used to seeing her in a party dress like this . . . or in *any* dress. A shirt and blue jeans had always been her style.

She smiled coquettishly at him.

Flustered a little he said, "I'm a pretty good pop seller. I've sold enough tonight to buy gas for the school bus from Rio Seco to San Angelo."

"That's a long way from Yellowstone."

"We'll get there. You want to buy a soda pop?"

"No, I just want to dance."

He sensed she was hinting. "Then go out there and get somebody to ask you."

"Why don't *you* ask me?"

He knew very well why he didn't ask her, but he said, "I never learned to dance."

"You need somebody to teach you."

"I'll get Anita to, sometime."

"Step out here and *I'll* teach you. A little bit. Most of it you've got to learn for yourself."

A faint alarm began ringing in the back of his mind. He tried to push her off by laughing gently at her. "I don't believe you can dance. I've seen you shoe a horse, but I've never seen you dance."

"You just come on out here and I'll show you."

He wondered what to do next; she was trapping him. "I don't want to, not in front of all these people. They'll laugh at me."

"There's nothin' to it. You just shove one foot forward and then the other. Anybody can do it . . . even you.

She caught his hand and pulled at him. He pulled

back, resisting. "Kathy, you're crazy. You know I can't do that."

"I don't know why not."

He pulled his hand free, feeling the warmth stronger in his face. He looked around to see if anyone was watching; so far as he could tell, no one was except sharp-eyed Chuy Garcia. Chuy Garcia saw everything, always.

Kathy Mauldin had never been one to mince words. "You mean because you're a Mexican?"

Reluctantly he said, "That's part of it." It was *all* of it.

"Does that give you an inferiority complex or somethin'?"

"No, but . . ."

"Your sister's dancin' with Buddy Thompson. If you're a Mexican, so is she."

"But it's different with her; she's a girl."

"So am I. Be damned if I see any sense in that."

Manuel's lips tightened. *He* never used that kind of language except with other boys of his own age; certainly he never used it around girls. "It's just the way people look at things. It's all right for Anita to dance with Buddy; she's a girl. But I can't dance with *you*."

"You *have* got an inferiority complex, Manuel."

"I haven't, either. But I just don't want people to talk."

"They've got to talk about somethin'. It'd just as well be us." She took his hand again and began to pull firmly.

He said, "Kathy, your head is as hard as a rock."

"I get that from my daddy. Come on, this is an easy step to learn."

He was out on the floor then, looking down at his feet as she tried to show him how to move them. He was conscious that two or three people besides Chuy were starting to look at him, and he imagined everybody was. "Kathy, I tell you they'll all be talkin'."

"Does it make your ears burn, or somethin'?"

"No."

"Then there's no way they can hurt you. As long as they're talkin' about us they're leavin' some other poor son of a bitch alone." She led him into the step. "If you'd been Page Mauldin's boy instead of Lupe Flores's, you'd be used to people talkin' about you. You'd of quit worryin' about it a long time ago."

The music ended, and he made a move as if to return to the concession stand. Kathy held onto him. "They can count their own change." The jukebox started another tune, a faster one. "Same step," she told him. "You just have to pick it up a little bit."

Gradually he lost some of the worry of being watched. He began to enjoy the feel of the girl, the easy touch of her hands, pressuring him one way or the other as dancers crowded around them. He stepped on her toe and apologized, his face warming. "I'm sorry."

She shrugged. "Happens to me when I shoe horses, too. Thing is, they weigh more."

"I'm not used to you lookin' like this. I wasn't sure you even knew how to put a dress on."

"You didn't think I knew how to dance, either. I don't spend *all* my time around horses."

The tune ended. Kathy smiled up at him. "There. That wasn't so bad, was it?"

"No," he admitted, "it was all right."

"All right hell, it was pretty damn good. *You* need to spend more time away from horses. You'd be surprised what I could teach you."

"Nothin' would surprise me very much."

She left him then with a promise that she would be back. He had mixed feelings about that, hoping she would and hoping she wouldn't.

Chuy Garcia came up to the concession stand, his face furrowed. Chuy always had the look of one who smelled onions burning. "What did you do that for, Manuel?"

"Do what?"

"Let a *gebacha* like that Kathy make fun of you."

The word was one in common usage among the Mexican people, referring to Anglos, and it had a slightly unpleasant connotation. The use of it in reference to Kathy brought an unexpected rise of anger in Manuel. "She didn't poke fun at me."

"They *always* make fun of us. Why else do you think she would dance with you in front of all these people? You don't think she wanted you in her arms just because she liked you, do you? You, a *damn Meskin*?"

Manuel had heard those words many times. From someone like Buddy Thompson they meant little because they were used in jest. But he had heard them from older Anglos like Buddy's father, and from them they stung like the popper on a whip. They stung a little now, coming from Chuy.

"You don't know Kathy," Manuel said defensively. "She's not like that."

"They're *all* like that. I hope someday you'll have the sense to see it." Chuy gave him a look of disgust, then walked away.

Manuel's face was warm. He had expected his dancing with Kathy to arouse some criticism, but he had expected it from the Anglos, not from his own. He began picking up Coke bottles and shoving them roughly into the empty wooden cases, making a lot of noise about it.

That damn Chuy, he hates harder than any gringo I ever saw, he thought harshly. Sometimes he felt like drawing back and punching Chuy in the nose. Yet he could not shake a gnawing suspicion that behind Chuy's constant smoldering anger lay a hard truth. Even in his sheltered life on Brushy Top, Manuel had seen and heard plenty. He knew that not all the Anglos were like Charlie Flagg. And even Charlie Flagg, he was gradually coming to realize, was not without his faults. Now that Manuel was old enough and experienced enough to detect them, he could see that even Charlie Flagg held some old-fashioned notions that dated back to the border wars.

"There's not a one of them," Chuy had told Manuel once, "that you'll ever want to turn your back on."

He heard laughter and looked up. He saw Buddy Thompson at the wall, sharing a joke of some kind with Paco Rodriguez. He realized Anita was no longer with Buddy. She stood in a dark corner with Danny Ortiz. The music was playing again so he could not hear what they were saying, but the jerky motions of Anita's hands told him she was angry, that she was arguing. Manuel watched for a minute, decided it was serious and walked directly across the floor, cutting through the dancers.

He heard Anita saying in Spanish, "I'm not dancing with you any more, Danny, not tonight. I've given you enough dances. Now leave me alone."

Laughter was much more a part of his sister's makeup than anger, but through the years Manuel had seen her flare into anger often enough to know she could do it, and to know it took considerable provocation.

Danny was saying something in a harsh voice when Manuel broke in, grabbing Danny's arm. "My sister says for you to leave her alone. Why don't you go pinch Luz Torres's butt some more?"

Danny turned, taken by surprise. His ill temper quickly transferred from Anita to Manuel. "You mind your own business, little brother. Go dance with that *gabacha* again."

Tears were in Anita's eyes. "Take me home, Manuel."

"All right. Go get your sweater."

Danny caught Anita's arm, but his eyes were still on Manuel. "You go peddle your Cokes, boy."

Manuel grasped Danny's wrist and dug his fingers in. He had a good grip that came from squeezing the teats of a Jersey cow twice a day. He gave Danny's wrist a hard twist that had to hurt, bad, then he flung it free.

He was aware that the commotion had attracted the attention of those near enough to hear it. Manuel glanced back and saw that his sister had picked up her sweater from the chair where she had draped it early in the evening. He gave Danny a final scowl and turned to follow Anita out the door.

The wind was blowing, and a strong smell of dust was in the air. He made his way to the old Flores family car and unlocked the door for Anita. She was sobbing a little. He said, "You ought never to've spoken to Danny in the first place. A dance or two and the damn creep thinks he owns you."

He heard a girl shout behind him, "Manuel, look out!" The voice was Kathy's.

A hand caught Manuel's shoulder and roughly spun him around. "A creep, am I?"

He saw the fist coming and turned quickly to one side. It struck him on the shoulder with a force that made the hat fly from his head. He staggered against the car, bringing his hands up defensively in front of him. His dust-burning eyes focused on Danny Ortiz, drawing back for another swing. Rage surged up in him like coffee bubbling from a big camp pot. He dropped low and jumped forward, meeting Danny more than halfway. He drove a fist into Danny's stomach with all the strength that years of hard work had given him. It felt as if it went in all the way to the wrist. He heard the breath go out of Danny. Danny stumbled back, almost falling. He crouched there, gasping.

Anita cried, "Let's go, Manuel. You've stopped him."

Manuel stood his ground. He had no intention of being accused of running away. "When *he* says."

Danny stayed put, glowering while he struggled to regain his breath. As his lungs started to fill he began cursing, in little more than a whisper at first, then louder, using words Manuel wished Anita couldn't hear.

Danny reached toward his pocket. Manuel thought with alarm, *A knife. He's always got a switchblade knife.* Mouth suddenly dry, Manuel backed up a step and found himself trapped against the car. He could only move to one side or the other but not away from Danny.

Danny was so intent on Manuel that he did not see Buddy Thompson step up beside him with a short piece of lumber. Buddy swung it, and Danny hit the ground like a sack of feed dropped from a pickup.

Buddy's voice was even and without sign of excitement. "Danny, you wiggle one finger and I'll bust you again." He stepped carefully around the prostrate Danny Ortiz and gave Manuel a quick scrutiny. "He didn't touch you with that frog-sticker, did he?"

Manuel shook his head. "He didn't even get it out of his pocket."

Buddy leaned over and felt of Danny's pockets. "He ain't even got one. I'd of swore he had it."

Manuel looked down at the stunned Danny Ortiz, then up at Buddy. He felt frustrated, somehow cheated. "What did you hit him for?"

"Looked like he was goin' for a knife."

"I could of handled him."

"Not if he'd cut you open."

Manuel felt a resentment he did not quite understand. "But he didn't even *have* a knife."

"He *might've* had one; there was no way to know." Buddy stared at him, puzzled. "Dammit, Meskin, I can't figure you out. I was just tryin' to take care of you."

The resentment colored Manuel's voice. "I don't need somebody fightin' my fights for me. I don't need a *gringo* to take care of me; I can take care of myself."

Buddy seemed inclined at first to continue the argument, but he shrugged in resignation. He still did not understand. "Aw hell. If I made you mad, I'm sorry. Anyway, if I hadn't hit him, Kathy would've."

Manuel glanced in surprise at the girl, who stood a little behind Buddy. "Kathy?"

Buddy said, "Where do you think I got that chunk of wood? She had it in her hands. I took it because I figured I could hit him harder than she could." Buddy turned to Anita, sitting in the car, badly shaken. "You take care of yourself, Anita. If you ever have any trouble this hard-headed brother of yours can't handle, you just whistle. I'll be in San Angelo."

Anita only nodded, her hands clasped in front of her chin in the aftermath of fear.

Manuel looked first at Danny, who still lay on the

ground, rubbing his head. Then he looked at Kathy, not quite believing. "*You* were fixin' to hit him?"

She had none of the brashness about her now that she had shown on the dancefloor. "Seemed like a good idea," she replied seriously. "I didn't want him to hurt you."

Manuel muttered a few strong words under his breath and got into the car.

Hands sticky with bread dough, Anita Flores stood on tiptoe to look out the kitchen window toward the barn. In the reddening glow of late afternoon she could see José Rivera loading heavy feed sacks onto the back of the blue pickup for the next day's feeding.

"The men must be in, Mama," she said. "I can see José."

Rosa Flores, a lock of black hair dangling down over her forehead, leaned forward to open the oven door of her butane stove and peek in at leftover roast kid she was warming for supper. She stepped back as the oven's heat rushed into her face. "Do you see your father?"

"No, only José."

"It seems to me you can always see José better than you can see anybody else. Hurry up with that bread."

Anita finished kneading the dough and spread it out in a flat pan without cutting it into biscuit shape as the Anglos would. Nor would she give it much time to rise. Mexican bread was customarily baked flat. Rosa Flores turned up the oven heat for bread-baking temperature and took out the roast. It was warm now, and it would hold its heat on the back of the stove.

Rosa said, "Miz Mary told me she heard in town

there was a little trouble at the dance. You didn't say anything to me about it."

"Trouble?" Anita kept her back turned. "What kind of trouble?" But she knew her mother must know much of it; it took something very serious to make Rosa Flores lapse back into Spanish with her children. Rosa was speaking Spanish now.

"Trouble between your brother and that Danny Ortiz. It is strange that neither one of you mentioned it to your father or me."

"It was nothing. Manuel was going to bring me home, and Danny did not want him to. They argued a little, that was all. Manuel was right in the matter."

"So right that he struck Danny with a piece of wood? It is said that Danny's head is bandaged today."

"It was Buddy Thompson who hit Danny with the wood."

"What has Buddy Thompson to do with you? I do not like you dallying with those Anglo boys. You know what they want from the Spanish girls."

"Buddy did not hit Danny for me; he hit him for Manuel." She suspected Rosa knew much of the story anyway and was simply trying to drag it out of her. She told the rest of it, her face flushing.

Rosa said something bitter under her breath. "That Ortiz family . . . like father, like son!" Her eyes were severe. "You could have gotten your brother hurt, even killed, do you know that? From now on you will have nothing to do with that Danny Ortiz—*nothing*. A boy like that can do whatever he wants to, so long as it is only to a Spanish girl. The law will pay no attention."

She was silent a minute, thinking. Finally: "Your brother, he really stood up to that Danny, did he?"

Anita nodded. "Yes, Mama. If Buddy had not hit him with the wood, Manuel would have beaten him."

Rosa looked out the window, watching for the men. She said, "He is a foolish boy." But Anita saw that her mother was smiling, a little.

Candelario pushed through the back door with a bucket about a third full of eggs. Grunting, he lifted the bucket up onto the cabinet, about chin high to him. Rosa glanced into the bucket and said without patience, "*Hijo*, that is not all of the eggs."

Quickly defensive, he replied, "That is all I could find."

"Then you didn't look."

"Mama, some of those old hens, they hide from me."

Rosa stared hard at him, then evidently figured the boy had done the best he could, for a boy. Probably had his mind on horses and cattle and ropes like Tom Flagg, instead of on something as lowly as chickens and eggs. The only use Candelario had for chickens was to practice roping at them—or Sundays, on the dinner table.

Anita suggested, "Mama, I think maybe a few of the hens have been going into the brush behind the barn. I've finished with the bread. I can take the bucket and go look." Her inflection asked permission.

Rosa looked out the window again. José was almost finished loading the pickup. "Don't you waste any time out there talking to that José. I can't feed all these hungry mouths without more eggs."

Bucket in her hand, Anita went first to the chicken house, for there was always a chance Candelario's mind had wandered to God knows where and he had simply missed some of the eggs. Fractious hens cackled and fluttered around in a wild flapping of wings as Anita entered the house. She poked two or three of the calmer ones up from their nests. One cantankerous old biddy fluffed her brown feathers and pecked irritably at Anita's hand. Anita found three eggs under her. She had probably kept Candelario so buffaloed that he hadn't tried to look.

From there Anita started toward the barn. José was too busy to have seen her yet. She liked to watch him when she could do so without his knowing it. Something about him stirred an interest in her that the boys in town never had. She sensed that he might feel the same, but he had done nothing and said nothing to give himself away. Sometimes she sensed his eyes following her, but when she turned to look, his gaze would shift elsewhere. But she could sense a hunger there that excited and pleased her. She had been tempted a time or two to try a little harmless coquetry on him, the kind she had learned to use on the boys in school. It meant nothing and was usually pleasant for both boy and girl, unless the boy took it to mean more than it did, as in Danny's case.

Something about José always stopped her. Perhaps it was the loneliness she saw in him.

José dropped a sack into place on the bed of the pickup and glanced around, catching sight of Anita. She gave him a cautious smile. "Hello, José."

He was a moment in answering. "*Buenos dias.*"

She paused, cautious because her mother might be watching through the window. Needlessly she asked, "What are you doing?"

"I am loading the feed so it will be ready in the morning."

He always spoke humbly, Anita thought, as if he regarded her of higher station. It was much like the deference the Texas Mexican people affected toward the Anglos, often without meaning it. Put-on, make-believe to get along better in a world where someone else had power over you. But she sensed that with José it was real. He had been here several weeks now, sleeping in a shed, eating with the Flores family. She had seen him at least twice a day—three times on Saturdays and Sundays—and she would have thought he would be over his shyness by now. At first she had enjoyed this deference, for no one had ever shown it to her before. It had been a tonic to her ego as a woman. Now she was tired of it. She wished he would talk to her easily and without reserve, as any Spanish boy in school would have done.

She said, "I am looking for eggs. I think some of the hens have been hiding around the barn to lay, perhaps in the mesquite. Have you seen any?"

"Yes, sometimes. There is one old red hen . . ."

For a moment she thought he would voluntarily climb down from the pickup and show her. He pointed. "Back behind the barn. I have seen this old hen go into the brush and I have thought, 'Watch out, *vieja*, one day you will find a coon or a badger waiting for you.'"

Anita at first resisted a temptation to feign helplessness, then yielded to it. "I don't know if I can find it myself."

Immediately she felt foolish. José jumped down and brushed some of the feed dust from his clothes. His sleeves were rolled up, and Anita could see how his arms had thickened and muscled since he had been here. Mister Charlie had brought José some new clothes from town and had burned the old ones that had been so loose.

He said, "Follow me. I will show you."

She had rather have walked beside him, but he

moved at such a fast pace that she couldn't keep up. She fell in behind him and contented herself with trying to walk in his tracks.

José pointed. "It was over there." He started into the tangle of mesquite and stopped, holding out his hand. "Give me the bucket. You should not walk out into these thorns."

"I do it all the time."

"Your legs are too pretty to be scratched." He said it without intending to. She could see sudden misgiving in his eyes. "I did not mean to speak that way. It is not my place."

He took the bucket from her hand and moved into the brush. She watched, shame touching her for ever having taken him lightly. She could see him moving around in the mesquite, bending now and again, pushing aside the green limbs into which the spring sap had brought life. When he came back and held out the bucket, she saw he had found six eggs.

"Some," he said, "have been there too long. Be careful when you break them."

She didn't care about the eggs. "José, are you afraid of me? Or is it that you do not like me?"

"I am not afraid of you. And I do like you. The trouble is . . . pardon me . . . I think I like you too much."

"Then why . . ."

"I am only a cowboy, and a Mexican."

"I am a Mexican too."

"But not the same. You are of this country. I am *mojado*. I have to run like a thief when I see dust on the road, when I see a stranger. It is not good for a man to run; it makes him less than a man. It is bad enough that I am only a cowboy, and you are the daughter of the *mayordomo*."

Mayordomo. To her the word conjured up the image of a manager on some great feudal cattle ranch, not the only hired hand of an outfit so small it could hardly afford to hire a second man unless he worked for wetback wages.

Anita spoke, "José . . ." and found herself run out of words.

Again he held out the bucket. This time she took it. She saw sadness in his dark eyes, then he bowed slightly and left her standing there by herself. His dignity remained intact, but hers was shattered as the eggs would be if she dropped them.

8

Dry weather had put no gray in Tom Flagg's hair. He listened to the roar of the rodeo crowd as he rode Prairie Dog in slow circles around an open field south of the arena, warming him up. The grandstands were packed for the afternoon performance, the dusty outer lot jammed with cars parked in lines suggestive of regimentation and therefore repellent to Tom. Whenever he went to a rodeo, he usually located a back entrance and parked along a fence or wherever the hell it suited him. It rankled for someone to tell him how and where to park, to be just another one of the crowd, herded around like a sheep. Occasionally when he arrived early enough, before the police, it pleased him to stop squarely in the middle of the lot and leave the car sitting there to foul up their parking arrangements.

From the loudspeakers' racketing echo he could tell the saddle-bronc riding had begun. Calf roping would be next. He reined the bay toward the car and trailer. Chunky Shorty Magee hunched there, smoking a cigarette and watching him quietly, listening to a Hank Williams song on the car radio. They traveled together—Tom, Shorty, and Chuck Dunn—sharing expenses.

Tom swung down from the saddle and reached into a big round aluminum can shaped like a hatbox. He brought out several coiled ropes and checked them one by one, like a baseball player trying the bats. Tom never put a spare rope on his saddle. Rules allowed a cowboy two loops provided he carried a second rope. Tom disdained the second loop. If he couldn't catch his calf the first time, he waved it goodbye.

Behind the chutes a pair of young contestants with bull ropes slung over their shoulders practiced at being bowlegged, as a cowboy was popularly supposed to be. Tom gave them a disdainful glance, regarding them as greenhorns out of some oilfield town or fugitives from a milking stool. Bronc riders tried out saddles, sitting in them on the ground and testing the length of the stirrups. An arena director yelled at them to hurry up, but they studiously ignored him. They were an inherently independent breed, these seasoned rodeo hands. They had twenty ways of telling a man to go to hell without speaking a word.

Tom listened to the rise and fall of the collective crowd voice as riders broke out of the chutes on twisting, snorting broncs. He did not have to hear the loudspeaker to know when a man rode well and when he bucked off the first jump or two out of the chute.

"Funny," said Shorty, "the way people enjoy it more when a cowboy gets throwed sky-high than when he fits a good ride."

Tom nodded. "Bloodthirsty, the whole damn bunch. People go to a baseball game, they like to watch a player show his skill. Go to a rodeo, all they want is to see somebody bust his butt."

It wasn't that Tom lost any sleep worrying about the bronc riders. Ropers and riders were two separate breeds, going their own way for the most part, each perhaps a little intolerant of the other, the riders considering roping too tame, the ropers considering the riders a shade crazy for letting those widow-makers stomp their brains out in the first place. A majority of the better bronc riders tended to be from the North and Northwest, the ropers from the Southwest. Thus they were divided by geography as well as by approach to their profession.

Two barefoot boys uneasily worked their way toward Tom. They stopped fifty feet away, watching him in some degree of awe. Their clothes were dirty, their hair long and uncombed. One wore what had once been a cowboy hat. The ragged brim sagged, as dead as an empty sack.

Shorty eyed them with amusement. "There's an audience for you, Tom."

Tom turned to the boys. "You buttons can't see nothin' from out here. You belong up in the grandstand."

The older boy came a little closer. The smaller one hesitantly followed a couple of paces behind. "They won't let us in. We got no money."

Tom frowned. "You boys ever seen a rodeo?"

The older one shook his head. "But we watch them rope out here sometimes on Sundays. We can see them through the fence."

"There's lots of things for a boy to see in a rodeo. Broncs, bulls, clowns, and stuff like that."

"We see the clowns out here ridin' around on their mules before they go into the arena."

Tom said ruefully, "You've missed the good part. Some clowns ain't very funny outside of the arena." He looked at the smaller boy. "Bet you're a pretty good rider." The boy said no, he had never been up on a horse. Tom asked, "Want to set a spell on mine?" The boy stepped forward eagerly. Tom lifted him into the saddle. "Don't you kick him, now. Prairie Dog's a ropin' horse. He takes off like a shot."

While the boy sat proudly, Tom fixed his rigging. He ran the end of the lariat beneath the neck rope and fastened it to the horn. He coiled the rest of the rope and tied it with the horn-string to stay until he was ready to use it.

He looked around then and saw the woman. She sat in a black Cadillac parked nearby, and she was watching him. She made no effort to look away when Tom gave her his attention.

"Shorty," he said, "don't look now, just ease around in a minute or so. Woman sittin' in that car yonder— you ever seen her before?"

Shorty didn't wait; he turned and looked boldly. "Can't say as I ever did. Wisht I had, though."

"She's been eyin' me for some reason. Noticed her out here this mornin'." He glanced at the oldest boy. "She live around here?"

The boy declared, "No, sir. I'd of sure remembered *her*."

Tom frowned to keep from grinning. "Button, you're too young to pay attention to women like that."

"I mean the car . . . I'd remember if I'd seen it before. Anyway, it's an out-of-town license plate."

Shorty said, "How come no woman like that ever watches *me*?"

Tom's frown deepened. "I'd give a pretty to know what she's got on her mind."

"Go ask her. Whatever it is, you might like it." Shorty looked again. "She's got a little touch of red in her hair. I always was a little partial to redheads myself. But I like blondes and brunettes just as good."

The bronc riding ended. Tom helped the boy down from his saddle. "Shorty, you ain't up this afternoon. Why don't you take these boys over to the contestants' stand and let them see the rest of the show?"

"Me?"

"You can use my pass for one of them and yours for the other."

"What if somebody gets the notion they're mine?"

"It'll just go to prove that some of the braggin' you been doin' is true." He pointed to the smaller boy. "Look at that grin, wider than a wave on a slop jar. You ought to be glad to make some kid that happy."

The boys grabbed the unenthusiastic Shorty by the hands and began to pull toward the grandstands. He looked back crossly at Tom but went on with them. He would sulk about it awhile, but he never had a bruise so deep that one beer would not pull the soreness out of it.

Tom swung into the saddle. He considered a moment, then rode by the Cadillac and tipped his hat for the hell of it. The woman gave him a brief, tentative smile that could be taken to mean anything or nothing. Riding toward the arena, he kept wondering. He was sure he had not seen her before; one like that he would be unlikely to forget. She looked like something out of those girly magazines except that she had more clothes on. That was no obstacle; Tom was a man with imagination.

Maybe she was celebrity-hunting. His name and picture had been in the papers lately because he was winning many of the rodeos. He had seen it happen to other rodeo hands; they would receive some notoriety and the girls would start hanging around them. Emptyheaded schoolgirls, mostly, the kind that can land a man so far back in jail that they have to shoot his beans to him with a slingshot. But this was no teenager; this was a full-grown woman, presumably old enough to know about birds and bees, bulls and bucks.

Tom moved the gray up into the arena gate where other ropers awaited their turn to ride in. He exchanged howdies and shook and joshed some of them a little. To one he said, "Bo, I notice you drew that Number 33 calf. I had him last go-round. He taken off out there thirty or forty feet and cut sharp to the left."

"Thanks, Tom. I'll sure watch him."

Tom caught a whiff of perfume over the rank smell of fresh horse droppings. He turned. There was the woman again, sitting atop a fence nearby, close enough that she could reach out and touch him if she were of a mind to. Or he could have touched her, and he *did* have a mind to. She wore red cowgirl pants and a pinkish Western blouse bought a size too tight. On purpose, he guessed. Bragging a little, and not lying either. She couldn't hide a figure like that if she wrapped it in a tarp.

Quietly he said, "Bo, you ever seen that filly before?"

Bo thought he meant a mare and started to give age, pedigree, and training of a sleek sorrel up by the gate. When Tom corrected him, he looked a moment. "That's Dolly Ellender. Sure does shine, don't she?"

Tom frowned. "She sure does. But the name don't register."

"You know of the Ellender Trailer Company, over in Dallas? Her daddy owns it, him and an uncle. Dolly there, seems like she's partial to rodeo hands. Went with Buzz Phelps some when he was takin' the steer wrestlin' so peart. I expect she was more fun to wrestle with than them steers. Used to go with Marty Sanders, too, when he stood high in the bull ridin'."

"Marty Sanders. Ain't he the one that got a horn through him in Houston?"

"Yeah. He'd fell apart by then, seemed like. Got afraid of the bulls, or somethin'."

Tom glanced at Dolly Ellender's left hand, on the top plank of the fence. No rings. That was good; he never had fancied hunting in the other man's pasture, not when there was game to be had without climbing any fences.

He turned his attention to the ropers then, putting the woman back in the warming oven. Most of the good ones were here. He watched them work and listened to the announcer call out their times. Jim McGinnis came up with the best one, 14.2.

"Next roper . . . Tom Flagg of Rio Seco," the announcer's voice came over the ill-adjusted loudspeaker. It was as if he were shouting through a box of wool fuzz. "You watch him, and you'll see a cowboy that's liable to be the world's champion calf roper in a year or two."

Tom always enjoyed talk like that; but he never let the enjoyment show in his face. He tucked the end of his pigging string under his belt and clamped the tiny loop of it in his teeth, where he would not waste a second getting to it when he needed it. He shook out a loop in his rope and backed the gray into the roper's box. A cowboy drew the spring-held barrier string across in front of him and fastened it. The Brahman calf was fighting in the chute. Tom could feel excitement building in the horse beneath him. A good roping horse became as addicted, sometimes, as his rider. The man in the chute got the calf quieted down. The gateman looked expectantly at Tom.

Tom said, "Let him out." The gate swung open. Seeing daylight and freedom, the calf dashed across the scoreline, its hoofs flinging up dust. The flagman's hand began to drop to spring the barrier open. Tom leaned down a little and gently tapped spurs to the gray. The horse's chest touched the barrier string as it gave way. Tom always rushed the barrier for the extra tenths of a second it gave him, risking the mandatory ten-second fine if he actually broke it. He was a man who never peacefully waited for anything.

The gray was fast; if he hadn't been, Tom would not have put up with him. He quickly overtook the calf. Tom swung a small loop over his head and cast it forward as he would throw a stone. The fit was perfect. As Tom yanked up the slack, the gray dug its hind feet into the ground, sliding to a stop. Tom swung his right foot over the horse's hip and jumped to the ground before the animal had stopped. The calf hit the end of the rope and flopped over backward. It let out a bellow and sprang to its feet. Tom was upon it as the calf made its first jump. He grabbed a foreleg and shoved his body into that of the Brahman. The calf fell again, on its side. Tom jerked the pigging string loop out of his mouth and dropped it over the foreleg. Almost before the calf could begin to kick, Tom gathered the two hind legs and drew them up to cross the foreleg. He made two quick wraps with the string and finished with the "hooey," a tie he must have practiced ten thousand times on anything that would hold still, even on his own booted foot. He sprang back, throwing his hands into the air to stop the judges' watches.

Without another glance at the calf he walked back to Prairie Dog. The horse had held the rope taut all the while. Tom swung into the saddle with a studied nonchalance, even a slouch, from the wrong side as if to show the crowd he could do any damn thing he was of a mind to.

He sensed that he had scored good time, and he could tell by the rising applause that the crowd knew it. A man who chased a calf halfway down the arena could usually count himself out of the prize money. Tom did not often go more than a third of the way. He rode the gray forward to give slack on the rope so the arena boys could free the calf. He coiled the rope and listened for the announcer.

"Well, folks," the word came from a loudspeaker atop a light pole, "here it is, the best time so far, 13.6. Told you that West Texas cowboy could rope."

Steak tonight, and not one of them cheap chicken-fries, either, Tom thought with satisfaction. The applause increased. It always made him feel nine feet tall. He glanced toward the contestants' area and saw the two boys jumping up and down, clapping their hands. He made an O with his thumb and forefinger and flashed it at them. Shorty Magee's sourness was gone; he was smiling.

The arena boys pitched Tom his pigging string as the calf got to its feet and trotted toward the back side of the arena, its hind legs momentarily stiff from being tied, its long Brahman ears flopping, its dignity violated. Tom rode out the gate, listening to the applause that followed him. A heady triumph coursed through him like a double shot of bourbon. Outside, he rode the gray a while, cooling him down slowly before he put him back into the trailer to haul him to a barn he was using. He listened to other ropers' times on the loudspeaker and noted with satisfaction that none had squeezed him out.

Shorty came eventually, the smile gone and his studied frown back in its accustomed place. Critically he said, "You strained hell out of that barrier again. You got to watch that."

Just as critically Tom said, "You got mustard on your shirt."

Shorty attempted to brush it off but only smeared it. He hadn't even noticed it before. "Tried to fill up them two buttons on hamburgers. If kids are that hungry all the time, I ain't ever gettin' married. I couldn't afford it."

Tom led the gray to the rear of the trailer and opened the tailgate. The horse stepped up and into the trailer like a trained dog. Tom shut the gate and fastened it with a hook, chain, and boomer.

Behind him a voice said, "That's a valuable animal you have, Tom. But I'll bet the trailer you haul him in isn't worth a hundred dollars."

Tom turned. The man he saw looked vaguely familiar, there were people who followed the rodeos as spectators and bettors whose faces became known but whose names remained always a vague blur. Tom was always a little distrustful of strangers who made free and easy with his first name; he had found they usually wanted to sell him something. "How do?" he spoke with reserve. His eyes widened as he saw the redhead standing just behind the man, smiling. "How *do*?" Tom said, a little friendlier.

The man said, "I'm Jason Ellender. You've heard of the Ellender Trailer Company? I'm the president of it. Like to talk some business with you."

Tom had much rather talk business with that redheaded woman. He was sure he could come up with an interesting proposition. He said, "I need to be feedin' this old gray horse." But he stood there looking at the woman. He didn't give a toodly damn about the man or his business.

Ellender saw where Tom's gaze was fastened. He turned. "Tom, this is my niece, Dolly Ellender. She's a fan of yours."

Tom grinned. "You don't know how tickled I am to hear that." He bowed slightly.

Ellender said, "Of course we're all fans. Nothing I like better than a good rodeo. Best show on earth, I always say."

"Yes, sir." Tom paid little attention as Ellender went on telling how long he had been an avid follower of the rodeo game, and how he always wished he might have contested some himself. Tom had immediately marked the man as a talker rather than a doer, and anyway he distrusted any man who wore a suit on weekdays. That much he had picked up from Charlie Flagg. Tom let his gaze drift slowly over the woman, giving her the careful appraisal he would give a young mare, though with somewhat different motives. He wondered idly if she could read his mind, if maybe a picture of his thoughts might hover over his head like the dialogue balloon in a comic strip. Well, maybe it would be a good thing if she *could* read his mind. There wouldn't be any room for innocent protestations later about misunderstanding.

He noticed that her hair wasn't really red, as he

had originally thought; it was more auburn. The sun, dropping now in the west, caught her hair and seemed to build a red halo in the edge of it.

He doubted that a halo was standard equipment with her; he hoped not.

Ellender pointed his chin toward Tom's old trailer; it was one Charlie had bought from a tin-barn welder, its running gear made from an old car chassis. It might not look like much, but it was hell for stout. Ellender said, "That trailer doesn't do justice to the fine horse you haul. How would you like a new one?"

"Mister, if you're tryin' to sell me a trailer, forget it. One of them good big ones you make costs too much money for me, and a cheap one wouldn't be half as good as what I got."

"It wouldn't have to cost nearly as much as you think. I spend a lot of money on advertising, Tom. And one of the best advertisements I can have is for good rodeo hands like you to be seen pulling my trailers to hell and gone. I think I've got a good offer for you."

Tom thought he would much rather hear an offer from Dolly Ellender than from her uncle, but maybe listening to one would help promote the other. "What's the proposition?"

"I'll sell you a trailer for cost. No profit, no dealer, no overhead . . . just cost."

Tom frowned. Before he would accept a stranger's definition of *cost* he would like to get well acquainted with the bookkeeper. With little effort to hide his suspicion he said, "In return for all this favor, what would you expect of me?"

"Nothing. We'd paint your name on the trailer in big letters where everybody could see them: TOM FLAGG. And below, much smaller, would be the company insignia. People would say to themselves, 'If an Ellender trailer is good enough for Tom Flagg, it's good enough for me.' And wherever you went, people would know Tom Flagg was in town."

That touched Tom in a tender spot. His mouth turned up in an ill-suppressed grin. "Can't say as I see anything bad wrong with that."

Shorty Magee warned, "Tom, don't you go and say yes to somethin' till you've scratched your head over it a little. Hell, there's other trailer companies, and maybe they'd sell you one at *less* than cost. Man never knows till he asks around."

Ellender's annoyance was not well hidden, but his mouth still smiled. "Your friend is right, of course. Tell you what, Tom . . . I'm having a little party for some people tonight after the show. What say you come out and join us? Plenty of drinks. Besides, it'd give Dolly a chance to get acquainted with you."

Tom said, "I'd be tickled."

Dolly held back as her uncle walked away. "Don't forget, now. We're at the Ranch Courts. Knock on the door of Suite 10."

"Brimmer bulls couldn't keep me away."

He let his eyes follow those tight britches till they disappeared into the Cadillac. He pushed his hat way back and whistled. "I swear, Shorty, yonder goes a *woman*!"

Shorty sniffed, suspicious. "I thought you had a woman back home in that dustbowl, Rio Seco."

Tom shrugged. "But I'm a long ways from home."

9

Charlie Flagg stopped his pickup in front of the wool warehouse and stepped out into the spring heat. An empty livestock truck passed. Charlie turned quickly away and shut his eyes against the dry dust that boiled from under it. Stepping through the big wide-open door, he blinked away the burn and saw a few men loafing in the rear of the building. He could hear Rounder Pike's loud voice winding up a windy yarn.

Pike turned to look at Charlie. "Charlie, I was just tellin' the boys here that I've made a bet with several people that it never *will* rain again in this country."

Charlie shook his head. "That's a silly bet."

"I don't know. Two of them have already paid me off." He took a good laugh at Charlie's expense, then eyed an empty coffee can that was being used as a spittoon. He reared back and took aim. A metallic thump testified that he was on target.

Warehouseman Jim Sweet didn't bother to get up. He motioned for Charlie to find himself a seat on a stack of sacked feed. Sweet said, "Charlie, I don't suppose you've met Bruce Hammond." He jerked his thumb toward a khaki-clad man. "Wool buyer out of Angelo."

Charlie shook the man's hand. "See your name in the paper once in a while. Pleased to meet you." From the fast clip of the buyer's speech, Charlie knew he was not a native. But Hammond was relaxed and seemed to feel at home. To buy wool in West Texas the Boston men had to learn to whittle and spit and horse-trade, forgetting they had ever read a clock. Sometimes it took as long to buy a little ranchman's ten-bag clip as to buy three carloads from Page Mauldin's big accumulation.

"How's wool?" Charlie asked, knowing what the answer would be. He had never met a wool buyer who didn't say the market was on the verge of going to hell.

"Mills haven't made a dime this year," Hammond said. "The futures market slipped three points yesterday. Grease prices are due for a drop."

Charlie nodded, his judgment vindicated. He had always observed that when the futures market was going up, wool buyers said it had no bearing on the spot market. But when it was going down they always mentioned it. He wished he had a dollar for every time he had heard a wool man predict hard times; he could buy a right smart of feed with the money. He asked Hammond, "They finished shearin' yet in the Del Rio country?"

"Just about. Wools are shrinking heavy this spring—too much dirt."

"No wonder. Every time a sheep puts its foot down it stirs up enough dust to choke itself to death. Gives you boys somethin' else to beat the price down with."

He smiled to indicate he didn't really mean it, but in fact he really did, and the wool buyer knew it.

Hammond said, "If you could find a way to keep the dirt out of that wool . . ."

"Can't keep the sheep indoors," Charlie said, "and there's damn little outdoors except dirt." He got up from his feed-sack seat and ambled curiously to a small bulletin board beside a wool scale. Tacked on it were two calendars—one a Western sheep scene, the other a buxom lass who seemed bewildered over the loss of all her clothes. Charlie spent about as long looking at the sheep as at the girl. They didn't paint girls as pretty any more as they used to, seemed like.

He came back and sat down again. "Gettin' hot already. We don't have much spring any more—just go from winter right into summer, and neither one of them any fun."

Rounder Pike worked his jaw to spit again. The bucket sang as he hit dead center. "Gettin' much green stuff up, Charlie?"

"Not grass. I'm gettin' up a way too much green stuff over at Big Emmett's bank and bringin' it over here to buy Jim Sweet's feed with." He smiled, but the smile did not cover the worry deep in his eyes. "Rounder, you seen any good sheep buyers lately?"

"Never seen a *good* sheep buyer. They're as rare as good wool buyers." Rounder glanced at Hammond, but the San Angelo man passed up the bait.

"I mean one with money."

"That's the rarest kind." Rounder dropped his attempt at humor. "You ain't taken a notion to sell out, have you, Charlie?"

"No, but I got some old ewes that need to go. Thought I'd be cagey last fall—keep them till it rained and the price went up. It never did. I fed them old nellies twice what I counted on, and they didn't shell out much of a lamb crop. Looks like I'll have to sell them out of the shearin' pen or I'll be feedin' them halfway into the summer."

Jim Sweet said soberly, "You don't need to feel like you got a patent on that problem. Been to any auction sales lately?"

"Ain't had time. By the livestock papers, though, looks like prices are droppin' bad. Sheep and cattle both." It usually went that way in a drouth; nobody had much room to buy anything, so the price went to hell.

Dead serious now, Rounder said, "You know Arlie White, over south of the divide? Sold everything he had last week and turned his lease back. He was made a fair offer last fall, but he figured it'd rain. Put a big feed bill into them ol' sheep, come up with a poor lamb crop and sold out for less than he'd of got in September. Sick? Arlie says to me, he says he's goin' to take what money he's got left and run like a thief. Never goin' to look another sheep in the mouth. Wants to buy him a tourist court over in Angelo and take things easy. But he's cowboyed since he was big enough to straddle a horse. He won't fit no-wheres else."

Rounder Pike's tobacco juice was too much for him again. He spat hard, but this time there was no metallic ring. Warehouseman Jim Sweet flinched.

Rounder said, "Ain't goin' to be enough ranchers left in this country to work up a decent poker game."

Jim Sweet's face twisted. That kind of talk made a townsman as nervous as a rancher, because without the ranchers there would be very little of a town. "A year from now we'll forget it was ever dry. We been through these spells before, lots of them, and this one has already lasted longer than most of them ever do. Bound to rain this summer."

Charlie nodded. "I guess." He tried to smile but couldn't. "Just the same, I wish I'd sold them ewes."

Across the street from the warehouse was the Lucindo Rodriguez pool hall, patronized mostly by the male Mexicans of the town. Walking out of the warehouse and pausing in the door to blink against the harsh glare of the sun and the caliche-packed roadway, Charlie heard the laughter of young men. He blinked again. In the shade of the Rodriguez porch four Mexican youths were horse-playing. Three smoked cigarettes. A fourth tried to light a cigar and was taking a ribbing because he couldn't get it fired up. He was too young to know how.

Charlie recognized him as Chuy Garcia, son of the shearing *capitán*, Teofilo Garcia. He took his watch from his pocket and squinted at it. No, school wasn't out yet; these buttons were playing hookey.

Darkly he thought, *Old Teofilo's out someplace sweatin' his soul away in a hot sheep pen so you can get an education, and look where you're at, and who you're with!*

Danny Ortiz! Charlie ground out a bitter "Damn!" He never had liked Old Man Ortiz, and he had long ago decided Danny wasn't worth the knife it would take to gut him with.

Well, Danny was almost grown. Maybe soon he would leave Rio Seco, looking for greener pastures, and then he would be someone else's concern. Chances were there was a prison cell somewhere, just waiting for him. One thing to be thankful for: Lupe's and Rosa's kids were beyond his reach out at the ranch. He couldn't do anything to hurt *them*.

Keeping his left hand on the steering wheel, Danny Ortiz touched Anita Flores's knee. She pulled away, her lips set tight and her eyes fixed on the ranch road which slowly passed under the beam of the headlights. Two more miles, that was all.

Danny said, "Come on, Anita, you don't have to sit so far away. Nothing's going to happen."

Coldly she replied, "That's what you said before. Keep both hands on the wheel."

Danny grinned. "It just takes one hand for a straight road."

"I wish you'd drive a little faster."

Danny shrugged. "It'll do a hundred and ten. Want me to show you?"

She quickly shook her head. She suspected he would do it if she gave him the least encouragement. "I just want to get home."

"I'm in no hurry."

"Just because I let you take me home from the movie doesn't give you any special privileges."

"There you go, always thinking bad things about me."

"What did you ever do to make anybody think different?"

"Look, if I hadn't found you standin' out in front of that picture show all by yourself, you'd have had to walk home."

She sat stiffly against the door, anger and suspicion building in her. "There's something very strange about all this. Mike Gonzales took me to the show.

He went out to get some popcorn and never came back. Don't you think that was strange, Danny?"

Danny shrugged. "Mike never was very dependable."

"What did you do to him, Danny? Did you beat him up, or get somebody to?"

Danny acted hurt. "Beat Mike up? He's a friend of mine. I wouldn't do anything like that to old Mike."

"What *did* you do, then?"

"Gave him ten dollars, told him to get lost before the roof fell in on him."

Anita gasped. "Ten dollars?"

"He wouldn't do it for five. Cost me ten."

She shrank back even harder against the door, as if she could get completely away from him. She folded her arms and held them tightly against her breasts. Genuine fear began to touch her. "What made you think I'd be worth ten dollars to you?"

"I'm a born gambler." His grin turned ugly. "You look like a good risk." He began slowing the car.

She tried to fight down a sudden panic. She knew she could not afford to let him see how frightened she was. "You keep going, Danny! Keep going, do you hear?"

But Danny was braking to a stop. She reached for the door handle. Danny caught her arm and gripped it so tightly she cried out in pain. "You stay here!" he said severely. Then he softened his voice. "You're the best-looking girl in Rio Seco, and you're bound to know it. But you've got your head too high and proud. Even the shiniest apple falls out of the tree sometime."

She struggled, trying to free her arm. He grinned at her futile effort. He switched off the ignition and lights. "I don't know what you want to fight for. Nothing's going to hurt you."

"Danny," she pleaded, "take me home."

"After a while. Good things ought not to be done in a hurry." He sat quietly a bit, holding onto her arm and staring at her in the moonlight that streamed silver through the windshield. "For a long time now I've wanted to have you alone like this, with no brother and no damn *gabacho* like Buddy Thompson in the way. God, you don't know how you've teased me."

"I've never teased you."

"You tease a man by just being there."

"Danny . . ."

His free hand touched her leg, and she trembled. "Don't tell me nobody's ever done that before; maybe one of those *gringos* you like so much." He leaned to kiss her, but she turned her head away. He took hold of her chin. Firmly he turned her face toward him. "I don't see what you want to fight about. I've never hurt a girl. I've made lots of them very happy." He kissed her fiercely. For a moment she braced herself against him, then she began to yield.

She could sense the heat rising in his face. He loosened the hold on her arm and reached up to grip her shoulder. He pressed her to the door, his lips firmly against hers until he had to break away for breath.

As he did, her clenched fist struck him on the throat. He jerked convulsively, instinctively grabbing at his throat with both hands. Suddenly free, Anita pushed the door handle. The door swung open. She half fell, half rolled out of the car, landing on hands and knees. She tried to jump to her feet, stumbled and fell again. She could hear Danny scrambling to get out. Heart in her throat, she pushed herself up and began to run.

Danny was coughing and cursing. "Damn you, come back here! Come back here, I tell you!"

Anita ran across the moonlit pasture as hard as she could go in her high heels. Ahead of her lay a dark mass that was a mesquite thicket. Once she was in that . . .

Looking back, she saw Danny Ortiz running after her. She had a good start, but he was closing up the distance.

"You're not getting away!" he shouted in fury. The sight of him brought a surge of panic and gave her fresh speed. Mouth open, throat dry, she found herself crying. She did not look back again, but she could hear him running, could hear him cursing, threatening her.

Then she was in the brush. She began to zigzag. She stopped to look back. She could hear him but could not see him. Her breath was almost gone. She moved deeper into the brush and dropped on her knees in the shadows, huddling close to the drouth-bared ground. Her heart pounded; her lungs ached for the breath she was afraid to draw. She trembled, and her eyes burned with tears. Never before in her life had she had reason to know terror.

"Anita?" he called from somewhere in the brush. "Where are you?"

She tried to draw herself into a tiny knot. Holding her breath, she thought sure he must hear the beating of her heart.

Danny's voice softened, coaxing. "Come on now, girl, you can't stay out in this brush all night. Come on and I'll take you home. I promise you, no rough stuff. Do you hear me? No rough stuff."

She could see him now, cautiously moving in her direction. He was little more than a shadow among shadows.

"Come on, girl," he said softly, curbing himself.

"Come on out and no hard feelings, okay? I'll be good." When that did not produce results, he loosed his rage. "Come on out here, you little bitch, or I'll drag you out, and I'll give you something you'll never forget!"

He was still moving toward her.

She lay huddled like a frightened little rabbit. She braced herself to jump and run again, but panic held her paralyzed. It was all she could do to choke off a cry.

She heard a sudden little scurrying noise and almost screamed. She realized it was a jackrabbit, startled by Danny's approach. Danny heard it too but did not recognize it for what it was. He moved off quickly after it, calling Anita's name.

For a long time she remained motionless, listening. She could hear him moving farther away, still calling her, alternately cajoling and then threatening, like a man afoot, trying to catch a horse that has gotten away from him. The panic slowly left her, and strength returned. When she was sure he could no longer see her, she moved. She dared not go directly toward the house. That was what he would have expected her to do, and he might intercept her. She headed away, staying in the mesquite. When she had walked perhaps a quarter of a mile, she paused. She could not hear him.

I'm free of him. Now I can go home. Thank God, I can go home.

It was a long walk, the better part of two miles. The high-heeled shoes made her feet ache. She stopped to roll down her stockings and take the shoes off. She walked barefoot awhile. Only then did she realize she had left her purse in Danny's car. But that was little enough price to pay just to get away from him.

The ground was mostly dust beneath her feet, no grass to cushion it. Dry mesquite thorns jabbed deep, causing more pain than the high heels. She stopped and put the shoes on her bleeding feet.

After what had seemed most of the night she could see the ranch headquarters in the moonlight. She was approaching by way of the corrals and barn. The fear was gone, but weariness was heavy on her shoulders. She paused at the last corral gate and leaned on it, relief washing over her as she drew deep breaths of the cool night air. She could see the Flores house lying dark a hundred yards beyond the barn.

Home, safe. All she wanted to do now was throw herself across her bed and sleep, hopefully to forget, to blot out the nightmare. Perhaps tomorrow that was all it would seem—a nightmare.

Rough hands grabbed her, yanked her off of her feet. She tried to scream, but a hand clapped painfully across her mouth, cutting off the cry almost before it started. She felt herself being dragged under an open lean-to that had been built against the shed.

Danny Ortiz snarled: "Thought you'd got away, did you? Well, you didn't. I knew you had to come here sooner or later. Scream now and I swear I'll break your pretty little neck."

He eased the pressure of his hand against her mouth. She tried to scream, but shock had robbed her of voice. She felt her dress tear as he dragged her toward a stack of baled hay.

"I'll teach you how to treat an Ortiz, by God! Who do you think you are, anyway? I'll tell you who you are—you're the daughter of a damn sheepherder, that's all. We can buy and sell a hundred like you. Do you hear that? You're nothing! *Nothing!*"

She sobbed, and the sob turned into a loud cry. She thrashed and fought, but he had a firm grip on her wrists. He let go with his right hand and slapped her across the mouth. "Shut up and quit fighting, or I swear by God I'll hurt you!"

He thrust her backward against the hay. Tears blinded her, but not before she saw the dark shape moving up behind Danny. She sank to her knees.

She heard a surprised "Huh?" from Danny, then a sudden frightened, "Who are *you*?" She heard the solid thump of the fist that drove Danny back against the hay. Danny grunted, and Anita heard the fist strike again.

"José!" Anita cried. "José!"

Jose Rivera grabbed Danny's shirt and hauled him to his feet. He struck Danny with his right fist, then caught him with the flat of his hand as he swung his arm back. Danny reached in his pocket and brought out his switchblade knife, but one blow sent it spinning into the hay. José slammed Danny to the ground. Danny lay a-tremble, hands in front of his face. "Leave me alone! Leave me alone!"

Anita swayed to her feet. José caught her, and Anita threw her arms around him. "José."

His arms held her gently. "*Está bien*," he breathed in her ear. "*Está bien*." She clung to him, tears burning her eyes.

Danny crouched on the ground. "A wetback!" he hissed. "A damn stinking wetback!" He pushed up onto his knees. "You acting high and mighty, and all the time you been carrying on with a lousy *mojado*."

José put Anita aside and turned toward Danny again, fists clenched. He knocked Danny rolling. Danny scurried out of his reach, crying, "You haven't heard the last of this. By God I know what to do about a damn wetback. I'll fix you, you tramp, do you hear? I'll fix you good!"

Jose closed in on him. Danny turned and ran away into the moonlight. José followed a few steps and halted.

At the Flagg house the porch light went on, then the yard lights. Charlie Flagg stepped sleepily out onto the porch in bare feet and khaki pants. Anita tugged at José's arm, moving him back into the shadow of the shed. Charlie stood on the porch a few minutes, looking around suspiciously. Eventually the lights winked off.

José turned, and Anita fell into his arms.

"Hold onto me, José," she cried. "Don't say anything, don't do anything. Just hold me."

Charlie Flagg paced the living room of the Flores house, angrily smacking his right fist into his left palm as he listened to Lupe talking with held-in rage. Anita sat on a small couch, her mother on one side of her, Mary Flagg on the other, last night's tears flowing again. The rest of the Flores young had been restricted to other rooms and the doors closed except for Manuel. He listened in silent fury. Charlie saw the Indian in Manuel's blood, showing now in his dark eyes. He could imagine that look of wrath in the eyes of the Comanches who had claimed these hills.

Charlie kept bringing his gaze back to Anita, wondering. Evidently Danny had been unsuccessful; nothing had happened between him and the girl. Charlie wished he could be that sure nothing had happened between José and Anita. There was some time here that he had heard no accounting for.

He turned and stared through the window at a far-off scattering of sheep, reddish in morning's first light. As Lupe finished, Charlie said tightly, "We ain't just settin' here and takin' this, Lupe, I promise you that." He looked then at Jose Rivera, who sat alone in brooding silence, halfway across the room. José did not understand the words, but he could have no doubt about their general meaning.

Charlie said, "I doubt that Danny let his shirttail touch him till he called the border patrol. Probably woke up a patrolman in the middle of the night. I wish to hell she'd told us sooner."

Lupe said, "She was ashamed."

"It wasn't *her* doin'." He turned to José and said in Spanish, "This means you will have to go."

José looked sadly at Anita Flores, who hid her face in her hands. "*Patrón,* I do not want to leave."

"You have no choice. Either you go of your own accord or you go under arrest in the back of a *chota*'s car."

José nodded woodenly.

Charlie went to Lupe's telephone, lifted the receiver and turned the crank. "Central, give me Rounder Pike, will you?" He turned and frowned thoughtfully at José Rivera as he waited. "Hello, Rounder? Charlie. Charlie Flagg ... Yes, I know what time it is, but I got an emergency here. I heard you say the other day you needed some help. I got an *hombre* here who needs a place to go. I'm afraid the *chotas* have got wind of him ... You can? I'll bring him right over ... Sure, I know it's risky if they catch him in the car with me, but they ain't goin' to catch me. You just set tight; I'll have him over there in an hour or so."

He hung up the receiver and gave the crank half

a turn. "José," he said in Spanish, "get your things together. I have found you a job."

José gave Anita one sad glance, then went out the door.

Charlie heard Anita sob. He looked in wonder as she stood up and hurried out after José. So far as he had noticed, she had hardly looked at José the whole time he had been here. Somehow, things seemed to get by him more than they used to.

"When I get José delivered," Charlie said angrily, "and out of the way of them *chotas,* I'll see if we can't get some law enforcement around here. I'm goin' to the sheriff. Boy like that Danny Ortiz has got no business runnin' around loose to prey on young girls."

Rosa said something quickly to Lupe, and Lupe Flores nodded. "Mister Charlie, you mean the right thing, but it is better you don't do this."

"Why not? He's got it comin' to him."

"People will make a lot of talk. Danny scared our girl, but he did not hurt her. Too much talk *will* hurt her. What do you think the sheriff will say? He will say she is just a Mexican girl out with a Mexican boy, and that's the way it is with Mexicans." He shrugged. "The sheriff will laugh at you, Mister Charlie."

Charlie clenched a fist. "I helped get him elected. He won't laugh at *me.*"

"Mister Charlie, you know Anita. But what if she was some other girl, some Spanish girl you don't know? What would you think?"

Hastily Charlie said, "I wouldn't think no different. I'd . . ." He trailed off.

"No offense, Mister Charlie, but you would think like the sheriff."

A sense of guilt came over Charlie, and he did

not like it. Lupe knew him in some ways better than
Charlie knew himself.

"But we can't just let him get away with it."

Lupe's mouth went grim. "We do not need a sheriff
to take care of family things."

For a few seconds Charlie blinked in puzzlement,
until he turned and saw the look in Manuel's eyes. At
this moment, Manuel could kill.

Oh my God, Charlie thought, *not that!*

With sudden apprehension he declared, "You're
not goin' anywhere, Lupe, you or Manuel either, not
in this mood. Anything to be done in town, *I'll* do it."

Lupe said evenly, "Anita is ours."

"And she needs you at home. Soon as I get José
taken care of, I'll go see Old Man Ortiz. I'll throw a
scare into him that he won't forget."

Charlie stomped out of the house, letting the screen
door slam. He heard it slam a second time and looked
back. Manuel Flores hurried after him. Charlie
stopped. "No use you arguin' with me, *muchacho.*"

"I want to go with you."

Charlie saw cold rage still in the lad's eyes. Afraid
he already knew, he demanded, "What you got in
mind to do?"

"I don't know yet. When I see Danny I'll know."

"They tell me he carries a mean knife. He'd gut
you."

"I wouldn't give him the chance."

Charlie shook his head. "I'm not lettin' you tangle
with him."

"I've tangled with him before."

Charlie rubbed his chin and stared hard at the boy.
This was a side of Manuel he had never seen. "You
don't know how cold and mean a knife can be till

you're lookin' at it from the other side. I faced the bayonets in World War I. *I* know."

"I'd take it away from him and do to him what we did to my colt. That'd fix him good."

"It'd fix you, too."

Stubbornly Manuel declared, "I want to go with you, Mister Charlie."

Charlie shook his head. "You and your folks are my responsibility, boy. I've always taken care of you. I'll take care of you now."

Flaring, Manuel said, "Dammit, don't you think we're men enough to take care of ourselves?"

Charlie stared in disbelief. This was the first time Manuel—or any Flores—had ever spoken up to him this way. His own voice took on an edge. "Boy, you're overwrought."

"Damn right I'm overwrought. The other time I tangled with Danny, it was Buddy Thompson who came in and took over. Now it's you. Won't you people ever decide we can do things for ourselves?"

Charlie blinked angrily, trying to excuse Manuel on grounds of strain. He didn't understand this reaction at all. "You could get in the hospital for yourself, or jail . . . one or the other. Is that what you want?"

"She's my sister."

"Don't you think I understand that? And she's a daughter to me, pretty near. *I* can take care of this thing for all of us, and I sure as hell won't wind up in jail over it, either."

Manuel's fists were clenched like live-oak knots. "Do you know what paternalism is, Mister Charlie?"

Charlie supposed he had heard the word, but he couldn't remember for sure. "No, what is it?"

Manuel shook his head. "No, I guess you *don't* understand. I guess that's why I can't talk to you."

Charlie muttered to himself. Later perhaps there would be time to study this thing out and try to understand what the boy was talking about. Right now there was no time for anything.

"Manuel, there's one thing you can do. Help José get ready. I'll run to the house and get my pickup."

The word *run* was an exaggeration. Charlie rarely ran anywhere any more, but he limped along at a good gait. Shortly he had the pickup idling in front of the shed where José had customarily slept. Manuel carried out a canvas bag that held all of José's belongings. He pitched it into the floorboard of the pickup, then stood and watched, still resentful.

Anita stood in the door of the shed, tears on her cheeks. José came to the pickup and stopped to look back at her. She said something to him, but Charlie could not make out what it was. José gave no answer. He climbed into the pickup and slammed the door. He looked straight ahead, face frozen like stone.

Mary came out. Charlie said, "Whatever you do, don't you let Lupe or Manuel leave this place till I get back."

He glanced once more at Anita and shook his head, still feeling a measure of wonder that he had never sensed anything between the boy and girl. Was he really that old? His foot was suddenly heavy, and he let the pickup lurch forward. He was doing thirty miles an hour before he reached the front gate, the dust boiling up behind him.

Neither man spoke as they lined out on the dirt road across the horse pasture toward the pavement that led to town. Charlie glanced once at José, wondering what thoughts must be racing through the mind hidden behind that mask of a face. He saw the bruised and torn knuckles and knew they must be paining José. It was pain in a good cause. Silently Charlie cursed Danny Ortiz; yet at the same time he speculated that Danny might have been of help in a way he would never have realized. Charlie had no way of knowing how deep a relationship might have developed between Anita and José. Maybe it was best it be broken off now before it led to the point of standing in front of a priest. José had no future in this country; probably his situation in his own country was little better.

The Lord moves in mysterious way, Charlie thought somberly. *But dammit, he could've found a better instrument than Danny Ortiz!*

Ahead lay a curve in the dirt road. An automobile appeared, coming rapidly toward Charlie's pickup. Charlie knew, somehow, even before he saw the green color. "*Chotas, José!* Down, quick!"

José ducked below the level of the dashboard. Charlie caught a glimpse of the border patrolmen as the two vehicles met. They were giving him a good looking-over.

Charlie said in English, "Five dollars says they turn around and come check us out." He remembered and repeated it in Spanish, the best he could. He pushed down harder on the accelerator. Just around the curve was a small culvert the county commissioner's court had built to prevent runoff water from washing out the road, back in the times when it used to rain. Charlie jammed on the brakes. In Spanish he said, "Quick, José, into the . . ." He was stuck; he couldn't remember the Spanish word for culvert, if he had ever even heard it.

But José sensed his meaning, for he grabbed his canvas bag and jumped out. Charlie said, "Wait for me. It may be awhile." Jose slammed the door, and

Charlie floor-boarded the gas pedal. He watched the rear-view mirror on the outside of his door, but he could see nothing except the dust behind him. That was good, for it meant the patrolmen could not have seen José jump out and hide.

Eventually, when the road made a turn to the left, he caught a glimpse of the green car rapidly overtaking him. He slowed, letting it happen. He heard a horn honking insistently. The car pulled abreast of him, and patrolman Nance motioned for him to pull over. Charlie let the pickup come to an easy stop on an area where the bar ditch was shallow and almost flat. He waited for the trailing dust to fog over him and settle. He opened the door and stepped out slowly, making a show of nonchalance, hoping his eyes did not give him away. The patrolmen had not waited for the dust to clear; they had jumped out as quickly as their car stopped. Nance was rubbing dirt from his eyes as he warily walked up.

"Mornin'," Charlie greeted him, lifting one hand.

Nance only nodded and walked around the pickup, peering into it. Charlie saw the man's disappointment, and he smiled a little. *Thought you had me, didn't you?*

The other patrolman came up, the one Charlie remembered as Parker. Charlie tried his greeting on him and found it a little better received. "Good morning, Mister Flagg. Out kind of early, aren't you?"

"In the ranch business you never let the sun catch you in bed." Charlie tried to be calm, but a knot was starting in his stomach. "You-all wanted to see me about somethin'?"

Parker said, "We received a telephone tip this morning. Man told us you are harboring a wetback at your headquarters. Would that be true, Mister Flagg?"

Charlie sighed. "Oh, that's what this is all about?

Well, there's no wetback out there that I know anything about."

Parker studied him closely. "Would you swear to
that?"

"On a stack of Bibles six feet high."

Parker wanted to believe him. "Mind if we go
look?"

"Help yourselves. You ought to find my foreman,
Lupe Flores, out there. Tell him I said for him to help
you look."

Parker studied Charlie's face. If he learned anything, it didn't show. "We never caught you working
a wetback, Mister Flagg. I'd hate for us to start now."

"So would I," Charlie told him.

The Anglo people of Rio Seco knew little of racial
distinctions and considered Old Man Ortiz as a Mexican. Ortiz regarded himself as a Spaniard, one of the
sangre puro, above the common herd. He lived in the
Little Mexico section of town, but outside of business
it was not his practice to socialize with the Mexican
people more than the Anglos did. He was keenly
aware where the line was drawn, and he stayed beyond it. His old house had a right to be the largest in
this part of town; it was built on the sweat and blood
of the Mexican people.

Charlie punched the doorbell, then looked around
while he waited for someone to answer. He could
recall that years ago these flower beds were always
abloom with something or other, like Mary's at the
ranch. That had been when Old Lady Ortiz was alive.
She had had plenty of time to cultivate her flowers, for
she could always afford to hire someone else to do the

heavy work, and Ortiz himself had little time for her. It was her function simply to grace the household and see to the raising of their son; it was said to have been a lasting bone of contention between them that she had given him but one child and afterward had lost the ability to bear. Even in his young married years, Ortiz was said to have maintained a *casa chica*— sometimes two—away from home to take care of needs which she never satisfied. That, of course, was not considered socializing. Charlie remembered Señora Ortiz as a woman prematurely old and terribly bitter, borne to the cemetery ahead of her time. The flower beds had died with her.

An attractive young woman opened the door a little way and gave Charlie a questioning look. He said, "I've come to see Danny Ortiz."

She showed no intention to open the door wider. She stared at him uncertainly, then looked back over her shoulder. Charlie heard a man's voice demanding, "*Quién es,* Panchita?"

In Spanish the young woman replied that it was some *guero* asking after Danny. Charlie could hear the voice ordering her to say that Danny was not home. But Charlie could see a sporty-looking red sedan parked in the garage, one he was sure he had seen Danny driving around town.

The woman gave Charlie the message in English and was about to shut him out when he opened the screen and placed his hand firmly against the door, pushing it open wider. "I come to see Danny, and I've got a few words to say to his daddy as well." He stepped into the tiled foyer before she had time to get over her surprise. The woman looked helplessly back over her shoulder. "*Señor* Ortiz . . ."

Ortiz stepped into the foyer from another room, which Charlie took to be a parlor. He was gray, his shoulders stooped, a crab of a man with skin as light as any Anglo's. His eyes were uneasy, but at sight of Charlie his mouth managed at least the semblance of a smile. "Ah," he said carefully, "come in." Charlie was already in. "There is something I can do for you?"

"I'm Charlie Flagg; you've seen me."

"Yes, Mister Flagg, I have seen you often. How may I be of service?"

"I come to have some words with your boy. Where's he at?"

"Danny has gone away."

"Afoot? I seen his car in the garage. You'd just as well call him. If he don't come out I'll search the house for him."

The forced smile left Ortiz's face. "You are abusing my hospitality, Mister Flagg. I must ask you to leave."

"Leave, hell! You trot that boy out here!"

"I want no trouble, sir, but if you do not leave, I shall have to call the sheriff."

Charlie's shoulders straightened a little. "That's a damn good idea. I'd like to talk to him myself. Suppose you go phone him."

The young woman made a move toward the front room; Charlie guessed she was headed for the telephone. Quickly Ortiz ordered her in Spanish to find something to do in the kitchen and to leave them alone.

Flushing, Ortiz turned to Charlie. "Sir, whatever little difficulty my son may have gotten himself into, it should not be enough to cause trouble between two adults like ourselves. If it is a question of damage, I shall be glad to pay." He turned into the parlor and walked to a small safe which stood beside a roll-top desk. Charlie had heard of that safe, and of the ledgers Ortiz kept inside it regarding loans to the Mexican people, their payments at a crushing rate of interest.

"Money won't pay for what he tried to do."

"Money," said Ortiz, "will pay for *anything*."

"Not this time. You callin' him out or do I have to go get him?"

Ortiz tried a moment to stare Charlie down, then gave it up and called his son. Charlie heard no answer. Ortiz called a second time, and a door creaked open somewhere down the hall. Charlie could hear the wooden floor protest a little beneath each slow step. Danny Ortiz stood in the doorway, crouched as if ready to turn and run.

The sight took Charlie by surprise. Danny's face was swollen, his eyes darkened. Two large bandages covered spots where he had suffered cuts, one on his right cheek and one above his eye.

Charlie wheezed, "I'll be damned! I *will* be damned! It's the first time I ever saw this kid that I could honestly say I liked his looks."

Ortiz said, "My boy has been badly injured, Mister Flagg."

"There's a little girl out at my ranch that always used to laugh a lot. She's not laughin' today. Whatever this boy got, he had comin' to him."

Ortiz said, "You have seen my son now, Mister Flagg. I am asking you now to leave this house." Charlie simply stood there, staring. Ortiz added, "You are in this house without invitation. You are trespassing."

"Your boy was trespassin' last night, on my place. I come here with half a notion of beatin' him into the floor myself, but I reckon the job's been done better than I could do it." He took two steps toward Danny, and Danny shrank back against the wall. Ortiz cried out in protest, expecting Danny to be struck. But Charlie simply raised his hand and pointed his finger, almost touching Danny's face.

"There's some people out at my ranch that want to kill you. I talked them out of it awhile ago, but I don't know how long I can hold them. If I was you I'd get out of town, and I wouldn't wait for dinner. I'd see how fast and how far that car would go. You hear me, boy?"

Danny Ortiz nodded, his mouth open. Charlie saw to his satisfaction a gap in the front teeth. So far as he had ever noticed, it had not been there before.

Charlie said, "All right, but so you don't forget, I'll tell you this: if you ever again set foot on my place . . . if you ever again touch that girl, or any of the rest of the Flores family . . . I'll come after you myself, with the double of a rope. And when I get through there won't be a piece of hide left on you bigger than a postage stamp. Do you understand me, you pepper-bellied son of a bitch?"

Danny made some gurgling sound deep in his throat.

Old Man Ortiz squared himself up to his full height. "Mister Flagg, we are not ordinary poor Mexicans that you can address us like this."

Charlie turned on the old man. "You're right about that. I got a lot of friends that are ordinary poor Mexicans, and the worst of them stands a head-and-a-half above *you*." He looked back at Danny. "You go, boy, *now!* And you be a long time in comin' back!"

He stamped out of the house, letting the door slam behind him.

* * *

At the ranch he found Manuel in the corral beside the barn, loving the neck of his bay colt. Manuel did not speak as Charlie opened the gate and walked in. He gave Charlie a quick glance and looked back at the colt.

Charlie said, "I seen Danny Ortiz."

Manuel did not reply.

Charlie walked up and ran his hand along the pony's withers. Manuel had this colt as gentle as Candelario's little black dog. "It's just as well you didn't go with me. There wasn't nothin' left for you to do to Danny. José had already done it all."

Manuel thought about it awhile. His voice was a little cold. "It was still my place to've gone. It was *my* place, not yours."

10

Summer was a dry disappointment. Thunderheads boiled out of nowhere, full of fury but devoid of rain, making their show and drifting away like a teasing girl. The scanty moisture evaporated from hot ground almost before the clouds were gone. Only the low swales showed any cast of green. Even there it faded pitifully through July, an empty promise gone without fulfillment. All summer Charlie had looked forward to the autumnal equinox to bring rain. Now he was saying, "Maybe there'll come a little moisture before the first hard freeze."

This morning he could sense the sharp breath of frost in the air. He skirted around the side roads that let him avoid passing the main square of Rio Seco; it depressed him to see the empty store buildings, a couple of them with their front glass broken out and nobody left with interest enough to replace them or even board up the opening. He parked his pickup by a railroad siding next to the wool warehouse and feedstore. There a couple of dozen ranchmen and farmers stood around with hands shoved deeply into warm pockets, awaiting the opening of a red boxcar.

As always, Rounder Pike had the floor. "Yes sir, grass has got so thin in my country that a cow's got to graze in a lope to stay ahead of starvation."

Charlie smiled in spite of himself, and he wondered about the others who laughed. The joke was too nearly true to be all that funny. But times it seemed that if a man couldn't find it in himself to laugh a little, he would break down and cry instead.

Warehouseman Jim Sweet leaned patiently against the boxcar, waiting. He waved Charlie a greeting and asked him, "You come to take a look at the government hay?"

Charlie shook his head. "Not on purpose; saw all the crowd gathered and thought maybe somebody got run over by a train."

Sweet slapped the palm of his hand against the boxcar. "Got the first shipment of disaster hay in here, Charlie. Government says it's goin' to save all the ranchers from the drouth. You better get your order in."

Charlie grimaced. "Reckon I'll wait." But he was curious now; he made up his mind to stay around and see.

A dust-grayed automobile pulled up to the siding, and square-shouldered Emil Deutscher climbed out stiff-legged, buttoning his coat against the chill. The farmers had elected him head of the county PMA committee for several consecutive years. The county PMA officer, March Nicholson, slid out from the other side of the car, clutching bills of lading and other papers. He paused and gazed at the boxcar, pride in his eyes. "Well, friends," he said cheerfully, "there it stands. I told you they'd listen up yonder." He looked over the men who gathered in around him, registering surprise as he saw Charlie. "Well, Mister Flagg, I didn't expect to see you here." All the chill was not in the air.

Charlie said, "Surprise to both of us, I reckon. As long as I was here, I thought I'd stay around and watch."

"You be sure and do that. You could've had some of this thirty-four-dollar hay yourself if you had applied for it."

Charlie knew everybody was listening. "I can still support myself."

Nicholson riffled the forms and invoices. He ignored a hoorawing comment from Rounder Pike that he ought to bale the papers along with the hay. Nicholson looked at the warehouseman.

"Jim, you do the honors."

Jim Sweet declined. "It's government feed. This is *your* show."

Nicholson nodded. "In that case . . ." He looked around. "Yancy Pike was the first man to sign up. Yancy, you come and break the seal."

Beside Charlie's pickup, Rounder Pike spat a brown tobacco stream and drawled, "Wonder if my big brother's the first one in line when they're takin' up collection for the Community Chest?"

Yancy Pike glared at moment at Rounder. "Some things ain't to be laughed about. These are hard times." He took a wrecking bar and twisted the metal seal. Nicholson had to hammer the door latch to work it loose. He put his shoulder against the door and slid it open, straining.

"Well, Yancy," he said, breathing a little hard, "back your truck up here and we'll fill your order."

Pike maneuvered his bobtail truck into place and cut the engine. He climbed up into the truckbed, waiting eagerly. Other men moved in close to see what this cut-rate government hay would look like. Nicholson and Emil Deutscher climbed into the boxcar.

Charlie thought he heard a woeful "Uh-oh" from Emil. Nicholson said, "Here it comes, Yancy." The two men caught hold of the baling wires and swung out the first bale. It landed with a thump in the bed of the truck, dust flying, the bale breaking open as one of the wires slipped off. Men nearby leaned forward to look, then went silent, disappointment pinching their faces.

Yancy Pike's voice lifted angrily. "What kind of a gyp is this? Let me into that boxcar! Let me see!"

He climbed up grunting and looked around sharp-eyed. He backed out cursing and shaking his head. "That damn stuff's five years old if it's a day! Just look at that crud—half weeds and the other half mold. Even been chickens roostin' all over it. See them feathers? A starved-out jackrabbit would pewk over that trash!" He jumped down to the bed of his truck and lifted the bale to pitch it back into the car. He could not get hold of it because of the loosened wire.

Nicholson protested, "Yancy, what're you doing?"

"Givin' you back this crap you're callin' hay."

"But you ordered it."

"I ordered *hay*! Step out of the way there!"

Nicholson moved. Yancy swung the bale up at the boxcar door, the hay stringing out. It balanced precariously. As Yancy angrily pulled his truck away the bale tumbled to the ground and broke wide open, black inside with mold.

"Yancy, you can't!" Nicholson cried out. But Yancy already had. Nicholson swallowed in agitation, then looked through his papers. "Henry Bunch," he read.

"Henry, you placed the second order. You can take your hay now."

Henry Bunch was not a man to talk much. He just stood there, looking first at the broken bale on the ground, then up at the open door of the car. "Emil," he called, "the rest of it look as bad as this?"

Deutscher only nodded. Bunch turned and walked out to his pickup. The rest of the crowd began to scatter slowly, some taking only enough time to file by and look at the bad bale. Shaken, Nicholson stood in the car door and called after them, "There's bound to be better hay in here, soon's we get a few of these bad bales off of the top."

A couple of stragglers paused to examine the hay on the ground, then they too walked away. Finally there were only Nicholson and Emil Deutscher in the boxcar, Jim Sweet on the ground, and Charlie Flagg standing to one side, apart from the rest. Charlie moved up and stirred the hay a little with the toe of his boot. He glanced at Jim Sweet. "They named it right. It's sure as hell a disaster."

Bitterly Nicholson said, "How can they know? They wouldn't even look at the rest of it."

Jim Sweet replied, "You don't have to eat a whole egg to tell it's rotten. Looks like you're stuck with it."

"Oh no," said Nicholson, "you ordered it. If you can't sell it, I guess it's your hay."

Sweet shrugged. "I'm only here to unload it. It never was my hay. It still belongs to the government, and that's you."

"We can't just leave it here and have to pay demurrage on this car. We've got to unload it somewhere."

Sweet conceded reluctantly, "I'll let you stack it in my shed, but what you do with it is your problem."

Nicholson's head was down. "I just never figured

on a thing like this. I'll have to call the state office. Bet they never thought of it either." He looked up, hope returning. "That's what I'll do. I'll call the state office and dump it in *their* lap. It was their job to think of things like this, not mine."

He got in his automobile and drove off, forgetting he had left Emil Deutscher in the boxcar afoot.

Walking toward the bank, Charlie paused to look in the darkened, dust-gathering window of Spruell's saddle shop. Spruell had moved out last summer after doing business in that location for twenty-five years. Charlie had always found pleasure in loafing around the shop when he had any time to kill in town, running his hands over the new saddles, enjoying the feel of the artistic stamping, savoring the pleasant smell of neat's-foot oil and new leather. Now the vacant building in the middle of the square was like a missing tooth in a woman's smile. Because of drouth, people weren't buying new saddles. They were making do with old boots they otherwise would throw away—ranch owners because money was tight and ranchhands because they didn't know how much longer their jobs might last. Charlie knew some small outfits which had played out their string; they had sold every animal they owned and let all the gates stand open.

He ran his hand across the back of his neck and thought about getting a haircut, but he remembered that his favorite barber had closed shop a while back and moved to San Angelo.

"So many people leavin' town," Rounder Pike had remarked, "it sure plays hell with our football team."

Big Emmett Rodale sat at his desk in the corner of the bank. He looked up over his spectacles as Charlie walked in. He offered no greeting beyond a quiet, "Mornin, Charlie." None of his customary badgering. Charlie took that as a bad sign.

"You look like they'd lowered the interest rate on you," he remarked.

Rodale grunted. "Been losin' collateral. Yancy Pike's sheep are dyin'. What this town needs is a veterinarian."

"It don't take a veterinarian to diagnose the hollow-belly."

Big motioned for Charlie to sit down. "Good to see you. No, I take it back, it ain't good to see you, but I felt like I ought to call you in to talk." His worried manner stirred uneasiness in Charlie. "Been lookin' over your accounts, Charlie. In fact, I been studyin' your books for the last three years' business."

Charlie frowned. "And you found I made some mistakes?"

"A year like this one, anything you do is a mistake. Just bein' a rancher is a mistake. Only real difference I see between ranchin' and poker is, with poker you got some chance."

Charlie stared somberly at a sheep picture behind Big's desk. It had been made in better times; it showed a huge flock watering at a big surface tank. Not many ranches around here any more, excepting perhaps Page Mauldin's, still had that many sheep. "I spent more money for feed this year than I ever did in my life. Looks like if I stay with it this winter I'll spend even more. I ain't got it, Big. If I get it, I got to borrow it from you."

Rodale studied him a long time. Charlie tried in vain to read what lay behind those poker-player eyes;

he had always wondered if this inscrutability was born into bankers or was an acquired art.

"Charlie, I'll tell you same as I've told others. Right now, before the winter sets in, you have a chance to make a decision. Go a little farther and there'll be no backin' out."

"What's the choice?"

"Sell all your livestock now, bank whatever you got left, and wait till the rain comes. Then you can buy back in—maybe. The other choice is: cull deep, then hang and rattle."

Charlie held his silence a while, squeezing his hands together. "Big, what would you do?"

"It's not my place to say. If I was smart, I'd be rich."

The idea was not new to Charlie; he had been considering it since late in the summer. "Either way, it's a gamble on the weather. If a man thought the drouth was fixin' to break pretty soon he'd be smart to hang on. If he thought it was goin' to last he ought to sell out and salvage what he could." He paused, the long-delayed decision weighing heavily upon him. "What do you think, Big? Reckon it'll rain?"

Big Emmett shook his bald head. "I was born here. I never predict the weather."

Charlie's face was deeply creased. He rubbed his knuckles so hard they popped. "When a cowboy sells his saddle, he's through."

Emmett made no comment. Those half-closed eyes were unchanged.

Charlie said, "We been through drouths before. Look at '33. That was a woolly booger, but we come out of it somehow. We'll come out of this one. It always rains in this country about ten minutes before everything goes to hell. Emmett, I'm goin' to hang and rattle!"

A change came to the banker's eyes, and a faint smile crossed his round face. "I don't know why you agonized so long over makin' a decision; I knew all the time what you'd say. It's the only way Charlie Flagg *could* go." The smile slowly faded. "Now, then, that we got the preliminaries out of the way, we'd best get down to the nut-cuttin'." He thumbed the papers on the desk. "First thing I tell most people is that they got to adjust themselves to a lower standard of livin'—cut out the frills."

"What can I cut, Big?"

"Damned if I know. You're like a sick man with no bad habits to give up, a sinkin' ship with no ballast to throw over." He scratched his shiny head. "Well, there is one thing that worries me, and that's Tom. I don't understand him, Charlie, or you either. He wins big at the rodeos, but still you're givin' him money."

"It costs a right smart to rodeo. Travel, entry fees, eatin' . . ."

"It don't cost that much. While you was teachin' him to rope, you ought to've taught him how to count his change, too. He throws it around like it was water and he was in a boat."

"I'll talk to him."

Big nodded. "Now for the ranch expenses. You'll need to cull deep—dig in for a long fight. Was I you, I'd ship every sheep that's a day over four years old. Might even trim them down to threes. I'd give the cows a real sharp goin'-over. Bad as the cow business looks, it wouldn't hurt you to cut that herd by fifty percent."

Charlie protested, "Big, I been half my life buildin' that bunch."

"And you could be one winter in losin' it. Keep the young ones and you'll still have the blood. You can hold all the heifer calves when it commences rainin' again."

"I got some old pet cows I sure would hate to sell."

Big showed a flare of impatience. "Why is it that a rancher can get so all-fired sentimental over a bunch of old mossy-horned cows? They never get that way over a set of ewes, and four years out of five the ewes'll make them more money."

Charlie said thoughtfully, "I reckon we just keep the ewes so we can afford the cows."

"Well, right now you *can't* afford the cows! Sell them!"

Charlie gave up reluctantly. "It'll be like pullin' my own teeth. But I'll cut the cow herd in two."

Big leaned back in his chair, looking past Charlie. "One more thing you *sure* won't like. I been savin' it for last."

Charlie braced himself. "Well, then, pull the trigger."

"It's Lupe Flores. He's taken a chunk out of your ranch income for years. You been payin' him a white man's wage."

"He's been *worth* a white man's wage. Besides, he's got a big family. Man with a big family, he needs a good wage."

"All Mexicans have got big families. I know Lupe's a good man, but I got to forget about men sometimes and look at the balance sheet. You're gettin' down to the point where there ain't no balance."

Charlie looked at his big hands. "I don't know how I could ask him to take a cut in wages. Nobody ever gets his wages cut in this country any more."

Rodale's voice went quieter. "I wasn't talkin' about cuttin' wages. I was talkin' about lettin' him go."

Charlie stiffened. "Hell's fire, Big! You know how long I've had Lupe with me?"

Big placed his palms together and spread his fingers, the tips touching. He didn't look at Charlie. "I didn't say it'd be easy. But consider this: you're fixin' to cut your livestock numbers way down. The ones you have left, you'll have to buy feed for . . . and with borrowed money. Lupe Flores is a luxury you can't afford."

Charlie sat in stunned silence.

Big said, "For a long time you been talkin' about makin' Tom a full partner with you. This'd be a good time. He could come home and take Lupe's place. He'd be a help instead of a drain on you."

Charlie couldn't remember when he had ever pleaded with anyone for anything. He was tempted to do so now; he was on the point of it, but he couldn't find it in him to say *please*. Instead, he clenched his fist. "Big, are you sayin' you won't back me if I don't get rid of Lupe?"

Big's eyes narrowed as he studied the resistance in Charlie's face. "Well . . ."

"I been bankin' with you since I first went to ranchin' for myself. I'd hate like hell to have to change banks."

Big rolled the cigar around in his mouth, his eyes unreadable again. "You threatenin' me, Charlie?"

"Depends on whether you're threatenin' *me*."

"I don't threaten people. I just lay the facts of life out there for them to see." He stared awhile in irritation, then finally shrugged. "All right, keep Lupe awhile longer and we'll see what happens. But if it don't rain, he's pavin' the road to the poor-house for you."

"Thanks, Big."

Rodale grunted. "I'm not doin' you no favor, lettin' you get by with this." He stared at Charlie a long time. "You was runnin' a bluff on me. You couldn't get credit at another bank and you know it. The shape you're in, they wouldn't have you."

"If I'm that bad off, why do *you* do it?"

"Stupid, I reckon. Hell, Charlie, I couldn't cut you off any more than you could cut off Lupe. We need you around here like beans need salt. You're one of the few men I know that'll stand up and give me an argument."

"It'll rain by spring, Big. I got a feelin'."

"You've had that feelin' the last three-four years."

Charlie managed a thin smile. "I reckon I have. I bet you think ranchers are a peculiar lot."

Big nodded gravely. "They *have* to be, to stay in the business. Everybody around this damn place is peculiar . . . except me."

If it had to be a dry winter, Charlie was glad it was an open one without undue cold weather to draw the livestock into a knot and make them suffer. True, just about everything the cattle and sheep ate was dry feed dribbled out the back end of Charlie's or Lupe's pickups, and paid for with a loan from Big Emmett. The old grass dwindled until Charlie knew he would have to begin feeding hay, at least on the bad days. When a man had to feed three times as much protein supplement as usual, and hay besides, he was burning both ends of the candle. Hay feeding on pasture was considered a shortcut to the poor-house. But he had it to do.

So once more he limped up the steps and into Jim Sweet's feedstore. He found Sweet stamping back and forth across the office floor, badly out of sorts.

"You'll have to pardon me if I look like I'm about to bite you, Charlie. I've spent an hour listenin' to Yancy Pike bitch at me about how poor the wool market is, like it was my fault. And him wearin' a *nylon* coat."

Another time Charlie might have smiled; today he didn't feel like it. He backed up for a minute to the old gas heater sitting near the middle of the linoleum-covered floor. He had always hated linoleum in the wintertime; bare wood seemed less cold. "Jim, I got to have some hay."

Sweet nodded. "First thing you do is apply through March Nicholson down at the PMA."

"I'm not talkin' about government hay. I'm payin' for my own."

Sweet misunderstood. "Charlie, the situation has straightened out some. You can get good hay through the program now, not junk like that first load still moldin' out yonder in my shed."

Charlie's voice sharpened. "I'll pick my own hay and pay my own money. You *got* some hay, ain't you?"

"Matter of fact, Charlie, I don't. I can get you some, but you may have to wait a spell."

"How come?"

"Government program, is why. Most everybody that's eligible is buyin' their hay through Uncle Sam. Got so they just about have to. Dealers like me, we can't afford to lay in a supply; we'd be apt to wind up stuck with it. We can't compete with Uncle Sam. Another thing, you'll have to pay a right smart more for it now."

Charlie's face was grim. "On account of the program again?"

"Yep. Government's been buyin' most of the hay and run the price up. Feller outside the program just can't afford to buy it; he's *got* to get in. You can't whip them, Charlie. You'd just as well join them."

Color spread in Charlie's face. "The hell I will! I'll just have to find me a substitute."

Since the time when Texas was still a part of Mexico, Mexican cart men had fed prickly pear to their oxen on the long trails during the wintertime. They would break off the thorny pads and hold them over a flame on a stick or a pitchfork to burn off the sharp spines. In later years Anglo stockmen had devised more efficient types of prickly pear burners, starting first with kerosene, developing gradually to butane units fueled from a tank on a pickup bed or truck. Resembling a military flamethrower, the device spewed a long, white-hot tongue of flame which in seconds curled the thorns and left only spots of white ash. Sheep and cattle learned to follow the men, eating the hot green pear leaves as a belly-filler in place of grass and hay. Once used to it, they liked it; some cows liked it so much they would even eat it with the thorns on, until their mouths were ruined and they starved from the pain of festering sores.

Charlie could not bring himself to burn pear. All his life he had fought prickly pear as an enemy to his grass. It strained his credulity that a cow or a sheep could actually eat cactus and get any good out of it. The concept ran counter to all his instincts.

Though other natural range feed was long since gone, Brushy Top still had tobosa grass on its open flats. Tobosa was highly seasonal in palatability; cattle and sheep liked it only when it was green, and it had not been green much the last few years. After frost and into spring it was of little value for grazing, as sterile as bedding-straw. It stood dry and coarse and tasteless, and nowadays covered by a thick coat of dust. Sometimes sheep would eat even the poisonous yellow bitterweed before they would graze dry tobosa.

But it stood there in the pastures, wasting, and Charlie Flagg could abide almost anything before he could abide waste. It dwelt heavily on his mind that this dusty-gray tobosa was good filler, if nothing else, to go with the protein pellets he was spilling on the ground at a bankrupting rate every day. The problem was to get the animals to eat it.

He had his pickup parked by the side of the ranch road in the edge of a large spread of half-brittle tobosa. Hitched behind the pickup was a trailer-mounted livestock sprayer that once had been red but now was sun-faded to a dull orange and had a fresh brown stain streaked down one side.

Experimenting with the sprayer nozzle, Charlie glanced up the road and saw a heavy cloud of dust. Beneath it was a familiar black Cadillac. Page Mauldin braked to a stop and sat at the roadside a moment, staring at Charlie. They hadn't seen each other in a month or more. The longer the drouth continued, the more miles Page bullied out of that automobile, rushing from one ranch to the next, from one piece of bad news to another.

Kathy sat in the front seat. This was Saturday, and school was out. Page opened the door and planted his boots solidly on the ground, then pushed himself to a stand. Kathy waved at Charlie but stayed in the car where it was warm. Page slammed the door shut and strode unhurriedly toward Charlie with his hand outstretched.

Charlie shook his head and turned his hand over, palm up. "Better not shake with you, Page. I got syrup all over my hands."

Mauldin eyed the sprayer critically and sniffed, trying to pin down the sweet smell. "What the Sam Hill you doin', anyway?"

Charlie looked smug. "Fixin' to try out a brainstorm. Looky yonder at all that tobosa grass. I got enough of it on this place to fill every barn in three counties if it was baled. It ain't worth a Mexican *centavo* piece the way it stands—like Shredded Wheat without milk or sugar. But I think I figured out how to bribe stock into eatin' it."

The tall old ranchman chewed his unlighted cigar and looked into the sprayer. He sniffed again. "You got molasses in there?"

"Puredee blackstrap molasses. I taken a bite of some cow cake one mornin' and got to thinkin' how they put molasses in feed to make cattle eat it better. You know how an old cow'll loll her tongue out after molasses. It came to me that a little *lick* might bribe them into eatin' this tobosa."

Page Mauldin frowned. "You goin' to put it on with this sprayer?"

"It's the only practical way I know to get coverage."

"Damn practical way to gum hell out of a good spray rig, if you ask me. But I reckon you didn't ask me."

"I cut the molasses with water to where it'll go through. I don't see any reason why it wouldn't work."

Mauldin studied the sprayer with worried eyes that

seemed sunk back into dark shadows. "Doesn't seem to me like *anything* works any more. A man struggles and tries, but everything goes to hell in front of him."

"So he struggles and tries some more. There's lots of things we haven't tried yet." Charlie looked across the pasture. "I got Lupe and Manuel out yonder roundin' up some stock. Time they push them over here, this stuff ought to've dried. Better stand back, Page, so you don't get it all over you."

Mauldin stepped away from the trailer and got up-wind. Charlie climbed onto the sprayer, wrapped a short rope around the starter and pulled. It sputtered but died the first two times. He cursed the man who first invented the gasoline engine, then tried a third time. It kicked off under protest. Charlie walked out into the grass and aimed the nozzle straight forward, then pressed the trigger. The water-thinned molasses began to spray, jerking the nozzle in his hand. As the wind shifted, some of the mixture drifted back onto him. His hands turned sticky. He licked his lips and tasted the raw sweetness. Not bad, not bad at all. Watching the molasses stain the grass, the little droplets rolling sluggishly down the stems, he felt proud of himself for the idea.

He was going to be in an awful mess before he was through, but clothes could be washed.

Gradually the stream shortened and choked down. He shook the hose and feverishly levered the trigger, but the flow continued to dwindle. He called to Page, "I haven't emptied that tank already, have I?"

Mauldin leaned to look down into the sprayer. "Still half full. Like I told you, the molasses has gummed up the works."

Charlie cursed a little under his breath. "I reckon

next time I'll have to cut it even thinner, and maybe find a bigger nozzle."

Page stood with hands shoved deep into his pockets, staring morosely. "Why, Charlie? Why do you do this?"

"Like I told you, a cow or a sheep is the same as a kid. Put a little sweetenin' in their feed and they'll lap it up."

"I don't mean that; I mean, you don't have to do it thisaway. You can get feed easier than this."

Charlie knew what Page was driving at and tried to head him off. He had had all the argument he wanted on this subject from Jim Sweet. "Tobosa will fill their bellies if I can get them to eat it."

"And if this don't work?"

"A man's got to try whatever he can think of. If the first thing don't work, try the next thing. If that don't work, go on to somethin' else. Minute a man quits tryin', he's blowed up."

Page lifted a water can out of the pickup to pour water over Charlie's hands. He grunted from its weight. Page didn't look strong any more. There was little of the cowboy left in him that Charlie remembered from so long ago; Page was grinding himself into the ground.

Charlie said, "Would you like to drive around a little while we wait for Lupe and Manuel?"

"I need to be gettin' on down the road," Page said. But Charlie sensed that the old ranchman yearned for a little visiting, a little bit of friendship. He hadn't taken time for much of it.

Charlie said, "Get in the pickup. I'll unhitch the sprayer."

He asked Kathy if she wanted to go along for a

bouncy ride in a dirty old pickup or sit and wait in
that nice clean car. She decided to wait.

There were many things Charlie would like to talk
to Page about, but each man held a solemn silence,
recognizing the other's presence, yet wrapped in his
own dark worries. There was little about the dry land
that made a man feel like talking. There was comfort
of sorts simply in silent sharing of the misery.

Moving across a bare, ashen pasture and remembering how green it used to be, Charlie found himself almost wondering if it was worth the fight. Who
knew how long it might be until it rained again? He
had read an article by a historian who said this region had known drouths of ten and fifteen years'
duration in the times of the nomadic Indians. They
could tell by tree rings and such. An Indian could
strike his tepee and take his horses and follow the rivers, the remnants of game, go as far as he needed to
escape the clutch of drouth. But the white man by his
acquisitive nature was tied to a piece of land.

Charlie had always believed a man should make
his own decisions, then stand by them without question, without regret. Lately he had found himself
looking back, wondering if he had been right to stay,
yet knowing he could have taken no other course. If
he abandoned this land he abandoned hope. Where
could he go? What could he do? What else did he
know except livestock? This land was no longer something apart from him, it was a part of him like his
arms and legs. His sweat and his blood were soaked
into it. Like an old tree, his roots went too deeply
into this ground for him ever to be transplanted. Pull
him up from here now and he could only die.

A man had to make his try, and when that didn't

work he had to try something else. Try and keep try-ing. Endure, and try again.

P age said, "Charlie, there was a time you had your deeded land all paid out clear of debt. Now I hear you've used it for security; you've gone in debt again."

Charlie shrugged. "A man has to, sometimes."

"I would; that's the way I operate. But you've told me many a time you'd rather own a little place free and clear than to be a big operator and owe it all."

"Times, a man can't have his druthers. He does what he has to, to stay."

"But you were out of debt." For a moment a dim spot of envy seemed to glow somewhere back in the darkness of those troubled eyes. "God, how I'd like to have that feelin' just once more in my life—to be free of debt. You don't know how heavy it can set on a man's shoulders. You don't know how it can drive him."

I know, thought Charlie. *I was there one time. But I was easier satisfied than some people. I quit reaching.*

Page said, "You're beatin' your head against the wall. You don't have to let it cost you this much. There's an open road ahead of you if you'd throw that fool pride out the window and do what everybody else does."

"Go beg for a government handout?"

"Not a handout. I'm talkin' about what's rightfully ours, about takin' your share before it's all gone. I'm talkin' about usin' your head to think with instead of to butt with. You remind me of an old bunch-quitter horse that can't get along with the others and always goes it alone. Pride won't buy you a cup of coffee, much less a barnful of feed."

"I don't believe in it, Page."

"That's all the argument you got?"

"That's all the argument there *is*."

"You know, Charlie, you make some of the rest of us look bad."

"I don't mean to do that. I'm not sayin' any man is wrong because he doesn't pattern himself after me; what anybody else wants to do is *his* business, not mine. I just want to live by my own lights and be left the hell alone."

They made a few windmills and looked at a few little bunches of cattle and sheep. Neither man needed to say much about them; that they were wintering hard was painfully obvious. No amount of conversation would do much about that.

When they returned to Page Mauldin's car, Lupe Flores was sitting on his horse by the spraying machine, his large body slumped, one leg thrown over the saddlehorn. Manuel was standing by the car, where Kathy had rolled the window down. The two were so deeply in conversation that they did not notice the pickup until Charlie came to a stop. Manuel looked around, startled, and Kathy quickly rolled the window up to keep the dust from fogging in.

Lupe had been loose-herding a little bunch of cattle and sheep on the sprayed tobosa. The animals began running toward Charlie's pickup; they were used to being fed from it. They crowded around, bleating and bawling as Charlie stepped to the ground.

He worked his way through them, slapping cows on the rump, pushing sheep out from in front of him. "Well, Lupe, how did it go? Did they like the molasses?"

Lupe swung his leg down. "Sure enough, Mister Charlie. They did like the molasses pretty good." He paused, his round face solemn. "But they don't eat much grass. Mostly they just lick."

Heart sinking, Charlie walked out into the tobosa. The animals had tromped a lot of it down as they pushed in to lick up the sweet, sticky spray. But it was evident they had not eaten much.

Lupe saw the disappointment that fell over Charlie.

"*No le hace*, Mister Charlie," he said with a naive confidence. "We will think of something else. Me and you, we will try again."

Charlie had drained the molasses from the sprayer in the pasture as well as he could. At headquarters he set in to hose down the tank and wash it out. He dreaded going up to the house. Mary had told him the idea wouldn't work, and she would probably remind him, in words or in look. It took him a long time to get the molasses washed clean and the tank spraying clear water again. By then Lupe and Manuel had ridden in from the pasture. Charlie looked up from his work to acknowledge their arrival. Lupe nodded, but Manuel made no gesture. He didn't even glance at Charlie.

Charlie frowned. There had been a strain between him and the boy since that incident with Danny Ortiz.

I always treated him good, Charlie thought, trying for the hundredth time to puzzle it out. *Must be a phase he's going through. Boys are that way.*

Anita stepped out onto the front porch of the Flores house, looking for the family menfolks. Probably waiting to start supper, Charlie reasoned. He stretched his aching back and looked at Anita across the distance of the yard. He had watched her worriedly for a time after José had left here, dreading a sign that she might be putting on weight. Eventually he had decided there was no change. Either nothing had happened between her and José, or they had been lucky. It had been a relief to Charlie. He had never spoken to Mary of his fears, but he knew from several guarded remarks that the same worry had weighed on her mind awhile.

José hadn't lasted more than three weeks at Rounder Pike's. The border patrol had picked him up and shipped him back across the river. Anita had grieved a few weeks, but of late she was laughing again.

Charlie could hear the sound of the horses Manuel and Lupe turned loose; he could hear the drag of girths and buckles across the wooden floor of the saddle shed. He heard Manuel fetching a bucket of oats and pouring them out in a trough for the horses. Then Manuel went whistling for his colt.

Charlie gave it little thought at first, until it occurred to him that Manuel had been whistling unusually long. Normally about this time of day that colt was up and hanging its head over the fence, looking for Manuel to come pet him, and feed him.

Manuel's voice came suddenly, high with alarm. "Papa! Papa!"

He wasn't calling Charlie, but Charlie dropped the water hose and stepped down from the sprayer. He trotted quickly to the hydrant and turned off the water because he could not afford to waste any. Then he half walked, half ran in the direction from which he had heard Manuel shout. He saw Lupe hurrying out a little way into the horse pasture. Charlie paused a moment, squinting. He made out something low against the ground . . . the colt, down, and Manuel kneeling beside him.

Charlie came as near running as he had in a long time. He had to go through a gate, and he left it open in his haste. He heard Manuel crying, "Papa, he's dyin'! Papa!"

Breathless, Charlie hauled up beside Manuel and Lupe and the colt. The little bay lay on its side, making a loud noise as it struggled for breath. It had been here awhile. Charlie could see marks on the ground where it had threshed with its feet and had slung its head.

Tears ran down Manuel's cheeks. "Papa, what's the matter with him?"

Lupe had no answer; he seemed as suddenly stricken as Manuel.

Charlie couldn't be sure, but he thought he knew the symptoms. "Poisoned."

Manuel seemed lost, bewildered. "But how?"

Charlie shook his head. "No way to know for sure. Somethin' the pony ate, some kind of poison weed, I'd judge. Drouth like this, you get all kinds of noxious plants. That kind grows when nothin' else will."

"But what'll we do?" Manuel pleaded. "We've got to do somethin'!"

Charlie's throat began to tighten. He could not remember a time he had ever saved an animal as far gone as this colt appeared to be. "You run up to the big house and tell Miz Mary to melt down all the bacon grease she's got. Hurry!"

Manuel hesitated. "Couldn't we take him to a vet?"

"Ain't no vet this side of San Angelo," Charlie said. "He'd never make the trip. You better go get that grease, boy."

Manuel took off in a hard run. Lupe Flores dropped

to his knees in Manuel's place and began rubbing the
pony's neck. His mouth was set in a grim line. "Bacon
grease don't save him no more, Mister Charlie."

"We've got to do *somethin'*. The boy's got to know
we tried."

The pony lifted its head and kicked its forefeet, a
terrible noise coming from its throat. Charlie knelt
and cradled the head in his lap. "You poor little bastard," he said softly. "You poor little bastard."

Manuel was back shortly, running as fast as he
could, carrying a bucket. Charlie could see Mary
coming down from the big house, a shawl wrapped
around her thin shoulders. "How is he, Mister Charlie?" Manuel demanded, shouting as he came through
the gate.

Charlie didn't answer. He didn't think he had to;
Manuel could see the answer for himself. He looked
at what was in the bucket. "Not enough," he said.
"Better go see what your mother has got. If it's no
more than this, get her to melt down some pure lard.
And get here with it while it's still hot and thin."

He wanted to keep Manuel busy, and keep him
away from here as much as he could. Lupe forced the
pony's mouth open, grabbing the tongue and holding
it while Charlie bent a point on the rim of the bucket
and began pouring the heat-thinned grease down the
bay's throat. He did it slowly, trying not to choke the
animal. When there were signs of choking, he let up.
When the choking stopped, he began pouring again.

"Grease is hardenin' up," he said. "We'll have to
build us a fire and heat it again."

That gave him something better to do than stand
here and watch the pony die. He gathered up some
dead brush from nearby. Candelario had arrived by
now, all big eyes and wet tears. Charlie sent him for

kerosene. By the time Manuel got back with the extra grease, Charlie had remelted the remnant in the first bucket and had gotten it down the colt's throat. He started with the new bucket, pouring gently. He was aware that he had a crowd around him now, a grave, silent crowd of Mary and Rosa and Anita and all the Flores children.

The grease hadn't helped; Charlie had known it probably wouldn't. He doubted that anything would have helped, as late as the colt had been found. The breathing was more painful, more labored.

Manuel sat and cradled the bay's head and tried to hide his face from the others. Charlie moved quietly over to Mary and Rosa. "There's nothin' you-all can do out here. Best everybody goes back to the house and leaves the boy alone. He won't want everybody to watch him cry."

The women and children slowly retreated. Lupe and Charlie stayed, but they had little to do. Lupe kept bringing a little wood periodically to keep the fire going because the night chill was beginning to bite.

"Why my pony?" Manuel cried. "Why just my pony and none of the others?"

Charlie studied the question a long time and had no fully satisfactory answer for it. "A colt is like a kid. It'll try things a grown horse would leave alone."

Lupe asked, "What do you think it ate, Mister Charlie?"

Charlie shrugged. "God knows. If there was a veterinarian here, maybe we could find out. Maybe we could go hunt it down and chop it out so nothin' else would ever eat it."

Manuel said, "Maybe if there had been a vet, we could save my pony."

Charlie doubted that, but the easiest thing was to agree. "Maybeso."

For a long time Manuel was silent. He broke that silence once to say, "That's what I'm goin' to be someday, Papa. I'm goin' to be a vet."

Charlie thought of the time and money it took for a young man to become a veterinarian. Manuel had no more chance than a snowball in hell. But it would be cruel to tell him so.

Charlie and Lupe sat there, periodically poking new wood into the fire. Hunger gnawed at Charlie, but he didn't give in to it. He didn't want to go off and leave this boy alone, to give him the feeling of being abandoned.

At length he realized he didn't hear the pony's heavy breathing any more. He saw no sign of movement. He pushed stiffly to his feet and walked over there, Lupe moving with him. Charlie knelt and put his hand on the pony's neck.

"It's over, boy. Your horse is gone."

Manuel nodded. He already knew. He laid the pony's head down gently, then turned away, still sitting on the ground, covering his face in his arms.

11

Tom Flagg had been silent ever since he had turned onto the ranch road from town. Nothing he had heard had prepared him for the dismal condition in which he found the country; he had seen starving jackrabbits stripping bark from cedar fence posts. He did not think he had been gone long enough to have forgotten how bad it was. Perhaps it had slipped a lot in a short time; or more likely, he had remembered it the way he wanted it to be.

What brought the realization to him with force was the auburn-haired woman who sat close beside him on the automobile seat. He could imagine how it must look to her. Dolly had held her silence too, and he was sure he knew the reason. He had described Brushy Top to her as he always saw it in his mind's eye, with perhaps an extra rosy hue. He had not especially intended to exaggerate, but exaggeration came easy when he was so eager to please her. He was afraid the reality now had thrown her into some minor state of shock.

"It'll be better," he said, his first words in ten nervous minutes.

She made no reply. She kept looking out the side window, so he could not quite see her face.

"We're almost there," he ventured again. "Just around the next curve and you'll see it."

"What's this I've been looking at?"

"Part of the ranch, since the last two cattleguards. Headquarters is just yonder a ways. You'll like that."

"I'm sure," she replied quietly, the tone of her voice giving lie to the words.

He put his big hand on her thigh. "Not nervous, are you?"

"No. Are you?"

"Not a bit."

She glanced at him, coming as near a smile as she had in an hour. "You're a damn liar."

"All right, I'm nervous, a little bit. I'd sooner take a whippin' with the double of a rope. But we got to face up to it sooner or later. Might as well be sooner." He slowed for the turn, then gestured with his hand as the houses and trees came into view. "There it is. What do you think?"

Dolly seemed to shrink a little. "It's . . . nice. Way you've talked, a girl would think the roofs were made out of gold, or something."

"Dry weather, is all. It'd look a lot different if things was green. Give this country three inches of good slow rain and it'd come alive like a flower garden."

Dolly grimaced. "It's got a long way to go."

"It'll grow on you."

Tom pulled up in front of the barn and sat a moment, letting the dust sweep by and settle before he opened the car door. He frowned. "The tank. I believe the bass tank has gone dry."

Dolly frowned at him, not understanding what he was talking about. He pointed to a motte of trees beyond the barns and corrals. "Surface tank down yonder. Dad had it built with mule teams and fresnos when I was just a button. He planted bass in it, and I've fished out of that tank almost ever since I can remember. Now it looks to me like the chinaberry trees around it are all dyin'. Tank must've dried up."

She touched his leg. "You didn't plan on doing much fishing for a while anyway, did you?"

He pinched her thigh. "I got better things to spend my time at."

"You damn betcha you have."

Tom stepped out and unlatched the endgate of the trailer he had gotten from Jason Ellender, the one with TOM FLAGG painted on it in fair-sized letters and ELLENDER TRAILER Co. just a little smaller . . . not as much smaller as Tom had been led to expect. The way the words were put together made it look as if he were a salesman or representative of the company. He backed Prairie Dog out and led him into a corral, where he noted that horses had chewed deep gaps in many of the planks. That was a sign they weren't getting the minerals they needed from the range feed. Tom wasn't surprised; he saw no range feed at all. He scooped up a bucketful of oats in the barn and poured them out in a wooden trough for the roping horse, shutting the gate behind him. He paused to unhook the trailer and leave it where it stood.

Dolly rolled her window down. "You're taking your sweet time. Stalling?"

Tom didn't answer. He got back into the car. Dolly pointed first at the big stone house, then at the white wooden frame. "Which one?"

"The rock house, of course."

"The frame looks the newest."

"It's been added to the most. About every time Rosa came up *preñada* they added another room to the house. Ol' Lupe, he was a pretty good carpenter till he finally ran out of buildin' material." Tom pointed his chin toward the rock house. "Dad's pickup is sittin' out in front. We'd just as well go on up and start the music."

Dolly said, "The way you've talked ever since I met you, you've never been scared of anything in your life. You're scared now."

He tried to laugh, but the effort came to no good result. "They're gettin' no younger, Dolly, and it takes older folks awhile to get used to a new idea."

"Everybody's boy comes home married sooner or later. You've held out longer than most."

Tom had no intention of telling her that Charlie and Mary had expected him to come home someday married to a different woman. He pulled in behind Charlie's pickup and stopped, sitting a moment with his hands idle on the wheel before he reached down and cut the ignition. He took a deep breath and stepped out onto the ground, walked around and opened Dolly's door. He caught a quick glimpse of leg far above the knee as she slid out; that was enough to reassure him—for the moment, at least—that he had not made any mistake. Dolly looked around for a minute, taking in Mary's fallow flower beds, the big rock house.

"Just how old is this place?" she asked.

Tom avoided a direct answer. "It was a German

built it. Them Germans, they always built everything to last."

Dolly frowned. "Whoever he was, he must've died before your time . . . of old age."

"The place has been well kept. You'll like it." Tom stared at the big house as if it were a jail. "We'd just as well go on in."

"You don't act like you think they'll take it good."

"They'll fall in love with you. *I* did, didn't I?"

"You had a stronger reason."

They walked up the steps together. Tom pulled the screen back just as his mother opened the front door. She had seen his car. "Tom?" Her voice was pleased and a little excited. "Is that Bess?" Mary Flagg's eyes widened as she got a better look at the young woman on the porch. She stammered, "W-w-why, hello."

Tom said quickly, "Mom, I want you to meet Dolly. Dolly, this here is *her*."

Mary's eyes reflected a big and urgent question. She tried to make her voice sound warm, but the surprise was too strong. "It's nice to know you, Dolly. You-all come on in." She hugged Tom, but her eyes were on Dolly.

Charlie Flagg stood in the doorway, a section of newspaper in his hand. He had trailed pages of the San Angelo *Standard-Times* all the way from his big rocking chair. Grinning, he shoved out his hand and gripped Tom's hand so hard that Tom flinched. Drouth hadn't done anything to Charlie's bone-crunching grip. "It's not even Christmas, son. What's the matter, bust your rope?"

Then he too saw Dolly. His eyes widened even more than Mary's. He did not yet have so much gray in his hair that he could not appreciate a fine-looking woman.

Tom fished desperately for words he had been re-
hearsing in his mind, but the hole had dried up. "Folks,
this here is Dolly Ellender. I mean, she *was* Dolly Ellender. Now she's Dolly Flagg." As if he feared they
wouldn't believe him, he lifted Dolly's left hand. "See
the ring? Two hundred and seventy-five dollars in El
Paso." He looked hopefully from one parent to the
other. "I'm a pretty good picker, wouldn't you say?"

Charlie and Mary stared as if Tom had struck them
with a club. Charlie let the rest of the paper trail onto
the floor. Finally he blurted, "You always *could* pick
the best-lookin' horse out of a bunch . . . or filly."
That was not the best thing to have said under the
circumstances, but it had to do. He rubbed his hand
over his reddening face, floundering. "No use you-
all standin' out here on this chilly porch. We got a
house."

They moved inside. Tom grinned awkwardly while
his parents looked at Dolly. It was not in his nature
to feel foolish about anything, and he felt a vague resentment against somebody—he was not sure who—
for being forced into that position now. His mother
hugged Dolly, then fluttered around her, trying to
make her feel at ease though she was lapsing into the
German accent which always broke through when
she was flustered or excited. Dolly was nervously sizing up the living room and presumably making up
her mind about the rest of the place. Now Tom was
uncomfortably aware how the room must look to
Dolly—big, clean but showing its age, the ceiling high
and old-fashioned, the way they were building them
when going to the toilet meant a venture outdoors.
The furniture was old and gross and overstuffed. The
wide mantelpiece was cluttered with photographs
and trinkets, mostly dear to Mary Flagg but a mess to

anyone else. Nothing like that fancy motel room in El Paso where Tom and Dolly had spent two nights after being married by that Mexican justice of the peace or whatever he was in Juarez.

He knew he had talked too much about this ranch, building it up in her imagination beyond all reality. But hell's bells, a woman ought to know a man is going to spread things thick when he is trying to sell her on a proposition; she ought to make allowances. He wouldn't have lied if it hadn't looked like he had to, to keep her interested.

Mary's old German accent broke out like a rash. "I don't know what's the matter with me . . . you must both be hungry. I'll get something on the table."

Tom protested that they had eaten in San Angelo, but his mother seemed not to hear. He decided she needed something to do with her hands while she tried to gather her wits. Mary said, "You want to come in the kitchen with me, Dolly? I'll throw some little thing together in a hurry. I hope you're a good cook."

Dolly cast a quick and pleading glance at Tom. "Well, not really . . ."

"You'll learn. Tom's a big eater. I'll teach you some of the things that he always likes . . . the German *Mehlspeisen* and all that."

Tom knew the last thing Dolly wanted to do right now was go into that kitchen. But he simply shrugged his shoulders to her silent call for help.

Charlie Flagg stood in his sock feet, staring after the two women. At length he said, "Well, I'll be damned. I'll be damned."

Tom studied his father's face for some indication of what Charlie was really thinking. "How do you like her, Dad?"

Charlie pondered his answer. "Like I said, you always had a good eye."

That was no real answer, certainly not the blanket approval Tom wanted. "You'll like her, Dad, when you get to know her."

"How long have you known her, son? I mean, this ain't somethin' that just sprung up all of a sudden, is it?"

"I've known her a good while."

"She a rodeo girl . . . a barrel racer or somethin'?"

"No, her old man . . . her daddy . . . has a big trailer outfit. You've seen the name . . . Ellender. He's the one built the trailer I been haulin'."

Charlie nodded thoughtfully. "I've seen the name. Rich feller then, I expect?"

Tom shrugged. "You know how it is with them big businessmen. They take in a lot of money, but they spend a lot too. Big income, big outgo . . . you never know where they stand."

"Just the same, she's probably been used to things awful nice. Reckon how she'll take to a greasy-sack outfit like this?"

"She'll do fine, Dad. She'll do real fine."

Charlie frowned deeply. "She's a good woman, I expect, else you wouldn't of married her." He walked over to the mantel and gently picked up a small framed picture of a woman. He glanced toward the kitchen, then carried the picture to a desk and slipped it into a drawer, face down. "Does Bess know about this?"

Tom avoided his father's eyes. "Not hardly anybody knows yet, except you-all and Dolly's folks. We ain't been in circulation much."

Charlie looked at the closed drawer. "Bess always had the idea . . . *we* always did . . ." He glanced up.

"Somebody's got to tell her. It ain't right that she finds out from gossip."

"Don't look at *me*. I can't go talk to Bess. What would Dolly think?"

"Does she even know about Bess?"

"She knows there's a girl here I used to go with a little, that's all. I reckon that's enough for her to know."

"I reckon." Charlie moved away from the desk but glanced back. "Well, I'll go talk to her in the mornin'. We just never figured there was any question . . ." He shrugged, leaving the rest unstated. "This girl must've taken a powerful hold on you."

"She sure did." Tom could not tell Charlie all of it. He figured his father was too old to understand how a woman could drive a man beyond all endurance by always being there, somewhere in sight but just out of reach, tempting him with her eyes and her voice and the way she moved, seeming always to invite him to reach and take but pulling away just as he tried, managing somehow always to leave the impression that the next time he reached, she might stand still. She had built his hunger until he could stand it no more. In desperation he had presented his proposition, and they had wound up signing a marriage document in Spanish just across the river, where he could have her back at the motel as fast as a Mexican taxi driver could make the run.

Charlie stood by the front window, looking toward the barn. He saw Lupe Flores come out of the horse pen and young Candelario walk out from the milking shed, meeting each other. At the distance Charlie had no idea what they said to each other, but he could tell they both were laughing. As they started toward their white frame home, Anita came to meet them from the chicken house, a basket of eggs on her arm. Candelario shared the joke with her, and all three were laughing when they went up the steps together.

Charlie could not remember when he had last found anything he and Tom could laugh at together. Maybe it was true what some people said, that Mexican families tended to be closer than Anglo families, that they shared a degree of understanding which most Anglos only wished for. He wondered if Manuel or Anita or Candelario would ever come home someday and dump a surprise in Lupe's and Rosa's laps like Tom had done here tonight. He doubted it.

Well, there was always a time for patching up past mistakes, or at least for trying to. He turned to face his son. "Tom, since you're married now, you've got to be thinkin' farther than you used to. It's time we had a talk, me and you, about this ranch."

Tom twisted uneasily. "I been lookin' at it. Looks like the devil's taken first lien."

"By rights this place is half yours. I've always promised you a partnership. You worked for it all the time you was growin' up. You got it comin' to you."

"We don't have to talk about that right now, Dad. We'll sit down someday and work it all out."

"No use puttin' it off any more. You've got a little woman in yonder now that deserves somethin' more than a car and a horse trailer. She deserves a *home*."

"Dolly won't worry about that for a while. She's got a different way of lookin' at things than most women."

"I doubt that. Every woman—I don't care how else she may talk—has got a nestin' instinct. Minute she gets a man she wants to start buildin' her a nest. Country woman, city woman, white, black, or brown—they all got that instinct about them. Yours'll build her a nest right here."

Tom lifted his hands, then dropped them in helplessness. "Dad . . ."

"I can sure use your help, son. There's a lot of work needs doin' on this place that me and Lupe just can't seem to get to any more. Feedin' these cattle and sheep takes so much time, and me and Lupe ain't either one as young as we used to be. I been watchin' some of the soil work that people have been doin' to help try to make the most out of the little rain we *do* get. I been thinkin' if I had me a little more help I'd run a pittin' machine over all the bare areas I could get to, and drop some grass seed in. Those pits would catch water from these little floatin' showers that come by once in a while, and that grass seed might germinate and give the old country a chance to hair over a little. And some of the places where the stock has packed the ground down so hard, I thought we could run a chisel through there and break up the hardpan so the moisture could get on down instead of runnin' off. Those are all things we could do around here, son, if we just had help. We'll bring this place back to what it used to be, and we'll split all the profits down the middle."

Tom said darkly, "Ain't been much profit lately, I'd judge."

"If we could run this place the way it ought to be, and if we'd just get a little rain . . ."

A woman's voice came from the kitchen doorway. "Mister Flagg, do you know how close Tom came this year to being the world's champion calf roper?"

Charlie nodded. "I read the papers."

"Next year he *will* be the champion," Dolly said. "I'm going to see to it."

Charlie said dubiously, "That'd be awful hard. Runnin' a ranch don't give a man much time . . ."

"He's not going to be running a ranch, Mister Flagg, not for a while yet. He's going to be out getting famous. *Everybody* is going to know Tom Flagg."

"Everybody *already* knows him ... everybody around Rio Seco."

"One little bitty town? That's not enough for us, Mister Flagg. It's nowhere near enough."

A touch of anger came to Charlie Flagg, and he struggled to put it down. "It's been pretty good for *me*."

"Everybody has his own standards, Mister Flagg. I married a man who's going to be a champion. *That's* what it's going to take to be good enough for Tom and me."

12

Another summer came. The brush was green—it reached deep and found moisture when nothing else did—but there was little grass and few weeds that a sheep or a cow would eat. Times, in the long, hot afternoons, a shimmering mirage lay just below the horizon, a silver phantom lake so real it made a man lick his dry lips though he knew it was a cruel lie, a deceit of a Nature adding mockery to injury against a land desperate for water.

Wherever Charlie drove to the accustomed feeding grounds, the cattle and sheep stood waiting. They had little reason to wander off into the pastures, for they found nothing there except exercise. They crowded around the pickup, bawling and bleating so that Charlie could hardly even hear the old pickup motor knocking. The young cows were thin enough that their hipbones stood out, the pattern of their ribs rippling beneath ragged hides as they walked, and this despite all the money he had borrowed and spent on them.

Charlie had seen poorer cattle, but he had never owned any. He had always said you couldn't starve a profit out of an animal, and he hadn't meant to try. But he had waited too long last fall to put the cattle on feed, hoping against hope for rain to bring on some winter picking. When they started downhill, they went fast. He was never able to feed the flesh back onto them. He studied them with hard-bitten eyes and knew nothing but green grass would ever cover those ribs with tallow again. There was no way a man could do it out of a feed sack.

He fed what he could afford, and more. When Jim Sweet suggested he could get it cheaper through drouth disaster relief, Charlie said, "Rain is what we need. Charity we've always lived without."

As summer went on and feeding continued with little slacking off, Charlie began dreading the fall confrontation with banker Big Emmett Rodale. He figured Big would hit him again with that damn foolishness about letting Lupe go and bringing Tom home to help take care of the business. Tom was a grown man; Charlie wouldn't try to make him do something against his will, even if he thought he could. From what he read of the rodeo standings, Tom was in a good position to move up and take the title this year; all he needed was to knock off two or three of those big-money shows late in the season. There was small chance he would willingly back away from that now and settle down to running a feed route on dusty ranch roads where hungry cattle and sheep made enough racket to drown out a rodeo crowd. Even smaller chance that Dolly would let him. From what little Charlie had seen of her, he judged she had become one of those stop-watch wives who sat in the contestant's grandstand, keeping her own

watch to check the time-judges and to analyze critically every move or gesture her man made that might
cost a tenth of a second here or half a second there,
lecturing him later about his errors.

One day Big phoned Charlie at dinner to ask him
to be there the following morning. Charlie spent a
sleepless night trying to find a spot in his mattress
that didn't seem to have a lump in it. Next morning
he had his pickup parked in front of the bank before
opening time, but he stalled long past nine o'clock,
waiting for Big to have plenty of time for his morning
elimination. That might not make much over-all difference, but every little bit helped.

As usual Charlie paused to weigh himself on the
bank scale. It was about the only thing in town that
was still free. To his surprise he found he had lost
weight through the summer. There was always a good
side to adversity if a man looked hard enough for it.

Big frowned as he beckoned Charlie to come over
to the big desk and sit down. They shook hands, and
Big said, "Haven't seen you much."

"Out of sight, out of mind, they say. I figured the
less you thought about me, the better."

"Oh," Big grunted, "I been thinkin' about you,
all right. Been doin' my homework on your financial statement. You remember what I said to you last
year?"

"And you remember what *I* said."

Big skirted any argument on those points. He
pushed his open folder of notes across the desk at
Charlie. "I wish you'd look at them figures. Especially the cattle."

Charlie gave them a perfunctory glance. "Nothin'
in there that's any news to me."

"I don't have to tell you that you've lost money

on everything you've touched. The sheep are bad enough; I doubt you could sell your ewes today and recover the feed bill you've got in them. But the cattle are three times worse. A sheep can root-hog for itself on short range better than a cow can. Those cows of yours are as poison as strychnine."

Charlie shrugged. "I don't know anything I can do about it."

"There's one thing: sell them."

Charlie's mouth popped open. "Sell my cows?"

"Sell them. There's no way a man can swim with a millstone tied around his neck. Those cows are the biggest millstone you ever saw."

All manner of protest stirred within Charlie, but somehow he managed to contain it. He glumly studied his sore, work-roughened hands. "You remember '33, don't you, Big? That was a rough time, roughest I ever had till I run into this one. I didn't sell my cows in '33."

"It finally rained in '33. It's beginnin' to look like it never *will* rain an end to this one."

"I was still workin' for cowboy wages out west of the Pecos River when I got my first cows. Some of these I have now, they're direct descendants of my first eighteen head. There's never been a day since I was good grown that I haven't owned some cattle."

"Tradition, Charlie. Tradition's fine as long as a man can afford it. You can't."

"What if I sold the last of them heifers and it came a good rain the next week? I'd never get that blood back."

"Every cow bleeds the same color of red. What goes into her stomach means more than what goes into her bloodline."

Charlie rubbed his knuckles so hard they turned

almost white. "I ain't arguin' with you about that. It's just that I sure hate to part with them. A rancher without any cows is like a man walkin' down the street without any pants on. He's just not respectable."

"Would you be any more respectable in the poorhouse?"

"It's all true what they say about bankers. You're a hard man, Big."

Big shook his head. "I'm the kindest man you ever saw, Charlie. I'm tryin' to save you from yourself." He took back the folder, lifting one sheet of paper from among the rest and handing it to Charlie. "I got a suggestion. You're goin' to jump six feet high when I tell you, but I want you to study on it till you see I'm right. There's one kind of animal that's kept right on payin' its way through this drouth, that's taken less feed and paid more dividends than sheep or cattle either one."

Charlie glanced at the paper, then looked up in protest. "Big, you tryin' to tell me to go out and buy me a bunch of *goats*?"

Big snorted. "Told you you'd jump. But you got to think of it from the money standpoint. That's no health resort you're runnin'."

"But *goats*! Outside of a few Spanish goats for meat, I never owned a goat in my life and I don't ever intend to. I'm no Ayrab."

Rodale's voice was dry. "You never used to have any gray hair, either. Now it's the only kind you've got. Time changes everything but economics. I know where there's a string of good young Angora muttons you could buy. Muttons are easier than nannies and kids. These goats'll shear you a mohair clip twice a year. Mohair's one of the finest fibers in the world, and it's outsellin' wool by a right smart here lately. The money you get out of those heifers will just about pay for the goats, and this bank'll stand you for the runnin' of them. You'll be doin' a favor for the man that wants to sell them and you'll be doin' a favor for yourself. What do you say?"

"What I'd say wouldn't do for these women to hear. But it looks like you've got me whipsawed." He looked around irritably. "Goats on Brushy Top! I'd about as soon be infected with lice."

"They'll grow on you."

"So will lice."

"You've got to change your attitude, Charlie. These aren't your old ordinary goats ... these are *mohair* goats, Angoras. They're aristocrat goats, and mortgage-lifters."

"A goat is a goat."

Sitting on the corral fence, his bootheels hooked over a lower plank, Charlie looked down gloomily at the Hereford cattle penned inside. He glanced up the road for the dust cloud that would mean the livestock trucks were coming. He didn't see it yet.

Beside Charlie sat Tooter Thomas, soft-bellied cattle trader out of Rio Seco, holding a tally book in his left hand and thoughtfully chewing a stub pencil. Charlie had phoned him before daylight this morning—told him he had two loads of goats coming in today and that he planned to ship his cattle out on the same trucks.

"I figured on sendin' them to the San Angelo auction," Charlie had said, "but I'll give you first refusal if you'll put your tradin' britches on."

Folks said the trader would buy a one-eyed tomcat

if he thought he could resell it for two-bits profit. He jotted figures in the book and mumbled to himself. Charlie let his gaze drift aimlessly across the corrals. These were all the cattle he owned except two milk cows, and they didn't count. His mind ran back down the hot, dusty, happy years he had worked to build his herd, both in numbers and in the blood. Big Emmett could say what he wanted to about bloodlines, but dammit, a man had to believe in *something*. Charlie remembered things long forgotten, hardships and joys, and an ache pulled in him at the idea of giving it all up.

These were good cattle, as good as had ever walked these hills. Charlie had always bought registered bulls to run with the cows, though he never kept up the papers. Many was the time Mary had set her heart on a piece of furniture or something else for the house, only to have to give it up because Charlie saw a good bull he thought he couldn't do without.

He knew most of the individual cattle. He could call to mind the mammies of them, and sometimes the grandmothers and great-grandmothers. That young cow with the stub tail—she had lost it as a calf when Tom had impatiently shut a trailer gate a little too fast. Her old mammy had had the same run of hard luck before her; she had had her tail eaten away in a bad screw-worm year. And her mammy, Charlie remembered, had been a salty old bitch they had to rope almost every time they needed to bring her in. Charlie would have sold her but Tom had been only a boy then, and that old cow was his favorite of all the herd. He had always loved to rope.

That heifer yonder with the small red spot around her eye had come from a cow that was the daughter of a dogie Mary had raised on a bottle. The dogie's mammy was a first-calf heifer that died giving birth. Charlie could remember how he and Lupe had cut into the still-warm heifer to save the half-born calf. They hadn't let Tom watch because they thought it was too bloody a sight for a boy. Didn't seem so long ago, really. But that little calf had been the grand-mother of this heifer here. Time sure had a way of slipping by a man.

Time and memories—so many good things and so many bad—but strange how the bad things seemed to fade so that you remembered mostly the good. Maybe that was one of life's main compensations, having those memories with the rough edges blunted down and the bright parts polished to a diamond gleam.

He wondered if someday he would even forget this son-of-a-bitching drouth.

Tooter Thomas mumbled louder, nodding in sat-isfaction. "Decent set of heifers, mostly. Of course, there's a few that need cullin', and we'd have to han-dle those at a packer price." A trader could not afford to concede perfection in anything, not even in Jesus Christ. "I've worked it up careful and been as gener-ous as I could." He handed the tallybook to Charlie and pointed with a thick, stubby finger. "How does that figger look to you?"

Charlie grunted. "Looks like hell!" Tooter was offering him only about a hundred dollars a head. Before the drouth there was a time they would have brought three times that much. "Give me that pencil."

He did some figuring of his own and handed back the book. "That's what it'll take to buy them."

Tooter shook his head in exaggerated disbelief. "Charlie, you're livin' in the past. They've wrote a whole new catalog. Did you hear about that cow

THE TIME IT NEVER RAINED

thief who got disgusted and gave himself up to the
law the other day in Angelo? He stole two heifers and
lost eighty dollars on the deal." Tooter bent over the
book and took back his pencil. He chewed on it as if
he were cutting teeth. Finally he handed the book to
Charlie again.

"There, Charlie, that's the very best I can do. You'll
just have to take it or I'll go on back to town."

Charlie frowned over it and shook his head. He
reached for the chewed-up pencil and figured some
more. He passed the book back. "That there's rock
bottom, absolutely the lowest I'll go. If you can't give
that, there's no use us wastin' any more of each other's time."

The trader looked at the book, then shrugged.
"Charlie, if you'd been in this country eighty years
ago they'd of hung you for robbin' stagecoaches."

Charlie said regretfully, "I've done the best I could."

The trader climbed down from the fence, looking
back to see if Charlie was weakening. "Well, 'bye,
Charlie."

"Take it easy, Tooter. Glad you could come out."

Thomas took his time walking to the car, and
Charlie was just as slow moving down off the fence.
Tooter opened the car door, fooling around a minute
getting the cushion fixed to suit him. He slowly slid
his bulk behind the wheel, carefully glancing back at
Charlie. He closed the door and started the car, racing the motor a moment before he backed out. He
was watching Charlie, and Charlie—standing by the
fence—was watching him. Tooter backed the car a
hundred feet, stopped, pulled forward again and cut
off the ignition. Charlie started walking toward him,
looking as uninterested as he could.

Tooter stepped out of the car. "Charlie, I've always

been a damn fool. Never was able to make any money because I got such a kind heart. I'll split the difference with you."

Charlie looked sadly at his cattle and said, "Get your checkbook."

Charlie had known from the day he lost his cows that he would lose Lupe Flores next. It happened after Tom stepped off of Prairie Dog a little too fast at a rodeo and broke a bone in his foot. The doctor put a walking cast on it, but that didn't help enough. Tom would be out of rodeo for a few months at least. Missing those big-money shows at the end of the season meant he was washed out of any chance at the title this year, and he wouldn't be able to start in time enough next year to catch up. So he came home; there was nowhere else to go. And with Tom here, even half crippled, Big Emmett made it clear that Charlie no longer had any excuse for keeping Lupe. Big had enough influence to find Lupe a job at a livestock yard in San Angelo; at least he wasn't turning him out to starve like some old used-up horse set loose on the desert.

The last thing Lupe put on the borrowed bobtail truck was a boxspring and mattress. He lashed a tarp down over them, then stepped to the ground to survey the job. The wind was blowing hard out of the west, carrying the dry taste of dust. A loose corner of the tarp flapped against the sideboards. All the property Lupe and Rosa owned was packed onto this truck, and into a cotton trailer Charlie had borrowed from Emil Deutscher. This was harvest time, but Emil didn't need the trailer. He hadn't made a crop.

The Flores family stood in an uneven line across

the front of their wind-swept yard—Lupe, Rosa, Anita, Luisa. Manuel was out past the barn, where they had buried his bay colt. The smallest boys, Candelario and Juan, knelt to pet the black dog they were having to leave behind.

Blinking back tears, Juan said, "I wish we could take him with us. I bet they've got dogs in Angelo."

Charlie put his hand on the boy's thatch of black hair. "He's a ranch dog, *hijo*. He's growed up out here where he's had the whole world to run in. He couldn't live cooped up. Town's no place for a dog." He added with a touch of bitterness, "Or a boy, either."

Lupe rubbed his neck and looked at the ground. He and Charlie had avoided each other's eyes. Mary stood beside Rosa, both women crushing handkerchiefs in their hands. Neither was talking. Tom stood to one side, leaning on his cane and watching soberly. Charlie looked around for Dolly; she was sitting on the front porch of the big house, watching from a distance. She hadn't come down to speak to Lupe's family, but he guessed she didn't really know them. Perhaps she felt this was a private farewell, best reserved to old friends. He *hoped* that was the way she looked at it. Ever since Tom had brought her home this time, the ice in her eyes had been thick enough to chill a man across the room.

"Just think, Lupe," Charlie said in a thin attempt at cheer, "regular hours from now on. You won't have to get up till six-thirty. Go to work at eight, get off at five, and it won't matter to you whether it rains or not." None of this was true; he had seen enough of the stockyards to know better.

Lupe was lost in gloom. "It will always matter to me, Mister Charlie. Any time I see a cloud, I will hope you got a big rain."

Charlie blinked and looked off toward the barn, toward Manuel. "I never thought it would wind up like this. I thought we was all fixed here for life."

Lupe shrugged. "God has His reasons. He knows that when we have our bellies full, we don't bother much with Him. He knows that we stop and listen to Him only when the trouble comes, so once in a while he sends trouble. Maybe He says to Himself, those people down there they think they are too big to need God any more. One time He made it rain for forty days and forty nights to punish the people. This time He made it dry. Someday when all the people learn to pray again He will make it rain." Lupe looked down. "I will pray, Mister Charlie."

"This is just temporary. It'll rain and everything'll be the way it was. You-all will be comin' back. You watch what I tell you—there won't be nothin' changed."

Lupe nodded, but Charlie saw the realization of truth in his dark eyes. Lupe knew—as Charlie knew—that times change, and people change. Lupe had been born on a ranch and had lived on one or another all his life. But put him in town awhile and there was little chance he would come back. He would accustom himself to new ways, set down new roots. He was far from being a young man any more. Once he changed he would not change back.

Charlie could talk about it all he wanted to, but nothing would ever be the same again.

He didn't notice the car on the town road until it came over the last cattleguard and pulled to a stop beside the truck. Kathy Mauldin stepped out and stood a moment, holding the open door, looking at the Flores family. She said quietly, "I was afraid I'd miss you." She put her arms around Rosa, then around Anita. She started looking then, for someone was missing.

Manuel trudged back from beyond the barn, his head down. He stopped beside Kathy, started to raise his hands and then self-consciously dropped them back to his sides. They stared at each other, not saying anything.

Finally Kathy spoke. "Angelo's not so far, really. You can drive down any time you take a notion."

Manuel glanced at Charlie, then cut his eyes quickly away. Charlie had seen resentment in them the last few days. Manuel had said nothing to him, but the message in his eyes had been plain to read: *You sold us out.*

Charlie didn't know how to explain it to him. He guessed he hadn't really tried. Now it was too late.

It was a long, silent, awkward moment, and Lupe finally broke it up by clearing his throat and getting into the truck. Manuel gave Kathy a last long look, then climbed up on the other side, sliding in with his father. Candelario followed him. One by one the rest of the family got into the old car.

Charlie kept looking at the truck, not wanting it to end this way with Manuel. He walked up and leaned against the door. "Manuel, I expect we can use a little help next spring at shearin'. I couldn't afford to pay you what I've paid your daddy, but I'll find a way to pay you somethin'. Reckon you can come?"

Manuel seemed surprised. Tightly he said, "Maybe. We'll see."

"I hope you can, boy."

Charlie couldn't reach Manuel, who sat in the middle, but he put his hand on top of Candelario's hat and gave the boy's head a gentle shake. Candelario began to cry. Charlie bit his lip as Lupe turned the ignition key and started the motor. He stepped back and lifted his hand in a half-hearted wave. The tears were working down his own cheeks as he could see them on Lupe's, and he didn't give a damn.

"*Vaya con Dios*, Lupe."

"*Adiós*, Mister Charlie."

He didn't move until the truck had disappeared behind the car and trailer, well down the road. The black dog chased after them all the way to the bend, then started walking back, panting hard. Charlie stood in silence, aching from the sudden emptiness inside. He blew his nose and delayed turning around to face the others until he could surreptitiously wipe his eyes.

When at last he turned, he found Mary watching him. He looked quickly away, not wanting her to see what was in his face; she would probably think him an old fool for letting the thing get to him the way it did.

She had never spoken reproachfully to him about this, but he had known the thought must be there. *I could have held onto them a little longer*, he knew. *I could have taken help like the others, and maybe I could have held onto them*. He wondered why she had never put the thought into words. It wasn't like her not to ache at him about something she didn't approve of.

To his surprise she slipped her hand into his and leaned against him in a way she hadn't done in years. He could feel her shoulders shake a little as she tried to hold it all inside.

"Mary," he said, knowing she must understand what he was talking about, "a man does what he feels is right, no matter what it costs him."

She nodded. Her voice was so soft he barely heard it. "I never said different."

Presently Mary asked Kathy to come on up to the house, but Kathy gave some quiet excuse that Charlie couldn't hear. She got back into the car and left. That, Charlie thought, was a wasted trip. Kathy hadn't spoken a dozen words during the short time she had been here. Or maybe it wasn't wasted. Sometimes a woman could say a lot and never open her mouth.

Tom moved up closer to his mother and father. Charlie brought himself to say, "Well, son, they're gone—gone with the wind and the dust and the drouth. Now it's just us . . . me and your mother and you."

Tom did not reply.

As the Flaggs turned back toward the big house, Dolly came down from the porch and walked out to meet Tom. She had nothing to say to the elder Flaggs as they passed her, and they were too somber to speak. She looked back after them a moment and finished moving to where Tom stood in front of the frame house. He said solemnly, "We just as well go in and take a look at the house. This'll be home for us."

Dolly looked down the road, where the dust was slowly clearing. "Seemed like a lot of fuss to make over some Mexicans."

"They were friends."

Her brow arched. "I just now got a good look at that oldest girl, Anita. I'll bet she was a *real* friend."

Tom's face colored. "What do you mean by that?"

"I know all about Mexican girls. Seemed to me when we got married, you brought a good education with you."

Tom's voice was acid. "I don't reckon me or you

either one was exactly an amateur. But whatever I knew, there didn't none of it come from Anita. She was like a little sister. I don't want you sayin' anything about that girl again. Now, you comin' into the house, or not?"

She followed him, pouting. Tom gave her a glance and looked away. He couldn't remember he had ever seen that pout before he married her. He was damn well getting used to it lately.

He stopped in the living room. The empty place was like a graveyard. "It's clean. Rosa always loved this house. She wouldn't of left it any way but clean."

Dolly's jaw took a firm set. "It's a Mexican house. It's got a Mexican smell to it."

"It's your house now. What kind of a smell *you* goin' to put in it?"

She turned her back on him and folded her arms across her breasts. She said tightly, "This wasn't part of the bargain when we married. You didn't say anything about taking me to live in a poverty hole like this."

"I can't help it if my luck went bad. I can't grow a new foot."

"You didn't have to break *that* one. If you hadn't gone off half-cocked and pulled a damnfool stunt . . ."

"All right, I was mad when I went after that calf, and I didn't have my mind on what I was doin'. But if you hadn't been chewin' on me so goddam hard just before I went out there . . ."

She turned on him, her eyes crackling. "Go ahead, try to blame your mistakes on me."

"I'm not puttin' all the blame on you; I'm blamin' myself too. I ought to've slapped your teeth out the first time you opened your mouth against me instead of just standin' there and listenin' to it." He took a step toward her and jabbed the tip of his finger at her breastbone. "So now we're here and the honeymoon is over and you'll by God make the best of it!"

She didn't cow. She lighted a filter-tip and drew on it slowly, her eyes burning like the end of the cigarette. She blew the smoke into his face. "We'll see," she said. "We'll see."

13

Despite the cast, Tom could drive a pickup if he took time and care. Keeping his weight on his good foot, he could help Charlie swing feed sacks up onto the bed of the vehicle. As he had done with Lupe in recent times since feeding had become such an encompassing chore, Charlie divided the feeding routes into two segments, one for himself, one for Tom. It was better that Tom not have to climb up and down into the bed of the pickup to rip the strings on feed sacks, so Charlie used the oldest of the two vehicles, the blue one Lupe had driven. Tom took Charlie's. It was not much better, but Charlie had had a shade-tree welder put a homemade bulk feeder onto the bed. All Tom had to do to distribute feed to the stock was to reach through his window and pull a rope. The pellets would spill out.

Charlie took over those chores which Tom couldn't manage. At such times he sorely missed Lupe. He had never fully realized before just how much heavy work Lupe had done for him.

They fed all winter and were still feeding when the scissor-tails returned, a sign spring had come to stay. Charlie did not look forward to shearing. No fresh green grass arose from the cracked earth. It looked as if his new crop of lambs would grow up without ever knowing the sweet taste of green feed—those that *did* grow up. Charlie's shearing-pen count of lambs would be considerably short of the one he had made at marking time, soon after they were born. More had died than he wanted to think about.

Many baby lambs became lost trying to follow their mothers in the wild melee around the feeding grounds. Some would never pair up again. Other lambs were simply abandoned. When a ewe was doing poorly, she might kick off her lamb in an instinctive move to conserve her own strength from the drain which milk production made upon it. It was a cruel thing but part of her nature. The lost or abandoned lamb would wander aimlessly in circles, bleating in hunger and bewilderment until its strength was gone. Then it would lie down under a bush to die in solitude in its own good time, giving up the struggle after a few harsh days of a futile life.

All his years in the sheep business had never steeled Charlie to the point that a dead lamb did not bring a wrench to his soul. In practice, however, he did not find a great many. Buzzards and other scavengers cleaned the pastures quickly and well. But Charlie did not have to see the bodies to know of the deaths; he could tell by the ever-increasing number of ewes that showed up with no trailing offspring.

Driving around the feeding ground, watching ewes with baby lambs tagging along sore-footed, trying to keep up as their mothers hurried in for their share of the pellets, Charlie sometimes felt himself slipping toward despair.

All of his life he had enjoyed what he had done. It had been fun being a wage-working cowboy out on the Pecos; with all the hardship, there had been more than enough offsetting compensations. Ranching, too, had always been enjoyable to him. Even during the hard years of the '30s there had been more pleasures than pain. But he had had his youth then, and a resilience the years had since stolen from him.

Now there was no longer any fun in it; now it was an ordeal.

He saw a ewe badly outdistancing her lamb in eagerness for feed. The lamb tottered along far behind, near exhaustion, bleating pitifully. Charlie rolled down the window and shouted in fruitless anger, "Slow down, old Nelly! There'll be a-plenty for all of you."

Instead the ewe broke into a run, following the pickup. "Damn sheep!" Charlie gritted. "Damn stupid sheep!"

The heedless ewe was headed for the other sheep and for the feed she knew would be there. In this wind and in the confusion around the feed grounds she would probably never find that lamb again.

An explosion of rage brought Charlie boiling out of the pickup. He reached down for rocks and hurled them at the ewe, shouting above the wind. "Get back there, damn you! Get back there and act like a mother!"

The ewe dodged around Charlie and hurried on toward the other sheep. "Damn you!" Charlie shouted. "Damn you!"

Tom had been out of practice at ranch work, but he was soon back into the swing of it. He said most ranch routine was like riding a bicycle; once learned, it was never forgotten. But Charlie had cause to wonder if Tom was really enjoying it, or if his mind was still out on the rodeo circuit, on the long highways and in the crowded fairgrounds. Tom never spoke of rodeo unless Charlie chanced to ask him something, and Charlie made it a point to mention the subject very seldom. The fact that Tom did not discuss it made Charlie suspect he was covering up the extent to which he missed it.

Doc Fancher declined to take the cast off Tom's foot when Tom wanted it removed; the doctor said it needed to stay awhile longer. When Tom got home he cut it off for himself. He showed little limp, but he could not hide the pain from his eyes as he walked.

"Just like you," Mary remarked to Charlie in her exasperation. "Nobody ever could tell *you* anything either."

At night was when Charlie missed the Flores family most. During the long years they had lived in that frame house, the lights in their windows had been a friendly beacon in the darkness. When Mary wasn't talkative or Charlie needed a change because she was talking *too* much, he would walk over to visit the Flores family. He would sip sweet coffee with Lupe and Rosa and listen to the cheerful racket of frisky children raising Billy Hell.

Now that Tom and Dolly lived in the Flores house, Charlie found no warmth in the place. Tom usually just sat there silent, his mind far away. Dolly never talked much to anybody. Nights, she sat watching a portable television set she had picked up on the rodeo circuit. The picture was fuzzy because the little rabbit-ear antenna did not pick up a good signal this far from San Angelo, but she seemed to prefer even

that to any kind of conversation. Charlie tried sometimes to get interested in the television and somehow
find himself a niche in that little world Dolly had
walled in around herself. But he found it no substitute for conversation, or for the laughter of children.
So far as he could tell, Dolly had no intention of providing either.

It occurred to Charlie that if Dolly was as cool in
the bedroom as in the sitting room, he never *would*
have any grandchildren.

He tried to hire temporary shearing-time help in
town, but it was not available. Too many people
had left. He borrowed Diego Escamillo from Page
Mauldin and a man from Rounder Pike. He phoned
San Angelo to see if Manuel Flores could work a few
days, but Manuel said he was busy in school. Charlie
received the uncomfortable impression that Manuel
didn't want to come.

He found a pair of wetbacks drifting through his
south pasture and hired them for the duration of
shearing, or until the border patrol came.

Big, fat Teofilo Garcia arrived early and set up his
shearing machine. Charlie noted that Teofilo had
brought only four shearers. Half the eight drops
would be idle.

"That ain't enough men to do a job," Charlie observed.

Teofilo shrugged. "Is not many shearers to find any
more. But with all this dry, is not so many sheep, either."

Charlie's own flock was cut to less than half what
it had been when the drouth had started . . . and how
many years ago was that? He had to stop and figure.

It stood to reason there was less work to hold the shearers. Increasingly they were abandoning this line of endeavor for something that offered more opportunity.

While Tom and the other riders were out in the pastures gathering more livestock, Charlie worked his way through the sheep already in the pens. Used to be that he would mark out some of the older dry ewes at shearing time and sell them to lighten the grazing load on the range. If a ewe was not delivering a lamb, there was no profit in keeping her after she had yielded up her fleece. But now it was hard to tell which ewes had never lambed at all and which ones had produced a lamb but lost it. As for older ewes, there weren't any. The old ones had long since made a one-way trip to town.

In an idle moment Teofilo walked out amid the bleating sheep and stood with Charlie beside the fence. He looked at the open sky, squinting his dark eyes at the harsh glare of the sun. "Brown in the west. Maybe this afternoon she blows up another duster."

Charlie turned to look. That brownish haze along the horizon was such a common sight he paid little attention any more. It was the *clear* days he noticed. "West Texas rain."

Teofilo did not smile; the old joke had stopped being funny.

Charlie stayed close to the tying table, making sure the fleeces were rolled and tied to suit him, and bagged as they were supposed to be. Wool was short in staple this year, and carried little grease. Times like this were hard on the clip's appearance. The shearers were good, though. All four were old hands who worked with a steady competence, if not with the flash and speed of youth.

It was awhile before Charlie noticed that one of
Teofilo's young tie-boys had picked up a shearing
head and joined the others. Of a sudden it occurred to
Charlie that five shearers were working. He stepped
to the machine and looked at the ewe the boy had
tied down. Seeing blood in a half dozen places, he
reached abruptly to shut off the shearing head.

"Get up from there!" he roared. The boy arose
wide-eyed. Charlie demanded, "What the hell you
doin', tryin' to kill that ewe?" The boy backed away
as Charlie dropped to one knee. Carefully Charlie's
fingers searched along the cut places where drops of
blood swelled like bright red rubies against white
skin.

"You're no shearer, you're a butcher! And look at
that ragged fleece! You've cut it up like it was a pile
of rags. Now, you take that shearin' head loose and
don't you let me catch you amongst my sheep again,
do you hear?"

Hurt and angry, the boy kept his head down. He
mumbled something Charlie could not hear over the
roar of the machine. That provoked Charlie even
more, for he liked to be looked in the eye by man or
boy. He pointed to the tie-stand. "You get back yonder where you belong!"

Up on the sacking frame, Teofilo's oldest son Chuy
was staring at Charlie, hostility in his eyes. From
what Charlie had heard around the wool warehouse,
that boy had turned into a *gringo*-hater. Probably
got it from running around with Danny Ortiz, Charlie figured. Well, that was his privilege and Teofilo's
problem. In his present mood Charlie didn't particularly give a damn.

"Boy," Charlie said again, "you better drag it!"

Shame-faced at being scolded in the presence of

his friends, the tie-boy put away the shearing head and returned to his normal station. Charlie could see Chuy talking to him, and he could well imagine what Teofilo's son was saying.

As his blood began to cool, Charlie started wishing he had taken the boy off to one side, out of earshot, before dressing him down. But it didn't help any to be thinking of that now.

One of the older shearers quietly finished the ewe's fleece and let her up. Charlie watched her rush bewildered into the bunch and shove her head down under other sheep's bellies in an effort to find shade from the hot May sun. With all those cuts he would have to watch her; she was likely to develop a bad case of screwworms.

Busy on the other side of the rig, Teofilo had missed the ruckus. Now he came around, and Charlie pointedly told him he didn't want any more kids butchering up his sheep.

Teofilo looked away and said quietly, "He is a boy, Mister Charlie. A boy has to learn."

"Be damned if he has to learn on *my* sheep!"

Noon came. The shearers dropped out one by one as they finished the last sheep in the pen. Teofilo Garcia shut off the machine. For a moment the corrals seemed in dead silence by contrast, though the ewes and lambs continued to bleat for each other. The shearers and tie-boys trailed down to the live oaks where Teofilo's old cook Mike had the chuckbox set up, waiting now with stewed goat, red beans, hot *jalapeno* peppers and the like.

The two wetbacks looked to Charlie, asking with their eyes if they were to follow the shearers. Charlie shook his head and pointed to his own house. "*Vamos por la casa grande. La madama tiene la comida.*"

Teofilo would have fed the *mojados* if Charlie had asked him to, but some of the crew would surely resent them. No use asking for ill will when good shearers were so hard to find; little by little, expedience was chewing away at the rancher's prerogatives. Charlie led the way to the house, followed by Tom, Diego, and Rounder Pike's man Anselmo. The two wetbacks stopped uncertainly to look at the door. At home they probably would not be invited into the house of the *patrón*.

Twenty years ago Charlie would not have asked even Diego or Anselmo into his house to eat. The line then between Mexican and Anglo had been sharply drawn. In recent times that line had become clouded and largely erased, so that Charlie rarely thought twice about asking a Mexican in. Somewhere along the way he had unconsciously drifted into acceptance of the idea so that now he did not remember it had been any other way.

The wetbacks gave him a moment's hesitation. Moving afoot across the country until they had lost count of the days, they had not had a bath in Lord knew how long. In close quarters their presence would have been hard to ignore. But to ask them to eat outside, apart from the others, would have been blatant discrimination, and would have been duly noted by Diego and Anselmo.

Charlie found that Mary had bailed him out of the dilemma without even being aware of it. She had moved a large table onto the big outdoor porch where the men could all eat together in the cool shade. Charlie figured he could put the *mojados* on the downwind side and no one need know he had ever been troubled. He showed them where to wash in the old German milkhouse while he went into the big kitchen for a look. He had seen Emil Deutscher's car parked in the yard. He hoped to find Emil, but he saw only Hildy Deutscher, an apron tied around her ample waist.

"*Wie geht's*, Hildy? Where's ol' Emil at?"

"He is at home planting cotton."

"Plantin', with the weather so dry? There won't a stalk of it ever come up."

Hildy Deutscher shrugged. "Just the same, the law says he has to. If he doesn't plant he will be penalized on next year's acreage allotments."

Charlie snorted. "Government lends the farmer drouth money to get by on, then makes him waste it on seed and gasoline to plant a crop that can't even grow."

Hildy smiled thinly. "Don't look at *me*; I don't make the laws."

"I wonder sometimes if *anybody* does. I get to thinkin' sometimes they just come out of a machine, untouched by human hands."

Dolly was in the kitchen pouring tea into ice-filled glasses. Charlie watched as Tom went in and spoke to her. If she said anything in reply, Charlie neither saw nor heard. Her auburn hair rolled up at the back of her neck and an apron tied around her slim waist, she looked tired and ill at ease. She didn't fit in this big kitchen. She seemed out of place alongside the comfortable-looking older women. It was probably the first time she had ever helped prepare a meal for a crowd of working men. Charlie could tell by looking and sniffing that the food bore Mary Flagg's trademarks, and perhaps some of Hildy's. Any help Dolly had given would have to be classed as unskilled labor. He had a notion she wouldn't take any prizes as a cook, because every time Tom came to the big house for anything, he raided the refrigerator.

Charlie made a crooked face as he noticed Mary had remembered to fix the turnip greens. When everybody else was eating cake, she would spoon out another helping of greens for Charlie and tell him in the presence of all that he needed to lose some weight.

He noted that Dolly walked a long way around the wetbacks, as well as the neighbor help. To her they were all the same.

By midafternoon he could tell the old shearers were tiring. They moved slower. One had begun feeling badly and had gone off to lie in the shade of the live oaks. That left only three to do the shearing.

This wouldn't of done in the old days, he thought, *not when we had so many sheep. We'd of been a week getting through.*

Even as it was, supper would come late if the men were to finish all the sheep in the pens. Charlie saw Teofilo pick up a shearing head and study it, evidently considering shearing a few himself. In his younger days he had been a powerhouse. But Teofilo put the implement down. At his weight he could not stand up to that kind of work any more.

Charlie motioned for Teofilo to move out away from the machine so they could talk. Leaning against a live-oak tree, Charlie rolled a Bull Durham cigarette. For sake of economy he had given up ready-rolls. He offered the sack to Teofilo, who accepted it and rolled a smoke for himself.

The brown haze Teofilo had pointed out this morning had turned into a duster, laying a golden mask across the sun. Charlie had to turn his back to the wind and cup his hands so he could keep a match burning long enough to light his cigarette. A roll-your-own was hell to light, and harder to keep burning.

"Teofilo," he asked impatiently, "what's the matter with that crew of yours? You got nothin' but old gray heads any more who can't put in a day's work. Why don't you hire you some young shearers?"

"You tell me where, Mister Charlie." Teofilo's round face showed futility. "You don't get no young men no more. Only these *viejos,* too worn out to shear and too old to start somethin' else. This drouth, she makes all the young men quit. You go out to a ranch where one time you shear five thousand sheep, now you shear maybeso two thousand. You go to a ranch where one time you get three days work without once you move the machine, now you get one day—maybe half a day. Not much money for a shearer that way. The rancher, he don't want to pay more because already he's lose his butt on these sheep. So the young shearer, he says *to hell with all this hard work.* He goes to the oilfield or to a filling station, or maybe in the Army. Pretty soon now nobody is left to shear sheep but the old men. And with *them* . . ." he paused sadly ". . . every once in a while we got to stop for a funeral."

"Looks like you could train a *few* young boys, at least. Don't look like *everybody* would quit."

Teofilo looked away discreetly. "Sure, Mister Charlie, I try. But it don't work so good. Young boy, he got to shear plenty sheep to learn. I don't have no sheep to teach him; he's got to learn on the rancher's. And he's make mistakes, and cut up some sheep. Pretty soon the rancher gets mad and says, 'Boy, you get the hell out of this pen and don't you ever come back.' A few times like that, the boy thinks maybe this shearin' ain't worth a damn anyhow, so he goes and looks for a job in town. It's close to the pool hall there, and no rancher to cuss him out."

Charlie cast a quick, suspicious glance at Teofilo. Garcia was gazing across the pasture, his face unreadable.

By four o'clock only two shearers were working at a time. The shearer who had dropped out first was still feeling badly and hadn't come back. The others wearily took turns about going to the chuckbox for rest and a cup of coffee. It looked as if the sheep never would get sheared.

Charlie stared at the young tie-boy, who wasn't being pressed much to keep up. The boy glanced now and again at the nearly idle machine, his hands making graceful little make-believe motions as he imagined himself shearing. It was, after all, an old craft and an honorable one that a skilled workman took pride in, and that a boy could admire.

Reluctantly Charlie shoved his hands deep into the pockets of his dusty khaki pants. With a jerk of his head he said, "Boy, come over here."

The youngster regarded him warily but took a few steps in Charlie's direction, stopping out of reach.

Gruffly Charlie said, "Boy, you really want to be a sheep shearer?"

The lad glanced at the fence; he was ready to run. "Yes, sir."

Charlie pulled out his right hand and rubbed it roughly across his chin, considering how much work it would be to keep a cut-up sheep from finding a place to lie down and die. He looked toward Teofilo Garcia to see if the *capitán* was watching, but Teofilo appeared to be busy moving sheep. Charlie pointed his chin at the shearing machine.

"All right, then, you can't learn nothin' standin' here. Get over yonder and go to work!"

Charlie was blue-lonesome the night the visitors came. Mary had cut down her club and church activities and was at home most of the time, but they seemed not to find much to talk about. Many nights they didn't pass a dozen words between supper and bedtime. Charlie seldom considered walking over to Tom's house; he knew he wouldn't find conversation there either.

Hearing the car, he dropped his newspaper on the floor and got up to snap on the big yard floodlights. He was so hungry for talk that lately even the border patrolmen had a hard time getting away from him.

"Who is it, Charlie?" Mary called from the kitchen.

He wondered how she managed to spend so much time in there, and why he saw so little come out of that kitchen any more. She hadn't baked him a cake in so long he couldn't remember what kind the last one was. Always had some of those damn greens ready for him, though, seemed like.

Charlie opened the front door and squinted. "Looks like a whole carload of them." The druggist Prentice Harpe slipped from behind the steering wheel. On the off side, Charlie saw the sour-faced Yancy Pike. Finally, from the rear seat, a tired, droop-shouldered Page Mauldin crawled slowly and painfully from the car.

"You better put some coffee on, woman," Charlie said over his shoulder, then stepped out onto the porch in his sock feet, pleasure rising warmly in him. Company was scarce. People had too much trouble on their minds to idle away the time visiting neighbors the way they used to. He called, "You-all light and come in this house."

They shook hands with him one by one, Page Mauldin the last. Charlie couldn't remember when Page had last set foot on this porch. In fact, he couldn't remember for sure when he had last seen Page anywhere. The old rancher had worn out two automobiles in the last three years.

"You-all sit down," he said, but Mary stood in the kitchen doorway and they had to file by and shake hands with her first, bowing slightly, most of them, in a manner that was dying out. They held their hats in their hands.

Page said, "Mary, I'd take a paralyzed oath . . . the years pass kindly over you. You're as pretty as I've ever seen you."

She smiled. "I wish I could say the same for you."

Page glanced at Charlie. "She's always been an honest woman, too. Never lies, even when a lie would help."

Charlie only grunted. "You-all sit down. We'll have coffee directly."

He saw a nervous eagerness in the face of Prentice Harpe. Now that the cattle business had gone into drastic decline, the druggist no longer wore his cowboy boots. It occurred to Charlie this was the first time Harpe had ever been out to this ranch. There had never been any reason for him to, Charlie supposed. But the thought set him to wondering: *Why now? Yancy Pike wouldn't of come, not without he wanted something. What have I got that anybody would want?*

Whatever it was, they didn't bring it up right at first. They started small talk about the last duster, comparing it to the big ones of the '30s. They talked lamb crops and livestock feed while the smell of coffee drifted out of the kitchen.

Tom had seen the car, and his curiosity got the better of him. He came over to see who was there. He apologized for Dolly's absence; she was awfully busy, he said. Charlie knew what she was busy at—that damn TV set. The hardest work she did, some days, was walking back and forth to turn that dial.

Presently Mary brought in a tray stacked with cups, and half of a chocolate cake. Charlie wondered where in the hell *that* had come from; he hadn't seen any of it. The small talk continued as the men sipped their coffee. Charlie noted that Tom took a big slice of the cake and ate it hungrily. *Cake is probably as scarce at his house as it is in this one*, he thought. He could sense nervousness increasing in Prentice Harpe, and a nagging impatience in Yancy Pike. They kept glancing at Page Mauldin as if waiting for him to start something. Page gave Charlie the strong impression he was putting off something unpleasant.

Finally Harpe said in an effort at humor, "Saw old Arch the other day. Told me anybody who said he'd ever seen a longer drouth than this one was either a liar or a hell of a lot older man than *he* is." He looked around expectantly, waiting for someone to laugh. The best he got was a half-hearted smile from Tom. Harpe went on, "Cattle market has sure gone to pieces. Worst it ever was, I guess."

Charlie didn't reply. Like a lot of people, Prentice Harpe had gone into cattle while the bloom was on the rose. He hadn't realized that when the bloom faded, the cattle business had traditionally had thorns that cut to the bone.

Harpe glanced expectantly at Page Mauldin. When Page said nothing, Harpe went on, "You know,

Charlie, they've got price supports on lots of farm commodities. Cotton ... wheat ... tobacco. And look at the feed grains. You go to buy a load of feed on the open market and you've got to pay somebody else's high support price to get it."

Charlie only nodded, convinced that Harpe was purposely working up to something.

Harpe said, "Then you go out and feed that supported grain to unsupported cattle. Doesn't seem fair, does it?"

"No, it sure doesn't."

Harpe looked once more at Page, and Charlie saw him jerk his chin as if prompting the old ranchman.

Page cleared his throat. "Charlie, what we come for is, a bunch of people all over the state are gettin' up a cattleman's caravan to go to Washington. We think Rio Seco ought to be represented in it."

Charlie said, "Sounds like a good idea. If they could get the support taken off of that feed ..."

Page gulped a big swallow of coffee. "Charlie, that ain't exactly what the caravan is about. We didn't intend to ask them to take the support off of feed. We're goin' to ask them to put a support price on cattle too."

Charlie frowned. That put a different complexion on things.

Harpe said quickly, "Charlie, we want you to go for us."

Charlie put his coffee cup aside and squeezed his hands together until a sharp pain lanced through one of them. He glanced first at Page, then at Pike, and finally back to Harpe. He could see they were not making idle talk. He said, "I got as much business in Washington as a boar hog has with a set of tits." He turned his attention to Page Mauldin. "Page, you got more cattle than anybody in this part of the country.

If this is what you really want, looks to me like you're the one that ought to go."

Page said, "That's the whole trouble of it, Charlie. I got the reputation of bein' a big rich rancher. That's a damn lie; you know it and I know it. But them *federales,* they don't know it. I owe more money than anybody in this country except the federal government. But anything I was to say, they'd discount because I'm supposed to be rich."

Charlie looked at Harpe. "Why don't you go, then?"

"Because I'm a drugstore cowboy. They'd sense it right off. We want somebody who *looks* the part, somebody who's always been a cowman, somebody who's got *ranch* burned on him like a brand burned on a bull. We want a man who—when he walks in there—will make everybody say, 'Now, there is the genuine article.' You're the one for that, Charlie. You've got *image.*"

Charlie's eyes narrowed. "Got what?"

"Image, Charlie. You're colorful."

Charlie rubbed his chin. "I been accused of lots of things, but this is the first time I've ever been accused of bein' colorful. Mostly what I am is *old.*"

Page said, "You'd be just right, Charlie. You're what they call a *little* rancher. Whatever you said, they'd listen to."

"I ain't got no cattle any more. I had to sell them all."

"So much the better. You're a perfect example of what's happenin' to all of us."

Yancy Pike had been sitting in the corner nervously rubbing his hands. Charlie noted that Yancy hadn't eaten much of his cake. "Charlie, we'd take it mighty kind of you. What do you say?"

Charlie looked a moment at Tom, and to his surprise he saw agreement in his son's face. "You never been to Washington, Dad. You'd enjoy the trip."

Charlie got up and paced the length of the floor a couple of times. He paused a moment to stare at the Remington painting of the Indian warrior defying the enemies who were about to overrun him. He walked on to the window and gazed out upon the lighted yard; he did not look at anything in particular. "Boys, you got a right to ask for anything you want to. But seems to me like the regular cattlemen's outfits like the Texas & Southwestern would oppose you on this; it goes against everything they stand for. They'll say things are bad enough now without gettin' the government mixed up in it too."

Harpe said, "The government is mixed up in it already. They've got all these drouth programs and support programs. When you're out, you have to help pay for the ones that are in. You'd just as well be *in* with the rest of them."

Charlie kept looking out the window. "Did you-all ever study what's happened to the ones that've been in for a long time?"

Yancy growled, "All I know is that the government keeps their crops from gettin' cheap the way cattle have done."

"You think so? Take cotton for instance. Government says, 'Boys, we're goin' to peg you a price and guarantee you prosperity.' The boys all say, 'Fine, let 'er rip.' Then Uncle Sam says, 'Boys, we're raisin' more cotton than the world wants to buy at our price, so we got to cut down.' This year you whittle off twenty percent and next year thirty percent and the next year forty. You whittle yourself half to death. Now you can't be trusted, so the government sends out a man with a search warrant—or what amounts to one—to check your place and be damn sure you don't overplant.

"Pretty soon it's like the dog chasin' after its own

tail. Government keeps cuttin' down the acres to cut down the cotton. You wind up gettin' less money because you've got less cotton, so you work harder on what acres you've got left. You put on extra fertilizer and raise more cotton on less land, so then the government's got to cut you down again. And all this time Uncle Sam has got the cotton pegged so high that it's priced out of the world market. Mexico and them other countries, they say to theirselves, 'Here's our chance to get in.' Every time Uncle Sam whittles off, they add on. One mornin' the fanner wakes up and finds out somebody else has got his market. He's worse off than he ever was, and infested with federates that don't know how to run their own business but are almighty free in tellin' him how to run his."

Charlie swung his gaze to Page Mauldin. "We've always had our up times and our down times in the cattle business. We take a stiff dose of medicine and then the thing gradually corrects itself. But you let a price-support crop get sick and it stays sick. The day the government goes to supportin' cattle, the cow business is lost, and the cowman is just another peon with his hand out to Washington."

Prentice Harpe said, "Charlie, all I know is that I worked for twenty years to save the money I sunk in those cattle. Now unless somebody does something, I've lost it. If price supports will bail me out, then price supports are what I want."

"But what about the future?"

"Let the future take care of itself. It's the present that's about to sink me. If I can ever get my money back I'll sell those cattle and never look at another cow."

Charlie looked again at Page. "I reckon I can understand Prentice, but I thought *you'd* see different. You used to."

Pain stirred in Page's deep-sunk eyes. "We're drownin', Charlie, all of us. We're grabbin' at whatever we can catch ahold of."

Yancy Pike stood up in stiff belligerence. "You got to do it for us, Charlie. You owe it to your friends."

A defensive anger began rising in Charlie. "If I owe anything to my friends, it's to do what's right. And this ain't right."

Page said, "Charlie, I know how you've always felt about these things. Believe me, I wouldn't ask you if I didn't feel like it was a case of have-to. But these are hard times. Hard times force a man to do things he might feel like otherwise was a little bit wrong."

"You can't be a little bit wrong any more than you can be a little bit pregnant."

Charlie could remember a few times, back when he was a cowboy kid and did something foolish, that Page Mauldin had shown anger at him. He hadn't seen that anger in thirty years. Now, here it was. Page said, "Charlie, you always did have a stiff back. But I thought maybe you could bend it a little for *us*."

Charlie shook his head. "I'd do anything I thought was right. I'm sorry that we don't see alike on what *right* is."

Yancy Pike stomped across the floor. He stopped at the front door and glowered. "I always said that when hard times come, a man finds out who his friends are."

Prentice Harpe's face was red, but he kept his lips sealed tight.

Page Mauldin struggled to his feet. He looked awfully old, pitifully weary. "Charlie, we'll have to find somebody else to go. I hope you don't intend to fight us on this thing."

Charlie shoved his hands deep into his pockets and

looked at the floor. "I won't do nothin' except what I think is right."

Page nodded grimly. "Then at least we all know where we stand."

Charlie followed the men out onto the porch but not into the yard. He wanted to say more, but he feared everything had already been said, and probably too much. He watched numbly as the car lights lanced through the darkness on the town road.

Tom Flagg said behind him, "I'd testify to anything for a free trip to Washington."

Charlie grumbled, "There's damn little in this life that ever comes free. One way or another, you pay for what you get."

Tom shrugged. "But sometimes it pays a man just to kind of play the game, and not go wavin' a red flag in people's faces."

Charlie turned impatiently. "I didn't wave a red flag, I just told them what I think. I've always told people what I think."

Tom didn't argue that point. "But there's times other people disagree with you."

"There's times other people are wrong."

Tom shrugged and walked out into the darkness toward the frame house. Charlie watched him awhile, then closed the door and went back into the living room. Mary's eyes were on him. Impatiently he said, "Well, you'd just as well speak your piece too."

Mary just stared. "There's still a slice of that chocolate cake left. You want it?"

Charlie looked at her a moment, trying vainly to read what was in her mind; he never could tell what she was thinking when she didn't want him to. He shook his head. "Don't you know it's fattenin'?"

14

Time was when an inch of rain would have brought fresh life, a greening to the land. But there had been grass then, a spongy turf to soak up and hold the moisture, and live roots to draw sustenance from it. Now the bare ground had nothing to soften the impact of rain, to catch and drink up the water. The first burst of precipitation would pack and seal the topsoil. The falling raindrops would strike hard and splash upward, brown with mud. Instead of soaking in, the water would swirl and run away, following the contours of the land, seeking out the draws and swales. Burdened by a heavy load of stolen soil, the rivulets swelled quickly into streams, the dry draws turned to rivers, and the muddy rivers bled away the vitality of a once-generous land.

When it was over, most of the water was gone, lost because the soil which thirsted so desperately could not capture and hold it. The sun and the hot wind would come and quickly steal back what moisture had managed to stay. Those grass roots which had

survived the long dry time would drink of the scant
moisture and send up fresh green leaves, only to have
them wilt and brown and retreat back to earth before
they had a decent chance at life. For a few days a thin
cast of green would buoy the ranchman's hopes, give
him a fresh surge of enthusiasm and encourage him
to take a deeper hold. Then, slowly, the hope would
die away under the hot west wind and the merciless
pressure of a hostile sun.

When the clouds had passed and the sun burst once
again into its accustomed place, Charlie Flagg drove
over his pastures, hoping that somewhere he had received and retained enough rain to do some good. At
intervals he would stop to stick a knife blade into the
ground and take out a plug of soil. An inch or two of
mud would stick to the blade. Below that, the dirt was
dry. He would look up to the open sky, hoping for a
sign that the clouds might come back. But there was
no sign. The skies were clear and the sun was hot.

Charlie and Tom managed to summer without
feeding in most pastures. But to keep the ewes from
drawing thin they had to wean the lambs and send
them to market in July, much earlier than Charlie
liked. "Damn lambs are so little they wouldn't make
a box lunch for a bobcat," he complained. They
brought little money . . . nowhere near enough to
pay for their mothers' feed bill last winter, or the bill
that continued into summer for some of the poor-
doers. Wool market was sluggish, too. When Charlie
added up the income from lambs and wool it fell far
short of what he had paid for feed, taxes, lease, and
interest.

Only the mohair goats had paid their way. Those
lousy goats! He had nourished a secret hope that they
would lose money so he could throw them up to Big

Emmett as an example of the banker's poor judgment. But contrary to other commodities, mohair remained in strong demand. The goats not only more than paid for the little amount of feed Charlie had grudgingly bought for them, but they subsidized a considerable share of the feed bill for the sheep.

It was hard to hate something that continued to pay when all else was going to hell. If they hadn't been bought at Big's stubborn insistence, Charlie might have begun to like them.

All summer he worriedly watched Tom. His son's foot had evidently healed; the limp was long forgotten. Evenings now, Tom would go out to a large pen that served as a practice arena. He had bought a dozen small Brahman calves which he kept around the milk lot, and which he daily crowded into a tight roping chute. Sometimes Shorty Dunn would come out and work the gate, turning the calves loose for him one at a time so Tom could make a run at them on gray Prairie Dog. Other times Dolly did it, though she showed no taste for touching the calves, or stepping into the dirt and fresh manure to crowd them into the chute.

Charlie never volunteered; that would have seemed a tacit approval. Every time he heard that chute gate fly open and the horse race out across the soft earth, he felt Tom slipping away from him a little.

Sitting at the roll-top desk, reading-glasses perched near the end of his nose, Charlie ran his hand through hair which turned grayer with each dusty, barren season. He looked up at Tom, who sat in a rawhide-bottomed chair, absently roping his own foot with a short pigging string.

Charlie knew the wish that lay behind every throw of that string. He riffled through the papers on the desk. "Tom," he said gravely, "you been partners with me now for a year, pretty near. I think it's time you taken a look at some figures."

"I never been very apt with figures."

"I think you ought to know where we stand."

"We don't stand very good; that's enough for me to know."

"It's *not* enough. You ought to know what we've took in and what we've put out and where it's gone. That's just sound business."

Tom shrugged and took the papers his father thrust at him. He mused over them and brought his finger to rest on a figure near the bottom of the last sheet. "Is this what we owe?"

Charlie nodded.

Tom said, "Goddam!" He tugged at his lower lip a minute. "How much deeper can we go?"

"That's up to Big, I reckon."

"Maybe it'd be better if we was to sell out and quit right now before we get in so deep that we never can get out."

"Look at them figures again. We're *already* in too far to quit."

"You mean we owe more than we could sell out for?"

"We still got an equity in our fee land. Other than that, our debt is bigger than the market value of all the livestock we own."

Tom began to look a little sick. "Appears to me this ranch life ain't all it's cracked up to be."

"It's a good life, son, but sometimes a damn thin *livin'*."

Tom didn't seem to believe, not entirely. "But, Dad, you was plumb clear of debt; I remember you sayin' you didn't owe a dime to nobody."

"There was a time I didn't. That was when it used to rain."

Tom handed the papers back to his father, his face gone sour. "Partner! Don't look like I'm a partner in *much*, does it?"

Severely Charlie said, "Don't be talkin' it down. This old country'll take care of you if you just hang in there with it and fight. Hell, don't you think I been in debt before? We bought this outfit on a shoestring, me and your mother. We come within an ace of losin' it . . . two–three times. We just hung and rattled. Times turned around, and we paid out and leased more land and got ahead. Times'll turn around again some of these days; they always have."

Tom muttered something about the faith of the mustard-seed. When Charlie demanded to know what he meant, Tom shrugged off an answer. He said, "Now we got another winter starin' at us pretty soon. What're we goin' to do?"

"Same as we always did. We'll face up to it."

"We'll have to feed like hell again unless it rains a lot in the fall; and me and you, we both know it ain't goin' to."

"We don't know that; it's got to rain *sometime*."

Now it was Tom who spoke sharply. "Dad, you got blinders on. It ain't goin' to rain this fall. For all we know, it may *never* rain again."

"We can't afford to be thinkin' like that. It always *did* rain here, eventually. A country don't change climate permanently, not all of a sudden."

"I been thinkin', Dad, there'll be some big-money shows comin' up before long. If I was there, I could be sendin' money home."

Charlie knew better. Tom never had sent money home, or saved any, during the times he had been winning well. "Son, everything you need, you've got right here. I know you been on short rations lately; everybody has. But any time now you'll see things start to change for the better. I know this country like I know myself. It's always been good to us."

"Maybe things never are goin' to be again what they was once. Big changes are comin' over the whole farmin' and ranchin' business. You can't expect that they'll pass us by."

"Don't you think I've seen a-plenty of changes in my day? Times are *always* changin'. I've managed to make the changes with them."

"But you were younger then." Tom flushed. "I mean . . . well, when a man gets set in his ways . . ."

"I'm not set in my ways. You show me a new idea and I'll grab at it."

"Them fellers with their cattleman's caravan . . . that was a new idea. Personally I think it's too bad it fell through."

"There was nothin' new about that idea. It's as old as mankind . . . the hope of gettin' somethin' for nothin' or of getting more out of the pot than you put in it. Nobody's ever made it work yet. Nobody ever will."

Dolly Flagg stepped out of her kitchen and stood in the living room with hands on her hips as Tom walked into the house. "Did you ask him?"

Tom side-stepped an answer. He tossed his hat into a corner, then dropped wearily upon a soft chair they had brought over from the big house. "We was doin' some figurin'. Ranch stood a bad loss again."

Dolly's eyes bored into him so hard that he turned away. "You never did ask him, did you?"

Tom shook his head. "No point in it. It can't be done."

"If you don't ask him, *I* will."

"Dolly, we can get along without it. That car of ours is still runnin'. It'll do till the rain comes."

She half shouted in derision. "Rain? I don't think it ever *did* rain in this God-forsaken desert."

Tom's chin dropped. "We're doin' the best we can. It'll rain one of these days."

"Now you're startin' to sound just like *him*. How long do we have to wait? How long do we have to go on living in this shack like Mexicans, using old furniture borrowed out of that mausoleum of a house, depending on your folks to bring us even the groceries we eat?"

"We're partners. We agreed we'd share the bad as well as the good."

"We've had our share of the bad. I'd like to see what some of the *good* looks like for a change." When she saw Tom had no reply to make, she went on: "When we were on the circuit we always had money. We had a good time. We were *somebody,* and people looked up to us. Where have we been lately besides that one-horse Rio Seco? I'm sick to death of it."

Tom's face was pinched. He didn't look at her.

Dolly said, "Let's blow this dump. Let's go back where we can live like *people,* where we can see things happen . . . *make* things happen."

"We got a stake here. Someday this'll be ours."

"Who the hell needs it?"

For a long time Charlie Flagg had watched other men burn the thorns from prickly pear so their live-stock could chew the pulpy green leaves. He had sworn that Rio Seco would have six inches of snow on the Fourth of July before he would subject his animals to eating cactus. Now he found himself face-to-face with necessity. The low-growing cactus he had fought for years was, finally, to be what saved him—if anything could. He swore some, and he pawed sand over it like an angry bull. But in the end he knew what he was going to have to do.

He bought the pear burner from Jim Sweet, and he hated it on sight.

"Dangerous contraptions, ain't they?" he demanded.

"A screwdriver is dangerous if you don't know how to use it," Sweet replied patiently. "Sure, this thing could burn a man alive if he got careless with it. The secret is, don't get careless."

The burner was simple, actually little more than a piece of steel tubing about five feet long, with a cutoff valve at one end, an S-curve and a funnel-like flame spreader on the other. Approximately in the center was a wooden handle which Charlie gripped with his right hand while holding the valve with his left. Because butane was extremely cold, the tubing itself was chilled almost down to the flame.

The first time Charlie lighted the burner, the sudden flash and the angry roar made him drop the thing and jump back. Jim Sweet picked it up. "It's as easy as pie, Charlie. To light it you just turn on the valve and let a little liquid butane drip out onto the ground, like this. You cut the valve off, then pitch a match down there and set that spot of butane on fire. Hold the end of the burner over it and turn the valve on again. Then the burner catches."

Charlie attacked the burner with a grim will to conquer it, the way he had gone after many a bronc in the days when all of his hair was still brown. In a few days he found himself reasonably proficient, and he began to lose his dread. But he never did learn to like the thing.

The burner was attached by a fifty-foot rubber hose to a large butane tank mounted in the bed of the blue pickup. The roaring flame flashed forward several feet, hot enough to fire a dry tree trunk in seconds. Charlie cut the flame back to size by adjusting the valve. He found that to hold the flame steady on a clump of pear could virtually destroy it, blistering the thick, watery leaves so that the sheep wouldn't eat them. But if he first made a slow, gentle pass with the flame, the thorn would burn back to a stub without the pear itself having time to singe. A second pass would burn the remainder of the thorn down to a spot of harmless white ash and yet leave the pear intact.

Charlie developed this technique by himself. Later, when he found that many experienced pear feeders did it the same way, he felt a glow of pride for having worked it out without being told about it.

Though he used the pear for feed, he did not give up his lifelong war against it. As livestock finished eating the burned cactus, he and Tom would grub up the stumps to retard regrowth and to clear the land of pear as best they could. Pear might be a life-saver in drouth, but it would be a moisture-robbing, encroaching pest like the mesquite when the rains came.

By early winter the Angora goats had finished working most of the live-oak brush. They had eaten the leaves off as high as they could reach, as much as five feet. Unlike a sheep, a goat could rear up on its hind legs, brace its forefeet on a limb for balance and stay there while it ate the high leaves. The live oaks remained green the year around. They held their old leaves all winter, dropping them only as the new leaves began to push out in the spring. To keep the goats in condition without a feed bill, Charlie and Tom began cutting high branches out of the live oaks, letting them fall to the ground so the goats could eat the leaves. The ranch had too many live oaks anyway. More benign than the insidious mesquite, they could nevertheless become a costly encroacher, stealing from the grass.

Charlie tried both jobs, burning pear and chopping live oak. Badly as he hated the burner, he decided Tom had a stronger back and better wind for swinging the ax. Charlie operated the burner most of the time.

It was arduous, unrelenting work, as hard as Charlie had ever done in his life. As the weeks dragged by with their drab sameness, he felt the effect in his aching muscles. He could see it wearing on Tom. Outlasting this eternal drouth had become the only thing that mattered any more to Charlie. All else faded from importance; it was a vendetta. He found little time to keep up with the magazines and newspapers as he used to do. He got up early and came in late, sometimes so weary he didn't care to eat. Even when he slept, he dreamed of dust and bleating sheep and mountains of feed. Of a morning before he put on his pants he would walk to the window and look out for a sign of a cloud in the flush of dawn. When he was dressed, he would step out on the porch and look again, hoping he had missed one in his restricted view from the window. The last thing he did most nights was to step out in his sock feet for a hopeful, futile search of the starry black skies.

The drouth was the beginning, the middle, and the end of his conscious thoughts.

He often wondered what there would be to talk about or even to think about when and if it ever started raining again. On reflection he knew he and Tom had never talked a great deal anyway. He could not recall that they had ever had a deep or serious conversation about anything other than horses or cattle or cowboys. They had never talked of politics or philosophy beyond some surface comment on news of the day, or some local development that touched them personally. He was not sure, when he let his mind run back over it, that Tom even *had* any politics, or any philosophy.

Times, Charlie tried to remember how things had been here in the good years when it used to rain; he found it increasingly difficult to pull up a picture in his mind's eye. It seemed twenty years since this land had been green with a thick turf of good cow-grass.

Gradually he sensed a darkness coming over Tom. Sometimes now when Tom spoke at all he did it curtly and with a brooding anger Charlie did not understand. He tried to remember what he might have said or done, but nothing came to mind.

One day he watched Tom up in a live-oak tree, swinging the ax, striking with such vengeance that the leaves went flying.

"Don't fight it so," Charlie warned him. "The work's hard enough without you fightin' it thataway."

"I'm gettin' them cut, ain't I?" Tom said sharply.

Charlie studied him in troubled silence, letting his pear burner wait cold. He watched the live-oak branches split off and crash to the ground, each one raising a puff of dry dust as it fell. The goats clustered a little out of harm's way, waiting patiently for the men to get done. Charlie had developed a respect of sorts for the intelligence of these Angoras. Sometimes

they would trail a man and watch him with a curiosity and an interest much like a dog's, something cattle
seldom did and sheep never.

Charlie stood by as Tom climbed down from what
was left of the live-oak tree. "Son, you got somethin'
troublin' you?"

Tom gave him only a glance, then turned away to
decide on another likely tree. He side-stepped the
question and asked one of his own: "What's the matter? That burner not workin'?"

"Tom, even as a boy you never was one to fret much
over things. Whatever you didn't like, you just turned
your back on and acted like it never existed. Lately I
get the feelin' you're turnin' your back on me."

"That wouldn't do any good. I'd know you existed.
And this damn ranch, I couldn't ignore that either."

"Am I supposed to take some kind of a meanin'
from that?"

Tom didn't look at him.

Charlie said, "Been a long time since I've noticed
you limpin'. That foot don't hurt you any more?"

"I've plumb forgot about it."

"Maybe that's what's eatin' on you, then. Now that
your foot's healed up you're thinkin' you could be
out on that rodeo circuit again if you wasn't saddled
down with all this."

"It *has* crossed my mind."

"If that's what you want to do, I wouldn't tell you
no. I'd just ask you to think hard on it first, and to
know your mind."

"I know my mind, and it ain't the rodeo that both-
ers me, not all that much. It's this place, and what
we're doin'."

"There's nothin' the matter with this place, nothin'
some good rain wouldn't fix."

Tom swung the ax with one hand and drove the bit into the trunk of a tree. There he left it. "Dad, I been home a year now . . . a year *past* . . . helpin' you."

"Helpin' *yourself*. Whatever we've got here, it's half yours."

"Big deal. What we got here is *nothin'*. For a whole year now we've done nothin' but work our butts off, and we're deeper in the hole than we was when I first come."

"I didn't tell you it'd be easy. Nothin' good in this life ever comes to a man easy. You just got to be patient, and give a little."

"Funny to hear you talkin' about givin' a little. *You* never give a particle."

"What do you mean?"

"I mean we have to sweat like a nigger at election and live tighter than the bark on that live oak yonder, and still you're throwin' money out every day because you won't give in and do what everybody else does."

Charlie thought he knew what was coming, but he didn't want to push it. He eased himself down onto a big live-oak branch and stretched his weak leg out in front of him. "I'm doin' the best I know how, son. That's all a man can do."

"You have any idea how much money we're spendin' every day to buy feed with? It's enough to scare a man out of his britches."

Charlie shrugged. "You can't starve a profit out of an animal."

"Do you know how much cheaper we could buy that feed if we'd get into the government program?"

"The feed wouldn't be cheaper. It'd just mean somebody else was helpin' pay for it, is all."

"I don't see nothin' wrong with that."

"I been makin' my own way since I was a kid. Nobody's ever had to pay my bills; I don't see where anybody ought to."

"You're livin' in the past. Drive by the employment commission office sometime and look at all them lazy sons of bitches lined up for relief checks when there's people tryin' to hire them for honest work. You think they worry about somebody else helpin' pay *their* bills?"

Charlie shook his head. "I'll let them wrestle with their own consciences; I don't intend to wrestle with mine."

"I don't see where conscience has got a damn thing to do with it. It's somethin' everybody else does any more; why shouldn't *we*?"

Charlie felt more disappointment than anger. "You know how I've always looked at things. Of all the people in the world, son, I'd of thought you'd be the last one I had to explain to."

"You never *have* explained it to me; you just throwed it out there and I accepted it. Now I don't accept it any more."

"You'd understand it if you'd known your great-granddaddy."

"You're fixin' to throw old Granddaddy up to me again. I remember all them stories about how he fought his way through the hard times and never would accept charity or take the pauper's oath. Maybe that was all right in Granddaddy's time, but people don't do it any more."

"Your great-granddaddy would, if he was still here."

"But he *ain't* here, and that's the point. The way I remember it, he spent the rest of his life with the seat hangin' out of his britches."

Charlie gritted his teeth. "He was poor, if that's what you mean."

"Damn right that's what I mean!"

"But by God he was still a man. They didn't take that away from him. He still had his pride."

"You ever try to cash in pride down at the bank?"

"It don't matter how much money a man puts together; if he loses his pride he's a poor man."

"Dad, you're livin' in the past. You've been sittin' here lookin' backwards at a time dead and gone. They've written a whole new set of rules."

"Their rules, not mine. I'll keep on livin' by mine."

Tom's eyes crackled from pent-up anger beginning to find release. "You think the rest of us ought to live by them too, just because they're yours?"

Of a sudden Charlie's weak leg seemed to be paining him. He turned away from Tom's demanding gaze. "You tryin' to say you want to quit?"

"I'm tryin' to say you ought to listen to somebody else awhile."

"I'm listenin'."

Tom studied him a long moment. "No you're not. I been talkin', but you ain't heard a thing I've said. And you never will."

"You're wrong; I've heard you. I don't agree with you, but I've heard you. And I suppose you've heard me the same way. Maybe I've done you an injustice, son."

"You see that, do you?"

Charlie nodded. "I oughtn't to've waited so long to talk things out with you. I ought to've talked to you more when you was a boy, so you'd of come up thinkin' right. I guess it's askin' too much to expect you to understand now."

Tom said in exasperation, "Aw, hell!" and yanked

the ax free from the live-oak trunk. He set in chopping the branches out of the trees. If anything, he swung the ax harder now than before.

Charlie was not surprised, after supper, when he heard the front door open and Tom stood there, absently holding onto the doorknob after he had closed the door behind him. Mary said something to Tom about having some coffee left if he wanted it, but Tom gave no sign he had even heard. His eyes were on Charlie. In those eyes, Charlie could see decision.

Tom said, "I been thinkin' over our talk, Dad, and I been talkin' to Dolly. I've decided there's no use us tryin' to go on the way we have."

They're leaving, Charlie thought, a little surprised that he felt no anger. Instead there was only an emptiness, a sad sense of loss.

Tom turned to his mother. "Maybe *you* can talk to him; I can't."

"About what, son?" Charlie had told her nothing of their argument.

"About us bein' the only damnfools left in this country, pretty near. About us backin' down and takin' some help on this feed business."

Mary nodded gravely. Charlie sensed that this was all the explanation she needed; she understood the rest of it. She said, "You think we ought to ask for help, do you?"

"When a man is drownin', he grabs any hand that reaches out to him."

"What if that hand asks a price too high for him to pay?"

"When it comes to a question of life and death, there ain't no price too high."

Mary studied Charlie, and he wished he could read what was hidden behind those blue eyes. He guessed she was siding with Tom and trying to figure out how best to say so. There was a time she would have understood Charlie and stuck by him, but he supposed that had been before they got so damn old. They hadn't talked things out much in recent years.

Mary said, "Son, when a man believes in a thing strongly enough, there is a price too high to pay. There is a point where compromise costs him too much."

Tom sagged a little. "Mom, he's wrong and you know it."

"Maybe I don't agree with him all the way, but that's not the point. I understand him. You can't understand him because you've never believed in *anything* as strong as he does. Maybe that's not your fault; maybe it's ours because we failed to teach you *how* to believe in something."

Charlie just looked at her and blinked.

Tom declared, "Mom, he's haulin' you down the road to the poorhouse."

She said, "He was a stubborn man when I met him. I've never asked him to change. As for the poorhouse, we've stood at the gates of it before; we've never gone inside."

Tom looked at his mother in surprise. "Never thought I'd see you take up for him in this. I swear, I believe you're as stubborn as he is."

"I always was. You'll find, son, that the world thinks more of a man who makes a mistake because he believes in it than of one who does the right thing because it comes easy, and without belief."

Shaking his head, Tom walked to the deep old-fashioned window and stared in the direction of his house. Charlie could see a dim light in the living room. Dolly and that damn television.

At length Tom turned around. "The way I understand partnerships, that means we own everything equal, fifty-fifty."

Charlie nodded. "That's the way it is."

"The way I see it, we don't agree on this thing now, and we never will. If we keep tryin' to work together it's just goin' to lead to a fight. Better we call a halt now. Divide now, so there won't be nobody mad."

Charlie's mouth went dry. "Divide?"

Tom pulled some folded papers from his shirt pocket. "I been doin' some figurin'. I tallied up how much livestock is left, and how much land. I figure if I take half the livestock and the O'Barr lease, that'd be fair. You keep the deeded land here and the rest of the lease country. The deeded is worth more than the lease, but I'd overlook that. I wouldn't want it ever said that I taken any unfair advantage."

Charlie just stared at him. He couldn't bring himself to answer.

Tom said, "There won't be no question of dividin' up the money, because there ain't any. I'll assume my share of the debts. You can run your part the way you want to, and I'll run mine. No arguments, no hard feelin's."

When Charlie said nothing, Mary asked, "Have you talked to Dolly about this? Do you know how she feels?"

Tom said reluctantly, "She'd as soon throw over the whole thing. I told her this way maybe we'd save the place yet." He looked at his father. "How about it? That suit you?"

The words came with pain. "If it's what you want . . ."

"Looks to me like the only way. We can go over the tallies and figure how to divide up the livestock without movin' more of them than necessary. No use chousin' the stock."

Charlie only nodded.

Tom said, "Been thinkin' I'd sell off a bunch of my goats and buy back some cattle. I never did figure you should've let them cows go."

Charlie looked at the floor. He saw no point in saying he had had little choice about it. He could also see that if he had kept the cattle until now he would be in even worse shape than he was, financially. The goats had been the only thing self-supporting. Weakly he said, "You do what suits you."

"It ain't that it suits me, Dad, you know that. But this looks to me like the only way to head off a fight. Better we do it like this and shake hands than wait till we're shakin' fists."

Charlie didn't look up. "There'll be a right smart of paperwork to do. Stock won't starve to death in one day. Best we skip feedin' in the mornin' and go to town. We'll need to make things right with Big at the bank."

"I was thinkin' I'd see if I could qualify for one of them FHA loans from the government. The interest is cheaper than we can get at the bank."

"Nothin' is cheaper. It's like the government feed . . . if you don't pay for the interest, somebody else has got to."

"Then let them. All the income tax we've paid through the years . . . we got somethin' comin' to us."

"And it'll come," Charlie said, a little bitterness creeping in. "One of these days, sure as all hell, it'll come."

Tom frowned. "Dad, I don't see any point in us arguin' about that. We ain't goin' to agree, so let it go."

Charlie was inclined to debate, but he saw the uselessness of it.

Tom said, "I'll have to find me and Dolly a rent house in town. Ought not to be hard, as many people as have left."

Mary spoke up quickly. "There's no need in that. Why not keep on living in the Flores house? It'd be less driving than from town, and it wouldn't cost you anything. It's a good house, son."

"It'd be kind of ticklish, don't you think, livin' so close after . . . Anyway, Dolly never has liked that house. I expect she'd be better contented livin' in town."

Charlie rubbed his rough hand across his face, realizing he was beaten but not quite willing to yield. He had a notion Dolly was at the foot of Tom's discontent. Tom never had been one to let things bother him much. If Dolly hadn't been punching the needles into him . . . "You sleep on this, son, and make sure it's what you want to do. We'll talk about it again in the mornin'."

"It'll be the same in the mornin' as it is tonight."

"We'll talk about it anyway."

When Tom was gone, Charlie got up and limped into the kitchen. He poured a liberal amount of bourbon into a cup and reached for the coffeepot. Then he thought *the hell with it* and drank the bourbon down straight. It burned like fire.

Turning, he saw Mary standing just inside the kitchen door, quietly staring at him. He saw worry in her eyes. He wondered who the worry was for . . . Tom . . . himself . . . or maybe everybody?

He gave the cup a fast circular motion, bringing

together the vagrant drops that had clung to the side, then he turned the cup up and drank the little that was left. He said, "I expected you'd take up for *him*."

"Why? When the chips were down, I was always on your side since the first time I met you."

He nodded, thinking back. She always was. "Been a long time since the chips was last down. I reckon I'd got used to the notion of us pullin' apart."

"If we have, I'm sorry. I didn't ever intend us to."

"We had good times for too long, I suppose. It takes bad times to pull people together."

Tears came into Mary's eyes, but she had too much self-control to let them spill over. "Maybe he'll come around after a time. Maybe he'll see for himself what you've been trying to say."

Charlie would like to believe that, but he didn't. "I thought I'd taught him everything I knew. I taught him how to ride and rope and judge stock. I taught him how to gauge his grass in the fall and how to bring an animal through a hard winter. But I forgot to teach him the way I think. Now it's too late for him to learn."

15

Charlie felt as though he had been to a funeral each time he saw a ranch fall idle somewhere around him, its gates flung open because there was no longer any livestock to confine. Lease contracts expired, or stockmen whittled down to the last thin shaving of their resources and faded away like a summer dew. Here and there some landlords voluntarily cut the lease rates, knowing a bankrupt lessee is no lessee at all.

Charlie saw Tom infrequently, occasionally coming upon him unexpectedly on one of the ranch roads. It was unexpected for Tom, at least. For Charlie, it was a result of conscious effort and a certain amount of planning. Any visiting was short and productive of little information. But Charlie could see enough to tell him what he needed to know: Tom was almost to the end of the string.

Charlie cornered Sam O'Barr one day in the domino hall and bought him a beer. Sam's red-veined face was without expression as he gulped the first bottle.

"About time for another payment on that lease, ain't it, Charlie?"

"That's how come me here." Charlie ordered a second beer for Sam. "You know my boy Tom is runnin' his stock on that land of yours."

O'Barr shrugged. "That don't make any difference. It's your name that's on the lease, and it's you I'll look to for the payment."

Charlie nodded. "But it's him that'll have to raise the money. I don't want him hurt any worse than he already is. You know, Sam, there's not enough feed out yonder to wad a shotgun. That whole nine sections of yours is just a big feedlot and little else. They got all the room in the world but nothin' to eat."

Sam gave no sign of interest in anything except the beer.

Charlie said, "Lots of landowners been cuttin' the price. They know their land ain't fit for much, and a broke leaseholder won't be worth a continental to them either. There's even been a few have written off the whole payment if the leaseholder agrees to idle the land and let it rest. God knows it needs it. I was hopin' you might work out somethin' for that boy of mine."

Sam stared across the room at a big calendar that featured a naked girl. He seemed more interested in the calendar than in what Charlie was saying. "Like what?"

"The sheep are cut to a fraction of what they used to be. Tom's bought him some cows, but nowhere near what that place once carried. It'd be mighty fair if you'd cut the lease rate down to fit the livestock."

Sam finished his beer and looked expectantly at Charlie. Charlie signaled the dirty-aproned proprietor to fetch Sam a third one. Sam said, "Charlie, the only livin' I got is what I get off of that land. Now, if I was to charge you or your boy half price, do you think the grocery store would cut my bill in two? Do you think I can live on half as much?"

"Everybody sacrifices at times like this."

Sam shook his head. "Not me. You signed a contract. Till that contract runs out you'll keep right on payin' what you agreed to and not one penny less."

"But, Sam, the others . . ."

"I don't give a damn what the others are doin'. Me and you, we got a contract."

"What if that boy goes broke?"

Sam shrugged. "I'd be right sorry about it, but business is business. I'd still have the land, and I'd find me somebody else that wanted it." Turning his back on Charlie, he picked up the beer bottle and squinted through its brown glass. "Empty again. I swear, they just don't put as much in these things as they used to."

In the weeks afterward, Charlie didn't have to ask anybody how Tom was doing. He could see for himself, watching across the fence. Tom somehow managed to borrow enough money to buy more sheep and cattle on the depressed market, and he concentrated them on the O'Barr land in a desperate attempt to wring more income from it. Charlie knew from experience this would be a futile effort. The more livestock Tom put on the pastures, the more the land would suffer. The more it suffered, the more feed he would be forced to buy to sustain the animals. It was an endless circle, like a man chasing himself around and around a hill and slipping farther into the depths with every round he made.

Charlie regarded this as an inherent evil of long-term

leases at high rates. When hard times and high lease backed a lessee against a wall, he felt compelled to overgraze the land in his struggle to meet the payments. Continued long enough, this abuse would make barren desert of pastures that once had grown tall grass. If one blamed the lessee for spoiling the land, he must also blame the landowner who drove him to it.

Charlie looked across the net fence at the trampled barrens that were Tom's feeding grounds. He felt no obligation to Sam O'Barr, but he felt a deep and binding obligation to the land itself. It mattered little who held the title; the land was a sacred thing. To see it bleed now brought him grief; it was like watching a friend waste away with a terminal cancer.

In his loneliness, Charlie usually took the Flores boys' black dog on his feeding rounds. He made him sit in the pickup cab where he wouldn't disturb the dog-fearing sheep. Charlie made it a point every day to drive along the fenceline he shared with Page Mauldin. He never saw Page, but often he came across Diego Escamillo or other Mexican hands burning pear. Talk-hungry, Charlie usually stopped. It didn't matter that he had to converse in Spanish sometimes, and that his own Spanish was fractured like a watermelon in a cowlot. He would talk with them about anything from women to the red pepper crop in Chihuahua. The subject didn't matter. The company was what counted.

It pleasured Charlie to pause awhile and watch the Mauldin cows trail in to the pear grounds. Some would follow the Mexicans' pickup. Others would come when they heard the roar of the burners. His own cows long gone, Charlie liked to feast his eyes on those of Page's. Page kept only black Angus, while Charlie's personal preference had always run to whitefaces. But hell, they were cows. Breed was a small matter, something to josh a competitor about— like wrangling over Fords and Chevrolets. It came down in the end to a matter of personal preference rather than any real superiority of one over the other.

Charlie always remembered what old-time cattle buyer E. W. Nicodemus had told him: "There's more difference *within* the breeds than there ever was *between* them."

Charlie marveled at the way these black cows would move in and start eating the hot pear while it still glowed from the flame. Many had all the hair burned away from around their mouths. They liked the pear, for it was green. Nothing else was.

Sometimes after school or on weekends, Charlie found Kathy Mauldin helping Diego with the feeding. She would be dressed like a boy in washed-out Levi's and a raveled wool coat, run-over boots and a floppy old hat. The sight of her always brought him a smile.

Good thing Mary can't see her thisaway. She'd blow a gasket.

Charlie would concede that Page Mauldin's lithe and slender daughter made no pretense about being a lady, and he would concede that she was not a particularly pretty girl according to the standards people seemed to go by any more. But he figured any man who judged a woman by a tape measure was fifty-seven varieties of a fool. He suspected that was the way Tom had chosen Dolly.

Kathy was, Charlie thought, an open and honest girl who didn't try to be something she wasn't; she led nobody down a false trail with phony affectations. You accepted her as she was or let her alone.

He decided she had turned out rather well, considering that she had spent years without her mother, and with a father who was always off to hell and gone. Maybe Diego Escamillo's old mother was a better teacher than Charlie had given her credit for.

But no matter how independent and self-assured she was, it disturbed Charlie to watch Kathy calmly light up a burner and move through the big clumps of green pear, that hellish flame leaping, roaring like something damned.

"That thing could burn you alive," he warned her. "You ought to leave this job to the Mexicans."

"Dad says this is my ranch. If I'm to accept the benefits, I ought to accept my share of the work."

"That sounds like somethin' Page Mauldin would say."

She smiled. "Or you, Uncle Charlie."

Through the long hot summer Charlie was able to cut his feeding some. He used the time to work on his windmills, releathering every one on the place. He talked of hiring help, but Mary told him they couldn't afford it. She went with him sometimes, as she had in the long-ago days, helping him rig the block and tackle in the windmill towers, driving the pickup that drew the sucker-rods up out of the wells, even grabbing onto the greasy wrenches and pipe tongs when she needed to. Charlie was surprised to find she hadn't forgotten much in twenty-odd years. The main difference was that she did jobs with a pickup now that she used to do on horseback. And she did them slower. But so did he.

It was hard work, sweaty work, and Charlie found himself losing more weight. It reached a point he couldn't wear his old khakis until Mary took up some slack in the seat.

Rain was still scarce as sheepherders at a cowboy convention. Even so, the goats did well. Charlie admitted grudgingly to himself—but to no one else—that they had been a smart buy. They could come as near fattening on nothing as any animal Charlie had ever seen except perhaps a prairie dog. Grass and weeds remained short all summer. Charlie turned out another crop of "jackrabbit" lambs twenty pounds lighter than they ought to be. What they brought him at the market wouldn't feed a pen of saddlehorses.

By September he saw he would soon have to begin feeding full force again. He hauled down the pear burner from its rack in the barn. By October he was burning pear and chopping live oak. Though he had culled his sheep deeply before, he culled again.

The first fall norther rolled in during the night with a choking pall of dust and a long wind that whipped limbs off Charlie's trees and shingles off his barn. It picked up his milk bucket from its rack just off the back steps and sent it bouncing and clanking across the yard. In the morning the wind stilled. Now there was an eerie silence, dust hanging so thickly in the air that Charlie could hardly see the barn from his front porch. Tumbleweeds had piled along the fences and against the buildings. It had been one of those high-rolling dusters spawned far to the north, the wind whipping up the plains soil, lifting it so high that airliners had to climb to avoid it. Now with the wind gone the fine dust would be a day or more settling gently to earth, possibly hundreds of miles from where it had lain during the eons before this granddaddy of all drouths had come to despoil the land.

Driving to the peargrounds, Charlie watched the

sun slowly climb in the east. Through the curtain of dust it was a cold copper ball, and it cast an unnatural sheen upon the surface of the land. Even the hood of the pickup reflected this ghostly glow. Days like this depressed Charlie most of all. He knew with a dreadful certainty that this was going to be another hard winter . . . the hardest he had ever seen.

The telephone rang one night about nine o'clock, just as Charlie was preparing to go to bed. The voice was Big Emmett Rodale's. He sounded angry.

"Charlie, I wish you'd told me what Tom was fixin' to do."

Charlie was a little sleepyheaded at first. He stammered something that didn't quite make sense, for what Big said made no sense either. "What do you mean, what he was fixin' to do?"

"To leave. I wisht you'd let me know he was fixin' to leave."

Charlie was suddenly awake. "He's, gone? Where'd he go?"

"I was hopin' you'd tell *me*. You didn't know about it?"

Charlie shook his head, though there was no way Big could see him; it was his habit to make head and hand gestures when he talked on the telephone, just as he did when he conversed with a man face to face. "I ain't seen Tom much lately. We ain't talked."

"Well, he's gone, Charlie. Best I can tell, they packed up what stuff was in the house and shipped it to his wife's home in Dallas. He loaded that girl into the car and that ropin' horse into the trailer, and he took off to find him a rodeo. He gave me a phone call as he was gassin' up at the fillin' station; said he

THE TIME IT NEVER RAINED   595

was checkin' it to me and the FHA to wrestle it out between us the best way we could."

Charlie just stood there with his shoulder against the wall, the thing running through his mind like some wild and implausible dream. He heard Big saying, "Charlie . . . Charlie . . . You haven't hung up on me, have you?"

Charlie managed to tell him he was still there. He chewed on the inside of his cheek while he tried to frame a question. "Big, what happened? There must of been somethin' happened."

"You know Sam O'Barr's lease was due. The FHA decided there was no way Tom could afford to pay it, so it canceled his line of credit."

Charlie said nothing. He just stood there.

Big said, "I expect they were right, Charlie. That lease was way too high."

"But without land to run on, there wasn't nothin' left but to close him out."

"The handwritin' on the wall. But he ought to've stayed and helped us."

Charlie turned and looked at Mary. She stood in the door, watching him. She had heard just enough to know something was badly wrong. He said, "Big, what can I do?"

"I don't know, Charlie, but I wish you'd come in and talk to me soon as you can."

"I'll feed in the mornin'. When I'm through I'll come see you." He hung up the receiver. He looked at Mary a minute, wondering how to tell her. He made it short.

She accepted it tight-lipped, showing no surprise. "I figured it would happen. I just didn't know when."

Charlie blinked. "I didn't. I had no idea but what he'd stay there same as I would."

"He's *not* the same as you; he never was. I don't

know why it's been so hard for you to see that. He
lives in a different world than you do."

Sadly he shook his head. "We're all livin' in a different world any more. I liked the old one better."

He went to bed, but he had as well have stayed
up. He lay in the darkness with his eyes wide open.
He relived again and again the arguments he had had
with Tom, listening to Tom's words in his mind, trying to fathom his son's thinking. He tried to visual-
ize what he might have done, what he should have
said that might have made things different, where he
should have yielded and where he should have stood
firm.

He lay awhile on his back, then awhile on one side
or the other, trying to find a comfortable place and
knowing there was none. At length he heard the floor
creak, and he saw Mary standing by his bed.

She said, "I could hear you to sing clear in yonder.
Can't you sleep at all?"

"I haven't yet. I don't know if I will."

Mary felt for the covers and crawled in beside him.
It surprised him; he couldn't remember *when* she had
ever come to his bed. It was seldom any more that he
ever went to hers. She laid her arm across him. "It'll
be all right, Charlie. We've had troubles before and
everything always turned out all right."

She kissed him on the forehead. He lay a moment,
wondering, then he reached for her as he used to do
a long time ago.

He was up before daylight, his mind a little foggy
from missing sleep. He fed the sheep, then drove up
the dim road that wound to the top of Warrior Hill.
The wind was raw, so he didn't stand out in it. He

sat in the pickup, staring through the windshield for an hour across his own land to that which belonged to Sam O'Barr. From here he could not see the fence, but he could easily tell where the fenceline was. If his own place looked bad, the O'Barr country looked far worse. He pondered what he could say to Big Emmett, what proposition he might be able to make that he could get the banker to accept. He thought about Tom's sheep and cattle, and the fact that if Tom was gone there was no one to feed them. They would be standing around the feeding grounds bleating and bawling.

He looked at the cairn of rocks where August Schmidt had buried that Indian eighty years ago. He said, "Old Warrior, I'm in trouble."

He ate dinner early and drove into town. Big was at his accustomed place, hunched over the old roll-top desk. The only thing that had changed in thirty years was that Big had gotten older and fatter. And lately he seemed to have gotten sadder. Charlie did not stop to weigh himself on the free scale; he walked straight to Big's desk. Neither man spoke. Big arose, and they gravely shook hands. Charlie sat down in the straight, hard chair and waited for Big to say something. Big seemed to be waiting on Charlie.

Charlie said, "Big, I'm sorry."

Rodale shrugged. "Feel sorry for Tom, not for us. This ain't the first time it's ever happened to us. It ain't even the first time it's happened to us *lately*."

"One way or another I'll see you don't lose nothin'. If the stock don't pay out what's owed, I'll do it."

"With what?"

"With time. Looks like that's all I got any more, is time."

Rodale gloomily shook his bald head. "It may take

more time than any of us have got left to bail us out of the trouble we're in. Not just Tom's outfit . . . *all* of them."

Charlie said, "I been thinkin', Big. I could take that O'Barr place back. Somehow or other I could manage, and if I'm lucky I might bail us out."

Rodale stared thoughtfully from behind half-closed lids. "That was the first thought that came to *me*. Then I got to thinkin' a little deeper." He leaned forward, closer to Charlie. "You taken a good look at yourself in the mirror lately?"

Charlie stared back. "You thinkin' I'm too old?"

"You'll never see sixty again, that's for damn sure."

"Don't sell me short. I can still do more work than most young men."

"Not as much as you think you can. You're already overburdened. Double the job and you'd be dead before spring. Anyway, the FHA was right about the O'Barr land. Bad as I hate to give credit to the *federales,* there's some of them pretty good with a calculator. There's no way a man could pay Suds's price and live with it."

Charlie tried to think of an argument. From outside, on a livestock truck passing through town, he could hear the bleating of sheep. That reminded him. "Them stock of Tom's, they'll need feedin'."

"I already sent a man out. Felipe Gonzales is a good hand, and he's been out of a job since the Hatcher ranch folded. He'll stay and feed till we can round up and sell the stock."

Charlie nodded, relieved on at least that one point. He rubbed his knuckles where the rheumatism was bothering him more of late. "I sure hate to see that land go. I had it a long time."

"You'll be better off without it. Let go, Charlie. Be

content with what you *can* do and don't fret yourself over what you can't."

Charlie argued a little more but to no avail. He would get nowhere wrangling with Big. He stared blankly at the floor, a kind of grief washing over him as he tried to reconcile himself to the loss of the land, and to the fact that he would probably never have it again. He stood up to go but had one more thing that needed saying. He cleared his throat. "Remember what I told you. If you come up short on Tom's debts, don't write them off. However long it takes, I'll pay you."

Rodale frowned. "You and the buffalo . . ."

"What do you mean?"

"I mean you're a relic of another age. Get out of here, Charlie, before they decide to stuff you and put you in a glass case."

Charlie paid little attention to the young man in the gray suit who got up from the waiting bench and followed him out the door. He heard someone call, "Mister Flagg," on the street and turned to look. He saw the young man hurrying to catch up, dropping a pad from his hand and stopping to pick it up, almost losing some pages that tore free in the wind.

"Mister Flagg," the young man said, a little out of breath, "my name is Johnson. I'd like to talk to you if you can spare a few minutes."

Charlie sized him up warily, fairly sure he had never seen him before. "I'm not in the market for anything," he said by way of caution.

"I'm not selling anything. I'm with the Associated Press, out of the Dallas bureau office."

Charlie nodded neutrally, not sure whether this was good or bad.

"I'm doing a series of stories on the effects of the drouth."

"You come to the right place at Rio Seco."

"I'd like to buy you a cup of coffee and talk a little."

Charlie saw no way any harm could come of it. It might be a good idea if more people realized what was going on here. He nodded and pointed his chin toward the coffee shop. "Girl named Bess Winfield takes care of that place. She makes about as good a cup of coffee as you'll find in a cafe, which ain't sayin' too much."

He pushed on the door but found it locked. He tried again before he was satisfied. He saw a sign in the front window: CLOSED. Peering through the glass, he saw that the floor was bare; all the tables and chairs had been removed, and all the equipment along the walls. The building had turned into a shell, like so many others. It took him so by surprise that he couldn't absorb the truth for a minute.

"I don't get to town much," he said finally. "I didn't know it had gone out of business. But I oughtn't to be surprised. We've lost over half the stores and shops in town since this drouth started. Anybody who thinks he can prosper when the farmer and rancher don't, all he's got to do is come look at this town. And you can write *that* in your story."

It bothered Charlie, finding out like this. Bess Winfield had probably left town.

The reporter asked, "If it started raining tomorrow, how long would it take the town to recover?"

Charlie frowned at the vacant buildings across the street. Sadly he said, "Did you ever see anything die and then come back to life?"

The only place he could think of which they could

handily reach afoot was Prentice Harpe's drugstore; it had started serving coffee the last couple of years . . . anything to help the store traffic. Prentice was standing at the cash register when Charlie walked in. He gave the ranchman a cold glance and turned his back. He hadn't spoken to Charlie since the collapse of the cattleman's caravan. He had sold out all his cattle shortly afterward and lost twenty years' savings. From what Charlie had heard, he was holding onto this drugstore by his toenails.

Charlie motioned toward a table, and Johnson sat down opposite him, laying out the note pad. The waitress who brought them coffee was vaguely familiar, though Charlie could not remember her name. He recognized her as the wife of a farmer out on Coyote Flat. A working wife was the only salvation now to many a small operator.

Johnson queried Charlie about the beginnings of the drouth, and its effect on him.

"Six years," Charlie said, counting on his fingers. "It's a blessin' the Lord never gave us the gift of prophecy. If we'd known when we started that we'd still be in it six years later, I think we'd of all gone and jumped into the Concho River. I get to thinkin' sometimes that maybe drouth is the normal condition here and the rainy years are the freaks."

"I suppose there have been drouths this long before."

"In Indian times, maybe; not since the white man has kept records. The Indian would take down his tepee and leave with the buffalo. It always rained *somewhere;* that's where he would go. We can't do that. Anywhere we went, somebody else would have a prior claim."

"What has been the drouth's effect on you?"

"It's aged me twenty years in the last six. It's cut me down to half the land I had to begin with. I had three sections of my own, deeded free and clear. Now there's mortgage paper on it again. I sold out all my cattle and I'm down to a fraction on my sheep. Once I had a son on the place with me, and a whole Mexican family. Now it's just me and my wife."

The reporter nodded sympathetically. "I was told about your son. He would make a good human-interest story, being so well-known in rodeo. People will know it *must* have been severe to force out a man of his qualifications."

Charlie looked down at his hands. "Anything you write about Tom, you tell them he tried awful hard."

"Perhaps he'll do well enough back in rodeo that someday he can get a fresh beginning on the ranch."

Charlie avoided Johnson's eyes. "Maybeso."

The reporter signaled the waitress to refill their coffee cups and asked Charlie if he would like some pie or something. Charlie shook his head. Because of the weight he had lost lately, Mary had quit pushing those damn turnip greens at him. He wanted to keep it that way.

Johnson said, "Perhaps what this part of the country needs is a good oilfield. That would pay off a lot of debts."

Charlie nodded dubiously. "Maybe, but you pay a price for it. An oilfield scars up the land. And them oil people, they don't care much about the land, most of them. They're only interested in what's under it. They'll use up your water or leave it polluted with salt if you don't watch them. There'll come a time in this country when a barrel of water is worth more than a barrel of oil."

"It appears to me the land is badly scarred-up anyway. Even with the best of rain, it may take years for it to recover from what has happened to it."

"We've done the best we knew how, most of us. Nobody goes in there on purpose to do damage to his country. We've grazed it too hard—we've made mistakes—but it wasn't because we meant to. It was because we didn't know enough. We had to guess sometimes, and we guessed wrong. We had to take chances sometimes, and we taken the wrong ones. But we've tried to do right. We *will* do right when we know how."

Johnson jotted some notes and turned a page. "Somebody was telling me you're unusual, Mister Flagg."

"Unusual?"

"They tell me you've gone this far through the drouth and have never taken emergency feed or gone in for any of the other government aid programs."

Charlie shrugged. "I expect there's others have done the same."

"I suppose. But it would interest me to know your motivations. I've always heard about the fierce independence of the pioneer cowman. Is this a latter-day manifestation of the same credo?"

Charlie blinked, some of the words going over his head. "I just don't believe in askin' somebody else to pay my way. I'll play my own cards or cash in my chips."

"But modern-day morality places no stigma on accepting assistance. It's the norm today; it's neighbor helping neighbor."

"And sometimes it's neighbor soakin' neighbor."

Johnson was writing rapidly.

Charlie said, "I'll give you an illustration. If you was to go out to my ranch and look around my barn, you'd find a bunch of cats. Feed barns and haystacks are bad about breedin' mice if you don't have cats to keep them thinned out. Now, if you'd go in my wife's kitchen you'd see an old pet cat curled up close to the stove. She's fat and lazy. If a mouse was to run across the kitchen floor that old cat wouldn't hardly stir a whisker. She's been fed everything she wanted. She depends on us. If we went off someday and left her she'd starve.

"But out at the barn there's cats that can spot a mouse across two corrals. I never feed them. They rustle for theirselves, and they do a damn good job of it. If I was to leave they'd never miss me. All they need is a chance to operate. They may not be as fat as the old pet, but I'd say they're healthier. And they don't have to rub somebody's leg for what they get. Now, you can call me old-fashioned if you want to— lots of people do—but I'd rather be classed with them go-getters out in the barn than with that old gravy-licker in the kitchen."

Johnson scribbled furiously, getting it all on paper. Presently he looked up. "A lot of honest people have taken drouth help and been glad to get it, Mister Flagg."

"I know. I got a-plenty of friends who've taken all they could get and were honest in figurin' they had it comin' to them. They've paid taxes for years and seen other people take the benefits. Now at least they're gettin' a little of it back. That's the whole point, though, that's what's wrong. There was a time when we looked up to Uncle Sam; he was somethin' to be proud of and respect. Now he's turned into some kind of muddle-brained Sugar Daddy givin' out goodies right and left in the hopes that everybody's goin' to love him. And people are playin' a selfish game with him, all tryin' to grab more than the next man, tryin' to get more out of the pot than they put in it. Let the other man pay. Gore the other man's ox but leave mine alone.

"It's divided us into little selfish groups, snarlin' and snappin' at each other like hungry dogs, grabbin' for what we can get and to hell with everybody else. We beg and fight and prostitute ourselves. We take charity and give it a sweeter name. And when we get what we ask for it's never what it looked like it was. The sweet milk generally always turns to clabber.

"Take the drouth program, for an instance. It's like haulin' a bucket up out of the well and findin' the water all leaked out on the way. They said they would help the rancher by givin' him ten dollars a ton to help pay for the hay he bought. Overnight the price of hay jumped fifteen dollars. The rancher was five dollars worse off than before, and the government was out ten. Congress agreed to refund two cents a gallon on tractor gasoline to help the farmers. The companies jumped the price of tank gas two cents a gallon delivered to the farm. Every time they set out to 'help' us, the price goes up enough to offset the aid. Somebody else steals all the sugar and the stockman is no better off. What's more, he's given up somethin' he can never get back. He's given up a little of his self-respect, a little of the pride he used to have in takin' care of himself by himself."

The reporter touched the tip of his pencil to his tongue. "Mister Flagg, I'm sure they've made mistakes. But doesn't it give you some satisfaction to know that the government at least had good intentions?"

"The road to hell is paved and bridged with good intentions. I'd be a lot more satisfied with Uncle Sam if he didn't hire so many left-handed nephews to run everybody's business."

A few days later Charlie stepped through the bank door and stopped to weigh himself on the free scale. From his desk Emmett Rodale rumbled, "I bet you weigh a lot less than you did when you talked to that reporter."

"How come?"

"Because you unburdened yourself of twenty or thirty pounds of opinions. I wouldn't of told him about you if I'd thought it'd get you in Dutch."

"In Dutch?" Charlie's mouth sagged open. "I don't know what you're talking about."

"I reckon you ain't seen today's Angelo paper." Rodale picked up a copy from the top of his desk and thrust it at Charlie. It was spread open to the livestock page. Charlie saw a three-column headline.

RANCHMAN URGES END TO DROUTH AID:
SAYS IT BRINGS MORE HARM THAN HELP

Charlie swallowed hard. "Have you read it?"

Big nodded his bald head. "Long before breakfast. And people been readin' it *to* me all day. It's an AP story; I expect it's bein' printed today in papers from Cape Cod to Hickory Bend."

Charlie sat down in the heavy wooden chair and hurriedly scanned the article. "He quoted me pretty much the way I said it. It's no different from what I've said to *you* a hundred times."

"But when you say it to me it don't get published." Big frowned. "Good thing for you that you ain't runnin' for office. Nobody would vote for you today but kinfolks, and maybe not all of *them*."

Charlie pitched the paper onto the heavy desk and sat in thoughtful silence, a little bewildered. "Who's mad at me?"

Big held up his stubby fingers as if he was about to begin counting on them. He switched his cigar to the other side of his mouth and scowled. "You're fixin' to hear from one of them right now. Here comes Yancy Pike like a bull on the prod."

Yancy slammed the front door shut behind him and strode toward Charlie, shaking a rolled-up newspaper at him. "Well, Charlie Flagg, I hope to hell you're satisfied!"

Charlie pushed to his feet, his nettle beginning to rise. "Now, Yancy, I'm not sure. Maybe you ought to make yourself clear."

"You made *yourself* clear enough. You as much as said we'd get along better if they just went and cut us adrift. What're you tryin' to do, ruin us? We got a long winter starin' us in the face. Just because you're too backward to take what's comin' to you don't mean you got to go and spoil it for the rest of us."

"The man asked me what I thought and I told him. One thing we can still do in this country is to say what we think."

"If them damnyankees up in Washington get ahold of that story, they're liable to say *you* did without, so we can all do it."

Charlie's fists were trying to knot. He shoved his hands into his pockets as a precaution. "Maybe you could, Yancy. You ever tried?"

Yancy pushed his face up to close to Charlie's. His breath was like something dead. "For years, Charlie

Flagg, I've listened to you spout a lot of damnfool notions and kept my mouth shut because I figured you was harmless. A fool, but harmless. Now I wisht I'd told you off a long time ago. You're a danger to every one of us."

Charlie had a hard time keeping his hands in his pockets. He was acutely aware that everybody in the building was watching and listening. "Anything you figured on doin' about me, Yancy?"

"I intend to raise some hell with this bank, for one thing. I'd like to know why Big keeps on backin' you. If he won't listen I'll go to the board of directors. If they don't do somethin' I'll see the examiners. They got no business standin' behind a man who ain't got sense enough to take somethin' when it's offered to him . . . a man who spouts off about things he don't understand and puts all of us in the shadow of the poorhouse!"

Charlie ground his teeth together. "I'm one man, Yancy, that's all . . . just one man. One man's words can't ruin anything that was worth a damn in the first place. Anyhow, they won't cut off your aid; they're too busy buyin' your vote with it."

Yancy Pike tried to stare him down but couldn't. He turned and stamped to the door. He stopped there to shake the newspaper at Charlie. "You mind what I tell you, Charlie Flagg!"

When Pike was gone, Charlie slumped back into the straight wooden chair. He had always suspected Big put an uncomfortable chair here on purpose to keep his borrowers at a disadvantage in dickering with him. "I wish to hell I'd never seen that reporter." He looked worriedly at Rodale. "Is this thing goin' to cause me trouble?"

"A man who snipes at Santa Claus can't expect any

brass bands. But Yancy Pike's not runnin' this bank. *I* am."

They talked about the feed needs for Brushy Top . . . what was left of it. Big gave Charlie a tentative approval for another winter's financing so long as every dollar spent was squeezed hard first. As Charlie stood up to go, Rodale said, "One last piece of advice, if you're in the market for any. Next time you run into a reporter, talk to him about football."

"I don't know nothin' about football."

"That's good."

As Charlie was about to reach for the door handle, the door swung open. Page Mauldin stopped in midstride, his tall frame bent, his dark-circled eyes fastened on Charlie Flagg. The two ranchmen stared a moment in surprise. Abruptly Page turned and started back out.

"Page," Charlie called, "whoa up a minute."

Page kept walking. Outside, Charlie called him again. Page stopped finally and turned. Charlie could see a stiff set to the old ranchman's jaw.

"Page, why the hurry? Ain't seen you in months."

Page didn't extend his hand as Charlie walked up. "Didn't know you'd been huntin' me."

Charlie awkwardly pulled back the hand he had held out. "I hope you're not still sore over that cattleman's caravan."

Mauldin flexed his fingers in silence, not looking at Charlie. "Can't say I'm happy about it. It failed, you know."

"I know. But that was months ago, Page. Anyway, I only did what I thought was right."

"So you did. And they whupped the britches off of us."

"I wish it could've been different."

"If it was to happen over again, Charlie, wouldn't your attitude still be the same?"

"You know it would."

"One thing about you, Charlie: you may not always be right, but you're never in doubt. A man can generally guess just about where you'll stand." Page brought himself to look at Charlie. His dark eyes smoldered. "But one thing I *didn't* expect . . . I didn't think you'd ever class me as a gravy-licker."

"Page, I never said no such-of-a-thing."

"You as much as said it. In the paper today."

"That's not what I . . ."

"If you don't mind, Charlie, I got business to take care of. See you sometime."

Page walked on down the street, forgetting or deferring whatever it was that had been about to take him into the bank. Charlie called, "Page, you got it all wrong."

Page gave no sign of hearing. Charlie watched helplessly, wanting to follow after him. But to argue with Page Mauldin now would be as futile as trying to hold back the wind with his hands.

Rounder Pike walked up beside Charlie and stood chewing his cud. "Charlie, don't you take it too hard. Page ain't hisself."

"He sure has got thin-skinned lately."

"For reason. You ever see a wounded bobcat backed into a corner? Page is on the edge, Charlie. He can feel the ice breakin' under his feet."

Charlie's chin fell. "I didn't know it was that bad."

"It's worse. You know what they say: the bigger they are, the harder they go down."

Charlie's mouth went grim. "Has he got a chance?"

"Awful thin. One little push now and everything he's got will go like a string of dominoes."

"Then pray he don't get that push."

"Big and the preacher have got a regular prayin' session every day. Page has got enough notes in that bank to paper half the houses in Little Mexico. And that bank's just one of the *small* ones."

"But how . . ."

"He's a builder, Charlie, but he's not a manager. There's a lot of difference. Thirty-forty years ago a man could be a builder and nothin' else. But this is a tight-margin world we've got today. The cowboy-rancher has had his day, Big says. It's a book-keeper's world from here on out."

Charlie felt a sour taste rise in his mouth. "Page wasn't the first man to eat my packin' out. Your brother Yancy took hide, hair, and all."

Rounder stepped to the curb and relieved himself of a wad of chewing tobacco. He paused, pensive. "Don't think too hard of us. We all want help. But there you stand like our own consciences talkin' to us, tellin' us how far we've strayed from what we believe in. Nobody likes his conscience naggin' at him, even though he knows he's wrong. We envy you for your guts, Charlie, but I reckon we resent you a little, too, for bein' stronger than the rest of us. Times past, they used to crucify the prophets."

16

Jim Sweet slumped at his feedstore desk, almost in a state of collapse. He seemed to be looking through Charlie without seeing him. "Thirty thousand dollars," he said over and over. "He says I owe the government thirty thousand dollars."

It had been a long time since Charlie had had thirty thousand dollars. Just the sound of it stunned him a little. "Who says?"

"That . . ." Jim's face clouded with helpless rage. He spat several smoky adjectives in a random mixture of English and Spanish. That was an underrated advantage of being bilingual; it gave a man a wider range of therapeutic outlet. "That goddam federal auditor, that shriveled-up son of a bitch you just met walkin' out of here."

Charlie turned to look. He had passed a stranger on the steps, but he had been too preoccupied to pay attention.

Jim said, "He was loaded for bear the first day he come here. As much as told me he was goin' to prove

I was a crook—all us feed dealers was crooks, and all the ranchers too. He's snarled and snapped and insulted the help around here for three weeks. He's been through every scrap of paper in the place except in the toilet. Now he tells me I been in violation of drouth feed regulations to the tune of thirty thousand dollars."

Charlie looked around for a chair and sat down heavily. He had already been jarred too much today. "You never cheated a man in your life, Jim."

Jim Sweet dropped his face into his hands. "You tried to tell me, but I didn't listen. It's easy for a politician to make promises when he's just passin' through and don't ever have to come back. Remember that time a bunch of Congressmen came through and made speeches over at Sonora about what all they was goin' to do to help people through the drouth? They talked about teamwork, about everybody pitchin' in together to help out. Said for us feed dealers and the county committees to go ahead and get the feed to the stockmen the best way we could; the government would see that we was taken care of.

"Well, it sure as hell *has*. We had to play it by ear. Department of Agriculture drug its feet for months till it finally come out with a full set of regulations. The county PMA committee would certify that a rancher needed a certain amount of feed, and we'd give it to him. The committee was supposed to allow them sixty days' supply at a time. Lots of ranchers didn't have that much storage; they'd take what they had room for and let us credit them for the rest. Sometimes they had credit left when the sixty days was up. We went ahead and gave them the feed. Other times they'd run short. We knew the committee would okay them the next time it met, so we advanced them the feed. Seemed like the logical thing to do. This ran on for months till the government finally got all its rules on paper. Now the auditors say the rules applied from the day the program started, and everything we done in those first months was illegal."

Charlie said, "They can't make regulations retroactive. That's against the United States Constitution."

"By God they've done it. That's where the thirty thousand dollars comes in. Nobody stole it. It was fed up just like them Congressmen said it ought to be. Now the Department says it wasn't legal because we didn't follow the rules they hadn't got around to writin' yet."

"The politician promiseth, and the bureaucrat taketh away." Charlie rubbed his face. "It won't stand up in court."

"Why not? It's *their* court." Sweet cursed and spun his chair around to stare out the window. "You'll want to know, Charlie . . . they're zeroed in on Page Mauldin."

A chill went through Charlie. "Page? How come?"

"That auditor you saw . . . he's pulled out all the certificates with Page's name on them. Told me Page shouldn't ever of been allowed to get any drouth feed. Said Page is a big operator who could afford to buy his own."

"What did the regulations say?"

"Anything, or nothin'. They write them regulations so a man's never sure what they mean; that way they can jump clear if the britches ever start to bind. County committee tried to get a rulin' on Page from the state office. State office just passed the buck, throwed all the responsibility back on the county committee. You take them men up in high office, they're slippery. They make sure it's always somebody else who gets burned." Jim Sweet's eyes bore a keen edge of pain. "Be glad you was smarter than the rest of us. Be glad you stayed out."

"I wasn't bein' smart. I just didn't believe in it, is all. I still don't."

"I wish I hadn't believed in it. I wouldn't be in all this trouble."

"It'll happen every time you hook up with them *federales*. There's too many of them got a brain like a pissant and a mouth like a foghorn."

A voice spoke behind him. "Are you referring to me?"

Turning, Charlie saw the man he had met on the steps, a thin, sharp-eyed man in his middle fifties who looked as if he had been chewing persimmons. Angrily the auditor said, "I believe you were referring to me!"

Charlie stood up, the blood rising in his face. "That's damn sure possible."

Jim Sweet pleaded, "Charlie, don't."

But it had been too long a day already. Charlie snapped at the auditor, "*You're* the one that's pullin' a fraud. There wasn't anything stolen here, and you know it!"

The auditor stood ramrod straight and faced him. "There were regulations and they were not followed. There have to be rules. It's my job to see that the rules are carried out to the letter."

The longer Charlie stared, the angrier he became. He thought he saw here the personification of a type he had always despised, a narrow-souled man in an untouchable position, flaunting his power. He had seen it in World War I in ninety-day wonders who used their commissions as a license for arrogance and cruelty. He had seen it in some ranchers contemptuous of their hired help and of anyone else forced to deal with them from a position of weakness. He had seen it in a few peace officers who covered their own moral weakness with the authority of the law. He saw it here, and instinctively he hated it.

"You figure you'll build your own prestige if you bring down a man the caliber of Page Mauldin. You're out for yourself, and you don't give a damn how many innocent men's hides you nail to the fence."

The auditor's eyes burned like two live coals. "There are no innocent men. Maybe I'd better look at *your* records again. I wonder how much *you* got away with?"

Charlie drew back his fist. He would have swung if Jim Sweet hadn't grabbed his arm. "Charlie, for God's sake . . ."

Charlie swayed. The fury swept through him like wildfire through dry grass. Before he realized it, Jim was rushing him out the big side door. Charlie dropped onto some feed stacked on the loading dock. An odd sickness swirled over him. His stomach was aboil. He felt a sharp pain in his chest.

Jim Sweet hovered over him anxiously. "Charlie, you got to be careful, lettin' yourself get carried away like this."

Charlie waved him off. "I'm all right. Leave me alone for a minute."

Jim watched him apprehensively. "You set there and rest a little. I better go back and try to soothe that *federale*. He can fair gut me if he takes a notion."

Charlie could hear Jim in the office, trying to placate the angry auditor. The auditor was demanding, "What's that man's name? I want to look at his records again."

"He ain't got any records."

"What do you mean he hasn't any? He's your customer, isn't he?"

"He never did take any drouth feed."

"Don't try to hand me that. Everybody lines up at the public trough when he gets the chance."

"Not Charlie Flagg. He never did."

The auditor mused a long time. "What is he, some kind of a nut?"

Page Mauldin was a dying man, suffocating in a swirling sandtrap of mortgages and due-notes, desperately clutching at anything that seemed to offer a hold. The awful weight of his empire was dragging him down.

It began with the federal auditor, who declared with official solemnity that Page never had been eligible for drouth aid and that he had therefore defrauded the government. Page snorted his contempt for any such notion. With the impatience which overworked, weather-beaten ranchmen usually have for people with clean suits, smooth hands and leather briefcases, Page simply told him to get the hell off of the ranch and stay off. When the auditor persisted, Page curtly ordered Diego Escamillo to throw him off.

Diego had always been a man who did what he was told, and did it with great efficiency.

Within a week the word spread across Texas. Tremors shook the marble halls of finance. Fearful the government's claim on Page might endanger their own, creditors converged on Rio Seco like a swarm of hungry locusts, each intent on getting his settlement first and escaping the fray with skin intact. With a numbing suddenness, Page Mauldin found his world crumbling down around him like a house built on sand.

Emmett Rodale had always cultivated a brooding appearance, for it invariably put the other man on the defensive from the start. That sourness came now without conscious effort. Gloom was like a dark cloud hovering over his head. He rubbed a ham-sized hand across his heavy face. "Charlie, we'll all suffer over this. When a man like Page Mauldin goes down, it's like the *Titanic* suckin' the lifeboats under. This'll take the starch out of people who've held on and fought. They'll say if he couldn't make it, what chance have they got?"

"Ain't there anything you can do?"

"Could I put out a brush fire with a canteen? Page got too big for this bank years ago."

"So what do *we* do?"

"Shore up our own, the best we can. And cry a little bit, maybe, for Page."

Charlie parked his pickup in front of the big Mauldin house. He stepped out into the winter sunshine and slammed the door. He stood a moment, looking, listening. He heard no sound except the chill, dusty wind rustling through the bare branches of the big old pecan trees and whistling mournfully among the electric and telephone wires. He saw no movement except a horse in a corral, poking his nose around an empty hayrack, looking for something to eat.

Diego was probably out in the pastures feeding, Charlie thought. Maybe Page was in the house.

He opened the cedar-picket yard gate and moved through. Rheumatism bothering him a little, he

limped up the rock walk to the front door. He hesitated a moment, then knocked.

In a minute Kathy Mauldin was staring at him in
surprise. "Uncle Charlie!"

Charlie had the odd feeling he was calling on a
house in bereavement. He took off his dusty hat.
"Hello, Kathy. You're lookin' good."

They stared at each other a long, awkward moment. Kathy swung the door wider. "It's windy out
there. Won't you come on in?"

Charlie said, "If you think it's all right . . ."

"Certainly it's all right."

"After that set-to with Page in town, I wasn't sure."
He walked in. "I tried to telephone first."

"We had to disconnect the line. So many calls, all
hours of day and night."

Charlie twisted his hat brim, unsure of himself.
"Maybe I oughtn't to've come, but I wanted to see
Page. I'd like to be his friend again."

"You never stopped bein' a friend, Uncle Charlie.
He never took time to cultivate friends much; there
weren't many. Right now he needs all there are, and
you're Number One."

Charlie looked around the pine-paneled living
room and past it into the hallway. "Where's he at?"

"At the barn, I think. He gets restless sittin' in the
house. But he keeps comin' back to it like a little boy
lost."

"I'll go find him."

"There's coffee on the stove if you'd like to warm
up first."

"Maybe I'll bring him back and we can drink it together." He turned at the door. "Page is takin' it hard,
I guess."

She nodded gravely. "Uncle Charlie, I think it's

worse even than when Mother died. I've told him over and over: we've still got each other. We've still got this home ranch because it was in Mother's name, and she willed it to me. It's awful little . . . a drop in the bucket compared to what he had. But it's a start. We can build on it."

Charlie studied Kathy Mauldin, realizing she was not a girl any longer. She was a woman, and she had a woman's instincts and wisdom. "What does he say to that?"

"Nothin'. It's like he can't even hear me. I'm scared."

So am I, thought Charlie. But he didn't tell her.

At the barn Charlie found Page had thrown a bundle of feed into the hayrack and sat hunched now on the barn steps, head bowed, squinted eyes solemnly watching the horse tear the bundle apart. Page gave no sign that he even noticed Charlie.

"Page, it's me. Charlie."

Page turned his head, his dark eyes slow to focus. He nodded, but he didn't speak.

"Page, I come over to talk to you. Come over to see if I couldn't square up whatever's gone wrong between us."

Page shook his head. "There ain't nothin' to square, Charlie. They've took it all away from me anyway. Nothin' matters now."

The old rancher hadn't shaved in three or four days. The gritty wind tugged at the brim of his felt hat, but he seemed oblivious to it. Charlie noticed that Page didn't even have his pants legs tucked into the tops of his boots.

"Page, it's chilly out here. Don't you think you ought to go back to the house and warm yourself?"

"There's no warmth in that house. No warmth anywhere."

"There's sure none in this drafty barn."

Page shrugged. "I used to be able to come out here and think. Quiet out here. A man's mind can find itself." He jerked his chin toward a shotgun that sat just inside the door. "Anyway, been some rats out here tearin' into the feed sacks. Thought I might shoot me one or two if they'd show theirselves."

Charlie sat down beside him, falling into a long, frowning silence. "Page, you didn't come here to think. You come to eat your heart out."

Page didn't answer.

"You got to let go. Make up your mind to accept what's happened and take a firm grip on what you got left. And you *have* got somethin' left. You've got this homeplace. You've got friends. Best of all, you've got yourself a daughter. All the drouthed-out land in West Texas ain't worth one tear in that girl's eye."

Page gave no sign of listening. He hunched with his elbows on his legs, his gnarled old hands hanging limp between his knees. "Did I ever tell you, Charlie, what started me to buildin'? It was hate. And, I reckon, envy. I never had no idea about tryin' to be the biggest rancher in West Texas till the time I went to work for a man down in Sutton County. Never mind his name; I've tried to forget it. This feller had inherited a ranch from his old daddy who had come in the early days and lived like a coyote while he tried to build himself somethin'. The boss had him an Eastern wife who didn't care beans about none of it. They had a fine big home they'd built out of the inheritance after the old man died. He'd lived in a frame shack all that time, you know.

"I was the foreman. One day I walked up to the front of the house to tell the boss about somethin' . . . sick cow, I think it was. His wife met me at the door. She looked at me like I'd crawled out from under a rock. She said, 'The hired help goes to the back door.' Well, sir, it flew all over me. Right then and there I quit. I swore that if it taken me the rest of my life I'd own that ranch. I'd buy it out from under them and slam that front door in their goddam faces.

"I went on my own after that. Started tradin' in cows and sheep. Luck was good to me. Leased up land, bought this homeplace. Depression come, and my old boss couldn't cut it. I scraped the money together and went and bought that place after the bank taken it over. I was there the day they moved out, him and his wife. I walked in the front door and stood there and watched them carry out the last of their stuff. I'd waited a long time for that day. But I didn't enjoy it the way I thought I would. I felt sorry for them, and maybe a little guilty. I never could bring myself to live in that house. I finally sold it to a feller who jacked it up and moved it into Sonora.

"I caught the land fever after that. Never could get enough. There was always one more ranch I wanted." He paused, pensive. "I've stepped on toes in my time. I expect there's people who felt about me the way I did about that old boy and his wife. You reckon any of them will feel sorry for *me*, Charlie?"

"Nobody really enjoys seein' somebody hurt."

"You want to bet? There's people would pay good money for a ticket to watch me go down." Page Mauldin clasped his hands together and brought them up to rest his chin. "I made some mistakes in my day, but that drouth program was the biggest one. If I hadn't ever touched it . . . if I'd stayed out of it like you done . . . maybe I wouldn't be sittin' here like this today, a ruined man. You was the smart one, Charlie."

"Not smart . . . just stubborn."

"I was sunk the day I taken the first load of feed. It never occurred to me somebody would want to crucify me for bein' big."

"Somebody's usin' you for a stepladder. But to hell with them, Page; you can make a comeback. All you got to do is make up your mind to it."

Page's voice sounded old and beaten. "Not any more. There ain't time enough. I ain't got the strength for the fight. They've whipped me, Charlie."

"You *have* the strength. All you need is the will. You don't have to have the whole pie. Settle for a slice of it; just be sure it's a *good* slice."

Page shook his head. "It's no good. I had the whole pie once. I couldn't settle for a slice any more."

Charlie stared at this gaunt ranchman who had been his friend for forty-odd years. He had taken advice from Page Mauldin many a time; he had seldom given any. He felt his throat tighten, and helplessness came over him like a shroud. Page looked eighty years old. "Page, quit thinkin' about yourself, then. Think of Kathy."

"It's late to start thinkin' about her now; I should've done that years ago. I cheated that girl, Charlie. For years I left her by herself. Didn't have time for her. Cheated her out of the attention a girl is supposed to get from her father. I told myself I was doin' it all for her sake, to leave her somethin' when I was gone. But I lied. I was doin' it all for myself."

"You gave her more than you realized. She's a levelheaded woman. And she's got your strength."

"She's got more strength than I have. And it's a

good thing, because she can stand up to what we've lost. I can't."

"You got to, Page. For herself and for you." Charlie pushed to his feet and glanced toward his pickup. "I got a right smart of feedin' to do. I'll be back, Page."

Page didn't reply. He wasn't even looking at Charlie. Charlie placed his hand on the thin shoulder, then turned and limped toward the house, helplessness and frustration heavy on him.

His hand was on the picket gate when he heard the shotgun blast. His first thought was that Page had seen one of those rats.

But realization struck him like a fist. He swayed, a chill running down his back. He started for the barn, half walking, half running, sharp pain lancing his bad leg. He heard the slam of a door and heard Kathy's fearful cry.

He reached the barn and started up the step. He grabbed at the doorjamb, his eyes wide, his stomach turning.

Sick, he backed away. He turned toward the house, toward Kathy. He caught her as she came by him. She struggled, but he managed to hold her. "Don't go over there, Kathy. For God's sake, don't go over there."

Lupe and Rosa Flores drove down from San Angelo early the day of the funeral, bringing Manuel with them. They came to Brushy Top first. Charlie tried to make small talk with Lupe awhile, discussing his job in Angelo, relating things that had happened to various people they had known in town and on the ranches. But the conversation was strained, made difficult by the sense of disaster which hung over them.

Manuel sat in dark and thoughtful silence. He said

nothing except when asked a direct question. As often as not he simply nodded his answer.

When the walls of the house closed in upon them to an intolerable degree, the three got into Charlie's old green pickup and drove over the ranch. Manuel sat in the middle, looking hard, saying little.

Lupe hammered the heel of his hand vainly against the dashboard in an effort to stop a persistent rattle. He looked at the mileage on the speedometer and remarked to Charlie that it was far past time to trade the pickup in on a new one.

Charlie shook his head. "You priced a pickup lately, Lupe? It'd knock your hat off. I remember when I used to buy a new pickup for the price of four or five good cows. Now it'd take nearer twenty cows, if I even had any. Seems like the higher the prices go on what we have to buy, the lower they go on what we sell."

When they returned to headquarters, Lupe strayed over to gaze pensively at the empty frame house he had lived in so long. Manuel hung back, looking at Charlie. Charlie sensed he was working up his nerve for something. He walked up to Manuel and asked him for the sixth or eighth time today, "You still doin' all right in school?"

Manuel nodded absently, then blurted, "Mister Charlie, you mean this is all that's left of the ranch, the part we just drove over?"

Charlie's eyes narrowed painfully. "That's it, *muchacho*. Just the tag end, that's all."

Manuel shook his head. "I guess I never quite realized . . ." His gaze drifted across the ranch yard and out over the horse pasture and on toward Warrior Hill. "Back yonder, there were things I didn't believe. I guess they were true after all."

Charlie puzzled. "I don't know what you mean."

Manuel shrugged. "I had some wrong ideas for a while. I hope you'll forgive me."

"How can I forgive you, son? I never blamed you for anything."

Kathy never did really break down and cry. From some deep resource she summoned up an iron will which held back the tears while the arrangements were being made. They buried Page Mauldin in the Rio Seco cemetery beside his wife, whose headstone already was darkening from the years. The crowd was large, but there were few genuine mourners beyond a close circle of friends and employees. Charlie sensed with resentment that many of the people were here more out of curiosity than from any desire to pay respects. It seemed to him there was more genuine grief among the dozen or fifteen Mexicans than in all the Anglos put together. Old Elvira Escamillo wore a black veil and wept more than Kathy did. Diego stood with his arm around his mother's shoulders, the tears running unashamed down his leathery cheeks.

Lupe and Rosa stood with Charlie and Mary, but at the graveside services Manuel stood near Kathy. Kathy held herself together stubbornly, determined to provide no spectacle for this crowd.

Later, when the grave had been filled in, a few of them returned to the cemetery. There was no crowd then . . . just Charlie and Mary, the Escamillos and a few other Mexican people who had worked for Page . . . the Flores family and Kathy. Now, with no strangers to watch, Kathy broke down and sobbed. Charlie's eyes burned, and he wanted to go to her, but he stood rooted in his tracks. Mary took a step toward the girl, then stopped as Kathy turned and buried her face against Manuel's chest. Manuel's arms went around her.

Mary seemed not surprised, but it caught Charlie unprepared. He stared, wondering if he had missed something somewhere.

They all stood awkwardly and let Kathy cry herself out. When she was done, Charlie painfully cleared his throat and said, "Girl, maybe you better come and stay with us a few days."

Kathy raised her chin. She glanced at the sorrowing Elvira and Diego. "Thanks, Uncle Charlie, but there's work to do and stock to feed."

"This once, they can do without you."

She shook her head. "You've taught me better than that, Uncle Charlie. It's my ranch. I'll take care of it myself." She clenched her small fists, her voice tight. "I'll not ever ask anybody for anything. I'll not ever let anybody *give* me anything. And no son of a bitch—*nobody*—will ever get a chance to take away what's mine. They'll never do to me what they did to my daddy!"

Charlie nodded, for that was talk he could understand.

Mary said, "Charlie, I think I'll go and stay with her a couple of days. I expect she and Elvira could use a little company."

Charlie agreed. He stood and watched as Manuel opened the car door for Kathy and the women. Diego crawled into the driver's seat of Page's brush-scarred car. Manuel closed the door, then leaned to the window and said something to Kathy. She touched his hand and gave him her thanks, then Diego slowly drove away. Manuel stood alone a little while, watching them go. Charlie had nothing to say; he simply watched Manuel, still wondering.

In a little while the Flores family was gone back to San Angelo. Charlie stood alone on the street, staring at the vacant store buildings, somberly realizing that after today—no matter how much it might rain, no matter how much the country might recover—it would never be the same to him again. There would always be an emptiness here, a scar that would never quite heal.

He became aware of two men walking slowly up the street toward him, a grave Emil Deutscher and a harried March Nicholson. Emil had been to the funeral; he wore an inexpensive blue suit from Montgomery Ward, one whose coat had never quite fit his broad, bony shoulders. He always looked ill at ease in a suit . . . in anything but his blue cotton work shirt and overalls. They stopped when they came up to Charlie, and Emil woodenly stuck out his hand. "Sad day, Charlie."

Charlie nodded. "Awful sad. You boys like some coffee? I need *somethin'*, and that's the strongest we can buy here."

He expected Nicholson to excuse himself, but Nicholson held the drugstore door open for them and followed them in. Emil dropped heavily into a chair, his face deeply furrowed. Charlie thought at first his melancholy mood was a carryover from the funeral, but he changed his mind. "Emil, you been sick?"

The cotton farmer grimaced. "You could say that, I suppose."

Yancy Pike was sitting at the marble counter. At the sound of Emil's voice he turned, saw who was at the table and strode over toward Charlie with a studied belligerence. No one invited Yancy to sit down, and he gave no sign that he wanted to.

"Well," he said, "ol' Page is no bigger than anybody else now. Just six feet of dirt, that's all he's got."

Charlie stiffened. "Somethin' eatin' you, Yancy?"

"Damn right somethin's eatin' me. *Your* friend Page Mauldin—the big man—he wrecked everything. On account of him they went and bore down on us little people too. They oughtn't to've ever let a big man like him in the program in the first place. That was for us poor folks."

Charlie thought angrily, *A man with no soul will always be a poor man, one way or another.* But he saw no gain in saying it.

Nicholson's voice was brittle. "*You* know why they cut you off, Yancy."

Yancy glared at Emil and Nicholson. "Somebody told them a bunch of lies about me. I got a pretty good notion who it was."

Nicholson glared back. "Any quarrel you've got, Yancy, you take it up with the state committee."

Yancy Pike pounded his fist into his palm. "I say if they're goin' to cut anybody off they ought to cut *everybody* off. Ain't fair, pickin' on some of us and lettin' the rest go on. I bet if somebody was to go and look into it they'd find there was a bunch of Communists at the foot of the whole mess." He stood in red-faced challenge, as if hoping somebody would stand up and contest him. Nobody did, but Charlie was tempted. Charlie simply said, "Best I remember, Yancy, you was the first one in. You didn't see no Communists then."

Yancy turned and stamped out, trying to slam the door behind him. He was foiled by its hydraulic closer.

Charlie stared after him. "There's always somethin' wrong with Yancy, but what is it this time?"

Nicholson said, "He's been cut off of the feed program. He reported livestock he didn't own and got more drouth feed than he was entitled to." He scowled. "Why is it that a man who abuses everything he touches is always the maddest when it catches up with him?"

Emil Deutscher sat in brooding silence, not listening. He blurted, "Word is come today from the state office, Charlie. They fired me off of the county committee."

"I thought the local farmers elected you."

"They elected me, but the state office fired me."

Charlie's face twisted. "It's a thankless job anyway. Was I you, I'd call it good news."

Nicholson put in, "It's not just being fired, Mister Flagg. It's the way it was done, and the reason. They threw him overboard."

Emil's eyes were bleak. "Charlie, they make out like something crooked we done, us on the committee."

"We all know better than that."

"We tried to do right. When we asked them for advice, they said it was for us to decide. Now they say we decided wrong. Why didn't they tell us *then*?"

Nicholson said acidly, "It's the system. An individual is always expendable to protect the system. When the drouth program started, we couldn't get the people higher up to make up their minds. We'd telephone and ask their opinion. Most of the time they wouldn't commit themselves. They dumped the responsibility back on us.

"Now comes some Eastern senator up for re-election. He wants to make a name with the homefolks as a watchdog over the people's tax money. It's dangerous to dig around in his own state, so he reaches off out here into something he knows nothing about. Who gives a damn if he hurts a few Texas clodhoppers and sheepherders, anyway? They don't count for much. Sure, some people cheated in the drouth deal. Some people would cheat in a church bingo game. But most of what has turned up here hasn't been dishonesty—it's been confusion—and it's been the fault of the brass who couldn't get off of their butts and make up their minds about anything. Now there's a rhubarb, and they've got to protect the system. So they throw a few Christians to the lions and go on about their business. The senator gets re-elected, and the auditors get a bigger appropriation."

Charlie's eyebrows arched. "March," he said, and realized he had never called the man by his first name before, "you're beginnin' to sound like me."

Nicholson pondered that proposition a moment. "No, not really. We still don't think alike. I still think the idea is good . . . it's the system that's at fault. *You'd* throw out the idea *and* the system."

"I damn sure would."

"There are lots of honest, dedicated men in the government service, Mister Flagg, trying to do what's right. They're usually defeated by the system. The idea is sound, but the ship goes aground on a reef of petty politics."

Charlie studied Emil's worried eyes and asked Nicholson, "Ain't there somethin' you can do for Emil?"

Nicholson shook his head. "I can't even do anything for myself. I'm in trouble for talking too much, and for being in the county where Page Mauldin headquartered. They'll transfer me now, or maybe fire me. I'm an embarrassment to them as long as I stay here."

Charlie said, "I'll hate to see you go, March. All of a sudden I think I'm beginnin' to like you."

Emil traced a meaningless pattern on the tabletop. Hopelessness was a dark shadow across his face. "Charlie, I am sellin' the farm."

"Emil!"

The farmer nodded painfully. "Too long already I've fought it."

"Stand up to them, Emil. They're sacrificin' you to keep their own ox out of the ditch. Tell them to go to hell."

"What happened today, that is not the only reason. It's just extra. For months now I have worked on a deal to sell the farm."

"But it's been in your family for sixty years!"

"That is time enough . . . and pain enough. You know, Charlie, how many years it is since we made a real crop, one to pay expenses? Now there's nothin' left to hold on to."

"It'll rain, Emil. Hang on a little longer."

"Always it is goin' to rain, and always it doesn't. What if it *does* rain? My cotton allotment is too small any more. Could I pay for a new tractor with the acres I am allowed? Cotton is the money crop here, and cotton only. One hope I'd have: to lease or buy enough extra land to build up a bigger allotment. But I got no money, Charlie. And even if I *did* get extra land, some other farmer I'd crowd out. *He* would move to town instead of me. The difference is the same." Emil brought the cup to his lips, but the coffee had gone cold. He grimaced. "What good is a high price support if always they cut your acres? From the start the little man is whipped. He can't get credit to expand. The big outfits, *they* can. You know who buys my land? A corporation called the Prairie Farm Development Company. It's not just *my* place they buy, either; they have bought many more. They buy up the good land and the bad land both, to get the cotton allotments. Then they will let the poor land go and plant cotton on the best. They will grow more cotton than *we* did, and always the government told us we grew too much.

"They will punch holes in the ground to find irrigation water. We have been too poor for that, us dirt farmers. *They* can get credit because with irrigation they know they can make a crop. The government will guarantee them a high price. With irrigation they will make four or five bales where we used to make one. For every acre they put in, some little dryland farmer will lose four or five." He made a bitter face. "A great big merry-go-round with lots of music. But it goes in a circle only, and when it stops you are still where you started. The wrong man gets the brass ring. And I helped make it so."

Charlie asked sadly, "Where'll you go, Emil?"

"I wish I knew. Farmin' is all ever I did. Maybe a job somewhere as a mechanic, or a carpenter. I don't know."

"We'll miss you."

"And we'll miss you, Charlie, you and Mary. But that old farm we won't miss. No sir, I'll never want to see that place again."

Tears welled into the farmer's eyes.

17

Three days after the funeral Charlie received a call from Big Emmett Rodale. "Come in as soon as you can, Charlie. I've got to talk to you."

His voice was grim, and Charlie felt a chill as he hung up the receiver, a chill not brought on by the north wind which whistled under the eaves.

Walking into the bank, he passed the free scale without even looking at it. He had a sense of dread, and he found himself hoping Big would be tied up with somebody else so Charlie had to sit awhile and wait. But Big had no one. He was sitting at his desk, watching the door. Charlie paused a moment, saw there was no excuse for stalling and walked slowly across the small lobby. Big's round face was deeply creased, and Charlie knew this frown was not feigned or exaggerated. It was real. Big stood up and silently shook hands with him, then motioned for Charlie to seat himself.

Big looked at him a minute, his eyes troubled. He picked up a box of cigars like the one he had clamped in his teeth, unlighted and cold. "Have one?" In all the years Charlie had known him, he could not remember Big ever offering him a cigar. He took this as a bad omen.

"I never smoke them, Big. Lately I even been rollin' my own cigarettes."

"I know," Big nodded. "It's been rough on everybody." He stared across the room, obviously doing some stalling himself. When he looked back, Charlie saw sadness in the banker's eyes. Big said, "It's fixin' to get rougher, Charlie. A whole lot rougher. This Page Mauldin bustup has raised hell and put a chunk under it."

Charlie murmured something to the effect that he was sure it had.

Big said, "All these years I ran this bank the way I wanted to, and nobody ever gave me any argument. If I wanted to make a loan a certain way, there wasn't nobody asked me any questions. If I *didn't* want to, nobody ever called me to account. But it's different now. This drouth has beaten us to the ground. We're a correspondent bank to one of the big ones in Fort Worth; you knew that. We could always farm out paper when it got to where we couldn't handle it all ourselves. They're lookin' a lot harder at us these days. Then there's the bank examiners. You think the Internal Revenue is rough? Try them examiners on for size. They been goin' over things with a fine-tooth comb since Page's deal turned sour. They been raisin' hell about a lot of our livestock accounts. It's been all I could do lately to keep the directors from foreclosin' on some of them."

He turned his eyes away from Charlie and shifted his cold cigar to the other side of his mouth. "Yours is one of them."

That hit Charlie like a kick in the stomach. He slumped in the hard, straight chair and clasped his hands together, tight. He took a long, deep breath and asked, "What can I do, Big? Or can I do *anything*?"

"Knowin' how you feel about things, I'd sooner take a whippin' with a wet rope than tell you, Charlie. Yancy Pike was agitatin' the board over it even before the bank examiners picked it up. Now they're all after *me*. They say you're a fool for not buyin' your feed through the government so you can get it cheaper; they say I'm a fool for backin' you."

"The feed would be a heap sight cheaper today if *nobody* had ever gone into the program."

"I won't argue that with you. But the graveyard is full of people who wouldn't of died *if . . .*" Big took out the cigar and used it for a pointer. "We got to live with what *is*, and not what might've been. There is a program, and you can get your feed cheaper through it than outside of it. Now I've got to put this thing to you the way they put it to me. Either you go into the program with everybody else, Charlie, or this bank will have to shut off your line of credit."

Charlie felt that kick in the stomach again, harder this time. He tried to say something, but no words came. He clasped his hands again, staring at them. Seemed he hadn't noticed how rough they had become, and how some of the cracks in the hard skin were so deep they must reach almost to the blood.

He managed the words, finally, but they came soft and strained. "No line of credit means no feed atall. My goats might get by without any bought feed, but the sheep would never make it."

Big didn't look at him. He had sagged in his chair and was staring across the room at nothing in particular. "This hurts me as bad as it hurts you, Charlie."

"Big, I find that hard to believe."

"Believe me, it *does* hurt. I wouldn't of thrown this at you if they hadn't forced me. If it was just me, the way it used to be, I'd back you till hell froze solid."

Charlie considered awhile. "I know you would, Big. I didn't go to job you none." He pulled a sack of Bull Durham from his shirt pocket and rolled a cigarette, his shaking hands spilling much of the tobacco on the floor. "I could sell some of the sheep to buy feed for the rest."

Big shook his head. "No you can't. They're already mortgaged for more than they'll bring. The only way you can sell them is if you turn all the proceeds over to this bank."

The thought had been a quick one on Charlie's part, and he realized now it was fallacious. He said, "All right, so I got no equity left in my sheep. Or in the goats either, because I've hocked them to buy sheep feed. But I still got equity in my sections of deeded land."

"Damn little, Charlie. You got enough left to borrow livin' expenses for a while yet, but not enough to buy feed. What's more, you got a lease comin' due on the land you're still operatin' outside of those three deeded sections. You can't do it, Charlie; there's just no way you can do it."

Charlie sat in silence, letting his mind run over all the possibilities he could think of. When he analyzed them, none worked. He felt like a rabbit trapped in the corner of a netwire fence; he couldn't go over, under, or through.

At length he cried, "God, Big, what am I goin' to do?"

"Give in, Charlie. It ain't no big thing, really. You've stood it off longer than almost anybody; you've made your point. There finally came a time Lee had to give in to Grant. He kept his dignity; so can you. Give in."

Charlie said, "If I'd done it right from the first, like most of the others, maybe it wouldn't of been so bad. But it was a thing that kind of built as it went along. The longer I stayed out, the more important it was to keep stayin' out . . . to show them I could . . . to show *myself* I could."

"You've showed them, Charlie. Now let it go."

"There's a big rain comin', just around the corner. I can feel it. Just give me a little more time."

"I been hearin' that for six years. There's already been many a good man gone under, waitin' for that big rain just around the corner. Face up to it, Charlie. It's whipped you; it's whipped us all."

Charlie's eyes burned like they had at Page Mauldin's funeral. He tried to blink away the sting. "If I *did* give in, what would you do?"

"I couldn't be generous; I'd have to cut you to the bone. But at least I could give you whatever you couldn't do without. Maybe I could see you through till that big rain *does* get here."

Charlie remembered his dignity and pulled himself up in the chair. He cleared his throat. "Can you give a few days to make up my mind?"

"I don't see where you got any choice. A few days won't help you."

"I got a few days' sheep feed in the barn. That'll buy me time to do some thinkin'."

Big seemed disappointed. He had probably wanted to get the decision over with and the trauma done; this left it hanging. "Anybody else, Charlie, I'd tell them *no*. But hell, go ahead and think about it."

Charlie nodded and pushed to his feet. He turned to go and was stunned by a sudden shortness of breath, a tightness in his chest. He sat back down, heavily.

Big got up and leaned over him. "You all right, Charlie?"

Charlie waved him away with his big hand. "I'm all right. Just got up a little sudden. Damn leg went to sleep."

It was a lie, but Rodale seemed to accept it. Charlie pushed to his feet again, slower this time. His breath was still labored, and he felt a burning in his chest. The shock of what Big had told him, he guessed.

Big said, "Old age, Charlie. Your circulation is slowin' down. Maybe that's a sign you better slow down with it."

"I'll still be ridin' rough horses when they've salted you away in a box." Charlie turned and walked deliberately to the door, trying to hide the fact that it hurt him to move. He thought about stopping to weigh himself, to show Big he was all right, but he decided it would be better to get the hell out of here and out of sight. He didn't stop until he reached his pickup and crawled in. He sat awhile, shivering a little in the cold, taking long and studied breaths until his lungs seemed to fill and the burning eased in his chest. He felt himself shaking, and not altogether from the chill. Alarm tingled through him.

What *was* that? he asked himself.

He didn't drive directly to the house. He cut out across the pasture and took the winding two-rut road that led him to the top of Warrior Hill. By now the physical pain was gone, but another pain had taken its place. He got slowly out of the pickup, buttoning his wool-lined coat against the cold north wind, pulling his hat down tight to keep it from blowing away. He walked out across the knob and looked down awhile across his ranch . . . what was left of it. He could vaguely see the windmills at headquarters through the haze of moving dust. He could see nothing where the O'Barr land lay; it was obscured by a heavy pall of brown.

He looked a moment at the cairn of rocks. "Old Warrior," he said slowly, "it don't look much like it did when you knew it. It must've been somethin' fine the day you came up here the last time. It must've been worth fightin' for then, and dyin' for. I'm beginnin' to wonder if it still is."

He stayed on the hill for perhaps half an hour, until he realized he was shivering all the way to his boots, chilled to the bone. Often when he had faced a decision, he had found it easier to make up his mind on this hill. Today he found no answer here; he was still as much in doubt when he drove off of the hill as he had been when he climbed it.

Two mornings later he took his customary look out the window before he put on his britches, and he saw what appeared to be clouds in the predawn sky. He dressed quickly and walked out onto the porch, afraid he had been mistaken. To his pleasure he saw that he had not been. Clouds were gathering in the north.

It had been his observation that most of the best rains to hit this country drifted in from the east, but he was willing to take a rain from whatever direction it chose to come.

By midmorning the clouds were shifting and becoming heavier, some dark-bottomed and beginning to look seriously like rain. He heard the pickup radio report that a moist frontal passage was due across West Texas with some prospects for precipitation. He hadn't paid much attention, for he had lost faith in weather predictions.

Can't afford to get excited, he told himself. He had been fooled too many times, had let his hopes build, only to be dashed to the ground.

But somehow this looked like the one. It smelled like it, felt like it. Charlie thought he could sense a change in the sheep. And he had seen the roan horse Wander run and pitch, even at his age. You might fool the Weather Bureau, but you didn't fool horses much.

Don't get excited, he told himself. *You don't count on a rain till it's floating chips up around your belly button.*

But at noon he was hardly able to eat. Twice he got up from the table and walked to the window to look out at the weather. By midafternoon the sky had clouded over solidly. The sun was gone. The clouds were drifting north toward the cold front the weathermen had talked about.

When these clouds hit that front, it's liable to be Katy-bar-the-door.

Charlie knew a jubilance he hadn't felt in a long time. He kept humming an old nonsense ditty that had been popular in his younger years: *It ain't gonna rain no more, no more, ain't a-gonna rain no more* . . . So hopeful was he that late in the afternoon he saddled Wander and hauled him in a trailer to the north mill. There he rounded up the yearling ewes that had been in a draw pasture and moved them into a small trap on higher ground. Most sheep were stupid about getting out of dangerous draws and onto safer footing when the rains came. Likely as not they would do the wrong thing, heading for protection of the brush in the low areas where flood water might trap them and carry them away.

Home for supper, Charlie stood on the porch and watched the clouds until Mary called him the third time to eat. Finally she went out to see about him.

"Just looky yonder, Mary. Don't it look good?"

"It hasn't rained yet. Come and eat your supper."

"It's goin' to, though. You can tell."

"And you'll starve unless you come in and eat. Afterwards you can sit out here and watch the clouds all night if you're of a mind to."

Charlie didn't eat much. He listened for the roll of thunder or the patter of rain. Finally he thought he heard thunder and stood up, pushing his plate aside. "Hear that? We're fixin' to get it this time." He moved out onto the porch and stood watching, waiting.

The smell of rain was so strong it went to his head like whiskey. "Looks like you could reach up and poke a hole in them clouds and they'd spill pure water."

Mary came out onto the porch, a plate in one hand and a cup towel in the other. She sniffed the air and looked at the clouds. She began finally to catch some of the excitement that had been building in Charlie. "You might be right. Maybe this is finally the time."

Thunder rolled. Lightning flashed to the north, small flashes at first and far away. Gradually they moved closer. The thunder crashed. Charlie could begin to smell the burn of the lightning.

Down at the corral Wander was nickering, trotting around with head high, anticipating the rain.

The first drop of water hit the porch steps. Charlie felt a tingle. He knelt to stick his finger in the spot, the size of a two-bit piece. He looked up and felt another drop strike him in the face. Jubilant, he moved down off the porch and out into the open, looking up at the near-black skies.

"Come on now," he cried out. "Rain! Rain!"

Mary called, "You better come back. You'll get soaked."

"I *want* to get soaked!"

He felt a few more drops and heard others strike around him. He stood expectantly, waiting for the drenching downpour.

Then he began to see a break in the clouds to the west, a tiny rent at first, gradually widening so he could make out the red tinge of last daylight through the opening. His mouth went dry.

"Come on," he cried. "Rain while you can!"

He stood waiting for the rain and watched the rent widen across the sky. Before long it extended overhead. The clouds began to split like breaking ice. Gradually the wind shifted to the west. Now it brought the familiar smell of dust.

There was an old saying in West Texas that it was a waste of the Lord's time to pray for rain when the wind was out of the west.

Charlie stood in the yard, unwilling to believe the clouds could build with such promise, then break apart with such heartbreaking speed. Finally the clouds were gone, just broken pieces still showing against the night sky. Stars began to twinkle.

"It's over, Charlie," Mary said at last.

Charlie dropped to one knee and stared at the walk, where the scattering of raindrops already had dried in the west wind.

He knelt there a long time, crushed. He felt something wet his face again and knew that this time it was not rain.

* * *

Charlie sat hunched two-thirds of the way up in the spectator section of the San Angelo auction arena, looking down over the front row of steel lawn chairs where the buyers sat. He could hear the wind howling outside, searching for a way under the eaves of the building, and it made him feel cold despite the heaters running at each end of the half-moon auction arena.

In times past he had always enjoyed coming to the auction. He almost always ran onto friends here. Today he had purposely found a place high in the stand and studiously avoided looking around him, afraid a glance in somebody's direction might be taken as an invitation to climb up and visit. He didn't feel like talking to anybody. He didn't trust himself to hold up his end of a conversation without his voice breaking.

A steel gate was flung open, and a near-white Spanish goat walked in with a tiny bell around its neck, leading a set of Rambouillet ewes. They plodded suspiciously, the first ones halting to look fearfully at the men sitting at ringside, just beyond the curved steel-pipe fence. Someone beside the gate shouted and popped an empty tow sack. The ewes jumped in fright and hurried to the far side of the ring, where a closed gate brought them up short.

The auctioneer leaned to his microphone. "Now, boys, these next few strings are all part of the Charlie Flagg sheep from down at Rio Seco. We've mouthed them, and we're sellin' them to you in age groups. These here are young ewes with a lot of good left in them, and bred to shell out a lamb crop before long. Anybody who wants to, just climb in the ring and take a look at their mouths."

A ring man jumped astraddle of a ewe and grabbed hold of her head, prying her lips open with his fingers and showing her teeth to the men sitting around the ring. "Boys," he shouted, "I just wisht you'd look at that ivory!" He glanced around quickly for sign of interest at ringside. "They're as good as walks, boys. We'll start them at seven."

The auctioneer took up the chant at seven dollars a head. Charlie hunched a little lower.

God, I bet I owe fifteen.

He would have taken it as a hopeful sign if anybody at ringside had gone in to look at the mouths for himself. No one did. For a time it didn't seem as if anyone would even raise the starter's bid. But eventually someone did, and someone else came in with a second bid just as the auctioneer was about to knock them down. It took a while, but the auctioneer finally got eight-fifty a head before he pronounced the ewes sold.

That's closer, Charlie thought. *But they started with the best ewes. The rest won't bring that much.*

In a way, considering that the drouth covered much of Texas and some of its neighboring states, it was a marvel to him that the ewes found takers at all. But somehow they did, one bunch after another, each string selling fifty cents or a dollar cheaper than the one before it. Every time that steel gate slammed shut behind a draft of ewes, Charlie hunched a little lower, and gloom settled darker and heavier on him.

A ponderous, familiar form moved through the open passage-way at the center of the arena beneath Charlie and stopped behind the buyers' chairs. Big Emmett Rodale looked up, searching the spectators until his gaze reached Charlie. Shifting his half-chewed cigar to the other side of his mouth, he laboriously started climbing the steps to the level where Charlie sat. Charlie moved over a little on the wooden bench to make room for him. It took a lot of room for the banker.

"What're you doin' here?" Charlie demanded, unable to keep a little resentment from coloring his voice. "Come to be sure you get your money?"

Rodale seated himself and fidgeted, trying vainly to find comfort. There wouldn't be any for him on that hard, flat bench. He had a hurt look. "You know better than that."

Charlie knew. He wished he hadn't spoken so sharply, but he wasn't given much to apology.

Big said, "I didn't think when it came to the nut-cuttin' that you'd really go through with this. I didn't think you'd really sell all your sheep."

"Told you I would. Did I ever tell you I'd do somethin' and then fail to do it?"

"Nope. I just hoped this one time you might. They sellin' any good?"

Charlie had been jotting the head counts and prices in a small shirt-pocket tallybook. He passed it over for the banker to read. Big frowned and shook his head. "That's a long ways from prosperity."

The ewes in the ring were knocked down at seven-forty. Charlie said, "This is about the tail end of them. They'll lack a lot settlin' what I owe."

"I told you that before you decided to sell them."

"I can't keep sheep if I can't buy feed."

"But you didn't have to do it this way. You could've bought feed; you could've kept the sheep. All you had to do was bend a little."

"I'm too old, Big, and too brittle to bend."

"Older men than you have done it. A man has to learn to change with the times. You're tryin' to live in a time that's dead and gone, Charlie. I wish it wasn't, but it is. There's no way a man can still make it all by himself."

Charlie gave him a long, challenging stare. "Bet you."

Big looked back at him, first in exasperation, then finally with a grudging admiration. "Anybody ever tell you, Charlie Flagg, that you're one stubborn son of a bitch?"

Charlie stood on top of Warrior Hill, the wind tugging at his hat, at the bottom of his heavy coat. It was less cold today than it had been. The dust seemed less heavy across the ranch, and he could even see one of the windmills on the Sam O'Barr country, vacant and unleased since Tom had let it go.

Charlie dropped down onto one knee to rest his weak leg, though the effort brought a stab of pain. His throat was tight as he looked across the remnant of his domain, the tattered leavings after all else had been taken away. He glanced at the cairn of rocks.

"Well, Old Warrior, they finally got me almost where they had *you*. First my cattle, then my son, then most of my land and all of my sheep. There's nothin' much left now but that bunch of damn goats, and Mary and me, and three sections of deeded land with a mortgage on it so heavy it'd kill the best horse you ever stole. But I swear, Indian, this is where it stops. This is as far as I back up. I'll stand here the way *you* stood, and if they take the rest of it they'll have to bury me here beside you!"

18

Not since the beginning of the drouth had Charlie found much time on his hands. Now, suddenly, he had it. The bounds of his range had contracted by half when he had split with Tom. Now, his sheep gone, he had turned back the rest of his leased land to its owners. He had only his own three sections left, a little more than a mile deep, hardly three miles across on the longest dimension. Hardly enough to break a sweat on the old roan horse, hardly enough to heat the radiator of his badly deteriorated old pickup. To a man used to operating far more country, it was almost as if he had been locked up in a small yard, the outside fence too high to climb. He felt a strong sense of being fettered, constrained, of choking for want of air.

He could not buy feed for the goats, so he had to rough them through on live-oak leaves and whatever else they could pick up. He realized he had his country overstocked, but he felt they would do no great harm between now and spring. Goats were far more a browse animal than grass and weed eaters. One of the failings of this area was that it had become too much of a browse country anyway, the brushy plants overtaking and crowding out the grass and desirable weeds. In that respect the goats would do his place good. If he could hold them until shearing time, that mohair clip would make a handsome dent in the debt the cattle and sheep had left him. After shearing he could sort off the older mutton goats and send them to market, whittling the herd to the right size for his three sections.

All his other livestock gone, he found himself coming to a greater admiration for these high-stepping, quick-eyed Angora goats. They followed him around somewhat like the black dog, their curiosity lively and persistent. They were bright and proud, as if they knew they were the only animals left in this country that still pulled their own weight. Mornings, Charlie chopped live-oak branches for them. This kind of feed cost him nothing beyond his own sweat, and he needed the live oak thinned anyway.

Afternoons or early evenings he went out with a backpack rig and made it a point to kerosene the base of a hundred mesquite trees every day. He figured if he could kill a hundred a day for a year, that would be 36,500 less mesquite trees. In a little less than three years, a hundred thousand. Someday perhaps, given rain, he could restore this range and make it appear again the way it must have been to draw that last Comanche back here for one final look. Lately a wish had begun to dwell on Charlie's mind, a hope he could live long enough to see this range better than it had been when he had taken it over.

He felt he owed that to somebody . . . to old August Schmidt, perhaps, or to God, or maybe just to the land itself.

Though the work was much less than he had been accustomed to doing, he found it uncommonly tiring. He would sometimes run out of breath and have to stop before the chopping was half finished. He would sit on the ground or on a fallen live-oak trunk, the ax at his feet. He would breathe heavily and watch the goats go after the old season's live-oak leaves while he regained the strength to finish the job.

Times he felt a little pain in his chest, or a touch of nausea. He was sure he knew what caused it: that damn coffee. With time to kill, he spent too much of it in the kitchen with a cup in his hands. It wasn't that he wanted coffee so much; it was just something to do. It was something almost everybody did. It had often seemed to him, watching other stockmen as well as himself, that the economy of the whole ranching industry was built around a coffeepot.

Well, he would cut down on it one of these days, soon as the weather warmed up and he didn't need hot coffee to thaw the chill from his bones.

The kitchen was a refuge of sorts. There he was not reminded so much how severely he had been crippled. There he did not have to look at distant windmills that he had long considered his own, or a hill that showed through the dusty haze, a hill that had been his but was no more.

Times he felt that his arms and legs had been chopped off and left lying there so that he had to keep looking at them.

He quit going up on Warrior Hill for that very reason. Up there he saw too much that he had lost.

At first he tried to busy himself catching up on chores long neglected because of their low priority. He tightened fences, replaced some bad posts. He re-leathered windmills that didn't need it. He curried

Wander so much it was fortunate the horse still had any roan hair left. He drove over onto Kathy Mauldin's place and talked with her while she burned pear for the cattle, or he passed the time of day with Diego. And times, when the place closed in on him too much, he drove to town. He had never been one of those ranchers who spent much time sitting around the coffee shop or the feedstore; he had never understood the ones who did. But anything beat sitting around the place with idle hands, eating his heart out.

On his way home one day he circled by what had been the Emil Deutscher farm. The Deutschers were gone now; they had sent Charlie and Mary a letter from Fort Worth, where Emil had found a job doing ordinary carpenter work around an aircraft plant.

Charlie saw a big landplane working in Emil's field, leveling it. He had never been a farmer but he recognized this as a preparation for irrigation. Dust rolled in a huge cloud. A man sat in a pickup at the edge of the field, his door swung open as he watched the moving machinery.

Reckon I ought to get acquainted, since they're going to neighbor us from now on, he thought, braking his rattling pickup to a stop. He let the dust pass, then got out and walked to the fence. The man in the other pickup looked at him a moment as if he hoped Charlie would go away, and Charlie almost did. Finally the man slid out onto the ground and ambled over to the fence with neither hostility nor any particular friendliness. "Hello. Something I can do for you, mister?"

Charlie was taken a little by surprise. That sort of coolness was unusual in this openhanded country. He extended his rough hand through the wire fence. "Name's Charlie Flagg. Live down yonder a piece. Thought I'd stop by and make your acquaintance."

"Oh yes, Mister Flagg. I've heard the name." The man took Charlie's hand. He was clad in dusty khakis, a pair of heavy, high-topped walking boots and a flat-brimmed hat crusted with sweat and dirt. "I'm Joe Fentress. I manage this property for the Prairie Farm Development Company." The man talked too fast to be a native here, but Charlie could not hazard a guess about his origins. To Charlie, anybody from outside of Texas was a foreigner more or less. Maybe an Okie wasn't, but just about anybody else . . .

Charlie said, "We used to be good friends with Emil Deutscher. Used to visit him at his house a right smart, me and my wife."

The man looked puzzled a moment. "Deutscher?" Realization slowly came. "Oh yes, the man who formerly owned this property. It's hard for me to remember so many, and what parcel belonged to which."

Charlie said, "I'll drop by the house sometime and get better acquainted."

"I live in town, Mister Flagg."

Charlie nodded glumly, taking that as a quiet way of saying *Thanks, but no thanks*. He began to wish he hadn't stopped, but it might seem unfriendly to break off and leave so quickly. "As many farms as you've bought here on the Flat, I reckon this'll be a right smart of an operation."

Fentress shook his head. "We won't intensify all of it. We bought up some poor land because it had cotton allotments on it. We'll use those allotments on the best land, like this tract. The rest we'll put in the soil bank. We can draw government money on that and help pay for the overall purchase."

"But you'll have to use it to rotate the cotton around, won't you?"

"Rotate? What for? We'll use fertilizer to keep it

producing. We can squeeze cotton out of this better land for a good many years."

"But eventually the land'll wear out."

The man shrugged. "By then we'll have amortized our investment. How do we know how long the irrigation water will hold up? We'll take our profit while we can get it. Farming is a business, you know. Just a business, and nothing else."

Charlie felt that nausea coming back, and he knew it wasn't just the coffee. He remembered the times he had watched Emil Deutscher kneel here and run his hands through the soil and take up a little and squeeze it. Emil had loved this land the way he loved his God. In a sense, he had seen God and the land as one and the same.

The noise of the landplane stopped. Fentress looked over his shoulder, then backed away from the fence. "My operator seems to be having some trouble. You'll have to excuse me, Mister Flagg."

Charlie nodded somberly. "Sure. You just go on about your . . . your *business*."

He turned and walked back to the pickup with his head down, trying not to think of Emil Deutscher.

Driving into the yard, he saw a dirty gray car parked in front of the stone house. It was several years old, and the license number had a local prefix, but he didn't recognize it. He figured someone was in the house with Mary. Then he saw a man raise up in the front seat, a beer can in his hand, and he knew. Sam "Suds" O'Barr had come to see him.

Charlie cursed under his breath. He still felt a lingering bitterness over his stop at the Deutscher place, and he sure as hell didn't need Sam O'Barr. But there he was, and it was hard to ignore a man like Sam. Charlie slammed his pickup door twice before it caught, and he walked up to O'Barr's car. O'Barr opened the front door and slid both feet out onto the ground, but he didn't get up. He sat hunched, cradling the cold can in both hands.

"Hello, Charlie. Want a beer? I got plenty."

Charlie would have taken a bet on that, sight unseen. "Never cared much for beer, Sam."

"I got a bottle of somethin' stronger in the glove compartment."

"Not right now, Sam. I still got things to do."

O'Barr looked around a minute, then tipped the can up for a couple of long swallows. "I come over to see you, Charlie."

"Glad you did, Sam," Charlie lied.

"I want to talk to you about that ol' country of mine."

"You'd just as well talk to a blind shoeshine boy. They've cut me off at the pockets."

"I heard. But I also heard they'd of stayed with you if you'd been willin' to see a thing or two their way. I was wonderin' if by now you've decided to go along with them. A man can't beat city hall."

"I don't reckon they've changed their minds. I ain't changed mine."

"But it's all so unnecessary, Charlie. I mean, takin' a little government money, that ain't no big thing. It ain't like you was a woman sellin' herself on the streets."

Charlie's stomach began to stir; the last thing he wanted right now was to argue with a drunk. Sam O'Barr was hard enough to reach when he was more or less sober; he was half a day past that point now. "I had all this out with Big awhile back. It's over and done. There's no use us talkin' about it, Sam."

"But I figure you owe me, Charlie."

Charlie's jaw began to tighten. "I owe several people, but I don't owe you nothin'."

"Years and years I let you have the use of that ol' country of mine. I could've leased it to other people many a time, but I always felt a loyalty to my old friend Charlie Flagg. Have you looked at that place lately, Charlie? Have you seen the shape your boy went and left it in?"

"I've seen it."

"It's a desert, that's all. I can't lease it to anybody. I'm starvin' to death, Charlie, because I can't lease out that land. Now I figure you owe it to me to lease it again yourself."

"What with, Sam? I'm on my back."

"Big'll lend you if you'll do right. That's all they've asked of you, Charlie, is that you do right."

Charlie felt the heat rising. His hands trembled from it, and he knew his face was going red. "Sam, you better get on back to town."

"It was your boy's fault. He made a desert out of that place."

Charlie poked his big forefinger at Sam O'Barr's chest. "Remember what I told you when that lease come up for renewal the last time? I told you the price was too high. I told you that if things went to the bad, a man'd ruin the place tryin' to make it pay your price. I told you it'd go to desert, and you said it didn't matter. You said you'd be dead before it come to that. Well, Sam, I'm afraid you lived too long!"

Tears were running down Sam O'Barr's flushed cheeks. "Charlie, I feel like I got somethin' comin' to me."

"So you have, Sam, but I'm a way too tired to give it to you. Get out of here before I change my mind."

Sam was still arguing when Charlie turned his back and limped up the front steps and into the house, closing the door firmly behind him. Standing in the middle of the living room, he could see through the big windows when O'Barr finally gave up and drove away.

Mary said, "He's been sitting out there waiting for you a couple of hours. I went out to invite him in and saw that he'd been drinking. I am *not* going to invite a drunken man into this house." Her voice was defensive, as if she were heading off rebuke.

"Damn good thing you didn't. I might've booted his butt down the steps."

The anger still boiled in him; his breath was a little short. He walked into the kitchen and fetched a bourbon bottle out of a cabinet. Pouring a stiff drink into a glass, he drank it without ice.

Mary stood in the doorway, watching with surprise and unspoken disapproval.

He said, "For my stomach. That Sam, he got my stomach goin'." Charlie walked into the living room and sat down, but his rump prickled with impatience, and his breath didn't come any easier. The whiskey seemed to ride along on the crest of a big wave. The house seemed overheated, all of a sudden.

"I got to go back out and get some air," he said, pushing to his feet. "I'm goin' to take a look at the goats."

"You've already chopped for them today."

"Well," he exploded, "I'll go back out and do it again. Have I got to explain every move I make around here?"

He slammed the door behind him and hobbled down the steps. He had to turn the ignition key the second time before the tired motor decided to run.

He drove out of the yard and across a cattleguard into the nearest pasture, the pickup bumping and clattering along the rough two-cut road. He muttered under his breath. There was lots of things this worn-out heap needed, but what it needed most of all was a good trading.

A loud and persistent rattle began somewhere behind the dash pane, near the glove compartment. Charlie stood it as long as he could, which in his present mood was a couple of minutes. He lifted his foot from the gas pedal and kicked the metal underside of the dash. "Cut it out, goddam you!"

The rattle stopped.

He felt foolish afterward. It was futile to loose his rage against an inanimate object like the pickup; he knew that, and he wondered why he had done it. He remembered how angry he had been at Sam O'Barr, but running the incident back through in his mind he could not see that he had had any reason to let things get away with him the way they had. Another time he might even have pitied Sam; however much the man might have been to blame for his own downfall in the years past, he was far beyond any question of personal responsibility now. He was as predictable as a child, and as helpless. Looking back, Charlie saw how near he had been to hitting him. It would have been a shameful thing, like striking a schoolboy.

And Mary. I like to've bitten her head off for nothing. What's got into me?

The pain started. It was dull at first, somewhere deep in his chest. In the beginning it did not bother him half so much as the shortness of his breath; his lungs felt compressed, suffering for air. Gradually the pain came sharper, and he felt another, a smaller one, in his left arm. He came to a bend in the road, and suddenly he lacked the strength in his arms to turn the wheel. The pickup jarred him severely as it jumped out of the ruts. He slammed against the wheel, losing much of the breath he *did* have. His head struck the top of the pickup, but his felt hat absorbed most of the blow. He managed somehow to throw the pickup out of gear and get his foot on the brake pedal. He brought the vehicle to a shuddering halt.

He leaned back, struggling for breath. The pain was sharper. Instinctively he wanted out, out into the fresh air. He leaned against the door handle, pushing it down. The door swung open, and Charlie fell out on his left shoulder. His head struck the ground, and he tasted dirt.

He lay there a little, his feet and legs still half in the pickup. He was afraid to move. Breath came slow and painfully.

He was soon aware of movement around him, and he raised his head. Standing almost within arm's reach were half a dozen long-haired Angora goats, eying him curiously.

Charlie finished falling out of the pickup. A goat snorted, and all of them ran off with a clatter of small hoofs, then turned again to watch from a safer distance of thirty or forty feet.

Charlie realized now what was happening to him. He realized Mary wouldn't start looking for him until dark, and then she probably couldn't find him. He had to get up and get out of here, because if his heart didn't kill him the chill of the night probably would.

The pressure seemed to ease a bit, once he had lain stretched out full length for a while. He pushed up onto his hands and knees. He tried to get to his feet but stumbled and went down again. Gasping, he crawled to the still-idling pickup. He pulled himself up a little at a time until he was on his legs, the upper half of his body lying on the pickup seat. He stayed that way a little, gathering strength, then got hold of the steering column and pulled himself up, gathering his legs under the wheel.

Through the pain he tried to put his mind into gear. He had driven nearly to the end of the big pasture; it was almost three miles back to the house. In his condition, three miles might be as much as three hundred.

In the back of his head, fighting its way through the pain, was the idea that Kathy Mauldin or Diego might be somewhere just beyond Warrior Hill, across the fence, feeding or burning pear.

He got the pickup into gear and let it lurch into motion. One of the goats was in the way. The vehicle bumped heavily as the wheels passed over the animal's body. Charlie had no real control on the pickup, plunging through the brush, smashing winter-brittle mesquite. Once he hit a dry wash and almost turned over.

If it goes, I'm finished, he thought helplessly.

But the pickup righted itself and rolled on. He could do little more than loose-herd it along. He blinked, trying to focus his gaze. He could see the fence ahead. He thought he could see a vehicle, but he wasn't sure. He laid his hand on the horn and held it there. He lifted his foot from the pedal and let the pickup coast in. He saw he was going to hit the fence, but he was powerless to stop. The fence stretched, and posts snapped. Then the pickup halted, jumping as the motor abruptly died in gear.

Over the blare of the horn he heard a shouting

voice. A hand touched his arm. He turned his head and looked into the wide-eyed face of Diego Escamillo.

The next days were no more than a painful haze to him. He was conscious, now and again, of someone jabbing him with a needle. He was dimly conscious of Mary beside him for long periods, but all his efforts to communicate with her evaporated in the heavy mist that kept settling over him. Ideas formed, but he could not put them into words. Words formed, but they never left him. The notion of death came to him sometimes, but he was too befogged to analyze it or to fear. The one strong feeling that returned to him again and again was that his ranch was slipping away from him, the little he still had left. That stirred fear where the sense of death never did.

Then one day he opened his eyes and saw plainly. He made an effort to speak and found to his amazement that the words came out. The sound of his own voice startled him. He thought a while about his right hand, then got up nerve to try it, to see if he could raise it. He could. He tried his left hand and found he could control it too.

Doc Fancher held a small bottle up to the light of the hospital window and drew something into a syringe. He withdrew the needle and turned toward Charlie, who lay watching him.

"Don't fuss at me," Fancher said. "It's not my fault you're in here. Now this is going"—he jabbed the needle into Charlie's arm—"to hurt a little. Some people would've died. You're too contrary."

"You'll *think* contrary," Charlie said, his voice weak. "How long you keepin' me?"

"Till I decide to let you go."

"I got work to do at the ranch."

"That ranch is the reason you're in here."

"It's all I've got."

"You've still got your life. Be thankful for small blessings." The doctor put away the syringe. "It wasn't much of a heart attack. It was so puny you ought to be ashamed of it."

"Next time I'll try to do better."

"This one was just a warning that you need to slack off. The next one might take you like Grant took Richmond."

"You've kept me so full of dope that I don't rightly know how long you've had me kidnapped in here."

"Four days, so far."

"Four days?" Charlie started to sit up, and the doctor firmly pushed him back down. "Doc, I bet I've got a bunch of goats starved plumb to death."

"Don't you worry about those goats. They're in better condition than you are. Now you lie still or I'll give you something that'll knock you out for four *more* days. I'm half-tempted to do it anyway. Things are dismal enough around this place without having to listen to you bitch."

"But my goats . . ."

"God knows why, but you have friends. They've taken care of your stock. Why any man can get himself worked up over a bunch of goats is something I'll never understand."

"You would if they was yours, and they was all you had left."

Fancher frowned. "I ran off one time to be a cowboy. My father caught me ten miles down the road, gave me the worst whipping I ever had and took me home. Luckiest day of my life."

"Maybe not so lucky. You might of made somethin' worthwhile out of yourself instead of jabbin' needles into people that can't defend theirselves."

Fancher glowered at him. "I doubt it'll help your disposition any, but I'll let you have a little company. Ten minutes, is all. Ten minutes and they leave here. If I hear you raise your voice, I'll run them out in five."

Fancher pushed the door open and nodded at someone outside. Mary walked in. She stood halfway across the room a moment, looking at Charlie, trying to hold back her tears and then giving up the effort. She took Charlie's hand and brought it to her breast and knelt to kiss him on the forehead.

Charlie's throat went tight, and his eyes started burning. "Careful," he said. "That old witch doctor'll chase you out of here for raisin' my temperature."

Mary blinked rapidly and managed a poor smile. "A kiss on the forehead hasn't raised your temperature in twenty years."

The doctor snorted. "And unlikely ever to do it again. You're used up, Flagg."

Charlie looked at Mary. "We could tell him a thing or two about that."

"Charlie!" she said, embarrassed. From out in the hallway came the faint sound of a bell, ringing three times to summon the doctor. Fancher left the room. Mary pulled up a chair beside the bed and held onto Charlie's hand. She asked him many questions about how he felt and whether there was still pain. He only half-answered them and finally raised his free hand in a gesture for her to hush up. "What about the ranch?" he demanded. "What about the goats?"

"Everything is all right. Diego came over the first couple of days. Those goats didn't even miss you."

"The first couple of days? But I been here *four* days, Doc says. What about the rest of the time?"

"I've had help."

The pleasure that showed in her eyes brought him a sudden hope. He tried to raise up a little. "Tom's come back?"

Mary shook her head. "No. Tom has called, but he hasn't come home. Ashamed to, I guess."

Disappointment was keen . . . as keen as his hope had been. He slumped back on the bed.

Mary went to the door and beckoned. "Manuel?"

Manuel Flores walked in, holding his hat in his hand. He seemed nervous, unsure of himself. He tried to smile, but it didn't work.

Charlie stared, incredulous. He had forgotten how tall Manuel had grown. "Manuel? Where did *you* come from?"

"From San Angelo."

"But you're in college . . ."

"This is the weekend. You lost track of the days, I guess."

Charlie couldn't bring the days into focus. "I'm still a little confused. The whole family with you?"

"Just me, Mister Charlie."

Charlie frowned. "You'll have to be gettin' back for classes. We got to find us somebody . . ."

"You don't have to find anybody. You've *got* somebody. Me."

"But school . . ."

"Semester's almost over. I can drive back and forth to Angelo the next couple of weeks if your old pickup will stand it. I'll lay out next semester and stay here till you're on your feet."

"You've got no call to do that."

"I want to. I've made up my mind."

"But why? I had a feelin' you'd given up on me."

"I decided I was wrong."

Charlie stared at the boy . . . no, not a boy any longer. Manuel was a man. "I'm broke, son. I don't know how I can pay you."

"Mister Charlie, don't you know you've already paid me? All those years—even when I didn't see it— you were payin' me. However long I stay here, I'm still ahead."

Charlie's eyes burned. He turned his head away for a minute. "It's not the place it was when you knew it, *muchacho*. It's shrunk to damn near nothin' now, and it's blown away, most of it."

"It's home."

Charlie couldn't say anything more. He felt choked, and he turned his head away again. When his voice came back he asked about the rest of the Flores family, one by one. Manuel said Lupe didn't enjoy the stockyards as much as ranch work, but at least it wasn't hard on him. He and Rosa had bought an old but solidly built house in south Angelo. "The kids are likin' it. You'd be surprised how many of their old friends from Rio Seco they find in Angelo. There's lots to do in school, more goin' on than there used to be here. Candelario's been goin' out for track. You ought to see him run."

"I'd like to, sometime. And what about Anita? She still laugh the way she used to?"

"More, if anything. She's goin' with a boy up there now, a real good boy. They talk about gettin' married when he finishes the university."

Charlie came near smiling. "I'm glad. I worried about her a long time after José . . ." The rest he left unsaid. "This new boy, she known him long?"

"Long enough. Before him, she went with Buddy Thompson awhile. You remember Buddy."

"Batch Thompson's boy? Sure, I remember him." A harsh thought struck Charlie. He remembered Buddy's father even better.

Manuel's face creased in remembered anger. "The old man didn't like it the least bit. Anita and Buddy, they never were serious like he thought in the first place; they just liked each other, is all. But old Batch Thompson, he was scared they'd run off and get married, or somethin'. They broke it up to keep from havin' trouble with him. Then Johnny Ramirez came along. He was serious and good-lookin' . . . kind of favored José Rivera, I always thought. Old Man Thompson was able to go back to livin' again."

"Don't think too hard of him. Old notions are slow to die. A man carries them to the grave with him, mostly. A thing like that—Buddy and Anita goin' together—it wouldn't of happened in *his* time."

"It's not his time any more."

Charlie grimaced. "No. I get to thinkin' it's not mine either."

"It'll be better. One of these days everything will turn around."

"Not all the way. I knew I wasn't young any more, but it never came to me I'd gone so far down the hill. Long as a man's young he can take trouble in stride. Time is with him no matter how bad a jam he's in. Then one day it slaps him in the face. It's not with him any more, it's workin' against him. His friends fall away . . . scattered, or dead, or just changed. His kids are grown up and gone from him. All the old principles that he anchored to, they've come a-loose; nobody's payin' attention to them any more. He's an old grayheaded man livin' in a young man's world, and all his benchmarks are gone."

"The *good* benchmarks are still there, Mister Charlie."

19

For a while Charlie was obliged to lie around the house. All he could see of the ranch was what was visible through the windows, and the substantial part of it that blew in around the old window casings to settle on the furniture. Gradually, on warm afternoons when the wind held no chill, he began venturing out onto the porch and even into the yard. It was a good day when Mary reluctantly gave her approval for him to walk to the barn with the black dog enthusiastically tagging at his heels. In other times he would have gone whether she liked it or not, but these days he could see the deep and genuine concern in her eyes when she looked at him. He could not bring himself to worry her more than she already was.

For years he had entertained some notion of tearing down that old barn and building a bigger, stronger one of steel. Now he could no longer afford to, and the barn looked good to him; he hadn't realized how much he was attached to that venerable old structure with its strong smell of horses and leather and alfalfa hay, its wooden floors stained by the long years' spillings of horse liniment and neat's-foot oil. It became routine for him to go to the barn late in the afternoons and pet the roan horse while Manuel did the chores. It made Charlie restless to watch someone else work; never in his life had he sat on the sideline. He badgered Doc Fancher until the doctor said it would be all right for him to ride with Manuel in the pickup so long as he didn't undertake any work, especially any heavy lifting.

It did Charlie good to set his boots on the land again. There had been a couple of light showers, and he could see sign of some winter weeds trying their damnedest to come up. If he squatted to the ground and took a low-angle look across a considerable expanse he could see a faint tinge of green. Standing up and looking straight down he could see no color at all.

"You know," he said to Manuel, "they always claim Texans are the biggest liars in the world. I believe they're right. A man has even got to lie to himself to find a reason for stayin' here."

"You lyin' to yourself, Mister Charlie?"

"I'm tellin' myself I can see somethin' green."

Manuel smiled as he looked over the pasture. "One of us needs glasses."

Manuel chopped a few live oaks for the goats that gathered around. Charlie walked out among the animals, talking to them as if they were children. He patted a couple that had become tame enough to walk up and let him rub them around their curved horns. Charlie had been forbidden to smoke, but he rolled a Bull Durham and took a few puffs for old-times' sake, snuffed out the fire and gave the cigarette to the tamest of the big muttons. The goat chewed up paper, tobacco and all, then rubbed its nose against Charlie's leg, wanting more.

Manuel said, "You're fixin' to corrupt these goats."

Charlie nodded. "A bad habit or two is good for man or beast. Did you ever know a man who didn't have any bad habits? I have, and I always hated the son of a bitch."

When Manuel had finished his job Charlie said, "Let's drive over by Warrior Hill and down to the fence. I'd like to see some of Kathy's cattle. Been weeks since I've feasted my eyes on a cow-brute."

Manuel seemed to find merit in the idea. He put the old pickup onto the fenceline road which Charlie had dragged years ago, both for travel and as a guard to prevent a chance grassfire from crossing the fence. It had been a long time since he had had it reworked; there had been nothing here to burn.

Charlie saw none of the black cattle along the fence; Diego and Kathy must be burning pear and feeding somewhere farther inside the pasture now. He could see the charred remnants of old pear-burning grounds, the stumps grubbed up to prevent their re-sprouting. If there was to be a benefit from this long drouth, it was that a lot of prickly pear would not survive it. When the rains came—if they ever did—the grass would have a chance to grow where prickly pear had once taken the dominant stand. On the other hand, he didn't know how some people would have survived this long if they had not had pear to burn for their livestock. One weighed the good points against the bad, and the conclusions remained always somewhat uncertain.

"Looks like we drew a blank," Charlie observed.

Manuel shook his head. "I see a pickup at that mill yonder."

Charlie squinted and decided Manuel's eyes were better than his. He could see the windmill, but that was all.

Manuel drove up to a wire gate and got out to open it. It was one of the old-fashioned jawbuster kind, made with a chain and a length of cedar stake. He laid the gate down, drove through, then got out and stretched the gate back into place, latching it with the stake and a loop of wire. Charlie had long intended to replace all those with modern steel gates, but there had always seemed to be something more important to do with the money. Now he would probably put up with them for however long the good Lord chose to leave him here.

As they clattered along the deep-rutted road, he could see a large pool of muddy water beside a round steel water trough, and someone working in the middle of this bog. He figured it was Diego. Then he recognized Kathy as she heard the rattle of the pickup and turned to look. Hell of a task for a girl, he thought. She wiped a muddy sleeve across her face and grinned as Manuel and Charlie crawled out of the pickup.

"You-all lookin' for a job?" she asked.

Charlie replied, "I'm retired. You might ask my helper."

He could see the trouble at a glance. The trough had spilled over, and milling cattle had churned the puddle into a loblolly.

Manuel laughed at the sight of her. "This is an awful mess."

"The trough, or me?" She looked down at her mud-spattered Levi's, the wet sleeves of her denim jumper, her boots sunk half-way into the muck. "Some stupid horse didn't have anything better to do than to stomp a float-pan into smithereens."

Manuel said, "Get out of that slop. I'll fix it for you."

"I've got it half done already. But you're welcome to it."

Manuel put on an old pair of boots he kept in the back of the pickup. He waded out into the muddy water past Kathy, touching her arm as he went by. He leaned over the control valve for an inspection. "You're right," he said, "you've almost got it. If we'd come along a few minutes later there wouldn't have been any use in me gettin' muddy."

"Told you," she said.

Manuel attached heavy new wire to the float lever, slipped the ends of the wire through the center hole of a new pan, then twisted them around a green mesquite stick to hold the pan in place. He untied a wire Kathy had put on to keep the lever up and the water shut off. He eased the float down toward the bottom of the trough to see if the water would run in properly, then raised it slowly to be sure it would shut off when the water reached the proper level.

"Looks like it ought to work. You're a lot of trouble, little girl."

"I didn't say you had to come and help me. I've done a pretty good job takin' care of myself."

Manuel walked out of the mud and up to the big concrete storage tank which caught the water as it was pumped by the windmill, releasing it on a controlled basis to the outlying water troughs. He peered over the rim. "It's lost about half of its water." Some times, some places that would be a tragedy.

Kathy said, "The well is strong, and the wind never stops. It'll refill."

Charlie felt tired. He seated himself on the pickup's bumper, easing his weak leg out straight in front of him. He had quickly decided those two didn't need him in their conversation.

Manuel looked critically at Kathy and touched the wet sleeve of her old blue jumper. "Look at you . . . wet and cold . . . mud all the way to your ears. Can't you let Diego take care of things like this?"

"He's busy doin' somethin' else. I couldn't let that water go to waste."

"Then maybe you need more help."

"I can't afford more help. Not unless I marry it."

Charlie looked up sharply. Most of the time he couldn't tell when Kathy was serious and when she was fooling. She was smiling a little now, but he couldn't shake a strong suspicion. She had never been bashful that he could remember.

Manuel let the remark pass. "Let's go to the tank and wash some of that mud off of you. You still won't look like a lady, but at least you'll be clean."

The steel windmill pumped a small gush of water into the concrete tank with each clanking stroke of the sucker-rod, and shuddered like a man swallowing bitter medicine. Manuel soaked a handkerchief and wiped the mud from Kathy's face. "Even got it in your hair," he said, trying less successfully to clean that too.

Kathy held her muddy hands under the pipe and rinsed them. She shivered, for the water was like ice.

Manuel caught one of her hands and held it up. "Bleedin'."

"Cut it on that old float-pan, I guess. It'll heal."

Manuel shook his head. "Kathy, you're . . ." He let it go for the moment, staring at her. "You're not a man, you're a woman. You shouldn't always be out doin' a man's work. You'll be old before your time."

Across the distance, Charlie stared at Kathy. Now

that Manuel mentioned it, she did appear thinner than she used to, and a little older perhaps than she really was. He had heard people say Kathy wasn't a pretty girl, but he guessed he had always been too close to look at her objectively. To Charlie she was pretty, especially when she smiled. He hadn't seen her smile much since her father died. Usually he saw a dark urgency that reminded him uncomfortably of Page Mauldin.

Manuel put into words the thought that ran through Charlie's mind. "Kathy, you've let this ranch weigh down on you just like it used to weigh down on your papa."

Kathy's eyes pinched as she gazed across the pasture at the dust haze lying like a rusty screen before the winter sun. "This drouth . . . this miserable drouth. Sometimes I think it'll last forever. Other kids grow up with a dog or a pony. Seems to me like I just grew up with a drouth."

"You don't have to fight it. You could lease this place to somebody else; you could go on to college and let somebody else have the work and the worry awhile."

Charlie saw a dark frown come over Kathy's face, and in her expression he saw Page Mauldin the way he had known him years ago. "No, this is my place, and it'll *stay* my place. Nobody's goin' to beat me out of what's mine . . . not any calculatin' banker, not any short-weightin' cow buyer, not any starch-shirted government man with a satchel full of papers. I'm stayin' right here."

Manuel didn't press the argument; he had as well have talked to a cedar post. "Any time you need help, just holler. I'll be over."

She touched Manuel's arm and looked into his face.

Charlie saw her give Manuel a kind of smile he had never seen before. "I'm glad you're back, Manuel. I'm real glad."

The two men were still there, Charlie sitting on the bumper, Manuel standing beside him, when Kathy drove away. They watched until she was gone in the dust. Manuel said, "You want to go look for some cattle?"

Charlie shook his head. "Reckon not. I'm tired."

He sat in silence as Manuel drove. Awhile after they went back through the wire gate Charlie said, "I never been one to poke my nose in where it don't belong, but sometimes I see things. I seen somethin' while ago that worries me."

Manuel asked him no foolish questions; he knew what Charlie was getting at. "We've always been friends, ever since we were kids."

"You're not kids any more."

Manuel nodded. "I know. I've thought about it a good deal. You think it's wrong, don't you?"

Charlie pondered the matter. "No, I wouldn't say it's wrong. But it *could* lead to some awful problems."

"Because I'm Mexican?"

"I'd be lyin' if I said it made no difference. A man has got to look at the world the way it is, not the way he wishes it was."

"Nothin' has ever happened between us, Mister Charlie. Even if I wanted it to, Kathy's lady enough to see that it wouldn't."

"That's where you misjudge her. If she decided she wanted you she'd climb up on the housetop and holler it to the world. Those that didn't like it, she'd tell them to go to hell. She's got that much of her old daddy in her. If it comes to that, son, it'll be *you* that stops it."

Manuel chewed his lip. "I'll face that when it comes."

Charlie said, "You still got a right smart of schoolin' ahead of you. You wouldn't want to mess that up."

Manuel shook his head. "I'm not kiddin' myself. I can get two years of college in Angelo because it's cheap; we're livin' there anyway, and I find work in my off times. But it's just a junior college. There won't be money to go somewhere else and finish. There *sure* won't be money for what I really wish I could do."

"You still wantin' to be a veterinarian?"

"It takes six or seven years to make a vet. Even when I finish in Angelo I'm still short four or five. I'd just as well wish to go to the moon."

"So what'll you do?"

Manuel let a little bitterness creep into his voice. "Study animal husbandry, and after two years I go out and hope I can get a ranch job as good as my papa had."

"He didn't have any college. He didn't even have high school."

Manuel nodded grimly. "Makes mine look like a waste, doesn't it?"

Teofilo Garcia's ancient shearing machine sounded as if it was trying to tear its own guts out. Charlie was surprised it even ran any more. He sat upon a freshly filled bag of mohair and watched Manuel and Diego Escamillo drive a fresh set of goats up into the small corral where the machine smoked and shuddered. The west wind was blowing twenty miles an hour. *I can sure pick the days*, he thought disgustedly. On reconsideration he realized he hadn't picked this shearing date. Teofilo had let him know when his rig would be available, and Charlie had to accept it on that date, come what may.

Given his choice, he had rather have waited a little longer, until the danger of cold rain was more nearly past. This was the big risk in keeping Angora goats. When other animals were trying to find a place to lie down and die on drouthy range, the hardy goat walked with head high. The goat could live with a measure of contentment where the cow went to bones and the sheep died. But the reason—the only reason—for keeping Angoras was to shear their silky fine hair. Goats would begin shedding their winter hair early, usually before winter was actually done. To get the mohair at its best, the ranchman had to shear before it started coming loose of its own accord and hanging in the brush. That meant while there was still a risk of bad weather. And though the goat otherwise had a strong constitution, he was poorly fitted to stand cold rain on a freshly shorn skin. A sensitive spine was his Achilles heel. The Angora could chill down and die in minutes.

That was the reason behind a grim old goat-country joke that shearing time came twice a year—just before the last cold rain in the spring and just before the first cold rain in the fall.

Charlie saw no sign that he needed to worry. All that appeared ahead of him was another duststorm. Tarps had been lashed to a rough framework of stretched ropes on the west side of the shearing pen to help reduce the wind problem on the shearing floor, but that was by no means a total solution. Wind still cut around the edges of the tarps and tugged at the bottoms, slipping under.

Mohair was considered one of the finest fibers in the world and went into the richest of fabrics. But

Charlie wondered what a French fashion designer would think if he could watch a rancher chasing handfuls of it across a goat pen in a high wind.

The Angora muttons bleated in fear as one by one they were dragged to the shearing board. Charlie noted with a frown that there were only four shearers, just half as many as the machine could accommodate. Old Teofilo must have seen Charlie counting, for he ambled over and slumped down beside him on the heavy bag. The *capitán* was not as fat as he used to be, and Charlie saw much gray amid the coarse black hair. It occurred to him that Teofilo looked unwell; he seemed terribly tired.

Time's catching up to all of us, he thought regretfully.

"Four men, Mister Charlie," Teofilo said. "Hard times."

"Mighty hard," Charlie nodded sympathetically. Teofilo had come to him three months ago to ask for an advance on the spring shearing. For the first time in upwards of twenty years, Charlie had not had it to give him.

"Teofilo," Charlie asked, "you been sick?"

Teofilo shrugged. "Not in bed. But lots of the time any more I don't feel very good. Too many years, Mister Charlie."

The thought came to Charlie that time might be running out for Teofilo; he had that look about him, that dullness of eye. The notion stung hard. *For God's sake*, he thought, *won't anything be left, or anybody?* Charlie clasped his hands together and looked away, blinking rapidly at the dust that stung his eyes. He had never fully realized before that he counted Teofilo as a friend.

Teofilo stared out across the pasture, what he could

see of it through the pall of gray. "I been thinkin', Mister Charlie, it is time for me to sell this old machine and maybe go to California."

Teofilo had as much business in California as Charlie did. He had been here too long; all his heritage, all his roots were here. He would not willingly leave Rio Seco any more than he would willingly sell this old machine except to replace it with a better one. Like Charlie, he was trapped here by tradition and memories, and by his age.

His son Chuy, working over there by the sacking frame, was young enough to pack up and leave; Charlie had sometimes wondered why he had not already done so. But Teofilo, like Charlie, was stuck with it. Both would stay and be buried here, even if the hearse had to pick them up at the county poor farm.

But Charlie did not say all that. He strung along with Teofilo, giving voice to an aborted dream of his own youth. "You could be right, Teofilo. When I was a young man it was always my ambition to move to Wyomin' or Montana. Lately I been thinkin' about it. I was up there one summer when I was seventeen or eighteen . . . worked for an outfit that ran cattle on an Indian reservation. Prettiest thing ever I seen, the way them prairies grew up so tall and green, and you could look and see an antelope three miles away like it was no more than three hundred yards."

Teofilo said, "I have been up there to shear sheep. I have seen the snow up to your belly in Wyoming. Better California, where all the time the sun is shining."

Charlie looked at him ruefully. "It shines here all the time too."

"But there it is not the same. There it is like a pretty woman's kiss. There the flowers grow and the wind is cool and everything is pretty and clean. I have seen it with my own eyes, Mister Charlie, when I was young."

"There's a lot of people in California now, from what I read. They've probably already beat us to all the good parts."

"If I get out there I will find a good place where the flowers bloom and a man can plant himself a garden and grow anything he wants, and the chill will never go to the bone. California is a good place for a Mexican; nobody looks down on us there. Once all of California belonged to us Mexicans."

Charlie slowly shook his head. "So did Texas."

Manuel shut the gate on a set of freshly shorn goats and picked up a can of black *tecole*, hanging by its bail on an old fencepost stained by the *tecole* and paint and blood of fifty other shearings. A paintbrush floated in the heavy liquid. He brushed off a little of the excess against the inside rim and began spotting it against shearing cuts on the goats crowded into the narrow alleyway.

A shadow fell across the bobbing heads and horns. Chuy Garcia leaned against the fence from the outside, watching. Manuel flashed him a quick grin. "I can get another can if you want to help."

Chuy shook his head. "I'm not paid for that."

"You don't know what you're missin'."

Chuy spat an oath. "I'll survive." He jerked his chin toward the two men sitting together on the mohair bag, well out of the way of the working crew. "Look at those two old farts. Did you ever see anything so worn-out and worthless?"

Manuel looked. "Worn-out maybe, but not worthless."

"You couldn't get an hour of honest work out of either one of them."

"They've worked hard in their time. They've earned the right to sit down."

Chuy shrugged. "What I can't understand is why the hell *you're* here. You got away from here once. Why didn't you stay?"

Manuel pointed the paintbrush toward Charlie. "He was sick and needed help."

"That old *gabacho*? You ought to let him drown in his own sweat. You'll never see a damn rancher go out of his way to help *you* when you need it."

"Mister Charlie would."

"*Mister* Charlie." Chuy spoke the words as if he were spitting a bad taste from his mouth. "Why don't you take off your hat when you say his name, and bow a little too?"

Heat began rising to Manuel's face. "I've got work to do, Chuy."

"Sure you have. These ranchers will always see that you have work to do. How much is he payin' you?"

Manuel hesitated to answer. "Nothin'."

Chuy exploded. "Nothin'? You goddam fool!"

"You always did say I was a fool. This shouldn't surprise you."

Chuy regarded him with disbelief. "You're lyin' to me. What's he really payin' you?"

"I sleep in the house where we used to live. Miz Mary feeds me. That's it."

"But why?"

"I told you. He was sick, and he needed help."

"My old man is sick too, and awhile back he needed help. Charlie Flagg didn't help him."

"What happened?"

"The old man went to him for a *regancho*. Flagg didn't give it to him."

"Mist . . ." Manuel caught himself. "Charlie didn't have it."

"These ranchers, they've *always* got it. They give you that poor-mouth so you'll leave them alone. So the old man, he went to Danny Ortiz."

Manuel stiffened. "To Danny?"

"Old Man Ortiz is dead."

Manuel nodded. Old Man Ortiz had died a few months ago, and from the accounts Manuel had heard he had the biggest funeral turnout of any Mexican in the history of Rio Seco. It was generally acknowledged that few came to mourn; most were there to be sure the old bastard was really dead.

Chuy said, "He got a loan from Danny, at Danny's interest rates. He's already paid back over half of what he borrowed, and he still owes more than he did to start with. Everywhere we go, Danny turns up, threatenin' to take this machine away from him."

"What're you goin' to do?"

"Keep stallin' him, that's all we can do. The old man has got a cancer eatin' at his gut. He won't make the summer. If I can stall Danny while the old man lives, then he can come take the son of a bitch. *I* don't want it."

Manuel stared open-mouthed at Teofilo, who was moving his hands in broad sweeping motions as he talked to Charlie. He swallowed hard, knowing how painfully his own father would take this news. Manuel couldn't remember when Teofilo Garcia hadn't been around; he was a fixture here, like Warrior Hill.

"I'm sorry about your papa, Chuy. I didn't know."

Chuy shrugged, a gesture of futility. "Nobody did

till lately; he didn't tell a soul. Now you can see it in his eyes when you look at him."

"I doubt that Mister Charlie knew."

"Wouldn't have made any difference if he *did* know; he wouldn't have lent the old man any money."

"If he couldn't lend it himself I'll bet he'd have hunted somebody who could. Did you-all try Old Man Rodale?"

"That *gringo* banker? We don't trust any of those."

"He would've been better than Danny."

"Danny is one of *us*." Chuy looked down at the goats Manuel was daubing with the black healer and fly repellent. "So here you are back with the rest of us poor Mexicans, workin' for the white man."

"Like I told you . . ."

"I know, he's sick. And you're sick, too, in the head." Chuy turned to stare disapprovingly at his father sitting beside Charlie. The two older men were adrift somewhere in a world of their own. "Look at him," Chuy complained. "You'd think him and old Flagg was brothers; you'd think he didn't have sense enough to realize that Flagg and all these others have used him all his life, and now that he's old and sick they'll just throw him away like a pair of worn-out boots."

"You're bein' too hard on Charlie. If he's ever caused harm to anybody, he didn't mean to."

"Listen to *you*, talkin' up for him. I remember when you came to me mad as a whipped pup because he patronized you—treated you like a pet dog."

Manuel shrugged. "Turnabout is fair play. Now I can patronize *him*."

"So you help him get back on his feet, and then he's the same hard-nosed old bigot that he always was."

Manuel pondered a moment. "I guess you could

call him a bigot. You could call us *all* bigots, one way or another. But he's gettin' better, Chuy. Are *you*?"

Manuel looked across the dusty pens at Charlie and Teofilo. Charlie was doing the talking now, using his hands to express himself the way Teofilo had done. It occurred to Manuel that neither of these two *viejos* ever realized how much they had in common, how much more they were alike than different. "He didn't ask for my help, Chuy. He didn't ask for anybody's help. If he hadn't gotten sick. I think he would have made it all by himself. It wasn't fair to see him go under just because he was sick. Whatever else he might be, he's a man."

The tail of his eye caught a movement, and he turned. A car was approaching on the road from town, the hard wind quickly floating its trailing dust far out into the pasture. Border patrol, Manuel thought at first. Shearing day drew border patrolmen like sugar draws flies. Well, they wouldn't get anything here today but a cup of stout coffee.

Chuy Garcia snarled, "It's that Danny. He's come to devil the old man again."

Danny. An old, remembered hatred stirred back to life. Fists flexing, Manuel squinted through the dust. He made out a red convertible. Danny had a new car since the last time Manuel had seen him; he had probably had several new cars.

Manuel glanced at Chuy, coming to a quick decision. "You used to count Danny as a friend of yours. I don't suppose you do any more?"

"Danny's only got one friend in the world, and that's himself."

"Good. Then you won't mind if I happen to deck him."

"I'd do it myself if the old man didn't owe him money. I'll do it anyway when the old man is gone."

Manuel hung the *tecole* can on a post and began climbing over panels. He had climbed over the last one when Charlie Flagg pushed himself to a stand from the mohair bag. Manuel could see anger building in Charlie's face. Charlie couldn't afford anger, not in his condition. He was saying, "That damn Danny Ortiz. I told him years ago, if he ever set foot on this place again . . ."

Manuel said, "Sit down, Mister Charlie. I'll talk to Danny."

Charlie showed no sign he had heard. Sterner, as a grown son might speak to a childish father, Manuel commanded, "You sit yourself down!"

Charlie blinked in surprise, but he sat down beside Teofilo, who looked suddenly very nervous.

Danny drove up at high speed and pushed on the brakes at the last possible moment. When the red convertible came to a stop, the front bumper was pushing into Charlie's netwire fence, stretching it a little. Danny stepped out of the car to find Manuel standing there waiting for him. He looked at Manuel in surprise.

Manuel said evenly, "You're not welcome, Danny. Drag it."

Danny gave him only contempt. "What are *you* doin' here?"

"I'm here to tell you to get back in that car. Nobody wants you."

"Who says?"

"Me for one. Charlie Flagg for another."

Danny snorted. "Who's Charlie Flagg? Just another broke rancher, flat on his ass. I don't have to worry about what *he* says. I could buy and sell him ten times over."

Manuel shook his head. "The whole United States government couldn't buy him. You'll never come close."

"I don't give a damn about Charlie Flagg anyway. I came to see Teofilo Garcia."

Manuel found himself staring hard at Danny. Somehow he had expected what he saw, yet it shocked him a little. Danny was matured, a man now where Manuel remembered him as an overgrown boy. The marks of dissolution were cut deeply into his face. There was a glassiness in his eyes that told Manuel that Danny was either drinking too much or was on narcotics, maybe both. Short of killing him, no one could have done as much damage to Danny as he had obviously done to himself.

Manuel said, "You're not goin' to bother Teofilo."

"What are *you*, some kind of Father Protector?"

"You'd better not try to find out."

Danny's eyes narrowed. "I'd have whipped you once if it hadn't been for that Buddy Thompson and his club. Are you movin' out of the way, or do I have to walk over you?"

"Your feet aren't big enough. The only thing big about you is your mouth."

Danny took a step forward, mouth open a little, his teeth set in challenge. Then it was the same face Manuel had always hated. He felt an exhilaration as he crouched a little, starting his fist from way down low and bringing it up, putting the power of his shoulder behind it. When it struck Danny under the chin, Danny's head snapped. A second later he was stretched out flat on his back, arms spread-eagled.

Manuel's knuckles were torn and starting to bleed, but all he felt was a wild soaring of spirit. "Get up from there, Danny. Get up, goddam you, so I can do it again."

Danny lay stunned. When he opened his eyes, they had a vacant look, a glassy stare that focused nowhere. Manuel reached down and grasped Danny's shirt, trying to pull him back to his feet. Danny grabbed desperately at Manuel's hand.

"Don't do it," he cried. "Don't do it. I'll have the law out here. I swear, I'll have the law out here."

It was an empty threat. If the sheriff was still the same as when Manuel knew him, he wouldn't get up from the supper table to keep someone from killing Danny in the middle of the street outside. Manuel drew back his fist to hit Danny again, but he stopped himself. He looked into Danny's frightened face and reconsidered. He somehow got Danny to his feet. He shoved him roughly back to the car. He opened the door and pushed Danny in. "Pick up your feet or I'll slam the door on them!"

Danny lifted his feet and pulled them inside. Manuel slammed the door hard. "I'm glad you came here, Danny. I'm glad I saw you again because now I can heal up a sore that's festered in me for years." He pointed at Charlie. "You see that old man over yonder? There was a time once I'd have killed you—or tried to. That old man kept me from it. I hated him for it at the time. Now I'm glad he did. You weren't worth it; you're *still* not worth it." He pointed at the road. "Now *git*, Danny! Travel before I change my mind and don't let you go!"

A trickle of blood ran down Danny's neck from the point of his chin where Manuel's fist had caught him. Fear was in his eyes. He got the engine started and backed the car out with violent speed. He jammed on the brakes, cut the wheel sharply, then stepped down hard on the accelerator. The tires squealed, spraying dust and gravel as he skidded into a turn, almost hooking an end-brace of the cattleguard.

Manuel stood sucking his torn knuckles as he watched Danny go. He had always figured someone would kill Danny someday, but now he decided no one had to. Danny would do that himself in his own good time.

Manuel turned, finally, and saw that no one was shearing goats. To a man, everyone was staring at him. He saw half a dozen broad grins, white teeth gleaming like flashlights through the dust.

He walked over to Charlie Flagg and Teofilo. The two older men were both standing in front of the stuffed mohair bag.

He said, "Danny decided not to stay."

A little later Charlie saw a long trail of dust on the town road again. His first thought was that Danny Ortiz had regained his nerve and was coming back for more trouble, but he knew that was unlikely. Danny didn't have to have a house fall on him to get a clear message.

Sitting on the bag with Teofilo, Charlie said, "Never saw it fail. Get busy shearin' and there's always company comes to drag you away from your work."

He pushed to his feet, his bad knee hurting from the effort. He studied Teofilo, who had not tried to get up this time. "You look like you could use a drink, *amigo*. Me and you, we'll sneak up to the house directly and see if Mary hasn't hidden all the bottles."

"The doctor lets you drink, Mister Charlie?"

"He don't *let* me do anything. I do what I damn please."

Teofilo nodded as if to say *You always did*.

Charlie recognized Big Emmett Rodale's old Chrysler, puttering along at a fat man's speed. Unhurrying, Charlie made his way through a wooden gate and limped out to meet Big as he drove up to the outside fence of the shearing pens. He turned away a moment to keep from facing the dust that fogged over him from the automobile. He worked up some saliva and tried to spit out the grit that stuck to his tongue and teeth.

The car raised up on its springs as Big laboriously crawled out from behind the wheel. "Shearin' goats, are you?" He had known that before he left town.

Charlie put on an exaggerated frown. "Ain't you afraid you'll be contaminated, gettin' this close to a bunch of workin' men? No tellin' what you might catch."

Big chewed his cold cigar and gave Charlie a long appraisal. "I doubt that *you've* done much work today. Your hands are as soft as a baby's butt. Let a man loaf around a hospital a day or two and it spoils him."

"I bet I done more work before breakfast than you'll do in a week."

Big came as near grinning as he allowed himself to any more. "It's always a pleasure to come visit you, Charlie. You make a man feel like he's welcome."

"Somethin' my ol' granddaddy taught me—always be nice to everybody, whether you want to or not. You come to count your collateral?"

Big shook his head. "If you say they're all here, Charlie, they're all here. Just thought I'd see how they're shearin'."

"We ain't weighed any fleeces, but it looks to me like a good clip."

"Mohair market strong as it is, it'll fetch you a fair price."

"Not enough to pay me out."

"Before you're paid out you'll be a lot older man."

"If I live that long."

Big's eyes showed sharp concern. "You feelin' all right?"

"I ain't fixin' to die if that's what you're worried about. I'm not ready yet."

"Nobody ever is."

Charlie cast a quick glance at Teofilo, who had never moved from his seat on the mohair bag. "And we're never ready to let them go."

Big followed Charlie's glance but not his thought; he knew little about Teofilo Garcia. Charlie let the matter drop. "There's coffee in the camp or somethin' stronger at the house."

Big shook his head. "You got no business drinkin' either one, the shape you're in. It's bad for the heart."

"Everything that's happened to me in this damn drouth has been bad for my heart. I don't see where a little coffee'll add much to the damage."

Big still declined. "No coffee, Charlie. Just want to talk a little. Let's get into my car and out of this wind."

Charlie noticed how the car sagged to the left when Big climbed in behind the wheel. Some loose mail on the front seat slid over under Big, and he had to raise his broad rump to retrieve it. Charlie saw that one envelope had a notation requesting that it not be folded, spindled, or mutilated. How about *crushed?* he thought.

He asked, "Any news in town?"

"Same old six and seven. Last barber we had left this week. If you need a haircut any more you'll have to go all the way to Angelo."

Charlie grimaced. "The big towns get bigger and the little ones die."

Gravely Big nodded. "Rio Seco's a shell now; that's all it'll ever be. The times, Charlie. Once the people leave, they won't ever come back. The drouth has made it go faster here, but it's happenin' all over the country, even where they've got no drouth. It's sort of a cannibalism . . . the big ones eat up the little ones. The little rancher and the little farmer are through. They've either got to get bigger or get out. Same thing happens to the towns."

Charlie took off his hat and ran his sleeve over his face, trying to wipe away some of the coating of dust. "There'll come a day when folks'll wish it hadn't. They'll wake up someday and wonder what in hell to do with all them people. They'll wish they'd found someway to keep them in the country where they belonged."

"But they'll never come back here, Charlie. We've lived through a pretty good time, me and you. Now we're watchin' it die."

"The land is still here. People may leave, but the land survives."

"It'll never support the families again that it used to. People in the cities, they want their food cheap. They don't want to pay what it takes to support a man on the land any more. I remember when a dryland farmer used to raise a family pretty good here on a hundred acres. Now it takes four or five hundred and he barely gets by. People in the cities feel like they got a right to keep their own pay goin' up, but they want food to stay down where it always

was. When they've driven the last of the little produc-
ers to the wall and it all falls into the hands of some
big food combine, *then* they'll have somethin' to cry
about. Pretty soon there won't be any little ones left
except the ones that have an outside job. Or the ones
too old to move away."

Charlie flinched. "Like me, you mean?"

Big shrugged. "And like me. You think at my age
I could get a place in a city bank? I'm stuck here,
Charlie, same as you. It's home for us, and we ain't
got many years left. One way or another we'll ride it
out. But what about the next generation?"

Charlie shook his head. He had no answer.

Big said, "The next generation is the main thing
that brought me out here." He swung his gaze to
Charlie's face. "You ever hear anything from that boy
of yours?"

"Tom? He called a few times while I was laid up;
he talked to Mary. One of his old travelin' partners,
Shorty Dunn, keeps us posted on him every so often."

"He must be doin' all right."

"Seems like. Except that wife of his, that Dolly . . .
She filed suit awhile back for divorce. Last I heard
from Shorty she was runnin' around with some steer
wrestler."

Big grunted. "Too bad."

"Maybe, maybe not. Probably better for Tom in
the long run. There always was a lot less to her than
showed on the surface. I have a feelin' that the poor
ol' boy she's goin' with had better enjoy wrestlin'
steers. Once the new wears off, that's about all the
wrestlin' he'll get to do."

Big picked up the bundle of mail and sorted through
it. "Thought you'd want to know, I heard from Tom."
He found an envelope and passed it to Charlie. Charlie

knew the handwriting. Big said, "There's a letter inside. Go ahead and read it."

Charlie's hands shook as he worried the letter out. He unfolded it and held it away from him as far as he could, but his eyes were blurry. He couldn't make out the words. "My glasses are up at the house."

Big took the letter, shaking his head. "Damn, but you *are* gettin' old. Well, what it amounts to is that he says he's been havin' pretty good luck on the rodeo circuit, and he got some money ahead. He sent me a check. Said he'd do it again as soon as he could, and keep on doin' it till he got his debt squared off."

Charlie's mouth was dry, and he ran the tip of his tongue along his lips. He looked out the side window at the goats in the shearing pen. He said nothing.

Big said, "All them lessons you taught him, they took better than you thought they did. He didn't stand hitched like you, but he hasn't turned his back on an obligation, either."

Charlie tried to speak, but nothing came. He swallowed and tried again. "He mention anything about comin' home?"

"No, just said he'd send more money as he could." Big looked at Charlie, then put a heavy hand on the rancher's shoulder. "Goes to show that a man shouldn't lose faith in his young just because they dance to a different music. They'll do the right thing in the end, most of them, if they've been brought up the proper way."

Charlie nodded. "I reckon." He sat looking out the window, blinking. Damn dust was sure working on his eyes. Finally he asked, "Big, you remember Bess Winfield, the girl that used to work in the coffee shop? The one Tom went with?"

"I remember."

"You have any idea where she went to?"

"No, Charlie, I don't. Why?"

"Nothin'. Just a thought, was all."

"If Tom wants to, he'll find her. Some things you got to leave the young ones to work out for themselves."

"I reckon."

"Don't worry about him, Charlie. You raised a good boy."

Charlie looked toward Manuel Flores, driving some hair-goats into the shearing pen. "I raised *two* good boys, Big." He studied Manuel a minute, an inspiration suddenly taking shape. He turned to stare at Big. The banker squirmed uncomfortably under Charlie's speculative gaze.

"You got a crazy look in your eye, Charlie."

"Not crazy atall. I was just rememberin' somethin' I've heard you say. You see that boy yonder?"

"Manuel?"

"Manuel. He's a good solid kid, Big. And smart? A's and B's . . . that's all he's ever made in school."

"All right, so he's smart. What's that got to do with anything?"

"I've heard you complain that Rio Seco is in bad need of a veterinarian. Ain't that right?"

"Well, we do. But I still don't see . . ."

"Does it need one bad enough for your bank to put a long-range investment into gettin' him?"

Big squirmed. "I don't know . . . maybe . . ."

"That boy yonder has wanted to be a vet ever since he was fourteen-fifteen years old. He's got a natural aptitude in that direction like no boy you ever saw. Rio Seco may lose most of its people, but *somebody*'ll operate the land and have livestock on it. And where there's livestock there'll always be need for a vet. This town can have one of its own raisin', Big. All you got to do is back him."

"I don't know, Charlie . . ."

"He'll work to help put himself through; you don't have to carry the whole load. All he needs is a chance."

"But dammit, Charlie, he's a Mexican."

"I don't see what difference that makes, so long as he's good."

"There'd be some people that wouldn't want to do business with a Mexican."

"Times are changin', Big. Most people are just goin' to ask if he's a good vet. If he is, they'll use him. As for them others they can do without, like they're doin' now. He'll be a *good* vet, you can bet your money on that."

"That's what you're askin' me to do, seems like, is bet my money." Big frowned. "I'll have to study on this some. You're askin' me to put a lot of faith in a Mexican boy."

"You've always said you had faith in my judgment. Well, my judgment says you ought to back Manuel as far as he needs to go."

Big grumbled to himself. Charlie started to go on with the argument, but Big raised his hands. "Don't badger me; I got to think on it."

"Think on it all you want to, but I don't aim to let you rest till you say you'll do it."

"I was just thinkin' what the sign would look like in front of his office. If it said Dr. Bill Brown or Dr. Jim Jones, that'd kind of fit. But Dr. *Manuel Flores?*"

"In a town with a name like Rio Seco, it'll fit."

20

The smell of rain brought Charlie suddenly awake. Rubbing one eye, he raised up to look at the luminous face of the alarm clock beside his bed. A shade past five in the morning. He heard the pat-pat of water striking the window. He swung up, his bare feet hitting the rug-covered floor.

Rain!

He had left a window partially open for fresh air, and the north wind came to him sharply cold.

The goats! Alarm hit him like an electric shock. It had been just two days since Teofilo's crew had shorn the goats. Now they stood out in the pasture, their bodies naked to the wind and rain. Barefoot and in his long underwear, Charlie padded through the house to the front porch for a look at the weather. The sky was still dark. He couldn't see much, but he could hear the increasing tempo of raindrops spattering against the roof and across the yard. He stepped close to the porch's edge and felt rain strike him in the face. It was cold rain, almost sleet.

"Mary," he shouted, "I got to do somethin' about them goats!"

Mary came hurrying, throwing a housecoat over her shoulders. "What does it look like out here, Charlie?"

"Too dark to see much, but you can smell it. This one could be an old-timey chip-floater. I got to get them goats up to shelter."

"Not you, Charlie; it's too much risk. I'll go wake up Manuel. Then we'll do it, he and I."

"I'm not stayin' here, woman. Them's my goats."

"*Our* goats," she corrected him.

Charlie dressed quickly. He was still buttoning his coat as he started running down the front steps and out toward the barn. Manuel was only a few steps behind him, fumbling with a slicker.

"Mister Charlie," Manuel protested, "you go back to the house. That doctor would throw a fit . . ."

"That doctor ain't in the goat business!" Charlie pointed at a corral. "You go saddle the night horse. I'll get the pickup out. We got to move the goats up here and put them in the sheds."

Charlie prayed that the motor would turn over and start the first time he tried it. It didn't. But the second time it began to turn sluggishly. He cursed with vigor, and it caught. He backed the pickup out, giving it plenty of gas to be sure the cold engine didn't die.

On a sudden thought he stopped by the gas pump and filled a five-gallon can with gasoline. Worst come to worst, it might help if he built a fire. And if this rain kept coming on the way it had started, nothing less than gasoline would start a fire on wet wood.

By the time they had loaded Wander into the trailer and headed out into the pasture where the goats were, Charlie could see a little. Daylight was coming.

The rain was still not falling hard, but he started the windshield wipers. They were so old and had been used so little that the rubber was hard and brittle. They left streaks of mud that Charlie could hardly see through. He cursed and stopped while Manuel jumped out and wiped the windshield down the best he could with an empty gunnysack, partially clearing it of an old accumulation of dust that was now brown mud. Charlie followed the dim tracks of a feeding road, worn into the sod by day-in-and-day-out usage for much of the last seven years.

"Wind's out of the north," he observed. "We ought to find them toward the north side someplace."

They saw the first of the goats, and Charlie braked the pickup to a stop. Hurriedly he got out and shuffled back to unfasten the boomer and chain that held the wooden gate of the home-built trailer.

"Don't run, Mister Charlie," Manuel advised him worriedly. "Take it easy."

"I'm all right," Charlie shouted. "Let's save these goats."

Manuel backed the horse out. Charlie unhooked the trailer and gave it a push with his shoulder. He knew he shouldn't strain himself, but he didn't want the trailer in his way while he drove across the pasture. "Push them hard, Manuel. Don't ever let them stop. I'll see how much I can do with the pickup."

"Mister Charlie," Manuel worried, "you watch yourself now."

"I said I'll be all right. You just worry about them goats!"

It would have been better, he thought, to have brought two horses. But it would have taken time to bring up a second one from the pasture, perhaps as long as it would take now to gather the goats.

The first he saw were older muttons, some of the ones he intended to sell as soon as they had grown enough hair to be marketable; nobody liked to buy goats straight out of the shearing pen because of the cold-rain hazard. The goats seemed to stand in an uncertain sort of battle formation, scattered a few feet apart, facing the wind. Charlie honked the horn to start them moving. They milled aimlessly at first, and he knew it was going to be hard to get them going south when the wind was out of the north. He kept honking the horn, and he could hear Manuel moving along behind him on the horse, shouting at others.

He couldn't tell that the rain was any harder, not yet. It hadn't really started with force. The goats were not soaked. If only it would hold off a while!

The goats began moving tentatively in the general direction of the house. Charlie made a run at them with the pickup, racing the motor and honking the horn, hoping to give them enough momentum to keep moving after he pulled away to look for more. They broke into a run.

He wheeled the pickup off to the left and went in search of more Angoras. The next bunch already were shivering. He honked the horn at them, but they paid little attention. He got out of the pickup and took an empty feed sack from the back and began to swing it, shouting obscenities at them in English and Spanish, slapping them across the faces. He could sense the fear that was taking hold of the animals. The goat was more sensitive, more perceptive than the sheep, more responsive to weather changes.

Charlie had heard old-timers claim the goat could tell hours ahead where a hail or a cold rain was going to fall, and they would move out of that area if they could. That sounded like superstition to him, and he put no stock in it. But now that he thought of it, he remembered he had sensed something vaguely wrong with the goats yesterday, a skittishness that was unlike them. They had drifted restlessly back and forth across this small pasture he had placed them in after shearing. He had attributed it to the natural stress that followed their being roughly handled and moved to a new place. But perhaps they had felt the weather coming on.

Charlie hadn't. There had been no sign at bedtime last night that anything strange was brewing. The Weather Bureau hadn't mentioned it on the radio except to say a cool front might move down from the Panhandle. No severe changes, the report had said. Charlie had only half listened, for he had been disappointed in rain reports too many times.

He had to fight the goats to keep them moving. He knew some weren't going to follow. He slapped at them with the sack, having to go from goat to goat to start them. Even then he was forced to keep moving back and forth, shouting, waving the sack. The goats wanted to stop and face back into the wind.

Presently Manuel got there on the horse, with the other goats. "Mister Charlie, you ought not to be walkin' that-away. Why don't you at least stay in the pickup?"

"Think you can get them movin' all right?"

"I'll start them. There's another bunch over yonder a way." He pointed.

Charlie got back in the pickup and went to them as fast as he could drive on the open ground, honking the horn.

The rain was falling harder. Daylight was coming on. Charlie could see big drops strike the bare earth so hard that little puffs of dust rose from the impact.

He found this set of goats easier to start moving, and he stayed behind them with the pickup, prodding them up with blasts of the horn. A few dropped out and started back the other way. He jumped out and tried to turn them afoot but couldn't. So long as the whole bunch didn't turn and follow them, he decided to let them go. Main thing now was to save as many as he could. A man couldn't expect to save them all.

Gradually the muttons he was driving with the pickup converged with the ones Manuel was pushing a-horseback. Now and then one stopped, arching its back against the chill. When one did this, there was little chance to move him again. Manuel would step down, lift the goat bodily and put it into the back of the pickup, pulling a loose tarp over it.

Through the rain Charlie could make out the dim shape of the buildings ahead. A little longer now—ten or fifteen minutes—and they would have the goats to safety.

The rain was driving harder. Gradually it became so dense that Charlie could no longer see the windmills and the barns. The north wind strengthened, its chill breaking straight out of the Panhandle. He had his window down so he could pound his hand against the pickup door. The wind cut through Charlie's coat like a sharp knife.

The goats slowed. Up front, some stopped. Those behind began piling up.

"Keep them movin', Manuel!" Charlie shouted. "If ever we let them stop, we'll have old Billy Hell gettin' them to move again!"

Through the downpour he saw someone running toward them, a gray, shadowy figure in the drenching blue of early-morning rain. It was Mary, an old felt hat pulled down over her head, an old slicker of

Charlie's over her shoulders. The black dog followed her, barking at the goats.

"Mary," Charlie shouted, "you get back to the house before you catch your death!"

She must have heard him, but she ignored him. She fell into the goats, yelling at them like a man.

Manuel spurred around toward the front of the herd to try to break up the jam. Charlie drove at the goats from behind, blasting the horn, leaning his head out the rolled-down window and yelling, beating against the door. The rain was falling so hard it was like thunder against the cab of the pickup. The water drove through the open window and soaked him. The wind lifted higher, driving the rain in sheets.

And there, no more than two hundred yards from the barns, the goats stopped. They balled up, milling senselessly, huddling together in an effort to warm themselves against each other.

Charlie jumped out and ran through the rain. "Don't let them pile up! They'll smother each other!"

But Manuel couldn't hear him in the wind, and there was little he could have done about it if he had.

All around the fringes of the herd, Charlie saw goats crumple, their bodies trembling. One after another they died. How many more must be dying in that mad pileup, trampled or smothered! A single mutton moved away from the others to stand in the only shelter he could see, a bare-limbed mesquite just now beginning to bud out and promise spring leaves. Other muttons followed him, but the tree was no protection. Gradually the goats began dropping, their bodies a-quiver.

Charlie remembered the gasoline can. Maybe if he could get a fire started . . .

He ran and fetched it. Yonder lay some dead brush

he had piled a long time ago to rot away. The rain slackened a little. He hurried with the can and began slinging gasoline over the dead wood. Wet as it was, there was only a slim chance it would burn. Charlie emptied the can, bent to shield the match with his body while he lighted it, then flipped the match at the brush. The first went out before it got there. The second one caught. Flames swept over the brush with a violent roar. Steam arose, and Charlie could hear the hiss of rainwater in the flames.

Chances were the fire would go out when it finished the gasoline. But just possibly the intense heat might evaporate the water from the surface of the wood and allow the flames to bite into the dry heart beneath the bark.

Manuel had tied his horse and was afoot now. At first he and Charlie and Mary tried driving the goats toward the fire, but the animals wouldn't go. They started seizing muttons by the hind legs and dragging them from the edge of the pileup, toward the warmth of the flames.

A pitiable cry arose from within the tangle of dying goats. Charlie had butchered many a goat to eat, and he knew the death cry. It came now, multiplied by twenty, thirty, forty. A chill went up his back, a chill that had little to do with the wind and the rain. He cried, he choked. He prayed, he cursed. He grabbed goats two at a time and dragged them toward the fire. He moved in desperation, like a man in a ghastly nightmare.

"Two hundred yards!" he heard himself crying aloud. "Two hundred more yards and we'd've made it!"

Some of the animals at the edge of the pileup began to see the fire and started following the goats Charlie and Manuel were dragging out. Now suddenly there was a rush by many to reach the warmth. The hope of salvation turned to horror, for the goats on the outside in their frantic struggle to get nearer began pushing the innermost goats into the fire. Charlie could hear the agonized cries of animals burning alive, cries that fused with the moaning of goats freezing to death.

Abruptly then, Charlie stopped fighting it. "Mary," he half-shouted in anguish, "they saved *me*, but I can't save *them!*" He stood there with his shoulders slumped in despair, his chest heaving in a painful struggle for breath. He looked upon the miserable huddles of death and felt too shattered even to cry.

Manuel was sobbing, still carrying on the struggle, his tears washed away by the rain that pelted his face.

Charlie was aware of two more people running toward them from the big barn—Kathy Mauldin and Diego Escamillo.

Kathy took a long look at the frightful scene, then turned her back on it. Head down, she said, "Looks like we're too late, Uncle Charlie."

He summoned voice from deep inside. It didn't sound like his own. "You came; that's what matters."

Mary moved up to Charlie, her old hat wilted, the sodden brim hanging down and almost covering her face. For a long time they stood together but not quite touching, trembling from the cold, helplessly watching the struggle of those goats that remained alive. When this was over they would be lucky to have one left out of three, or one out of five.

Kathy put her arms around Manuel, and the two young people leaned their heads together, saying nothing.

Charlie watched them a moment, shaking his head. He had been through his hell already; theirs might not yet have started.

He found his voice. "Rain's comin' even harder. We'd just as well get out of it."

Manuel trembled. Charlie wondered whether it came from cold or from emotion. "After all the time you waited for rain, Mister Charlie . . . why did it have to come like this?"

"I've lived through other drouths, son. They usually break hard."

"But why? It already robbed you of most everything you owned. Why take what little you have left?"

Numb, Charlie said, "I'm not a prayin' man, especially. I couldn't claim to know. In olden times when the Indians really wanted somethin' they made a sacrifice. Maybe this was our sacrifice. Maybe now we'll get the rains."

"What good will they do you? You can't start again."

Charlie lifted Mary's heavy hat brim and looked at her eyes. He saw little hope there now, but he remembered other times when there had been little hope. He knew how it would be. Today those blue eyes would cry. Tomorrow the life would start showing again, and they would begin to hope, to calculate, to plan.

"There's still the land," Charlie said, more to Mary than to Manuel. "A man can always start again. A *man* always *has* to."

He didn't think what he said was reaching her now, but it would. Tomorrow it would.

Diego drove the Mauldin pickup down from the barn, a long trailer behind it that he and Kathy had used to haul their horses here. He began grabbing up live goats and shoving them into the trailer, motioning for Manuel to help him, and Kathy. They would haul the goats up to the barns a load at a time. They would save some that way. Not most, not even half, but *some*.

Charlie knew he could be no help. He was incredibly tired now, and chilled to the bone. He laid his heavy arm around Mary's shoulder. "I think me and you need some hot coffee. Come on, woman, let's go to the house."

He turned his back on all he had lost, and they walked together through the cold rain.

AFTERWORD

Elmer Kelton is a son of the West Texas ranch country that he brings so vividly to life in his fiction. Born on a ranch in Andrews County, Kelton grew up among stockmen and dryland farmers. He left his native precincts for military service during World War II, but after acquiring a degree in journalism from the University of Texas at Austin, he returned to West Texas to pursue newspaper work. From 1968 to 1990 he was associate editor of *Livestock Weekly*, published in San Angelo. In his spare time Kelton writes fiction—in all, more than three dozen novels since 1955. He has written formula western novels, and he has written "serious" western novels. Six of his books have won prizes and awards of various kinds. But Kelton has said that, of all his works, *The Time It Never Rained* is his favorite because "it was the most personal one I've ever done." It is my favorite, too. And the reason it is my favorite is its central character, Charlie Flagg.

Charlie is one of the most remarkable and memorable characters I have encountered in twentieth-century American fiction. I will readily corroborate Kelton's experience, recounted in his introduction, that many readers have believed the character of Charlie to be based upon their fathers. When I first read *The Time It Never Rained* several years ago, Charlie's integrity and stubbornness reminded me of my father; he was a farmer rather than a rancher, but he loved and fought and suffered with the land very much as Charlie did. Just recently an older student, at my urging, read the novel. She immediately became convinced that Charlie was modeled after her father-in-law, who had ranched down in the San Saba country during the great drouth of the 1950s, and no amount of diplomatic argument on my part could convince her otherwise.

Westerners—Texans, in particular—tend to identify strongly with Charlie Flagg and with what he represents. Charlie is, to use J. Frank Dobie's phrase, "out of the old rock." He embodies what we believe were the best qualities of the legendary Texan rancher: strength of will, independence, self-sufficiency. He loves and respects the land, harsh and unyielding as it is. His sense of right does not waver. He opposes equally the inert, clotted force of bureaucratic regulation and the evil of untrammeled power that too often crushes the powerless. Part of the appeal of Charlie lies in the fact that he is an anachronism, one of the last survivors of a dying breed. He springs from an older, better time—a time when, it is widely thought, our forebears acted from a deep conviction that seems increasingly implausible in the gray, ambiguous morality of the modern world. Charlie is our symbolic father, and we honor him for his courage. As we turn the novel's pages, we can only affirm the cliché: they don't make men like Charlie Flagg anymore.

But while Charlie may be a genuine hero, commanding our respect and admiration, he is also a thoroughly believable human being. He is sketched in the novel with warts and wrinkles intact; his flaws show clearly. Far from being the slim young giant that Owen Wister's *The Virginian* branded into the American consciousness as the cowboy archetype, Charlie is old and overweight. He is contrary and more than a touch cantankerous, taking secret delight in his reputation as someone who is *different*. Most disturbing are Charlie's difficulties in communicating with his wife, Mary, and with Mexican-Americans. The cowboy's code is essentially a masculine code, and it offers few helpful guidelines for the interaction of male and female. The tension of those long, silent evenings when Charlie and Mary speak hardly a half-dozen words to each other is excruciating; such scenes provide a striking illustration of what Larry McMurtry has called the "domestic tragedy" of the ranch household. Charlie's position as *el patrón* among the brown underclass of the area inevitably generates a degree of condescension on his part. Though he treats Mexican-Americans kindly and his relationship with Manuel Flores ends happily, he is unquestionably guilty of the paternalistic attitude of which Manuel accuses him.

So Charlie is no saint. He is, however, a man of principles—of principles rooted in the West Texas land and culture. His unbending resistance to federal drouth relief issues from the rancher's fierce self-reliance and a suspicion of interference from outlanders bred of generations of proud isolation. But it would be a mistake, I think, to read into the novel a specific political message—that all government aid should be sternly and righteously rejected. The real lesson of Charlie's story is that, no matter the circumstances of our lives, we should never give up. "Minute a man quits tryin', he's blowed up," says Charlie: "A man had to make his try, and when that didn't work he had to try something else. Try and keep trying. Endure, and try again." At novel's end there appears little hope for a new beginning—at least not for Charlie. He is too old and too debilitated. But he has triumphed nonetheless; he has endured. The future of Charlie's beloved region is deeded to Kathy and Manuel, who becomes Charlie's spiritual son, filling a role that his biological son Tom has, for the present anyway, abdicated.

Though the people of the novel constitute its most impressive aspect, other elements of *The Time It Never Rained* were also fashioned by an expert craftsman. The narrative spans several years, but plot development never seems halting or disjointed. Time passes, the seasons come and go, and gradually the cumulative weight of the drouth's disastrous impact sinks deeply in the reader's consciousness. Kelton's style, in this novel as in the rest of his fiction, is beautifully understated. He has mastered the West Texas stockman's laconic, pithy way of speaking better than any writer I know of. That manner of speech is shown best in the book's colorful dialogue. But even in the third-person narration enough of it is injected to suggest the rhythm and flavor of the region—without becoming annoying dialect.

Deservedly, *The Time It Never Rained* has been widely acclaimed for its high merit as a work of literary art. Upon its original publication in 1973, the